TWO FATHERLANDS

THE RESCHEN VALLEY SERIES – PART 4

Chrystyna Lucyk-Berger

Chrystyna Lucyk-Berger / Inktreks Dornbirn, Austria www.inktreks.com

Publisher's Note: This is a work of fiction. Names, characters, places, and incidents are a product of the author's imagination. Locales and public names are sometimes used for atmospheric purposes. Any resemblance to actual people, living or dead, or to businesses, companies, events, institutions, or locales is completely coincidental.

Book cover design by Ursula Hechenberger-Schwärzler (ursulahechenberger.com)

James Wheeler on Unsplash, Eugene Triguba on Unsplash, and Ursula Hechenberger-Schwärzler

Cover model: Kathrin Maier

Two Fatherlands, a Reschen Valley Novel Part 4/ Chrystyna Lucyk-Berger. – 1st ed.

ASIN: B08K7MC83C

ISBN: 978-3-903748-15-6

TO MY BROTHER, STEFAN—

It's two sides of the same coin.

Welcome to the Reschen Valley series. Though *Two Fatherlands* could stand alone, readers would benefit from reading the previous books. Recommended is to at least begin with *Bolzano* (Part 3). However, if you are inclined to begin here, please know that some of the details may not be clear at the start. They will, however, come to light as the story continues.

Thank you for choosing this book.
Chrystyna Lucyk-Berger

For a complete guide to this series, including maps, glossaries, character lists, etc., please see www.inktreks.com/guide-reschen.

Please be so kind as to share your experience in the form of a book review or rating on platforms such as Goodreads, Bookbub and where you shop online.

BOOKS IN THIS SERIES

Other Books by the Author

CONTENTS

PART I

1938

THEY CAME DRESSED FOR CHAOS.

—Vanessa Friedman,
New York Times, Jan. 7, 2021

1

GRAUN, APRIL 1938

K atharina was fixing the wiring on the chicken coop when she heard the gunfire. From below the ridge, surprised shrieks, like panicked birds startled from the brush. A second shot. Silence.

By the time she came around to the front of the house, Manuel appeared at the top of the road, furiously pushing the bicycle pedals. Even from a distance, she saw the way her youngest son's face was pulled tight with sorrow. Bernd and he had been racing up and down the farm road, cheering one another on as they took turns with the bicycle. It had been a scene of peace and unity, of a normalcy so distant these last months that it nearly made everything all right again. Surely, Katharina thought, that squealing had simply come from something Florian had not properly oiled. Manuel was probably distressed because he thought he might have broken the old contraption.

Before he reached the barnyard, Manuel jumped off and dropped the bicycle to the ground—exactly what his father had told him not to do—before throwing himself on Katharina.

"Mutti! They shot Hildi!"

"Who did?" But before Manuel could name the Italian police guards, Katharina was already running for the ridge.

Behind her, a tool clattered in the workshop, where Florian was mending the pushcart wheel, but she did not stop to see whether her husband was on her heels. She had to reach the *carabinieri* before they hurt anyone else.

At last sight, Katharina had seen Hildi's black-and-white tail swinging wildly in circles as she had chased after Bernd on the bicycle. Hildi—God knew how much Bernd loved that dog—had kept up with him, but not because she'd been on a lead. Bernd must have removed it.

When she reached the scene, a policeman was fastening handcuffs onto Bernd. Her son's head drooped over his heaving chest. Katharina rushed at the two policemen, intent on pulling her son out of their grips, but at the sight of the prostrate dog in the field, she pulled up short and covered her mouth.

"*Sentite, è davvero necessario?*" she demanded. Was this necessary?

Florian now pushed towards the *carabinieri*, hands up. "*Vi prego*, he's upset about the dog."

"Yes," Katharina reasoned with the smaller policeman, "you've shot his dog. Naturally he's upset."

With a crushed expression, Bernd looked down at Hildi, then up at Katharina. He wrenched himself from the policemen's hold. There were always two of them: one to read and one to write— that was the joke. By the way they gripped Katharina's son again and shook him into stillness, however, these two made it clear they were not joking.

"He came after us," the shorter one replied, indignant. "He's not allowed to strike at the police." To Bernd, he added, "You know that. This is not the first time you've crossed the line of the law."

Katharina started again, as did Florian, the two of them talking over each other.

"Don't you dare beg them," Bernd growled in German. Behind those eyes—so much like his great-grandfather's had been—anger flared dark blue.

The policemen swung Bernd to the road and marched him towards town.

Katharina rushed for her boy, but Florian pulled her back. She twisted out of her husband's grip, his interference making it all the more urgent that she fight harder. She grabbed the first policeman by the arm and pleaded again for Bernd's release.

"Please! Fine us. The dog should have been on a lead, I know. We'll pay whatever you want. Just don't take my son to Captain Basso."

The man's expression wavered. "*Signora* Steinhauser, my mother is a lioness too. I'll tell you what I tell her: you cannot fix everything for your children. Bernd is old enough to take responsibility for his actions, for his life."

Katharina glared at him.

"Take the dog," the presumptuous policeman said. "Bury it. Then come to the station and pick up your son. But only after he has learned his lesson."

Florian came to her side and muttered something, but she wasn't listening. She watched the two *carabinieri* stride off with her son still defiant between them. Florian then marched back up the road and to the farm.

Katharina followed her husband, Manuel, at her side. Only a few weeks ago, the authorities had fetched Florian in the middle of the night. He'd undergone questioning—questioning that had chilled Katharina. Captain Basso had made it clear that the authorities had information about the family, information that Katharina and Florian had carefully kept from the boys. Florian said Basso had seemed disappointed, angry even, that Florian had not reacted more surprised or vehement about Basso's knowledge. Katharina could easily imagine the police captain would break open the truth to Bernd.

By the time she reached the top of the road, Florian had disappeared into the workshop. He returned with his hat.

"I'll take care of this," he said.

"I'm coming with you."

He put a hand against her shoulder before she could move into the house. "Stay here." He indicated the ridge. "You and Manuel should bury Hildi. I'll come back with Bernd."

"I want to go with you."

"You offered to pay a fine. I'm going to need the emergency money."

It wasn't just Hildi running around without a lead. Accosting a *carabinieri* was a serious matter. Bernd could be sent to prison, as far as to Bolzano, unless they could pay. Katharina knew Vincenzo Basso well enough to know they could never pay enough to keep him quiet. He'd had his reasons for testing Florian. *Divide et impera.* Divide and conquer. That was Basso's tactic. His and the other Fascists'.

"I'll get the tin." Katharina went into the house.

Above the stove, tucked away in the alcove, was the container of matches and the extra lire they'd saved for a rainy day. Florian would also need Bernd's papers. She took the tin into the sitting room with her and pulled open the drawer of the writing credenza, removed the envelope with all their documents, and found Bernd's. Before she put the envelope back, she noticed the edge of a picture frame sticking out from between old letters and newspaper clippings. Puzzled, she reached for it and then remembered. She dropped her hand.

That frame was empty now. It had once held the photo of Annamarie dressed in her blue-gingham smock and a white blouse. Katharina recalled the beginning of her daughter's smile, the reason for it. Manuel and Bernd had dashed out, dressed up in capes and silly hats, swinging wooden swords and trying to get their older sister to laugh over made-up rhymes. Beyond that moment—beyond that photo—Katharina remembered her daughter's eyes yearning for something far away, remembered how that child loved to run, bounding through the fields, abandoning her chores. How many times had that girl scorched the milk? She remembered her daughter's crushed expression, the shame on Annamarie's face, the day she'd returned from Bolzano, hoping for forgiveness. Instead, it was Katharina who had begged to be forgiven, and denied it.

Annamarie. She was in Innsbruck, across the border now, leaving Katharina and Florian to wrestle with the past, with the lies that had compounded over the years and that Annamarie had learned about in the most heartbreaking revelation.

The frame was empty, the photo in Angelo Grimani's possession. Katharina had pleaded with him to search for their daughter, to be more than a politician and to finally take responsibility. He'd returned empty handed, remorseful, and far too late.

She stuffed the envelope into the drawer and slammed it shut, angry now. At the *carabinieri.* At Bernd. At the dog. At Florian for refurbishing the cursed bicycle. At herself, most of all, for all that she had managed to undo in the last year.

Hildi was lying on her side in a bed of crocus and snowdrops, head angled upward, neck stretched out, as if she were simply enjoying the midday spring sun. Her tongue poked out from between her teeth, turning violet, the only sign that something was wrong.

With Manuel sniffling next to her, Katharina bent to roll the dog onto an old blanket and lifted the animal into her arms. Hildi's long black-and-white fur was matted in two places with blood—one bullet wound to her chest and one to the side of her head.

"We'll bury her with the other dogs," she said.

Manuel made a small noise in the back of his throat as he stroked the animal's rump. "She was just playing with us. She saw the *carabinieri* coming up the road and ran straight for them."

"Was she barking?"

He shrugged. "She didn't mean anything by it. You know how she is. She runs around strangers in circles, like when she herds the cattle..." His voice trailed off, as if he realised he was still talking about the dog in the present tense.

A cuckoo called from the wood above them, and a breeze brushed across the meadow. Katharina lifted the animal closer to her and started the walk up the road. Poor Hildi! From the time the dog had arrived on the *Hof*, there had not been a day that Bernd and she hadn't marched off together to do chores. In the beginning, where Florian had scratched in the sizes of the children on the doorway of his workshop, Bernd had insisted his father add Hildi's measurements to the marks. At some point, the dog had stopped growing, but their son had not. He was now fifteen, old enough to know better than to provoke the authorities. Now Florian and she were part of the half dozen families to whom this fate had befallen. It was meant to teach them all a lesson about what would happen if they misstepped. The dogs weren't the problem, after all. It was the Tyroleans the authorities wanted to keep on a lead. Since the village men had become emboldened by Hitler's march into Austria and come to blows with the Italian authorities in the churchyard, the *carabinieri* were on a rampage. Then there was the night the swastikas burned on the hillsides. She still could not believe the authorities had picked Florian up for questioning. Florian! Of all people!

How was shooting people's dogs supposed to convert dissenters of Il Duce into supporters? Instead, some of the valley residents, who'd previously remained neutral, were now talking about how Hitler would set his sights on this part of Tyrol. They were Germans, after all. They speculated that the

Führer would do as he had done with Austria and force another Anschluss.

Katharina jerked her head at the barn. "Manuel, go get the shovel."

She went to the walnut tree. Her shoulders ached from the weight of the dog. She lay Hildi gently to the ground and pulled the blanket's corners over her before stepping away to look at the two markings on the tree: Bello, barely three years old, who had been crushed by a cow, and Hund, Katharina's beloved old dog.

Manuel slowly returned and extended the shovel to her, and Katharina etched out a rectangle into the ground before stomping onto the shovel's edge. Grunting, she pushed the dirt up. Just then, one of the boys' riddles popped into her head.

Annamarie, here's one! Here's one! All the kids are standing in the fern, watching the roof burn. Except for Klaus—he's still in the house.

It was a perfect description of the condition in which they found themselves. Everyone in Rome was standing on the outside looking in, while the valley's folk were trapped inside, with nowhere to go and no choices left. She grimaced and threw a big heap of earth to the side, then stopped to look at it. Whole families on both borders had been uprooted by systems and politics. Mussolini. Hitler. A poor economy. Heavy debts. Banks foreclosing on their mortgages. Government officials seizing their properties. The reservoir.

Katharina straightened and thrust the shovel back at Manuel. "Finish this off. I'll leave you some food in the house."

"Where are you going?"

"To Graun. I'm going to get your brother out." Before the price became too steep.

Katharina took the back road from Arlund to Graun. The valley floor was mostly tilled, and farmers were out sowing the fields with rye, wheat, barley, and flax. The surface of the two lakes rippled on the spring breeze. South of Graun was the third lake. The reservoir would connect all three bodies of water, which meant the hamlets from east to west would disappear beneath. This included Arlund. It included Katharinahof, her farm, if Angelo Grimani did not manage to stop the construction.

The bells of the church tolled twice. Half past one. Next door, smoke rose from the chimney of Jutta's inn. The town hall stood on the other side of the church and served as the police headquarters. There was a single room for detainees.

She pictured Captain Basso questioning Bernd. Basso would rather chew nails than let Bernd off easily. Her son had a record. He'd been caught painting graffiti on the walls in the Italian quarter, had had fights, and pulled pranks that went over line.

The gloves and socks sent to the school had started Bernd's capers. The pupils whose parents were registered nationalists and who took part in the paramilitary youth group received the coveted clothing along with copies of that macabre story about a wooden puppet and how his nose grew every time he lied.

Bernd had bullied one of the boys to hand over his pair of woollen mittens and woollen socks to Manuel. But subsequently, together with two of his friends, Bernd had ambushed one boy after another over the next week and passed the goods on to their classmates whose parents were steadfast pro-Germans. The same ones who sent their children to the illicit German lessons with Maria Plangger, which was a matter of contention between Florian and Katharina.

Captain Basso had shown up at the *Hof* not long after that, dragging Bernd home by the ear.

"Your boy," Basso had sneered, "thinks he is some kind of vigilante for you Germans."

Basso had the meanness of someone who felt entitled. Entitled to his position. Entitled to his political loyalty. Entitled to reigning over the Tyroleans in this valley. He was the same man who had gone and broken all of Jutta's dishes at the inn one day because they'd been made in Austria.

With great disgust, Basso had sworn that if he ever got his hands on Bernd again, he would make sure the young man stayed in jail. He'd shoved Bernd so hard into the house that Bernd toppled straight into the wall of hanging coats and slunk to the floor.

Katharina now reached the bottom of the road and picked up her pace. She had to get her son out of Basso's hands and back home. Bernd would face his own house arrest from now on. Florian would accuse her of meddling, but her husband's tactics of trying to win over his opponents with charming diplomacy would likely fuel Basso's mean spiritedness.

"Katharina! Is that you?"

Katharina whirled around to face Jutta coming out of the millinery.

"I'm glad to see you," Jutta said, her voice too high pitched. "I need to speak to you."

Alongside, Alois waddled on his thick legs, unable to keep up with his mother's quick pace. His smile widened at the sight of Katharina. He was not yet thirty and was losing his hair to a high forehead, but one patch stood straight up near the back of his head.

By Jutta's demeanour—examining, probing, obviously mulling over an approach in the short distance between them— Katharina knew the innkeeper had something up her sleeve. Katharina stopped to wait for her. Maybe a little distraction, a chance to calm down, would make her discussion with Basso more productive. Katharina noticed that the gash Jutta had suffered to her forehead during the skirmish in the churchyard was now a shiny scar.

"How are you?" Katharina asked. She nodded at Alois, his smile contagious.

"Fine." Jutta turned sideways, as if to get Katharina to follow her towards the inn, or perhaps to block Alois from their discussion. "I'm glad to see you."

"So you said." Katharina stayed put and glanced at the town hall ahead. A man came out, but he was not Florian or Bernd. "I can tell you're up to something, so get on with it."

Jutta's look darted about. "That night, the night they questioned me? You know, the same night as they did Florian?"

Katharina nodded.

"They talk too much, that Basso and his men. They talk Italian and think I don't understand." Jutta shifted on her legs, leaning in closer. "You see, we now kow that we have to find a new… embroiderer. For the church altar. To cover the relics."

Katharina stiffened. Jutta was referring to the clandestine German lessons with the children. Jutta couldn't mean that she wanted Katharina to take over. She shook her head. "I thought Maria Plangger was doing that. She's been embroidering all winter."

Jutta glanced surreptitiously over her shoulder. "That's right. But she's taken ill." She stressed the last word. She meant Maria was suspected—that the authorities were keeping an eye on her. "She hasn't been able to work for a few weeks now, and we," Jutta said meaningfully, "thought of you."

"We" was the "committee." She knew what people said about her behind her back. Her friendship with Iris Hanny, the *Italian* schoolteacher and Dr Hanny's *Italian* wife, had labelled Katharina an *Italian* lover. Her ability to speak the language made her an *Italian* sympathiser. Suddenly Katharina was their best option? She nearly laughed aloud. She was the last person anyone in this valley—especially the Italians—expected to hoist a swastika up a pole. But to teach the children their language, their culture, and their traditions—all forbidden by Mussolini's government—she was good enough for that. If caught, she'd be taken to Bolzano and imprisoned.

"I can't," she said. "We've the planting to get through. I'm already behind on the things I have to get done." She looked over Jutta's shoulder. Still no sign of Florian or Bernd. "I have to go."

"Wait," Jutta pleaded. "Think about it. You wouldn't have to start until after the harvest." Her eyes darted about again. "And the committee has arranged for a small stipend."

Just then Florian and Bernd stepped out of the town hall. Florian put his hat on his head and jogged down the steps ahead of Bernd, who took his time descending. Was he limping? Jesus and Mary, if they hurt her son…

She did not care what Jutta saw now. "I'll let you know."

Alois looked relieved the conversation was over.

Katharina hurried to her husband and son. She took Bernd by the shoulders and assessed him, but there were no bruises, no marks she could see. "Are you all right?"

Bernd shrugged. "Please. Don't make a scene."

Katharina tried to reach for him, but Florian put a hand on her shoulder.

"He's fine." He gently steered her for home. "They took our money. All of it."

Behind them, Jutta called. "You'll think about it, Katharina? Promise? And I can help you choose the pattern."

Katharina ignored her. "We'll talk about everything at home, Bernd. I'm sorry about Hildi. Manuel and I buried her."

Bernd's head shot up. "I wanted to do that. She was my dog."

Katharina halted, but her son kept walking. "I'm sorry, Bernd. I just—"

Her husband wore that confounding expression of endless patience and understanding.

"I did what you told me to," she said. "You told me to stay home and bury the dog. I should've known better—"

"He's upset. Give him some time."

"And the money?" she asked when she reached him. "All of our emergency money?"

When Florian did not answer right away, she knew more bad news was coming.

"We still owe them," he finally said.

Katharina stopped in her tracks again. Florian returned to her.

"How much?" she asked.

"Fifty lire, based on today's inflation rate. Due after this year's harvest."

She pressed a hand over her mouth. It was almost a third of what they earned in a season. She spent months stretching every *centesimo* to provide for their basic needs and save a little something.

"Don't worry," her husband said again. "I told Basso I'm going to make Bernd earn it. He'll have to look for a job, that's all. Manuel will simply have to do more on the farm with me."

And risk having Bernd out of their sight? Like Annamarie? "A job? Where? How? Nobody can find a job around here. He's fifteen, Florian. The only job he can get will be under a *capo*, somewhere south. You and I both know that will only provoke him. How can you imagine sending him out of the valley to work for the people he hates?"

Florian's jaw tightened, and he picked up speed. "What was Jutta talking about back there?"

He was changing the subject. She hated that. "You know Jutta. Always something happening. She wants me to embroider something for the church."

"Again?"

She did not reply. He did not know what the code meant.

Before her, hanging in the window of the Farmer's Bank building, was a poster for a play to be performed in Reschen by a travelling amateur theatre. Now it was her turn to change the subject. She hurried to catch up to her husband.

"How many theatres do you think there are in Innsbruck?"

she asked. "A half dozen? Maybe a dozen? It's not an overwhelming number, right?"

Florian slowed down. "Annamarie?"

"I could write to Tante Rosa, my mother's aunt. I haven't seen her since I was a child, when we were living in Innsbruck, but I could write to her. She could visit the theatres. See whether she could find Annamarie."

"That's a good idea." Florian took her hand. "Problem is, we don't have a *centesimo* to our name left. We can't pay for a phone call. We can't even pay for postage." He squeezed her hand and smiled. It was a sad smile for a sad joke.

Katharina kept pace with him. Jutta had mentioned a stipend for teaching German in secret. But that would not come until the fall. Fifty lire was a lot of money. She could not be certain that the committee could scrape that much together from the families in Graun. Unless she offered to teach children in neighbouring Reschen or St Valentin. But it was so dangerous.

Above them, Bernd was already climbing the road to Arlund, his hands shoved into the pockets of his *Lederhosen*.

On the other hand, if she did teach, it would be a way to keep her eye on her son. Maybe even influence him down a different path. That, in itself, was almost a good enough reason.

2

INNSBRUCK, MAY 1938

The cramped apartment on Kaiserjägerstrasse was bursting at the seams with the post-show party. Bodies collided in the middle of the sitting room as they danced to jazz music. Earlier that day, they had rolled up the carpet to save it from the drinks that would surely spill over from the revellers. Moving between the partygoers, Annamarie went to the windows and threw them open. She hung out of the last one to take in some air. The neighbouring roofs were glossy from the mist that had been falling all day. Electric lamps, reminiscent of another age, cast small spotlights on the street three stories below. A few blocks away, she heard the distant rumble of a tram. Turning back to the room, she realised the city's damp air was doing little to relieve the stuffiness. Between the people's heads and the ceiling was a thick cloud of cigarette smoke, and Annamarie caught the now familiar sweet whiff of cannabis.

Across the way, in a quiet corner near her bedroom, Sepp examined something in his hands. It had to be the new movie camera. New to him, that was. She wandered over and leaned against the frame of her closed bedroom door. His notorious bright-green scarf was wrapped around his skinny neck, his spectacles were resting on the middle of his forehead, and a cigarette was dangling from the side of his mouth.

"Are you going to quit lighting design for the theatre and go into the movies?" she asked.

Sepp grinned as he wound the handheld movie camera. "Why not? You're the one who keeps saying film is the way to go, that theatre's for old people."

Annamarie crinkled her eyes and glanced to where Lisi was dancing, her arms raised above her head, her red hair still coifed in the style of her current role. Next to her was Veronika, Lisi's understudy and a cast member. She usually got the smallest roles.

"Go into filmmaking and you'll never see Lisi again," she teased.

Sepp glanced over his shoulder and grinned back. As always, any time he gazed at Lisi, he looked afflicted.

Annamarie raised her empty glass and wiggled it in front of Sepp. "I could use another one."

He grinned again, lifting the camera's lens to his eye and turning to the crowd. "Are you offering to get me one?"

"Always the gentleman," Annamarie teased. She headed to the kitchen.

As Annamarie tried to move past Lisi, she raised her own empty glass, and Annamarie grabbed it, then bumped hips with her. Laughing, she moved to where they had set up the drinks, greeting those she knew and basking in the limelight. She was roommates with the star of the State Theatre. She waited as people jostled against one another, trying to refill drinks, passing cigarettes along like bonbons and lighting up. Annamarie took it all in.

This was freedom. This was living. Never in her seventeen years had she imagined how much fun life could be. This was nothing like the farm in Arlund. Nothing like Bolzano, where she'd mistakenly believed she had found her destiny, painful as that lesson had been. Innsbruck was far from where she planned to stop though. It was just a springboard to Berlin, to get into the film business. Berlin was where everything was happening. Everyone who was anyone was either heading to Berlin or returning from Berlin, only to complain about how provincial Innsbruck was.

"One step at a time," Lisi had warned not even a week ago. Then with a lot of forced cheer, she had announced, "There's a private theatre looking for someone your type. It's a small part, but you need to put something on your résumé." She'd examined Annamarie up and down. "You need to learn how to move and how to speak. We have to polish off that accent of yours. I promised the director that, if he gives you a chance, I will personally work with you."

It was a generous offer considering that the first time they had met, Annamarie had done everything to cover up her real story. She had lied about where she'd come from, her training and experience in theatre, which was near to none. She had even lied about her last name and why she was in Innsbruck. Yes, Annamarie had a distant aunt or cousin or something from her mother's side, but in the two months since her arrival, Annamarie had not even tried to get in touch with Tante Rosa, and certainly not when Lisi offered a room in her apartment. Because the first thing Annamarie saw was the opportunity to pursue her acting career through the Innsbruck State Theatre starlet. Until Lisi uncovered the imaginary story Annamarie had created about herself.

First Annamarie had botched the cabaret theatre audition, and Lisi had expressed measured sympathy, chalking it up to nerves. But when she accompanied Annamarie to the registrar's office—something Annamarie had not calculated on—and Annamarie had to produce her identity papers, Elisabeth von Brandt the Actress wanted nothing more to do with Annamarie the Liar. Thankfully, Lisi the Roommate was kind enough not to throw Annamarie out on the street. When she, however, offered

Annamarie this second chance, she followed Lisi's instructions to the letter and rehearsed as if it were a new religion. As of tomorrow, and because of Elisabeth von Brandt's name, Annamarie was going to start her career.

Space cleared, and Annamarie lifted a fresh bottle of sparkling wine. Headily, she popped the cork, poured three glasses and some elderberry syrup, mixed them, and placed them on a small tray to deliver to Lisi and Sepp. She found them together, Sepp with the camera lens pointed at Annamarie. She served their drinks then glided through the dancers.

"When's your audition?" he called out to her.

Annamarie grinned. "Tomorrow at eleven in the morning."

"Say that with a little drama," he instructed and backed up a few steps, bumping into two dancers.

Annamarie flung her arms in the air. "Tomorrow, darling! At eleven in the morning!" She caught her reflection in the window. Dark hair, slight figure, and the skinny arms a whole shade darker than most of the people in the room. She dropped them and took a step back.

Lisi reached out and stroked the black leathery sides of the film camera. "This is so exciting. How could you have possibly afforded it?"

Sepp lowered the contraption, his goofy grin appearing, as it always did in Lisi's presence. Annamarie moved in closer, wishing he had kept going. She wanted to perform her lines and maybe see how she appeared later.

"The professor you told me about," Sepp said. "He was desperate for cash. I got it for a song." He showed Lisi the boxy device. "It's a Siemens Model C. Almost ten years old, but it works quite well. Sixteen millimetres and can take up to fifty feet of film."

Lisi grinned at Annamarie. "You should have Sepp film your lines for tomorrow."

"Yes, do!" Annamarie raised her glass while he righted the camera back onto her.

As she moved away so that he could get more of her in the picture, violent pounding on the door made her jump. Men's voices ordered to open up. Annamarie thought of the neighbours, but most of them were here at the party, a trick that Lisi used to her advantage. Annamarie saw Veronika move behind a group of carpenters who worked on the theatre's sets.

Lisi laughed airily. "It's nobody. It's only Franz. It's my brother. Open up."

Annamarie went to the record player. Franz was all right if he was not drunk, but some of his fellow Brown Shirts left a bad taste in the mouth. She watched as four of them stepped into the room, bottles of beer in their hands, grimacing and laughing at how they had scared them all. Annamarie recognised Mean Mouth Simon, a real piece of work she avoided at all costs.

"Hey, Annamarie." Franz headed her way with a bottle of schnapps that must have replaced his beer. "How's it going under my sister's tutelage?"

Annamarie shrugged. "Good."

"You still cleaning houses to pay the rent?" He took a swig before handing her the bottle.

He knew well enough what she was doing to earn her few Reichsmark. "I've got an audition tomorrow."

"Really?" He looked surprised, but a sly smile crept across his face. Franz brushed the long blond fringe out of his face and looked over his shoulder. Mean Mouth Simon was coming right for them. "Hear that, Simon? The South Tyrolean's got an audition tomorrow."

Mean Mouth Simon grimaced. He was tall and bulky, with a face full of scars from what must have been horrible acne when he was younger. Annamarie imagined him as a child, pulling off insects' legs or drowning kittens for sport.

"Is that right?" he slurred. "You find someone who needs a bad impersonation of the Führer?"

Franz laughed and tipped the rim of his beer bottle under her nose. "That was certainly ballsy of you!" He cackled again and swigged his beer.

"It sure was." Lisi was at her side and added lightly, "Loads of cabaretists have done it, but never a girl. It would have been great, but your timing was all wrong, Annamarie."

"It was not," Annamarie protested. "Besides, you said I made a brilliant Mussolini when I imitated him at the Iron Rooster."

Lisi poked her side. "He did not just annex Austria to Germany, you silly goose."

"Serves you right," Franz jeered. "The Reschen Valley? Bozen's Fascist university theatre club? How did you ever think you'd measure up? Especially against my sister?"

Annamarie's face seared hot. She barely managed to register Sepp, who was standing outside their circle, the camera aimed at them.

"Well, she did have you all fooled," Sepp said. "Even me, and I'm from South Tyrol too." He swung the lens at Lisi. "And you. What's your excuse? Don't recognise an act when you see one?"

Lisi scoffed, and Annamarie forced a smile. She put a heavy arm around Lisi's shoulders, asking the camera, "Does that mean I have potential? Fooling the starlet?"

"If nothing else, you do know how to give a performance," Lisi mocked.

"Or go back to the cabaret," Mean Mouth Simon said. He lifted a lock of her hair. "Italians and Jews, that's where they belong."

Annamarie jerked away from him. She was so angry, she could spit.

Sepp lowered the camera. "She's not Italian. She's Tyrolean like you and me."

Mean Mouth Simon snorted.

"You should talk—" Annamarie started, but Franz raised the bottle between them.

"Come now. We're teasing." He looked nervously at the partygoers, who had grown quiet with disapproval. "We're all friends." He took a swig and handed it over to Mean Mouth Simon.

Annamarie snatched it from Franz's hand and tipped the bottle to her mouth. She gulped down the stinging liquid.

"Annamarie," Lisi said sharply. "What are you doing?"

Franz whooped and laughed again, calling to the others in the room to watch. Mean Mouth Simon made to retrieve the bottle from Annamarie, but she swung away from him, drank more, then stared him down, eyes bugging out, and made as if to spit the last mouthful into his face.

He backed off, fanning his hands. "You—"

"You know whom I just imitated?" She sneered and wiped her mouth on the back of her sleeve. She lifted her shoulders, made herself bulkier, and stood on tiptoe. "I'm Mean Mouth Simon," she bellowed. "Turn off that music! We don't tolerate those *Neger* playing that crap. Put some good Bavarian tunes on! Come on, everyone. Let's do the polka. No, wait. That's Polish."

Lisi made to grab for her, but Annamarie swung away, tipped the bottle once more, growing into her role.

"Let's sing to our Fatherland!" Annamarie broke into the Horst Wessel song.

Out of the corner of her eye, she saw Veronika's face freeze, her eyes grow wide. Someone else protested. Franz had both hands up against Simon's chest, holding him back. To Annamarie's surprise, Lisi, still glaring at her, started to sing as well. Then Sepp joined in.

Annamarie marched around, growing louder and pumping her arms into the air. The partygoers backed away from her, some with nervous smiles, others with uncertain giggles. But everyone gave way to her. She took another long drink from the flask, thirsty now and wishing it was water, not schnapps. By the second stanza, almost everyone was singing. Even a shell-shocked Mean Mouth Simon stood with his mouth agape, but he was singing.

She made her voice louder, deeper, conducting the choir around her. Franz also walked around, gesticulating for everyone to raise their voices.

"Our sword is truth. Our shield is faith and honour. In age or youth, our hearts and minds we pledge!"

Lisi gestured for the bottle, but Annamarie backed away, the room spinning. She swayed to the small dining table and propped herself. With flat palms, she drummed to keep herself steady. Soon anyone who could find a flat surface was following the beat. She had to admit, there was something powerful in the melody, the rhythm, even the words.

"Though we may die to save our people and our land, this cause will stand, our millions marching on!"

Annamarie looked up and saw that Sepp had his finger on the camera again, like on a trigger of a gun. She raised her right arm straight into the air and goose-stepped before the lens.

"Sieg! Heil!" She snapped her salute before Franz and Simon. They barked it back, and Annamarie dropped the bottle onto the floor between them, empty.

Fists beat on the door once more. This time Annamarie was certain it was the police. She stumbled towards the kitchen. Everything within her peripheral vision careened this way and that, as if she were standing on a ship in a great storm. She barely reached the water closet before vomiting everything up.

With her face in the toilet, Annamarie was aware that Lisi and Sepp were there with her, but she could not get up. A commotion came from the sitting room, shouts and grumbles, and finally the door slammed shut and only a few murmurs remained. She felt herself being lifted up, the haven of the toilet falling away. She stumbled over something and hit the floor. There was nowhere else to go but into the waiting abyss.

It felt as if someone was pulling her eyes open by tugging the skin from the front of her skull to the back of her neck. The roof of her mouth and tongue were stuck together with what felt and tasted like cotton wool balls. Annamarie groaned and rolled over onto her side. She blinked, recognising the threshold beneath her. She was lying between the kitchen and the water-stained floor of the toilet. Moaning, she struggled to sit up, but the room spun and someone shouted at her. She put her hands over her ears to keep the noise down. Outside the tiny crack of a window, a tram thundered by, and Annamarie wondered when the city had put a line right into their alley.

"What a mess. All that confessing! Honestly, Annamarie. Who knew?" It was Lisi, her voice echoing, her tone was severe.

Outside the kitchen window, Annamarie saw the early morning light over the neighbouring roofs.

"It's a good thing," Lisi continued more gently, "that Sepp stopped the camera, though he was pretty certain you might want to see yourself in the tragic state you were in."

"Research. It would have been good research," Sepp said to Annamarie's left.

She moaned again. "What happened?"

"You fell on all fours," Sepp said. "And never got back up."

They were crossing through the sitting room, and Annamarie gagged at the sight of bottles and strewn glasses and cigarette butts. Someone lay on the small sofa, head hanging on the far edge. A woman in a navy-blue dress, her bare thighs exposed to the world, Sepp's bright-green scarf draped over her middle.

"Who is that?" Annamarie peered at the headless body as the other two guided her to the bedroom.

"Veronika," Sepp said.

Her bedroom door wide open, her bed had never looked more inviting.

Lisi stepped back as Annamarie propped herself on her knees, wearing an expression of half-amusement, half-worry. "Don't trouble your broken head. Your secrets are safe with us."

"What did I say?" Annamarie groaned.

"All sorts of things," Lisi promised. "But thank goodness, Sepp is the only one who understood what you were going on about."

Annamarie glanced up at Sepp. "Why?"

He pushed his spectacles up his nose, the lenses smeared. "Because you were speaking Italian."

Annamarie fell backwards and moaned. The bed spun, and her peripheral vision was a dark smudge of grey. She closed her eyes, not able to even open them, when Lisi said, "That's right. Sleep a little. You've got three hours before we have to get you ready for the audition."

The raw egg Lisi had made Annamarie swallow made her break out into a cold sweat. She took in a deep breath, brushed down her skirt, and stepped into the limelight of the empty stage. She raised a hand to her eyes to shade the glare and saw the silhouettes of two people sitting about eight rows deep.

"Good morning, sirs."

"Good morning." A woman's voice, like chalk scraping across a blackboard.

Annamarie corrected herself. "Madame. Good morning."

There was an indignant snort and then a man's voice—the second person—answered good morning as well. "And what's your name?" he asked with anything but interest.

"Annamarie Steinhauser." She raised her hand again to shade

her eyes, when she noticed movement. The two silhouettes were whispering.

"Elisabeth von Brandt sent you?" the woman shrilled.

Annamarie glanced uncertainly to where Lisi stood stage left. Lisi nodded encouragingly.

"Yes, ma'am."

"So you will perform what today?" the woman asked.

"Desdemona, from Othello," Annamarie said.

"Fine," the woman responded, this time an octave lower.

Annamarie glanced again in Lisi's direction, and Lisi mouthed, *Go on.*

"Go on," the man's voice called.

Annamarie cleared her throat. "My noble father," she squeaked. "My noble father," she tried again. "I do perceive here a divided duty: To you I am bound for life and education. My life and education both do teach me."

"Learn me," boomed the man's voice.

"Pardon?"

"It's *learn me*, not *teach me*," the woman explained. "What is that accent of yours? I can't quite place it."

"Tyrolean, madame."

"Stop calling me madame. I'm Frau Direktorin Weisgarber. Tyrolean, you say? From which provincial town? Isn't it provincial, Herr Falkner? There's something else. I can't quite put my finger on it."

"I haven't even begun," Annamarie said. She now knew which of the bodies belonged to whom. Frau Direktorin Weisgarber was directly before Annamarie, her arms crossed before her.

Weisgarber's head jerked back in the shadows, turned to Herr Falkner. "Awful, really. Can you stand listening to it?"

"Try high German, my dear," Herr Falkner called out. "Please. We might be a small theatre, but we do expect some class."

"Yes, Herr Direktor," Annamarie said weakly. "Shall I begin at the beginning?"

"Heaven's no," the woman said, rubbing the sides of her head. "Start where you left off."

From stage left, Lisi hissed, "My life and education both you learn me—"

"How to respect you," Annamarie continued, taking on her father's German accent. "How to respect you: you are the lord of duty—"

"My goodness," Herr Falkner called out.

"What's that?" Weisgarber shrilled. "Wait. Where are you?"

"Do you hear that, Frau Direktorin? She can go from provincial to Nuremberger at the push of a button."

"I didn't ask for Nuremberger," the Frau Director shrilled back. "I asked for proper German. She's to be performing Shakespeare. Shakespeare! This is not a provincial farmer's theatre!"

That was the last straw. Annamarie felt the sulphuric taste of egg coming up. She covered her mouth, tears springing to her eyes. This was a disaster. A real catastrophe. Worse than the cabaret.

"Now, child! You're not going to be sick, are you?" the man called out. "You are looking quite green."

"Green around the ears," the woman scoffed.

"I can do this. I know I can." Annamarie swallowed, fighting desperately not to vomit onto the stage, but the tears were uncontrollable.

"Fräulein von Brandt," the woman called out, panic in her voice. "Fräulein von Brandt, I know you're backstage. Come out here, please."

"Young lady," Herr Falkner said to Annamarie, "stay with us please."

Annamarie was shaking. When she saw the disappointment on Lisi's face, all she wanted was to run backstage. She had to choke back bile again.

Lisi stood in the spotlight. "Yes, Frau Direktorin?"

"Fräulein von Brandt," Weisgarber continued, this time in a placating tone. "We agreed to take a look at your friend, but it seems she is unable to withstand even the slightest of criticism. How does she expect to work with any director if she cannot take even the simplest direction? Who is this young lady?"

Lisi took in a deep breath. "She promises to have talent. I know she does."

The woman sighed with such drama, Annamarie imagined she might faint in her own seat. "So you said. What she suffers from, and projects upon us, is overinflated and misplaced confidence."

Herr Falkner lifted a hand. "You also indicated you would work with her, Fräulein von Brandt. I assume you prepared her for this audition."

Lisi nodded.

"It's obvious she cannot even take your direction," Weisgarber jabbed.

"She really needs training," Lisi explained. "Voice, dance—"

"Acting," Herr Falkner pitched in. "What training has she had?"

Lisi dropped her head. "As I discovered recently, none at all except with that of the Fascist youth group in Bolzano. For women."

Even Frau Direktorin Weisgarber was silent. Annamarie wilted.

"Take her away," Herr Falkner finally said, his voice flat. "She's not one of us."

For someone with such a thick Italian-Tyrolean dialect, for someone so *provincial*, for someone so ridiculous, the only job Annamarie could get was that with the Rampenlicht Theatre, cleaning up after the cabaret performers, the actors, the musicians who came through to put on popular performances.

Lisi had brought her to Herr Baumgärtner, the owner, the day after the miserable Desdemona audition, after Annamarie had recovered enough to not cry at the drop of a hat.

"You're a miserable loser, Annamarie," Lisi scolded gently. "Honestly. Do you believe that I won my first role at my first audition?"

"I'll ruin your relationships if you keep this up."

"Nonsense. I don't care about that old bat. She really is as unpleasant as her reputation precedes her."

But nothing Lisi said or did could console Annamarie, and when Lisi told her she had a job at the Rampenlicht for her, Annamarie dragged her feet to the interview, defeated.

Baumgärtner was a gentleman and a gentle man through and through. Lisi knew his wife, who played the cello in the state orchestra. He took Annamarie on for twenty Reichsmark a month.

Two days later, Lisi and she sat down to go over her expenses and how much she would have to save for the voice, the dialect, the singing, and the acting lessons.

"This is for stage acting," Lisi said. "Not playacting to get away from whatever you're running from. You understand?"

It was still not clear what it was Annamarie had exactly said in her drunken state, how much of her story she had spilled, and as long as Lisi did not ask about it, Annamarie was not going to either. She went to work, came home, closed the door, and went to sleep. Even when Sepp or Franz came to visit, Annamarie made her excuses to hide in her bedroom. Because when Annamarie did the calculations —her income minus her expenses—the time it would take to afford any private lessons would take forever and ever. She would be an old woman before she became a properly trained actress.

At the end of the week, however, Annamarie overheard Lisi

and Herr Baumgärtner speaking. Lisi said she was just coming by to walk home with her, maybe grab a drink and something to eat at the Iron Rooster, to which Annamarie was prepared to make her excuses again. But the discussion presented a silver lining in Annamarie's drab and grey future.

"There are opportunities for Annamarie," Herr Baumgärtner said, "if she rubs shoulders with the right people. Makes connections. There's something about her—"

Lisi nodded enthusiastically. "She's good at that, that's for certain. She can get entire crowds to eat out of the palm of her hand. Why the other night, we had a party and she had the whole room singing those Brown Shirts songs. Can you imagine? My theatre people singing Horst Wessel's song with enthusiasm and real gusto?"

Baumgärtner looked dubious and then laughed. "Then I am not wrong."

Annamarie understood. It was up to her now to look for any door that stood ajar, one that she could knock down to grab the opportunity that waited inside. Something, anything, to propel her forward.

A few days later, Herr Baumgärtner popped his head into the room where Annamarie was cleaning up. A wine bottle, a broken glass with lipstick on the rim, someone's single black sock draped over a broken lightbulb on the mirror—typical fare.

"Annamarie? Lisi's here asking for you."

"Could you please tell her I'm staying until after the show tonight? She should go on without me."

Herr Baumgärtner opened the door farther. "I think she needs to see you right away. She has someone with her."

Curious, Annamarie headed for the green room, where eclectic couches were laid out, most with burn holes from cigarettes and stains from spilled wine or beer, or whatever it was that landed on the couch in the early morning hours. Lisi was there with an older woman. The woman, Annamarie guessed, was in her sixties. She had grey-blonde hair beneath a pale-blue hat and was wearing matching gloves. Despite the warm weather outside, she also wore a fur stole around the collar of her cream-coloured dress.

"Annamarie?" the woman said with an irritated tone. "I've been looking all over Innsbruck for you."

Annamarie gave Lisi a questioning look, who in turn looked rather chagrined.

"I'm sorry. I don't know who you are," Annamarie said cautiously.

"Of course you don't know who I am," the woman said with exasperation. "And why should you? I've never met you in my entire life, but your mother sent me a photo and the awful assignment to go looking for you."

This was the aunt Annamarie had always known about, had even told the Austrian border patrols she was going to visit and stay with, but had never done so. Because she knew that exactly this would happen: the old woman would send her packing back to the Reschen Valley.

"I'm your—"

"Tante Rosa. I know."

"Well, third cousin to be exact, but call me what you will. I have found you and now expect you will come with me, and we shall finally settle this matter between you and your parents. They're worried sick about you."

Annamarie stared at Lisi. How could she? "No," she said so strongly she even surprised herself. "I won't. I mean, you're free to inform them I am doing well. You may even promise them I'll write. When I am ready. You can't just come here and fetch me. I have a life here."

"A life? Here?" The woman's shrill voice reminded Annamarie of Frau Direktorin Weisgarber.

"Yes, here." She felt a sharp pain in her chest. She had done this before, had said this before. But that time it had been to her father, who had travelled from the valley to Bolzano, looking for her, begging her to return home. With a stab, she realised her circumstances had not been all that different then either.

Annamarie noticed Lisi nodding encouragingly. It drove her on. "And later," she added, "maybe I'll be in Vienna. Or Berlin."

Tante Rosa took a step forward, hand outstretched. "Child, go home. I beg you." She'd dropped her voice, and the anxiety was unmistakable. "These are not good times for us here. Go home and wait this out. You're young. You have time. But on this side of the border…"

Annamarie frowned. "I don't know what my mother told you, but one thing is for certain. Times are much, much worse where she is. Much worse on the Italian side."

The older woman retreated. She patted the stole around her neck, straightening it. "Yes. Well. How shall I explain this to your family, then?"

"I just told you. Tell them what you like. Tell my mother you found me working at a theatre. Tell her I am perfectly fine. Tell her you found my roommate. I have no idea how—"

At the same time, Lisi and Tante Rosa answered, "Looking for you in every theatre…"

Annamarie smiled. "Excellent. Then tell them that you have accomplished your mission."

Tante Rosa looked Annamarie up and down, then set her mouth into a grim line. "Are you certain? Is that what you really want me to do? Why can't you go back?"

"Believe me," she said, still smiling, "you do not wish to hear the reason. Hold on to the belief that your niece, or cousin, whatever my mother is to you, is a good person. All right?"

With a deep breath, Tante Rosa opened her purse, took out a pencil and a piece of paper, and wrote something down. She handed the slip to Annamarie. "This is where I live. If you need anything, anything at all, please come to me. I'll at least assure your mother of that."

Annamarie glanced at the address. The one person connected to her family did not live more than four blocks away from the theatre. She gazed at the woman. She was well off. She had money. This made her curious.

Annamarie smiled once more, opened her arms, and took the few steps between them to hug her briefly. "Thank you for finding me. Let them know that I am all right. We'll talk soon."

After Tante Rosa left, Annamarie carefully folded the paper and glanced up at Lisi. "How?"

"She was asking about you at the State Theatre, and Veronika mentioned she knew you and brought her to me."

"And you brought her here."

Lisi shrugged. "You really should let your parents know you are all right."

"I just did. Anything else?"

"There is one more thing."

Annamarie sank onto the couch, irritated. "What? What do you want to know now?"

"Who is Marco Grimani?"

3

BOLZANO/BOZEN, MAY 1938

The aroma of freshly ground coffee was irresistible. Angelo stepped into the newly opened Caffè dei Ritti, just before city hall, and ordered a double espresso and a brioche. He watched the steam, admiring the way the contraption worked. The barista—a tall, square-shouldered man with bushy eyebrows —reached over the counter to shake Angelo's hand. He explained that he had moved from Florence to Bolzano the year before.

"Nice to meet you. Minister Angelo Grimani." Angelo pointed over his left shoulder. "I work over there. The Office of Civil Engineering."

"It's your roads then that helped me make my way up here," the barista joked. He tapped the coffee into place and twisted the filter into the machine.

Angelo thought how he would like to take the credit for the vast improvements to the region's infrastructure, but much of it was thanks to the visionary new magistrate, Giuseppe Mastromattei. The new magistrate had proven himself skilled in more than just military and governance matters. He and Angelo shared a deep appreciation for function and form; aesthetics were just as important as the purpose of a

36

construction. Just like the espresso machine the barista operated.

As people popped their heads into the café, commenting and curious but not quite ready to come in, Angelo faced the outdoors. The Saturday morning market was picking up. The vendors, their stalls set up hours earlier, called to the first shoppers filtering into Piazza Vittorio Emanuele. Across the way, cobblers were setting in new pavement stones. By the workers' hats—a mix of feathered caps and tweed *coppole*—he noted that the crew was made up of Tyrolean and southern Italian labourers.

The barista placed the warmed espresso cup on the counter and the brioche on a plate. Angelo faced the man again.

Angelo said, indicating the bar. "It's an interesting concept."

"The idea comes from the American saloons. Wild, wild west, you see?" The barista stuck his index fingers into his waistband, then withdrew them just as quickly, making pistol shots. "In Florence you find many espresso bars like these. But me? I'm the first here. I like being the first. You like it, Minister Grimani? You think the people will like it?"

"I'll be sure to tell everyone at the city offices to come." Angelo saluted him with the brioche and drew the espresso closer.

The cathedral's bell rang twice; it was half past eight. He tipped the cup and emptied it in one swallow, wrapped the brioche in paper, and pointed to the abandoned newspaper next to him. "Mind if I take that with me?"

The barista grinned. "Go ahead."

Angelo paid the man and slipped the newspaper under his arm. He headed for the four-story neo-Baroque building, its back facing the square. On the third floor, two long windows with Juliet balconies marked his office. He rounded the corner and unlocked the front entrance before climbing the polished wood staircase to his floor. He looked forward to reading his newspapers and catching up on his paperwork without the phone ringing every few minutes, or Miss Medici asking whether he needed anything, or any other number of people interrupting his day. Besides, he was going to miss this place. In another month or so, the ministry was relocating to a building on Via Dante. The expanding police department needed more room now that Bolzano's population was bursting at the seams. In under two years, the number of residents had more than tripled to over one hundred thousand.

Angelo unlocked the door to the ministry's offices and entered his secretary's front room. The scent of lily of the valley permeated each corner. Miss Medici's workspace was tastefully furnished in mahogany and a small red oriental carpet. Her own eclectic additions—a potted fern, a cloisonné pencil holder, a silver tray etched with swirling patterns that held various pins and clips and other things secretaries apparently needed—created a homey atmosphere. The telephone, however, was his addition and was state of the art. Miss Medici called it "the Monster."

He moved through into his own high-ceilinged office and opened the two windows to let the air in. The muslin curtains filled like sails with the breeze. The espresso bar stood at the top of the market square. The beat of ceramic cups and hissing steam had picked up in tempo. Apparently, the passersby risked trying the place out. Opposite the square came a dull clanking sound. Angelo watched the cobblers—only Tyroleans—knock back heavy mugs of beer.

This was the problem with the economy: beer breaks before nine o'clock, as if the Germans had no idea the nation was crawling out of a severe depression. But if he were honest, he could not blame them. Everywhere Angelo looked, buildings were under construction and expansions were being made to the city. The German residents, in the meantime, protested that the Italian regime was colonising the Alto Adige with Italians in order to make a minority group out of them. They could complain all they wanted; Angelo could not take them seriously. In fact, he marvelled at how the Tyroleans always managed to turn the situation to their advantage. With the supply and demand for real estate at an uneven scale, the Tyroleans had taken to charging the influx of migrant workers extortionist's rates for even the most cramped space, no running water, and no heat. Business owners, such as his father, had taken it to the senate. The government stepped in and appropriated property to house those who came to work for the industries at the BIZ. The industrial zone, including the new apartments, developed and grew upon generous government subsidies, a good portion of it now supported by a new real estate tax exacted on property owners earning anything over a set cap. In other words, on the back of those high Tyrolean rents. It was not subtle, but it did the trick. Rental rates had begun dropping, and now the Italians had the advantage again. But how long before they found another way? The Tyroleans were innovative, Angelo had to give them that.

He left the din of the market and took a seat at his desk. There was a note from Miss Medici that the office relocation was now set for the middle of June. Angelo sighed. He cast an eye over all the things that he would have to move. To his right was the bookshelf with a rolling ladder. His massive mahogany desk and the two black leather upholstered armchairs across from him would come along as well. The blue oriental carpet that composed a vast island on the parquet floor. There was an array of commodes and cabinets, many that he had inherited from his father-in-law when Angelo took over as minister. To the far left stood the models of the various dam projects, reservoirs, roads and railroads. Maps, charts, and other statistics hung on the wall, providing a colour-coded overview of all that was coming, in progress, or near completion.

The idea of moving his entire office as well as setting up a new residence in parallel drained his energies. The Laurin Hotel had been his home for four months, offering him a reasonable discount for his extended stay since Chiara had thrown him out of Villa Adige months earlier. He had come to terms with it but his separation with his wife and his estrangement with Marco left him in limbo. His son had still not forgiven him for the catastrophe, for the secret that was Annamarie Steinhauser. Both his children were unreachable to him now. Annamarie, thanks to him, had been swallowed up somewhere in Austria, and Marco was buried in his studies in Bergamo. Perhaps, Angelo thought, he should focus on only the things within his control. Gina, for example.

He nearly laughed aloud. Gina Conti might be in his corner now, but Angelo would never presume he could control anything about her.

The memory of her in his arms the night before sent another thrill through him. He was *innamorato perdutamente*—head over heels in love. He knew it, but damned if he would tell Gina Conti that anytime soon.

"Start with something you can manage, like the move to your new office." He chuckled at his own joke. The espresso—or the barista—had put him in a good mood.

He put the note about the move off to the side, and before organising his work for the day, he opened the early edition of *Corriere della Sera*.

The headline was about a paper written by government-funded scientists, called the "Manifest of Race." Two politicians, who had made their antisemitism well known to the public, were pushing for laws that would ban mixed marriages between Jews and Gentiles. Angelo did not know any Jews, nor anyone married to one. He wondered whether Jews could divorce more easily than Catholics, because that was what he wanted: a divorce. Chiara had made it painfully clear she was not interested in reconciliation. But a divorce was practically unheard of amongst

Catholics; annulments, yes, but try explaining to the church what he'd done to his family. Even Mussolini had succumbed to the authority of organised religion, drawing up a treaty with the pope in a move to win support. However, Angelo mused, unheard of did not mean impossible.

He snapped the paper and folded it to reveal the next page. There he was, the magistrate, Giuseppe Mastromattei, shaking Adolf Hitler's hand. In the photo, Mastromattei—wearing an officer's fez—towered over the German chancellor. The caption indicated that the meeting between the two had taken place at the Brenner earlier in the week.

It was then that Angelo realised he had not voiced his admiration for Mastromattei with the barista. Mastromattei meeting Hitler simply symbolised how much confidence Il Duce had in the man. He was efficient, brilliant really. He executed orders with genius strokes. When Mastromattei had been given the task to see to the BIZ, he had called upon the expertise from the largest industrialists in Italy, converting the BIZ into a national model for all future industrial zones.

Together with Angelo, Mastromattei focussed on the modernization of the region, but it was the magistrate who courted the industries, who used his political wiles and counted on them to establish the three million square metres that made up the BIZ. Because hydroelectric power was key and Mastromattei was determined to produce as much power as possible to supply his great visions for the Alto Adige, he had helped get investors for the Colonel's power plant, and this helped Angelo's father reinvent himself under the new name of Monte Fulmini Electrical, or MFE.

Angelo recalled the first time he'd met Mastromattei. It was in the stairwell, shortly after the magistrate's new appointment last September. Mastromattei had opened with, "So I hear you also fought with the Alpini." They had then introduced themselves officially and soon established that their units had essentially fought right next to one another during the Great War. The conversation—short but pleasant with the typical camaraderie Angelo experienced amongst veterans—had ended with a polite promise to meet for supper one evening. To date, that had not happened. They worked together but had not yet socialised together—something that could build an even more fortuitous relationship.

Angelo withdrew a pad of paper and a pen from his desk drawer and wrote a note to Miss Medici to make such arrangements. If the magistrate was going to be taking over his office, the least Angelo could do was have a bite to eat with the man in a less formal capacity.

He was just about to settle into the news of the football when someone rapped on the door. He lifted his eyes from the newspaper and tried to smooth the irritation from his face. Saturdays were his days to hide away and get things done, including catching up on the football.

"Yes?"

The Colonel popped his head in. "I thought I saw you slinking in here." He did not wait for an invitation but entered and examined the bookcase as if he had never spent a minute in Angelo's office before. It struck Angelo that his father had shrunk.

Angelo sucked back a sigh of frustration as he stood to greet his father. "Good morning. How did you—"

"Find you? I was just returning from my walk before breakfast when I saw you going in." The Colonel swung to him. "Your mother wants to know whether you will join us for dinner this evening."

His mother wanted to know when Chiara and he would settle their marriage "problem."

Angelo indicated the seat across from him. "Espresso? I can make us one."

"Dinner?"

"I can't. I have plans."

"I see." The accusation was syrupy. Angelo braced himself for it, and the Colonel did not disappoint. "With that woman?"

Angelo went to the sideboard at the far end of the room, where he kept the makings for coffee, though the Colonel's presence always triggered the need for something stronger. He unscrewed the mocha pot and poured water from a glass decanter, spooned in the coffee, twisted the pot back together, and lit the gas burner.

Behind him, the Colonel pressed the issue. "We haven't seen you since the incident."

"Is that what you are all calling it? The incident?" That horrible night when all hell had broken loose around him and his family at the discovery that Annamarie Steinhauser was his daughter? Or was the Colonel referring to how he had used Angelo's former chief engineer to spy on ministry activities?

Angelo stared at the old man's back, daring him to turn around. *Say the word and I'll pull off the gloves.* The Colonel, however, seemed content to gaze at Angelo's empty desk chair. The coffee boiled, and Angelo pushed himself away from the sideboard. He poured two cups and placed them on the tray.

"Your mother wants you to—"

"Face the firing squad," Angelo said. "Yes, I know. Is she taking special requests for my last meal?"

The Colonel was silent for a moment. "I told her you would get to it when you're ready."

Was that sympathy? Some sort of attempt at empathy?

"But she is very concerned about this…this rumour about you and, well, the general's widow."

No, it was the old man fishing. Angelo forced the corners of his mouth to turn up as he handed a cup to his father. He stood over him. It was ironic considering it was the Colonel who had introduced Angelo to Gina Conti. Now the old man was concerned about a liaison? There was one, true. Gina was working on assessing Angelo's position on how to make good on the promise he'd made to the Steinhausers on his last visit there. If there was anyone who could help him, it was "the woman who made men," as his father had so aptly described her. And the idea that Gina might be working on Angelo's "making" likely bothered the Colonel more than anything.

Let him squirm. It was time for Angelo to fish. "And I thought you had come to apologise."

The Colonel frowned. "For what?"

Angelo took a seat behind his desk and waited for his father to concede. He did not. "Fine, let's talk about the incident. Not that incident—my wife and my son are none of your business. I will handle it the way I feel it needs handling. I'm talking about the other incident. I'm talking about Stefano Accosi. I was told you made him MFE's new head engineer."

The Colonel pursed his lips and steepled his hands. "That... was business."

Angelo laughed, astounded. "Business? Really?" Stefano had not only been the one friend Angelo thought he'd had but the best damned chief engineer he knew. "You sent my most trusted man to sabotage the ministry's project."

"You were going to undermine the largest project in this province, and someone had to stop you," his father said. "The only thing you wanted was to downscale the reservoir. Stefano proved to us that the locals are prepared to sell out."

"Stefano sold out," Angelo snapped. "That's the only person who sold out. And willingly, I might add."

The Colonel narrowed his eyes. "Why were you in Reschen Valley last month?"

"Who told you that?" Angelo laughed bitterly. "Wait. Of course. Your spies."

Angelo rose and went to the window, everything outside veiled beneath the sheen of muslin.

"You saw the girl's mother," the Colonel said. "Did you go see them about Annamarie, or were you there to discuss the fact that the Steinhausers are on our list of dissenters?"

Angelo rubbed his neck. There was silence for a long moment.

The Colonel moved behind him. "I understand, Angelo. Family is family. It must have been quite the shock for you to discover that you have an illegitimate daughter and that she was…" He cleared his throat. "Right under your nose."

"You took her in! You also knew that, after Marco met her in the Reschen Valley, I had forbidden him to see her."

"You have your way. I have mine."

Angelo bristled.

"That is what you told me a long time ago, remember?" His father was moving, his voice coming from somewhere else in the room. "Also, you did stab Stefano Accosi in the back the day you agreed to blame him for Gleno Dam break."

Angelo whirled to see the man standing over the model of the Reschen Lake reservoir, adjusted to MFE's project scale now. "You gave me no choice."

"I gave you no choice," the Colonel mused as he moved something on the model. "We always have a choice. You still have to learn to live with yours." He strode back to Angelo's desk and leaned on it. "Perhaps you will learn to make better ones in the future."

Angelo balled his hands into fists. "Why are you here?"

"I'm irritated." The Colonel sat down again. "I received word that we must, once more, notify the locals of the official scale, as well as present our draft of the water rights, fishing rights, road rights, railroad plans to and from the Reschen Valley, and so on. Your people up there will have an opportunity to protest anything they want. Again. They haven't been able to collect themselves thus far. What makes anyone think they will this time? Especially after Stefano has already managed to help us acquire the most immediate lands that will be affected?"

"Because it's the law."

The Colonel scoffed. "Yes, the one you helped put through. The one I'm going to make sure gets amended. This project will be staked out by next year. You can take my word for it." His father straightened, his look boring into Angelo. "I'm prepared to offer the Steinhausers a substantial amount for their farm if they agree not to share the details with anyone else in their community."

"They won't take it."

"You seem so sure."

"And you seem to believe that everyone can simply be bought out."

Blinking, the Colonel said, "But they can."

"Not the Steinhausers."

The Colonel crossed his leg, brushed something off his suit coat. "The husband. He's German. I mean, really German, not Tyrolean. From Nuremberg? He had a house there. Shame he sold it."

Angelo did not reply.

His father studied him. "Where is the girl? Annamarie?"

"What does it matter?"

"Well, when she was living with your mother and me, she was attending university. Perhaps the Steinhausers would be interested if Annamarie could continue her studies. Acting, wasn't it?" He laughed a little. "She certainly did put on the best show with us, didn't she?"

Angelo doubted Annamarie had ever truly fooled his father.

Rising, the Colonel shrugged. "Anyway, if you do know how to get ahold of her, find out whether she is still pursuing that chimera of hers. But maybe there's a way we could help her."

"This is my affair, not yours."

"Angelo, you have a lot of reconciliation to do. You can't just stick your head in the sand and hope it all goes away. Family is family."

"Coming from you—"

The Colonel placed a hand on Angelo's shoulder. "Yes, coming from me. Especially from me, Angelo. Take your father's word. You cannot hide away forever. And"—he dropped his arm and jerked a head out the window—"you cannot simply replace your old family with a new one."

The Colonel gave him a hard look, then strode out.

Angelo sank against the edge of the desk. What did the Colonel know about family? Nothing.

4

GRAUN, JUNE 1938

The air was saturated by the scent of freshly mown grass and wildflowers. Katharina's bare arms itched beneath the stray bits of hay. She stopped to wipe the sweat off her brow and pushed her headscarf back, damp hair sticking to her neck. She considered cutting it all off. In the magazines that lay around in Jutta's inn, women were wearing their hair shorter, shoulder length, rather than long and coifed at the back of the neck. But that was an Italian look.

She leaned on the pitchfork and watched Florian and the boys piling hay into the V-carts. She lifted the canteen from the ground, unscrewed the top, and took a long gulp. The water was lukewarm. From where she stood, she could see the roofs of the small hamlet and the gravel road that rose up over the ridge and to their *Hof*. A warm wind rounded up dust devils, and just as quickly, a second gust demolished them with a downward stroke. She replaced the cap on the canteen and looked south. The Ortlers bordered the horizon, but the sky above the peaks were hazy yellow. The sands of the Sahara were coming right for them. The *foehn* lifted grains of dust and carried them north over the African continent, over the Mediterranean and all the way north to the Reschen Valley. The wind would blow hot and oppressive for the next day or two, and that sand—all of it—would reach the walls of their mountains and drop onto their crops, onto their meadows and fields, coat the vegetables in her garden, and the animals' fur, feathers, and hides. And then it would rain for days, but that sand would take ages to wash away.

Katharina whistled, and Manuel looked up first, shaded his eyes, and waved. In those simple movements, she saw herself in him. Blond and gangly and sweet natured. He was reserved like she was—even more unassuming. Next to Manuel, Bernd was pure Thaler, just like her grandfather, but with Florian's looks. He glanced at his brother, then at her, this very gesture already signalling impatience. What did she want? She had interrupted his workflow. She pointed to the sky. Bernd frowned before calling to his father. She couldn't hear the words though. Florian also looked up, nodded, and waved to her. She had to hurry and get this last row together, or the hay would be sacrificed to the wind.

Nothing good ever comes from the south

That was what Jutta always said. It was her bitter joke. It wasn't true though, not when Katharina considered some of the Italian people who had come here. There were plenty of the Tyrolean farmers profiting from extra hands, especially after losing fathers, sons, and husbands to the war. Some of the transplanted families were victims of the circumstances themselves. Border patrols and the authorities excluded. The postmaster, Matteo, for example, had obviously been punished when he'd been assigned the post office in Graun. Katharina imagined he was a dissender and that was why. She actually quite liked him.Then there were people like Iris. Katharina remembered meeting her the first time. Iris had hoped for a teaching appointment near Venice or Verona, even nearer to her own village. She certainly had not expected to be sent to the hinterlands. But Iris had found love here, married Dr Hanny, and Katharina was happy to call her a friend.

Katharina could hear Jutta now. *Iris is all right. For an Italian.*

When the wind picked up, it sounded like a far-off steam locomotive, charging unhindered up the narrow valley. Florian and the boys were furiously trying to weigh the hay down before it could blow away. Manuel leapt off after securing one side of the tarpaulin and dashed down to the barnyard. Florian waved at Katharina and indicated he was taking the hay in. He pulled on the oxen's lead and aimed for the back of the barn, where he could unload it into the loft. The pile Katharina had managed for their easy picking started swirling around her as the wind charged up the slope. She stood above it, trying to keep it together.

Bernd met her and began laying out stones from his cone-shaped basket just as Manuel returned with another tarpaulin. The southern horizon was turning into a churning, living thing. Dust began to settle on the fir trees along the southern ridges, turning them ashen orange. The steeple of St Anna's chapel on the ridge across from them was hidden in the haze.

"I need something heavier to keep this down," Bernd said after placing the tarp over her pile. "We won't get this in."

Manuel took off towards the edge of the wood. A moment later, he was dragging two large logs, one hitched under each arm. They arranged the weights, then shifted their attention to the *Hof*.

The empty milk canisters, piled up on the drive earlier, were rolling about like scattered chickens. Another strong gust sent Katharina's skirt flapping wildly over her knees. Manuel helped her secure the house. The windows. The barn. The animals. In the meantime, Bernd helped Florian get the last of the hay in.

Later, as the wind whipped and howled outside, Katharina set out the midday meal. She was about to call Florian and the boys to come to the table, when someone pounded on the front door.

Katharina hurried, wondering who would be out in this weather, and threw it open to Patricia Ritsch. Squinting, their neighbour held her headscarf down with one hand and a letter pressed to her breast with the other.

"This came for you." Patricia thrust the envelope at Katharina. "I just made it back from Graun, and Jutta wanted to make sure you got this." She looked up at the sky. "Rain's coming. All this dust is going to turn into sludge and just leave a stain everywhere you look."

Patricia ducked out from under the eaves and hurried around the corner of the house, leaving Katharina to call out her appreciation to her neighbour's back.

Katharina closed the door and looked at the envelope. Tante Rosa's address. Innsbruck.

Heart lodged in her throat, Katharina tore open the letter and unfolded the two pages.

My dear cousin,

I found Annamarie. She is well. I want those to be the first words you read to ease your aching heart. I do have to say, however, that the child has no idea what she is on about or with whom she is truly dealing with. As you said, she is young and naïve. She's skinny but not on the streets, as you might have feared.

Indeed, she is working in a small theatre, and not as an actress either. From what I could gather, Annamarie is helping to clean, keep things orderly, etc. I worry about the security of the position. The owner is not a Gentile, you understand. I'm sure you've heard of the Nuremberger laws. They are being severely enforced here too. Annamarie is, however, rooming with a very well-known actress in this city, by the name of Elisabeth von Brandt. I must say, it is rather admirable that your daughter has made such a connection. The von Brandt family is one of most powerful in the city, if not the most powerful. They are loyal party members and, from that information, I will have you draw your own conclusions. Annamarie, you see, has expressed an unwillingness to return home or to have contact with her family again. I have offered to take her in, but even I am apparently too close to the situation (which I find utterly ridiculous).

I understand this part of my letter must pain you. I promise, however, to keep an eye on her in these very uncertain times. As you know, there is talk of the Sudetenland and of expanding the Reich's reach in order to make room for us Germans. The only reason I can think of uniting South Tyrol to the rest of the Reich is, dear cousin, so that your daughter is at least back "home." I will write if anything further develops. I can only imagine how much this distresses you. I wish I knew what this was all about, but neither you nor Annamarie seem inclined to share the details with me, which makes me a rather impotent advisor.

Katharina folded the letter and put it in her pocket. Florian and the boys came down the stairs, and they ate their midday meal, without speaking, amid the rattling and banging of the insistent wind. By the time they finished, the roofs, the outside walls and windows, and even the letters of the wood-cut sign above the door, which read *Katharinahof*, were caked in a yellow-orange dust. When the boys pulled out the deck of cards and began playing, Katharina handed Florian the letter and put on the coffee. What was coming from the north—the storm gathering beyond the Italian-Austrian border—sounded just as bad, if not worse.

The day after the rain, the wind turned and brought a freak snowstorm from the northwest. The snow lasted only a day but caused such a mess on the *Hof* that it was not until the end of the week that Katharina found time to get down to Graun. She nearly ran straight into Iris Hanny coming out of the milliner's store. She was dressed in a fur-trimmed coat, her hair freshly coiffed beneath a wool hat.

"*Come stai,*" Iris greeted her. "It's been too long, dear friend."

Katharina hugged her. "We've been better. That storm! It's set us back. We can't take the animals up to the pastures as planned. I imagine there's still snow piled all the way up to the hut."

"It will be fine," Iris tut-tutted. "Dr Hanny says warm weather is heading our way again."

"Where are you off to? You look beautiful."

"Friends of ours are getting married tomorrow, and we're all here in town for a little get-together."

"So Dr Hanny is with you? How is he?"

Iris, a sly smile spreading across her face, pointed to the Il Dante, the Italian guesthouse. "Frederick's playing bocce with some of the gentlemen."

"In this cold?"

Iris laughed. "He brought cigars, and they're celebrating. I imagine the grappa is keeping them warm. We're invited to the dinner tonight with visiting guests." Iris nodded at the bundle in Katharina's hand. "What have you here?"

Katharina unwrapped the top layer and showed Iris the bricks of butter. Each one had a beautiful pattern pressed into it, one with hearts, others with flowers. "Jutta orders them on a regular basis now."

Iris looked up, her eyes alight. "You are really putting your ideas to use, aren't you? The dried flowers, the herbs. Your cheese wheels are the fanciest around."

Katharina smiled. "It took me a while, but yes. I've got a real production line going." She laughed and reached into her bag, retrieving a hand-labelled packet of hay-flower tea. "These too."

"They're very pretty." Iris looked at the butter again. "Did Florian make the moulds?"

Katharina nodded, and then Iris placed a hand on hers.

"How many more do you have? These, with the hearts?"

Katharina shrugged. "Maybe a dozen or so?"

"What if I ask the wedding party whether they would like to

have your butter for the reception dinner? I'll ask them to talk to the owner of the Il Dante."

"What a nice idea. But if they say yes, we can't let Jutta find out." Katharina glanced over her shoulder at the Post Inn to make her point. What she saw made her turn and face it head on.

"What is it, Katharina?"

She pointed past the garden fence and into Jutta's yard. "There's a hole in the landscape."

"A hole in the landscape?"

But Katharina was already marching to the back gate, and only as she neared it did she see the fallen apple tree, already sawed up and stacked against the house in manageable chunks. Where the tree's roots had been, the earth lay gaping towards the sky. The sight of it almost made her cry.

At her elbow, Iris said, "The wind. It was very, very bad the other day. And then the heavy snow on those branches. It must have knocked it down."

"More like yanked it out."

There was a tap above them, and Katharina glanced up to see Jutta standing in the kitchen window. She then appeared at the back door. Katharina gave her a sympathetic look, and Jutta indicated the remains of the apple tree, hands on her hips, dish towel hanging from one. Her black-and-grey hair was swept back in a disarrayed bun.

In greeting, Katharina said, "Under that tree, that's where Florian and I first met. When the children were throwing apples at Alois."

"That's right. I almost forgot about that." Jutta crossed her arms and looked Iris up and down. "Good day."

"Good day," Iris replied in German.

To Katharina, Jutta said, "Well, they've been at it again with Alois."

"Who?"

"Some Balilla boys, young cadets." She threw daggers with her

54

glance at Iris. "Been taunting my Alois, calling him Luigi." She jerked her chin at Katharina. "Bernd came to his rescue."

Katharina was taken aback. "He did?"

Jutta's eyebrows jerked up. "Pummelled two of them good. The little Fascist Walsch bastards deserved it though."

"You know how I feel about violence," Katharina muttered.

Jutta smirked at Iris.

To change the subject, Katharina lifted her package. "I've brought the butter."

"Well, come in then." Jutta disappeared through the door again.

Iris shifted. "I have to go. I'm expected—"

"Nonsense," Jutta's voice barked from inside. "Iris, you'll come in for tea. Or coffee. Or whatever it is you drink."

Katharina took Iris by the elbow and gave her an encouraging smile. The women went up the stoop and were just about to go in, when Katharina heard a man's voice calling.

"Lucia! Lucia! Sweetheart, where are you?" It was the *podestá*. Ghirardelli came around the corner of the guesthouse, heading towards the churchyard, hands cupped around his mouth. He walked right past Iris and Katharina and into the cemetery opposite.

Jutta poked her head back out, and Katharina threw her and Iris each a questioning look. The three women stepped to the landing, and each stretched up on tiptoe to peer over the cemetery wall. Katharina could only make out Ghirardelli's hat and his deeply furrowed brow. When he looked up, he noticed them, raised his fez, and came back around to Jutta's back fence.

"*Come stai?*" he greeted. "Goat?" he asked in German.

"Goat?" Jutta and Katharina asked together.

"*Sí.* I, goat. You, goat?"

Jutta looked first astounded, then amused, and Katharina turned her face away. It was impossible not to smile.

Iris spoke slowly in Italian, as if to an idiot. "Who is a goat? Or what do you mean? Whose goat?"

Ghirardelli spoke fast, but clarity dawned on Katharina. The men in the valley joked about the prefect's beloved Lucia. She had always believed he was in love with some woman she'd never met, but Jutta had once told her that Lisl Roeschen, who had a direct view into Ghirardelli's garden, saw the prefect swooning over a white goat, milking her with the reverence of a lover. At Jutta's retelling, Katharina had laughed, and now she felt that very same tittering bubbling up in her when Iris attempted to keep a straight face.

"Lucia comes all the way from Istria," Iris announced importantly in German. "And the little white goat makes the best cheese."

Jutta clicked her tongue and pulled a face. Katharina snorted with laughter. The only thing that made her straighten herself out was Ghirardelli's genuine distress. There was no hint of embarrassment or suspicion that he was becoming the laughingstock of this little party on the stoop.

"I not see your goat," Jutta said in Italian.

Katharina dropped her hand away from her mouth to reveal a sympathetic look. "Me either. I'm sorry."

Ghirardelli smiled uncertainly, then touched his fez and walked on.

Jutta jerked her head in the direction of the door, and the three scurried through into the steaming kitchen. Katharina fell against the kitchen door as they doubled over in laughter. Iris and Jutta cooed Lucia's name over and over, between peals of merriment. Katharina's sides ached.

See, she wanted to say. *See? We really can all get along.*

"And?" Jutta held the kettle of water above Katharina's cup as if to hold the tea hostage until her question was answered.

Katharina shook her head.

Jutta poured. "She'll come around."

Katharina bit her bottom lip and glanced at Iris in apology for the way Jutta was purposefully excluding her from the conversation.

"She will," Jutta stressed. "They always come home. Like cows." She topped off Katharina's mug and then moved behind Iris, who covered her cup.

Iris held Katharina's look and mouthed, *An-na-ma-rie?*

Katharina nodded.

Iris looked up at Jutta, who still hovered dangerously over her head. "Thank you, Jutta. No more. I am expected at a dinner. I'm already late, but thank you."

"You have that wedding, of course. Exclusive party." Jutta waved the kettle away and moved towards the stove, then into the pantry, where she scolded Iris. "You know, in this valley— amongst our people—everyone is always invited to everything. That's the way things are done."

"As if I can control what other people do," Iris whispered in Italian. "Jutta wouldn't come anyway." She looked questioningly at Katharina. "What about your daughter?"

"Annamarie's in Innsbruck. Tante Rosa found her. She's well, but she won't have anything to do with me." She had told Iris everything after Angelo Grimani had shown up in Arlund that one day. It was the only way Katharina had managed to relieve some of her distress.

Jutta returned with a few dried figs and sat down between them. She pulled her mug to her and blew into her tea. "I'm old, but I'm not deaf," she muttered.

"Surely the border will open soon," Iris said in a normal voice. "Italy and the Third Reich will work it all out, and it will be like in the old days. We'll all be allies and free to come and go."

Jutta clicked her tongue and slammed her cup onto the saucer.

Iris looked at both of them. "Did I say something wrong?"

"The Italians understand their own version of history," Jutta scoffed. "Hitler is no Kaiser Franz Josef either."

Katharina rolled her eyes.

Jutta rose. "I have to milk the cow."

Iris also stood and reached for her coat. "I really do have to go. Thank you so much for the tea, Jutta."

"I'll come with you," Katharina said to Jutta. She saw Iris to the door and kissed her on both cheeks, then followed Jutta out to the barn.

"You make up your mind?" Jutta asked. "You know, about Maria?"

The teaching, she meant, the clandestine German lessons. Katharina was about to answer, when she heard the muffled bleat of a goat outside. Voices followed—young men's voices—from behind the tall fence at the back of the chicken coop. She stepped out and listened. They spoke in German.

"Come on. He's left ages ago," one whispered.

Another, "Come on..."

"Hurry up!"

That one was Bernd.

Before Katharina could peer through the cracks in the boards, she knew it was Ghirardelli's goat, the one the prefect had been looking for earlier, that the boys were herding along. A snow-white flash of fur and the pungent smell of the animal confirmed it. Then three sets of legs in *Lederhosen* and muddy boots. Katharina recognised Andreas Ritsch first, their neighbour's firstborn. As the boys scurried down the narrow path between the cemetery and Jutta's garden with Ghirardelli's goat between them, Katharina picked out Ulrich Noggler, then her son.

Before Katharina could call after them, Jutta poked her side and put a finger to her lips.

"Follow me."

Hurrying out of the yard, they moved up the alleyway in the direction of the lakes. Katharina dreaded finding out what the boys were up to. Bernd's last arrest had left the family in debt.

"They're going to the Nogglers'," Jutta said at Katharina's elbow.

Before the blacksmith's barn, the two women hung back. The boys opened the gate to Ulrich's yard and tugged the goat in by the halter. The animal bleated again before disappearing behind the hedges. Bent over, Jutta and Katharina slid along the fence and peered through the branches.

The boys were muttering between themselves, but Katharina heard Andreas say, "You do it."

The three of them had circled Lucia, and Andreas had a knife in his hand, the type used to whittle sticks and slice small branches. He was holding it out to Ulrich, but it was Bernd who reached for it.

Katharina grabbed the prickly hedge and shook its branches. "What in God's name?"

All three boys sprang away from the goat, and the animal skittered off towards the gate but came up short when Jutta blocked their way. Rushing into the yard, Katharina took hold of Lucia's halter.

Bernd was staring wide eyed, his face gradually pink, then red.

"Have you boys lost your minds?" Katharina demanded. "Bernd!"

"What do you think you're doing?" Jutta cried at Andreas and grabbed for the knife.

But he twisted away from her and held the weapon high in the air before spitting on the ground. His saliva landed on Jutta's left shoe. "Mind your own business, you nosy hag."

"Bernd Steinhauser," Katharina hissed. Her son took a step

back. "Shame on you. Your father just paid a fortune for your last act of defiance."

Ulrich and Andreas both sniggered. The prefect's goat skittered behind Katharina, bleating as if to scold the boys or dare them to come after her again.

"We weren't going to kill it," Bernd said to her.

"No?" Jutta addressed Andreas. "It looked to me as if you were going to butcher the creature."

"Honest, Mrs Hanny," Ulrich said shakily, "we were just going to nick it and use the blood for…" He was easing his way to the gate.

Jutta grabbed hold of Ulrich's arm. "What were you going to use the blood for?"

Ulrich shook his head, his eyes wide and fearful.

Forgetting the goat, Katharina marched to her son and grabbed his shirt collar. Not a day in her life had she ever raised a hand to her children, but when he tried to wrench away and make a dash for the gate, she itched to thrash him right there in the blacksmith's garden.

Andreas glared. "Let go of him."

Katharina was about to ask who he thought he was giving her orders, when Bernd tried to pull out of her grasp. She clutched harder but turned her anger on Toni Ritsch's son. "This is all you, Andreas Ritsch. You should be ashamed of yourself."

"The Walscher killed our dog," Bernd cried. "They deserve it!"

Katharina whirled on her son and shook him. "And Ulrich's family? Do you know what would happen to them if you were to do this in their garden?"

"We weren't going to kill it. I swear," Ulrich sobbed again. He tore out of Jutta's grasp and burst out the gate as if demons were on his heels.

"Sissy!" Andreas laughed after him. "Come back here, you sissy!"

"We'll deal with you later," Katharina snapped to Andreas. "Your father will hear about this."

Andreas looked Katharina up and down. "My father doesn't care two licks about Ghirardelli's stupid goat. He doesn't care what you think, either, you Italian lover." He scoffed at Jutta. "And you? Why don't you go home and get your mongoloid son to shut his mouth?"

Jutta's face flushed bright red. "How dare you?"

Andreas laughed. "You're nobodies. A stupid old cow whose husband went mad." He glared at Katharina once more. "And you don't even belong to this valley. Got nobody left here. Why don't you pack up your things and go to Germany?"

He dashed for the gate, and neither Katharina nor Jutta tried to stop him. All that was left was his pounding footsteps on the cobblestones and the sound of something liquid hitting the paving stones. The goat was relieving herself.

Chilled by Andreas's words, Katharina wrenched Bernd to face her. "Your father will put an end to this and whatever you have with these boys."

Jutta snatched the rope and led the *podestá's* goat out into the alleyway. Katharina shoved Bernd in front of her and marched him in the opposite direction.

"You don't fool me, Bernd Steinhauser," Jutta chided behind their backs.

When Katharina looked over her shoulder, Jutta pointed at Bernd.

"He's a long way from being as rotten as that Ritsch boy," she said.

"My father did not fight in the Great War to get shit on by a bunch of Italians," Bernd shouted. "Better a Nazi than a traitor Fascist like my sister."

It happened fast. Katharina spun her son around and, with all the strength she had, slapped him so hard he stumbled backwards. "You!" She raised a shaking finger at him. "You should have been the one to run away and leave us in peace!"

Bernd straightened himself, touched his face, and gave Katharina a look of such pain it nearly took her breath away.

"All right, Mutti," he said quietly. "You'll be sorry. I'm going to make sure of it."

He pushed past Jutta and her, headed in the opposite direction.

5

INNSBRUCK, JUNE 1938

After paying the utility bills, the grocery money she owed Lisi, and the rent, Annamarie was left with exactly eight Reichsmark to her name until the following month, and this paired with the bad news that Herr Baumgärtner would be cutting her hours by half. Twelve hours a week was going to get her nowhere. She inserted the key into the apartment door, ready to crawl into bed and bury herself beneath the blankets, but the apartment was already unlocked.

Lisi stood in the kitchen doorway as Annamarie walked in. "Franz is here."

Annamarie slumped against the door. "I just want to go to bed."

"Franz," Lisi called back into the kitchen. "Annamarie's home."

A chair slid across the linoleum floor, and Franz rose with his Hitler salute when Annamarie came in. He was dressed in the brown uniform, and suddenly Marco Grimani flashed before her. Like Franz in Austria, Marco had led his local paramilitary group under Mussolini's government. His and Franz's features might be completely different, but Franz was just as enthusiastic with the training he received as leader of the Hitler Jugend troop. She wondered whether this was what every young man between Germany and Italy did these days. Not Sepp though. Not the barkeep at the Iron Rooster. So maybe not everyone, but just about.

Lisi popped open a bottle of *Sekt*. "We're celebrating."

"Are we?" Annamarie sank onto one of the seats.

Lisi poured wine into the teacup Annamarie had left on the kitchen counter that morning. She seemed to enjoy being uncouth—something that must have occurred the moment she broke out of the von Brandts' cocooned and blue-blooded world.

"Franz has quite some news," Lisi said.

"That's right," Franz said. "I've joined the SA and have been assigned to security detail for Gauleiter Hofer. He's arriving next week."

Annamarie did not know who that was and shrugged, unimpressed.

Franz narrowed his eyes. "Gauleiter Hofer? He's responsible for all of Tyrol and Vorarlberg."

"I guess that's a big deal to you," Annamarie said. "Congratulations." She took a sip of the wine, but it tasted flat. Her bedroom was just around the corner, just a few steps away. Was he finished with his bragging yet?

"There's something else." Lisi tipped her head at her brother.

Franz got his footing beneath him again, cleared his throat, and said lightly, "I'm engaged."

Annamarie looked up from her cup. "Engaged?" A few months ago, when she'd first met the von Brandts at the Iron Rooster, Franz had been flirting with her, his hands all over her, and now he was engaged? She hadn't even known he was seriously seeing anyone.

"Margit Rainer." Franz positioned his chair to face Annamarie. "I'd like you to meet her."

"Me? What in heaven's for?"

"Because she might have a job for you."

"What does she do?"

"She's head of the Innsbruck division of the BDM."

Annamarie frowned. "The BDM?"

"Bund Deutscher Mädel. It's the League of German Girls, like the Hitler Jugend but, you know, for girls."

Annamarie scoffed. "I'm nineteen. Hardly a girl any longer."

Lisi cleared her throat and gave her a look.

"Fine. Seventeen." Annamarie was indignant. "And even so, too old to be marching around, doing gymnastics, and singing with a bunch of little girls. What could I possibly do for the BDM?" She regretted the question immediately.

Franz crossed his arms, looking satisfied. "Margit is heading the new Faith and Beauty Society. It's for women ages seventeen to twenty-one years old, and the program will be better than a university education. You can take part in anything that interests you, in anything that you're talented in." He laughed a little and looked at them nervously. "Women with talents and strengths to help the German nation—that's what the society will produce. Strong women with a purpose, with a role."

It sounded more like a factory. Annamarie looked at Lisi with disbelief.

"Tell her what she'd be doing," Lisi urged.

"Margit needs someone to set up and run the theatre and acting department."

Lisi looked expectantly at Annamarie.

"Why don't you do it?" Annamarie asked her.

Lisi scoffed. "Because I have a job—a good job—and I've outgrown all that." She looked at Franz. "What? Stop that. I'm not interested."

"What makes you think I would be?" Annamarie asked.

"Because," Lisi sighed, "you have the experience with the, you know…" She waved a hand downwards. She was referring to Annamarie's activities with the Fascist youth group in Bolzano.

Annamarie stood and dumped the wine down the sink, leaned

against the counter, and faced her. When Lisi had asked about Marco Grimani, there was only one way to respond in order for Annamarie to keep her secret *her* secret. Marco, she had told Lisi, had introduced her to the women's Fascist youth group, that was true and simple enough, and she had taken part in order to attend the free university. Lisi had not left it at that. She'd said that Annamarie had cried when she mentioned his name the night of the party—the night Annamarie had drunk too much. She then flipped the story and told Lisi how her youth group leader, Filipa, had been betrayed by Marco.

"It was traumatic for all of us," Annamarie had explained. "They were engaged, and he was, well, you know…"

"Did he…did he try something with you?"

One hard meaningful look was all Annamarie had managed. Lisi could interpret it any way she wanted—and when Lisi had sighed and patted her hand, Annamarie knew she was off the hook.

Lisi grabbed her by the wrist now. "This thing with the BDM is my idea. I thought you'd like being in charge—that's the first thing. And the next thing, well… Go on, Franz. You tell her."

Franz grinned. "Margit's just returned from leadership training in Brunswick. She's the district leader. Margit is recruiting section group leaders, for hire."

"It's a real job, Annamarie," Lisi interrupted. "Group leaders get two hundred Reichsmark a month."

Two hundred Reichsmark! Annamarie sat up straight and looked from Lisi to Franz and back to Lisi. Her mind reeled with the list of things she could afford with ten times her current salary. She could get out of here, for starters, and begin anew, get her stories straight, and maybe finally make some headway with the acting.

They were waiting for her, watching her, their eyes shining bright, as if listening in on Annamarie's plans in her head.

"When can I meet her?" she asked.

If anyone could have been the perfect poster model for the pure-blooded Aryan woman, Margit Rainer was it. Dressed in a slim skirt and fitted blazer with the BDM insignia on her right shoulder, Margit was an athletically fit, blue-eyed blonde with a welcoming and confident smile. When Margit met Annamarie in the entryway of the new BDM headquarters, Annamarie could not help smiling back. Margit's warm and accessible nature was in direct contrast to the immaculate and starched uniform.

She invited Annamarie on a tour of the building and its grounds. "Isn't this house marvellous? It used to belong to a state-court judge, and now it's all ours. You know…" She gazed at Annamarie, decided something, and put a warm hand on Annamarie's shoulder to steer her into another room, one with a Baroque ceiling and oil paintings of statesmen on the floor and on the walls.

Three men in HJ uniforms were removing a portrait. Three other paintings were leaning against the walls.

"We've been waiting for years for this opportunity," Margit said.

"To take down these paintings?"

Margit laughed. She also did not offer any further explanation.

Annamarie followed her to the end of the salon and entered the next room. She was startled by the open space and how it had been transformed into a gymnasium. It reminded her of the one in Bolzano, near the city hall. Here, young girls were doing all sorts of gymnastics on thick mats, jumping the pommel horse, swinging from rings hanging from the ceilings, doing somersaults and cartwheels. When Annamarie had taken part in the Giovani Italiane, the girls were fit, but these here? They were like machines. Trim, fit, muscular, each one. They were like the young warriors of ancient Sparta.

"I thought I would get you started with the younger girls." Margit interrupted her thoughts. "The ones who will be transitioning into the BDM Faith and Beauty Society in the autumn. In this way, you can get to know them. We've got the rest of the summer to organise the new curriculum, to get everything on track and running smoothly. That's my job now, to make the transitions flawless and to establish the programmes."

At the shriek of a whistle, each BDM girl somehow landed out of the air and onto her feet and positioned herself almost immediately in an orderly line before a tough-looking woman. She could not have been older than twenty-five, but her severely scraped-back dark-blonde hair lent her a matronly air.

Annamarie had been right. The Faith and Beauty factory was what this was going to be. Yet she had to admire it. It was impressive. Nobody in this lineup giggled, as Annamarie had done with her friends in Bolzano. Each was serious and attentive. The discipline was impressive…and intimidating.

Margit was waiting for her. Her smile had been replaced by an expression of pride, of daring. "I'd like to start you off as this troop's leader."

This troop? These girls would laugh her out of the room. Annamarie weakly gestured to the woman leading the girls out. "What's wrong with her?"

"That's Hanni," Margit said. "She's getting married next month, and, you know, you can't be a wife, mother, and a career woman. It's the rules. Anyone who gets married must resign."

Annamarie frowned and followed Margit through the Baroque hall. "Aren't you and Franz getting married soon?"

"We're engaged, yes. But I'm only twenty. I told him he has to wait at least three or four years. I just received this position, and I want to be able to spend some time working for the nation, be a part of all this. He understands. He's doing the same thing. Besides, Franz is working his way to officer status. We said it would be better for both of us if we achieve these things first."

Annamarie pictured Franz and Margit designing their futures as they would the architectural plan of a house.

Margit was hurrying Annamarie into the next part of the building. "My idea is to have you work with the current leader and her troop, and then, in the fall, you can take the girls over as they transition into the Faith and Beauty Society. And if you work hard and prove yourself, I'll put you in for a promotion and training for January in Brunswick next year. How does that sound?"

This was not quite what Franz had talked to Annamarie about. Certainly one thing was missing. "Do I get paid as a troop leader with the younger girls too?"

Margit smiled. "Of course. One hundred twenty Reichsmark a month to start."

It was still a lot more than twenty a month, or ten, now that Herr Baumgärtner had reduced her work schedule.

The tour continued whilst Margit rattled off the anticipated Faith and Beauty Society's weekly routine, an entire curriculum devoted to a well-rounded education and training, including literature, sports, homemaking, fashion designing, the arts, and even nursing. A special area of the house was set up for "home evenings," where the young women would cook, bake, learn to set dinner party tables, dress appropriately, and keep house in general. They would rotate the groups Mondays through Fridays. On Saturdays it was time to look after one's health and fitness. Strenuous outdoor activities, including track and field, marching, hiking, swimming, and gymnastics, took place, and each woman could choose what she wanted to specialise in. Sundays were usually dedicated to national music, folklore and culture, and race education. The remaining days were for the young women to choose from a variety of activities that interested them.

"Any questions?" Margit finished.

Annamarie knew she was gaping. "It's truly amazing."

Margit laughed, obviously pleased by the effect. Annamarie

looked at the pretty woman again, thought of how easy it must have been for Franz to choose her. Margit on his side would probably further his career with the Nazi party. That he had ever flirted with Annamarie at the Iron Rooster seemed remotely ridiculous now.

"Are you from Innsbruck, Margit?" she asked.

"Yes. My family is one of the better established here, meaning we have a long history in the city. Just like the von Brandts. Franz and I have known each other for ages, but it wasn't until we were in Brunswick that we really..." She winked. Her eyes stayed on Annamarie, and then she took in a breath. "Can I trust you with a secret?"

"Of course."

"My brothers and I have been active with the party for years, but underground. That's what I was referring to earlier when I said we've been waiting. My family have been National Socialist Democrats since the beginning, but we weren't allowed to take part or be active here in Austria." Margit put an arm around Annamarie's shoulder. "I mean, it's not a terribly interesting secret now, I suppose. I'm simply excited to finally do what we've been hoping to do for years, and that is to create a Reich, a glorious nation. The Führer is leading us there. Trust me. We will be the greatest power on earth!"

Margit's enthusiasm—not necessarily her words—drove Annamarie to happily follow her to a small but neat room. There was a desk next to a sun-filled window. Stacks of papers, files, and evenly spaced books were arranged in what Annamarie guessed to be in all the right places. They sat opposite each other as Margit launched into showing Annamarie the organisation's structure and hierarchy. The league was set up in two distinct groups. The younger girls received their education over the Jungmädelbund. From ages fourteen to eighteen, the girls were then encouraged to transfer into the BDM.

"One idea," Margit explained, "is to also have all the girls do mandatory land service, such as helping harvest on a farm, or plant, or help with dairy production or with cooking preserves." Margit paused. "Franz says you have an agricultural background?"

"My family has a dairy farm in South Tyrol."

Margit leaned back and grinned. "South Tyrol? Now I understand that accent."

Annamarie bit the side of her cheek.

"It's sweet...I mean, very exotic. How did you manage to—"

"I have an aunt here in Innsbruck," Annamarie rushed. "My parents wanted to make sure that I was on the north side of the border. We don't know what's going to happen with the pact between Italy and the Reich..."

Margit looked somewhat relieved. "So your people are pro-German. That's wonderful. South Tyrol will reunite with us. It is their duty, and thanks to the pro-Germans there, it will happen."

Annamarie sensed that the sentiment was more hyperbole than genuine commitment. In her months in Innsbruck, she had learned that—very much like back home—there was an even split between the Tyroleans here. Some fervently hoped to reunite the old province's territories, but Annamarie had seen how the few "Italian" migrants, who trickled in from the south, were treated by their "fellow" Tyroleans. Like rubbish. Like the worst kind of invader. She had heard men and women complain that the "southerners" took away jobs and homes, and in such lean times, what were they even hoping to find up here? One group had even cornered an elderly couple and heckled them, telling them to go back to where they'd come from. Annamarie did not want that to be her. She did not want to be told to "go home" when all she had been given to understand was that "home" was the most unwelcoming place too.

Margit reached over and opened a desk drawer on her right and withdrew a sheet of paper. "These are the instructions for registering with the BDM. You don't officially have to be a party member, but it would be helpful. What I will need, however, is proof that the last three generations of your family are of Aryan descent." She searched Annamarie's face and then smiled hesitatingly. "Can you do that for me?"

Annamarie took the paper but could not focus on the words. When Lisi had asked about Marco Grimani, the one thing Annamarie had not shared were the macabre details about how her mother had lied to her, had kept secret that Annamarie had a different father, the same father as Marco's.

She swallowed. "How do I go about doing that? I'd have to... I'd have to go home and get my birth certificate, find the church records, or ask the registrars..."

"Then take the time and go home. It's only a few hours away." Margit must have seen Annamarie's expression of horror, because she paused. "I know it's labour intensive. The authorities will have to certify your birth certificates and the marriage and birth certificates from both sides of your families. Maybe you can ask your mother and father to do it for you and just send the paperwork back? It's going to be an important document, Annamarie." Margit waved towards the window. "At some point, I imagine, everyone will need one no matter what they do. What is your history, anyway? You said your mother's family is from Innsbruck. So her paperwork should be here. What part of South Tyrol is your father then from?"

Which one? The man she had grown up to know as her father or that man whom she looked most like? Annamarie's chest constricted. She could not even be certain who was listed on her birth certificate, Angelo Grimani or Florian Steinhauser? Then she remembered the day she had returned home, the day her mother had told her everything. Florian had been the man who had taken care of her, raised her, disciplined her, loved her. And he was German through and through as far as she knew.

"Nuremberg," Annamarie finally said. "He comes from Nuremberg, but my paternal grandmother comes from Meran, in

South Tyrol. She met my grandfather when he was working in Tyrol."

"That's fascinating!" Margit's beautiful forehead rumpled as her eyes flitted over Annamarie's face and head. "So your grandmother, she's Tyrolean or Italian?"

Annamarie frowned. "Tyrolean."

"I meant," Margit said hastily, "I know Italians have lived there too and, well, never mind." She laughed. "It would explain your look, that's all. Never mind. I'll let you get to that then."

Margit stood, and Annamarie took that to be the end of their interview, if that was what this had been. She took the form off the desk and folded it. How could one sheet of paper weigh so heavily?

She followed Margit to the door, who then turned to her with the same warm smile as when they had started.

"You've only been in Innsbruck a few months, right? How about dinner with us tonight at our home?"

"I couldn't."

"You must. My parents are in Vienna, and Maxi's just came back from Berlin. He's been assigned as Gauleiter Hofer's driver, and he promised to bring us some new music records. I'm excited to see him. Franz will be there too."

If only Margit knew how unappetising the idea of seeing Franz again was.

As if she could read Annamarie's mind, Margit laughed and waved a hand. "Who cares if my fiancé is there." She hooked her arm into Annamarie's and led her outside. "I want you to meet Maxi. He's been spending all his free time in the cabarets and the Berlin scene. You're definitely going to want to talk to him."

Back at the apartment, Annamarie rushed up the same stairwell she had clomped down earlier that day. Margit had been wonderful to her, genuine, Annamarie thought. She would find a way to obtain the records she needed for the *Ahnenpass*, even had ideas of where she could start. The job—if she got it—would be the best opportunity to afford the theatre and film training she needed, and then there was the promise of meeting someone who had been to Berlin, who knew the theatre and entertainment scene.

She threw open the door to Lisi dressed in a loose kimono of dark-blue satin. Her hair was wrapped up in a turban, and she wore several beaded necklaces around her neck.

Annamarie—after being surrounded by the uniforms all day—came to a halt in front of her and nearly laughed. "What's this costume?"

Lisi rolled her eyes. "Honestly, Annamarie. Did you forget already? Karl's surprise birthday party? Sepp and Veronika are coming, the whole crowd."

Annamarie moaned. "Margit's invited us to dinner at their home. She extended an invitation to you as well. She wants me to meet Maximilian."

Lisi smirked. "Ah, Maxi. He was in Berlin. How could I forget?"

"Have you met him?"

Lisi's eyebrows shot up, and she turned away. "Am I to assume things went rather well today? You are certainly cheerful."

Annamarie shrugged and sat down to pull off her shoes. Lisi removed a cigarette from her case and lit it, then strolled to the sideboard, where she kept the spirits. It was filled with new bottles.

"Drink?"

Annamarie shook her head. "I'll excuse myself right after dinner, Lisi, and then come back here."

"Take your time." Lisi smiled, but there was nothing genuine about it as she mixed herself a cocktail.

Was Lisi hoping she would stay away? Annamarie had made a

fool of herself at the last party. Maybe her roommate was relieved to be rid of her.

"I really liked Margit," Annamarie said, and bit her tongue before adding how she could not imagine Franz had managed to win her over as a fiancé. It would not do to insult Lisi.

"I'm sure," Lisi said coolly. "She's a very pretty girl, a very likable sort." She disappeared into the tiny kitchenette, her fresh drink swirling in her upheld hand.

Annamarie remembered what Margit had said. The two families had a history.

In her room, she stood before the half-empty wardrobe. Nothing looked fit for the occasion. A well-established family in Innsbruck meant the Rainers were wealthy. She could ask Lisi to lend her something, but Annamarie was certain it would start an unpleasant discussion. Annamarie sensed that she had possibly worn out her welcome, had—with her lies—damaged any chances at an honest friendship with Lisi. Besides, she now had a chance to win over someone completely different, to start with a clean slate. A new position meant a new start. A new circle of friends maybe. They would have to accept her for who she was.

Annamarie changed and said her goodbyes. At the address that Margit had given her, Annamarie rang the buzzer. The house was a stately Habsburger manor with turrets and ivy growing all over the facade. It reminded her of the villas in Marco's neighbourhood in Bolzano.

She was taken aback when Margit opened the door. She was wearing a stunning dress, but more surprising was Franz, who was standing right behind her, as if the two of them were already married and welcoming guests together. *Playing house*, Annamarie thought. Not unlike what the BDM would be preparing for.

"Goodness, Margit," Annamarie said after they had greeted one another. She reluctantly removed her summer coat and handed it to Franz. "Your dress is really beautiful."

"Thank you." Margit brushed a hand over the front of the tailored white dress with delicate pearl beads along the collar. "I made it in Brunswick in the BDM fashion course."

To avoid any polite compliment Margit might make about her plain navy-blue dress, Annamarie handed her the cheap bouquet of flowers.

From a room to her right, a young man strolled out, hands in his trouser pockets, like the American stars in the movies. He leaned in the doorjamb and cocked his head at Annamarie with a mildly curious look. He had dark-blond hair with a perfect side part and dark-brown eyes. But it was his mouth that Annamarie fixated on. The left side curved up a little, as if he were either amused, confident, or ready to sneer. They locked eyes briefly, and now his smile balanced out. She saw a flash of recognition in his eyes, as if he knew his effect on her. Her cheeks grew warm, and the back of her neck tingled. This had to be Margit's brother, the one who had been in Berlin.

As if he remembered himself, he shook himself away from the door and pulled his right hand out of his pocket, extending it to her. "Maximilian. But you can call me Maxi. You must be Annamarie."

"I've been gushing about you since I got home," Margit said.

Maximilian withdrew his hand from Annamarie's. "Pleasure to meet you. My sister was certainly right about one thing." His mouth curved up, then back down again, and his intensity returned, but it was not hard, nor soft. It was excruciatingly penetrating.

"And what's that?" Annamarie asked quietly.

"Hmm?" He raised an eyebrow, bent down to her.

"Quit your flirting, Max," Franz said with a hint of annoyance. "Annamarie, where's Lisi?"

"I should have remembered when Margit extended the invitation," Annamarie replied. "Lisi and I were supposed to host a party for the crowd. It's Karl's birthday today, and we had planned a surprise party. It was silly of me to forget."

"Who's the crowd?" Maximilian's eyes narrowed again, that half grin making the back of Annamarie's knees tingle.

"Just the people from the theatre," Annamarie said.

"A bunch of freaks," Franz chided.

Maximilian softened, laughed. "Lisi, yes. God, do you remember when she...she always had that... Never mind. I shouldn't talk about your sister that way. Besides, Annamarie seems far from a freak, Franz. You've always been so quick to judge. You're in the theatre too, then, Annamarie?"

"I want to be a screen actress," she said quickly. "That's something different to what the others..."

Maximillian's eyes darted up and down her. It was a split second, but she knew he'd assessed all of her. "I suppose it is. Saw a lot of films when I was up in Berlin."

"Will you tell me about them?"

Margit's look darted between Maximilian and Annamarie. "Yes, do, Maxi. But first, let's go into the dining room. We've got some champagne, and I've made a gorgeous dinner."

Annamarie followed everyone into a room where an intimate table had been set. "Shall I help you?" she asked Margit.

Margit twirled towards a door, a kitchen beyond. "I've cooked the whole meal myself. I've made *Sauerbraten* and fresh vegetables and an apple strudel for dessert." She put a hand on Annamarie's arm and squeezed. "And just for you, I made some *Schlutzkrapfen*."

Annamarie laughed. She loved the filled dough pockets. They looked like giant ravioli. That was not what was making her giddy, however. "How can I help?"

In the well-appointed kitchen, Margit handed Annamarie a carving knife. They arranged the food on the plates. Annamarie was dying to ask about Maximilian, but Margit spoke first.

"So Maxi seems to really like you."

Annamarie blushed. "What was he doing in Berlin?"

Piano music suddenly came through into the kitchen. The boys were singing loudly along with it, but Annamarie could not catch the words. She paused, and Margit and she shared a smile.

"It's the new record," Margit said. "Anyway, Maxi's been training with the National Socialist Motor Corps. He'll be Gauleiter Hofer's driver starting next month."

"My mother used to make this all the time," Annamarie said as Margit handed over the platter of *Schlutzkrapfen*. They were perfect and beautiful.

Margit chopped up fresh chives to sprinkle on top, then glanced at her. "You must miss her, but you'll see her soon enough again, right?"

Annamarie caught her bottom lip between her teeth.

"When was the last time you heard from her?"

"My Tante Rosa and she communicate about me."

"You're not speaking?"

Annamarie shook her head.

"I'm sorry to hear that. Mothers and daughters, very complicated. I know."

"You too?" Annamarie asked only to be polite. She could not imagine that Frau Rainer had remotely done anything comparable.

"My mother and I combat over silly things. But never to the point that I would not talk to her." Margit stopped carving. "I know you can't choose your relatives, but you can choose your friends. Annamarie, you're welcome here anytime."

Her throat constricted. "Thank you."

"You know what I think," Margit added lightly. "I think the reason we have conflicts with our parents is so that we are forced to seek out our own friends. Don't you?"

Annamarie finished the platter of beef and lifted it to carry it out.

"We should honour our mothers either way," Margit continued. "Maybe, now you have the opportunity to make up with her." She cocked her head towards the dining room and smiled wickedly. "Come on—the boys are starving."

In the dining room, Annamarie took the seat opposite Maximilian. He looked up from his conversation with Franz and flashed her that lopsided grin. It was the wink that sent the blood to her head.

As she and Margit passed the platters around, Maximilian and Franz discussed engines, fast cars, and motorbikes.

Following Margit's example, Annamarie poised her knife and fork over her plate before cutting into her roast. "Motorbikes? I've never been on one."

Maximilian's eyes flicked over her, but she was certain he'd read her message loud and clear.

"Isn't that a shame." He toyed with the stem of his wineglass, then raised the glass to drink.

Annamarie wondered whether he was put off by her now. When he set his wine down, he seemed to examine his food before finally choosing the *Schlutzkrapfen*. He looked at Annamarie again, one eyebrow raised, that confident mouth curving upwards. "I'll have to take you out for a ride then, won't I?"

He'd seen through to her intention and accepted. She took a gulp of wine and swallowed down the need to cheer.

6

BOLZANO, JUNE 1938

The only reason Angelo tolerated Gina's cigarettes was because she only lit them after sex. Lying on the bed together, the smoke curled up into the weak light beyond the half-opened curtains. It was a cloudy Saturday morning. Below the hotel window came the din of slow-moving, lazy weekend traffic. When the phone rang, Angelo jerked out of half sleep and, regrettably, pushed Gina off him to reach for the receiver.

"Grimani, *pronto.*"

The intake of breath on the other line was followed by Chiara's voice. "I hope I'm not calling too early." A hint of derision, as if she suspected Gina was lying next to him. She probably sensed it more than presumed it. Women were like that.

"I'm awake. What is it?" He sat up to put more authority in his voice, and Gina extinguished her cigarette, one eyebrow arched into a question mark.

When Chiara spoke again, Gina must have heard it coming through the receiver, because she tossed her head. She slid away from him and draped her satin robe over herself before going into the suite beyond.

Angelo turned back to the receiver. Chiara was in the middle of a sentence.

"...they're going to release him later today. The doctor says he needs his rest, and of course we're all worried about him. I thought you might want to know."

"I'm sorry, Chiara. I missed all that. Who?"

"My father." She was irritated. "It's his heart."

"*Managgia!* When?"

"Last week, Angelo. For heaven's sake, don't curse like that."

Now it was his turn to be accusatory. "Because you're telling me this just now!"

She made a smacking sound and exhaled. "I'm calling because Marco's arriving at the train station today."

Either she was ignoring him or—

"I have to go to the hospital, and your son needs someone to pick him up, what with his luggage for the summer and everything. I'm quite overwhelmed. I wouldn't call otherwise."

She was ignoring him. She was not going to apologise for not informing him about Pietro's heart attack.

Angelo rubbed his face. "I'll do whatever you need."

In the far room, Gina snorted.

"Are you sure I'm not inconveniencing you?"

Chiara knew she was.

"Would you rather have me at the hospital?" he asked with maybe too much hope. "Or at the train station?"

If she wasn't going make this comfortable for him, he couldn't blame her. In fact, he admired her when she asked him to fetch Marco. Chiara would wait at the hospital until the doctors released Pietro. Angelo agreed and replaced the receiver into its cradle. A part of him was relieved that Chiara—although it would likely create fireworks—supported some sort of reconciliation between Angelo and their son.

Outside, it had begun to rain. He could hear the swish of water as the cars passed by. Gina entered the bedroom a minute later with a tray of coffee and pastries but stopped when she saw him rising. "I suppose our relaxing day has been interrupted by family and duty."

Angelo went to her and took the tray. He kissed her before setting it on the writing table. "Marco's arriving today. I'm going to fetch him."

"Then…" She picked up the espresso cup and sipped. "I'll go home and do what a widow does."

"And what's that?"

"Now that you've sensibly decided against running for the senate, and Mastromattei keeps putting off your dinner plans, I'm going to look into what our magistrate has up his sleeve. Why does Il Duce trust him enough to send him to meet Hitler, that kind of thing. Things to help your cause."

Angelo chuckled and drew her to him, kissing the top of her head. "*Our* cause."

She rested on his breastbone. "Yesterday you said you want to be close to the Steinhausers. I've been wondering about that since. Did you mean near them or close to them?"

He shrugged. "What's the difference?"

"I'm talking about your relationship with them versus the geographic proximity, Angelo." She pulled away. "You know what I suspect?"

Angelo shook his head, trying to keep an amused look on his face.

"I suspect you're trying to prove to everyone that you're the good guy, and that way your estranged family—families—may love you again. At least hold you in esteem."

He snorted. "I'm not trying to prove anything to anyone."

Her eyebrow arched. "All right. Neither is Chiara, I suppose."

"I can't speak for Chiara."

Gina nodded and studied the tray. "Have you written to them —the Steinhausers—yet?"

"No."

"When will you?" she challenged. "The news is not good. MFE will stake that ground with or without the Tyroleans on it—you know that."

"Soon." Again the scrutiny from her. "Soon, I promise. As soon as you get more information about Mastromattei for me. As soon as I actually have a plan. If you're so eager, you could draft the letter yourself."

She narrowed her eyes. "I'm not your secretary."

"I always wanted you to be that for me," he teased. "I always imagined you on the desk—"

"You know how I hate clichés."

He laughed softly. "The reason I never offered."

Gina tucked a wavy strand of dark hair behind her ear, the robe falling over her left shoulder as she looked down at the sheets of hotel paper and a pen. "Tell me you'll talk to her again about a divorce."

She meant Chiara, of course.

"Make me into an honest woman again, Angelo. Move into the Conti villa and stop living in this hotel."

He did not answer. There was no need to. This rare vulnerability had only to do with the fact that Chiara had asked; Chiara had reached out first. He knew the minute he would take Gina up on her offer, she would find an excuse to postpone it. The Grimani children. The Grimani in-laws. The party. The church. Gina wasn't ready. Instead, Angelo told her that his father-in-law had had a heart attack.

"Pietro d'Oro? I am sorry to hear that."

"I might be all day. Don't wait for me. I'm going to lend Chiara a hand, see what needs doing."

Gina headed for the bathroom. "You mean the infamous father-in-law you stabbed in the back in order to get his position? You're now going to help nurse him back to health?"

"Ouch," Angelo said. "That was aimed below the belt."

She swung to him, unsmiling. "No, darling." She winked.

"That was my left hook. When I'm disappointed, I don't let you see it coming."

~

Marco was not at the train station when Angelo arrived ten minutes late. The drizzle had turned to rain, and he had forgotten his umbrella. Shaking off his coat, Angelo checked his watch, checked the clock, asked the stationmaster, who said the train had come in a few minutes early. Of course it had. Why would it come late like it always did?

Angelo searched the train station again but did not find Marco. He groaned. One thing! He had one thing to do and that was to pick up his son so that his estranged wife could take care of her father. Why couldn't the boy have just been a little more patient? Angelo strode across the road, heading back the other way through town and to Villa Adige.

A car horn honked and nearly missed him. Angelo jumped back, but water splashed his trousers. He cursed under his breath and moved on. Perhaps he would run into Marco, the boy dragging his cases and pouting. If that happened, if Marco realised it was Angelo who was supposed to have fetched him, Marco would probably release a stream of complaints and accusations. Or more likely, bitter silence. Either way Angelo was prepared to take it. He hadn't seen or spoken to his son in months. It was high time, though the words still failed him.

Angelo hurried, but the more ground he covered without running into Marco along the way, the angrier he got. The boy had taken a taxi. Of course he had. It was raining, and Marco had no regard for expenses. Indeed, when he arrived at the villa, Angelo saw the abandoned suitcases by the door. A man picked them up, and at first Angelo thought it was a taxi driver or someone new to the household staff, but when the stranger straightened with one case in hand, Angelo stopped in the middle of the flagstone walkway.

Michael Innerhofer did not smile. In fact, he seemed as surprised to see Angelo on the premises as Angelo was to see the journalist in his entryway.

"Is he upstairs?" Angelo demanded. "Did you pick him up?"

Michael shook his head. In flawless Italian he said, "I just arrived myself. Marco said nobody came for him."

"I was supposed to meet him, but his train arrived early. I missed him."

"No need to be accusatory."

"I'm not being…" He was. He was being accusatory. He looked Michael up and down. "My wife," he said pointedly, "asked me to help."

Michael squared himself with Marco's suitcase in hand, his eyes darting to Angelo's puddle-stained trousers. "I just arrived with her from the hospital."

Michael had been with her at the hospital? Angelo could spit. "Fine."

The journalist made room in the doorway. "You want to come upstairs? They're both upstairs."

"No. You've obviously got everything in hand."

Michael made a sympathetic face, pointed to the third case, and shrugged.

Angelo gritted his teeth. "My father-in-law?"

"Is that your way of asking where he is? He's on the veranda."

"I'll go see him." Angelo nodded curtly.

He started around the garden to the front of the house but turned to watch the journalist struggle with Marco's two biggest cases before disappearing, his footfalls going up the stairs to the apartments above. Angelo shook his head. His mother worried about *his* reputation? If she saw this, she'd march to the priest herself and demand an annulment for Angelo and Chiara.

On impulse, he stomped to the stoop and snatched the last case. He had every right to take it upstairs, but after he visited Pietro.

His father-in-law was, as Michael had said, on the veranda. In a wheelchair. Pietro's head drooped in sleep, a woollen blanket on his lap. Laces of fog and low rain clouds hovered over the vines and roses. The misty day made it seem more like September than June. At the sound of a French door opening above, Angelo set Marco's suitcase down and glanced upwards. Chiara was leaning over the far banister, cutting climbing roses for the vases she loved to arrange.

Angelo ducked beneath the veranda. If she caught him, she'd be angry for two things: missing Marco and waking Pietro. When he heard her go inside, Angelo looked at Pietro again and softened. The old man's pallor was less than healthy, his skin grey. He missed the familiar friendship with his father-in-law, his former mentor and boss, but also the father figure Angelo had always wished he'd had in the Colonel.

Angelo lowered himself into the lounging chair next to the old man. When it creaked, Pietro stirred, blinked, and straightened.

"I didn't mean to wake you."

"Angelo, you're here. That's fine. Good. Marco?"

"Gone upstairs to his mother." There was no need to share the details.

His father-in-law shuffled his legs beneath the blanket, as if his knees were paining him. "Old men like me no longer keep regular hours. I get up in the middle of the night and nap all through the day." Pietro pointed to the suitcase. "Are you moving back in?"

Angelo laughed softly. "It's Marco's. Though I am moving. Just not to this villa, I'm afraid. How are you?"

Pietro waved a hand, reached into the breast pocket of his coat, and pulled out a handkerchief before discreetly wiping his nose. "Close call. Enough to make me sit up and pay attention, I suppose. They've put me on bed rest for at least another week. Stop scrutinising me like that. Something was bound to happen at my age. I'm almost eighty, you know." Pietro raised his chin and pointed to the veranda above them. "Have you spoken with her yet?"

Angelo shrugged.

"And Marco? Did you have an opportunity to speak with your son?"

"Train arrived early. Marco had no idea I was picking him up. He took a taxi." Besides, how could Angelo reconcile with anyone with Innerhofer underfoot now? Angelo had always suspected that Chiara had feelings for the Tyrolean journalist—the martyr, her childhood friend, that pain in the arse. Angelo did have to admit, however, that Michael's Italian had become good enough to make him almost witty.

Angelo slumped forward, resting his elbows on his thighs. "Things have changed. Neither one is going to forgive me for the way my...the way things came to light. I tried with Annamarie, but I was too late. Instead, Pietro, I've made promises I don't know if I'll be able to keep."

Pietro bobbed his head and fidgeted with the blanket in his lap. "Such as?"

"I promised to support the Steinhausers and the locals when the offers for their land come in. That I would advise them. None of them speak Italian well enough, you know?"

"And what about your political ambitions?"

Angelo straightened. "How did you hear about that?"

Pietro closed his eyes and shook his head. "I told you a long time ago, you ought to go into politics. I did not think you'd ever listen to me. You never have before."

"Then you'll be glad to hear I have chosen not to run for the senate. I won't beat Tolomei. I may as well finish what I started. I thought joining the senate was the only way I could make a difference, but working with Mastromattei—"

"Now he's a politician. I'm not sure whether to admire the man or be terrified of him."

Angelo shared the same sentiment sometimes. "I'm not a politician, Pietro. You aren't often wrong, but on this count you were. I thought being a minister was a tough, dirty business, but getting into that wrestling ring they call a parliament?"

Pietro laughed. "You're right there. You're no diplomat."

"No. My people skills…"

He and Pietro smiled at each other.

"So you'll stick to engineering," Pietro said. "It's not a bad thing."

"Maybe I'll be more like Chiara and become an activist." He beamed at Pietro's surprised look. "I don't want to—I can't—play the games. I'm too straight. But I do know what I want."

Pietro folded his arms, waiting.

"Whatever options we present the Tyroleans up in the Reschen Valley, all I want is that they are treated fairly, as we would any of Italy's citizens."

Pietro made a low whistle. "Are you listening to yourself?"

Angelo glanced at him questioningly.

"The reason I was tossed out of the ministry is exactly for the same reason they will get rid of you," Pietro warned. "Activist? Yes. And that's the problem. You're making your sympathies too obvious. That would make you a dissenter. They won't even involve you in the process if they suspect you of that."

"I'm doing things differently."

"Are you? Because you have a Tyrolean daughter?"

"Nobody outside the family knows about that."

"So you'll risk your job for your daughter?"

Angelo shook his head.

"What about your son? He needs you especially right now. He has some tough decisions to take now that he's finished with his studies."

Angelo threw a look up at the ceiling. "He doesn't need me.

The Colonel has already secured his future with a position at MFE."

"He does not wish to be an engineer."

Angelo threw up his arms. "Since when? He's just done years of studying to become one."

Pietro opened his hands. "He's been saying for over a year that he wants to do something else."

"That being?"

"Talk to him."

The French doors above them flew open, and someone crossed the space above their heads before stopping at the banister.

"Angelo?" Chiara called down. "Is that you there?"

Angelo rolled his eyes at Pietro, stood, and took the steps to the garden so he could look up. "I'm here."

"Michael said you were downstairs. Are you coming up? He says you have Marco's last case."

"I'll be right there."

She exuded no warmth, kept her eyes on him as she called down to Pietro. "Papá, I'll come to you in a moment."

"I'm fine," Pietro responded. "Take your time."

Chiara turned away, and Angelo listened until he heard the doors close again. The mist had lifted, and dull sunshine broke through.

There was a moment of uncomfortable silence before Pietro cleared his throat.

"Listen, Angelo, here's what I would do differently if I had a second chance. I'd play the political game better. Never, ever do the things that will jeopardise the confidence that comes with your position. But if you know someone willing to do the dirty work for you? Don't allow yourself to look bad. Don't get in the papers. You've been your father's pawn many times. If you do one thing right, it's turn the tables and hire the hands that must get dirty. Even bloody. Don't learn from me. Learn from him. It's the only way you're going to be able to put this plan of yours together. Do you understand?"

Angelo did not agree, but he did not want to argue.

"What is the latest then?" Pietro asked. "On the Reschen Valley, that is?"

"MFE is getting everything ready for staking out the ground. There are still several land disputes, paperwork to overcome regarding land rights and water rights."

"On the one hand, that's good. You could use the time to your advantage."

"How?"

"Go talk to Mr Innherhofer."

"Michael? Why?"

Pietro shrugged. "He's working on something. Something about the hardliners trying to get rid of the Tyroleans once and for all. At least that's what I overheard when he and Chiara thought I was sleeping."

Angelo was about to ask what was going on with the journalist and Chiara anyway, but he stopped himself. "And why on earth should he help me?"

"I just have a feeling your interests might be similar."

"Is that so?"

Pietro's eyes danced over him. "No, Angelo, Mr Innerhofer and I don't hold fireside chats over grappa. Unlike with you, my daughter still confides in me. But not enough to really share the details." He put a hand to his left breast. "She doesn't think my heart can take it. But I can tell that, from what I gather between the lines, it might be useful for you to make his better acquaintance."

Angelo rubbed a hand over his beard.

Pietro chuckled. The old man was having fun with this. "You need someone who knows people. Someone willing to put himself on the line. A martyr."

Angelo stared at him. Martyrs did know other martyrs, didn't they? "I need to go." He rose.

Pietro shifted in the wheelchair. "Don't do it today. Today, you go talk to your son."

Angelo patted the man's shoulder. "Anything I can do before I go?"

"I'll do that."

Angelo spun around at the sound of Marco's voice.

His son walked over and fussed over Pietro, tucking in the blanket, moving the wheelchair farther back from the veranda's edge. Anything, it seemed, to avoid looking at Angelo.

He was the same, but edgier, more muscular. His dark curly mop of hair had been cut. His chin was sharper. There was nothing of the usual mirth or kindness in the bright-green eyes, however. Pure accusation. Angelo had done that to him. It was his fault.

"I was looking forward to seeing you," Angelo tried. "I'm sorry I missed you at the station."

Marco glanced up, already turning Pietro towards the parlour. "Nonno," he said to Pietro, "Mama wants me to take you inside now."

Angelo's son backed the wheelchair into the parlour, Pietro facing Angelo once more.

The old man patted Marco's hand. "Tell your father what you want to do."

"You're tired now, Nonno." Marco pulled Pietro and the chair into the room and disappeared behind the muslin curtains.

Angelo lifted the suitcase and was about to follow them, but Marco appeared in the doorway again and indicated the case in Angelo's hand.

"I'll take that," Marco said.

Angelo handed it to him. "Look, I'm sorry I was late. Maybe we could talk about—"

"I'm starting at MFE at the beginning of next week. I'll see you around, all right?"

"You are going to work for the Colonel then."

Marco studied him for a minute. "Why wouldn't I? It's what I went to school for, right?"

"I suppose I mean… Look, if you want to discuss other options, I'm happy to talk to you." He took a step forward and indicated the chairs on the veranda.

Marco tossed his head. "There is absolutely nothing, and I mean nothing, I want to discuss with you."

Angelo froze. "All right, son."

The boy closed the parlour doors before disappearing once more.

Heavy-hearted, Angelo left the property. He faced a long walk back to the Laurin and briefly considered going to Gina's. Instead, he stopped for a quick bite to eat at a restaurant he had never before visited, and still someone recognised him. After shaking hands with a gentleman and his wife and exchanging superficial pleasantries, Angelo took a table in the back, ordered a simple meal he barely tasted, and tried to distract himself with the newspaper.

He was at a loss as to how to reach his son. The letters Angelo had written to him in Bergamo had been left unanswered. Chiara censored everything to glossy generalisations anytime Angelo asked about Marco. *He's fine. He's studying for his exams. He's passed. He's graduated.* Angelo had ruined all he had ever had, and he wondered whether the answer was not to simply let go and forget about it. Marco was old enough to decide for himself with whom he wanted his relationships. *Family is family.* Only, sometimes, it was not.

Over the aching heart, he read the news from Rome. Pietro's suggestion that Michael might have something worthwhile for Angelo needled its way through and stabbed him with irritation. He paid the check before he was finished.

After leaving the restaurant, Angelo walked past the military barracks before turning into the next street. The Conti villa appeared before him, lemon yellow with the bright-green shutters and the brick tower.

Gina buzzed him through the gate on the second ring and opened the door. "Thank goodness you got my message."

"Actually, no. I wasn't at the hotel. What's happened?"

She let him in and drew him into the salon. She was taut, jittery. He was barely seated before she launched in.

"I had lunch with someone close to Mastromattei. Angelo, it's a good thing you're not running for the senate. There's nothing you can change from Rome. It's a real cesspool of chopped-off heads."

Angelo was about to comment, but Gina lifted a palm. "Listen to me. You wanted to know why Hitler was in Rome in May and then on the Brenner, right?"

Angelo pictured the photograph of Mastromattei and Hitler shaking hands. "Right."

"Mastromattei accompanied Foreign Minister Ciano on the Brenner. Do you know the reason for the meeting?" Angelo did not react, and she ploughed forward. "Hitler refused to let Il Duce make a public announcement about Germany sacrificing any claims beyond the Brenner. Mastromattei was suspicious. He warned Ciano this sounded like Hitler was having second thoughts about leaving the Alto Adige alone. You understand? That maybe he would indeed be interested in annexing it as well."

"That probably did not sit well with Il Duce."

"No, I can't imagine. Anyway," Gina continued, "they met with the German delegation, and Mastromattei returned with the idea that there ought to be a German-Italian commission to finalise, once and for all, the Tyrolean question."

Angelo waited, allowing Gina to fit the last pieces of the puzzle together, although he had already seen the big picture.

"When he came back, however, Senator Tolomei and he had a

vehement argument behind closed doors. Angelo, do you see? Mastromattei does not see eye to eye with the harder nationalists." She sat back and let that sink in. When Angelo smiled, she said, "That's not all. Mastromattei has decided that he will be accelerating the rate at which the Italianisation programme is to take place. He's gotten permission to establish twelve new settlements for over fifteen hundred Italians between Bolzano and Merano."

Angelo was astounded. "What? With whom?"

"With the ONC—the veterans' association."

He tilted his head. "They're going to put veteran combatants onto farms?"

Gina nodded slowly.

"And intermix relocated Tyroleans…"

"Possibly."

Angelo put his face in his hands. Some areas of land there had been drained by the redirected rivers for the first dams the Italian government had ordered. There was plenty of space available.

"Angelo, you need to find a way to get Mastromattei to cooperate with you. The good news is, he's not a hardliner. Not like Tolomei. And if we work this properly, we could very well find an incentive for him to…" She paused, and when Angelo looked up, she had a wicked grin on her face. "I don't know. Jab him, needle him, really put Tolomei into his place."

Angelo chuckled sadly. "Pietro said something today. He said I should find someone to do the dirty work for me."

Gina crossed her arms. "How was it? Seeing Marco and Pietro? And Chiara?"

"Pietro is the only one who still behaves as if he might like me. The others—" He waved a hand. "Forget it. My son is not interested in reconciling with me. At some point you need to accept that your children have chosen their own paths."

Gina made a noise, and he cocked his head at her.

"You disagree?"

"No." She shrugged. "Do what you think is right, until you find out that it's not that either."

Angelo rose and went to the window. Gina left the room, and he could hear her heading for the back of the house, probably to the kitchen. He would have to tell her that he'd already eaten without her. He sighed. He was tired of disappointing people.

7

ARLUND, SEPTEMBER 1938

Short brown trousers and a tan long-sleeved shirt, wrinkled where the sleeves had been rolled up. A square cap, a tie, and a belt with a plain brass buckle.

Katharina sat sullenly at the kitchen table, Bernd's discovered uniform spread on top. It looked like a wake, but the corpse was missing. The boy to whom the uniform belonged was sitting before her, very much alive and fuming in protest. Manuel, with hurt, red-rimmed eyes, sat next to her, whilst upstairs Florian rummaged through Manuel's bedroom. Her youngest son's meek protests about hiding anything from them had nearly finished breaking Katharina's heart.

At the sound of Florian's footsteps in the stairwell, Katharina straightened. She watched as her husband descended. Florian met her questioning look and shook his head. Relieved, she put an arm around Manuel.

"It's good," she whispered. What she wanted to say was that she was sorry for not believing him, but that would mean putting her husband's authority into question. And Florian was angry enough as it was.

Face blank, the boys' father took his seat at the head of the table. She could have mistaken it for calm, but Katharina knew better. She could smell the disappointment, the anger. It culminated into the stink of fear, and she shared it with him. He took out his pipe, considered it, and indicated the uniform between them.

"Tell me again," her husband started, "how this is Andreas's uniform and you are just keeping it for him."

Bernd opened his mouth, but Florian jabbed the stem of the pipe at him, his eyes flashing. "Think, boy. You think before you open that mouth of yours, because if you lie to me one more time..."

Katharina squirmed at the sight of one angry tear rolling over Bernd's right cheek.

"Go ahead, son." Florian's voice was just a little softer, almost regretful.

"It doesn't matter what I say," Bernd muttered. "You won't believe me anyway."

"Where did you get the uniform?"

"From Andreas. I already told you."

That part was most certainly true.

"Meant for Andreas?" Florian prodded.

Bernd did not answer, his eyes cast down somewhere to his left. Just the slightest lift of his shoulders.

"All right," Florian said. "Who else?"

Bernd's eyes flicked upwards but away from her, away from Florian. He hunched into himself. "I don't know. Nobody."

"Ulrich, for instance," Florian said. "Andreas, I'm going to guess, is likely your leader. You just let me know when I'm wrong, Bernd. Tell me if I don't understand what is happening here." Florian's voice was strained, challenging again. "Someone managed to get hold of these uniforms for the purpose of recruiting you boys into the Hitler Youth. Now, I was in Germany last year, Bernd. I know that parents have to sign a permission slip for minors, that you have to be registered, that it requires party membership. How did you get party membership? And these uniforms cost something. So tell me how it is that you have one in your possession. And don't you dare tell me it's Andreas's again, because I swear to the good Lord that I will march you over to the Ritsches and demand that Toni show me his son's uniform. And he will, by God. He will, Bernd. Because he'll be more than happy to prove his involvement in this and test our"—he waved the pipe around the table—"loyalties on top of it all."

Looking Florian in the eye, Bernd sat up straight. "If you know everything already, why are you asking me?"

Whack! Katharina and Manuel both jumped. Florian's hand vibrated on the table.

"Go," he breathed. "Upstairs. I don't want to see your face. You disgust me."

Bernd shoved himself away from the table. "When Hitler comes to take South Tyrol, you'll be sorry! You'll be sorry for taking sides with the Walscher." He ran up the stairs, and a door slammed above them.

Her throat tight, Katharina studied her youngest. "Go on up to your room. I want to talk to your father."

Manuel's face flooded with relief. He left quietly, but at the stairs he asked, "Mama? Does this mean I can get the guitar?"

"We'll talk about this later."

Florian was staring straight ahead, his hand flat on the table. "He's right, you know?"

"Who? About what?"

Florian shook his head in disbelief. "Bernd was here when Angelo... When Minister Grimani...just appeared that one day. Remember? He's not stupid, Katharina. If that night in Basso's office didn't convince you, maybe I can. Your secret—the one you've been so careful to hide—it's not a secret anymore. Basso? Ghirardelli? They know, but how do they know? They used Grimani's name with me. They asked where Annamarie was.

They wanted me to know they know there is a connection between the two. The question is, how did they get the information? Who told them?"

Katharina cupped a hand over her mouth.

"The day they shot Hildi? Bernd was in Basso's office when I got there," Florian continued. He rose. "They're going to use this against us, mark my word. And we will be judged."

"By what jury?" Katharina snapped.

Florian stared at her. "The committee, that's who. The same committee you want me to convince to rally against MFE if they just"—he bent his head to whisper—"help Angelo Grimani."

Now it was her turn to bang the table. "Everyone knows where I stand! I stand for this land. On this land! This is my home, for better or for worse." She stilled her bouncing knee and lowered her voice. "Do you think Bernd knows Grimani is Annamarie's father?"

Florian looked up at the ceiling, breathing in deeply. "No. I think he suspects, and that makes things worse. He knows we're lying—"

"We're not lying! We're just not telling."

His face softened. "You believe there's a difference?"

Katharina bit her lip. "What are we going to do with Bernd? His behaviour with me..." It still stung her that she had struck her son, and in public. Florian had said little over the incident, but his disapproval still hung there, right before her. She had challenged her husband after returning home and asked him what he would have done. What was he going to do now, she wanted to know. "You must talk to him."

Florian faced her. "Klaus Foglio said the government is going to make the Italian youth group mandatory for all the boys, like military service." He strode into the *Stube* and looked out the window, hands on his waist.

Katharina rose and went to him so that he would keep his voice down. "We have to remain politically neutral. That's the only way we're going to get the locals to work with us and with Minister Grimani. We take the middle road."

"Politically neutral?" Florian laughed. "Katharina, are you listening to me? Basso and Ghirardelli, they know. Something is going on that neither you nor I understand, but I suspect it is to make certain that nothing further prevents MFE from building that reservoir. Nobody on the committee is going to listen to us when they connect you…and me…to Minister Grimani." He took her by the shoulders. "I can already hear the committee. We're leading the sheep to slaughter, that's what they'll say. Grimani has the knife, and his father, that company of his, will do the processing."

"Then we need to find someone who will really understand." She slipped away from him. "Someone the committee all trust."

She pictured the group, measured them in her mind's eye. Hans Glockner, who did just about anything Jutta or Florian advised, was loyal to them. If she could convince Jutta that working with Angelo Grimani was to their benefit, Jutta would convince Hans. Walter Plangger, Maria's husband, was known to be vehemently against anything that would help the Italians in any way. Fine. She knew that. But if she were to begin teaching German? Maybe she could gain their trust that way. Martin Noggler had made a bad deal for his land, one of the first to be purchased by the bank. And they had told him he could stay as long as he needed, at least until the reservoir's construction began, but now MFE—Angelo's father's company—had given the Nogglers notice. They had to be off their land by late spring the following year. Martin would likely set his blacksmithing hammer to any Grimani head before joining forces. Father Wilhelm was also on the committee, the most sensible of them all. He would be easy enough to convince—anything to keep the peace. There was Dr Hanny, who, after marrying Iris, had silently withdrawn from the many conflicts the valley faced. He seemed resigned to living a quiet life, and Katharina could not really blame him. That left the Roeschens.

She took her husband's hands in hers. "We have to pay off Bernd's fine by next month, and before you sell off another two calves, I could earn some money and get the committee to work together with us."

Florian looked dubious, but he waited.

"Maria Plangger is being watched by the authorities. Jutta's asked me to replace her."

The way Florian's eyes widened, she knew he understood she was referring to the secret German lessons. "There's a little money in it, maybe enough. I'm going to try and strike a bargain. If there's anyone this valley trusts, it's—"

"Mayor Roeschen."

Katharina nodded. "Strength in numbers. Angelo Grimani is not wrong about that. You and I know it, and we'll get the rest to understand it. Especially if it's Georg who does the convincing."

The next day, Florian offered to go with Katharina to speak with Georg Roeschen about the German schooling, but she insisted he stay and find a way to reach Bernd. Still fuming about their involvement with her son's transgressions, she avoided the Ritsches and took the more direct route to Graun. Ahead of her was the chapel of St Anna, lit up by the afternoon sun. She noted the angle of it in the sky. In the next days, they and their neighbours would hike to the alp to fetch the cows and put them in the lower fields. Another season, another full cycle, was coming to a close. She could hardly believe it. The fields in the valley showed golden, just like the grasses that were taking on the shades of autumn.

Boats dotted the eastern shore of Reschen Lake. A few farmers worked out in their meadows, pulling in the last of the hay. As she reached the bottom of the hill, she could hear the steady steel-on-steel clanging from Martin Noggler's blacksmithing. On the main road to the centre of town, two cats —one black, one grey and white—tore their stares away from one another to slink off in opposite directions. The sound of a cart reached her ears before she got around the corner and recognised Hans Glockner, navigating his ox towards the inn. She called to him in greeting, and he slowed to a stop.

"On your way to Jutta?" Katharina asked.

"I am." He pointed to the back of the cart, which held a pile of logs. "Alois and I are setting to mend the fence."

She hesitated, considering whether to speak to Jutta first before going to the Roeschens. She could advise Katharina how to best approach the sensitive subject.

Hans interrupted her thoughts. "I'll be going back later this afternoon, if you want a lift back."

"I'm fine to walk. Tell her I said hello."

Hans dipped his head and clucked the old ox to move on. Katharina continued on the road to her left.

She passed Ghirardelli's home and peeked over the fence to see whether Lucia, the goat from Istria, was in her pen. She was.

"Come here," she said to the goat.

It took a few tentative steps towards her but no farther. Katharina tried again and was forced to admit that the goat was just a way to prolong her journey to the Roeschens. The closer she came to reaching their house, the less confident she felt about her chances at negotiating the terms she wanted. When Lucia no longer responded to her coaxing, Katharina moved on around the corner.

At the sight of two *carabinieri* in Lisl's garden, Katharina halted. They were the same two who had arrested Bernd in the spring. Lisl was standing with her hands on her hips, Georg right in front of her, shaking a finger at the authorities, his voice raised.

Katharina hurried up the hard-packed road and stopped at the gate. It was then that she saw, on the far end of the house, a third policeman she did not recognise. He was on his knees in the flowerbed, ripping Lisl's flowers out of the ground.

Georg shouted in German. The *carabinieri* gazed at him with scepticism or boredom. Katharina unlatched the gate.

"What's happening here?" she asked in Italian.

The policeman, who had mentioned his mother during the incident with Bernd's dog, seemed almost relieved to see her. "Tell them the Austrian colours are illegal here."

"The Austrian colours?" Katharina looked around, looked for a flagpole, a flag, anything. In German, she asked Lisl and Georg, "Are you flying the Austrian colours?"

Lisl guffawed and pointed at the destroyed garden. The uprooted and torn flowers lay in heaps along the beds. "If red and white dahlia are flying a flag, then I suppose I'm guilty!" She shouted at the third policeman, now brushing off his trousers. "They're flowers, you idiot! *Fiori, capsice? Idiota!*"

The second policeman indicated Georg but spoke to Katharina. "Tell him we know about their connection to the VKS. Tell him we have our eyes on them. And if we catch their son in any illegal assemblies, we have every right to arrest him for disrupting the peace. Go on—tell them." He eyed the flowerbeds, then Lisl, as Katharina translated.

"What in heaven's name does he mean?" Katharina asked Lisl.

But the officer interrupted them, glaring at Lisl. "*Capisce, regina dei fiori?*" You understand, queen of flowers?

The three *carabinieri* left, affixing their caps onto their heads. Katharina, Georg, and Lisl watched them go before turning to one another.

"For heaven's sake," Katharina said, but Lisl stood above the uprooted plants. She brushed an arm across her brow before looking at her husband in despair. "Just like when they go and ransack Jutta's inn, Georg. Just like that."

Georg took in a deep breath and headed into the house without a word of greeting.

Katharina picked up the debris. "You could replant the bulbs. They'll grow back next year again."

Lisl sniffed. "And have those mobsters come back? No thank you."

Katharina bent to pick some flowers up. "I don't understand what they're going on about. Look, it's really the *tricolore* if they looked at it right. Red. White. And the stems are green. See?"

Lisl first looked as if she'd been slapped, and then her hands dropped and she laughed sadly. After a moment she said, "Why are you here, Katharina? Besides to translate?"

"I wanted to speak to Georg." Katharina shrugged, chastened by his lack of greeting and Lisl's mocking. "Though it's not a good time. I can see that."

Lisl hesitated the slightest. "Come along. Maybe you can cheer him up."

Katharina sincerely doubted it.

A clock on the wall ticked in the library, where Katharina waited at the bay window, the torn-up flowerbed before her. The surface of Graun Lake was mottled in sun and shadow. The wind came up, as it did most afternoons. Someone moved on the floors above, and she heard deep voices. It had to be Georg, and perhaps the second voice—a young man's—was David, the Roeschens' youngest son.

What had that all been about with the *carabinieri*, really? Florian had said that he'd seen both Georg and David brought into the station the day of the fires last spring. The whole incident had set the locals on edge, and it seemed they wanted to keep it that way. First Hildi. Then Martin Noggler's eviction notice, which he was fighting now with little hope of getting an extension. Jutta had mentioned that she always felt as if the authorities were lurking about her home. Father Wilhelm reported he received occasional visits from the authorities, asking seemingly banal questions. Even Iris had told Katharina how one patrol had marched up to a toddler, grabbed him by the chin, and scolded him for saying "*wau wau*" when the child had pointed out a dog to its mother.

"We say *bau bau* in Italian," he'd reprimanded.

When the door behind her opened, Katharina faced Lisl. She had obviously freshened up her face. It was not blotched with anger, and her hair was patted into place. Though she came in with a tray of tea and sliced apples, Katharina had the impression, by the way Lisl avoided looking at her, that something else was wrong, as if Katharina had somehow offended her.

"Georg will be down in a moment."

Katharina glanced at the ceiling. The conversation had indeed come to an end above them.

Lisl poured the tea, her hand shaking.

Katharina rose. "Here, let me do that. You're still very upset."

Lisl resisted with a taut smile. "I'll manage. Thank you."

"Maybe I should come another time?" Katharina swallowed.

Lisl passed her the teacup and cleared her throat. "I think Georg would like to see you now."

She returned to the sofa. "Do you mind me asking? What's brought on this trouble? What's this about, Lisl?"

Shadows flitted over Lisl's face, and she concentrated on her tea. "It's David they want to scare."

Katharina did not understand at all. What had David done? He was a kind young man. Her family had relied on him for years. He always went up to the alp with them, helped with the milking, the herding, and anything else they needed. Tomorrow, he was supposed to head for Graun's Head again to help close out the season. "What reason do they have to badger David?"

"Because we are patriots." Lisl pursed her lips and held her look.

Was Katharina? That was what Lisl wanted to know.

She jumped when Georg entered, his brow furrowed, tie loosened. He studied Katharina for a second, then approached, hand outstretched. "I'm sorry you had to see all that. It's a terrible thing. I will put in a complaint with the prefect. It will do no good, but it's the principle of the matter."

Katharina sat again. Lisl poured tea into a third cup.

"What can I do for you?" Georg settled into one of the chairs.

"Jutta has asked me to speak to you, to the committee. About your need for a German instructor."

Lisl shifted a little, cleared her throat.

Katharina glanced at each of them. "I've given it a lot of thought."

"And?" Georg might as well have said, "So what?"

Uncertain now, Katharina said, "If you have someone else... What I mean is, if you feel there is someone more qualified, more willing to—"

"Take the risks," Lisl interjected.

What did they expect from her? "Yes, there is great risk if I get caught."

Georg crossed his legs and leaned back. "There is. That is why we have pulled Maria out of it. We have no one else. Jutta insists you are our best and safest option. You're the one who would be least suspected."

"Mmmm," Lisl said.

Katharina felt a prick of alarm. Something had changed for Lisl, and most especially between them. When did that happen, and most importantly, why?

"I have some..." Katharina drew in a deep breath. "I have some conditions I'd like to discuss with you."

"Conditions?" Lisl asked sharply.

"Go on," Georg said.

Katharina settled onto the sofa and smoothed her skirt. "I don't really understand what has happened these last few months, what the *carabinieri*, the authorities, and the like are trying to do, but Georg, Lisl, what I do know is that they are driving a wedge between us all here. We have a very serious problem coming our way with the reservoir."

Georg showed patient interest.

"You must know by now that Minister Angelo Grimani visited our farm this past March."

"Do tell," Lisl said icily.

Georg folded his hands. "It's nice to know that you are finally sharing this with the rest of us."

"Surely," Katharina said, "if you had suspected anything wrong, you could have asked Florian."

"We prefer that people are forthcoming on their own accord," Lisl said. "Maybe that's not how they do it in Nuremberg, but it is how we do it here. You should know that."

So that was what they had done wrong. Florian and she had kept Angelo's visit to themselves for too long. The suspicion had grown the longer they had been quiet about it. *Do you really believe that not telling is not lying? They don't know which side we stand on. They don't know whom to trust.*

Katharina opened her hands. "We never had any intention of going over the committee's heads about this. We just were not sure what we needed to do, how to approach this, that's all."

Georg rubbed a hand over his face and looked apologetic. Lisl took in a deep breath.

"Why don't you tell us what is happening, then?" Georg said.

She had to. Katharina started with the day she had found Angelo in Karl Spinner's hut and stuck only to the details regarding Angelo's injuries, his connection to Fritz Hanny, and his role in the reservoir's plans. Bringing up her grandfather's role seemed to lend credit rather than more suspicion, and she stressed how it was Opa had been afraid to put the *carabinieri* on the trail of one of their own locals as the possible perpetrator in Angelo's stabbing. Dr Hanny had also been involved in the secret, and she reasoned with the Roeschens about the purposes of keeping it so. She finished with simply, "Minister Grimani feels he owes us for his life. He came to ask how he might help."

Georg and Lisl looked at each other before Georg asked what their answer had been.

"We need someone who will lead a front against MFE when the time comes. It won't be for months yet, maybe a year or two," she said. "But Minister Grimani is prepared to assist us when the time comes to negotiate for the values on our land, for restitution, and for planning and designing the new land that we will need to rebuild on. We don't know what's coming, but Grimani has warned me it's not any good. He's willing to stick his neck out and help us negotiate better deals." Better than what Martin Noggler had gotten, she wanted to say. She checked their expressions. "If we choose to do so. But we need to work together."

"Of course we will rebuild," Georg said.

"I think you should be the face of this effort, not me, not Florian." She looked sympathetically at Lisl. "You see how quickly we seem to attract mistrust."

Lisl sighed but looked away and nodded.

"And this is your condition?" Georg asked. "That I rally our locals into a unified front, and you will teach German?"

Katharina smiled wanly. It did seem rather ridiculous now. There was something else, however, and she felt suddenly that she could really trust the Roeschens, the way she always had before. "Georg, we need the money I might make from teaching. Bernd…"

Georg closed his eyes, nodding. "That hasn't escaped us either. He's trying to find his way."

How he looked up at the ceiling, Katharina wondered whether he meant his own son as well. Had the VKS reached

David too? But he was much older. Certainly Bernd and he had little to do with each other. She remembered then how the two of them had gone off into the wood on the alp a few times, talking intently as they disappeared into the stand of pines. Maybe they did share more in common. The Roeschens were patriots. But so were she and Florian.

"I'll teach the schoolchildren," she said. "With no conditions. Will you help us, however, to convince the locals that Minister Grimani is truly on our side? That his concerns and commitment are genuine?"

Georg rose. "You'll get the money you need to pay off Bernd's fine. The committee will see to that. No protest, please. Katharina, it's the least we can do. You want us to look out for one another, then allow us look out for one another. You let us know where you want the students to come for their lessons. It cannot be in Arlund. It will be too obvious when a group of children go marching up to Katharinahof. Jutta has offered to find a place more guarded. And I will canvass the locals about their concerns regarding the reservoir, start dropping in Grimani's name. It's rather unfortunate he is the son of Colonel Nicolo Grimani."

Katharina rose. "Minister Grimani has promised to alert me as soon as he hears any further developments. So far I have heard nothing."

Lisl seemed to be considering something. "And you're sure he's to be trusted?"

"Absolutely certain." He was Annamarie's father, after all. He was doing this for her as much as for them. But that was one secret she would not air to the Roeschens. Ever.

On Katharina's way back home, Jutta stood outside the inn as Alois and Hans worked on putting together the new garden fence. As Katharina drew nearer, Alois straightened from where he was holding a log into place and waved to her, smiling with that wide-toothed grin. He removed his spectacles and wiped them on the corner of his shirt, then returned to work.

Katharina walked over and stood next to Jutta. "Alois has lost a lot of hair."

"He woke up one morning, and it was all lying on his pillow." Jutta faced her. "I was going to go up to Arlund, but Hans said he saw you earlier. A letter's come for you. I think it's your aunt."

"Cousin, though I've always called her Tante Rosa." Katharina hurried behind Jutta, heart racing. She hoped it was not bad news. When Jutta handed her the post, she recognised Tante Rosa's handwriting and opened it quickly.

Dearest Katharina,

Annamarie has requested that I write to you. It took me quite some time to process her unusual request, and all I can say is that I suspect that she is not only involved in theatre but has now entered the political arena. I could not get the details out of her, Katharina. I can only fathom she is somehow involved with the party. Why else would she require an Ahnenpass? *The document is necessary in the Reich only for those who want to become members or who are working in some branch of government. I can share my trepidation with you. Starting this month, the young girls who have taken part in the League of German Girls have been offered an opportunity to attend an academy called Faith and Beauty. She came in uniform to me but was tight lipped. Katharina, they are forcing the boys and girls in these groups to report on their own parents should they exhibit any treasonous behaviour. Neighbours of mine have been brought in for questioning. A friend of mine said her teacher's daughter disappeared. Just disappeared after such an incident. I fear this letter will not reach you, should it be censored. I hope that we are not yet that far, but if we are, this might be the last you hear from me.*

Here is your daughter's request: she requires a certified copy of her birth certificate and the marriage records between you and your husband, as well as your mother and your father, and then the next two generations of grandparents. She is truly insistent that I help her to get the information from our side of the family here, in Innsbruck. Katharina, she plans to travel to Nuremberg at some point in the future to fetch your husband's records for his side of the family. I implore you to write her, or even come here, before it is too late. I do not like the shape of things.

With most tender greetings,

Rosa

Katharina chewed her bottom lip.

"What's happened?" Jutta rubbed her shoulders. "Child? Tell me."

Katharina shook her head and pressed the paper to her breast. She hugged Jutta close and whispered, "I am very afraid."

8

INNSBRUCK, NOVEMBER 1938

Outside of Nuremberg, the landscape along the Bavarian roads raced by at a breathtaking speed. Annamarie held fast to Max's waist. Snaking its way through the dales and sentries of stripped-bare trees, the Danube was matte grey with cold. Max whooped when they hit the winding, hilly roads. He steered the motorcycle in a wide berth around Munich, and Annamarie read signs for Chiemsee. She smiled. Max was lingering with her. He did not want her to board the train to Innsbruck either.

Annamarie closed the distance between their bodies on the motorcycle, wrapped herself securely around him, revelling in the act of intimacy.

After that first dinner with the Rainers, Max regularly took Annamarie for drives around the mountains of Innsbruck and Tyrol. Annamarie had fought to keep her distance—even their first kiss had forced herself to imagine this was something else. She had given in to his lips, pictured them as a romantic couple on a movie screen, but that was the actress in her. What she had really felt was caution, hesitation, a violent conflict within that prevented her from growing too close.

The more time she spent with the BDM, leading her troop under Margit's guiding hand, the more convinced Annamarie was about the necessity of the *Ahnenpass*—the paper that would seal her identity once and for all. It was the most important document she could own.

When Annamarie expressed her frustration at getting no word back from South Tyrol about her request, Margit had dismissed it with a quick smile.

"These things can take time," she'd said. "Sometimes the only thing that gets us through the bureaucracy and over the hurdles are relationships. The *right* relationships."

The following morning, Annamarie sought out a different route. When she had wistfully told Max her father was from Nuremberg and that she could at least get his side of the pass done if she could just get up to Germany, Max had quickly packed her up onto the motorcycle and driven half the day to get her there. He first checked them into a room reserved for members of the party, then—and with little ordeal—he succeeded in getting the booklet filled with the information and official stamps. He then offered to pay her party membership when the pass was all complete. As quickly as Maxi had managed the affair in Nuremberg, Annamarie realised Margit had been right. Knowing the right people—aligning yourself with the proper people—was what opened doors. That night, she had given herself to Max to seal her loyalty and to reward his.

Now, if only Mother would finally reply to Tante Rosa's request. It had been two months with no word. Annamarie decided her mother was showing her true self now. She was stubborn, unforgiving, and a liar.

Annamarie scrunched the helmet onto her head and encircled Max's waist again, using the windbreak that his body was. His left hand moved from the motorcycle handle and pressed against her right forearm. A reassuring squeeze. Fear and excitement pricked her belly. She would make this work, this thing between

Maximilian Rainer and herself. This time she would make it work.

The city limits were in sight. The countryside disappeared, and large buildings took its place. Max was heading for the train station, following the signs, crossing over tram tracks, and dodging the people and carts. At the *Hauptbahnhof*, Max switched off the motor and kicked the stand down before lifting his helmet off his head and helping Annamarie off the motorbike. Their leather gloves creaked as they gripped each other.

She shook out her hair and smiled. "How long will you be in Munich?"

"The week. The anniversary of the Putsch is a huge affair. Then Gauleiter Hofer will be welcoming everyone in Innsbruck on the fourteenth. I'm helping to coordinate the motorcade for the Führer and the whole entourage. There will be a lot of work for me. I'm afraid no more rides before winter."

Annamarie kissed him. "Thank you for your help. It was a really...lovely time." She blushed at the memory of their lovemaking.

Max stroked her hair, lifted her chin, and kissed her again. "I will miss you. Be a good girl, will you?"

She hugged him one last time, and hurried to the platform where the train to Innsbruck hissed as if with impatience.

Lisi was at the door, blocking the way. "Maximilian with you? No?" She let Annamarie in. "You're home late."

Suspicious, Annamarie slid out of her coat and laid it on the back of the chair in the kitchen before searching for a clean glass amongst the dirty dishes. She found one and turned on the tap.

"Maximilian had to stay in Munich for the gala," Annamarie called out. "It's freezing. Have you got tea on?"

She confirmed Lisi was listening, and was so shocked to find

Veronika standing behind her that Annamarie nearly dropped her water glass. "I didn't know anyone else was here."

"Keep your voice down," Lisi said.

"Why?" Annamarie drank deeply from the glass—parched from the journey—then filled the teakettle. "You want a cup of tea, Veronika?"

Lisi grabbed the kettle from her hand. "She's not here for a cosy cup of tea."

Annamarie took the actress in more closely. Veronika's face was splotched red, and she looked as if she had been crying. Annamarie shivered as much from the cold as from the woman's ominous state. "You two look as if the theatre's just burned down."

Lisi led Veronika to the kitchen table. The two kitchen chairs, standing askew on the blue-and-white linoleum floor were positioned such that Annamarie assumed the two women had been sitting there before her arrival. A plate of biscuits looked untouched. The two must have scattered when they heard Annamarie at the door. She looked at them with renewed interest.

Veronika gingerly took the far seat. "The theatre's let me go."

"No," Annamarie said. "That's terrible."

The theatre was opening Schiller's *Mary Stuart* that weekend. Lisi had the title role, but Veronika—who'd spent over a year as Lisi's understudy—had won her first big role opposite the starlet. Annamarie started to commiserate, but Lisi shoved a chair aside.

"We're opening on Friday," she said. "How the devil are we going to get a new Elizabeth I in five days?"

"What happened?" Annamarie took the kettle from Lisi and lit the hob.

Lisi was seething as she pointed at Veronika. "She—and her understudy!—are Jewish. Do you think anyone knew? No. Not until the SS arrived in the middle of rehearsal and demanded that all Jews rise. And they stood up, like idiots. You all stood up as if your name had been drawn for a grand prize in a raffle. For what? *Heil Hitler!*" Lisi kicked the chair leg in front of her. "Had you told me...had you simply told me back when the Nuremberger laws were passed..."

Veronika dropped her head into her hands and whimpered. "Franz—"

"To hell with Franz, Veronika! Fuck him! It's me! You know?"

The kettle screamed.

Lisi sighed with exasperation and strode over, yanking it off the burner. She reached for the packet of cigarettes above the stove and fished out a match from the sugar canister—long emptied of sugar. She lit the cigarette, inhaled, and exhaled with exasperation. "I can't handle him now. I can't tell my baby brother anything any longer. To hell with it!"

"No," Veronika whispered. "You can't. He's out of control."

"*It's* out of control." Lisi ran a hand through her hair. "You know, I bought into it all too. In the beginning, anyway. My parents have been drilling this all into our heads since I was a child. We're better than anyone. We're the master race. Our family can trace its blue blood centuries back." She looked at Veronika. "I read Goethe, Voss...Jerschke. And I fought my family tooth and nail to become an actress. I began thinking for myself. And living a dual life."

Lisi turned on Annamarie and challenged her with a distorted smile. "And you?"

Annamarie stepped back. "What about me?"

"You need to leave the BDM."

"You were the one who made me join them! You and your *baby* brother."

For the first time since she had known her, Annamarie saw true fear in Lisi's eyes. "I was wrong. God, Annamarie, I was really wrong. I just thought maybe it would help you, you know?"

Annamarie looked at Veronika in disbelief, but the unveiled Jewess only mirrored Lisi's despair.

"What will you do about Friday's opening?" Annamarie asked. As soon as she said it, she knew what would happen next.

Veronika's face fell. "I have to go." Without looking at Lisi or Annamarie, she picked up her coat. "It's not my business anymore what the theatre does. It's men like your brother who are carrying this torch, Lisi. And if you want to do something about it, stop trying to help me and put an end to his activities."

Veronika then stopped before Annamarie. "And your boyfriend? Margit? You..." She smirked. "Don't forget to report this tomorrow. Elisabeth von Brandt was harbouring a Jew in this apartment today."

Annamarie gaped at her. "I would never—" She looked to Lisi for support, but Lisi pushed by her and followed Veronika to the door.

Annamarie listened from the kitchen doorway.

"She could do it. You practice your lines with her anyway," Veronika said, jutting her chin at Annamarie. "Tell the Herr Direktor to hire her. It's what she's always wanted anyway. And now that she's an active party member, the SS can install her as my replacement."

Chilled, Annamarie jumped when the door slammed shut.

Annamarie waited for Margit in her office, still trying to formulate what she'd come to tell her, but at the sight of her, she kept her mouth shut. Margit was bursting with news. Franz and she would marry in the spring with plans to honeymoon in Paris.

"April in Paris." Margit sighed. "Cherry blossoms and the Sienne, the Notre Dame, cheese and wine. Did you hear about the Jew who assassinated Ernst vom Rath in Paris? Two days ago. It's just terrible! Some Polish-Jewish refugee. He and his family were relocated to Hannover, and this is how he repays the German people? Thank goodness the Gestapo arrested him.

Honestly, what is this world coming to? And in the city of love!"

"Terrible," Annamarie muttered. So this was the crackdown? Max and she had missed the news for being on the road. Her thoughts turned to Veronika. Nobody was safe—not the Jews, not the Germans. She could not say what came first, the problems Jews had with the Germans or the problems the Germans had with Jews.

Margit had apparently run her course with her news, and Annamarie was about to tell her that the State Theatre had taken her on for Veronika's role, but before Annamarie could formulate her request, Margit rushed on.

"How did it go in Nuremberg?"

Annamarie reached into her purse and removed the stamped booklet. "All settled. At least on my father's side."

Margit flipped through it, her smile conspiratorial as she handed it back to Annamarie. "And how was it with Maxi? He's really taken by you. Wouldn't it be wonderful if we were sisters-in-law?"

"Yes, well, we still have time." Annamarie picked at the cover of the *Ahnenpass* before putting it back in her purse. "Margit, I need to tell you something. I'm going to need some time off. I know I just had some, but I have a really great opportunity."

Dull sunlight streamed through the window behind Margit as another cloud moved on. Farther to the north, the sky was the colour of steel wool, with more clouds piling up on the horizon. They probably carried snow.

"What do you need the time off for?" Margit sounded conspiratorial.

Annamarie requested permission to take part in the play, finishing with a promise to make up for it in some way. Whatever Margit wanted.

Margit crossed her arms and leaned back in her chair. "You really want this, don't you, this role, the theatre?"

"I do." Annamarie realised she was bouncing her knee, and she placed a hand on it to still herself.

Margit leaned in then. "I have something better. I mean, yes, go ahead and do the State Theatre if you'd like, but I have something better."

Annamarie frowned. "Better?"

"Maxi told me that he's coming back with Gauleiter Hofer and with..." She squealed a little. "Joseph Goebbels! Yes, *the* Goebbels is coming to Innsbruck. Maxi wanted to surprise you, but I feel you will want time to be prepared. Don't you?"

Annamarie knew she was gawping. "Prepare? How?"

Margit grinned. "Well, we always said you would help set up our theatre and acting division here. I have it on good word, according to the last memorandum, that it's going to be a very important one. The Ministry of Propaganda wants to expand the number of Italian-German propaganda films in Division Five. Yes, Annamarie, the division responsible for films. Of course"— she opened her hands—"I dropped your name as someone who should be involved in that meeting. I mean, with your connections to Italy and everything."

Annamarie placed her hand on her chest, fearing her heart would jump right out. "A film division here, in Innsbruck?"

"You would be perfect for the job. You are familiar with the unique culture that is Italian Fascism. You'll have a lot to offer Goebbels. UFA is a union of actors and actresses and you would, of course, need a union card. Annamarie, this is it! Get that *Ahnenpass* all filled in."

Annamarie nodded, her imagination reeling. The sets. The locations. Berlin. Rome. She wanted this. She wanted this more than anything. "What do I have to do?"

Margit lifted her head, pursed her lips. "Be a loyal party member."

That was easy, too easy. "Is there any doubt I am?"

"It's not you, Annamarie." Margit shuffled some papers on her desk, then looked at her knowingly.

"I don't understand."

Margit leaned back in her chair and glanced out the window. "I love Franz very much, you know. But there's something that he's not able to do. He can rise through the ranks of the SA all he wants, but when it comes to his sister—when it comes to the great Elisabeth von Brandt—he's not himself." Margit's smile wobbled. "She is his one weakness."

Annamarie felt caught. Caught and guilty.

"She's involved where she ought not be," Margit said. "These Jewish artists—it's all unfortunate, but we must protect the safety of our nation. I wish my future sister-in-law would see how necessary this is. I'll just point to the tragedy in Paris once more." She leaned in, lowering her voice even further. "She should have denounced this. Veronika before the SS had to go into the theatre. She was aware of who was who."

"She wasn't though," Annamarie said.

Margit tipped her head. "Really?"

Annamarie shrugged. "That's what she told me. She was surprised to find out Veronika was…"

"You silly goose. She had you fooled, didn't she?"

Annamarie did not know what she meant.

"Don't be confused. This is exactly what I mean about Lisi. They know which side you are on. If Lisi admitted that she knew about Veronika's…race…you would have to report her, right?"

Annamarie searched Margit's face. Was Lisi playing Annamarie like a stringed instrument? She thought of the setup in the kitchen. It was so much like a theatre set. Annamarie could picture the curtain going up, and the way the chairs had been positioned, the biscuits spilled out onto the plate. A set up.

Margit leaned in. "Both Maximilian and I have our doubts that Franz would ever be able to…let's just say, do the duty he has sworn to do. But you, Annamarie, you have access to her every day. Steer her onto the right path. Her job at the State Theatre will be at risk, as well as with the Actors' Guild, if she does not…" Margit smiled, then drew a finger over firmly pressed lips. "Show me that you can bring Lisi back on track, and there will be no question who I put in charge. Consider it a test, your way of earning a badge of honour." She clapped her hands, bright again. "A special UFA badge!"

Annamarie looked down at her lap. If Lisi had lied about Veronika, what else had she lied about? If her roommate did not trust her enough to stop playing games then… Annamarie assured herself that Lisi would certainly want to keep her job at the theatre. She had said so herself. Some things were necessary to just get through a bad situation. Veronika would be all right. Lisi had to watch herself. Franz was in question too. And Lisi would definitely not want to put her brother at risk.

"I'll talk to her after rehearsals tonight," Annamarie said. "I can't imagine she'll say no when she understands the situation."

Rehearsals that week were gruelling. So much so that Annamarie and Lisi hardly had a moment alone, and when they did, it was just enough time to brush their teeth and fall into bed. Veronika was not the only one who had been let go. There had been at least two other minor actors and several backstage hands the SS had escorted off the theatre property. The troupe was in chaos, and the atmosphere was one of gloom and trepidation, something Annamarie found difficult to navigate.

On Wednesday night, two nights before they were to open and were conducting their dress rehearsals, they discovered that the costumes were incomplete. Herr Kern, the director, lost his patience.

"People, if we have to be here all night, we will be. I don't want to hear a single complaint. The curtain goes up in two nights. Everyone pulls their weight here. Who can sew?"

The seamstress, it turned out, had been a Jewess.

Annamarie raised her hand and scooted into the backroom to pin up hems and sew on feathers and other baubles needed for the costumes for Mary Stuart, Robert Dudley, and Elizabeth I. Lisi appeared in the backroom shortly after midnight.

"Herr Kern wants you to run through the next scene with the Earl of Leiceister. I'm exhausted and need a break."

Annamarie took the pins out of her mouth, looked around, and found someone to take over. She straightened her clothes and ran a hand over her hair before hurrying onto the stage. Despite the hour, she felt energetic and fresh. The scenes went rather smoothly. She did everything Herr Kern told her, and even his voice lost some of the edge he'd permanently had since the beginning of the week.

It was long after two in the morning when they left the theatre. In the cold night, Lisi lit a cigarette before they walked along Adolf Hitler Platz, then turned into Universitätsstrasse. Although exhausted, Annamarie's thoughts rattled, searching for the words to test Lisi's opinion about keeping her mouth shut. But Annamarie was losing her confidence. A few of her roommate's snippets during rehearsal were cause for alarm. Sure, Lisi was a little Bohemian, maybe acting out her rebellion against the von Brandt family name. Margit had been right. Lisi had indeed drifted far away from the party's rhetoric. The party provided security and access to the circles of power, but if one slipped outside the circle, one was at risk of being ostracised. And then it dawned on Annamarie. She almost laughed aloud with relief. If there was one thing she knew for certain about Lisi, it was this: Lisi did not like to be excluded from anything.

She watched Lisi light another cigarette. Annamarie would wait until after opening night and rehearse her approach. The air smelled of smoke, and Annamarie frowned.

Lisi blew out some. "What?"

"Nothing. It's just especially strong tonight."

"This?" Lisi looked at her cigarette. "You want one?"

Annamarie nodded. She did not usually, but today it seemed necessary. She waited until Lisi had lit it, then they walked on. They reached the next corner and were about to turn up Kaiserjäger when, to their right, they saw an orange-yellow glow consuming the roofs of several buildings. A thick cloud of smoke poured upwards into the sky, blotting out the starry night. The sound of engines roared from behind them, and headlights blinded Annamarie for a moment. One sedan and a transport wagon rushed by. Police and Wehrmacht. Lisi and Annamarie exchanged a look.

"That looked like it was the Gauleiter's car, no?" Lisi asked.

"It can't be. They're still in Munich."

Beneath the streetlamp, Lisi narrowed her eyes. "Veronika lives up that way." She snatched Annamarie's hand and dragged her in the opposite direction of home.

Annamarie's first thought came unbidden. Since when had Lisi had this much affection for the strange girl? Was this worth it? There was a sign in Yiddish. They were in the Jewish neighbourhood. The synagogue was down the road and to the right. And with a sickening blow, Annamarie knew they were heading for trouble.

The entire street was on fire or exploding. Apparently, help had arrived too late. The scene that Annamarie and Lisi came upon was of utter panic. Men, women, and children huddled in their nightclothes in the cold early morning as flames spit out of windows and licked up the walls of buildings. This had been going on for some time.

"Where is the fire brigade?" someone called next to her.

Two young men with clubs took a swing at a shop window across the street. Although Annamarie anticipated the. explosion —the impact—she screamed and ducked, yanking Lisi with her.

But Lisi wrested her arm away from Annamarie's grip and ran down the road.

Annamarie sank into the crowd of onlookers. With truncheons, Wehrmacht soldiers shoved a small group of bearded men together. Annamarie stopped as she caught sight of Franz exiting the automobile that had inched up to the scene. He opened the back door, unaware of her presence, unaware that she was witness to this.

A man dressed in an SS uniform stepped out, was approached by a Wehrmacht soldier, who nodded brusquely. The SS man raised a revolver into the air. He fired one shot, and people screamed. Annamarie flinched. The quiet that followed was chilling. Only the fire crackled and snapped and hissed, devouring people's livelihoods and homes with a merciless fury.

The SS officer then strode to a group of soldiers who were holding on to two men. They were speaking, but she heard nothing. One of the men, clad in a robe and nightclothes, nodded violently. She recognised the insignia on the uniformed officer. Obersturmbannführer. Gauleiter Hofer's second-in-command. He jerked his chin at one of the transport trucks, and the man was marched over and shoved inside the back.

"Annamarie!" Lisi hissed into her ear. "Come with me. Now."

She whirled around to see Lisi standing there with Veronika. Both faces were etched with fear.

"We have to go," Lisi said louder. "Now!"

The second man before the Obersturmbannführer was now also being loaded onto the transport vehicle. On the fringe of the crowd, Annamarie saw that the patrols were shuffling through the onlookers, asking for papers. Who was going to have papers here, in their nightclothes? In the middle of the night? With their houses burning?

Lisi was already moving along the walls of the buildings. In the shadows, where no fires burned, where the light did not reach them, Lisi was making her escape with the Jewess. They were heading back to the main intersection, and Annamarie determined they'd go to the apartment. She slowed down and threw one more look at the oncoming patrols and gasped. Franz was shoving his way through the crowd, his cap tipped back. He stopped, craning his neck. Only when she realised that he was heading for her did she run. She ran as fast as she could, clinging to the shadows, as Lisi had done. At the intersection, she searched for the two women, squinting beneath the dull light of the streetlamps, her eyes still adjusting to the new light after the hot, bright blazes. Before her, their street, the park to the left, the bridge up ahead. She saw no movement. Annamarie, so jumpy her feet hardly touched the ground, attempted a normal tempo all the way to the apartment. Still no sign of Lisi or Veronika. No lights were on inside when she made it upstairs. Had they been stopped? Picked up?

Only after Annamarie had dropped her coat on the settee was there any sign of life. A key in the door. Her heart leapt. And then Lisi and Veronika slipped in, Lisi immediately sliding the bolt, at the same time saying in dull, flat voice, "Turn off the light."

In the dark, the three women breathed.

"Franz saw me," Annamarie whispered.

Nobody said anything, but she could tell Lisi was thinking. Finally, "Did he see me?"

"I don't think so. But he'll want to know what I was doing there."

Veronika spoke next. "We'll come up with a story."

"We'll?" Annamarie asked, incredulous. "What the devil was that all about anyway?"

She did not finish the thought, as someone moved in front of her. "We're going to hide her, Annamarie." Lisi's determination sent chills running down Annamarie's back. "For as long as it takes for the Nazi's anger to cool down. All Veronika knows right now is that several of her neighbours have been rounded up and arrested—"

"They put them into one of those canvas-covered trucks," Annamarie balked.

"I'll talk to Franz." Lisi wheeled in the dark back to Veronika.

Annamarie groaned. "You can't, Lisi. You're in danger."

She heard her roommate take a step towards her. The streetlamp from outside the building was enough to give Annamarie a glimpse at how Lisi was searching Annamarie's face.

"I'm in danger? What on earth do you mean? From whom? You?" Lisi grabbed Annamarie's neck so fast, Annamarie had no time to react. Lisi's hand tightened on her throat, but Annamarie remained unnaturally calm.

"You will keep your mouth shut," Lisi whispered dangerously. "Or you can start looking for a new place."

When Lisi let her go, Annamarie backed away to the door.

"Where do you think you're going?" Veronika asked in the dark.

Home. I'm going home, was what Annamarie wanted to say. And she meant it. She would take the next bus or train, even walk, to the border. Annamarie turned the knob. It was locked. When she spun back, Lisi chuckled.

"The key is safe," she said. "For the time being, you stay here. All of us will just stay right here."

She was in front of Annamarie again and took her by the shoulders. "We need to learn to trust one another, or none of this is going to work. Relax. We've got a show to put on tomorrow. It's your big break."

Annamarie bit her bottom lip. She was terrified, but losing the opportunity to perform with Lisi was even more frightening.

9

BOLZANO, NOVEMBER 1938

Three hundred buildings. One thousand domiciles to accommodate five and a half thousand transplanted Italians who'd come to work at the Bolzano Industrial Zone—the celebrated BIZ. Angelo waited for Giuseppe Mastromattei on the Semirurali settlement site, the plans laid out before him in the hazy fall sunshine. Around him, the sounds of construction: shovels scraping the earth, hammers clacking against wooden frames, metal rods pinging along the gravel. Muddy water from the rain days earlier splashed up as a line of trucks rolled past. Angelo stepped away and around the table to protect his trousers and shoes, then went back to studying the project plans.

The settlement was designed on a grid system to stimulate order and structure. The distant location from Bolzano's centre and the BIZ—but the near proximity to the military base— supported segregation and control. Mastromattei had designed the settlement in order to keep the Italian workers away from the Italian nationalists already deeply rooted in Bolzano, the ones who were already affixed Fascists; those who had already proven their loyalty to the ruling government. The working class who would move here leaned towards more liberal, more social, more unionised tendencies. Socialists. Communists. And Mastromattei intended to control them. They would come and go under the watchful eye of the authorities. The men would have to hike some thirty minutes to work at any number of companies located at the Bolzano Industrial Zone, whilst the women and children would remain under constant guard. For their own safety, that was what Mastromattei communicated, but should there ever be any hint of a workers' revolt, the military could quickly shut down the Semirurali streets and isolate those working men from their families. For as long as it was necessary.

A black limousine pulled up, and Angelo straightened to greet the magistrate. Mastromattei stepped out from the back, wearing his double-breasted grey overcoat and black fez. The military dress indicated that today they would be addressing each other in official capacities. Even Mastromattei's expression—the dark eyebrows knitted together, the mouth turned down, the square jaw set—signalled a sense of decorum was required. Or maybe something was not up to par.

"Magistrate." Angelo shook Mastromattei's hand firmly. "It's looking very well."

Mastromattei cast an appraising eye over the grounds but then appeared distracted, again. "Have you seen to the waterlines?"

"I have," Angelo said. "They're all laid out to plan. The second phase is coming along smoothly, considering the shortages we experienced in September."

Mastromattei nodded at the sprawling construction site, then laid eyes on Angelo, as if finally taking in his presence. "Let's take a walk."

Angelo followed him along the muddy boardwalk between the foundations of several housing units. He waited for the magistrate to speak.

"I've just given a tour of the BIZ to Galeazzo Ciano," Mastromattei said.

"The foreign secretary is here, in the Alto Adige?"

"He was on his way back to Rome from Vienna." Mastromattei concluded there, as if his meeting with the foreign secretary was enough to explain his distracted behaviour.

Angelo did not press the issue, but Mastromattei stopped, turning abruptly to him, as if he waited for Angelo to do exactly that.

"What did he have to say about the industrial zone?" Angelo tried.

Mastromattei smiled before returning to his sombre state. "He feels the BIZ is a fantastic mosaic piece in the overall Italian landscape. Then he said he was astounded at how the city has lost its Nordic flair, has become more Mediterranean in style. He said in ten years nobody would be able to say that this is Bozen anymore. Only Bolzano, a true Italian city."

Angelo nodded. "This is true."

Yet this did not seem to be the topic preoccupying the magistrate. Angelo's head swam with the possibilities. Ciano had been in Vienna. There was the issue with Czechoslovakia and Hungary, but Angelo hardly believed that affected anything the magistrate had a hand in.

Mastromattei was watching Angelo, as if attempting to read those swirling thoughts. "I stopped the foreign secretary right there," he said. "I explained to Ciano that when I arrived in Bolzano, the Germans had already established, in very short time, a Nazi presence."

"The VKS." Now Angelo understood where this conversation was going.

Mastromattei nodded. "Thus *Südtirol*"—the magistrate raised an eyebrow, as if to challenge Angelo to correct his German reference to the province—"finds itself between two tendencies. One consists of the old Austrians, the second Nazi. And the latter are mostly made up of the younger generations. It's always the younger generations that let their emotions rule over their heads.

Maybe it's their lack of experience." He squinted. "I explained to the foreign secretary that if Bolzano is to enjoy its natural Roman state, become a true Italian metropolis, we must take greater measures to control the Nazis here." He winced. "In other words —and Ciano agreed—it's time to crack down on them. And I know just how."

Two workers pushed past them with wheelbarrows filled with mortar, cigarettes dangling from their mouths.

Mastromattei followed them. "One thing at a time," he said more lightly. "First, let's see to our Italian question. Then we'll take on the *allogeni*."

The *allogeni*. The others. Cigarette smoke lingered in Angelo's nostrils. He shivered in his overcoat. Now the magistrate was attending to his inspection of the site. They walked on, stopping to talk to the foreman, asking questions and assessing the answers. Still, the magistrate was holding something back for later. When they reached the table where they had begun, the sun was almost setting.

Mastromattei looked Angelo up and down. "Let me drive you back into the centre. There's something I want to talk to you about."

Angelo suggested they warm up at the Laurin. Mastromattei agreed, and they climbed into the limousine, but the magistrate was quiet all the way into the city centre. By the time they reached the hotel, Angelo's anticipation had risen to a nervous peak.

The maître d' showed them to a corner lounge in the bar, and Angelo ordered two coffees with Strega and instructed the waiter to put them on his room tab. His new apartment would be ready before Christmas, and he was looking forward to moving in, but he was going to miss the service and convenience of the Laurin.

Mastromattei crossed his legs and seemed to finally relax. "Tell me how this Reschen Valley project is coming along, Angelo."

Unsure whether the question was just polite chitchat or whether this was the magistrate's agenda, Angelo started with the simple facts. "The electrical society has given MFE permission to dam up the Reschen and Graun Lakes—"

"Is the Colonel still running things with that group?"

Angelo confirmed he was, sensing that Mastromattei was smirking inwardly.

"There will be a smaller inflow into Haider Lake," Angelo added, his way of sharing how he had prevented the third lake from being integrated into the general reservoir.

"How much power is this project going to bring?"

Of course Mastromattei would be interested. It was the electricity they needed for the BIZ. "Over thirty-three thousand kilowatts to the first plant in Sluderno."

"I've heard"—Mastromattei smiled more than he had since arriving at the construction site—"that MFE has also managed to secure the diversion of the Adige River to Lasa, and Plima Creek to Castelbello."

"You're well informed, as usual," Angelo said. "Altogether, we're hoping for approximately eighty-five thousand kilowatts per day."

"We're going to need that power," Mastromattei said.

Their coffee arrived, and the magistrate beckoned the waiter to him and whispered something into his ear. The waiter nodded and hurried away towards the main lobby.

Angelo picked up where they'd left off. "Plans are to finish expropriating all the necessary land by next spring."

Mastromattei leaned forward to stir the whipped cream on his coffee. It curdled beneath the alcohol.

"Germany is gearing up for war," he said. "They're shitting on the Versailles Treaty. Ciano says that Britain has proven too weak with the infighting taking place in parliament. They and France could have put a stop to Germany's sufferings years ago. Instead, together with the United States, they are now trying to outbid each other on who can sell the most aeroplane engines and parts to the one country determined to win back its former glory." Mastromattei gazed at Angelo, his spoon tapping on the rim of the glass. "Hitler's army will require bodies. Soldiers. And they will pull Italy into this."

The Colonel had predicted this would happen almost as soon as the Great War was over.

Mastromattei made a regretful noise before taking another drink. "The Nazis will try to recruit the Tyroleans northwards first. We must crush the VKS if we're to net our most valuable commodity."

"White gold," Angelo muttered. It was the new term. Italy, poor in natural resources such as oil and metal, had gained, with the annexation of South Tyrol, the one thing that other countries needed, namely energy. Energy that came from the province's alpine rivers and lakes.

Mastromattei looked appreciatively at Angelo. "Yes, white gold and our citizens."

Angelo leaned forward, his coffee still untouched. "What are you suggesting?"

Mastromattei suddenly looked up. "Ah! There you are."

It was the waiter. He held out a newspaper to Mastromattei, who then gave the waiter a few coins. "Good man."

He placed the copy of the day's *Archivio per l'Alto Adige* on the table. "Angelo, what do you think about the Libyan resettlement project?"

Angelo's pulse quickened. "The one that Tolomei says we should all celebrate?" He pictured the distinguished and arrogant senator, the self-proclaimed designer of the Italianisation programme. "His plan is to transplant twenty thousand settlers to our colony in North Africa."

"We've taken many Italians from the south into Bolzano, as many as we can accommodate," Mastromattei said. "The Semirurali will take another year before we can move anyone in, and we'll be planning another one right afterward. But what Tolomei and his other hardliners have failed to see is the opportunity to have integration work the other way around." Mastromattei rubbed his chin. "You are still mediating the expropriated lands and the restitutions for the Reschen Valley population, right?"

Angelo picked up his coffee, pushed the whipped cream aside with the spoon, and took a long sip. The Strega warmed him. He nodded. "Problem is the veterans' administration is stalling with their offers."

"As is MFE."

To avoid scoffing, Angelo took another long drink before answering. "There's not enough land to relocate the hundreds of families. They can't very well make their living off the side of a mountain slope."

"I have a solution," Mastromattei said. "You know the twelve hamlets I allotted between Bolzano and Merano—"

"The Italian settlements. Are they proving prosperous?"

"They're doing well, yes," the magistrate said. "Yet our esteemed senator claims the borderlands are still—after almost twenty years—tenuous at best."

Because, Angelo thought, *the people living there are not self-evidently Italian.*

"What is the goal of Italianisation?" Mastromattei propped his elbow on the arm of his chair and leaned his temple against his index finger. His square chin rested on his thumb.

Angelo played along. "Italianisation means integrating the two cultures so that we can't tell who is who. Especially those living in the community. It might take a couple of generations, but soon enough they'll all feel Italian."

"Exactly. This reservoir is massive. If we push the citizens— Italian citizens!—off their land and north into Hitler's arms, we'll be losing a lot to the efforts I have taken great pains to establish here. Our economic base. Our productivity." He pointed to the wall behind him—the direction of the BIZ beyond. "We'll lose the consumers for those goods we're producing over there."

Angelo's skin prickled. Gina had been right. Mastromattei could be the one to cooperate with. Maybe this was the news he could share with the Steinhausers and the Roeschens and the Hannys. By God, for a price they could finally move forward. "You're suggesting moving the locals out of their valley and into the new hamlets south. If the restitution is fair—"

"They'll find any expropriation unfair." Mastromattei looked amused. "I want them all out. All of them. As far south of the border as possible."

Angelo winced inside. "And if they don't want to go? What other choices can we offer them?"

Mastromattei's look darted to the newspaper between them. He released his index finger from his temple and pointed at it, the amusement gone. "They're Italian citizens. We could resettle them to Libya."

He couldn't be serious. "That's an...extreme move. Can we not explore all our alternatives before we do that?"

Mastromattei leaned back in the plush chair, the leather creaking beneath him. "Then call a meeting with everyone involved."

Now they were onto something. Open discussions. "Good. It will take some time to get the representatives from the Reschen Valley—"

"No. Call a meeting with your father's company, the electrical society, and the veterans' administration. The people in the Reschen Valley will get offers for their land and get instructions for resettlement after the stakeholders agree on a procedure. There is no need to involve the population in this yet. It's only one idea of how we could proceed, correct?"

"Surely the residents could stay in the valley if they choose to. All they want is a fair offer. What is the worst they can do? Tie us up in legal battles?" Angelo laughed drily. "There isn't a lawyer around who would take up that fight."

Mastromattei leaned forward, eyes narrowed. "There is no court in the nation that would accept the case." He slapped his thigh and straightened. "They can do what they want. But perhaps you should inform them of the consequences. These days Rome is coming down hard on those who revolt." He drained his glass and stood. "I'd prefer to save those bullets for the war we'll be dragged into and not defending ourselves against a bunch of farmers who still haven't accepted the fact that they are Italians first."

Angelo rose with him and soberly took the magistrate's offered hand. He understood the warning.

Dismissively, Mastromattei said, "Let me know when you've coordinated with everyone else."

Angelo nodded and watched the man weave his way through the room, greeting the people he passed. The magistrate's populace, all of them, showed great respect to the man, though respect was simply a thin veil over fear.

He drained his coffee and leaned his head back, staring at the rich wood-panelled ceiling and the wainscoting. The bar was filling up. He imagined Gina next to him, what she would say at this very moment. If she were not visiting Filipa in Rome, he would call her now and talk this out. Better yet, just head over to the villa.

This was not going to work. That was what she would say. A resettlement to the south was an easy solution, she would say, but the Hannys, the Roeschens, and the Steinhausers were not looking for an easy solution. A revolt—Mastromattei had made that clear—would be quashed with blood and violence. Besides, the magistrate's design for the Semirurali settlement had proven that he was ahead of all games. He could anticipate and prevent.

Angelo heard Gina's voice loud and clear. *You'll have to tell the*

Steinhausers about this. Don't you dare keep them in the dark. You promised them that.

They would shoot the messenger, that was what they would do. He remembered the meeting in March, the way Katharina had pointed the rifle at him when she found him sitting on the bench outside her house.

"She's not here," she'd said. "You're too late."

Annamarie was gone, presumably in Austria. Except he really had not been too late, had he? Because Katharina offered him the opportunity to set things right. He was still astounded by the memory of meeting her husband then. The man had walked up to him, introduced himself as Florian Steinhauser, and—as if this were an everyday occurrence—invited Angelo into the house. Angelo remembered their two boys, curiosity overcoming the initial hostility and suspicion. He, Katharina, and that husband of hers had been careful to keep Annamarie's name out of the conversation, but between the lines and in front of their sons, Katharina and Florian had made one thing clear that day: Angelo owed them. It was time to pay his dues.

"We can learn to live under Italian law," Katharina had said, "even be loyal citizens, but not if the government pulls our land out from beneath our feet. We won't accept it, Angelo. You must help us. We need someone who can negotiate in our favour."

Except there were dangers involved. He had to be smart. He had to play the game. And that was why he also needed Gina.

Mastromattei was now talking about war, about keeping the Tyroleans here because they needed them. The Fascist hardliners would probably do everything in their power to get rid of the Tyroleans but keep the land. Neither party wanted Hitler to renege on the deal with Mussolini. The Alto Adige would remain Italian. But those hardliners...he could imagine Tolomei gleefully escorting the Tyroleans over the northern border himself.

Angelo shot up. He waved the waiter over, paid his bill, and strode into the lobby. At the front desk, he requested a free line on a telephone. He gave the operator the instructions, waited, and finally heard the ring.

"Chiara," Angelo said when she picked up, "I need to see you. Urgently. Can we meet on neutral ground?"

Neutral ground was the café in the park along the Talavera River the next day. In the distance, Castel Roncolo overlooked the bluffs. To Angelo's right, the Three Chimneys of the Dolomites shimmered in the midafternoon sun. It was late November, but the palm trees and plane trees that lined the walking paths waved gently in the breeze.

He caught sight of Chiara as she made her way from where she would have taken the shortcut from their neighbourhood. She wore a fur-lined coat and a close-fitting cap, beneath which her red curls had been elegantly fashioned to shoulder length. He could see the line of her mouth and how she was uncertain about how to form it, her expression wavering between cool and aloof to a kind of pitying politeness, to curiosity and annoyance all at once. Angelo stood and took her hand, then led her to a chair at the table. When he settled in himself, he tried to get her to look at him, but her eyes darted nervously between the tables, the other patrons, the mountains she faced, the waiter whose attention she must have hoped to get as an excuse to avoid looking at Angelo.

He finally waved over the waiter himself. "Espresso?" he confirmed with his wife.

"Tea," she said. "Herbal."

The waiter asked about pastries, and she waved him off before turning to Angelo. "So. Here I am." She lay her hands in her lap.

"Chiara, can we move past this?" The awkwardness, he meant. How often would he have to say he was sorry? He really was. He was not going to get the help he needed as long as the hurt and the anger and the resentment still lay between them.

"What is it that you expect of me, Angelo? You called me. I'm here. What is it that you want?"

"I want to know how you are."

"You want a divorce. How am I supposed to be?"

He drew in a breath, tapped the serviette next to his plate. "I'm not here to talk about that."

"And why not, Angelo?" Her voice was low but sharp. A hard jab.

"We can talk about it another day. That's not why I called."

She undid the top two buttons of her coat and opened them up. She wore a lace blouse beneath. "It's hot in the sun."

"So it is."

She pulled impatiently at her gloves and removed them when the waiter brought her tea. She looked up at Angelo. "Fine. We're not talking about a divorce. I don't want one. I want an annulment. And that will mean you will simply have to own up to what you did. If you would ask me—just once—what I want, that would be my answer. To stand before our priest and tell him what you did and why it justifies an annulment."

"Done."

Chiara stared at him.

"I'm serious. I'll do it. I have no problem with paying my penance. Let's do it, Chiara. An annulment, and then let's move on with our lives."

The handle of her teacup kept her occupied. "That easily?"

"It's been almost a year, Chiara."

"Marco…"

Angelo tipped his head. He wanted to reach out for her hand —her voice had been so sad. "I promise to find a way to him. He's not ready. That's all."

"He's going into the military in January." her tone was choked. She looked at Angelo. "There's going to be a war."

Now he did reach out for her hand and held it. "It's terrible timing, I know. Has he been through the musters yet?"

"Yes. And wants to be a pilot."

Angelo was stunned. "A pilot?"

"Mechanical engineering. That's what he says he's always wanted to do. Not civil engineering, but then…" She shrugged. "He decided he wants to operate the plane."

"Do you want me to talk to him?"

Chiara laughed aloud, withdrawing her hand from his. "Why would he listen to you, Angelo?"

"Fine." The back of his neck grew hot.

"No," Chiara said, straight faced again. "He won't listen to you, but he might listen to the Colonel."

"My father would never try and talk him out of it. You can forget it."

She nodded. She still had not drunk her tea. "Yes, your father doesn't listen to you either."

Angelo took in a deep breath.

This time it was she who reached for his hand. "But I am listening. Talk to me. That's why I came. I'll hear out what you have to say."

Angelo swallowed. "All right, then let me say I'm sorry."

"I know that already." She lifted her chin towards the Three Chimneys. "So am I."

He remembered a particular day they had spent here together. One fall day, a picnic, Marco just a toddler, their cares and concerns—Pietro's detention, the Colonel's moves to make Angelo minister without his consent—had dissipated that day, and Angelo had loved her fiercely all the more because that was also the day he'd recognised that they had drifted worlds apart.

"I tried so hard to hang on to you," he said.

"You betrayed me with a young woman up north." She tried to pull away, but he grasped tighter. She looked defiant. "You did not tell me about it for sixteen years, and I had to find out in the most embarrassing, devastating, and shameful way I can imagine. You did that to me."

He squeezed her hand. "I did all that. And much more, Chiara. Much more. It's unforgivable, what I did. I want to know how we can"—and he was surprised by the revelation that this was the true reason why he'd called her—"continue to be friends. To end our marriage officially and remain Marco's parents. In order for me to win back my son, I need you to stand by me. At least in this respect."

Chiara dropped her eyes but he'd seen the tears well up. "Then you agree. There is nothing left to salvage between us."

"Do you understand how much I have always loved you? That it was killing me to hide what I did? That I admired you so much I almost hated you?"

Revelation bloomed in her expression.

"I was," he continued. "I was jealous that you were in love with all your causes more than with me—"

"Never! I never loved my activism more than you, Angelo."

He gently let go of her hand. "But you did, Chiara. You did."

She toyed with the teacup handle.

"Maybe I'm not wholly correct. If I look back, you were fighting to be my equal. But you were asking for the impossible. Look—"

"Enough, Angelo." She closed her eyes. "I can't listen to this."

"But I mean it. Look at me. I mean it. I am not saying these things to try and make things better or to lay the blame one way or the other. I'm telling you what it is that I finally understand about myself. I know how I came to make my mistakes."

"And the benefit of these lessons learned?" she asked sourly. "Gina Conti receives the prize, or what?"

Angelo sighed. He placed his hand on the table, open. An offering. "This has nothing to do with her. Not this."

"Then what does?"

"Chiara." His voice was low, warning. "Keep her out of this.

I'm going to tell you one more time. She has nothing to do with you or me."

His wife's hand disappeared beneath the table before she held his look. He saw concession. "Fine. She's not our topic of discussion. Why did you call me? What is it that you need?"

Angelo proceeded cautiously. "Pietro told me you and Michael Innerhofer have something you're working on."

"What do you mean?" she asked sharply.

Angelo leaned in, kept his voice low. "I need your help. I need your help, and I need Michael Innerhofer's help. And there's something in it for both of you."

Chiara's green eyes flashed. "Really, like what?"

"Well, if I were to tell you that the South Tyrolean might put up a statue in your name in the end, would that make a difference?"

Chiara huffed. "What makes you think I'm interested in… Angelo, that's ridiculous." But her face had flushed. Gina had been right all those months ago. Chiara wanted to be loved by them, the Italian light for the South Tyroleans. She and Michael recognised as leaders of a peaceful, intermixed society.

Angelo kept his look steady on her.

"It's ridiculous," she repeated. "But I'm listening."

Angelo smiled. "Good."

10

RESCHEN VALLEY, NOVEMBER 1938

T he smell of warm chestnuts filled the Planggers' *Stube* as Katharina unravelled the red-and-white-chequered dishcloth. The children gathered around the table for Katharina's special surprise, chattering with anticipation. She set the cloth in the middle, and the other five children snatched at the warm chestnuts. Little Anna cautiously poked at one before Katharina handed it to her. The child juggled the chestnut between her palms, blowing on it, though after Katharina's long walk across the valley, it could not be so hot anymore.

Out of habit, Katharina checked the window to make certain nobody had followed her to the Planggers' or were sneaking about. Even in the darkness she could see the snow illuminated on the peaks above. The sky was light with clouds. It would snow once more.

She held two lessons a week here in the Planggers' *Stube*. One group from seven to eight and the second for an hour thereafter. On Tuesdays she met with a dozen children at another home in Reschen, except then she had four groups. Each for half an hour, the children weaving their way back to their homes between the backs of houses and alleys to avoid the roads. They were that close to the military barracks, right under the Italians' noses. Georg claimed the Italians would never suspect they were that stupid. It made sense, but still, Katharina hated Tuesdays.

Back at the table, the children cradled the warm nuts between their hands before cracking the shells open and popping the starchy nuts into their mouths.

"Today," Katharina announced, "we're going to talk about the different traditions that we celebrate. In three weeks, children, what holiday will we be celebrating?"

"Christmas?" one child cried.

"That's in six weeks, not in three," Katharina corrected. "What comes before Christmas? Anyone know?"

Manuel's arm shot up, but she frowned and shook her head. He knew what she was referring to. He'd just seen Bernd trying out the Krampus costume Katharina had fashioned from lambskins. Then Florian had carved and painted a grotesque but artful wooden mask, affixed with deer antlers.

Peter Plangger raised his hand uncertainly. "Is it St Niklaus?"

"That's right," Katharina said.

She looked sternly at Manuel when he whispered to his friend. She had instructed him to keep the secret to himself. Since last year, Manuel had learned that St Niklaus was really Florian dressed up in a fake white beard and wig. As Florian disguised his voice into something more gruff as he read the poems they had written for the children, Manuel had come to her and whispered in her ear.

"That's Father, isn't it? I recognise that voice when he reads the pirate story to me."

That was when Katharina knew her youngest had grown too old to believe in the magic of St Niklaus.

"Mrs Steinhauser?" One boy now wiggled his arm wildly. "Peter wants to know how St Niklaus knows everything?"

"The Walscher tell him," another boy said, and some of the children gasped.

Katharina bit her lip. Children were much more insightful than the adults cared to admit.

Manuel protested. "Nah-ah. The only ones who tell St Niklaus anything—"

"St Niklaus," Katharina interjected loudly and gave Manuel that warning look again, "is all knowing. He sees everything. That is why he knows who's been good and who deserves lumps of coal."

"Which Krampus brings," Little Anna said wisely.

The boy who'd guessed that the Italians informed St Niklaus shivered. "Krampus is scary. Scarier than the Walscher. Those chains dragging on the ground. And that awful face." He stood, held his arms up wide, and limped a few steps, as if dragging chains.

There was more tittering and speculation about St Niklaus's dark shadow. Peter Plangger still looked stricken.

Katharina glanced at Manuel, who looked bored. He, of course, now suspected the truth—that each verse that Florian had read as St Niklaus contained information gathered from the parents. That day Manuel had recognised Florian, Katharina had tried to get her youngest to believe in magic again and made up a story of how St Niklaus always chose an adult in each village to represent him. With that, he then provided that representative with a report on the children. Manuel had thrown her a look of disbelief, but then Bernd had jumped in and confirmed Katharina's information, ruffling his brother's head.

"Even I know that," he'd boasted.

And whatever the older brother said, Manuel believed was set in stone. Until a few weeks ago when Bernd revealed he wanted to be Krampus this year. Now Manuel knew only the adults were behind the legendary saint.

With the chestnuts almost gone now, Katharina pulled the children's attention to her once more. "So what else do you know about St Niklaus's story?"

"He brings cookies and nuts," one child cried.

"And Krampus comes with him and leaves coal in our shoes if we've been naughty," Peter Plangger said soberly.

"*Ja*," said another child, "like when you break the law!"

Katharina laughed and glanced at Peter again. With no empty shells before him, she realised Peter had not yet taken a chestnut.

"Peter," she urged. "Take one. Go ahead before all the others eat them up."

But Peter shook his head.

"Aren't you hungry?"

He shrugged.

Of course they were hungry. Everyone was hungry almost all the time, especially children. She frowned and placed a chestnut before him to make sure he got at least one. "Then eat it when you are, all right?"

"Frau Steinhauser," he said so softly that she had to bend to hear him. "St Niklaus is dangerous, isn't he?"

"But, Peter, why would you say that?"

"Because just like the Walscher, he knows everything about everyone."

Katharina squatted next to him. "I suppose, in a way, that's true. But he has other reasons for knowing so much."

Peter looked at the chestnut. "Yes, but if the Walscher give him enough cookies, he might just report what he sees here every week."

Katharina stared at the boy, at a loss for words.

Snow was falling when Florian picked Katharina and Manuel up at the Planggers' to take them back to Arlund. He always waited in Graun at the inn during Katharina's lessons. They took the road that cut through the fields between Reschen Lake and Graun Lake.

"Jutta and Hans have asked me to bring you by before we go on home," Florian said.

"Must we?" Katharina was tired.

"They insisted."

"Why tonight of all nights?" She just wanted to get warm and into bed.

Florian turned his head, and even in the dark she caught his mischievous look.

Katharina halted. "They haven't! Is it finally going to happen? They're going to get married?"

Florian laughed. "It's supposed to be a surprise. Can you at least pretend like it is when they tell you themselves?"

Katharina laughed, and Manuel tugged away from her hand. He ran ahead of her in the luminous snowy landscape. When he was far enough away, she told Florian about Peter Plangger.

"From the mouths of babes," Florian said.

Katharina chewed her bottom lip. "Where's Bernd?"

Florian did not answer right away, and when he told her that he'd taken the Krampus costume to show "the boys," Katharina groaned.

"He's most certainly gone off with Ulrich and Andreas again," she said.

"I can't put him under house arrest for the rest of his young life," Florian said. "Besides, he said something about meeting with David Roeschen. He wants to find out whether he can join the carnival club, wanted to show the costume. He could use it again then."

Katharina tried to assume the best. David Roeschen was the least of her worries; she'd prefer it if Bernd would spend more time with him.

"What about Annamarie?" Florian broke the silence through the falling snow. "Have you decided how you want to go about this?"

Katharina thought of Tante Rosa's last postcard. It was cryptic only on the surface, but Katharina was certain it was Tante Rosa's way of telling her it was time to fetch Annamarie home as soon as possible.

We'd love to see you here at Christmas, it had said. *Your old cousin is not getting any younger. We could have a lovely reunion for the holidays.* They'd never spent a holiday together. Katharina had also made it clear she would not help Annamarie fill out anything on that *Ahnenpass*. Not without seeing the child for herself.

"I'll go to the town hall tomorrow," she finally said, "and try to get a travel permit."

Florian nodded. "If you can't, I will. I'm still a German citizen."

In answer, she wrapped her arm in his. One of them would bring Annamarie home, and before Christmas. Katharina imagined having all her children around her.

The church steeple in Graun tolled the half hour by the time they reached the village. The lights at Jutta's inn illuminated the drifts of snow. Even from where they approached, Katharina could see the *Stube* was full, and she heard muffled laughter coming from inside. Against the windows where the benches lined up, heads bobbed and she heard people clapping. It was a real celebration, like in the old days.

Manuel pushed the door open, and Katharina and Florian followed him in. Jutta came into the hallway as they shook out their coats. Behind her, music poured out of the *Stube*, and Katharina caught sight of Hans, grinning all the way past his beard as he clinked mugs with the regulars.

"What is everyone celebrating?" she asked innocently.

Jutta put her hands on her hips and tilted her head in Florian's direction. "You told her, didn't you?"

Florian shrugged. "She guessed. You know how she is. Can't get anything past her."

"Come here." Katharina hugged Jutta to her. "Congratulations. I'm really happy for you. Now how did he propose?"

147

Jutta laughed. "He didn't! I did."

"What?" Katharina whirled on Florian in surprise. "Now that part he did not tell me about."

She followed Jutta into the *Stube* and listened to the story, which Jutta must have told a few times before that night already, so smoothly did it come out.

"*Bratäpfel*," Jutta started. "All because of *Bratäpfel*. Hans was helping me peel and stuff the apples, and then he asked me where I keep the sugar, and I said, 'If you don't know by now where my pantry is, then maybe it's time we get married so you can find out.' And he said"—Jutta put her hands on her hips, puffed up her chest, and tucked her chin in—"'Now Jutta Hanny, that sounds like you're making a marriage proposal.' And I said, 'Well, Hans Glockner, I am. What do you say to that?' And that man over there"—she pointed to Hans—"dropped onto both of his aching knees, took my hand, and said, 'It would be my honour to finally be your husband. What took you so long?' And then, Katharina, he reminded me that he had asked me all those years ago, when I tried to, oh, you know, give him some money to save his old farm. And I had refused him, and we argued about that for about ten minutes while the apples wilted, and until I finally kissed him and said, 'Shut up, already, and let's go get the priest.'"

Katharina laughed. "You two have been beating around the bush with this for decades."

Jutta's face smoothed out, and she looked wistful. "Not necessarily decades. It took a while for me to get over your uncle, you know?"

Katharina nodded and hugged Jutta to her. Behind her was a large pop, and then a second one. She and Jutta pulled apart, and people exclaimed around them.

"Who's popping champagne corks?" someone called out.

Next to Katharina, Jutta muttered, "I haven't had champagne in this house in I don't know how long..." She moved to the back of the room, towards the door that led to the kitchen. When she opened it, there was another pop, and this time a muffled explosion. Katharina could see directly through the kitchen window facing the back of the inn's garden and the church. The unmistakable glow of flames appeared on the ground floor of the town hall.

Others had sensed something was not right, some leaving the *Stube* and stepping outside and around back. Katharina stood next to Jutta and Florian in the kitchen, and she quickly looked for Manuel. She found him squeezing through the bodies, eyes wide with fright.

Another explosion, and a collective gasp. The windows to Basso's office exploded, and now the flames licked outwards and upwards. Snow still drifted lazily in contrast to the urgent fire.

"Hans," Florian called, "let's get a line going from the well and put this out."

Everyone pushed out the back door, and Katharina followed Jutta and the men into the barn, looking for every possible vessel they could get water into. Katharina searched through for anything left over, anything at all. A metallic sound coming from a dark corner in the barn made her stop.

"Hello?" She listened. Nothing.

"Katharina," Florian called from outside, "hurry up."

Beyond, voices rose. High pitched with outrage and cursing in Italian. Several *carabinieri* got into line with them. The air was thick with greasy smoke. As Katharina hurried out of the barn with a shallow feed dish—useless really, but the only thing she could find—Father Wilhelm ran from the parish home in his cassock, like a dark specter against the snowy landscape. Across from Jutta's inn, the Prieths' curtains pulled open. Herr Prieth's son and his wife stared out at the assembled group from Jutta's inn, already passing buckets and jugs filled with water as fast as they could fill them. Several men faced off against the fire, and the uniformed *carabinieri* worked side by side with members of the committee: Georg Roeschen, Martin Noggler, Hans and

Florian, and now Father Wilhelm. When Katharina looked back at the bakers' home, the curtains had dropped and the lights turned off.

The fire took on another form—raging from within, flames now at the roof. The town hall would burn to the ground if the militia did not arrive soon. And then there they were. They took their place next to the others and reorganised the line, pulling hoses out and connecting them to the water tanks on the vehicles. Then they doused the fire, but Katharina and the others did not stop passing the water buckets from Jutta's well. It took an agonizingly long time and a second truck of water to put the fire out. By that time, the church bell had already rung eleven and the snow had stopped.

Katharina saw Florian making his way back to her. When he reached her, the *carabinieri* were already organising everyone into smaller groups and questioning people about what they had seen.

Katharina grasped Florian's arms. "Where's Manuel?"

Florian scanned the crowd of people. "I thought he was with you."

Katharina called for her youngest, but what she really wanted to know was where Bernd was. Her gut told her this fire was no accident. And that her son was somehow involved.

Just as she found Manuel with Jutta and Hans, Captain Basso came striding over. "Everyone stays here for questioning. Signora Hanny, we will use your inn."

"Certainly we can pick this up in the morning," Jutta argued. "Everyone's exhausted. We fought this fire with you, in case you haven't noticed."

But the captain ignored Jutta and told his men to funnel them all into the inn. A half hour later, the investigating *carabinieri* grew bored when everyone had the same thing to say: they'd been celebrating Hans and Jutta's engagement, heard popping noises, and went to look. They'd seen a fire, organised themselves to put it out, and now were answering the investigators' questions. They were tired. Could they go home now?

"Go on—let them go," a policeman said.

"I'm worried about Bernd," Katharina said to Florian.

He closed his eyes briefly and said to Hans, "Do you mind taking us up to Arlund?"

She lifted Manuel into her arms, and Hans steered Katharina out of the *Stube*. Her son weighed heavily, and he fell against her. Shivering, they climbed into the cart. Because the snow was too deep for the shorter and steeper route, Hans took the long way back to Katharinahof. When they reached the ridge, Katharina's heart leapt at the sight of several policemen standing in lamplight in their front yard. Pushed into the circle of light, Katharina saw two figures. Bernd she recognised right away, but it took her a while to see that the second person was Andreas Ritsch. Both were dressed in lambskins and chain-link draped all the way down their arms. Two Krampusses surrounded by the *carabinieri*.

A policeman laughed. "*Molto appropriato da parte vostra essere vestiti come i diavoli che siete!*" Very appropriate of you two to be dressed up as the devils you are.

This was the same guard Katharina seemed to cross paths with over and over, the one who had told her she needed to let her children grow up and take responsibility. Lorenzo Tocci. That was his name.

Florian was out of the wagon before Hans rolled to a stop. This time her husband was not placating. He charged into the circle. "What's happening here?" he asked in Italian. "Bernd? What's happened? What have you done?"

"These two were caught hiding in the cellar here," Tocci said angrily. "Someone reported seeing these two devils throwing burning bottles at the town hall. They're coming with us."

Florian pushed his chest forward, but Hans, who stood behind him, clapped a hand on his shoulder. Katharina yanked Manuel to her and demanded that Bernd deny it, but her son did not even look her way. The police hustled him and Andreas to the waiting vehicle. Both boys were in the back of the car when Toni and Patricia Ritsch came around the corner of the house.

"Release my son now," Toni demanded of the *carabinieri*.

Katharina pointed at Toni. "This is all Andreas's fault! He's the one who gets our Bernd into trouble. He's the one with the stupid ideas!"

Toni's face twisted. "Florian, get your wife under control here."

The police were leaving, and Katharina rushed to one of them. "Where are you taking my son?"

"Tonight, to the barracks. They'll stay the night there. First thing tomorrow, they'll be transported to Bolzano for sentencing."

"Bolzano?" Patricia cried in disbelief.

"How can I see him?" Katharina pleaded with Tocci.

He grimaced. "Sorry, Signora, but you won't be able to see him. Unless, of course, you travel to Bolzano."

Patricia was saying something to her, but Katharina pushed her to the side. "Get off my property," she snapped. "Go on. Go home!"

She watched as the vehicles pulled away, skidding on the icy roads. Manuel cried after his brother. Katharina shovelled him inside, leaving Florian arguing with the Ritsches. By the time he was through, Katharina was already curled up in bed, weeping.

"Toni and I will go to Bolzano, follow the transport down."

She sat up. "Over my dead body. And we can't afford it. We could barely afford to get up to Innsbruck if I'd gotten the permission!"

Florian cleared his throat. "I'm going to ask the committee to lend us the money."

Katharina stared at him in the flickering lamplight. She pointed a finger at him. "If the committee even pulls that kind of money together, I'm telling you right now, it will not be Toni travelling to Bolzano, but me. You do not go without me. You understand?"

Florian took in a deep breath and sank down next to her on the bed.

"I mean it," she said.

He scooped her into his arms and smoothed her hair. "I know you do. I know."

As Florian rocked her back and forth, she grieved for her children.

11

INNSBRUCK, NOVEMBER 1938

Applause. Cheering. The crowd was on their feet. Lined up on stage with the whole cast, Annamarie waited for Lisi's signal, then raised her hands with the rest to step forward for the final encore. For a second, her heart froze at the sight of four SS men in the crowd. She stepped back into the limelight, searching for Margit and Franz. When Lisi moved forward to take another bow, Annamarie was surprised to hear Max amongst the voices. She found him, grinned, and tore her hand out of the actor's to her right to throw Max kisses.

The curtain fell and the entire cast, Annamarie included, broke into excited chatter until the director appeared. Unsmiling, he pecked Lisi's cheek and congratulated the others, but his demeanour was—as it had been all week—of one who was attending a funeral.

In the dressing room, Annamarie was quick about changing, eager to see Maxi. She stood over Lisi and squeezed her shoulder. "It was marvellous, was it not?"

Lisi, too, seemed sobered by the success. She rubbed her face furiously, as if she wanted to scrape deep beneath the makeup. "You've gotten better with every show." She set the washcloth down and picked up a brush. Her gaze landed on something beyond the mirror. "The gang is going to want to celebrate. We need to convince them to go out, not to our—"

Annamarie swung towards the door, expecting to see Margit or Max or Franz, but no one was there. She faced the mirror again, and Lisi shared a look with her in the reflection.

"The Iron Rooster?" Annamarie asked.

What lay between them, between the play on stage and their real-life drama, was Veronika. Quite literally, for Veronika was, despite Annamarie's misgivings, still hiding in their apartment. It had made for a terrible, nerve-wracking week.

Before Lisi could reply, the gang barged in, laughing and applauding, and Lisi twitched beneath Annamarie's hand.

Cradling a bottle of champagne. Max sauntered over and kissed Annamarie whilst Margit and Franz fell upon Lisi.

"Are you surprised to see me?" Max beamed. "I was able to get back from Munich in time."

"I am. Wasn't it wonderful? Maxi, I could do this forever. I was born to be an actress. I really was."

His expression wavered. "Forever's a long time, *Schätzchen*. Anyway, you certainly outshine that Jewess."

Annamarie's smile cracked.

"Franz reported they haven't managed to find her since she was tossed out of the theatre," Max said. "What's her name? Veronika Fuchs? Shame, really. Gauleiter Hofer is ordering another crackdown, and Franz has got a quota to meet."

Annamarie could not move a muscle, did not trust her voice.

Max shrugged. "The authorities have her parents, right? Maybe she'll turn up."

Margit moved in and embraced Annamarie, but Annamarie did not register her words. Instead, she looked to Lisi for help. Franz was crouching at the dressing table, one arm around his sister's shoulder and twirling a cigar in his other hand. He behaved as if he'd never shared a drink with Veronika, had never joked with her, danced with her, or teased her.

"I told the gang," Franz said to Lisi, "that you throw the most marvellous parties, sister heart. We're all joining you tonight."

Lisi smiled wanly. "We're celebrating at the Iron Rooster."

"But why?" Franz protested. "You've been at the Rooster after each show. That's not like you." His eyes searched hers in the mirror, and something about him frightened Annamarie.

When Lisi stood, he feigned a pout. "Come now, Lisi. I promised Max and Margit they'd finally get a taste of your Bohemian-styled parties."

"But we haven't prepared anything," Annamarie interjected. How could Lisi smile so coolly?

"Nonsense." Franz laughed. He rubbed his sister's shoulders so hard, she swayed back and forth. "The best parties you've ever thrown were the spontaneous ones."

As if to prove his point, when a few of the cast and crew passed by the door, he stepped into the hallway and announced that the post-show party would be at Lisi's apartment. Annamarie listened with horror as most whooped with delight.

"I'm tired tonight," Annamarie whispered into Max's ear, "and I haven't seen you in a week. Why don't we go somewhere where we can be alone?"

"You have an apartment, and I don't," Max whispered back. "They can celebrate without us, and we'll just lock your bedroom door." He pulled away and gave her that trademark smile of his. With a jolt, it repulsed her. The smile wasn't sexy. It was sinister.

Annamarie followed everyone to the exit, her mind spinning with the worst possible scenario, but the door flew open and a surprised Sepp stood before them, rain falling in such a drizzle it almost looked like snow beneath the streetlights.

"I was coming to look for you," Sepp said to Lisi, his expression one of mortification. "There is an SS higher-up asking for you." He glanced over his shoulder. "Four, to be exact."

Lisi swayed a little, but Sepp's brow knitted.

"They're here with flowers, Elisabeth." He held her arm before whispering, "They've brought flowers, not handcuffs."

Just then, the four men Annamarie had seen in the audience stepped around the door and in front of Sepp. Max, Franz, and Margit snapped to attention and saluted them. Lisi donned a coy manner as one of the officers presented her with an armful of roses.

"Fräulein von Brandt," he said, clicking his heels and bowing, "SS-Untersturmführer Gustav Schwarz at your service. We would like to invite you to dinner at Otto's Cellar." He introduced the three other officers and eyed the rest of the group before adding, "Bring your friends here."

"Otto's Cellar," Lisi said brightly. "How delightful. I'd be most honoured." She turned to her brother. "You know the place, Franz. It will be grand. There's music and dancing, and," she trilled lightly, "we mustn't disappoint these gentlemen here."

Annamarie's heart thundered, and a hysterical laugh bubbled up. She clung to Max's arm. "Let's go to Otto's. I'm starving." She nodded at Margit to gain immediate agreement.

Max looked put out. Just as quickly, he flashed her the one-sided smile and jerked his head at Franz. They were outranked, and they knew it.

Lisi hooked her arm into Schwarz's offered elbow and swept out into the rain, but not before flashing Sepp a grateful look that Annamarie could not miss. Could it be that there was one more person who knew about Veronika? She did not care. For the moment, these SS men had saved their skins. And only by a hair.

Veronika had taken to locking herself in Lisi's room whenever she was left alone in the apartment, and also to sleeping in Lisi's bed with her. Annamarie padded into the sour-smelling kitchen the day after the celebration in Otto's Cellar, bracing herself for a cosy scene between Lisi and Veronika at breakfast. But only a sleepy Lisi was sitting there with her back to Annamarie, smoke from her cigarette drifting out of the cracked-open window. Annamarie wished they would stop smoking in the apartment.

A pot of coffee was on the table. Annamarie took a cup and saucer out of the kitchen cabinet.

"This was in the pile of post." Lisi yawned and held an envelope out.

Annamarie took it from her and glanced at the postmark. Graun. She sank into the seat at the end of the table, and the coffee cup rattled in its saucer. Tante Rosa must have shared Annmarie's address with her mother. She looked at Lisi meaningfully, but Lisi seemed oblivious to the significance of the letter. It was too thin to contain the documents she had requested. Her mother's defiance was the last thing Annamarie needed on this day.

The door to Lisi's bedroom opened, and Veronika came in, pecked Lisi on the cheek, and gave Annamarie a cautious good morning before pouring herself the rest of the coffee.

"Sorry," she said to Annamarie as she caught sight of the clean cup. "You didn't get any."

Annamarie fought her annoyance. "I'll just make some more. Anyone else?" she asked pointedly.

She folded the unopened letter into her pocket and went to the stove to make hot water.

Veronika whispered something to Lisi about how she hadn't meant to pour all the coffee for herself before loudly announcing, "I'll be leaving this afternoon. You two needn't worry about me being here. I'll go tonight when you're at the show. Annamarie is right. Last night was too close of a call."

Annamarie stifled the thrill, feeling guilty about being happy that Veronika would finally leave. It had been just over a week since the Nazis had burned the synagogue down. The fire brigades, they found out, had been ordered to stay away. The city was still coming to grips with the violence, this little party in the kitchen included. Her presence posed a great danger.

"You can't just leave." Lisi was fuming. "Where will you go?"

"I have family in Dresden," Veronika said.

Her relief checked, Annamarie faced them. "She has to go. What if people want to come over again? They always do."

Lisi scoffed. "Let's not forget Max and how eager he is to escape his male-dominated sleeping quarters." She turned to Veronika. "You're safer here than anywhere. Trust me on this. Dresden is out of the question too. What happened here has happened everywhere."

"Goebbels ordered a nationwide pogrom," Annamarie said.

Lisi shot her a look of disgust. "You ought to know. You'll be meeting him tonight anyway, after the parade."

Annamarie marched to the table and pushed the morning paper to Veronika. "It's the headline," she snapped. "And yes, Margit and I are guests at Gauleiter Hofer's tonight, but, as you know from your SS admirers, Goebbels's interests are widespread."

Lisi leaned over the article, then stood only to drop before Veronika and pull her into her arms. They embraced for a long time.

"Just wait a few days," Lisi pleaded. "I'll talk to Franz tonight. I know he suspects, but I'll come up with something that will keep him at bay. This will run its course, and by then your family will be back home. I'm sure of it."

Annamarie felt sorry for Veronika. She did. She felt that punishing the local Jews for a crime committed by one passionate vagrant refugee in Paris was ridiculous. And very serious. Which was why her heart fell when Veronika agreed she would stay.

"And if Franz suspects enough to come looking for her?" Annamarie demanded.

Lisi studied Veronika. "I've already got ideas for an escape plan. Trust me."

Veronika sat stock still in the chair, like a child terrified into obedience.

The hysteria. Annamarie was jostled on every side as each girl in her troop shrieked at the sight of the black sedan pulling into their street. It crept slowly behind the marching Wehrmacht. Annamarie believed thousands of men were goose-stepping in straight, thick black columns, leading the Führer on a procession of fawning and bliss.

Annamarie caught sight of Margit, who always cut the perfect image of a conservative Aryan woman, but now even she exhibited excitement. The bouquet of red and white roses quivered against her bosom, her gaze trained on the topless automobile creeping towards them. The Führer was perched on top of the backseat, waving at the crowd. When the vehicle finally reached Margit, she stepped forward and presented the bouquet—perhaps the hundredth, the thousandth of such flowers that filled the sedan—and swooned as the Führer patted her hand and glided by. When he was level with Annamarie a moment later, his head, his attention, switched from the group of BDM girls to the Hitler Jugend on the other side of the street. Just as the boys were segregated from the girls in most activities, so were they separated on the parade route. Only fifty metres later did the Führer's head turn back to her side of the road. Annamarie covered her ears as the young women keened and cried, hoping for a nod of acknowledgment from the man leading their Fatherland to greatness.

Just like Mussolini is doing in Italy. Annamarie shook off the feeling of déjà vu and the images: the parades, the white blouses, black skirts. The banners. The fawning and swooning girls. Marco.

The parade's end appeared, a troop of alpinists taking up the rear. The BDM troops and their members fell in step behind them and followed the convoy to the square renamed after the Führer. Annamarie's eyes widened as she recognised Goebbels taking the podium. A breathless Margit appeared at her side and squeezed Annamarie's hand.

"Isn't he wonderful?" Margit swooned. "Isn't it exciting? We're going to see him up close at tonight's dinner!"

Annamarie bit her bottom lip and hopped on the balls of her feet. "I still can't believe Max got us invited. Well, you, yes. But me?"

Margit laughed. "And why not? Goebbels will certainly be interested in meeting the new theatre and acting director of Division Five."

Annamarie blushed. "I'm not yet."

Margit winked, dropping to a whisper as Goebbels began to talk. "Two months. You'll be in Brunswick for your training, and that's close enough to hop over to Berlin for a visit."

Goebbels thanked Gauleiter Hofer and began his speech, shouting into the microphone. It was about the Jew in Paris. Annamarie could not tune in. It was difficult to make out his words, though she could see him waving his arms, punctuating his speech. He was saying something about the Jews, something about the assassination and Greenspan's arrest.

Suddenly, clear as day, his voice rang out. "You must be fighters! Our enemies consist of legions, and they are not prepared to tolerate a strong Germany! They prevent our folk from unification! They prevent our citizens from defending themselves! They prevent our freedom!"

His manner reminded Annamarie of Il Duce once more, and she frowned. As the crowd up front, those who could hear and understand, roared with support, Annamarie shouted with them, just as all the people around her did. Then she burst out laughing, remembering how she had mocked Mussolini at the Iron Rooster when she'd first met Lisi and the others.

Margit grinned, but her brow crumpled with confusion. "What's so funny?" she shouted over the roaring and applause.

"Nothing," Annamarie said, clapping harder, making her palms sting. "He just reminds me of someone."

The humour would be lost on Margit. Lisi would understand and laugh with Annamarie. So would Sepp, mostly because Lisi would laugh. That thought made Annamarie laugh even more.

Margit scrutinised her, looking uncertain.

"I'm just so happy," Annamarie shouted over the crowd. "This is just so, I don't know…euphoric."

"Isn't it though?" Margit threw her arms around Annamarie, laughing too now. But the joke was on her.

When the speeches were over, Margit and Annamarie walked to the café where they had arranged to meet with the boys afterwards. They took a seat and ordered two coffees. The waiter returned just as Annamarie spotted Max, but he was alone.

"Where's Franz?" she asked Margit.

"Franz has been called to a scene."

It was the way Margit said it—the way her eyebrows curved upwards and the way she sat back satisfactorily—that gave Annamarie pause.

Max reached them, and Annamarie stood to peck his cheek. Before he could even order his own coffee, Margit launched into reviewing the parade and the speeches, gushing with excitement. Annamarie waited until she had taken a breath before laying some coins next to her cup and standing up.

"I need to get ready for tonight," she explained. "I'll see you at the Gauhaus then?"

Max rose. "I'll come with you."

"No, finish your coffee. I want to take a bath, and I need to find something to wear."

But Max was not listening. "Margit, I'll see you tonight."

"Are you going in uniform then?" Annamarie tried.

He smiled at her. "Of course. Come." In her ear, he whispered, "I'll scrub your back."

Annamarie's pulse raced as she frantically tried to figure out a way to avoid bringing him back to the apartment. She barely said goodbye to Margit as Max wheeled her back through the square. Then Annamarie remembered the crafts market.

"Max, let's walk to Bismarck Platz first."

"But that's in the opposite direction."

Annamarie squeezed his arm. "My troop is setting up their stand for the weekend. I want to make sure they don't need anything."

Max did not look pleased, but he gave in. They walked the few blocks to the square, and Annamarie found her group, her mind still racing at how she might get rid of Max. She lingered over the handmade wares, the candies, the candles, the fleece slippers. It was when she held up a child's vest that she got the idea.

"You know what, Max? I've nothing to wear for tonight, but maybe I can borrow something from the costume department at the theatre. Come with me? You can help me choose."

"I feel like you're avoiding me," he said.

Annamarie put on a brave smile. "Never. It's just that I'm so nervous about meeting Goebbels, Max. It's almost the only thing on my mind."

"Almost the only thing?"

She flushed. "Lisi's certainly home. Besides, I want to make you proud tonight."

Grunting, he finally gave in. They walked back to the State Theatre, Annamarie congratulating herself only partially. She would still have to convince someone to lend her a dress, and even then she was not certain she would find something fitting for tonight, but it was a delay.

Before they were even a block away, Annamarie spotted the milling crowd in front of the theatre. She stopped, recognising the SS guard uniforms. And Franz. Then Lisi. The front theatre doors swung open, and Annamarie swallowed hard when she spotted Veronika between two uniformed policemen. Max was pulling her along before she could even react. They went straight to Lisi, whose face was pulled tight and narrow. She was standing next to Franz, but when her eyes landed on Max, Lisi's face darkened.

Franz greeted Max first. "Lisi found her hiding in the theatre, in the cellar, and reported her. Took us a while to get here with the parade and all, but we kept an eye on the exits."

"This the one whose parents you have?" Max asked.

Franz nodded.

"Did you know her?" Max asked Annamarie.

Annamarie did not know where to look. "I…I don't," she stammered. "I mean, sure I knew her. From the crowd, you know. But I haven't seen her in… Not since the Jews were, you know, no longer permitted to work here."

Max had his eyes on Lisi as the car pulled away. Veronika, in the backseat and with a terrified expression, slid past them.

"You did the right thing," Max said.

Lisi looked as if he'd slapped her. Then her mouth spread into a gruesome smile. "Yes, Max. You know me. I always do the right thing. Especially by you."

Annamarie wanted to yell at them all, to demand they tell her what in God's name was going on. She whirled on Lisi, her question muted when Franz put an arm around his sister's shoulder. He drew her to him, as if he were tussling with one of his pals. Lisi was stiff as a board.

Franz tossed them all a smile. "That was a great show,

wasn't it? I love surprise endings. Now, wait until we tell Goebbels about this tonight. I can hardly wait. You, Annamarie?"

"I need to go home," Annamarie said. And in her heart, she meant South Tyrol. It was then that she remembered the letter from her mother.

"You know," Max said, "I think I'll just pick you up later. Go get ready. Lisi looks like she needs a drink. Lisi? Can I buy you a drink?"

Annamarie was prepared to offer Lisi moral support. She would bring her home. They could talk.

Instead, Lisi seemed to shrink into herself. "Sure, Max," she whispered. "Let's go get a drink."

Franz rubbed his sister's shoulders. "They'll want to question you at the station. I'll let them know you're coming a little later."

Lisi still did not make eye contact with anyone.

Dragging her way through the streets, Annamarie racked her mind to understand what had just happened, what was happening. Who had betrayed Veronika? Lisi did not show up by the time Annamarie had to leave for the Gauhaus. And neither had Max. She waited until half past the hour, uncertain whether she should go to the Gauhaus at all. A few minutes later, she swept up her coat and left.

On the way into town, dressed in one of Lisi's gowns, Annamarie's jaw ached from the stress. She arrived at the modern building, where a red carpet had been rolled up the stairs, and people milled about in the foyer and the entryway. One Mercedes after another rolled to a stop in front of the building. Annamarie stared at the entryway and realised she could not go inside. Not alone.

"Annamarie!" A breathless Max dashed up the road to her. "I'm sorry. I'm so sorry I was late. We got carried away."

"How's Lisi?"

He shrugged. "I left her at the station."

"I waited for you, but I thought…" She had no idea what she'd thought. There was something different about him.

Max frowned and cupped her chin, his thumb and forefinger squeezing. "Don't give me this Italian temperament of yours tonight." He dropped his hand, but Annamarie rubbed where he'd grabbed her.

"My Italian what?" she muttered.

"Let's go." He offered his arm, but his smile was terse. "And just be a good girl tonight, would you? This is important."

Annamarie's cheeks flushed as she hooked her arm in his and climbed the stairs to the entrance. Inside, the room swirled with ball gowns, music, lights bouncing off the crystal chandeliers and glasses of champagne. There were groups toasting the great nation, and then the crescendo of the entourage's entrance. The Führer and Goebbels, the power and prestige, created such a heady atmosphere, Annamarie felt as if she were drunk already.

Margit appeared with Franz in tow. "Annamarie, hurry up. We're to present ourselves now."

Annamarie followed as if in a dream. Someone laughed, and Annamarie saw a large, rotund man doubled over in laughter, his champagne glass tilting dangerously, and a butler eyeing it, as if ready to capture the liquid into his hands if need be. Another group—women this time—burst into giggles, all eyes on Hitler and Goebbels at the front of the room. Suddenly, Goebbels was alone, dressed in a white smoking jacket, and Annamarie was so close now she could see he had a pockmarked face, that he limped, and that his hand appeared deformed.

A couple approached, speaking to Goebbels and drawing his rapt attention.

"Mother? *Vati?*" Margit addressed the man and woman with the minister.

"*Schätzchen*," the woman exclaimed. "Minister Goebbels, this is our daughter, Margit. And this is…"

"Annamarie Steinhauser," Margit said, pushing Annamarie

forward. "Annamarie, this is my mother, Hilda Rainer, and my father, Werner Rainer. Minister Goebbels, a pleasure to meet you in person. Annamarie is the one I have recommended to assist with your aim to build up the film industry in both Italy and Austria."

Annamarie raised her hand, felt him take it in his. His eyes assessed her. She heard the noise in his head, but not a single comprehensive thought that she could interpret. It was like trying to break code, until he smiled and said, "Annamarie Steinhauser. A pleasure. You must come and visit the UFA building, tour the sets, and meet our people the next time you're in Berlin."

Margit agreed politely. She squeezed Annamarie's hand. "She'll be in Brunswick for BDM leadership training in January. She could pop into Berlin anytime in between."

12

BOLZANO, NOVEMBER 1938

The victory monument on Piazza della Vittoria in Bolzano was a nineteen-metre-wide gate, over twenty metres high, eight metres deep, and bedecked with solid white marble, as was the Fascist style. Add pictorial pillars—fourteen here—and a superhuman, bare-chested woman over Latin script to finish off Il Duce's signature.

Angelo stepped back, hand raised against the midday sun, so that he could translate the provocative lines. *Here at the border of the fatherland set down the banner. From this point on we ennobled the others with language, law and culture.*

The past tense was not a slip of the marble cutter's chisel. It was there to make the reader hover between past and present, to create undertones of a before and after. To cause controversy. On the day of the monument's inauguration, ten thousand Tyroleans protested in Innsbruck. The Italian authorities took little heed. The nationalists believed that the *allogeni*, the "others," were in their hearts Italian, after all. They had already been educated in the Italian ways once and, having relapsed into otherness, merely needed to be "recovered," or redeemed. *Ennobled* referred to the idea that the Roman imperial empire had already managed to tame the barbarians of the North long before Italy claimed the hinterland and planted its banners. German civility, the words claimed, stemmed from the close contact of its dignified neighbours. Why should they not be grateful to be under Italian rule?

Angelo faced the road. Across the street, Gina came around the corner. He watched her. He never tired of watching her. She was a petite powerhouse, and she always looked good. Today, she was wearing a russet, orange, and pomegranate-red striped coat with a dark-brown fur trim. Possibly beaver. They were her colours, her style. Her dark wavy hair was set in large curls and pinned up just at the sides. Angelo realised with a jolt that she had changed little in all the years since he'd met her. She was still gorgeous—small and curved—and she impacted all his senses in one heavy punch to the beltline.

When she spotted him, she gave him a wan smile, then crossed the road. He kissed her cheek, lingering just a little longer than customary. She smelled of autumn spices.

"I've reserved a table at Due Platani." Angelo offered her his arm.

A few steps away, Gina looked up at the monument Angelo had been reading shortly before. "You actually read the inscriptions?"

"Don't you?"

She smiled crookedly and pointed to her eyes. "Nearsighted."

Angelo chuckled. There was nothing wrong with her eyes. If one thing had changed about her in all these years, it was her disenchantment with Fascism. She had gradually moved to more moderate political rhetoric. Discreetly, anyway.

"How was the meeting?" she asked.

"The ONC wants as few Tyroleans as possible, the veterans saying they cannot imagine a peaceful cohabitation. My father found it to be a grand idea, moving the affected Tyroleans all into Mastromattei's hamlets, and the electrical society kept pointing out the legalities, much to the Colonel's consternation. It sounded like a lover's quarrel."

Behind the monument, Angelo steered Gina across the street to the café. Evenly spaced tables and chairs had been set out beneath the two large plane trees the café was named after. "Is it too cold for you to sit outside?"

"Nonsense. I have my coat." She took the seat at the one table fully bathed in sunshine. "So the result was?"

"I'm to mediate the situation with the Steinhausers and their little committee. Mastromattei said that if they are the good Italian citizens I have made them out to be, then they will understand that by leaving their homesteads, they are improving the country. It is—in other words—their patriotic duty to accept fair and balanced offers. Or else…"

Gina's left eyebrow arched. "Libya?"

"Mastromattei did not say it. I think he was afraid to throw himself into the camp of the hardliners, but my father did. Explicitly. The Colonel suggested that MFE would see to it that the *allogeni* understood their choices."

He did not tell her the most biting of the Colonel's comments, when Angelo's father had said, "These people will be found guilty of resisting public authorities. Detain them for crimes against the state, if you must! Put them all in a penal colony if barbarians so badly want to be together."

Gina's forehead creased. "I see. And how did Mastromattei take that?"

Angelo smirked. "You can imagine. But he did confirm the rumour that Hitler is making noises about taking back the Alto Adige."

Angelo set his briefcase aside as a matronly waitress took their orders. Gina and he ordered the menu of the day.

"Hitler's not the problem," Gina said thoughtfully. "I have it on good authority that the Duce has no intention of letting go of the province. The land anyway. The people? Well, that's a different issue altogether."

"What?"

"Not what. Who. Adriano Colocci-Vespucci."

The special attaché to culture in the Alto Adige. He'd stepped in when Tolomei vacated the role to take his position on the senate. Colocci-Vespucci was the most vocal about the "barking tribes"—the Germans and the Ladins. Angelo recalled how Colocci-Vespucci had called for the Italian government to expel all the Tyroleans immediately after the treaty had been signed. Whereas Tolomei believed the two nationalities had fluctuated so much in the centuries that it would be easy for the Tyroleans to simply accept themselves as Italian, Colocci-Vespucci once declared that the ideal situation would to be expel all non-Italians from Italy. When asked whether he really believed that would be possible, he admitted that modern humanitarian sentiments stood in the way and international opinion ruled out subjugation as well. He finally settled on coexistence as the final option with the hope that the *allogeni* would adapt or leave on their own accord.

"Now," Gina said, "Colocci-Vespucci is proposing that the Tyroleans be prevented from acquiring any more property and that all immigration of non-Italians be halted. And if *that* doesn't work..." Her left eyebrow curved upwards. "Label them as illegal inhabitants. That's what he wants to achieve. I have it on good authority—"

"Your contact."

"Yes, my contact." She grinned but returned to business. "There's a new bill for Tolomei to draft and present to the senate. The bill would assign illegal immigration status to all Tyroleans. Those who do not assimilate, cooperate, and accept their lot in life will be deported."

Angelo sat back in his chair. "So now we're throwing them together with the Jews."

Gina nodded soberly. "Colocci-Vespucci is suggesting that instead of trying to resettle the *allogeni* to Libya, send them all back to Germany. I don't think we'll be able to tell the difference between Hitler's government and Mussolini's soon."

Angelo whistled softly and rubbed a hand through his hair. "The first thing the Steinhausers and their people will say is Hitler should recognise the Alto Adige as part of the Reich."

"Exactly. I don't believe that's going to be plausible. Or come into question."

Angelo could not believe it. "The Steinhausers assured me they would gain the valley's cooperation overall. If they catch wind of these plans, it would set them back, sabotage everything we've been working toward."

"It does not help us that the VKS is gaining in popularity either." Gina shrugged. "I don't know, Angelo. Maybe that is what we need to consider. If Italy asked the Tyroleans to determine for themselves what it means to be Italian, what would they say?"

"Mastromattei would be proven right. We'd lose a rich economic base, a rich population." And Angelo would lose any contact he had left to his daughter.

Gina leaned in. "Look, the lands to the north, we call them redeemed. It's been almost twenty years, and the majority still don't speak Italian. This may indicate that they don't want to be Italian, and certainly the nationalists will see it that way. But if there is one thing you know about your Steinhausers, what is it?" Gina looked at him meaningfully.

Angelo thought for a moment. "They want to keep their land. And so do many others. Or they at least want to stay in the area." He paused. "Gina, are you suggesting that we provide them with the choice but manage to convince them to voluntarily choose Italian citizenship?"

Gina touched his hand. "I think Mastromattei might be hoping for exactly that."

Angelo was curious. "Who is your contact anyway? Where are you getting all this information? That is, if you can say?"

Gina's eyes darted playfully between the tables before she leaned in. "Tolomei's secretary."

Angelo was astounded. "I didn't think women liked you."

"*Pah!* Who said?" She smiled slyly. "Besides, who said Tolomei's secretary is a woman?"

"Ha!" But she had him.

"It's Tolomei who doesn't like women." Gina winked.

"He's married."

Gina tilted her head back and laughed. "In the history of the Roman Empire, since when, Angelo, has that ever made a difference?" She raised a hand. "It's only a rumour, but…"

They were interrupted by the delivery of their food, a simple pasta with tomato sauce followed by a fish platter. They ate in silence until Gina asked him about his move to his apartment. Angelo had checked out of the Laurin already but discovered that the workers had come back to repair some wiring in his apartment.

"So you're without lodging for the night?" she asked.

"I'm sure I can spend another night at the hotel." It irritated him. He wanted to move on.

"Why don't you just stay at my place?" Gina took a sip of her espresso. Dessert was a small slice of Tiramisu. "The house is empty. None of the children are around. Come after work."

Angelo groaned. "I have a meeting with Michael Innerhofer this evening."

"Ah! And Chiara."

Angelo shook his head. "No, she said she would not attend this one. Something about letting the two of us slice up the thick air between us."

Now it was Gina who sat back, folded her arms, and assessed him. "I see."

"Every time you say that, I know there's something more."

She tilted her head and spooned another mouthful of her dessert. "Maybe it's time the two of you—if you're going to partner up, anyway—have a good old-fashioned tavern fight, you know? What is it about men anyway that they need to knock each other's heads in before they can be friends?"

Angelo chuckled and wiped his mouth.

"So what is it that they are bringing to the table, your activist and your journalist martyr?"

"Peter Hofer."

Gina ducked her chin and stared at him with disbelief. "The VKS ring leader?"

Angelo nodded.

"And what is the reporter-activist duo's objective?"

"Interestingly enough, they're fishing for dirt on the VKS here. Apparently, there's quite some infighting going on between the German League and the VKS."

"I imagine," Gina said slowly, her brow furrowed, "the only way to control the VKS is via direct orders from the top."

"From whom?"

"I don't know." She paused and twisted her spoon in the glass bowl before putting it down. "Do you believe Hitler really aims to wrangle back the Alto Adige?"

"What are you getting at?"

Gina looked sober. "I mean, is it really in his political interest? Or is he just trying to drum up support from our Tyroleans, who are still disgruntled about losing their province?"

Angelo considered it. "You might have a point."

"I'd wait and see. I'd wait until the foreign minister reports on his next visit. I simply have a feeling Hitler needs Italy more than he's letting on." She shrugged nonchalantly. "It's just a feeling."

Angelo gazed at her admiringly. "Your instincts, Gina, have never been wrong."

~

Before meeting with Michael Innerhofer, Angelo had work to get done. He returned to the office and stopped outside the new building. He sometimes missed the character and elegance of city hall, the old smells. He went to the second floor and found Miss Medici on the telephone.

She sat up with a look of relief and raised a finger. "Just a moment, Signora. He has just walked in."

Angelo waved his hand. He did not wish to be disturbed. He had things to do.

"One moment, please." Miss Medici fumbled with the Monster. She looked apologetic but also prepared to stand her ground. "Signora Steinhauser is on the line. This is the third attempt to connect here. She is at the Post Inn in Graun."

It was the only telephone line near Arlund.

"Fine. Put her through." There was no time to be delicate about the situation. If the Steinhausers wanted any chance at a fair deal, it was time they took the bull by the horns and got their people to clean their hands of all that pro-German rhetoric.

He went into the office, closed the door. The line was already buzzing before he'd taken a seat at his desk.

"Signora Steinhauser—Katharina—I'm sorry to hear you've been trying to reach me. Next time, may I suggest you send a telex and we can arrange to telephone when it's convenient for everyone?"

"There's no time to make formal arrangements, Angelo." Katharina's voice was strained.

"I'm working on all this, really. I'm sorry that I haven't contacted you earlier. I just had a meeting with the electrical society and the ONC—that's the veterans' association—as well as with MFE and Mastromattei this morning. I was going to write to you in the next days, but since you're on the telephone, here's what I can tell you. Katharina, if you can deliver a representative committee that proves they are interested in their patriotic duty to the Italian nation—what I mean is, if you are prepared to behave as Italian citizens, we might be able to relocate all of you to new hamlets not too far apart and not too far from home. Now before you—"

"Angelo, I'm not calling about the project." Her voice had dropped a decibel.

It had to be about Annamarie. "What's happened?"

"We had a…we had an incident, Angelo."

He hated that word. It made his head hurt. "Go on."

"Bernd and two others have been arrested by Basso's men."

"Bernd? Your older son?" Angelo pictured the sandy-brown-haired boy he'd met the past spring. His countenance, his suspicion.

"Yes, Angelo. They're bringing him and the neighbour's eldest son down to Bolzano."

"Bolzano? But that must be very serious if they're moving them to the prison."

"They're charged with setting the town hall on fire and…"

Angelo groaned. In the background, he heard voices, male and female.

Katharina came back on, obviously unmuffling the mouthpiece. "And of being members of the VKS. Dr Hanny spoke with the authorities, and they mentioned something about a tribunal. But in Rome."

Ice shot through his veins. There it was again. Someone mentioned something—his father had just spoken of such charges this morning—and somewhere down the line, it would pop up again. "This is serious, Katharina. The only reason the authorities would take them to Rome is because they are charging the boys with offenses against the state." He rubbed a hand over his head.

"Dr Hanny said that there will be a preliminary instruction in Bolzano first."

"Yes, they will conduct an investigation, and the prosecuting attorney has the right to judge them, Katharina. He could—"

"They've searched our homes already. Just came in and threw everything around. We need someone who can help us, Angelo."

"Katharina, this is exactly—and I mean exactly—what MFE is waiting for." He cradled the receiver against his ear and stood up. "And from you, the Steinhausers, who are supposed to lead this damned campaign. Damn it! I can't be anywhere near this!"

"Damn it?" Katharina bit back. "Damn it is all you say, Angelo Grimani?"

He held the receiver away from his ear and gaped at it. She had some nerve! He suddenly remembered an echo from the past. Katharina wrapping a bandage around the stab wounds. The pig's fat she'd smeared on his skin. Hadn't she said something like that then with a wry smile?

Angelo put the receiver back to his ear.

"Are you there?" she asked.

"How much time have we got?"

"Dr Hanny says nothing may happen before Christmas. Christmas! That's weeks away. It could be anywhere from six to eight weeks by the time they see the inside of a courtroom. We want to come down to Bolzano, but we don't have the money. And we're farmers, Angelo. We can't just leave the farm for two months. The committee is asking for donations for both families, but it's a lot. Angelo, I'm calling because we need your help."

He could wire them the money. He was already reaching for a sheet of paper and a pen. "Go ahead. Give me the bank's address and information. How much do you need?"

Katharina stammered on the other end. Again, she covered the mouthpiece. Again, some muffled voices. "Angelo, we don't need your money. Please, that's not why I called."

"Then what is it?"

"Please go see him. Please make sure that the authorities treat the boys decently. Is there any way you could do that? And then we need special counsel."

Angelo yanked at his tie and loosened it. "Katharina—" He

sighed. "Listen, if I go to the prison, I have to register my name there, and there will be a record that I'm visiting. I can't associate myself with suspected Nazi supporters. I'll be accused of supporting national terrorists, because that's what Mastromattei is calling those involved with the VKS. Do you understand the predicament? Nobody will take me seriously when I try to mediate the project between you and the other stakeholders. You're putting everything in jeopardy by asking me this." He realised he was talking fast, trying to convince her. Katharina's end was silent. "Katharina? Are you still there?"

"I think I understood everything you said," she said slowly. "You said you won't do this for us. For me. Is that right?"

"That's correct."

"I don't give a damn, Angelo Grimani, how it looks," Katharina said with venom. "Make it look as if you are there to rehabilitate him if you must. I'm asking you to go check on my son. Please." Her voice broke. "We weren't planning…I was trying to get to Innsbruck."

Angelo shifted the receiver. "What's in Innsbruck? Annamarie?"

He could hear her struggling to keep the emotion out of her voice. "I was hoping to get permission to travel. I know where she is, but, Angelo…"

He waited. When she spoke again, she sounded defeated.

"She's been asking me to fill out an *Ahnenpass* for her. She's already had Florian's information entered. Angelo, she went up to Nuremberg to do it herself, but she refuses to come here to have her mother's side of the pass filled out. She says she won't see me."

"I don't understand. What is this pass?"

"It's the document she needs to prove her ancestral purity." Her breath hitched, and he could tell she was covering the mouthpiece even though she was speaking in Italian. Who was with her? "She needs it in order to join the Nazi party."

Christ! "Katharina." Angelo shouted down the line now. "You need to put a lead on your children. What is going on up there? Have I made myself clear yet? Mastromattei has absolutely no tolerance for the VKS or the Nazis. This does not fit into his agenda. And if you do not fit into his agenda, you will—"

"Funnily enough," Katharina sounded scornful, "everyone else has been telling me I need to allow my children to take responsibility for themselves."

"Is that right? And do you feel that is working to the benefit of your community?"

There was silence on her end. Angelo looked up at the ceiling. He should apologise, but her voice came back on, and it was snide.

"How's your relationship with Marco? How under control do you have that?"

Angelo wanted to slam the phone down. *Switch tactics. Now.* "Is Annamarie at least all right? Is someone watching over her?"

"My cousin Rosa," Katharina said measuredly, "is keeping an eye on her."

"Fine. Then get down here as soon as you can arrange it, and we'll discuss the tribunal. When that's over, I'll arrange the travel documents for you to get over the border. But, Katharina, you do not—I repeat, do not—fill out that pass for her." *Stupid girl. What was Annamarie up to anyway?*

"And in the meantime?" Katharina asked plaintively.

"Let me wire the money for you and your husband. I'll get my secretary to arrange accommodation as well."

"I told you, the committee would support us. Nobody wants your money."

"Give the donations to the other family. Let me help you, Katharina. Please."

"Angelo," she said, "we appreciate your offer, but please go see Bernd. Please. He only knows you as someone who is trying to help us. Maybe he will listen to you."

Angelo shook his head. "I'll see what I can do. I'm late for another meeting. I'm going to give you back to Miss Medici, and she will take the bank information down and arrange accommodation for you. Just let her know when you are ready. I'll be in touch, all right? Promise."

She finally agreed, and Angelo pushed the button, sending the call down the Monster's throat and out of his hands. At least for the interim. He gathered his things to go to Innerhofer's.

How was he doing with Marco? Marco wanted to be a pilot. That was the big surprise. Had signed up with the Royal Air Force. Come spring, Marco would head down to Rome. As a veteran himself, Angelo knew he ought to be proud of his son. Yet with Italy still helping Spain in their civil war, and with conflicts looming in the Mediterranean, something in Angelo resisted the very idea of his son fighting for this government.

As he stepped outside the ministry building, a cold wind gusted down the narrow road. The flag lifted from up against the building and billowed in undulating waves. He recalled his father's words before the Colonel had made the suggestion to commit the Reschen Valley residents to a penal colony.

"A Fascist," the Colonel had reminded them, "subordinates himself to the state by moral law. He leaves his superfluous ideas of liberalistic autonomy. The individual must sacrifice his personal interest, not his collective interests. He foregoes any natural right to an autonomous existence. If the Tyroleans cannot abide by that, then they are not to be given any incentive to call themselves citizens of this country!"

Angelo blew into his hands and rubbed them. It was going to be a long and difficult winter.

"Why on earth ought the VKS be interested in what the Italians want?" Michael asked.

Angelo pursed his lips. "Because if the wind blows the way it's being forecasted, it may well come down to Hitler *wanting* them to cooperate."

Michael flung his hands up. "I might be the one who composes stories for a living, but this one tops them all. Are you saying that—"

"What I'm saying," Angelo said impatiently, "is that the VKS will be quashed just like the German League, and if Peter Hofer wants to remain in *this country*, in *Italy*, then he needs to take it down a few notches. Now."

Michael sat back, his fingers touching various sheets of paper before him. Angelo let him digest the news.

They were in the rounded alcove of a modestly appointed library where the smell of paper and old leather mingled with the scent of the polished wood table. Michael's things had been hurriedly gathered and piled into unceremonious stacks onto one end of the round table, save for the few sheets before him. A simple vase with a single orange chrysanthemum looked lost among the towers of journals and papers.

Angelo shifted in the uncomfortable wooden chair, his coat draped over his arm. Outside the window, the branches of a maple waved in the wind, scattering a number of its curled burgundy leaves. He felt the draft of it coming through the window frame.

"The reservoir will happen," Angelo insisted again. "And now I want to see the locals have a fair chance at recouping their losses, of having homes that they can relocate to and establish new farms on. I'll grant you access to all the information we get if you find someone who will publish it. Exclusively. I want to keep things open and show the Tyrolean people that we are doing our damndest to play fair. And I want you to work this in a way that will lessen the hold the VKS has on the people."

Michael snorted and looked over Angelo's head. He then patted around his coat and reached into his left breast pocket.

He withdrew a cigarette case—Angelo noted it was new. Michael lit the cigarette with a match and waved it out before inhaling the cigarette. "I'd offer you one, but I know you don't smoke."

Angelo swiped his nose.

"And what do you want in return?" Michael asked.

"I want firsthand information about what the VKS is up to."

Michael looked out the window. "And Chiara is prepared to agree to this? To spying?"

"Yes. And I would not call it spying."

Someone knocked on the door, and Michael called for them to come in. A woman—blonde, middle aged, and well groomed—smiled shyly at Angelo from the door. Behind her, the smell of frying meat wafted in.

"Will your guest be staying for dinner?" she asked.

Michael rose. "Minister Angelo Grimani, my wife, Evi."

Masking his surprise, Angelo stood and greeted her. He politely declined the invitation, and she left after Michael told her they needed about another half hour.

Angelo put his coat on the back of the chair and lowered himself into his seat. His right knee popped. "I had no idea you were married."

"I am."

This changed so much. Perhaps everything, really. Or maybe nothing. Angelo bit back his questions.

"Who believes," Michael asked, flicking his cigarette into the ashtray, "that Hitler will pull Italy into some sort of alliance?"

"Signora Conti and I."

Michael's eyebrows shot up. His eyes shifted away from Angelo to his cigarette.

Angelo could imagine the man was fighting the urge to ask his own questions now. *Fine. It's time to get this out in the open.*

"What is the nature of your relationship with my wife?" Angelo demanded.

Michael frowned behind the cigarette. "Are you being serious, Minister? Wait. Is this the real reason for your visit?"

"No, but by the look on your face, you would love to know whether the rubbish thrown about Signora Conti and myself is true."

Michael laughed, narrowed his eyes. "I am a journalist, you know."

"Are you mocking me?"

The man shook his head but was still chuckling.

"I am her husband, you know," Angelo retorted. "I believe the issue with Chiara is relevant if we're to…to work together."

"Work together?" Michael stopped laughing, stunned again. "Relevant to what?"

"To whether I can trust you."

Michael inhaled, his eyes narrowing. "I see. Is that what we're doing?"

"Can I? Trust you?"

"You are flustered, aren't you? Yes. Yes, you can."

"Why?"

Michael smiled crookedly. "Good question. That is a good question. But isn't it obvious?"

"You'd like your countrymen to be treated fairly," Angelo listed. "You have an interest in justice. And it makes for a sensational story."

Michael's face softened, and he gazed at Angelo in the least defensive manner the man had ever shown towards him. "That's right."

"So do I. Well, save for the juicy story, that is."

Michael laughed abruptly. He stabbed out his cigarette. "Here's another thing. That woman you just met, the one who has so kindly invited you to dinner this evening? That's my wife, and I love her. Always have. You can ask your own wife just how much."

"What is it with you two, then? Really?"

"Chiara and me? We're close."

"Close."

"I give you my word. I've been a gentleman and nothing but." His look was questioning. *And you?* That was what he wanted to know.

Angelo straightened and dropped his hands to his side. *Go ahead. Ask.*

Michael rested his arms on the table. "Why is Signora Conti even involved? What's her interest?"

"She likes me."

Michael huffed an appreciative laugh.

"And maybe she's bored. Maybe she does it to prove she can."

"Sounds a bit like a woman fighting to be emancipated."

"You should know what that looks like. You've been dealing with my wife even longer than I have."

Michael blew softly and fiddled with the cigarette case.

Angelo straightened and smoothed down his tie. "I appreciate your being so forthcoming. And so accommodating. It's a mess, this thing between Chiara and me, I'll admit. One of my own doing. At some point, I imagine, she'll be ready to speak to me about it, to forge a new way."

"I think you'll be surprised to know she's been ready for some time. She is wondering whether you are."

"What do you mean, whether I am?"

Michael shifted his eyes over his desk and rubbed his jaw. "Whether this...well, the rumours thereof...this thing with Signora Conti..." He took a deep breath. "Well, man, whether this is just a passing phase or whether it's serious. An affair or...the beginning of the end? For Chiara, I mean."

Angelo blinked.

"Anyway, it's none of my business." Michael brushed off the front of his double-breasted suit coat.

"What a mess." Angelo smoothed his hair back with both

hands. "I'm sorry, Michael. I'm sorry you have to be witness to it all."

Michael nodded, then scribbled on a sheet of blank paper. When he was finished, he handed it to Angelo.

VKS | Tyroleans | Fascists

"Where do you and Signora Conti fit in?" Michael asked.

Angelo looked up. He gestured for the pen. Wrote a plus next to *Tyroleans* and then the word *Italians* and handed it back to Michael. "With you."

"And Mastromattei?"

"If you don't push him, he's going to remain in the middle. Like me, he serves the country, but he's going to see to it that it's a long-term solution and not…" Angelo did not even know how to describe it.

Michael took in a deep breath. "As some have said up north, 'this' can't last long."

"Nothing this extreme ever does."

Michael sniffed. "It will, however, leave an indelible mark upon us. It will change everything. Forever."

They were silent for a moment, then Angelo made the decision. "I have another story for you. Something you can use in reverse, so to speak."

Michael shook his head. "Sounds like you're trying to form me into some other kind of journalist."

"No," Angelo said quietly. "This story is one you won't want to miss." He told him about the Steinhausers in Arlund and then about Bernd and the prison in Bolzano.

Michael looked sombre. "Do you know when the preliminary examination will take place?"

"I have no idea."

"The families need to get the charges reduced if the authorities are even considering the penal law. Once the instruction is complete, they have fifteen days to hold the *citazione*. When the indictment is heard, then they'll set a trial date. Angelo, the Steinhausers must get their son to be tried in Bolzano. Not in Rome. They'll be court-martialled in Rome and..."

Michael did not have to say it. There was only one sentence. Death. Angelo's only option was to perhaps approach Mastromattei. It was a risk. For himself and anyone else involved.

"You could go see this boy," Angelo said. "You could ask for permission to visit them, check on the two and how they're being treated."

Michael nodded, but his eyes never left Angelo. "You want me to go do your dirty work? I mean, it is a good story, but I'm not going to visit Bernd in the prison for you, Angelo. Besides, until they've been arraigned, no investigating magistrate is going to allow a journalist near them."

"Not if you say you are a family friend."

"This is not my story. It's yours."

Angelo picked at a loose thread on the seam of his trousers.

"Tell me." Michael folded his arms. "Does this Bernd know that you're Annamarie's father?"

Angelo shook his head. "Frau Steinhauser says he doesn't."

"But you suspect he does."

Angelo shrugged. Yes, he did. He suspected that Bernd at least knew Angelo was not all his mother said he was.

"I mean, if we're going to be honest with each other, if we're going to be working together, then I daresay I'm going to be direct with you. I think you can finally make good on what this Katharina Steinhauser has done for you. It would be a shame. And..."

Angelo looked up.

"It might give you some practice for when you're ready to set things right with Marco." Michael slapped the table and stood.

"All right. You feed me information about what the Fascists are up to, and I'll keep you informed of the VKS's actions. It's a deal." He extended his hand.

Angelo rose and grasped it. "Thank you." He put on his coat and followed Michael to the door, taking the man's hand again, more firmly this time.

Michael winked. "All right then, partner."

Angelo chuckled, surprised. "All right."

When he left, Angelo found a taxi around the corner from the house. It had begun to rain. He gave the driver directions to the Conti villa and sat back, brushing the droplets off his coat and letting the conversation run through his head. Between Gina, Michael, and Chiara, he now had information flowing to him, allowing him to stay ahead of the politicians.

The taxi stopped at the corner near the main square, and a police vehicle rushed past them, then took a right into the next street. As the taxi rolled past city hall, Angelo saw several *carabinieri* gathered at the front. The red-striped trousers, the brass epaulettes, the navy-blue uniforms. He pictured Bernd in his knee-high breeches.

Angelo leaned forward. "I need to change course," he said. "Take me to the Bolzano prison, please."

PART II

1939

13

BOLZANO, JANUARY 1939

The bus from Graun pulled up to the train station in Merano just in time. Katharina and Florian raced to the platform and managed to hop on to their assigned carriage right before the train to Bolzano pulled away. Katharina caught her breath and watched the landscape slide by. The last time she had been on a train was when she'd been a small child on her way to the Reschen Valley. Her mother had stared out at the passing landscape on their way from Innsbruck to Landeck. On occasion, a look had passed between Katharina's father and her mother. From her father, something grateful and also regretful. From her mother, a look of martyrdom. Katharina's mother had left her home and her family, as so many women had done over the centuries. Still did even now. Obey thy husband. Follow him. Unquestioningly. The farm had needed Katharina's father. Only now did she realise that he too had bent beneath the yoke of obligation. He'd gone to Innsbruck to be something other than a farmer in the first place. Nobody knew any longer what he'd wanted. Except maybe Jutta.

Katharina cast a look at her own husband. Florian was watching her. They shared their thoughts as they often did—in silence. What was not uttered aloud could not hurt anyone. No words, no accusations. It was better this way.

She looked out the window again, the steep and towering mountain peaks stepping back, opening them up onto a broader valley where apple orchards and vineyards outnumbered the winter-covered grain fields. The Etsch River ran alongside the track, whitewater scrabbling over stony beds.

It was not until the train had passed through Lana, a half hour from Bolzano, that Katharina asked Florian a question.

"Is it much different than what you remember? I mean, when you spent time here as a child?"

Florian looked out the window. "A little. I was more shocked by the changes in Bolzano last year."

Katharina tipped her head. He'd called the city Bolzano without even wincing. Was this how it worked then, this constant infusion of Italian? With a start she remembered that her husband had left the valley to search for Annamarie in the city almost exactly a year ago. So much had happened since then. So impossibly much.

She finally did utter that which was between them, the feeling that if she did not, she would implode. "I'm worried about these people Angelo wants to introduce to us. I feel a bit helpless. Do you feel we can trust him? And them?"

With a reassuring squeeze, Florian nodded. "I do, but not blindly. We do everything with a grain of salt. Those are our boys there."

Katharina frowned. She had never really thought about Andreas as being her responsibility, but Florian was right. They ought to consider both boys. She could hardly wait to see Bernd, and she stilled her bouncing knee to hide her anxiety.

To distract herself, she patted the outside pocket of her rucksack under the latch and removed the small pocketbook that contained the address of the pension Miss Medici had booked for them. Angelo had made the offer that they stay in some grand hotel. Florian had scoffed at the invitation, and Katharina had politely declined. She'd heard relief in Angelo's voice thereafter. The proximity of their connection to each other was more than ample; there was no need to pretend there was more.

When the train rolled into the Bolzano station, Katharina leaned forward to take it in. Chaos. That was her first impression. So much activity and so many people. She was again taken back to Innsbruck, remembered the crush of people at the market or when riding on a tram. The scents and sounds of people living on top of one another. But Bolzano was twice the size, or perhaps even three times.

Outside their carriage, she saw the shapes of buildings and smokestacks against the backdrop of the Dolomites. She pointed at the ascending wall of rock behind what seemed an impossible landscape of industry. "That's the Rose Garden, isn't it?"

Florian confirmed it was.

On the other side of the train where the centre was, she saw the grand old architecture intermingled with modern designs—she'd forgotten how tall buildings could be—and the streets! Automobiles were everywhere. Overwhelmed by the feeling that she had experienced nothing, had lived no life beyond the valley, Katharina wondered whether she had ever risked anything in her life. Like Annamarie was doing. Like Bernd had done. Her heart wrenched in empathy for her daughter. The girl had fled the valley. That was what they had believed. But all Annamarie had wanted was discovery. Adventure. To find herself and the place where she belonged.

Helping her gather up their cases, Florian cleared a passage off the train. They stepped down, and Katharina took it all in. The station doors were shut tight against the cold. The air here was damp too, more so than in the mountains. On the other side, facing the street, automobiles pushed their way through the throng. It seemed as if there was no order to how one drove or where one crossed the street. People just ran out in the middle of traffic. Florian hailed a cab, and when it stopped for them, the driver spoke rapid Italian. Katharina handed him the address for city hall, and the man grumbled something, then threw open the boot of the vehicle and piled their two cases into the cramped space. They climbed in, Katharina relieved to be in the vehicle with someone who hopefully knew where he was going.

What were Florian and she anyway? A couple of farmers, their lives nothing as important as all this—these people here were coming and going, doing important things, building important places, producing goods and services, learning or teaching at the university, running the government—Fascist or not, it was all still impressive. Katharina tended to some chickens, a few hares, had a garden, a dozen or so cows, and a horse. And three children. Only one of which remained in that sheltered place they called home.

Those feelings of foreignness followed Katharina to city hall, where Florian and she were to meet with Angelo and some other people. Florian pointed to a building across the way.

"Behind that fountain there? That apartment building is where Annamarie had been staying when she was here. It belongs to Colonel Grimani."

Katharina eyed the three-storyed building, connected to another one via an arch, under which a street ran. "That's where Angelo's father lives, then?" She still did not understand how Annamarie had landed accommodation with the owner of Monte Fulmini Electrical. She did not understand a lot of things about her daughter. And she wanted to. She wanted to gather up her children from the corners of the world and get them back beneath home, where they belonged. Where had she—and Florian—gone wrong?

As she entered the atrium, Katharine gaped. City hall was lush with beautiful details, such as the chequered floor, the polished wooden stairs, the palm trees and plants in the atrium and the courtyard in the middle of the building. Realising she must have looked like a fish out of water, she closed her mouth as they climbed the staircase to the second floor, just as Angelo had instructed. She marvelled at how Florian moved through all of it with ease, as if he'd been in this city at least once a year. He'd grown up in Nuremberg. He'd been in Paris. He was a city dweller. Even after twenty years on Katharinahof, he'd never really fit into its provinciality.

They reached the rooms that housed the local police, were told to move on to the next room for the national police, where they were then ordered to wait. The worn benches on the train had not been as hard on Katharina as these in the police station. She watched as plainclothes and uniformed police went back and forth. As Florian and she waited for someone to finally recognise their distress, Katharina sighed with impatience. Were they invisible? She jumped when someone shouted in Italian behind a closed door. She looked at Florian, once again picturing her son with a pummelled face, skinny from lack of good food and sickly from the cold prison cots and damp walls. Katharina covered her face with her hands.

"How much longer do they expect us to wait," she muttered none too quietly.

Her husband rose and went to the desk. She ought to go with him, help him with the Italian, but she could not bring herself to. Instead, she searched for a hint of where the water closet might be, but Florian returned, dejected.

"They said it will be impossible to see Bernd today."

She jumped up. "We did not wait all this time… Someone could have told us earlier." She moved toward the clerk behind the desk. "*Scuzi*, Signore."

The man looked up from a document, disinterested. "Signora, I told your husband. I'm sorry. We could not have known. We put the call in, but the prison authorities have just now said it is impossible to see these boys today." He shuffled the sheets of paper. "Benito Steinhauser and Andrea Ritsch? They are in pretrial consultation at the moment."

He was trying to provoke her by Italianising the boys' names.

"With whom are they meeting?" Katharina demanded.

"I assume with an attorney, *Signora*, but how am I to know?" He waved his hand around him. He was just a clerk, was what he was saying.

"I don't know anything about an attorney. I want to know who is consulting my son."

The policeman looked at her wearily.

"Then when?" Katharina demanded. "When can we see our son?"

"Tomorrow morning. Between nine and ten o'clock." He looked back down at the papers and crossed things out.

Florian put an arm around her shoulder. "Come now. Let's check into the pension, get something to eat, and rest. It's been a long day."

"Our meeting with Angelo is at nine o'clock tomorrow," she said.

Florian pulled away. "Then we'll have to reschedule."

Katharina checked the clock on the far wall. The ministry would be closed. Back on the *Hof*, last spring, when she had politely enquired about Angelo's family in Bolzano, he'd been surprisingly forthcoming about the details of how Annamarie had discovered he was her father. Perhaps his openness was understandable. His entire trip to Arlund had been fuelled by the need to confess and seek forgiveness. Later, he'd made a sad joke about his estranged marriage and the fact that he had taken up residence at a hotel. Katharina remembered the literary reference of the hotel's name: King Laurin, who had gone searching for his daughter, whom the dwarf king had kidnapped and hidden in the crags of the Rose Garden.

"I know where we might find Angelo." After gathering up her coat, the rucksack, and her case, Katharina strode out of the police waiting room and into the hallway. Back on the street, she asked for directions to the Laurin Hotel.

≈

The interior of the hotel made Katharina gape as well. It was posh and decadent, unlike anything she had ever experienced.

"Excuse me," she said to the hotel clerk. "I'm looking for Signor Grimani—Minister Grimani, that is."

"*Sí*. We know Minister Grimani well, but he is no longer a guest here." He shrugged and turned away to sort keys into their respective boxes.

Florian put a hand on her arm. It was his way, she noted, of keeping her from succumbing to exasperation. She pushed away from the walnut desk, wondering where they might look next.

A short older man in a smoking jacket glided from her left and behind the desk. He placed a stack of receipts onto the counter and riffled through them. He glanced up, his eyes grazing Katharina, then scouring both her and Florian, until she could feel his look beneath her heavy coat, the coat that revealed that *they don't belong here.* He smiled with polite concern, the sincerity not quite reaching the bristling look.

"Signora? Is someone helping you? Are you lost?"

The man's colleague turned away from the keys and explained that "these people" were looking for Minister Grimani.

Something on the second man's face made Katharina ask, "Is he here?"

She did not wait for the answer. They were not going to tell her anyway. The clerk had come from the restaurant. The clock read five. There were a few guests inside. She ignored Florian calling to her, ignored the suspicious and questioning looks from the waiters. She pulled herself up straight and walked into the restaurant as if she were simply going into the Post Inn.

Behind two potted palms, there he was. Angelo Grimani.

Before Katharina's eyes, their history flickered at light speed. This was the man with whom her life had become entwined in one single moment. She remembered the blood stains in the snow, how Hund had led her to the Spinners' hut. How Angelo had lain on the floor, as if already dead. How she had turned him over, surprised by the foreign look of him. His wounds had been deep. And she had not escaped injury either.

She had run to get Opa, told her grandfather that an Italian man was dying up on the mountain. And she had tended to him as she had done with stray cats and fallen birds, with. love and attention, hungry for reciprocation. She'd been so lonely then. So terribly devastated by the losses of her family. He'd become so much more than a victim in need. The night his fever spiked and he had reached for her—how foolish, how young and stupid she had been to think he was calling for her. She had wilfully lain with him. And that one single action had changed her entire life for good.

Now here they were, except they were not alone. A woman in a trim navy-blue suit with gold-leaf print on the padded shoulders sat next to Angelo. She was dark haired, small, and had large, vivacious eyes. She was digesting Katharina the way Katharina had just digested Angelo and his history with her. And just as rapidly.

Two other men were there as well. One with dark-brown hair, a chequered suit jacket, double-breasted, and the other a sharp-nosed balding man with a high forehead. He wore black-rimmed glasses and a serious countenance.

Everyone except the woman was engrossed in conversation, but when Katharina stopped next to their table, one man after the other looked up. Only Angelo showed immediate recognition, and he struggled to mask his surprise.

He rose. "Frau Steinhauser. Herr Steinhauser. This is unexpected. How did you—"

"We've come a very long way," Katharina said tersely. "Only to be turned away again and again. My husband and I need an invitation to stay."

The hotel staff accommodated them by moving the group to a quiet room in the back of the dining area. Katharina hung off to the side with Florian as Angelo spoke with the head waiter. Angelo had not changed in appearance much in the past year, save for the taut lines at the corners of his lips and other lines etched deep into his forehead. Lines of worry. As she watched Angelo, the dark-haired woman studied her once more. Her look revealed everything she presumed to know about Florian and Katharina. It was unnerving. Every time their eyes met, the woman smiled. She examined Katharina with such interest that Katharina had to wonder whether the woman was privy to more than the most superficial details about Angelo's relationship to Katharina. And if so, why had Angelo shared that information with this woman?

Angelo finally turned his attention from the restaurant staff to the party. First he introduced the curious woman as Signora Gina Conti, who gripped Katharina's hand firmly, and this time her smile was more than just curious. It was strangely comforting. Angelo next presented a Tyrolean journalist, Michael Innerhofer.

"Don't we know you?" Katharina asked.

"That could very well be," Innerhofer replied. "I've written about your valley in the past. I visited the valley some time ago."

"I remember." Florian shook his hand. "I don't think we met personally, but it's nice to have someone in our corner."

Innerhofer's mouth twitched. "I assure you that everyone at this table is here because of your son first, and the valley's circumstances as second. You can turn to me if there is something you do not understand in Italian."

Katharina smiled gratefully, and then Angelo presented the second man.

"Dr Ercole Ubaldi," Angelo said as the man dipped his head at Katharina. "He's the attorney who has agreed to represent your son and his friend."

They were interrupted when the maître de announced the table was ready. Angelo motioned for Katharina to slip into the curved booth, Florian following. Gina Conti sat to Katharina's left, Ubaldi next to her. Katharina and Florian were in the middle, surrounded by strangers. Even Angelo, sitting at the other end, was still a stranger to her.

"You saw my son, today," Katharina said to Dr Ubaldi. "The police told us we could not see Bernd today because you were with them."

Florian's leg pressed into her right thigh. She did not flinch.

"*Sì*, Signora Steinhauser. Today I advised your boys about the tribunal next Tuesday."

Katharina looked to Angelo, then back to Ubaldi. "And what, may I ask, did you advise them? I thought this was the reason we were going to meet tomorrow. Why is this happening without us?"

Angelo indicated the group. "Katharina, you requested my help. These people are here to help."

Florian nudged her again before he spoke to the journalist. "Please, we don't wish to offend. We are simply concerned. We have not seen our son in two months. How is he? That's what we want to know."

Innerhofer translated.

"They are fine, considering the circumstances," Ubaldi said.

Katharina looked at him with disbelief. "Circumstances? Which circumstances? The tribunal? The condition of the prison?"

Ubaldi looked uncertain and seemed about to speak, when Signora Conti placed her hand on the table at the same time as a platter of antipasti and bread arrived. Another waiter brought a bottle of wine and began pouring.

"Excuse me." Katharina motioned that she had to leave. In all this time she had still not managed to find a toilet. "I really must."

"I'll join you." Signora Conti moved with Katharina. "I can show you to the powder room."

Resentfully, Katharina followed the woman. She was not prepared for the lavish room and the modern toilet facilities. Signora Conti showed her to a small enclosure, and Katharina went inside, tense with the fact that the woman appeared not to require a toilet at all. When Katharina came out to wash her hands, Gina Conti was waiting for her.

"Forgive us, please," Signora Conti said. "We were all a little surprised, as Minister Grimani had just mentioned your names a moment before you appeared."

Katharina dried her hands and crossed her arms. "Who are you? I don't understand what everyone's role is in our...situation."

The smile was placating. "Of course you do not. I am a friend of the minister. We move in the same, we'll simply say, political circles."

"Fascist."

Signora Conti slowly tipped her head side to side. "If we must, yes. It is always about who one knows. And I know a lot of people. Ubaldi is a colleague of mine."

"Is he a Black Shirt as well?" Katharina asked bitterly.

Signora Conti glanced at the door before her expression smoothed. "Signora Steinhauser, he must be. He is not allowed into the courtroom if he is not a member of the party. You understand?" She turned to the mirror and washed her hands as well, shaking them slightly before patting them dry on the towel. "He was a socialist," she added.

"Was?"

"A friend of *avvocato* Ubaldi was murdered many years ago.

Fascists shot and left the man to die in a ditch. A good man. An eloquent man. Ubaldi, however, decided to find a different way to work against the forces that be. For now, anyway."

Katharina frowned.

"Not everyone, Signora Steinhauser, who wears the black shirt sleeps in it. You understand? Sometimes one must dress appropriately for certain occasions, and then, when one is within their four walls, they change into the clothing that they are more comfortable in, yes?"

Katharina stared at her. "Why do so at all? Why be..." She struggled to find the right word in Italian, and then it was there. "Complacent?"

Signora Conti smiled again, this time as if to let Katharina in on a secret. "So that we can be invited to the party," she said. "Without an invitation, no source of information. No source of information, Signora, no way to take action. Without information, we cannot protect the people we love, the children we are meant to protect."

Katharina bit her lip. She understood. She understood all too well.

"Come, Signora Steinhauser. I will bring you back to the table. And then we must discuss what it is that Magistrate Mastromattei wants to achieve with your son's tribunal. It is time to talk about strategy."

"The magistrate? What does he have to do with this?"

Signora Conti took in a deep breath and patted Katharina's hand. "Much. Much more than he perhaps should. And I want you to eat. Eat with us. Break bread with us. Promise?"

Katharina reddened. "Yes. Yes, I will."

Back at the table, everyone rose again, and Katharina saw that Florian had prepared a plate of antipasti and bread for her.

"Signora Steinhauser and I will sit on the end," Gina Conti said. "Please, gentlemen, sit back down."

As Florian passed her the plate, Katharina faced Angelo

directly across from her. His eyes darted between her and Signora Conti, but Signora Conti was already speaking, slowly, checking to see whether Katharina was following.

"*Avvocato* Ubaldi has met with the boys to discuss Mastromattei's demands. I was explaining to Signora Steinhauser that the magistrate has a heavy hand in this matter, and it's twofold." She waited until Michael finished translating for Florian. "Mastromattei has arranged to make a proposal to the families that will be affected by the reservoir's construction. That proposal includes finding new homesteads for you to the south—"

"That's what Minister Grimani told me on the phone when I rang," Katharina said.

"That's correct," Angelo said. "Those proposals will be going out in the next couple of months. Mastromattei is waiting to see how you will cooperate with the tribunal."

"What does he want?" Florian asked.

Michael Innerhofer cleared his throat. "To crush the VKS, and he will begin in the Reschen Valley if he must. He wants the name of the ringleader. He wants your boys to give up the boy who recruited them."

Katharina gasped and leaned over to look at Florian. If she were asked to guess, she would name Toni Ritsch.

"Never," Florian said angrily. "My son does not rat on anyone to anyone, and certainly not for your political theatre here."

Ubaldi shifted next to Florian, glanced at Angelo, and slowly said, "Then your son and his friend will be sentenced to hard labour for seven years."

"Except," Angelo said, "there is a hitch. The first boy to give him up will be released and sent to a military school for young boys. The other will be sentenced to hard labour. Ubaldi left them with that choice. Whichever one gives up the name first will be spared the prison sentence."

Florian shoved his plate away from him. "Excuse me. Katharina, it's time to go. Now."

Katharina moved, but Gina put a hand on her arm.

"Please, Signora Steinhauser—"

Angelo had also not moved. "Please sit, Herr Steinhauser. Please. This is very serious, and you must have the entire story."

Florian's face turned pink, and Katharina shared his distress.

"I sent you to Bernd," she said to Angelo, "to help my son. Not make him into an informer."

Angelo sighed. "Katharina, I cannot apologise, because it will make no difference. Please hear us out."

Ubaldi withdrew a sheet of paper from a small file. "Signor and Signora Steinhauser, this is the first offer made by the prosecutors of this case." He turned the sheet to Florian, and Michael leaned over to look at it too. He nodded at first glance and turned to Katharina's husband.

"This was the first letter. Andreas Ritsch would be hanged—"

Katharina cried in protest. The colour now drained from Florian's face.

"And your son would be sentenced to prison," Michael finished. "However, Mastromattei's concerns are twofold. Italy will be dragged into a war together with Germany. His aim is to keep enough peace between the Tyroleans in order to make certain they are prepared to pick up arms when the time comes and to fight for their country."

"Your country," Florian bit back.

Michael's face twisted. "Tyrol is as much my home as it is yours. From what I understand, your mother was from Meran."

This threw Florian back into his seat. He glanced at Katharina, and his eyes were shining. she understood the emotion. It was the first time anyone had acknowledged Florian as Tyrolean, and not just some German from Nuremberg come to pretend to be one.

"Mastromattei worries more than anything about the Italian

military's future," Gina said. "I suggested that both boys be released and sent to a military academy. What Ubaldi has given them today is the prosecutor's begrudged and negotiated terms."

Ubaldi removed his glasses and rubbed his eyes. "Now, Signor and Signora Steinhauser, are you prepared to listen to what I have to say? I will go with you to the prison tomorrow—it will make things easier for you."

"I will be there as well," Angelo said.

Katharina threw him a grateful glance.

Florian shook his head. "I don't know what to say."

Katharina knew his heart was breaking.

"We must do what's best for the boys. We don't want either of them to hang," Katharina said.

It took another hour for Katharina and Florian to establish all the facts and to understand what to expect from the tribunal the following week. Katharina was so desperate to see Bernd that when Angelo began telling them about his last visit with her son, Katharina could no longer hold back the tears. She rose and excused herself, miffed that Gina Conti once more followed her to the fancy powder room.

She hurried ahead, relieved to find it empty, and ducked into the enclosure to collect herself. Gina stood outside offering words of reassurance, but Katharina did not want to hear from this woman.

When she had washed her face, still flushed from crying, she glanced at Gina in the mirror. "Why are you here? I mean, really? What is it that makes you want to help us?"

"I am a mother as well. To four children. Minister Grimani and I are…close," Gina said softly.

Katharina looked at her reflection. Gina's expression was, for the first time, not carefully composed, not cool and focussed. It was soft, and the way her voice had dropped, Katharina knew Gina and Angelo were lovers.

Gina's eyes stayed steady on Katharina.

"You know then?"

Gina's lids fluttered. "I never met Annamarie, but my daughter Filipa and your daughter were in the same Fascist troop. Filipa was Annamarie's leader, and Marco and she were, well, I think they were in love. At least somewhat. As I understand it now, Annamarie and Marco met up in your valley, and he teased her. She was smitten enough with Marco to come to Bolzano and find him."

Katharina paled, embarrassed that this stranger knew the pieced-together horror story. The role of deception that each of the parties played, leading Annamarie into their labyrinth of secrets.

Gina took Katharina's upper arms and squeezed gently. "It was nobody's fault."

"It was mine," Katharina said. "I should have told my daughter about Angelo the moment he returned to the Reschen Valley. I suspected that Annamarie had met him, and the son, and I did not stop it. For me to believe that Angelo would have told her the moment he found her in Bolzano—"

"He couldn't," Gina said firmly. "Angelo was not capable. He had so many things to overcome, and he was trying to save his own marriage."

Katharina huffed. "Well, that didn't work out well at all."

Gina briefly closed her eyes. "It did not. Now all we can do is move on."

"Where is Marco now?" Katharina asked.

"He's not yet reconciled with Angelo. I think that's one of the reasons Angelo is so desperate to help you save Bernd. Signora Steinhauser, is there any way that Bernd would give up the person who had recruited him and the other boy?"

Katharina felt the tears rising again, and Gina clucked sympathetically.

"Then let's sleep on this tonight, all right? Tomorrow you will finally see your son, and we will then see what happens." She steered Katharina outside.

When they returned to the table, Florian was waiting for her.

"Michael Innerhofer has invited us to stay with them in his home. He insists. He won't have it any other way."

"You've had a long journey here," Angelo interjected. "Michael is a good man. You will be in good hands."

Katharina blindly shook hands with Ubaldi, then Gina, and finally Angelo. Michael led them out and helped them into a taxi. As they pulled away from the Laurin Hotel, Katharina thought of Angelo's words. Indeed, it had been a long, long journey to where they were now. And still, she felt they were only at the beginning.

14

BERLIN, JANUARY 1939

Berlin! She was in Berlin!

Margit had been right to talk Annamarie out of returning to the Reschen Valley. Home would always be there, but a chance for a well-funded trip to Berlin and the UFA studios? That only came once in a lifetime. Besides, Annamarie's family was busy with Bernd's upcoming tribunal.

In the crush of people waiting to disembark the train, Annamarie used her case to clear a way. She finally reached the steps, using the small case as a shield against the boarding passengers. She landed on the platform, relatively unharmed. This was *Berlin*! The capital of entertainment, of avant-garde culture and... She stepped away from the crowd and looked around her.

A sea of red banners and flags stood out against the winter fog. At the front of the train several men were disembarking, dressed in an array of black, white, and brown uniforms. They waited until the last of the officers had stepped down, then with sombre purpose they strode around the station to where Annamarie could see the last of a row of motorcars waiting. The men slid into the automobiles, the doors sealing with a *rat-tat-tat* of slams.

Berlin. The Führer's capital now.

Annamarie placed her small suitcase on the platform, glad she had forwarded her boxes to Brunswick in advance. She studied the map Max had provided her one more time. The most important address was circled in her red lipstick in the middle of the city, just over half an hour's walk from the train station. It was an address on the map to her new beginning: UFA—the film production company.

Annamarie made her way through the station, the smell of roasting sausages causing her mouth to water but the idea of finding the studios immediately curbed her hunger. Outside the train station, she looked for a sign to let her know that she was on Invalidenstrasse. To her right was a harbour and the River Spree. From the map, she knew the river wound its way all round Berlin. She looked for signs for the Tiergarten or the Brandenburg Gate, the first two indicators that would lead her to the UFA compound.

Someone stopped in front of her, and she recognised the green scarf before she did his face. "Sepp Greil! What are you doing here?"

Sepp pushed his glasses up onto his forehead and hitched his rucksack onto his right shoulder. "I should ask you the same question, except that I am pretty sure I know what you're doing here."

Annamarie laughed abruptly, both giddy and relieved to see him. Maybe she could finally find out why Lisi had become so withdrawn that Annamarie had left to live with the Rainer family since just before Christmas.

"I'm on my way to Brunswick," she said.

Sepp's eyebrows knitted together beneath his glasses. "So you decided to go. Even after what happened to Veronika."

Annamarie took a step back. "Sepp, the BDM pays me very well. I need the money."

"Right," he said sarcastically. "That makes it all right then."

His words stung. Coolly, she said, "And you? Dodging musters?"

He clicked his tongue. "How did you know?"

"Not really?"

He eyed her once more and shrugged. "Italy or Germany, one of them will want me. Unless you're a student. So I applied to the university."

Annamarie had to give him credit. "In what program?"

"Filmmaking."

She grabbed hold of his upper arms. "Really? You're going to make films?"

"I'm thinking more in journalism terms." Sepp gently shook her off and swept a hand over the landscape of red flags, uniforms, and the bustling street. "I want to capture all this on camera. So not the kind of films you're looking to make, no. Documentaries and that sort of thing."

She thought about the news reels she saw in the cinemas. She was suddenly glad he was here. "Sepp, come with me to the UFA offices. I'm going to apply for the summer internship. It won't start until after I'm done with Brunswick, but I want to make sure I get my application in early. Come with me."

Sepp chuckled and scratched his head, his glasses plopping back onto the bridge of his nose. "No, Annamarie. I'm not the one with a personal invitation from Dr Goebbels."

Annamarie bit her lip.

"Look." He shifted on his feet. "It's not my thing. Entertainment is great and all that—you know I love the theatre —but the glitz and glamour and the, I don't know, strict nationalistic regimen mixing into the arts is not my thing. I'm looking to study history through the lens and get it permanently down on record. Even if it's only for me. Even if it's just so that maybe I can understand it."

Just as Annamarie believed he was going to go his way and leave her to her own devices, he invited her to walk with him. "The Brandenburg Gate is just that way, and we can walk through the Tierpark too. When do you have to be at the offices?"

"I have some time." Annamarie did not have an appointment. She did not even have a contact.

She started for the harbour, thinking they could walk along the river, but Sepp pulled her to the main bridge. Trams rumbled by, and motorcars puttered and weaved their way between the tracks. A motorcycle with a sidecar zipped past. Annamarie followed Sepp as he cut through Königsplatz, where the traffic was reduced to pedestrians and bicyclers. A little while later Annamarie spotted the top of Brandenburg Gate. Between each column, swastika flags hung in the soupy grey air. Sepp and she hardly spoke. He stopped and removed his camera from his rucksack and panned the camera over the cityscape. As they closed in on the famous monument, Annamarie saw that along the entire length of Unter den Linden, white pillars stood like the leftover ruins of Roman villas. The Reich's flags were stuck atop the edges. She'd visited a Greek Orthodox church in Innsbruck once, where she'd seen prayer candles pressed haphazardly upon sandy tiers. That was what this looked like. It was certainly worship.

Sepp guided her but Annamarie stopped before a pillar at the park's entrance, higher than the others. A gold eagle with a swastika at its feet was mounted atop. The black streetlamps along the avenue were reminiscent of the gaslights they used to be. Each contained two cylindrical bulbs on either side of the posts. They looked like skinny priests standing in benediction over the spectacle along the avenue.

She shared her observations with Sepp, and he lowered his camera.

"That's really good, Annamarie."

"What is?"

"Your descriptions. You ought to write those things down."

Annamarie flushed. She set her suitcase down. It was getting heavy, even if there were only a few things inside. "Are you going to trying to make a writer out of me now?"

Sepp shrugged before raising the eye of the camera again. "You do love to make up stories."

"You always call it lying," Annamarie retorted.

"Depends on which end of the story you're standing at I suppose."

They walked on, and Annamarie thought about what he'd said. All of it. "You know I used the opportunity to do something in theatre, to study, but had to be part of the *fascisti* in Bolzano, right?"

Sepp nodded.

"I can't change anything about the way politics are or what I have to do to make something of myself. The leaders and authorities are always so angry, so depressing. I don't even understand it. What am I supposed to do about it?"

Sepp started to speak, but Annamarie stopped him.

"I've spent my entire life adapting and adjusting to what the rules are. First to the Italian ones. In public we had to speak Italian, but at home my parents made us speak German, and in secret. Don't do this. Don't do that. You're Tyrolean, so you can't do this. And you can't do that. You're Tyrolean. Remember who you are and the centuries of traditions that we must now practice but from prying eyes. But wait. The Walscher says, if we join them, we can be a part of everything."

Sepp nodded. "I know. I grew up there too, remember?"

She laughed. "Even my body adapted to Italian society."

He pushed his spectacles up his forehead again and narrowed his eyes. "What do you mean?"

"When I was little, I had lighter hair colour. The more Italian our valley got, the darker my hair seemed to turn. Well, I learned the real reason for that later on." She snatched up the case and walked fast, the suitcase banging against the side of her knee. Why had she broached the topic?

"Are you going to tell me that reason?" He caught up to her.

She'd spilled it because she had to tell someone. "My father is Italian. My mother and he"—she glanced at Sepp—"had an intimate history."

"Did you know him?"

"He's a big shot in Bolzano. No."

Sepp's glasses shot higher up his forehead. He placed them back on his nose. "Wow. And your mother?"

"I don't want anything more to do with any of them." Her chest constricted. She was like Pinocchio, the puppet whose nose grew long when he lied, except that it was her chest that hurt with every lie. "My mother wrote to me in November and said she refused to help me with the *Ahnenpass* without seeing me. She said she would come to Innsbruck and have the documents I needed with her. Whatever she could salvage from this supposed fire."

"And?"

Annamarie walked faster. "She never came. First, she couldn't get the permission to travel across the border. I figured she was just stalling. Then I got a telegram. My brother was apparently running around with the VKS and burned down that stupid town hall."

Sepp blew softly. "Did he get caught?"

Annamarie nodded. "He's in prison, awaiting a tribunal."

"And you don't want to go down there?"

She had planned to. She especially wanted to see Manuel, to hug her baby brother, to say she was sorry to everyone. But now she would have to admit to Sepp that she had chosen a paid trip to Berlin over her family. She'd broken everyone's heart and done this to herself.

"My mother's busy now with my brother."

"And the *Ahnenpass*?"

"Margit's parents helped. They got special concessions. My brother's story—pro-German and all that—worked in my favour, and now it's filled out."

They walked along the street. To their left were rows of shops with flats above them.

"So you just crossed the border into Austria and decided to become a Nazi? Because your father's Italian?"

Annamarie scoffed. "You know I didn't, Sepp."

"So, what are you doing, Annamarie?"

"It's a job. These are the times. What do you expect me to do? I'm just going to get through these months in Brunswick and hope I get the internship in the film business. Then we'll see." She was eighteen, and there was only one thing she wanted, and it would start right here, in Berlin.

"It's my birthday today," she said.

"Really?" Sepp stopped her. "I mean really?"

She nodded. "Eighteen now. Really. No lies. Promise."

Sepp pulled her against him, and it surprised her. She set her suitcase down and tentatively wrapped her arms around him. It felt good.

"It's nice that you're here, Sepp. Another Tyrolean on the run."

He looked sternly at her. "You're wrong, Annamarie. There is something else that you can do."

"What? Resist?"

"Naturally."

"That day when they arrested Veronika, you weren't even there. You didn't see Lisi's face. You know how she always talks big? I saw her looking helpless, Sepp. Elisabeth von Brandt was helpless. Helpless against the brother she believed she could control. Helpless against all those men in uniforms, with badges, with…" Annamarie threw up her hands and spun around. "Look where we are Sepp. Look at all this. Why would we want to resist this? Don't you feel the energy? The togetherness? The victory of this all? We know who we are. We all just want to have an identity, to belong. Things are going well, aren't they? I have work. You had a great position at the theatre, and now you're going to study again. The youth has a future ahead of them. We're learning practical things, and even the women here are encouraged to contribute, to be valuable assets to society."

Sepp shook his head. "You sound like a socialist playbook. You're not smiling, but you've got to be joking. I never know whether to believe you. This is why Lisi can't trust you."

Annamarie dropped her hands. "Lisi can't trust me?" she asked brokenly. "Why? She created this. She was the one who said, 'Take the job, Annamarie. Take the money.'"

"But you're eighteen now," Sepp said sharply. "Take some accountability. Go to UFA and get an internship but—"

"Sepp," Annamarie exclaimed, "you have to be a party member to even be considered. You have to be a party member because you have to join the union. These are the rules! Look, I speak exactly two languages, Tyrolean German and Tyrolean Italian. Italy is run by Fascists. Germany is run by Fascists. Tell me what am I supposed to do? Just give up my biggest dream because of stupid politics? You're right—I do have some control, but not over the government. I don't have control over who runs the country—"

"We can change that."

"I'm eighteen," Annamarie bit back. "I didn't do this. And neither did you! You were still in Italy when you turned old enough. But here we are, stuck with it. Sepp, I can still control what I do, what steps I will take, when an opportunity in all this madness is offered to me. And if I have to buy the ticket to enter, I will."

Sepp looked up suddenly and shuffled her to the side. Across the street, two men stumbled out of a beer hall, shouting and swinging at each other. Both were older and dressed like tradesmen. Sepp pulled Annamarie closer to the kerb, directly across from the fight. He lifted the camera and got it rolling again. From a distance, someone blew a whistle, and two SD men ran around the corner. They shoved their way through the onlookers and tackled the wrestling men. One of the tradesmen fell towards the street, with an SD man on top of him. Annamarie heard a sickening crack as the tradesman's head hit the edge of the pavement. She stepped behind Sepp and bit her lip so hard she tasted blood.

The policeman pulled at the fallen man's collar, but the head came up limp on the neck. It was then that Annamarie saw the blood pooling.

A woman screeched, and the patrons from the beer hall and the tobacco shop next door spilled out and surrounded the fallen man. She heard the SD men swear as the man's head lolled back into the gutter. As the crowd gathered, they blocked the victim from Annamarie's view, but there was more shoving and yelling. A man with a thick neck and shaved head grabbed one of the SD men and put a chokehold on him. The other police officer raised a pistol and shot into the air. Annamarie ducked.

A moment later a vehicle pulled up, and two men stepped out and elbowed the onlookers out of the way. Gestapo. Sepp's camera continued rolling. He took a few steps closer and panned the scene around the bleeding man. Annamarie decided the tradesman was dead.

Suddenly, Sepp pulled on Annamarie's elbow. "Come on. Let's get out of here."

She could hear the sirens pealing across the road behind them. But Sepp was anxious, and only after he put his camera back into the rucksack did Annamarie notice that one of the plainclothes policemen was watching them. He tucked something into his breast pocket and pressed his way through the crowd of onlookers.

"You there," he shouted at Sepp.

Sepp grappled for Annamarie's suitcase and walked quickly away. He pulled up the collar of his coat with his other hand. She could do nothing but follow him.

They hurried across the road, and Annamarie read a sign for Potsdamer Platz. Sepp lifted the case high and scrambled through some close-growing hedges and into the park beyond. Annamarie's coat caught on a branch, and she yanked it out with her free hand, nearly falling forward. She heard another shout.

"Why are we running?" she called to Sepp.

He slowed then. They were on the path with signs indicating the river ahead. "We're not."

But they were. She looked over her shoulder. There were just people, people in yet another Berlin park. A woman hurried by with a pram, bent over the handles as if to shield what was inside. It drizzled so lightly Annamarie didn't think she could get wet no matter how long she stood there. She could smell the river. Two young boys ran by with square book bags slung over their shoulders and a leather ball between them. A man in a dark coat turned up the same path they were on.

"I think he's still following us," she warned.

Sepp did not turn around. "Just keep walking. I'm going to get you to the train station."

"What did we do?"

"We witnessed all that, that's what. He's Gestapo." He yanked her down a little alley between two buildings, and now she, too, was running. What did she have to fear? Beneath her wool coat, she wore a BDM blouse, her proof of compliance. The mark that signalled she stood on the obedient side of the regime.

Sepp stopped when they reached a broad street again. He stuffed the camera back into his rucksack. Across the road, Annamarie recognised nothing.

"He's just going to ask questions, and he'll want my film reel," Sepp said hurriedly. "I don't want to give it up. I've got to keep going, Annamarie. When will you be done at the UFA?" He handed her the suitcase.

"I don't know. I just know that my train for Brunswick leaves around six."

Sepp looked around and then over her shoulder. She turned. There was nobody there. Maybe they'd shaken him off. Maybe the Gestapo man had given up. Or maybe Sepp was just being paranoid.

"You think he's gone?" Annamarie asked.

"Let's split up here to be safe." Sepp undid his scarf, unwrapped it from his neck, and shoved it into his rucksack before dropping it to his side. He told her he would head to the university and settle in at his accommodations.

"Meet me at the Café König," he said. "It's in Unter der Linden, just a few metres from the gate. Just ask someone. I'll be there by four. We'll drink to your birthday."

Annamarie said she would.

He leaned in and pecked her cheek. "I'll see you later."

Facing the road, she watched him walk away. She needed to get to the centre, somewhere in the direction of the Spreeinsel. "Sepp," she called to his retreating figure. He was too far away to ask for directions now. "Café König?"

He whirled around and raised a hand. "Good luck, Annamarie."

She walked in the direction she thought might be correct, when she stopped again. How did Sepp know Berlin so well anyway? Sometimes she felt like she'd never done anything in her life at all. She would have to ask him that and not forget to ask him about Lisi this time.

The blue-and-red diamond logo on the five-storeyed building in Victoriastrasse was a beacon. UFA—Universal Film Limited. The offices were on the upper floors above a high-ceilinged first storey with arched windows. Heart beating in her throat, Annamarie tried to look as if she belonged there. In the foyer was a large front desk and two well-dressed women behind it. Both were blondes, both wore fitted blazers and skirts—one in burgundy, the other in green blue—and both began looking busier as Annamarie neared the desk. It was like approaching an altar and the priestesses were sharpening their daggers.

The woman on Annamarie's left was Burgundy. She looked up from whatever she was doing behind the deep desk and held a pen in midair, her eyebrows arched into question marks.

"I'm here to see Dr Goebbels," Annamarie said. The suitcase landed with a click on the stone floor.

The question marks exploded into exclamation marks. "Dr Goebbels is not here. Do you have an appointment?"

"If I did, would he be here?"

The woman tutted.

Blue Green looked up and tucked her chin, as if to say, *Glad it's not me who has to deal with this.*

"What do you need?" Burgundy asked.

"I'm Annamarie Steinhauser, and I'll be working in the film division in Innsbruck. Dr Goebbels offered a personal tour of the studio lots should I ever come to Berlin."

The woman blinked. "And did you make arrangements for this personal tour?"

"He said the next time I'm in Berlin…" Annamarie turned to her left, the sound of excited chatter spilling out into the hallway.

A group of people stepped from behind a door. Two women broke away from the group and approached the desk. One had wavy shoulder-length strawberry-blonde hair, dark intense eyes, and a wide mouth. Annamarie took in a deep breath and straightened herself. It was Leni Riefenstahl. Actress, dancer, film director.

Stepping aside to allow Riefenstahl and her companion space

at the reception desk, Annamarie said as graciously as she could, "Please, go ahead. I'll wait."

Miss Riefenstahl's companion smiled gratefully at Annamarie. She had light-brown hair, appeared to be in her mid-twenties, had high cheekbones on a diamond-shaped face, and her nose was a little upturned.

"Miss Riefenstahl, it's so very nice to see you," Burgundy behind the desk said, as if she were addressing the British queen. "How was the tour in America?"

"Very fine, thank you. Miss Mainz here will take over the press reports now." Riefenstahl indicated the second woman and threw Annamarie a quick glance. "I won't take up your time. Please make sure Miss Mainz gets what she needs."

"Certainly, Miss Riefenstahl."

Riefenstahl dipped her head at Annamarie and turned away. The second woman—Miss Mainz—then asked for a room and mentioned some names and numbers. When she was finished, she faced Annamarie.

"Thank you for waiting. Is there something I can help you with?"

Burgundy huffed softly. "This woman here says she met Dr Goebbels in Innsbruck and he invited her to visit the set when she was in Berlin."

Miss Mainz smiled broadly. "But Miss Grünberg, that's nothing unusual."

It was now Annamarie's turn to be surprised.

Miss Mainz stuck out her hand. "I'm Charlotte Mainz. I do a little bit of everything around here, but mostly I handle international publicity. Miss Grünberg, I'll take it from here. Thank you."

Annamarie grasped Charlotte's hand and shook it energetically.

"So you're from Innsbruck?"

"South Tyrol, actually. I'll be working in the film division in Innsbruck."

"Really! That's wonderful. Why, Miss Riefenstahl met Mr Luis Trenker in South Tyrol. She loves those mountain films." Charlotte moved away from the desk and toward the hallway where Riefenstahl had gone. "How long will you be in Berlin? I could arrange a tour for you, say in a couple of days?"

Annamarie's heart sank. "I'm leaving tonight."

Charlotte looked disappointed. "I'm afraid we're all tied up. Miss Riefenstahl's return from America is big news today, and we're handling quite a number of interviews and press releases at the moment."

Annamarie finally found the courage. "Dr Goebbels mentioned that it might be beneficial for me if I won an internship here. Before I get to work in Innsbruck, that is. He said the company takes on new interns in the spring?"

"Yes, we start looking for applicants in the early spring, and the internship goes over the summer. There are quite a lot of applicants, however." Charlotte tipped her head. "What experience do you have in the industry?"

"I'm training to be an actress."

"Anything in an office? A job behind the scenes, so to speak? The internship will not offer acting roles, but you would learn about everything that goes on behind the scenes."

The door down the hall opened again, and Leni Riefenstahl stepped out once more. "There you are, Charlotte. Can you join us now?"

This time the film director looked more intently at Annamarie.

"This is Miss Annamarie Steinhauser," Charlotte said. "She's from South Tyrol."

Riefenstahl flashed Annamarie an acknowledging smile. "Luis Trenker. Wonderful director. Good friend."

Annamarie broke away from Charlotte. She marched up to Riefenstahl and stuck out her hand. "So very nice to meet you. I've never seen a Trenker film, but I have heard much about him. All I know is that your movies are wonderful. Your eye for storytelling, your ability to capture action and emotion all on film, it's admirable."

Riefenstahl blinked, her smile frozen. She looked at Miss Mainz. "Do you hear that accent?"

Annamarie cringed but Riefenstahl grasped her hand, and without looking at her asked Charlotte, "What is she here for?"

Charlotte grinned broadly. "To apply for the summer internship programme."

Riefenstahl looked at Annamarie and then at Charlotte. "She'd be perfect for the project in Spain." She studied Annamarie again. "Yes, you apply for that internship. Charlotte, bring me her application directly. Then closer to summer, Miss Steinhauser and I will talk."

Annamarie exhaled slowly, her thanks breathy. She shook the director's hand vigorously, and Riefenstahl cast her one more appraising look.

"You're quite a brave young woman, aren't you? I can see that. I like that."

Charlotte swept Annamarie away, leaned over to Miss Grünberg behind the reception desk, and asked for an application form. Fifteen minutes later, Annamarie pressed it into Charlotte's hands.

"We'll see you in summer, then." Charlotte winked. "Look forward to it."

"Will I get that tour?"

Charlotte laughed. "You'll know the lots and studios like the back of your hand. Make sure you have a decent pair of walking shoes with you."

Annamarie floated out the building. Outside, the drizzle had turned to snow. As soon as she was out of the way, Annamarie whooped and skipped in the chill damp. She headed north for the swastika-draped boulevard of Unter den Linden. She could not stop smiling, even at the stony-faced strangers who averted their looks. The more they tried, the broader she smiled and laughed aloud. A singer outside a U-bahn exit extended a hand to her, and she fished for a single coin out of her pocket.

Annamarie found the Café König in plenty of time before four. The café smelled of hot coffee and crisped cheese. She ordered a sandwich and a cup of cocoa, and she shivered against the counter. Positioned at a high table along the windows, Annamarie had a view onto the street and the passersby. What light was left was already dimming into early winter night. The snow was turning into slush, and the vehicles that drove by made wet swishy sounds she could hear even through the windowpanes. She wiped her greasy fingers on a napkin and waited for Sepp, bursting with the news.

It was five o'clock before she began to worry. Had the Gestapo man accosted Sepp? Had there been an altercation? She had no idea where to look for him. He had not mentioned which university he was at. She had not asked. She'd talked about herself the entire time. She had to get back to the train station, which was a half hour walk away. And if she missed her train and had no place to stay, it would be a long, cold night. At half past five, Annamarie asked for a piece of paper and a pen and left Sepp a note.

It was already dark when she reached Brandenburg Gate. Music and laughter, glasses clinking, and singing seeped out of the cracks of bar doors before she cut across Königsplatz again. The wind blew off the Spree, and she pulled her coat collar up and wrapped her arms around herself to keep the heat in. Her ankles were wet from the slush that splashed up from the street as she walked. She turned around a couple of times, wondering whether she would spot Sepp's figure, or maybe he would come across her now, knowing she had to catch her train.

Maybe he'd said it all. Maybe his one message was,

"Annamarie, you're a fake, and we don't trust you," and he wanted nothing more to do with her. Either way, she felt a terrible sadness for having missed him. For not having been able to better explain herself. For not being able to share the news with him and expect the kind of happiness from him that she'd felt.

But Sepp had been kind to her, as if he'd been trying to understand her. As if he were putting the puzzle pieces together, finally, after what? A year? Good old Sepp. He was loyal and true. And she'd done him wrong.

A bookshop was still open in the station that sold magazines and wares alongside *Pfennig* sweets and day-old pastries. She found a notebook and purchased a pencil, an eraser, and a sharpener and asked for them to be wrapped up. The shopkeeper did so and handed her the parcel.

She was going to write down what she observed. If nothing else than to preserve this time for herself. And maybe, like Sepp, to better understand it.

In Brunswick, she was met by a woman who took her to the training facilities. Annamarie was astounded by the modern building, still lit up from the outside. The woman led her through the common rooms where, the Gruppenführerin told her, both the women and the men could mingle. The canteen, where Annamarie was offered a hot drink and a bowl of soup as well as a fresh pretzel, was spic and span. The woman patiently explained the house rules as Annamarie ate, rapt with attention and barely tasting the soup.

She was then led through the large gymnasium, with every kind of equipment for performance and sports one could imagine, and into an attached building of the women's dormitories. The men's dormitories, her leader told her with a conspiratorial wink, were in the next one-story building and were connected by a tunnel.

The woman handed Annamarie her key at the door to her room. She waited until Annamarie had pushed it open, then flicked on the lights. Annamarie had her own room, a bed, cabinets, bookshelves, a welcome packet, including her agenda for tomorrow. And a telephone.

"Is this for internal calls?"

The Gruppenführerin shook her head. "Internal, external. It's a phone. Ring anyone you like. Your direct number is listed right next to it."

She said good night to Annamarie and closed the door. Annamarie's box of things had arrived. On top was a note with a message: *Elisabeth von Brandt rang.*

Annamarie's first thought was that Lisi was calling about Sepp, but the next lines made it clear that it had not been the reason.

Your mother tried to reach you in Innsbruck. Your brother's tribunal is on the 23rd.

That was tomorrow.

Annamarie sat on the edge of her bed and looked around the room. If Bernd could see her now, he wouldn't believe it. She lay on her back, holding the note.

Bernd had called her a Fascist, an Italian lover, a Walscher. The fact that he was probably going to prison for his actions whilst she was here, getting rewarded in all sorts of ways, left her feeling sick. And wondering even more about what had happened to Sepp.

Outside the window, it was dark. She could make nothing out. She saw only her reflection and the room. She reached for her bag and unpacked the parcel with the notebook, sharpened the pencil, and tapped the first page with the tip before the first thoughts poured out onto the page.

15

BOLZANO, JANUARY 1939

Outside the Bolzano prison, Angelo met Katharina and Florian. They were to see their son for the second time in a week. He led them through the door and signed them all in, and a guard escorted them to the visitation room. At the sight of Bernd, Katharina slumped into herself. Her son was sitting in a cage again in the middle of the room.

"The charges were reduced," she cried. "My son is not an animal."

Angelo was sympathetic. "It's the system." They had all been surprised and relieved when Ubaldi announced that the intent to harm was reduced to endangering the general public rather than the police or politicians. The latter would have put the boys in Rome for a deadly tribunal.

Bernd was a well-built youngster, muscular and square, the physique of a hardworking farmer. Since his incarceration, however, he had lost weight. His light-brown hair, curly like Florian's, was hanging in greasy strands. He wore an expression of permanent shame and fear, not the mask of defiance Angelo had seen the first time he'd visited the youth.

Bernd rose and clutched the bars. Angelo stood off to the side. He'd told the Steinhausers they could call on him when needed, but otherwise he'd done all he could.

"What did you decide?" Florian started evenly. "Whatever you want to do, Bernd, this has to be your decision."

Katharina's hand twitched, and Angelo sensed she wanted nothing more than to reach into that cage and yank her child out.

Bernd's eyes were dull with repentance. "I'll do anything I need to get out of this prison. But nobody ever spoke to me directly about the VKS. Not specifically. It was all Andreas. So now what should I do?"

Katharina and Florian shared a look. Angelo knew Bernd was not telling the truth.

Florian turned to Angelo. "If he names Andreas, it will kill what fragile relationship we have left with the Ritsches."

It was not Angelo's place to advise them on how to handle that.

Someone knocked on the door, and the guard checked through the peephole, then opened it. Ubaldi strode in and dropped the dossier onto the table, then took a deep breath and scratched his brow. "I met the Ritsches on the way in. They told me in no uncertain terms that I would not be representing their son."

After translating for Florian, Katharina asked, "Do the Ritsches understand the seriousness of the penalties?"

Ubaldi cleared his throat. "They do not want to understand."

"I'll talk to them," Florian said. "I'll get them to understand."

"What about you?" Ubaldi said to Bernd. "Are you still resistant to my help?"

Bernd hung his head.

"Good," Ubaldi said. "Then let's clear the room. This is a confidential discussion."

Katharina leaned over the table, stretching a hand into the

cage and grasping her son's forearm. "Bernd, we'll be there tomorrow. We'll be right behind you the entire time. All right?"

Bernd looked wildly at Florian as Florian rose as well. He quickly spoke in German. All Angelo understood was, *Father, I promise.*

Florian pressed his eyes closed and ran a hand over his face. Angelo imagined the boy was pleading for a way to get home, that if he could just get home, he would do nothing like this again. If the tables were turned and it was Marco in there, Angelo wondered what he would advise his son.

They left Bernd with Ubaldi, and Angelo accompanied the Steinhausers outside.

"We need to speak to Toni and Patricia," Florian said.

"I don't think that's a good idea," Katharina said to him before turning to Angelo. "They already hate us for being down here, for having spoken to Andreas at all about denouncing their group leader."

Angelo cleared his throat. "Why don't we get some fresh air? It's going to be a long few days. A walk along the river?"

Florian glanced at him, then at his wife. His fingers brushed Katharina's shoulder, and he whispered something to her.

Katharina nodded. "Florian is going to wait here for the Ritsches. But I will take you up on that walk."

"I'll bring her right back."

Florian nodded stiffly, but his expression was one of acquiescence.

As Angelo led Katharina to the promenade, the sun fought through thick white and grey clouds. The river slugged its way through the cold. Katharina fidgeted with her mittens.

"Your husband is a very generous man," Angelo said.

Katharina dropped her hands. "He is exceptional in many ways, yes."

"How are you? I mean, truly, how are you doing?"

She clicked her tongue. "It's all rather strange, don't you find?"

He agreed with her.

"How do you think we'll fare tomorrow?" she asked.

"I honestly don't know. And I feel speculating too much is not going to help. Ubaldi means to do right by Bernd. He would have by Andreas as well."

"We're very grateful to you for acquiring the attorney for us."

"It was Signora Conti who managed it all."

Katharina's sideways glance was questioning. She folded her arms around herself and her look averted to the park across the river.

"We're practically strangers," she said.

Angelo wanted her to know that they all—he, Gina, and Michael—meant well by the Steinhausers. "You're right. We are. The one thing—"

"Two."

His hesitation lasted a second before he understood. "Yes, two. Annamarie and the reservoir. But, Katharina…" His hand hovered over her arm, asking permission. "I have no regrets."

She turned away and continued walking, her pace slow.

He followed. "May I ask about Annamarie? How she is?"

"The reservoir is easier to talk about."

"All right."

"Georg Roeschen has managed to talk the villagers into at least considering Mastromattei's proposal regarding the hamlets. But I had another idea." She looked earnest, but her eyes were heavy. "The committee is keen about it too. You see, we once had many tourists to the valley who enjoyed the fresh air, the hiking, and the lakes. *Sommerfrishler* is what we call them. And I thought, well, what if we started thinking differently about commerce? What if we built on the idea that we could still offer a wonderful place for tourists? And that would allow us to at least stay in our valley?"

Angelo frowned. "Is that what the community wants? To stay?"

"Of course."

"And you too?"

"Yes, me too. If Florian and I can find another way to earn a living, if there is any way to stay, I beg for your department to manage a new deal. We are putting our trust in you." There was something else.

"But?"

"If our boys are imprisoned," she said slowly, "we'll never manage to keep everyone together, Angelo. We won't have a chance at resolving this peacefully. It's not us against the Fascists any longer. There is infighting, and our own people are split into two camps. If one or both of our boys are imprisoned, I can't guarantee any semblance of cooperation."

Angelo sighed. "We're doing all that we can to prevent that. But if the Ritsches refuse Ubaldi's help and Andreas tries to defend himself at the trial, or your son does not at least identify one person…" He did not complete the thought.

She knew what he was implying. "I hope Toni wisens up," she said bitterly.

"What about Annamarie? I have arranged for your travel permits. Will you go to her?"

Katharina looked pained. "I tried to reach her. I wanted to let her know that I've been delayed. When she found out that many of the town hall records were destroyed, she accused me of lying. We still have the church documents, but I did not want to tell her that. I said if I could travel to Innsbruck, I'd help her with that pass. I have a number now to the BDM headquarters there. A young woman, Margit Rainer, told me that Annamarie is in Brunswick."

"In Brunswick? That's near Hamburg! What is she doing all the way up there?"

Katharina sounded as if she were choking the words out. "I

don't know. She will stay there for four months, according to Miss Rainer. She's simply moving farther and farther away, Angelo. I just want to see her. I want to understand what she is running after."

They paused at a bench just as the sun broke out. Neither of them sat.

"She's searching for her identity," Angelo said. "Why do you think she enjoys acting so much? She can try on as many masks as she would like."

Katharina walked to the edge of the riverbank, and Angelo followed her.

"I believe we know when we are incomplete," she said after a moment. "When we feel we are missing a part of ourselves. I was certain that was why she was always running. Always."

"How can I help?"

Katharina bit her lip before answering. "She needs her mother. Like you are to me, you're a stranger to her. And let's not forget, you are also Marco's father. She's in great pain, Angelo."

And shame, Angelo thought. He understood what shame could do. The girl was weighted down by shame. Just like Bernd was now. It could work for you or against you, but usually it worked against you.

"Give her time," he said. "I truly believe that sometimes we need to sink to the very bottom to get back up again. You and Florian have raised good children."

Katharina narrowed her eyes.

"No, the environment they are growing up in is not conducive to our intentions. They will navigate their way through it, however."

"Have they any other choice?" Katharina said softly. She faced him. "I have to go back."

"Certainly." He turned to lead her back to the prison, but Katharina raised a mittened palm. "You've done enough. I'll find my own way."

He nodded, relieved. He was drained from the events of the last few days. "I'll see you in court tomorrow."

For a moment, he watched her before changing course for his office. He weaved his way through the outdoor market as a shortcut and stopped when he spotted Chiara at a wool socks stand. Still, after all these years, he could pick her out in the densest crowd, and still, despite everything that had driven them apart, she made his heart skip a beat. He found it remarkable. A person next to her stepped out from behind a rack of woollen scarves, and Angelo's heart felt a different kind of pain. Marco was with her. Steeling himself, Angelo closed the gap between them and greeted them.

Chiara said in a telltale tone, "We saw you along the river." Her eyes asked the question—*was that Katharina he'd been with?*

Angelo confirmed without a word.

Next to her, Marco was hunched into his coat, looking down at the ground.

"We're shopping," Chiara announced, "for things Marco needs before he goes to Rome next month."

"May I join you? Invite you for lunch?" Angelo asked.

"Don't you have to work?" Marco asked acidly.

Chiara pushed their son forward. "I want this, Marco. I want the three of us to have lunch together. If your father can take the time—"

"I can take the whole day."

Chiara looked surprised. "Well, we have a few things to get yet." Purposefully she walked down the row of stalls.

Angelo matched Marco's tempo. "How's the job been at MFE?"

"Fine."

"Where did you work?"

"Wherever Chief Engineer Accosi needed me."

This irked Angelo, knowing that the man who had betrayed

him was now closer to his son than Angelo had been in over a year.

"What did you do with him?" Angelo asked.

"Mostly surveyed."

"Like you did with me?"

Marco did not answer.

Angelo reminded himself to ask open questions. "What kinds of drawings did you have to produce?"

"I didn't. I'm more interested in mechanical engineering anyway."

They halted suddenly as Chiara veered to a stall with leather belts. She took a few off the hooks and wrapped one after the other around Marco's waist, tutting about how thin he had become.

Angelo continued pressing his son. "What division are you going to be in?"

Marco told his mother any of the belts were fine. He turned to Angelo. "The Sixty-First. Now you'll ask me how long my training is going to be. Three years. What am I hoping to be? A fighter pilot. And if that doesn't work out? An aeroplane mechanic."

Angelo did not know whether to ruffle his son's hair the way he'd done when they'd sparred and joked in the past, or whether to be disappointed in the insolent tone. He chose to spar. "All right. What is your favourite aeroplane?"

Marco rolled his eyes, but the corners of his mouth did twitch upwards.

They continued like this all the way back to the piazza, and Angelo decided to introduce him to the stand-up café.

"It's like a saloon in the westerns," he explained.

Marco muttered something about how his father was with the times.

The barista greeted Angelo boisterously and reached over the counter to shake his hand. "And this is your family?"

"Yes," Angelo said.

But a dark shadow passed over Marco's face. Angelo quickly ordered three espressos and steered "his family" to the end of the bar. They downed their demitasses in uncomfortable silence. Forcing a light tone, Angelo asked Marco when it was that he'd decided mechanical engineering was more interesting, but Marco shot him a piercing look.

His son pointed to a chemist's shop across the way. "I need to pick something up."

"Let me come with you," Chiara said.

"No need."

Angelo stood with her outside the espresso bar and waited.

"Don't push him too hard," Chiara said. "Go gently."

"I was making progress."

The rims of Chiara's lips were turning white.

Angelo sighed, checked his watch, and was about to fetch his son, but Marco came out and they continued to the restaurant. At the trattoria, after they were seated, Chiara removed her coat and gloves. Angelo hung their coats and pulled out Chiara's chair. When she was settled, she said much too cheerily for the announcement, "I saw your mother the other day."

Except for the Colonel, Angelo had not seen his family since Christmas Eve. That too had been a tense and miserable affair. The three of them and Pietro had joined the Grimanis. Everyone was there including Angelo's sisters and their families. They had all crammed into the Grimani parlour, everyone injecting the tense silence with trivial updates.

Angelo, your niece is teething.

Marco's progressing so well at work.

Have you heard Mama's latest doctor report?

Any trivia to avoid speaking about the herd of white elephants in the room.

During the third course, Angelo's sisters had launched into a debate about which dress shop had the best bargains. That was when Marco had risen from the dinner table, drained his wineglass, and announced he'd had enough of the family farces. As soon as Marco had stormed out, the tension erupted. Every family member hurled accusations at Angelo the way one would hurl *zabaglione* in a food fight. Angelo had helped Pietro out of his chair, and he, Chiara, and the old man made a hurried exit.

"And how is my mother?" Angelo now asked.

"Your mother is her usual self." Chiara fussed with the napkin. "She has a new ailment, however. Nothing serious, we've been assured. I don't even remember what it is."

The waiter took their order. Angelo ordered a half bottle of white wine after asking Marco and Chiara whether they would share it with him. Marco ordered the tomato soup to start and Chiara an antipasti. Angelo asked whether they ought to share that as well. She agreed. The waiter left, and Marco was looking at the two of them, a sick grin on his face.

"You know what I like about floatplanes the best?" Marco asked. "They can fly over seven hundred kilometres an hour. I can imagine flying at seven hundred kilometres an hour to get away from hearing the two of you prattling on about white wine and whether an antipasti platter is large enough to split."

Chiara tucked in her chin and made a noise.

Leaning across the table, Angelo kept his voice low and stern. "What do I have to do to set things right between us?"

Marco glared at him. "There's nothing you can do. You might have Mother dancing to your tune, but—"

"Marco," Chiara warned.

The waiter returned much faster than Angelo could have anticipated. He set the bowl of soup before Marco, followed by the antipasti platter and two plates.

Marco ploughed on. "But you won't have that with me. The moment you saw Annamarie at the house, you should've fessed up. Instead you allowed me to—"

"Stop it," Angelo snapped. "You weren't exactly innocent in

any of it. You defied me." He yanked the spoon out of Marco's hand. The table trembled. "Your behaviour was the least gentlemanly I've encountered in a long time. I understand why you defied me as you did, but that was the reason it got out of control."

Marco's jaw clenched, but his voice was still higher pitched than usual. "You knew who she was when you caught us messing about in that field."

"I suspected," Angelo corrected. "I did not know."

Chiara sat back in her chair, her hands falling into her lap.

Marco was sulking now, the fury flaming up his neck to the tips of his earlobes.

"I suspected, Marco," Angelo said again. "I admit, I denied the entire plausibility of it all, and that was my mistake. Signora Steinhauser—"

"Must we?" Chiara protested.

Angelo ignored her. "Signora Steinhauser did not involve me. She found a different way to handle her burden. Only when Annamarie had run off to Bolzano did I discover the truth. Marco, listen to me."

Chiara placed a hand on the table. "Keep it down. Both of you."

One of the waiters approached, as if to rescue the family, and she waved him away. Marco toyed with the knife to his right. But he was listening.

"I had no idea," Angelo repeated, more softly this time. "That you were hiding her away."

"I wasn't," Marco snapped. "She followed me here because of one stupid kiss."

"And you," Chiara said sternly, "took advantage of her."

"Like father, like son," Marco retorted.

Angelo's hand itched to slap him. Instead, he silently pleaded with Chiara. Reminding Marco of his deepest shame would only make things worse.

She leaned back in her chair.

"Marco," Angelo said, "what is done is done."

"Really?" His son looked up. "And when will you finally set Mama free? Just give her a divorce already."

"Marco, I don't want—"

"Why?" The boy glared at his mother. "It's embarrassing. Both of you are embarrassing. You should be ashamed of yourselves. Everyone talks about you behind your backs. Only you two aren't aware of what pariahs you are."

He rose, and Angelo knew this was going to end like Christmas once more. But Marco placed his napkin gently on the table, pushed the chair in, and raised an eyebrow at Angelo.

"I can't wait to leave for Rome. I can't wait to show you my back. So I'm going to do it now. Good luck at your other family's tribunal tomorrow."

Marco snatched his coat off the rack and veered between the restaurant tables. He could not reach the door fast enough.

Chiara's face was pulled taut.

Angelo sighed. "Well, I think that went rather well, don't you?"

She scoffed and smoothed the napkin in her lap. "At least you got your say." She lifted the corner of it and dabbed at her eyes. "I don't have an appetite. Can we please leave, Angelo?"

He'd hurt her too. No matter which direction he moved, he pierced someone and drew blood. Angelo motioned to the waiter, cancelled their order, and paid the bill.

Outside, Chiara said, "Marco's right though. We ought to get on with it. The annulment, I mean."

"Would that suffice?"

She nodded. "It will be easier to get than a divorce."

"Do you want me to arrange it?"

She nodded again.

"The military is going to change him," Angelo said. "Maybe it's what he needs. Order. Discipline. A total diversion from the past and perhaps a better sense of duty and honour to the family."

"It's a terrible time to be in the military," she said.

"He has three years of training ahead of him. Maybe England and France will finally step in and quash Hitler before we get dragged into anything."

"Your attempt to reassure me is admirable. Thank you."

He took her hand and held it in his palm for a moment before she gently withdrew.

"I'm going to be at the tribunal tomorrow," she said measuredly. "I do not want to meet the Steinhausers."

"I understand."

She shifted her purse to her other arm. "And I'll be there with Peter Hofer."

"No." Angelo grasped her arm. "Chiara, you cannot."

She frowned.

"He will be arrested. I promise you that. Mastromattei is looking to chop off heads. If the boys choose to give up their own group leader to save their skins, and Hofer appears—the head of the VKS—I can guarantee they will change their minds. And Hofer will not walk out of that tribunal a free man either."

Chiara glanced over her shoulder. "What am I to do, then?"

"Talk to him. He should not use this situation to create a protest." Angelo thought of the Ritsches, who were already going to make the tribunal all the more challenging. "Get Michael to help. He'll know what I'm talking about. All right?"

Chiara laughed airily, but her face contorted. "The day that you send me to Innerhofer for advice? I never, ever..." She covered her mouth and shook her head. As she walked away, her shoulders were still shaking.

~

On the day of the tribunal, Angelo stepped inside the courtroom and assessed the situation. Even the gallery was packed with people, but the air was subdued. The two boys were already in the barred pen in the middle of the courtroom. It was the first time Angelo laid eyes on Andreas Ritsch. He had scruffy black hair and a broad back, and his trousers hung loosely as if they were too large. When Andreas turned his head, Angelo saw his mouth pulled down into a mean line.

Ubaldi walked in and the attorney acknowledged Angelo with a quick handshake before moving on to where Katharina and Florian were sitting up front in the left row. Behind them, a couple turned their heads away at the sight of Ubaldi. Angelo assumed that the dark-haired man with the heavy beard and the thin-faced woman next to him were the Ritsches. They had obviously not changed their minds about allowing an Italian attorney to represent Andreas.

The courtroom door opened once more, and Chiara sidled in to the left, opposite Angelo. He was relieved she had not brought Peter Hofer with her. He caught her attention and pointed to a row with two seats left. She nodded and eased her way over, but the door was pushed open once more and Chiara stopped in her tracks.

Gina appeared, stepped straight up to Angelo's wife, and extended her hand to Chiara. Angelo moved to them, anxious to keep them apart or to rescue one or the other if need be, but Chiara slowly raised her hand and accepted Gina's peace offering.

"Signora Conti," he greeted Gina.

"Oh, stop it," Chiara hissed. "Or is that what you call her in your most intimate moments?"

Gina smiled broadly.

Chiara straightened and took Angelo's arm. "You were going to show me to my seat."

"May I have a word with the two of you?" Gina was serious

again. "I have news about Foreign Minister Ciano." She indicated Chiara. "It would interest you as well."

Chiara dropped her guard.

Gina let someone else squeeze by them before quietly explaining. "I was at a dinner party yesterday evening. Mastromattei and the foreign minister were also in attendance."

Angelo could imagine Gina floating from one to the other, information magnetised to her the way a bee collects pollen.

"I managed to steer the conversation to the Reschen Valley," she said. "Ciano would be very interested in visiting it himself. Mastromattei however—" She dipped her head, and Angelo and Chiara both bent towards her. Angelo saw a shadow of fear pass over Gina's face. "Mastromattei cornered me afterwards and warned me. If this tribunal does not produce the leaders of the VKS in the Reschen Valley, he will make certain that Ciano never finds his way to the Reschen Pass. He said if I had any way to make that happen, he would"—she swallowed—"do his best to lose interest in my activities." She looked up at Angelo. He saw she was truly shaken. "And yours."

"Damn it," Angelo muttered. He wanted to put a hand on her arm.

Gina raised her chin. "Why would Mastromattei care whether I was getting information about Tolomei and Colocci-Vespucci?"

"It's a good question. I'm not certain he is. I think he's looking for an opportunity to have one hand wash the other."

"You think that's all it is?" Chiara asked.

Angelo nodded.

There was a rustling sound as people settled into their seats. The clock on the wall read nine sharp, and the door at the far end of the room opened. Angelo watched as Michael Innerhofer hurried into the courtroom from the side door and beelined to the front rows. He greeted Katharina and Florian. Now there was only standing room. The two seats Angelo had previously aimed for were taken. Three judges glided to their seats and settled into a variety of poses. The first rested his chin in his hand, eyes scanning the spectacle before him. The second sifted papers from the dossier, and the one on the far right appraised the two accused. The praetor rose and read the *lettura*, listing the accusations submitted by the public minister and ranging from the destruction of property to endangering the public to all counts of arson.

The middle judge spoke next. "I see that counsel is on hand. Whom do you represent?"

Ubaldi rose. "I represent the accused, Bernd Steinhauser."

"And the other one?" The judge waved a hand towards the cage without looking up.

"The parents of Andreas Ritsch have refused counsel for their son," Ubaldi said.

"Is this what you want, Mr Ritsch?" the judge asked Andreas. "You wish to represent yourself?"

"I am not guilty," Andreas snarled in a gravelly voice.

"Not guilty of what?" the judge asked.

The other two judges were also paying attention now.

Andreas Ritsch shifted in the cage and stammered. "Of anything. Of any of your charges."

The questioning judge rested his brow in his hand as he read the dossier. "I have here witness testimonies that place you at the scene—"

"Lies," Andreas called. "All of them."

The judge stared at him, took a breath, and turned to Ubaldi. "And your client?"

"He pleads guilty, Your Honours, to the charges of destruction to property and to third-degree arson. But not guilty to first- or second-degree arson."

The judge levelled his look on Bernd. "You believed nobody was in the building? Captain Vincenzo Basso said the lights were still on."

Bernd shook his head. "We believed it was empty. The whole

building. We would not have thrown the flaming bottles if we had believed there were people inside."

The judge nodded. "You were dressed in costumes. Of the devil?"

"As Krampus," Bernd said. "He helps St Niklaus."

The judge looked askance at him.

Bernd hung his head.

The judge turned back to Andreas. "And you? Did you know that people were in the building?"

Andreas shook his head vigorously.

The judge pursed his lips. "We have testimonies here that claim the opposite to be true. And you both have records for disobeying the law. Quite a list here, as a matter of fact. Graffiti. Theft of property. Resisting arrest. It's a wonder we haven't seen you two here before."

"Your Honours," Bernd pleaded uncertainly. "I can explain my ways."

The judges looked at one another. Angelo caught sight of Mastromattei in the front row on the far right. He leaned forward.

"Go on," the judge said.

"I'm guilty of throwing those bottles. We filled them with alcohol, stuffed them with scraps of cloth, and lit them."

"You said *we*. Was your friend here an accomplice or the main perpetrator?"

Bernd hesitated, and Ubaldi began rising, but Bernd stammered, "I did not throw at any of the windows that had a light burning inside."

"Your Honours—" Ubaldi began.

The questioning judge held up a hand. "You said, Mr Steinhauser, that the place was dark. That you believed nobody was inside. You just said that."

Bernd took a step back inside the cage. He looked at Ubaldi, but Ubaldi was rubbing his brow furiously. The boy had done himself in.

"I threw those flaming bottles because I was angry," Bernd cried. "The *carabinieri* shot my dog, Your Honours. The officials mistreat us. Everywhere I go, I get harassed. Any time I'm outside our home, I don't feel safe. Even our schoolteachers make sure to beat us every day with their sticks. The authorities ridicule me and my family. The government is trying to take our farm away. And nobody is doing anything to stop it. Nobody. Not our leaders. Not our families." Bernd ran a hand over his head and dropped his arms to the sides. "I am to live in Italy, and this is the way you treat us Italians. You beat us to the ground and then demand that we love our nation. I do not know how you can expect that from us."

Ubaldi sat back down, pointedly staring at Bernd in the cage.

Bernd threw him a look, took in a deep breath, and continued, but this time he sounded impassionate, as if he were reciting from memory. "I am trying to understand, and I am trying to be a better Italian, Your Honours. These past ten weeks in prison have shown me the errors in my ways. I understand that law and order are important. I understand. And I swear to you, if you let me go, I will be a model citizen."

"There is a matter on record in the investigations against you," the middle judge started, "that you are a member of an illegal group called the *Völkischer Kampfring Südtirol.*"

Bernd shook his head. "Andreas and I have always been friends. We have always gotten into trouble together." There were a few chuckles in the room. "He talked about the VKS, but he is the only one, and there was nothing official."

"We are looking for a name, Mr Steinhauser. Of the group leader in your area. Do you know who that is?"

Bernd slumped. "No, Your Honours."

"Lying to the court is only going to make it worse for you, young man."

"I'm not lying, sir."

Andreas was gripping the bars now, and he stepped forward, almost shoving Bernd to the side. "Yes, he is. He's lying because he knows exactly who the ringleader is."

Bernd faced Andreas as if he had been slapped.

The judge swung his look to the Ritsch boy. "And that means you do as well, then. Are you prepared to cooperate with this court now and tell us who it is?"

Andreas pushed away from the bars. "Walscher traitor," he snarled at Bernd.

Angelo looked at the Ritsches. The father was gripping the back of the Steinhausers' bench, glaring at the judges. Andreas's mother was tugging at the collar of her coat, as if she wished to disappear.

Meanwhile, Michael Innerhofer was translating everything for Florian and Katharina, and then Andreas's father leaned over and poked Innerhofer in the shoulder. Innerhofer looked at the man with distaste. They whispered back and forth, and Innerhofer seemed to give in. He was explaining something to the Ritsches.

The judges gave the reins over to the public minister, who got up to speak, repeating the cases against the two boys. Then it was Ubaldi's turn.

He rose, scratched his forehead, and leaned against the table. "Your Honours, my client understands that he has gone too far. Boys have a tendency to push the boundaries. And as you have heard, he has felt unjustly treated. His dog was shot by the local authorities. He worries about his family. He does what any good young man does—he contemplates where he fits in society and what the expectations are. And he has been steered in the wrong direction by outside influences." He turned a little toward Katharina and Florian. "I have met the parents, Your Honours. They are good people. They are solid people. And they have three children. Their daughter attended the university here in Bolzano and was a member of the local *Giovani Italiane* troop. Bernd Steinhauser has also expressed sincere regret for his actions, and we are proposing that he be taken under the wing of the GIL in Orvietto. With regular court monitoring, he will be re-educated. If it pleases the court."

The judge on the far left spoke for the first time. He leaned forward, addressing Bernd. "You would attend a military school? Fight for Italy should the day come?"

Bernd nodded. Andreas scoffed and backed into the far corner of the cage. Bernd looked at him briefly, then at his parents before facing the judges once more.

"Yes, Your Honours."

"Is there anything else?" the head judge asked Ubaldi.

Ubaldi launched into his speech. The judges asked afterwards whether the public minister had anything further to say or argue. He declined.

"What about me?" Andreas Ritsch cried.

The head judge folded his hands before him. "We have already heard your plea. Not guilty, you said. Or have you changed your mind?"

Andreas looked at his parents, and his father looked uncertain. The boy made a hissing sound. "No, I have not changed my mind."

Mastromattei slammed back into his seat. Nobody was giving up any names.

The judges announced that they would deliberate and asked the public to remain in the courtroom. It would not take long, they promised.

Indeed, it was no more than ten minutes before they all returned, took their seats, and announced sentencing would proceed.

"We will begin with Bernd Steinhauser," the judge launched in. "You are charged as guilty to second- and third-degree arson, as well as destruction to state property, for which the penalties are very severe."

Katharina moaned and slumped against Florian. People stirred and whispered.

"However," the judge said loudly over the disturbance, "we see that you are repentant and have accepted counsel's advice. We will give you one more chance, young man. You have a duty to your country, to your nation. You are to obey. You are to cooperate and to follow orders. This court sentences you to nine months of penal servitude, after which time you will be enrolled with the Giovanni Fascisti at the Gioventù Italiana del Littorio—the GIL—in Orvieto. You must achieve high marks, young man, and you will be checked routinely with a report due to this court until you have graduated at the age of twenty-one or have been enlisted into service, whichever comes first."

Bernd twisted to his parents and to Ubaldi. From where Angelo stood, he could see the boy was distressed. Ubaldi signalled Bernd to stay calm.

"Andreas Ritsch," the judge continued. "For your refusal to cooperate in this court and in the investigation of the public magistrate, of which we have a number of documented accounts notarised by this court, you are charged with arson in the first degree, the destruction of state property, and we sentence you to seven years penal servitude."

Michael Innerhofer leaned over to the Ritsches, and the mother keened. The judges rose and filed back into their chambers. The police guards removed the boys out of the cage, each of the accused shouting something in German.

Mastromattei stood up then.

"*Vater!*" Andreas shouted. "*Sag es ihnen schon! Sag ihnen, wer es ist!*"

Angelo watched Ubaldi pass behind the cage and head to Mastromattei. Ubaldi whispered into the magistrate's ear, and

Mastromattei tipped his head, nodded, and shook Ubaldi's hand. Angelo frowned at the magistrate's quick grin.

"Will you walk me out?" Chiara interrupted. "I don't want to meet the Steinhausers, Angelo. I'd like to leave, all right?"

"Just a minute," he said.

When the boys were escorted by the guards out of the room, Mastromattei placed his fez on his head and was at Angelo's elbow a moment later. He gave Chiara a polite but cursory acknowledgment.

"Very interesting events," Mastromattei said. He narrowed his eyes and appraised Gina as she stepped into hearing range. "It seems that the foreign minister is interested in visiting the Reschen Valley. I don't know what you and Signora Conti are up to, but it's now your job to see to it that the welcoming committee you choose is made up of the most cooperative representatives. Do you understand me?"

"When?" Gina said.

"May, June is what Minister Ciano suggested." Mastromattei touched Angelo's arm. "Are we clear, Minister?"

Angelo nodded, although he was not. On the contrary, he had questions. Lots of them. Why the change of heart? What had Ubaldi said to him? Were the two things even related?

As the Ritsches stormed out the courtroom, Angelo looked back to see that Katharina and Florian were approaching. He broke away and went to them.

"That was a good sentence for Bernd," Angelo said when he reached them.

Florian winced. "Not for Andreas."

"There was nothing more we could do about that," Angelo said, "and you both know it. Listen, I have just been told that Foreign Minister Ciano intends to visit the Reschen Valley."

"Il Duce's son-in-law?" Katharina's eyes widened.

"Yes," Angelo said. "Believe me, this could be good."

Katharina's eyes flicked behind his shoulder, and Angelo froze when he saw that Chiara had moved behind him. She stepped forward, her hands grasping her purse.

"I'm Signora Grimani." Her voice was steady. "I think it's time we finally meet."

Katharina offered her hand, and Chiara took it, followed by Florian, just as Michael stepped next to her.

"Good luck," Chiara said to the Steinhausers. "To all of you up north."

It was Michael who escorted her out of the courtroom.

16

RESCHEN VALLEY, MAY 1939

I t was Katharina's last evening to teach the children in Reschen. After Bernd's and Andreas's trial, the families in the communities were wary, and sometimes Katharina was told not to come at all. Often, only one or two children met with her. She did what she could, though she could not shake the feeling that she was being watched by the authorities. It was the things Captain Basso sometimes said in passing to Florian or even to Jutta, such as asking whether Katharina was slinking along the alleyways with her butter moulds again. Or whether she was planning on moving to Spinn with how often she crossed the valley floor. Katharina informed Georg and the committee that she would no longer be teaching come spring.

Just down the road from the Pichlers, Katharina passed a group of boys, all dressed in Balilla uniforms, consisting of black britches, black shirts, and bright-blue scarves. They carried carabiners and sang, saluting her with those axe-chopping motions, "We are little Italians. Youth, youth! Viva, Mussolini!"

As she had feared, the door to the Pichler family did not open to her. The lights were not on inside. She'd made the trip to Reschen for nothing. Katharina turned away and looked at the lake. She could walk to Iris and Dr Hanny's house and pay them a visit. She was just about to cross the alley when two *carabinieri* stepped from between the Pichlers and the next house.

"*Buonasera*, Signora Steinhauser," they greeted her, their palms held up to stop her.

"Good evening," she replied.

"Captain Basso has announced a curfew," the first policeman said.

"I had no idea." She glanced back where she'd seen the young boys. With Bernd's case, who knew whether they were just looking to get her into trouble? "From what time?"

He glanced at his watch. "From right now."

"Is that so? Since when?"

"Since yesterday."

"I have honestly not heard anything about it."

"That is awkward," the second *carabinieri* said. "We have to take you in."

"Surely not." Katharina thought quickly. "I was only on my way to the Hannys'."

The two men looked uncertainly at each other, their faces shadowed by the falling dusk. Dr Hanny was, after all, one of the most respected residents. But the policemen decided against it. They asked her to follow them to the town hall.

Katharina was about to submit when she heard an automobile engine. She stepped aside just as Dr Hanny's vehicle turned into the narrow street. It slowed to a stop as it drew level with Katharina and the policemen. Dr Hanny leaned over the passenger side and flung the door open. He locked eyes with Katharina.

"I was looking for you."

Katharina frowned.

"Iris is waiting for you," Dr Hanny rushed. "We'd forgotten about the curfew and that it might have prevented you from joining us tonight. Gentlemen, surely you'll disregard this, this one time. Signora Steinhauser was invited some time ago to join us this evening."

"*Dottore*," the second officer said, "we cannot make exceptions. Captain Basso's orders."

"I understand," Dr Hanny said. "I do. Then allow me to bring Signora Steinhauser home, please, and we'll pretend this never happened. Iris will be very sad, Katharina. She made cannelloni this evening. You're from Sicily, is that not right, Officer Di Mauro?"

The first officer nodded at Dr Hanny. "That's correct."

"And you, Officer Rizzo, from Calabria?"

The second officer nodded.

"Iris made her wonderful baked cannelloni with pork. And her tomato sauce, gentlemen—you know that tomato sauce of hers."

The men squirmed next to Katharina and protested again, but Dr Hanny interjected.

"Well, Katharina, I suppose tonight is not your night for Iris's cannelloni."

"But I was so looking forward to it," Katharina said with cautious disappointment.

Rizzo cleared his throat. "Please take Signora Steinhauser directly home." He glanced at Katharina, and she swore he looked pained. "There is a curfew. Orders are orders."

The *carabinieri* stepped away, and Katharina climbed into the vehicle. Dr Hanny shifted gears, reversed the automobile, and turned it around in the Pichlers' stable yard, pointing it back towards Graun.

When he was on the main road, he asked her whether she was all right.

"I arrived at the Pichlers, but... When did this curfew take effect? We heard nothing about it. Not a word."

"The authorities were out nailing flyers on every door in the valley all day yesterday."

"We were in the fields, but surely we would have received something. It's a good thing you came when you did. And cannelloni!" Katharina laughed nervously.

Dr Hanny smiled, but he looked worried. "There's something I need to speak to you and Florian about. Rizzo and Di Mauro will be waiting to see that I make it home soon, so I will tell you, and then I want you to inform Florian. All right?"

Katharina sobered. This sounded serious.

"Basso and Ghirardelli are looking for David Roeschen."

"Why?"

"My nephew's on the run," Dr Hanny said, "because he is the VKS *Gruppenführer* here."

Katharina covered her mouth. "So it *is* David." She rubbed her face, the car bumping and jostling up the hill to Arlund. "I suspected, but I could not believe it. David is the most mild young man."

"Still waters and all that, I suppose. Apparently the authorities have been keeping an eye on him for some time. They learned of a meeting in the woods near the border. The boys were surrounded."

"How many?"

Dr Hanny scoffed. "Nobody knows, really."

"They're all on the run?" Katharina exclaimed. They pulled into the *Hof*.

"Our boys know these mountains like the backs of their hands. Ghirardelli ordered an immediate curfew. The one you were not informed of."

Katharina narrowed her eyes as he turned off the engine. The lights were on in the *Stube*, and she saw Manuel plopping himself into one of the chairs, with a bowl of something. She had a good idea of who might have removed the notice from her door. Just so that they might get into trouble like this.

Dr Hanny looked at her askance. "Georg and Lisl are very distraught."

"I can imagine," Katharina said. "Is Henri with them?"

"He is."

The door opened, and Florian stepped out, bent down, and waved at Dr Hanny. Dr Hanny raised his hand in return, then turned to Katharina.

"Katharina, they're blaming you and Florian."

She stared at him. "For what?"

"For giving up David Roeschen."

"Why? Why in heaven would I give the boy up?"

"Not you. But maybe Bernd. Maybe that was the deal."

"Who would say such a thing?"

Florian pulled the door open, and Dr Hanny dipped down again, looking at them both. "Toni," he said, as if in greeting. "Toni's been saying it."

Katharina scrambled out of the vehicle and whirled back to Dr Hanny. "And you? Do you believe him?"

Dr Hanny slowly shook his head. "You know I don't, Katharina. But you have to put on their shoes and take a look at it from their perspective. Bernd got off relatively easily compared to Andreas. And that does not bode well."

Divide and conquer. Katharina felt stone cold. She straightened herself and took a few steps back so that she could see Dr Hanny's face clearly. "I'll take care of this."

Even her husband understood what this was about. By the way he grasped her arm as if to steady her, she knew he understood.

The early morning birdsong did not match Katharina's mood one bit as she marched around the back of her farm and to the Ritsches' home. Florian was on her heels, muttering how she ought to approach this better, but she closed her ears to him. As soon as she reached the door, she pounded on it.

Florian grasped her elbow, but she yanked it away.

"Let me do this," he hissed.

"He expects that, Florian. He expects you to stand up to me. Because he knows that when you're with him, you lose yourself and behave like the idiot he is. Just like all his friends."

Florian looked stunned. "What are you talking about?"

Katharina stuck her hands on her hips. "You begin talking like them, joking like them, and being rude like them. What is it you always say?"

Florian's jaw worked beneath his beard, and he rubbed a hand over it, as if to prevent his next words.

"Then I'll tell you." Katharina pounded on the door again. She could hear footsteps approaching. "It's boys just being boys. We can't—God forbid!—make enemies of our neighbours, you say. And why not, when they are doing their damndest to be ours?"

The door was yanked open, and Katharina faced Patricia Ritsch. They might have seen each other every day, and usually from afar, but today Katharina was taken aback by the deep lines around the woman's mouth, the quickly brushed-back hair streaked with ash-coloured strands. Patricia looked as if she had aged twenty years in the span of a few weeks.

"*Grüß-enk*, Patricia," Katharina said.

She was guarded. And why not? The Steinhausers rarely came by. Together, anyway.

"Katharina? Florian? Is something the matter? Have you heard something from Bolzano?"

"Toni here?" Katharina snapped.

"He is. We were just about to have breakfast."

"I'll only be a minute." She stepped in without further invitation. Florian, gratefully, remained mute behind her.

Toni sat at the table, expectant. There was a rucksack propped up against the tiled oven, with Toni's coat slung over the top. Their four other children—two boys, two girls—were at the table and twisted in their seats to watch her silently.

She greeted Toni stiffly and acknowledged the children. Toni's look flitted between her and Florian. She knew what he was thinking. He was accusing Florian of not having his wife under control. Well, she was not about to be browbeaten and trodden upon like Patricia. Not now, not ever.

Katharina eyed the rucksack more carefully.

Toni scowled. "What do you want, woman?"

"Toni, you've gone too far this time,"

Toni blew out an exasperated sigh. He waved his hand at the brood of children, and they all scattered from the table to a back room.

"You really know how to ruin someone's appetite." Toni said. "I don't welcome collaborators into my house."

Collaborators? Collaborators! Katharina widened her stance in front of him and clenched her fists. "You have no right to blame us for what happened to Andreas, Toni. You were the stubborn mule who refused any help." She scanned the *Stube* and found what she was looking for. Two sheets of paper. One with a tear at the top where it had likely been nailed to her front door. She glanced down at it and read *Coprifuoco*—curfew. She held it up to Florian, and he sighed and shuffled his feet.

Fine. She would take care of this.

"Did you think this was harmless fun, Toni?"

Toni huffed. "That was on our door."

"Two, Toni. Two notices. And we had none." Katharina drew a forearm across her brow. The room was hot and steamy and sour from stale-cooked cabbage and warmed milk. "And these rumours that you've been spreading?"

"I have no idea what you're talking about."

Katharina bent towards him. "Our son denounced no one. Not a single name. Seeing as it's your boy who landed ours in this situation, refused to cooperate with the investigation, it's no wonder they gave him a stiffer penalty."

"Is that so?" Toni scowled down at his whey soup and pushed

it aside. "Seems to me, Katharina, that both you and your son denounced Andreas to get Bernd a lighter sentence. The *carabinieri* keep coming up here and sniffing around my place, but you knew all the time, didn't you? You knew that it was David Roeschen the whole time, but you needed the mayor's help, so of course you'd tell Bernd to turn us in."

Florian moved next to her. "Now, Toni—"

"That rucksack," Katharina trilled. "You were up there on that mountain, weren't you? Suddenly, I'm not so sure it really is David they should be after."

Toni's dark eyes shifted to the rucksack and back to her. He shoved his chair back and rose. "You barge into my house, make accusations, and make yourself a fool. You have no idea what you're talking about."

Florian moved a little between Toni and her, already beginning some sort of pacification speech, but Katharina rounded on him and stopped him short with a piercing look. Patricia hung back near the door, an expression of dismay on her face.

Katharina faced Toni, again. She was shaking and could not focus on him, but in her mind everything was clear. "You gave him up," she said. "You gave David Roeschen up so that Andreas might get his sentence reduced."

Toni's face turned crimson. She took a single step back, but only to assess him and the rucksack better.

She was right. She nearly laughed with the revelation. "Deny it, Toni. Go ahead. Nobody will believe you when Andreas suddenly shows up, a free man. If you ever drag my name through the mud again, Toni Ritsch…" she snarled. "Remember the night you found Opa and me in the back of the barn with that huge wolf? The one I shot dead? In the pitch dark of night?"

Toni's rage gave way to a momentary look of confusion, as if he were trying to connect the two things together. Katharina did not wait for him to figure it out.

"I shoot predators, Toni. Remember that. Your son crossed the line. Andreas and you have nobody to blame but yourselves."

Toni spewed a mouthful of sharp protests, but they landed on deaf ears. She was done. She turned to storm out, but Patricia stood before her, stone faced and apparently not willing to move out of Katharina's way.

Florian's tone was dangerous. "Patricia, step out of the way and let us through."

"Seven years, Katharina," Patricia pleaded. "In an Italian prison. He would grow into a man amongst Walscher."

"Woman, keep your mouth shut," Toni shouted behind Katharina. "And you two Walscher traitors, get out!"

Later that morning, Florian was out turning the clumps of hay to dry in the early summer sun before Katharina could exchange any words with him. Breakfast had been tense, and he had pulled her into their bedroom, reprimanding her and asking her, more than once, what in God's name had gotten into her.

"They're our neighbours, Katharina. One of two that we have, and certainly not the ones we want to be on the wrong side of."

"Take a bottle of schnapps over to him tomorrow then," she had snapped in response. "And it will all be set right."

Florian had shaken his head in disbelief, or maybe it was distaste, and marched back downstairs, took Manuel with him, and banged the door shut behind them.

She went out into the hall. Manuel had left his bedroom door ajar, where he now slept in Opa's former room to be closer to Florian and her. Bernd's things remained in his old bedroom. Katharina opened the door, looked in, and sighed. The next room was Annamarie's, the same one where Angelo had recovered from his injuries.

Katharina stood at the foot of Annamarie's bed, gazing out the window. It revealed the garden out back and the forest on the slope beyond. Even through the windowpanes, she could hear the rushing Karlinbach. She bent and peeked out to the left, where she could see the Ritsches' farm. She had never really cared for Toni Ritsch. His father, Kaspar—God rest his soul—had been good friends with Opa, but even now Katharina wondered whether the only reason for that had been because they all lived in such close proximity to one another. Either way, Katharina was finished placating the family. When it came to her children, to their health and safety, she would build a barrier to prevent that Ritsch venom from poisoning her boys. She could still remember how rude Toni had been at her grandfather's funeral, the mean things he'd said about Florian, his behaviour at her wedding. No, there was no love lost between them.

She looked at the room again, Annamarie on her mind. There was no way for the Steinhausers to travel as far as Berlin now. They had an entire farm to run, would be up on the alp soon. Every season brought with it the same cycle of responsibilities and obligations. She could not just pick up and leave and try chasing down her daughter all across the Third Reich.

Below, someone knocked on the front door. Katharina hurried downstairs and opened it to Patricia. Her heart lurched. She was not prepared for another confrontation, but Patricia extended a cloth-covered basket.

"I had planned on bringing over some cake today. Wild strawberries. I had too many, and I just want you to have it. As I'd planned."

Katharina stared at it, grasping for her resolve. "Patricia, I know you want me to say sorry about this morning. But Toni's gone far too far this time. The police wanted to detain me last night!"

Patricia bowed her head. "It was a prank, Katharina. He didn't mean anything by it really. Toni certainly was not thinking about...you know?"

She could not begrudge the woman. She opened the door wider. "Come in. You're avenging yourself. I was just about to get started on the butter."

"I can come back later."

"No, no. Come in. Please."

Katharina poured Patricia a glass of milk, which the woman accepted.

"I won't be long, Katharina. To be honest—and Toni would be furious if he knew I was saying this—I'm glad that you've finally given him a piece of your mind. Sure, he was up there on the mountain, meeting with the others, but he wasn't the Judas who turned David in to the authorities. If you spread that around the valley, he'll never forgive you."

Katharina looked down at her lap and bit her bottom lip. It was Toni who had done it. And it was Toni who'd sent Patricia here.

Oh, Patricia, the minute he threw you down on the ground under the Planggers' tree, he had you, didn't he? We were just children, but he pinned you down, hacked and spit on you. And then he kissed you, and you thought it was love.

"Florian and I have raised our boys to be law-abiding citizens, Patricia. And I have tried to raise them with an open view, with some tolerance. I don't know how it all went so wrong, but I aim to fix it."

Patricia's mouth pressed together, the source of those deep lines around her mouth. "Toni says you're too strict with the boys, that since Annamarie ran off, you should have learned your lesson."

"Toni can say what he wants," Katharina snapped.

"I came here," Patricia urged, "to convince you to take a kinder way with us. It's important that we remain good neighbours, don't you think? You've said so yourself so often— anytime we have to talk about the reservoir plans or the next measures taken by the Walscher. You are the first to say we need to stick together."

Katharina closed her eyes and took in a deep breath. She wanted to say it wasn't she who championed that neighbourly cause, but Florian. Always Florian. "Patricia, I know you love your son but—"

"Stop blaming Andreas for everything Bernd does wrong," Patricia cried. "Take your grief to the Roeschens. That David is the one you ought to be angry with. Not with us. He was at your alp every summer, practically since he could walk. He's the one who influenced your son. Andreas just went along with it all."

Katharina wanted to laugh aloud. She studied Patricia, but it was useless trying to convince her. She stood up. "All right. I'll speak with the Roeschens." She had no such intention, except to offer her support and comfort.

She saw Patricia to the door. The woman was about to take her leave, when Florian and Manuel jogged down from the meadows and into the *Hof*.

Patricia greeted them. Florian looked questioningly at Katharina.

"Toni sent her here with cake," she said with saccharine sweetness.

"Thank you," Florian said.

Unsmiling, Patricia faced Katharina. "Just making up, is all. Right?"

Florian grinned, as if his day had just been made. "That's very fine. Tell Toni he's welcome to my schnapps. He should come by tonight."

Katharina threw him a piercing glare.

"Or I'll come to him," Florian corrected.

"I'll tell him." Patricia took her leave.

Katharina pushed inside the house before Manuel or Florian could, stalked over to the plate of sliced cake, and—despite Manuel's and Florian's loud protests—tipped the whole thing into the compost pail, where it nestled between the potato and onion peels.

"You should be thanking me," she said. "Toni probably made her poison it."

~

The next day, Katharina finished the milking as quickly as she could and grabbed a basket. Behind the house, she had several frames and screens set up to dry the rose petals she would deliver to the church later that day. Iris and Lisl had brought baskets full of roses from their gardens, which they had then pulled apart and set to air drying. Between their two gardens and Katharina's, they had plenty to shower from the choir loft on Pentecost. At the sound of someone coming around the house, she quickly flipped the last few petals on the screen before her, expecting Toni or Patricia again. But it was Jutta, come down from Hans's field.

"Good morning, neighbour," Katharina said brightly. "How are the newlyweds?"

Jutta wrinkled her nose. "Newlyweds? Now that tops my morning. Hans and I are a pair of oldyweds if anything."

Katharina chuckled. "Well, you should've married him decades ago."

Jutta huffed and sifted through the rose petals. "This for the church? Father Wilhelm gives in way too much to the Italian tradition, this rose petal stuff."

"But it's beautiful," Katharina said matter of factly. "And it makes people happy."

"Except for the person who has to clean up afterwards."

"Oh, Jutta," Katharina groaned. "You're not two months newly married and already complaining like a fishwife."

Jutta blinked. "I'm heading down to Graun. You want me to take these?"

Katharina determined they were dried well enough. "I have a

better idea. Why don't I come with you?" She jutted her chin towards the Ritsches. "I could put a little distance between us today."

Eyebrow arched, Jutta reached for another basket and began collecting the petals. When they finished, they took the front road and followed the Karlinbach gorge. The creek roared with whitewater, and Katharina stopped to pick daisies and lupus for the Post Inn tables. A few snowdrops and cowslips were still blooming too.

"What news have you from your children?" Jutta asked. "How are they? How are all of you?"

Katharina fingered the flowers she'd placed into the basket. "Annamarie writes to Manuel, the postcards you know about. I can't help but think she is reaching out to me, to us—to me and Florian. She doesn't write much, but there are little things, like asking about any new kittens or whether I'm still scorching milk. Nostalgic things, you know?" She hitched the basket back into the crook of her arm. "I write back, of course, via Manuel. I don't know, Jutta. Maybe I can get away in the summer. Berlin is so far away though."

Jutta jostled her arm. "You should go. As soon as you can."

Katharina nodded. She was actually terrified of being turned away, like Annamarie had done to Florian when he'd chased after her all the way to Bolzano.

"And Bernd?"

"We get regular letters. He says the fellow inmates are actually kind to them most of the time. Andreas gets into trouble, but Bernd said he doesn't really cross paths with him." She laughed sadly. "He actually said he can hardly wait to get out and go to that military school."

Jutta sympathised. "Your Bernd? Can't wait for school?"

"It's Florian, though, who keeps me awake at night."

"Wait a moment," Jutta quipped. "I'm the newlywed here."

Katharina shook her head. It was no joking matter. "I've never seen him so disappointed in me. I confronted Toni Ritsch."

"I heard. Florian told Hans. Nasty thing Toni did, however."

"It is wholly plausible that he is the one who gave away David's name."

Jutta gritted her teeth. "Far more plausible than your Bernd. Or you, for that matter."

"Anyway, Florian's difficult to get through to when he's bitter. He did not stand up to Toni, you know? He went right over the same night and had schnapps with him."

Jutta grunted. "The big diplomat."

Katharina rolled her eyes.

They reached the bottom of the road and turned into Graun, following the lake.

"Alois is looking forward to getting back up to the alp," Jutta said.

"Three weeks," Katharina said.

"He's getting quite good with Hans's sheep," Jutta added. "Calls Hans his father now."

That was the sweetest thing Katharina had heard in a long time. "And?" she prodded. "Quit avoiding my question. How is married life?"

Jutta blushed a little and waved a dismissive hand, then a slow grin cracked the scowl. "I do have to admit, we had to find our way, but it is quite nice. Hans"—she rolled her eyes heavenwards —"is quite nice."

Katharina laughed and linked Jutta's arm in hers. Before they reached the inn, however, Jutta unwound herself from Katharina. Three men were running towards the church. Something was happening. Behind the inn, the women found a group of men scuffling in the churchyard. Young boys were hollering and cheering, standing on the bench beneath the oak tree and whipping pebbles at a group of younger Balilla boys. Father

Wilhelm stood in the church entrance shouting at everyone to stop. A whistle sounded. The *carabinieri* were already coming.

Walter Plangger shoved Klaus Foglio, the butcher. "You sold us out, you damned Walsch-lover!"

Klaus Foglio, who towered over Walter in both height and girth, hardly moved. "He wasn't interested in us from the very beginning," he sneered. "How am I at fault for Hitler's decisions? Do you think I get a private line up to Berlin, or what?"

"Not again," Katharina groaned. "Why must they always fight?"

Jutta tugged at Katharina's arm. "Come along. Leave them to their own devices. I don't have the energy for this any longer."

The scuffle was already breaking apart. Katharina spotted Iris making her way to her, nervously skirting around the crowd. Iris held a newspaper in her hand.

"Did you see this?" She held it up so that Katharina could read the headline.

Jutta scowled. "And? What does it say?"

"Hitler and Mussolini have signed a pact. They're allies now," Iris said in German. "They're calling it an axis."

"Yes," Jutta snapped. She looked at the fighting men. "And we South Tyroleans are the oil to grease it."

Understanding now why everyone was upset, Katharina gave Iris the paper back. "We're doomed if we keep fighting like this. Plangger and Noggler will be the first to abandon any support for our cooperation with Grimani."

"They'll be the first to write to Hofer directly," Jutta said, "and demand Hitler find us new land."

Katharina blew softly.

"The foreign minister is coming, no?" Iris said. "Is he not interested in the valley?"

Jutta scoffed. "It's going to be fanfare and hot air. That's all."

"Then you must plead with Georg to bring them back together," Iris said. "He's always come through as your last hope."

Katharina and Jutta shared a look.

With David on the run and the authorities after him, and now the accusations and lies spreading around, Katharina was certain Georg could not—and would not—do anything more for them. Their cards were now in Angelo's hands and the group of people he supposedly trusted.

17

BERLIN, MAY 1939

On the last day in Brunswick, Annamarie received her leadership certification and her party card, stamped with all the necessary approvals and all on the same day. Whereas everyone else's families were present for the closing ceremonies of the training program, Annamarie only received notice from Max that he would not be able to attend and would come to see her in Berlin as soon as possible. Margit had also sent word that she would not manage the trip. *We are so busy here in Innsbruck. I am excited to show you what we are up to. Come back soon.*

After Franz's and Margit's wedding the month before, Annamarie was relieved they were not coming. A distance had grown between Margit and her in the past half year, and most especially between Annamarie and Lisi. She never said anything, but Annamarie just knew that Lisi blamed her for Veronika's arrest. It hurt her. And it drove her to find new friends.

On either side of Annamarie were Silke and Ulli, young women also from less-privileged families like Annamarie's. Both girls had also managed to work their way up in the BDM. Such things were possible now, their Gruppenführerin reminded them. Every Aryan had an opportunity and a duty to lift the nation. But Annamarie's two friends and she had another understanding as well. Like Annamarie, they enjoyed the camaraderie, the sports, the independence, the telephones, and yet there was an underlying scepticism that had slowly crystallised into muted fear.

During the final dress rehearsals, in their short white BDM skirts and halter tops, Annamarie had moved through her gymnastic routine with her group, demonstrating light athletics and dance with large airy balls. When they were finished, Annamarie and her friends then watched the other troupes rehearse with ribbons or with hoops. Each time, Silke, Ulli and she had marvelled at how beautiful the spectacle was, and how intimidating. Everyone moved as one. Everyone performed as one single unit with machinelike precision. When her group was called up again for their next routine, Annamarie had considered making fun of it—of purposefully slipping out of the disciplined movements—but it was only a passing thought. There was no fun in provocation any longer. As she and forty-nine other girls lifted their balls into the air, she mused how the BDM had pummelled the rebel out of her and created her into two separate people with alter egos. And she was not the only one.

It had taken a few weeks into the training before Silke, Ulli, and Annamarie admitted to one another that, on the inside, they had reached a boundary when it came to the lectures on race. The Jewish race, the Slavic race, gypsies, and the physically and mentally deformed—like Alois Hanny—were subhumans, beneath the Aryan. Annamarie and her family had been treated this way in the Reschen Valley. She knew what it felt like. Silke had only recently admitted that her best friend had been Jewish. Ulli, who would rescue a hurt fly, admitted that she had never wanted to join the BDM, that it was her father's ambition to have his entire family be personally commended by Hitler.

But Silke's and Ulli's families were here at the closing ceremonies now, looking on and beaming with pride and anticipation. And Annamarie knew that when they left for their individual corners of the Reich, one way or another, Silke and Ulli would at least have their families to turn to, to dispel the doubt—that what they were doing was the right thing for the Fatherland.

All Annamarie had was a pile of postcards from Manuel and the words she knew her mother and Florian passed along through him. They were subtle, and each one generically indicated that they missed her, wished her well, and hoped to see her again soon. It had given Annamarie four months of comfort and four months of remorse. She even missed Bernd, about whom she spent occasional nights worrying. When she had been studying her folk history and political lessons, the content had often left her feeling queasy, and she wondered whether Bernd was really swallowing and digesting the same information and finding fulfilment. She wanted to reach out to him, to tell him she knew better. She'd seen both sides of the Fascist line. It was ugly, thin, and cruel. And something told her it would ensnare her brother, shape him, and change him. Now that Italy and the Third Reich were united, neither one of them had a chance to escape.

As the entire campus—hundreds of young, new, and enthusiastic Nazi youth leaders—paraded by the stands, Annamarie remembered how Bernd and Manuel had dragged her up to near Graun's Head to show her a cave they'd discovered. They'd climbed over rushing streams and waterfalls, sometimes tying themselves to one another, lest one slipped. When they'd reached the deep, dark cave, the top of the cliffs were just above them. Manuel had excitedly told her they'd found old canning jars and sheep's bones, bits of crates, and the oldest embers from a fire. But best of all, the boys told her that they could climb in and would come out on top of the plateau of Graun's Head.

Hesitant to follow them, Annamarie watched them scramble

over the rubble of rock to just below the cavern. She was amazed at how tiny they were compared to the dark overhang that made up the cave's entrance. They called to her, and she started to follow but then recognised potato plants growing around the fallen rock.

"Someone lived here," she'd said. Or still did.

"I know," Bernd had called, his authoritative self. "Father said that some relation to the Hannys' lived here." He waved a hand before his face. "He didn't have all his teacups in the cupboard."

Despite her protests, Annamarie had clambered into the cave after the boys. She had done it because standing alone outside the cave seemed a miserable idea. She hated the dark and the cold, damp space. Bernd had carried one of their ancient oil lanterns. Manuel called out that a spring was up ahead, and Annamarie closed her eyes to the dark pool of water when she reached it.

Bernd held the lantern over his head, taunting. "Look, there are things swimming inside."

She had not wanted to look. She had walked by, her eyes shaded and half-closed, and she slipped. She sprawled sideways towards the water. Her scream echoed and bounced in the cavern. Only her foot landed in the pool, but before she could look away, she caught sight of leeches groping the rock bed.

Excited by his own fear, it was her baby brother who'd grabbed her hand as Bernd, at the same time, scolded Annamarie for being an idiot. Annamarie had trusted Manuel to bring her to the top then.

She had held on to that in her four months at Brunswick as well, that it was Manuel who would help her

After the ceremonies, Annamarie said goodbye to her comrades, but Silke and Ulli were the ones she called friends.

"Don't forget us when you become a famous movie star," Ulli said.

Silke laughed. "Of course she will forget us."

"I won't." Annamarie hugged both tightly again. She would take them with her if she could.

That evening, Annamarie boarded the train to Berlin. She would begin her internship at UFA in just five days. She had her party card. She had credentials. All she needed now was to duck her head, break through the cracked-open doors, and convince everyone she was worthy.

The boarding house in the Lichtenberg District of Berlin reminded Annamarie of a run-down shack surrounded by newly installed and modern blocks of flats. Her room was in the attic, where the roof sloped on one side and the window provided a view to the upper stories of a row of townhouses. Her bedroom contained two beds, a dressing table, two cupboards for clothes, a simple, straight wardrobe with no frills, and a night table between the two beds. One bed was made up with mint-green linens and white lace, the other in a Prussian trellis floral print in blue and grey shades. Annamarie set her suitcase on that bed, the mattress sagging already, when Charlotte Mainz knocked softly and came in.

"Welcome, Annamarie."

"Thank you so much for arranging this for me," Annamarie said.

Charlotte looked around the room. "It's not the prettiest place, but you'll be treated well, and Frau Tannenhof, the landlady, is kind. The other girl has just returned to Pottsdam to work at the headquarters, so you'll be alone for the first few weeks. We've got another intern coming in June."

"Fine," Annamarie said.

Charlotte perched on the other bed, which was just as saggy. "How was Brunswick?"

Annamarie pushed herself up against the headboard and told

her about the campus facilities and how one night the boys had decided to raid the girls' dormitories. They had come in the middle of the night, through the tunnel that connected the two buildings, and hollered out orders to get dressed and assemble for a drill. She had been dead asleep and missed the entire thing. She told Charlotte about the theatre and the plays Annamarie had been involved in, as well.

"And I saw Leni Riefenstahl there," Annamarie said. "She came to film us, and, Charlotte, she recognised me again and mentioned that I should come see her when I arrive. Is she in Berlin now?"

Charlotte shook her head. "She's currently in Spain filming *Lowlands*, but I do have instructions to get you oriented at the studios and then"—she smiled broadly—"send you to Spain to join her. I don't know for what exactly. She was being rather secretive."

Annamarie laughed. "That is so exciting!"

"When is your boyfriend coming to visit you?"

"Max is coming the day after tomorrow."

Charlotte shared a few tips about where they might go, then invited Annamarie to visit Berlin with her the next day. "Frau Tannenhof is strict about dinnertime here, but we can maybe go to one of the dance halls afterwards?"

Annamarie agreed, and when Charlotte left, she looked at herself in the dressing table mirror. She picked up a brush and tried straightening the waves, something niggling in the back of her mind. She reminded herself she was no longer in Brunswick. She would work her way to the UFA union card and be settled.

She grinned at her reflection. "You are simply going to love Berlin, aren't you?"

After Charlotte's whirlwind tour of the city over the next few days, Annamarie met Max with feverish excitement, wanting to relive with him everything she had experienced. She hopped from one foot to the next trying to find him amongst the crowd disembarking the train. Finally, she recognised his gait in the mix of uniforms and caps, that swagger and his lopsided smile. She could pick him out of a crowd with those two things. But when he caught sight of her, his smile seemed to freeze. Something was wrong. It was the way he looked at her but did not appear to see her, as if she were hidden behind something. That invisible wall was what she felt when she embraced him.

"Max," she gushed into his shoulder. She peppered his face with kisses, willing her feeling of dread to go away, to yank down whatever it was that had wedged itself between them.

Max kissed her cheeks and held her by the shoulders. "Greetings from everyone, Annamarie."

"How are Franz and Margit?"

"Good. And greetings from Lisi."

She frowned. "You saw her? How nice."

Max nodded, then placed his cap on his head. On his collar, the black square with the silver stripes had been replaced by a black square with a silver square in the middle. Squad leader.

"You've been promoted to Scharfführer." She tried to sound happy.

"Among other things," Max said flatly. "You're not the only one who was in training." He gave her a friendly shake before putting an arm around her shoulder.

She tried to find comfort in the gesture, so she chattered away about her tour of Berlin with Charlotte, but Max was only half listening. He interrupted her with comments about the streets, or the weather, or an observation about a building. At some point, he stopped before a café.

"This is my favourite place. I want a coffee," he said.

"But I wanted to take you somewhere special," Annamarie said. "And if we hurry, we'll get in before the prices go up."

Max winced. "Look, I've been in Berlin countless of times. I doubt there's any place that you can show me that I don't already know. I want to go in here."

He nearly shoved her through the door. They took a table way in the back of the café, beneath autographed photos of famous stars and musicians. Annamarie was embarrassed that she did not recognise half of them yet, but one she did.

"Look," she said. "That's Dr Goebbels and Lída Baarová."

Max narrowed his eyes as he glanced up at the photo behind her. "She's gorgeous, isn't she? There are rumours, you know?"

Annamarie's exaggerated her surprise.

The waitress came and took their orders for two beers. Max toyed with the napkin holder and looked about, as if searching for an exit.

"Maxi?" She cringed. She rarely used Margit's nickname for him. "You seem preoccupied. What's the matter?"

Max shook his head and gazed at the patrons around them, but his fingers were drumming on the table, and not to the beat of the song on the radio. "Everything's fine."

He was bored with her. Or the distance had been bad for their relationship.

"I'll be here for only two months," she said. "If that's what's bothering you."

Max's look grazed her. "That's not what's bothering me."

"Good. I guess. And then I'll come back to Innsbruck."

He grunted.

The waitress carried a tray filled with mugs of beer. She stopped at a table before theirs.

Annamarie reached across the table and placed a hand over his. "I'm excited to get started and really look forward to when we don't have all this distance between us."

"Mmm-hmm."

Annamarie slid her hand away. "Tell me what is wrong already."

But the waitress now swung towards their table and placed a mug of beer before each of them. Max, his gaze on the bar beyond, raised his glass, held up a hand to the waitress, and downed the entire beer.

"Another one." He pointed to two remaining mugs on the tray. "That will do."

"But it's for the next table," the waitress argued.

Max leaned forward, one eyebrow cocked, that sneer at the ready. "I don't give a shit who it's for. Give me one of those mugs and go fetch them another one."

The waitress's look landed on his lapel. She placed the mug down with a hefty sigh and rolled her eyes at Annamarie before moving on.

"That was rude, Max."

Ignoring her, Max raised his glass, gestured for her to do the same, and said, *"Zum Wohl,"* before drinking half his mug. Now his leg was moving to the beat of the music, shaking the whole table.

Annamarie carefully set her glass back down. "You're here to break up with me, aren't you?"

Max flashed that smile, but his eyes were dark with something he was holding back. "Finally. You get it. Spares me having to explain."

Annamarie slid out of her chair. She snatched her beer mug, raised it over Max's head, and tipped it to slowly pour the beer over him.

He did not resist. He let the beer rain down over his face, wiping his eyes and nose with the back of his hand. Then he chuckled. "Yeah. Yeah. I probably deserved that."

Tears rose as she set the glass down and manoeuvred around the tables and out of the café.

As she hurried back to the U-bahn station, a voice in her head asked whether she was absolutely certain that was what Max had intended.

"What? Don't you remember Marco?" she responded aloud.

Neither Charlotte, the job, or all the activity at UFA could balm Annamarie's bruised spirits. She was melancholy and avoided Frau Tannenhof's mothering. Instead, she escaped into her miserable little room. But she could not sleep at night, so she would get up and visit the cabarets and shows. She was at yet another seedy show, sipping beers to make them last, and let the stupor come over her. The bartender handed her a fresh glass when she was finished, and Annamarie swung unsteadily to face the stage. A man dressed as Marlene Dietrich was crooning at the microphone. Just another random place in a random crowd of people. Or so she thought until she recognised a certain forehead with a pair of glasses resting upon them.

"Sepp, my goodness!" Annamarie set her glass on the bar and rushed up to him, throwing her arms around his neck.

He staggered backwards and spluttered. "Annamarie, you're back."

"I thought they had arrested you," she cried. Someone shushed her from the crowd. She lowered her voice. "I thought you got caught by that Gestapo man."

Sepp chuckled as he pulled her off him. "Dramatic as usual."

"What happened to you?" she demanded. "I waited in that café for ages. Did you get my note? Why didn't you show up?"

Sepp frowned. "That? Your birthday? I'm so sorry. I had troubles with the student dormitories. It was pretty terrible of me, I know, especially after that chase scene."

She rubbed his upper arm before wrapping herself around it to hold herself steady. "What's new with you?"

"Studying, but I've already got a job as a cameraman's assistant. I'm learning the business."

Annamarie accepted a drink from him, something fruity and sweet, and told him briefly about Brunswick and her boarding house, the job at UFA, where she was still getting oriented on all the ropes. She was learning a little bit about everything.

"And Max was here," she said, taking a big gulp of the cocktail. It was hot in the bar, and the drink made her feel sick on top of the beers.

Sepp's face went slack. "Max came to see you? Here?"

Annamarie nodded and swirled the pieces of fruit. "He's a squad leader now. And he broke up with me."

Sepp's eyebrows flinched.

"You don't seem surprised." Annamarie lifted her head to study him. "Wait. You expected this?"

There was no way Sepp could have known or have anticipated, Annamarie thought, because there was nothing that connected Sepp to Max except... Annamarie's eyes widened. Sepp looked as if he were about to deflect a punch.

"Annamarie, he didn't tell you, did he?"

She could not see clearly. "Tell me what?" But she knew. Lisi and Max had had a history long before Annamarie came onto the scene.

She remembered Lisi's take on Max once. *Oh, he's back in Berlin?* Max's remarks about Lisi, *Do you remember when we... Oh never mind.* And he'd been to Berlin so often. As had Lisi.

Annamarie downed the drink in one gulp and slammed the glass on the bar, turning her back to the dancers and music.

"God, Annamarie." Sepp waved the barkeep over and ordered two more drinks before looking at her. He put his glasses back on. "It's really crappy of him to not have told you."

"Tell me what?" Annamarie demanded.

"Really? You want me to be the one who spills the beans?"

Annamarie narrowed her eyes. She knew she was slurring when she said, "If you are a true friend, you will."

Sepp sighed and rubbed a hand over his head. "I am your friend. I'm also Lisi's friend—"

"Don't we all know!"

He frowned. "Fine, Annamarie. Lisi's pregnant. And her family and Max's family are making them, you know, get married. Make the whole thing honourable. Damned family reputations and all that. You know?"

Annamarie clamped her hands over her mouth as bile rose up her throat. When it receded, she jabbed at Sepp's chest. "Take that back."

But Sepp shook his head slowly. "The night Veronika was arrested…"

Max was late to the dinner with Goebbels. Annamarie pushed away from the bar and shoved her way through the crowd of people. At the door, she looked left and right, her head spinning. One place? Was there one place where she was safe from pain? One person who had never betrayed her? Everywhere she went, people lied to her.

Annamarie stopped beneath a streetlamp. She laughed. Lying was her forte. Why wouldn't she attract others who lied to her? *You make your bed, you lie in it.* Her father had always said that. Florian.

She needed that voice, for her father to take her into his arms and tell her what an absolute idiot she had been all these years. And to tell her that all was forgiven, that he loved her anyway. Annamarie lurched and stumbled through the street, vaguely aware that Sepp was calling her name behind her.

The Hotel Adlon was across the road. She marched over, yanked the door open, and spilled into the lobby.

"Telephone," she hollered, unable to control the pitch of her voice. "Where are the telephones? I need you to please put a call through."

The receptionist widened her eyes but took down the details after Annamarie dumped a pile of coins onto the desk. She then pointed Annamarie to an empty booth and told her to wait there.

Annamarie slammed into the seat and caught sight of the clock on the wall. It was past ten in the evening. Her heart sank. When the telephone rang, she lifted the receiver, slowly sobering up.

"Post Inn. Who's calling this late?"

Annamarie nearly laughed, picturing Jutta Hanny's stern face and no-nonsense pose, hands on her hips, her hand flicking either a dishtowel or that keyring like an irritated cat's tail

"Tante Hanny?" Annamarie's voice was tinny through her constricted throat.

She vaguely heard someone else speaking with a South Tyrolean dialect, but it was coming from outside the booth. Tante Hanny's shrill voice pulled Annamarie's attention back to the receiver though.

"Who's this? Annamarie? Is that you? Jesus, Mary, and Josef! Where are you? No. Are you all right? That's what I mean to ask first."

Annamarie sobbed down the line as Jutta Hanny shouted at someone, probably Hans Glockner or maybe Henri Roeschen, because her parents were likely no longer there this late, if they had been there at all.

"Annamarie is on the line," Tante Hanny shouted again. "Something's the matter."

"I'm fine, Tante Hanny. Nothing is wrong," Annamarie tried. But everything was wrong.

Sepp appeared outside the telephone booth, his face scrunched with worry. She turned away to face the wall.

"I just wanted my mother. My…" Florian. She really wanted Florian. "I wanted to speak to my father. Is he there?"

Jutta's voice dropped. "Annamarie, they're not here right now. They're at the Il Dante."

Sepp was knocking gently, and she finally slid the folding door open for him.

"What are they doing at the Italian guesthouse, Jutta?" she asked.

"Because, oh, I don't know. You know. They're with...with Iris."

Annamarie sat up. Jutta was lying. This was where she'd learned it from. From these people. All liars. The line crackled.

"Annamarie," Jutta shouted. "Can you hear me? What are you doing these days? Where are you? Let me go fetch your parents and you can call back. Or tell me how to reach you and I'll put the call through."

Annamarie faced Sepp and the rucksack he carried his camera in.

"No, don't disturb them," she said more soberly. "Just tell them I called. What am I doing these days? Tell them I'm making movies."

Sepp cocked his head.

"Yes," she added. "Tell my father that, please. Tell him I'm recording stories."

"That's all? Just that?" Jutta asked shrilly. "After all this time—"

"Yes. That's all." Annamarie slammed the mouthpiece back into its place and rose.

"You lied," Sepp said.

"They all lie. Everyone lies. Max did. Lisi did. Tante Hanny just did."

Sepp grabbed her and spun her just before she went out the door of the hotel. He pulled her to him and spoke into her ear. "Max raped her, Annamarie. In the holding cell. He went in under the pretence that as her friend, he could get her to reveal more information about Veronika and her family."

Annamarie shivered uncontrollably. "And now you're lying too."

Sepp made a deep noise and held her tighter, his grief so genuine that Annamarie knew she was wrong. He was right.

She yanked away and pushed past him, the alcohol haze completely dissipated now. A tram came around the corner, and she quickly ran to the stop and boarded it, not caring where it was heading. She just wanted to get away. By the time she reached the boarding house again, she had made the decision to tell Charlotte Mainz that she would quit the internship. She was going home. To South Tyrol.

The next morning, Charlotte was in the lobby when Annamarie came in, and did not even greet her. "They've derailed the movie in Spain, and Leni Riefenstahl is really upset. She had a big fight with Dr Goebbels."

"Really?" This was Annamarie's chance to get out.

Charlotte looked conspiratorial. "Truly. And now Frau Riefenstahl has asked specifically for you."

"Me? But why?"

Charlotte winked. "She's calling in all the troops today to help look for new funding. Including in Italy. She needs you to help her with the pitches."

By midday Annamarie had been assigned the job of typing letters to a whole list of important people in Italy and on Leni Riefenstahl's behalf. And by the end of the week, Frau Riefenstahl sought Annamarie out, had Annamarie stand before her, and said, "And when I get the funds for this project, Annamarie, I think we should have you try on a role. In front of the camera."

18

BOLZANO, JUNE 20, 1939

The role of diplomat had never suited Angelo. As he buttoned his shirt in frustration, only to find that he'd done the top ones askew, he yanked at the shirt so hard that a button popped off and rolled beneath the bed. He cursed and dropped onto his knees, but it had rolled all the way into the corner to join the dust mites and God knew what else the hotel's cleaners had missed.

No, the role of diplomat did not suit him, and now here he was again, up north at the Il Dante, trying to weave through the labyrinth of political agendas. Gina ought to be here, but she was keeping her head low, and not because of the Tyroleans but because there were ever more alarming signals that people were turning against her. Some of her sources had stopped talking to her. Others completely ignored her. She later reported that in Rome and to the south, bodies were turning up. One wrong word about—one discerning look at—the government and *poof!* The person was suddenly gone, their remains turning up weeks later.

Giving up on the button, Angelo ripped the dress shirt off, sniffed at the one from yesterday, and opened the window to the cool mountain air. The Il Dante was still nestled deep in the shadows on the valley floor, the morning sun just hitting the western peaks, but it did not feel like early summer by the chill in the air. God knew he was not going to find any real warmth in today's discussions either. Unless he could jockey all the players onto his—and the Steinhausers'—team. Unless he stayed one step ahead and convinced Mastromattei that building a liveable area around the reservoir was a viable, and preferred, option.

From where he stood, he could also see Reschen Lake. Beyond was a wide expanse of fields, some of it swampy. A lone willow stood in the far distance. He knew that tree. It was between two creeks and a pond. On the map, it was named Plangger's Pond. It was there that he'd discovered Marco with Annamarie, before he'd known that she was his daughter. The daughter who was now in Berlin, "making films," Katharina had said. At least she had called. At least they knew she was well.

He shook yesterday's shirt out and hung it on the open frame of the window, hoping the cold air would quickly freshen it. He knelt on his knees again, and his right one protested. The bed frame was a thick wooden board attached to the wall. He could not have moved it if he'd wanted to. He found a coat hanger and finally managed to ease the button out from beneath the bed. He placed it on the table with the shirt and a note to have someone please mend it.

Angelo went and shaved. He looked at himself in the mirror, once again glad that he'd rid himself of the beard after the winter. It had gone grey, just as his hair had. Without the beard, he had managed to recover a few years.

He checked his watch—quarter to seven. He had to meet Mastromattei for breakfast, and the foreign minister was due to arrive in Graun at eleven. Before all that, Angelo was also to play welcoming committee to the ONC, the SEAA, and the Colonel. Stefan Accosi would also be there. It was going to be a hard day of butting heads.

Something brushed by his bedroom door. He stepped into the

hall and found the day's newspaper propped up against the wall. The headline caught his attention: GERMANS GET OUT! SEN. TOLOMEI INTRODUCES BILL TO PARLIAMENT.

"Damn it." Angelo tossed the newspaper onto the bed, grabbed the shirt from the window, and put it on.

After what Katharina and Florian had shared with him about the fighting going on amongst the residents, Angelo wondered what would become of Mastromattei's settlement plan. He had four hours to figure it out.

Downstairs, Mastromattei held up the same newspaper with the front page. "This is not helping matters."

They walked into the breakfast room, which was just one designated corner in the otherwise spacious bar. The air was stale with tobacco smoke and espresso fumes. A string of coloured lightbulbs, meant to make the place festive, hung loosely and haphazardly across the ceiling.

Mastromattei smoothed his uniform jacket as he sat down. He raised one eyebrow at Angelo. "These discussions last night about wanting money to rebuild the towns just above the lakes? That's not what we came here for. We came to convince these people to move into the hamlets where we have already appropriated homes for them. The ONC has managed enough for eighty families across the twelve hamlets."

"That's still too few," Angelo said. "What about the others? They want to stay together or not go at all."

Angelo had listened to the community's heartfelt pleas. And their demands. They expected the government to pay not only for new roads and residential grids, but for all of it. He had already told them—diplomatically—that no way in hell was that going to happen. But he could help negotiate the best deal.

"The best deal," Florian had said, also diplomatically, "is that it's all paid for."

"They have to agree to my proposal or it's nothing at all," Mastromattei grumbled. He sighed and glanced at the ceiling, then back at Angelo. "Why? Why do they all insist on staying together? Are they really such good neighbours—all of them—that they'd miss one another?"

Angelo unfolded his napkin as the innkeeper brought two coffees, one espresso and one larger cup.

Before Mastromattei could catch him scrutinising the man's coffee, Angelo said, "There's a sign on the wall at the Post Inn that I find quite fitting. The good Lord knows everything"—he paused for effect—"and the neighbours even more."

Mastromattei chuckled. "Speaking of knowing everything, your father is arriving today as well?"

Angelo appreciated the joke. Mastromattei was one of the few who seemed to really see through the Colonel. "Yes. He doesn't trust me to show Foreign Minister Ciano the full extent of the project without being able to defend himself."

Mastromattei grunted appreciatively and dumped milk and three teaspoons of sugar into his coffee. He stirred the cup and looked up. "My wife," he said, indicating the concoction. "She convinced me to try this, and I say, I do prefer a sweet, milky cup of coffee in the morning." He patted his middle, which was not what Angelo would consider lacking.

Angelo poured olive oil onto his plate, drizzled some salt, and dunked the semi-dry slice of bread into it. "Do you think parliament will pass Tolomei's bill? Make the Tyroleans illegal immigrants?"

Mastromattei smirked. "Not if I have anything to do with it, and frankly I will. I'm headed to Berlin after this to hold that very discussion. My goal is to keep our economic base here. Almost the entire Alto Adige is mountainous farmland. The farmers pull up rocks like we do potatoes. It's backbreaking work to eke out a living here. Tell me which Italian will want this? Who will want to move up from the plains in order to farm the mountainsides? And even those who must leave their farms are finding factory jobs that offer better conditions."

Angelo heard it coming. "But?"

"But Ciano has hinted that the Germans are developing a different plan in regard to The Question of this province. Is it rightfully Italian or is it rightfully Austrian?"

"Certainly we won't give up the province now."

"Certainly not."

The door to the inn opened, and Angelo recognised the prefect and the police captain. These were the two men who had taken Angelo's report about the attack on him the first time he'd ever visited the valley.

Angelo rose. "Podestá Ghirardelli. Captain Basso."

Ghirardelli shook his hand first. "We've come to talk to the magistrate." The men took a seat across from Angelo.

Still chewing, Mastromattei wiped his mouth with a napkin and indicated he was listening.

"We've detained the boy," Basso said. "The Swiss border patrols caught him trying to sneak over. They returned him to us, though he kept claiming he was an Austrian citizen."

They were speaking of David Roeschen then. Angelo groaned inwardly. This was not going to help keep matters light and simple. Not with Georg still steering the committee's wills.

"What's going to happen to him?" Angelo asked.

Basso's face smoothed, and he studied Angelo with interest. "You know the boy?"

"I know of him."

"He's an enemy of the state," Basso said. "What do we do with enemies of the state?"

Mastromattei was reaching for something in his breast pocket and handed Basso a folded packet of paper. "Make sure it's taken care of swiftly. We don't have much time before a bunch of former Kaiser lovers make a big stink about it." He glanced at Angelo before he continued. "And keep it quiet. Don't inform the family until after today's delegation has left. We need these people to cooperate today."

"Agreed." Basso stuffed the papers into his own breast pocket and rose.

An hour later, Angelo was at the Graun Town Hall. The paint was fresh, most of the windows new. He'd seen the photographs that had shown how the fire had ruined a good portion of the building, but now it stood in gleaming defiance. The double staircase—one on each side of the door—led to a new rounded oak door with ironwork. Around each window and the door, someone had painted a Roman-like pattern in oxblood red.

A motorcar honked, and Angelo turned around to face the oncoming vehicles, three of them. The doors opened, and he recognised the four members from the veterans' association, then two from the electrical society, and finally his father and Stefano Accosi. Stefano was the tallest of the entire group, and he had a habit of pushing up his wire-rimmed spectacles before meeting anyone, as if he were farsighted and could not see anyone from so far above. Stefan, too, had turned grey. He took Angelo's hand, his mouth grim and his eyes everywhere but on Angelo's steady gaze. It gave Angelo a little thrill to know that Stefano was uncomfortable. In contrast, the Colonel stood before the town hall as if gloating. This was his day.

A truck drove slowly by. In the back, several workers. The driver honked and waved to the delegation before heading onwards to the town of Reschen. Angelo saw the pile of wooden stakes in the back.

He took in a deep breath and followed Accosi and the Colonel to Ghirardelli's office.

"As the Romans always say," Angelo said behind Stefano, "let the games begin."

He grinned to himself when Stefano frowned.

~

Angelo's first impression of Galeazzo Ciano was overwhelmingly positive. The foreign minister was an elegant man, about Angelo's height, with a sympathetic face and statesman's manner. Angelo shook the man's hand firmly and appreciated that Ciano appeared keen to see everything, meet everyone, and to listen. He asked people for their names twice, repeated them, and thanked them for taking the time to meet with him. Angelo could see why Edda Mussolini was said to be head over heels in love with the man. Rumours were that Ciano shared the same strong affection for Il Duce's daughter.

"I was advised to bring appropriate footwear." Ciano said to Angelo and lifted his trousers to expose a handsome pair of mountain boots.

The group chuckled.

"We can arrange to have you brought up to St Anna's chapel by car for the majority of the way, but then, yes, it's a walk," Mastromattei said. "We have an oxcart available, should you wish."

Ciano bowed his head. "I'm happy to take a walk." He looked around the rest of the group. "Anyone else?"

Angelo volunteered, and he nearly laughed aloud when the Colonel shoved Accosi forward. His father was not going to trust Angelo with any politician alone, especially this one, whose sole purpose was to assess the circumstances of the valley. Ciano would make his recommendations to Rome based on what impacts the reservoir would make on the residents.

Not paying attention to whether Accosi was following or not, Angelo began the short hike. Behind them, car doors slammed and motors revved as the remainder of the group took the road towards Arlund, where they would then have to walk along a path to the chapel. They had luck with the weather. A blue early summer sky where only thin white wisps trailed across it.

Ciano asked questions about Angelo's work first, then said to Accosi, "Tell me something about the reservoir."

"This will be the first-ever earth-filled dam," Accosi rushed.

"The proposal is to connect the two lakes of Graun here and Reschen back there," Angelo said and stopped to point out the gleaming lakeshore in the distance. Dr Hanny's villa was a dot on the hill above the north end. "MFE's plan is to also join Haider Lake farther down as a reserve. Total capacity will be about one hundred and ten cubic metres of water."

Ciano looked impressed. "And where will all this energy go?"

"Southwards," Accosi interjected. "To the industries, to supply necessary electricity."

"The Glurns power plant is already in operation," Angelo said.

Ciano nodded. "I saw that on the way up here." He stopped on the edge of the lake, waves lapping at the shore. They were just beneath St Anna's hill. The footpath wound upwards to the chapel above. "It's beautiful country here."

He then turned to the hill and began climbing. Angelo followed, Accosi behind him. Ciano stopped on three occasions during the short climb to look out onto the valley. Each time, his expression grew harder, and by the time he reached a point where he could see all three lakes, he blew softly.

"This is quite a project," he said to Angelo. "What is the budget?"

"The entire complex will cost twenty-five billion lire."

Ciano looked out onto the valley, green from new shoots just breaking through the surface of that rich earth below.

The rest of the group had also just arrived. The Colonel licked his lips and stood abreast with Ciano. He pointed toward St Katharina's church. "That cemetery there in Graun? We've put in plans to exhume all the bodies and relocate them here to St Anna's."

Ciano's gaze followed between the cemetery below and the one next to the chapel. "How will you even fit all of them up here?"

The Colonel crossed his arms. "We'll only be taking the most recent bodies."

Ciano looked aghast. "Surely the families will be against that."

"With their agreements, of course," Accosi said. "Some of the relatives are no longer in the valley."

"But the community—"

"We're looking into other options to relocate the buried," the Colonel said. "We will definitely find a place for each of those memorials down there."

Ciano did not look placated.

Mastromattei stepped in. "Foreign Minister, it's time we head to Arlund. The residents are awaiting us there and would like to show you another view."

Angelo smirked inwardly at the final word. Yes, the Tyrolean committee would certainly be providing a different perspective.

But when they all arrived by car to the Steinhausers' farm, Angelo was pleasantly surprised. Only the Steinhausers, Georg Roeschen, and Dr Hanny were on site. Roeschen introduced himself and the others, finishing with Katharina and Florian.

Ciano looked up at the wooden sign above the Steinhausers' door. "Katharinahof. That's nice. Named after you?" he asked her.

"Thank you, yes," Katharina said. "Recently we realised it is apt, as it also honours our church." She gazed at him pleadingly. "The one that MFE plans to detonate."

Ciano straightened but his smile wavered. "Would you be so kind as to lead the way, Signora Steinhauser?"

Now it was Katharina at the forefront with the foreign minister. Angelo hung just behind them, trying to listen in. Next to him, Dr Hanny and Georg Roeschen fixed their sights on the trail ahead. Katharina called this the back road to Graun. They soon came upon a wayward crucifix where everyone stopped. Someone had filled a jar with fresh meadow flowers and placed it at Christ's feet. Ciano made the sign of the cross and turned to the landscape below him. They were now between Graun and

Reschen, and Dr Hanny's *Schlößl*, all its turrets and towers, was close enough to make out the details. Flowers bloomed in the Hannys' garden facing the lake.

Angelo took out his map and unfolded it where Katharina and Florian had made a rough table of logs and boards. He spread it out, and Ciano, the Colonel, Accosi, and Mastromattei approached. The members of the valley's committee hovered near Angelo.

"This is where I first surveyed the land." Angelo indicated the mountain behind him. "And up there." Katharina and he shared a look. "Up there" was also the place where he'd been attacked by Fritz Hanny. "My first proposals to the ministry included raising Graun Lake by five metres to connect it to Reschen and then leaving this farmland alone." He pointed to the fields on the map.

Ciano leaned over it, tracing where Angelo had compared it to the landscape around them.

"The river and lake beds are relatively wide and flat," Angelo continued. "There might be a slight problem if the water rises too quickly, and will affect Haider Lake, but if we're careful, it should be all right. You see here, here, and here? These are biotopes. These are swampy, unproductive tracts. I proposed redirecting the river here so as to take these farrow lands into the reservoir system. The ground here is spongy—the water gets sucked right in."

"Sounds reasonable," Ciano said. "But that's not the scope of the project now."

"No," the Colonel said. "Our project will raise the lakes twenty-two metres. His project would have supplied enough electricity locally, but we need much more for the BIZ."

Ciano, still propped against the table, gazed at the Colonel, then at Accosi.

"Will the reservoir hold?" he asked them.

Accosi pushed his spectacles up his nose. "Yes, sir. It will hold."

Georg Roeschen glowered at Accosi. Under his breath, he said, "*Verräter.*"

Angelo knew that word well enough. It was painted on walls and monuments all over Bolzano.

"Yes," he said quickly. "Since my first assessment, there have been new engineering developments in which we can divert the river."

He removed the first map and revealed the one beneath it, with the topographical lines. The reservoir's size and the hamlets ensnared within it—five of them plus Reschen and Graun—were within that circle. Dr Hanny's villa would be located on the new boundaries of the northern lakeshore, just a few metres above the lake's surface.

Ciano studied the map. Angelo realised they were all holding their breaths.

He looked at Katharina and Florian first. "This is your hamlet here?" He tapped Arlund within the circle.

They nodded.

Ciano turned and looked in the direction of where they had come, then back at the valley. He straightened and walked away from the table. Nobody moved except Angelo and Mastromattei.

"He seems sympathetic," Katharina whispered to him.

When Angelo approached, he saw Ciano's face had grown pale.

"How will you flood this all?" the foreign minister asked quietly.

"MFE will detonate all the buildings," Angelo said.

"Including the church?" Ciano asked, voice still flat. "How old is it?"

"Fifteenth century."

"And then?"

"We release the river. The water will rise slowly. The reservoir will fill."

"And this will all be gone."

Below them, livestock roamed the fertile valley. Fishermen had their boats in the water. The sun played the surface like the strings of an instrument. Smoke rose from the chimneys, and the bells of St Katharina tolled a quarter of the hour.

Angelo was taken aback when he glanced at Ciano again. Tears rolled down the foreign minister's face. Maybe Katharina was right. Ciano brushed them gently away and turned back to the group at the table. The Tyroleans and the Italian delegation had drifted several metres apart from one another.

"Why did Mr Roeschen call the engineer Accosi a traitor?" Ciano asked Angelo.

He hesitated. "They know him."

"How?"

"He used certain tactics to acquire information. Early on in the process."

Ciano looked questioningly at him. "Please. Elaborate."

"They were not entirely honest means. He began using that information to acquire property, using the owners' weaknesses. And he was, unfortunately, doing it while he was my chief engineer at the ministry."

Ciano narrowed his eyes and glanced at Accosi. "I see. But why *traitor*? He's Italian. Why not Walscher?"

Angelo shook his head. "His mother is Tyrolean. And the residents found that out."

Ciano pursed his lips then strode back to the table. "Let's finish this."

He waited until Angelo and Mastromattei rejoined him. "You've had an offer to relocate to any number of hamlets between Bolzano and Meran," he said to the Tyroleans. "And what do you say?"

Katharina spoke. "We want to stay together and…"

Angelo encouraged her with a nod.

"And we'd prefer it if the government would consider funding an alternative town and extending Reschen's remains up the mountain slopes, to higher ground."

Ciano turned to Mastromattei and Angelo. "Is that an option?"

Mastromattei began to shake his head, but Angelo broke in.

"It is, Foreign Minister. I've made initial projections for new roads and a grid system."

"But," Mastromattei interjected, "we have already allocated the necessary housing for the families in those hamlets."

"Except for about twenty families," Angelo pointed out. "Who may be resettled as far as south of Bolzano."

"If you would excuse me," Katharina said. "We are only a small group today. Too many heads can be more like a hot keg of gunpowder." She smiled at Angelo gratefully before confirming, "But we can assure you, Foreign Minister, that our intention is to all stay together. It is not an option to have us spread throughout Italy. If you want our land, then you must find a suitable place where we can rebuild. Together. We are a community."

Ciano gestured to the fields below, the roaming cattle, the green of promising crops. "But what will you do when this is all gone?"

Katharina smiled brightly. "Some of us will find new farmland. It will be hard work. Up to now, the government was claiming that we can't farm over fifteen hundred metres, but we can. We must just learn to do it differently. And others of us will start a new kind of industry. We will live from *Sommerfrischler*."

Ciano shook his head. "What is that?"

"Tourists," Katharina said.

Ciano nodded and shook her hand. "Thank you for sharing all of this with me. I will write up a report and share it with Rome."

Together with Mastromattei, Ciano returned to the vehicles. The rest of the Italian party slowly followed.

The two men spoke quietly before the driver opened the door

for Ciano, and the foreign minister stepped away to shake hands with everyone once more, thanking them all for coming.

Later, when Angelo was alone with Mastromattei in their vehicle, he asked him what the result was without directly requesting to know what the two men had talked about.

"Ciano gave me instructions for Berlin," Mastromattei said. "He wants me to negotiate a *special* option for the Tyroleans."

"How's that?" Angelo asked.

"He wants them to choose for themselves whether they want to be German or Italian. He instructed that I talk the Germans into a special vote and leave it in the hands of the citizens to figure out whether they want to assimilate to the Fascist Italian nation or to the Fascist German nation. But if they stay..." Mastromattei looked out the window. They were rolling into the Italian quarter.

Angelo waited.

Mastromattei turned back to him. "If they choose to be Italian, they must be prepared to give up the German language completely. They must be Italians. And then he will make a proposal that you and I help build their new towns and village along the lakes. You and your committee get what they want, and I maintain my economic base with loyal citizens."

Angelo sucked in a breath. "Do you think it will work? I think they're going to all flock to Hitler."

Mastromattei pinched his nose. The car stopped. He dropped his hand and sighed. "The foreign minister claims that nobody chooses to leave their home if they have the option. Nobody."

19

RESCHEN VALLEY, JULY 5, 1939

The Post Inn was filled with people, the entire wall of the dining room was lined with benches and tables, and people were forced to take spots in the centre of the room. There were representatives from as far as St Valentin who had come to hear the latest news about the reservoir and a proposal the committee in Graun had for the government officials in Bolzano. It was Katharina's idea, but she was not prepared to claim it as hers. Not at the risk of sabotaging the entire project. Who wanted to hear from a woman? And one whose reputation was now in question, thanks to the Ritsches, and to Bernd's arrest, and to Annamarie absconding to the Third Reich? No, it was better if Georg Roeschen or Dr Hanny presented the idea and convinced the communities that it was their proposal.

She and Florian had pitched in to help Jutta and Henri carry in wooden serving boards piled high with thinly sliced *Speck* and onions. Each board also contained wedges of cheese and dried sausages alongside baskets of bread. At the tables, Katharina was able to catch snippets of conversation. It was a mixed mood.

"Have you seen Georg or Lisl?" Katharina asked Henri as he headed for the kitchen.

Henri stopped. "I wouldn't count on my parents today. With David's trial coming up, I doubt they can take another thing on."

Florian patted Katharina's shoulder. "Leave it be. We'll tell them everything they need to know."

Katharina moved aside as Alois passed by with a tray of drinks.

"Are you ready?" Florian asked her. "You look a little nervous."

She laughed abruptly. "You think so? With this crowd?" She glanced around. Many, like her family, had come down from the high summer meadows for this, and they were eager to get back up to their herds.

"I'm not the orator or storyteller in the family," Katharina added.

Florian sighed and squeezed her shoulder.

"I miss her, you know? I'm still angry that we missed her call. I wish she would return ours."

"Concentrate on what we have to do just now," Florian said softly. "If Georg does not come, I'll step up with Hans and Frederick. We'll make it irresistible." He pecked her cheek and went behind the bar, where he grabbed another pitcher filled with red wine.

The door to the *Stube* swung open, and an immediate hush settled on the room. Katharina glanced over her shoulder to see who had come in. It was George and Lisl, already greeting some of the committee members. Father Wilhelm strode over and lay a hand on Georg's shoulder. The priest leaned in and said something, including Lisl in whatever he was saying. Georg shook the priest's hand, and stepped into the middle of the room.

"I've just been to the town hall," he said. People perked up. David's trial information would have been pinned there. "I not only found the information I was looking for—David, as you all know, will be on trial within the month—but I found information that I was not looking for. Namely, the details about the water rights and fishing rights and the land rights—the one that allowed us two weeks to raise any further objections—has been removed from the notice board. And then a convoy of trucks passed us by. I asked one of the *carabinieri* what was happening. What were these trucks? Who were these people? MFE, he says to me. They're off to build up the workers' barracks, he says to me. Naturally, Lisl and I went to the *podestá* to ask whether there have been changes now made, and Podestá Ghirardelli informed us that the deadline has already come and gone."

People murmured in confusion and asked Georg to repeat the news, to confirm what he had said. Katharina frowned at Florian. Two weeks. They had been given two weeks, had they not? Only a few had seen the notice, as the officials had hung it up at Pentecost weekend and everyone else was prepared to take their herds to the alps. There had been no official announcement from Ghirardelli, who seemed to live for making such announcements. And now Georg was saying they'd already taken it down?

Georg cleared his throat. "Well, I said in no uncertain terms to the *podestá*, you must be mistaken. The law was changed from one month to a fortnight some time back, and that was our last understanding. So that means we would have eight more days to make any formal objections. No, he said to me. We had five working days. That's what the notice said."

Angry voices rose above Georg's, but he raised a hand. Even Dr Hanny looked upset.

Jutta walked around shushing small groups of people. "And now what?" she demanded of Georg.

Lisl looked at her husband, her expression stricken.

Georg shook his head. "I then asked the *podestá* about any other changes we should be aware of. And he reminded me that under this government, if we question any authority figure, we will also find ourselves arrested and tried as enemies of the state."

People burst into angry shouts, and Lisl shook Georg's arm. He raised a hand, and the room quieted. Hans rose and came to stand next to Jutta. He whispered something to her, and she nodded, her brows stitching together. Georg rose on tiptoe and turned, scanning the crowded room before pointing his hat first at the Ritsches, then at Katharina and Florian. "Good. You're all here."

He moved to the middle of the room. "The, uh, information I received about David..." His head bobbed up and down as he looked at the floor. He took a deep breath and lifted it again. "There is an offer, and it has to do with all of us. With all our boys."

Katharina clutched Florian's hand. She took a step forward. Toni edged closer to the middle as well.

"Mastromattei said we have two days to make up our minds," Georg continued, "but if we choose to relocate to the hamlets, if we all choose to relocate..." He looked around the crowd of people. "He'll let all our boys go."

Katharina gasped.

"I won't be held hostage," Florian said loudly. "Neither Katharina nor I will allow Mastromattei to do this to our community. Toni, sit back down. Our boys are fine. They are doing fine, and they committed a crime. They will serve out their sentences. That's all." He turned to Georg and Lisl. "I'm very, very sorry, but I will not—no, I can't—make that kind of decision."

Georg was nodding, and Lisl looked as if she were about to break down in tears.

"They're going to execute our son," she cried.

"No." Katharina rushed to Lisl's side and hugged her. "They will not, Lisl. We'll do everything we can to stop it. Really. We'll write to the German Reich's head of security in Bolzano. We'll write to Peter Hofer directly. I know someone in Bolzano—a Tyrolean journalist—who can help us make contact with all of them. Someone from the VKS, from the German Reich, must step forward and protect him."

"Katharina," Georg said. "What good will that do? Do you not see that the Italian authorities have all the power they need to pull the wool over our eyes?" He whirled on Dr Hanny. "Frederick and I were there, watching as that foreign minister—Il Duce's son-in-law —cried crocodile tears at the sight of our valley. I'll write a report to Rome, he said. And we believed we'd won. Well, we haven't won a darned thing. And now they've taken our sons as ransom. And they want you all to agree to their ridiculous resettlement proposal."

Lisl stepped away and turned her back on the crowd, sobbing. Katharina's anger rose as she drew Lisl protectively to her. Jutta also came and whispered something to Lisl, but the poor woman only sobbed harder.

Georg looked around the room, his expression drawn. He raised his voice over those offering suggestions or decrying the Italian authorities.

"I cannot let them win like this," Georg said. "If we accept, what guarantee is there that they will hold to their promises? Or just make a new law to fit their agenda?" He hung his head. "There are no guarantees except that they will flood this valley."

"MFE is going to get what they want," Dr Hanny grumbled. "Access to land for dirt cheap."

"That's right," Jutta said. "Just look outside your doorsteps. Those stakes they pounded into the ground? That's our daily reminder that the water is coming."

"Have you seen the stakes they've pounded in?" Iris asked behind them. "All the way to edge of our garden."

"All the way above Arlund," Katharina said. "Above Hans and Jutta's house and the garden. And the inn…"

Katharina tore away from Lisl. She held Georg's look, his plea for support.

"This is bribery," she said angrily. "Do you understand why Mastromattei wants us in those hamlets?"

Katharina stood before another group and repeated the

question. She stood before Toni, who glared at her. "Do you? Do you understand?"

She returned to Georg and pointed to the door. "Their one and only goal is to separate us and remove any history we have together. They want to make certain we can't stand on the new edges of the lake and point to the surface and say, 'Do you remember when this was our home? Do you remember the community we had here? That centuries of Tyroleans lived and died here?' They don't want Italians standing on the edge of this new lake and having us say, 'This is what you did to us. This is what you did to your own citizens.' They want us to forget that this is our home. Our home! Our country! And I don't care which side of the border I'm on. One Fascist regime is just as bad as the other. This"—she stamped her foot—"this is my country. I don't belong to the Italian fatherland. Nor to the German fatherland. I belong to this land, to Tyrolean land. I am the daughter of Andreas Hofer. Not Hitler! Not Mussolini!"

Martin Noggler, red faced, burst out with a half-hearted, "Hear, hear."

Her heart went out to him. He and his entire family had had to move off their land and settle in with relatives in Spinn as they searched for an appropriate farm to take over.

Jutta raised her voice. "Katharina has great ideas. Go on, Katharina. Tell them. It makes no difference if it's Frederick or Georg proposing it. Katharina here has come up with an excellent plan for these communities, and I think you should all hear her out." She indicated the menfolk—Hans, Georg, Florian, Dr Hanny, and Father Wilhelm—and added, "And she has all our support. The entire committee."

"Go on, Katharina," Maria Plangger said. She elbowed her husband, and Walter Plangger turned to the others at Toni Ritsch's table, shushing everyone.

"Hear her out," he said.

The Pichlers also called for everyone to pay attention. Then other families whose children Katharina had taught in secret also shouted encouragement.

Katharina turned to Florian, and he smiled. She saw the pride in his eyes. Why not? Why not take accountability for these ideas of hers? Share them honestly with everyone?

She hurried to the bar and grabbed the letter of intent from the Royal Corps of Civil Engineers. A good majority of those here had already received them. She held up the envelope and received knowing looks. She withdrew the letter and pointed to the official stamp.

"Did you see how much this stamp costs? Eight lire. Eight! And how much are they offering for our land? How much are they offering per hectare?"

"My letter of intent," Walter Plangger called, "is missing at least fourteen hectares in the calculation."

"They counted over sixty as forest on mine," someone else called. "Instead of my fields, which of course would get me more."

"They put a value of only half of my herd. What about the rest?" another farmer piped up.

There were now more agreements, more complaints.

Katharina scoffed. "It would cost us more to go down to Bolzano to pick up our money than the value they've placed for our land." There was a flutter of appreciative chuckles and cries. She waved the paper. "You know what the answer was when I put in a complaint? The answer was, but we are providing you with free homes in lower plains with easier land to farm."

Hans crossed his arms and took a wider stance. "I like my land just fine, thank you very much." He twisted both ways without moving from his spot and said pointedly, "Me, my family, and my five sheep."

People laughed. Everyone knew Hans had a healthy herd of at least forty sheep now.

"We stay here," Katharina cried. "We don't budge. And we

301

demand that the government build us new housing and new places to live."

"But, Katharina," Patricia called. "Where?"

Others also wanted to know, and Katharina narrowed her eyes. "That's right. Where are we going to farm? There are tracts of land that would still be farmable higher up—" Dismissive waves. She tried again. "And some of us, some of us—" She looked at the Planggers, and at Patricia, and then at some of the men who loved mountain climbing and whose fathers had once worked as guides, taking *Sommerfrischler* up to the peaks for hikes. "We have other talents we can put to use. They're going to build those barracks out there. They're going to build this reservoir. No matter what. Like Georg says, this valley will be flooded. But what we can do is stay and tell about it and make sure that nobody ever forgets how large industry, how big companies, can quash us little people. We stay here in testament, and we invite people to come and visit this enormous reservoir they've planned. And the more people who come to see us, the more will know what they need to do. And that is to end authoritarian governments once and for all!"

The cheers and clapping made Katharina so giddy, laughter bubbled up. "So who wants to run an inn? A guesthouse? A restaurant? And we'll need people who will supply us with goods and materials. Runners who will go pick those things up in the cities and bring them back for us. Dr Hanny once told me that a blessing amongst the living is that we can always start over. I'm here to tell you that we are alive! And we can recreate the Reschen Valley to suit our purposes. That purpose..." She scanned the people standing in the room. "That purpose is to stay home!"

The majority cheered and applauded, but Katharina was not fooled. They weren't all won over. Not completely, for some rose from their seats and patted Katharina on the back, but it felt as if they were only placating her. Dr Hanny was already urging others to seriously consider her proposal. A small group of farmers approached Georg and asked whether he really supported this, and he confirmed that he did. But when Toni rose, slamming his hat onto his head, the room froze. He walked up to Katharina, Patricia just behind him, and poked her in the breastbone.

"I want my son back," he spat. "You going to do that? Get my son back, Katharina?" He swung to the muted crowd. "This is all bull crap, and every single one of you here knows it."

The *Stube* door creaked open, and those nearest to the entry shifted uneasily or dropped their heads. Toni glared directly at the door. Ghirardelli and Basso appeared. Ghirardelli had a habit of pulling his fez off his head before delivering bad news, like a mourner at a funeral paying his respects. Now he walked in holding it in his hands already.

"*Buonosera*," he said.

Toni dropped his hands to his sides.

Some people who had been standing now sat. Others shuffled farther into the corners.

"Good evening," Ghirardelli said again, switching to German. "We have very important announcement."

Katharina glanced worriedly at Florian as he moved to stand beside her.

Captain Basso handed Ghirardelli a document. In Italian, Ghirardelli read, "Magistrate Mastromattei has officially announced an agreement made between Germany and Italy regarding the debate about to whom the Alto Adige should belong."

Basso rocked on his feet and placed his hands on his belly, jeering. "Or what you insist on calling, *Südtirol*."

"Frederick?" someone said. "Translate, please."

Dr Hanny repeated Basso's words, and the air was electric as everyone directed their attention to the two officials.

Ghirardelli looked down at his document again. "All German-speaking and German descendants will have the option of choosing German or Italian citizenship."

Dr Hanny translated with cautious optimism. Katharina watched as the faces became less grim. Basso was also studying the faces in the room.

"You will be provided with further instructions in the coming months regarding an official vote." Ghirardelli cleared his throat and lowered the document.

"You choose Germany, you belong to Hitler. Hitler's problem," Basso said in German.

Ghirardelli placed his fez back on his head, nodded, and turned to exit. As the door closed behind them, the entire room seemed to take in a collective breath.

"There you have it." Father Wilhelm stood from his chair at the end of the row. "I was wrong. You folks were right. Hitler has come for you."

Toni raised his hands and cast Katharina a triumphant grin. "Now we know what we need to do. We all vote German and make certain we are returned to Tyrol." To Georg he said, "Now your boy won't be a traitor. He'll be a hero."

He stepped up to Florian. "Your wife's ideas are irrelevant. Nobody here is interested in serving a bunch of ridiculous tourists. Everything you discussed tonight is null and void. Including this." He reached into his breast pocket and removed an envelope. Then Toni took the candle off the *Stammtisch* table and placed it beneath the letters of intent until it caught fire. It blazed. He held it up higher and then dropped it into the small serving plate that the candle had been on. Snatching Patricia's hand, he yanked her out the door after him.

20

BERLIN, AUGUST 1939

Two weeks before Annamarie's internship came to an end, she received word from Margit that Lisi had given birth to a baby boy, whom Max named Karl.

On the telephone, Margit gushed, "He's absolutely gorgeous, Annamarie. Such a sweet baby. Lisi calls him Charlie, of course. Anything to drive Maxi out of his head."

Annamarie had said little. Why Margit found it necessary to rub salt into her wounds was beyond her. After that call, Annamarie spent the entire weekend in bed. When Charlotte appeared at the boarding house, asking why Annamarie had missed the latest UFA screening party, Annamarie told her about how Max had broken up with her, or she with him, and about his baby.

Charlotte gasped at the part about Annamarie pouring beer on his head and laughed gleefully. "Annamarie, my goodness. Remind me to never get on your bad side."

"I don't think I can go back to Innsbruck," Annamarie said. She pulled the covers up high again. "I just can't face them. It's an awful situation, and I considered them all my friends. And poor

Lisi. Really, I cannot imagine what she is going through. Margit said she's lost her job at the State Theatre."

Charlotte seemed to mull something over, then brightened. "Let's go to that pastry shop you love so much. It's time to celebrate."

Annamarie scoffed. "Celebrate what?"

Charlotte put a friendly arm around her shoulder. "Your successful internship. And our friendship."

Annamarie did not much feel like celebrating, but she got out of bed for the first time in two days.

They took the tram to the city centre, and Annamarie ordered a slice of wild berry torte with cream. Charlotte predictably ordered the *Bienenstich*.

When they were settled in, Charlotte dangled the fork over her pastry. "So you don't want to return to Innsbruck."

"No." Annamarie took a bite of her pastry but did not taste it. She could not bring herself to tell Charlotte the entire story, how her former boyfriend had allegedly raped Annamarie's roommate.

"Frau Riefenstahl has managed to get new interest drummed up for *Lowlands*." Charlotte cut through the caramelised crust of almonds with the side of her fork. Custard oozed out the sides. "She went directly to the Führer to get around Dr Goebbels. There are rumours that she is getting private funding for the production."

Annamarie widened her eyes. "Will she go back to Spain?"

Charlotte smiled. "Probably. Anyway, she's hoping to get back to filming it next year. *Schätzchen*, I know that she promised you a role eventually, but I don't believe it's going to happen right away. So the best thing for us to do is to get you on the crew. Make sure she doesn't forget that promise she made."

Annamarie tapped her fork on the plate. "Does she have a habit of breaking her promises?"

Charlotte winced. "You know Leni."

"I know Leni? No, I don't know Leni."

"All right, then I'll tell you. She talks a lot, and then she gets buried in her work, and she forgets. That's why it's best if you are under her nose. You know what I mean?"

Annamarie laid her fork onto the plate. "All right. I understand."

"Thing is, I know you want to act, Annamarie."

She had thought so as well. Truly believed it. She studied Charlotte.

Her friend frowned. "What is it?"

"Can I make another confession? A little one this time?"

"Go ahead." Charlotte forked a mouthful of cake and rolled her eyes. "Heaven."

Annamarie reached into her satchel and withdrew the third journal she had nearly filled since arriving in Germany.

Charlotte eyed the notebook. "Is that your collection of autographs?"

"My writing."

"You want to be a writer?"

Annamarie shook her head. "I've been writing my thoughts and ideas, my observations, that kind of thing. I've filled almost two books just since the internship. Thing is, I think I might want to work behind the camera."

On occasion, Annamarie had run into Sepp, and one day when she was feeling particularly happy, she'd snatched his camera from him and ran off with it into the Tiergarten. He'd been angry with her, but when she'd pleaded for him to let her have a try, he calmed down and gave her instructions. As a late birthday gift and to make up for not having shown up at Café König in January, he'd edited the film for her and put on a little show at the boarding house for everyone, her own screening party. The gesture had touched her, and she spent the night listening to Sepp talk about his film studies.

"Now that's definitely something new." Charlotte took another bite of cake.

"This internship has shown me the ins and outs of filmmaking, and when I worked on Herr Jacoby's set of *Women Are Better Diplomats*—"

Charlotte waved her fork at Annamarie. "With your love for comedy and farce, I thought that assignment was a match made in heaven."

Annamarie leaned on her elbows. "He was very generous with me. I mean, meeting all the stars and watching how things unfold, it was all fascinating. But when he allowed me to sit in on the screenwriter's meetings, I was amazed at all the ways a film has to be organised just for the storytelling. What was really fun was when Herr Jacoby allowed me to sit behind the camera. Or in the editing room. How they cut the film! Charlotte, that was truly magic. One snip in the wrong direction and you could change everything. And of course, you can also ruin it."

Charlotte pointed the fork at her. "Your eyes are on fire."

Annamarie clasped Charlotte's forearm. "Everything that goes into producing a film! Choosing the music scores! And the location scouts. I spent an entire luncheon talking with someone whose job is to travel to locations and find the exact right place for creating a screenplay's world. That job must simply be amazing!"

Charlotte wriggled away and scraped her plate clean. "I daresay you have fallen in love with the whole show. Maybe you want to be a director."

Annamarie flushed.

"My goodness." Charlotte grinned. "You do! You've been thinking about becoming a director!"

"Would it be so bad?"

Charlotte cut into her cake again and collected the custard with her fork. "Nope. Frau Riefenstahl has certainly proven it's possible. She's a hard woman though. She's got remarkable drive and ambition. I admire her, but I'm not sure I'd want to be in front of the camera with her." She popped the piece into her mouth, still grinning.

Annamarie smiled back slyly. "Frau Riefenstahl casts herself in roles for her own films. If I directed, I could finally act without having to go through an audition."

Charlotte laughed.

"I just don't know where to start."

Her friend pointed to the journal and swallowed. "What do your head and heart say?"

Annamarie shrugged. "All of it. I want all of it."

"Then"—Charlotte flourished her fork—"we need to find you a permanent position at the studios. Or…" She winked. "We march up to Frau Riefenstahl and tell her she has a new protege. I mean, why not?"

Suddenly everything seemed possible. All of it. Annamarie could simply chuck the job in Innsbruck. She would get Margit to explain, to pass along the information that Annamarie had received a better opportunity in Berlin. Margit would understand, and even if she didn't, Annamarie no longer cared. She dove into her cake and ate it with gusto.

The day after Annamarie's internship ended, Germany was at war with Poland. The radio was crackling when Annamarie came down to the breakfast table. Not only were all the boarders gathered around the contraption, but Frau Tannenhof's neighbours had come to listen, perched in chairs like a murder of crows on a pylon.

Polish troops had crippled installations along the border, one of the neighbours declared to Annamarie. This act of aggression alone justified the Reich's immediate invasion. For weeks, Annamarie had heard people complaining about how Poland was treating its German residents. They were no longer allowed to speak their language and were oppressed by the Polish regime, and Annamarie had felt anger. She understood what that meant for the German people there. She had seen it well and good in South Tyrol under the Italians. Hitler had laid claim to protecting his people. Yes, Germans should be allowed to live in peace wherever they were. Every news report held some semblance of threat: the Third Reich was surrounded by foreign enemies, by aggressors everywhere, trying to eradicate their culture and their race.

She thought of Franz, who'd been stationed near Silesia, and wondered whether he had already been mobilised to the border.

"It won't last long," Frau Tannenhof said. "We'll secure the German people within Poland's borders like we did in the Sudetenland, and that will be the end of it."

Except two days later everyone realised it was only the beginning. By the time Annamarie had reached the UFA studios to submit her completion documents for her internship, France and Britain had declared war on Germany.

Clipboard hugged to her chest, Charlotte met Annamarie in the foyer, her face grim. She hurried her into one of the smaller conference rooms. "Annamarie, I'm so sorry. There's an emergency meeting right now, but I know this much—our foreign productions have all but been frozen. Dr Goebbels is upstairs with everyone. Crews are being put together to go to Poland to record the war for the news offices. But I've already been informed that all open positions are now to be cancelled in the interim. None of the departments here or in Potsdam are hiring right now."

Annamarie slumped in her seat. "I have no choice then, do I? I have to return to Innsbruck." At least she had not yet called Margit. She'd wanted to right after she and Charlotte returned from the pastry shop, but something had held her back. Sepp, she smirked to herself, would have called it maturity.

Someone knocked, and Frau Riefenstahl stood in the doorway, her wavy blonde hair a tad disarrayed, as if she'd been rubbing her scalp.

"There you are, Fräulein Mainz. I've been looking for you."

Charlotte jumped up. Frau Riefenstahl glanced at Annamarie and looked as if she were trying to place her.

"You're done with the meeting?" Charlotte asked her.

"Yes. I've been let go, but I want you to do a couple of things for me before I leave. Can you do that?"

Charlotte looked stricken.

"Good." Riefenstahl looked at Annamarie more closely. "You're the South Tyrolean, aren't you?"

Annamarie stood. "Yes."

"BDM girl?"

"Yes."

Riefenstahl crossed her arms. "Your internship is complete now, correct?"

"Yes."

"Plans?"

Annamarie hesitated for only a second. "None."

"Good." Riefenstahl dropped her arms. "Pack your bags. I'm going to Poland. There's a crew of BDM girls and Hitler Jugend headed out with the security service to requisition houses for Germans. I've got a news agency interested. We're going to record history together." She turned to Charlotte. "Put a crew together. I'm going to need a cameraman. Alexei's just been called to the front."

Charlotte nodded and wrote it down onto the sheet on her clipboard.

"I know someone," Annamarie called.

Riefenstahl faced her. "You do?"

"Yes. Sepp—Josep Greil. He's also from South Tyrol. From the Eisack Valley. I know him from Innsbruck. He worked as a light designer and technician for the State Theatre and is completing his programme in filming just now."

Riefenstahl cocked her head. "How fast can you get to him?"

Annamarie looked at Charlotte, her heart racing. "Now. I can go get him now."

Riefenstahl pointed at her. "Be at the train station tomorrow morning at six. Train to Krakow leaves at ten to seven. Don't be late. Charlotte, let's get the rest of the crew together."

Charlotte threw Annamarie a broad smile before hurrying after the director.

Annamarie assumed she would find Sepp in the editing studio at his university, and she was right. He was incredulous.

"Riefenstahl wants me?"

"Well, she didn't ask for you specifically by name." Annamarie grinned. "I told her about you."

Sepp threw his arms around her neck and kissed her cheek. "You're truly a wonder, Annamarie."

She flushed and awkwardly pulled away before warning him. "It's going to be political."

"I don't care." Sepp kissed her cheek again, and they both laughed.

Back at her boarding house, Annamarie called Margit, who immediately lay on the guilt.

"I'm disappointed, Annamarie. We were all expecting you here next week," she said flatly.

"I don't know what will come of this," Annamarie said. "But maybe you can just delay it for a few weeks. A month. I need this, Margit. I'm going to be with Riefenstahl for weeks."

Margit said she could not commit to it but would send word. "Let me know when you've made a decision. And this will be the last time I try to help you in any way, understand?" Margit hung up without saying goodbye.

Sepp and Annamarie were at the train station on time the next morning. She pointed out the group with Riefenstahl and

Charlotte buzzing around, getting everyone's baggage sorted for the train and then herding everyone into the carriages. Annamarie introduced Sepp to Riefenstahl herself. She could have kissed Charlotte for assigning Sepp and her to Riefenstahl's carriage. Riefenstahl and Charlotte took seats across from Annamarie, Sepp next to her. He immediately set to playing with his new toy, a Leica. Riefenstahl watched him with interest.

As they left Berlin, Annamarie found the courage to ask the director about the *Lowlands* project.

"If I get the funding," Riefenstahl said, "I'll try to shoot it in Spain again. But that is still questionable."

"Are there interested parties?" Annamarie asked.

"The funding is not the question. It's Spain in and of itself. With the civil war, we're not sure whether we'll manage to pull together enough locals to help with the production in the Pyrenees."

Annamarie asked how Riefenstahl came to have the script. The director explained she had written it several years before, based on a play and an opera. "It's been filmed twice. Once in America and once by a Russian Jew."

Annamarie waited, but Riefenstahl said nothing more. As if that was enough reason for her to rewrite the script. An Aryan, Riefenstahl seemed to suggest, would do the story more justice.

"So it takes place in the mountains?"

"In the Pyrenees, yes," Riefenstahl said. "Do you know the storyline?"

Annamarie shook her head.

Riefenstahl brightened. "It's a love triangle across the classes. Pedro is a simple shepherd, falls in love with a beggar dancer— that's Martha—except that the landowner Don Sebastian also falls in love with her. Don Sebastian is a real bastard. He gambles and has debts. Instead of taking care of his peasants, he squanders away money and is courting a rich woman, Amelia. When he sees Martha dancing in a tavern, he kidnaps her and takes her to his castle. Martha wants the don to create better conditions for the peasants, and they get into a quarrel. She tries to run away, and from exhaustion, collapses in the mountains. Pedro finds her, takes her to his hut, and revives her. Don Sebastian then sends his men to retrieve her. He marries Amelia but wants to keep Martha as his mistress, so he makes Pedro marry Martha."

Annamarie nodded, smiling.

Riefenstahl hesitated. "I should not give it all away"—she grinned—"or you won't go watch it."

"But I do want to watch it," Annamarie ventured. "I want to watch it while you make it."

Riefenstahl's face smoothed. "You are an ambitious young woman, aren't you?"

Sepp cleared his throat. Annamarie looked down at her hands. She remembered something. A connection to the Tyrolean filmmaker Luis Trenker. Since Annamarie's first encounter with Riefenstahl, Charlotte had told her that Trenker and the German actress were rumoured to have once been lovers, that Trenker had managed to get Riefenstahl important roles for many of the mountain films that had been produced in the twenties. Riefenstahl was reputed to have had many lovers. All handsome, all athletic. All with some sort of prestige to propel Riefenstahl forward. Especially the Führer, though no one dared to suggest that the two had been or were romantically involved.

When Annamarie looked up, Riefenstahl was reaching over the aisle to Sepp.

"May I?"

Sepp handed her the Leica.

"I've got a Zeiss with me," Riefenstahl said.

"Black-and-white or colour film?" Sepp asked.

"Black-and-white. I prefer black-and-white."

He nodded. "So do I sometimes. It challenges me to really pay attention to the light."

Riefenstahl's eyes creased when she smiled. "That's right."

"What if," Annamarie said carefully, "you can't film *Lowlands* in Spain? Have you considered the Dolomites?" She could imagine being one of those location scouts for Riefenstahl. And it would give her an opportunity to maybe at least visit Manuel. To stop at home briefly and test the waters with her family.

Riefenstahl grinned broadly. "I like the way you think. Actually, I have."

"I lived in Bolzano for a while," Annamarie said hopefully. "Did some acting there."

"Is that what you want to be? An actress?"

Charlotte shifted next to the director. Annamarie was not going to stop now.

"I think I want to be more like you. I want to do it all." She checked Riefenstahl's expression. It was intent. "Act. Direct. Produce."

"And you want to learn it from me."

Annamarie smiled.

Riefenstahl did as well. The woman looked out the window, and Annamarie followed her gaze. The countryside was turning from late-summer colour to early fall already.

"I want to film it in black-and-white," Riefenstahl said finally. "Like Trenker. My God, he has an eye for capturing the most majestic scenes and making them come alive, even in black-and-white. And the lighting…" She looked at Sepp then. "You understand what I mean?"

Sepp cleared his throat again. "Yes, Frau Riefenstahl, I absolutely do."

"Good."

Annamarie ducked her head to hide the giddy smile. It could work, and maybe, just maybe, she'd have a chance to smooth a thing or two over with her family. When Riefenstahl turned to ask Charlotte something, Annamarie bumped him lightly with her elbow. Sepp bumped back.

After several checkpoints at the border and beyond, Annamarie and the crew arrived in Krakow. The Reich's colours already hung from every pillar and column. Riefenstahl excused herself to use the facilities in the station, and she later strode out wearing military garb, including a holster with a pistol.

Annamarie's mouth dropped open. Sepp put a finger beneath her chin and closed it. Riefenstahl held court with the more veteran crew.

Charlotte approached Annamarie and Sepp. "We've got permission to travel to Warsaw, but we have to wait awhile. In the meantime, we're staying at a villa not too far from the old town. One of Frau Riefenstahl's acquaintances."

Annamarie wondered whether he was good looking and athletic. She lifted her case, and Sepp slung his large rucksack over his shoulder. Outside the station, they hailed taxis.

The next days, Annamarie was busy helping with equipment, with following the crew around as they filmed Krakow and its sights. Like Charlotte, she coordinated timetables and locations, tables at cafés for the crew and in restaurants. At the castle, they filmed the unfurling of the Reich's banners. Sepp switched constantly between cameras—filming and taking photos everywhere they went and trying to stay out of the way of the big shots who were sometimes patient enough to provide instructions and mostly telling him to get out of the way.

Riefenstahl's true personality shone as well, and Annamarie was not certain whether to admire the woman or fear her. She was demanding, worked to achieve perfection, and was obsessed with details. Which might have accounted for her short temper. On rare occasions she might have caught Annamarie in her sights and acknowledged her, but it was usually to ask whether she had nothing better to do than stand around and gape.

At least that was what it felt like to Annamarie. Gone was the

316

camaraderie she'd experienced on the train. Gone was any hint that Riefenstahl might take Annamarie under her wing and teach her the ropes.

"Watch and learn," Sepp whispered to Annamarie in passing. "Stop being a dolt, and take this all in. Lower your expectations of the woman. Just be happy to be here."

Whereas Riefenstahl aimed to capture the victory and glory of the Wehrmacht and the regime over Poland, Annamarie observed something different, something happening on the periphery of the camera lenses. When she found herself waiting at a café for the crew to arrive, Annamarie noted the shell-shocked faces of the residents. People spoke to her with wary spite and in a language she could not understand. But Annamarie understood the melody. It was the sound of fury. *Szołdry*, they called the crew, which Annamarie later discovered meant *pigs*. *Fryc* was another word she heard whenever they appeared.

Annamarie would take out her journal and write, casting a surreptitious glance around and noting what the Poles looked like, how they reacted, and their behaviours. She even bought a dress from a local shop, used and in good shape, with embroidered flowers. The next place where she reserved the table for the crew, she pretended to be mute, and the owner was kind, spoke Polish to her, and helped her to move several tables together. She had only been in the city for a few days, but she had learned enough to understand the basic questions. Only when the crew arrived, all speaking German and bossing the waitstaff about, did the owner glower at her. Annamarie recorded everything, including the vocabulary.

On September 11, when the newspapers made it clear that Britain's and France's declarations of war were nothing more than hot air save for the few attacks on German marine craft, Riefenstahl announced they would be taking a bus to Warsaw, with one stop in a town called Końskie.

"There's a BDM troop that's been called in to help with inventory," she said. "I want to get that."

"Inventory for what?" Annamarie whispered to Charlotte.

Charlotte's mouth puckered with uncertainty. "I guess when they requisition the homes, we need to list the contents. Something like that?"

Annamarie frowned. "That's not going to be very exciting on film. Watching a bunch of girls cleaning up rooms."

Sepp was suddenly at her shoulder and sniggered. "Men fantasise about all sorts of things."

That was not all Riefenstahl was capturing. Annamarie figured it would end up as one small scene in the entire kaleidoscope. Besides, the woman had a knack for making the most routine things unique. During dinner one evening, the air filled with cigarette smoke, Riefenstahl recalled the aerial feats and different angles used in *Triumph of the Will*, where she had filmed the Nazi Party Congress in Nuremberg five years earlier. The cinematography was gorgeous. Shots of BDM girls dancing, the beautiful black-and-white photos of athletic women and men throwing javelins and disks, performing gymnastics and the precise routines Annamarie had taken part in her own BDM career. Sometimes Annamarie smirked when she listened to Sepp speak with Riefenstahl about her work. To the woman's face, he called it "fine art," though in Innsbruck he'd called it "horrendous propaganda." But Annamarie decided that he, too, had a right to examine the other sides of things, to review from different perspectives.

The next day, with the rest of the crew, Annamarie boarded the bus to Warsaw, a rickety old thing with hard wooden seats. Annamarie pushed the dingy curtains aside and watched the landscape of fields and poplars roll by. Here there no swastikas, but on occasion military vehicles overtook them. It was a warm day, and great white clouds drifted across the sky.

Annamarie wondered how many Poles had taken to the

woods. The newspapers were reporting that the majority of the Polish soldiers had simply given up, and Sepp ventured to say many others had fled to the southern border and were collecting themselves. She did not know what to think about the idea of organised resistance. Or that the Wehrmacht would anticipate it. Then it was far from over, wasn't it? The countryside, however, continued to roll by. Pastoral. Peaceful.

"Are we at war with France and Britain or not?" she asked Sepp suddenly.

Seated directly behind her, he leaned in to talk to her in the crack between the window and her seat. "A couple of skirmishes were reported on the French border, but nothing else. It looks like we've picked off Poland as easily as the Sudetenland."

Annamarie nodded. Next to her, Charlotte snored lightly, her head bouncing with each bump—and there were many. Her hair was flattened at the back. She had been knocked out since the bus had left Krakow. Last night Annamarie had seen her sneaking off with one of the cameramen after the group had opened what might have been a second case of wine.

About three hours later, the bus pulled up alongside a park next to a palace that looked like a Roman building with a triangular roof and six carved pillars in the front. Again, the Nazi flag claimed its spot there. Annamarie read the plaque on the gate: *pałac Małachowskich*. Everyone began to move, and she shook Charlotte awake, who wiped her mouth and smiled weakly.

"Did I drool?"

Annamarie brushed her left shoulder. "I'm all wet."

"Really?"

"No. Not really. Come on. I need to get off this bus."

Annamarie set her case on one of the palace steps and sat down to unbuckle her shoes. Sepp stood before her. Across the street, a group of BDM girls—white blouses, black skirts, clipboards hugged to their middles—hurried down the block, following their troop leader.

"Looks like they've already gone to work."

Riefenstahl shaded her eyes just as the sun came out from behind a cloud. "Let's follow them."

They were not far behind when the BDM girls reached the checkpoint set up in the middle of the road. Several Wehrmacht soldiers stepped forward and checked the girls' identification cards. Riefenstahl pushed ahead, the journalist passes and documents at the ready. She spoke with one of the soldiers just as the BDM leader turned away from the checkpoint and herded the troop's girls back in the direction they'd come.

"What's going on?" Charlotte asked one of the young women.

"We were supposed to clear out a residence," she said. "On the next street, but we've been told that the Wehrmacht has taken over."

Meanwhile, Riefenstahl returned to the group, handed Charlotte the packet of documents, and waved the crew over to her.

"Apparently there was an attack on a few soldiers yesterday," Riefenstahl said in a low voice. Everyone moved in closer. "They don't want the girls to be in danger, so the Wehrmacht has taken over in vacating the premises. They're going to let us through, but with a soldier to accompany us. For our own safety."

Everyone agreed, and Sepp checked his camera, fiddled with something, and then began shooting photos of the checkpoint.

Annamarie waited for him.

"Sorry." He forwarded the film. "Leni asked me to take stills today."

The group followed a young soldier around the corner from the checkpoint, but as soon as Annamarie had cleared it, she heard men's voices shouting orders. A woman screamed and begged. Annamarie lurched to a stop. She stood at the end of the street, along the right side. It was lined with a row of houses and shops. The one before her had a beautiful arched wooden door and arched windows. There was a shopfront and the scent of something sweet. The architecture in Poland might have been different, but the scene was the same as the night Annamarie had witnessed the Jewish synagogue burn in Innsbruck. The crying woman, on her knees in the street, reminded Annamarie of Veronika dragged out of the State Theatre.

Trucks were lined up in the middle of the road, and soldiers were loading them with everything from suitcases, to candelabras, to chairs and tables, to goods straight out of the shops. Two women in headscarves and an old man were shoved out from one shop and into the middle of the street. Others soon followed. Another man was flung out only a couple of doors away from Annamarie. She pressed herself against the wall of the nearest building. The Wehrmacht went in pairs, from one door to the next, banging them with the butts of their rifles before barging in. From inside a ground-floor apartment, opposite Annamarie, came the sound of breaking glass.

The film crew had halted at various points along the block, and the soldier who had escorted them was far ahead and no longer paying attention to them. Charlotte and Sepp were just ahead of Annamarie. Riefenstahl, however, was in the middle of those trucks, turning slowly around—wearing that uniform, wearing that holster. When she faced Annamarie, her face was aghast. Riefenstahl motioned to her first cameraman, and he dug out his equipment. Over the voices of the Wehrmacht officers, Riefenstahl shouted her own orders. Annamarie did not move.

From the home where Annamarie had heard glass breaking, a Wehrmacht soldier yanked a little girl and her mother out onto the road. He tossed the child onto the kerb and slammed the woman onto her knees in front of the door. The soldier's beret flew off, exposing a high forehead. A second soldier, beefy and barrel chested, wrestled a bearded man out, young enough that Annamarie guessed it was the woman's husband. The beefier

Wehrmacht shoved the poor civilian up against the shop, but the man flailed and kicked wildly. The soldier stepped away just in time and yanked his pistol out of his holster. Annamarie leapt back against the wall at the sound of the shot. The man's wife howled and flung herself on top of her husband, but the soldier yanked her up and aimed the revolver at her head. The child wailed in the street on all fours.

"*Halt!*" It was Riefenstahl. She charged the few metres across the street, withdrawing her own pistol from her holster. "Stop right there!"

The soldier with the high forehead tackled Riefenstahl and yanked her away. He grabbed her pistol and—like in a western— flipped the barrel onto her and pressed it to her right temple. Riefenstahl's face fell, the colour draining as she slowly raised her hands.

Annamarie's knees buckled. "She's a journalist! Don't shoot."

Another shot blasted, and Annamarie screamed. But Riefenstahl was still standing. The woman—the mother of the child in the street—was the one who slumped against the shop and onto the ground next to her dead husband.

The soldier who had Riefenstahl rolled his eyes wildly. He jabbed the barrel into her head. "On your knees!"

"I'm Leni Riefenstahl," she cried, but she slowly lowered herself onto the pavement, her hands up. "Don't shoot. We're filming a documentary for Dr Goebbels. This is my film crew, to document your victories."

The soldier looked over his shoulder and manoeuvred around Riefenstahl in a way so that he could see the entire crew. Everyone gathered in a semicircle on the street. Annamarie raised her hands. In her periphery, she could account for everyone but Sepp. Where was Sepp?

"Charlotte," she said shakily. "Give me the documents. Go find our escort." To the two soldiers across from her, she called, "I'm bringing you the documents."

Paper rustled, and Charlotte pressed the packet into Annamarie's raised hand. Annamarie grasped it, her pulse racing at the base of her neck. She swallowed.

"Sepp," Annamarie called, keeping eye contact with the man holding Riefenstahl hostage. "Sepp? Where are you?"

"I'm here," Sepp called back.

She heard the camera clicking.

"Stop taking photos," the beefier soldier shouted. But doubt had settled into his expression. "Bring the camera here."

"We're journalists," Riefenstahl said again. "This is my crew. Dr Goebbels wants us to document everything."

"I think she's telling the truth," the short one said. "I think I recognise her."

The one with the gun to Riefenstahl's head looked less frightened, and he glanced at his comrade. The child was still curled up on the street, wailing. It took all Annamarie had to pass her by. Another pistol shot and screams down the street. Annamarie's bowels turned liquid.

The short soldier snatched the papers from Annamarie and riffled through them, then nodded to his partner, who pressed the barrel of the gun to Riefenstahl's temple and swung her toward the blood-stained wall.

"You were standing up for Jews! These are filthy Jews. You nearly lost your life for a bunch of filthy Jews!" He yanked Riefenstahl off her knees and shoved her back towards Annamarie and the crew.

The child, maybe two years old, was trying to get up, blinded by tears, her mouth wide open in terror. Annamarie bent down to lift her, but someone yanked her backwards. She whirled around. It was their military escort.

He wheeled Annamarie back across the road. She vaguely heard Sepp cry out in protest, but the soldier shouted orders, and soon enough the crew was herded all the way back to the other side of the block and surrounded by Wehrmacht. Annamarie watched the soldier who'd held the gun to Riefenstahl's head retrieve his beret next to the man's body. He brushed an arm across his forehead and began striding across the street. At the child, he stopped and pointed his sidearm. Annamarie screamed before the child's wails ceased and stumbled, but Sepp's voice urged her in a whisper, "Get up. Get up. I've got you."

She let him lift her, falling against him, and when they were marched back to the checkpoint, back to the palace, he had his arms around her the entire way.

As the bus pulled away from Końskie, Annamarie watched the Wehrmacht shove a group of Jewish men down onto the ground around a tree. Another crew was unloading shovels from a truck.

Shock settled over the passengers of the bus as it rocked and jerked with each gear shift. They were still heading north, towards Warsaw. Riefenstahl sat rigid in the front row with one of the cameramen. It was not possible to read her thoughts. Charlotte silently wept in the seat ahead of Annamarie, and Annamarie placed a hand on her shoulder even as she continued leaning against Sepp. Since they had fled the scene, his arm had essentially glued itself to Annamarie. When the bus backfired, she yelped and Charlotte sobbed loudly.

Riefenstahl turned to face them, her eyes stone cold until they landed on Charlotte, and then they flashed with emotion. The woman leapt up, using the tops of the seats to make her way over to Charlotte, who moved over against the window as Riefenstahl slid in next to her. Like Sepp was doing with Annamarie, Riefenstahl shielded Charlotte in her arms.

"Those sons of bitches," Riefenstahl burst out.

The whole bus turned to her.

"Those sons of fucking bitches! Damn them! Who do they think they are? Damn them! When the Führer hears about this!"

Her arms swung away from Charlotte, and Riefenstahl pounded on the back of the seat before her. Charlotte curled into herself, wailing now.

Riefenstahl rose and stood in the aisle, turning to all of them. "Who the fuck do they think they are! I want an answer!"

One of the cameramen muttered something, and she swung to him. "What? What did you say?"

Annamarie did not hear what he repeated, but Riefenstahl deflated. She rubbed her face with her hands, swaying and dangerously off balance. She sank onto the seat across from Charlotte's. Riefenstahl hung her head and cried.

A tear rolled down Annamarie's cheek as she whispered to Sepp, "This is nothing like back home. Nothing. We were never treated this badly by the Walscher."

"We don't know what it's like now," Sepp said.

"Not like this." She shifted so she could look at him. "Never."

He still looked doubtful.

In Warsaw, Riefenstahl ordered the bus driver to go directly to the train station and insisted that Charlotte, Sepp, and Annamarie leave Poland and return to Berlin. She and the others would continue onwards after she put a call in to the office. She hugged each of them stiffly, rubbing Charlotte's hair and whispering to her. Charlotte nodded against the woman's shoulder as they hugged again.

Clutching Annamarie next, Riefenstahl said, "What you did back there? Showing him our credentials? Standing up to them? That was brave. It was quick thinking. Get back to where you are safe. People are not themselves."

Annamarie nodded woodenly, and Riefenstahl touched each of them one more time before boarding the bus again. Annamarie led the other two to the ticket counter, where they purchased the tickets to Berlin, but she was no longer certain she could call Berlin home. She was no longer certain that it was where she wanted to return. For the time being, however, she had nowhere else to go, and she did not want to leave Charlotte or Sepp. Ever.

Their train was not leaving for hours, and nobody wanted to eat, so they found a bench in the foyer and waited. After a while, Sepp excused himself and returned with lemonade and pretzels.

"You have to eat. We haven't had anything since breakfast."

Quietly they nibbled their pretzels and butter, but Annamarie felt the tears welling again. She laid the pretzel off to the side and covered her face.

"Come on," Charlotte whispered. "Let's find the toilets."

Annamarie left with her, and when they were in the ladies' room, they clutched each other and sobbed.

Riefenstahl had given them enough money to purchase a carriage with two sets of bunkbeds. Relieved to finally be alone and moving back towards Berlin, the three of them stumbled into the carriage, put their cases on top of the extra bunkbed, and perched on the two lower bunkbeds—Sepp on one end with the cases above his head, and Annamarie and Charlotte on the other.

"Do you want top or bottom?" Annamarie asked Charlotte. Her muscles ached, her jaw ached, and she could hardly breathe, her nasal passages were so swollen from crying.

Charlotte asked to sleep above, pleading claustrophobia. Annamarie agreed.

They each shimmied onto their cots, but nobody had turned off the light. Annamarie could only see the reflection of the carriage in the window against the darkness outside. She turned her head and caught Sepp watching her on his side. His left arm was outstretched across the narrow aisle, his eyeglasses dangling in his hand.

"How are you?" he asked softly.

"I don't feel anything right now."

He nodded into his pillow and closed his eyes, but his brow remained furrowed.

"Sepp?"

He opened his eyes. They were bloodshot.

"Who would want to live in strangers' houses anyway?"

"Germans."

"From where?"

Sepp raised himself on his elbow. "Didn't you hear about the Option?"

Annamarie blinked.

"Our parents will have an opportunity to choose whether to be German or Italian. They can actually vote on it."

Annamarie mirrored him as she propped herself. "I didn't hear anything about that."

"You're old enough to vote for yourself."

"And if I vote German, I get to move to Poland?" she asked, astonished.

Sepp sniffed. "Weird, no?"

"How is that any different to what the Italians are trying to do to us South Tyroleans? Just coming and taking our homes away?"

He raised his eyebrows and put his glasses on. "There isn't," he said softly.

Annamarie's head fell back onto the pillow, and she stared at the bottom of Charlotte's bunk. Tears welled again.

"Hey," Sepp called gently. "Hey."

She heard him rising, but she ducked her head beneath the thin, sour-smelling blanket. He crouched next to her in the aisle, put an arm over her again. Annamarie tried not to alarm Charlotte, and she sobbed into her pillow. She felt Sepp gently pushing her to move against the wall. He then lay down next to her and pulled her to him. Her hair and pillow were wet with tears.

"I don't know where I belong," she whispered hoarsely. "I don't know."

"This isn't going to last forever," Sepp said. "It isn't, Annamarie. We need to get through this. And listen." He pulled back, his face blurred before her. "Listen to me. I'm voting for Italian citizenship, because when this is all over, at least I have a home to go back to."

"I want to go home," Annamarie pleaded. "I'm tired of all this."

Sepp made a noise in the back of his throat. Into her hair he muttered, "I think it's only getting started."

21

BOLZANO, SEPTEMBER 1939

With a team of builders and engineers around the table, Angelo cut up Stefano Accosi's model of the Reschen Valley like a celebratory cake. The engineer had built it before Angelo had tossed him out of the ministry. Pointing out the villages of Graun and Reschen, then the remaining five hamlets, Angelo made sure the group understood what they were looking at. He then lay a flat piece of glass across the valley floor, supported by the edges of terraced hills on either side. Across the beam, in red lettering, *+22m* indicated the new level of the valley floor and the reservoir's surface. Everything except St Katharina's tower was located beneath it. He moved a couple of farmhouses from the "old" valley floor and set them along the "new" lakeshore. To the landscape above Graun, he transferred some tiny blocks that represented the individual homes and began establishing a new town behind St Anna's hill and up along the Karlinbach. A path that led into Langlaufertal to the east was now a road. He described the area. It was usually only accessible on foot, but there were plenty of sunny slopes and plateaus where the farmers could plant grain. In other words, they could transplant a few of the hardest-hit farms to the area here.

Angelo finished. "This is the rough idea. Now I require the statistics and costs. I want the first calculations and plans within a fortnight. And..." He eyed each of the seven men individually. "I want it to be a feasible project. This must work."

The team broke up. Lastra, a road engineer Angelo knew only too well, pursed his lips. Lastra always asked questions and had tried to undermine Angelo's authority several times. Before the group could leave, Angelo called Lastra back to him. He needed a consensus. And he needed to know what Lastra held against him or the project, or both.

Angelo invited the man to sit. He'd learned from Gina that if he kept his mouth shut, waited long enough, people would just start talking, and they usually started with the information you were looking for anyway. Angelo pretended to be searching for something on his desk. He let the silence weigh down on the road engineer.

"Why are we even bothering with this?" Lastra finally blurted.

"We owe it to our citizens." Angelo knew he was provoking, but he had no time to waste. Lastra should get it out, be put back into his place, and then they could get on with it.

But Lastra looked at him with disbelief. "Our citizens? Come December thirty-first, the Tyroleans will have all chosen to be German. You know what they think? They think that if they all— and I mean *all*—vote German, Hitler will have no choice but to declare the Alto Adige as German soil." Lastra pointed towards Angelo's door. "You know what Hitler did in the Sudetenland? In Poland? That's what the Tyroleans want."

Angelo folded his hands. "The magistrate and I are committed to two things. Keeping the Tyroleans here and, secondly, finding a solution for the Reschen Valley residents. He wants to go about it a different way, and the Tyroleans—and I—believe there is another. We keep them where they are. We not only keep them there, we make certain they continue to thrive and improve. And that is why you will do as I request and put together a plan and a cost estimate so that we may weigh our options. Now, if that's all?"

Lastra sniffed and looked down at the floor. "Mark my words —it's a waste of my time, as well as the other six men's time, who were here. A waste of resources. The *allogeni* will all be gone by next spring."

"Nobody," Angelo said, echoing Ciano's words, "chooses to leave their home if they do not have to."

Lastra shrugged. "I'm from Calabria. And now I'm here."

When the door closed behind the engineer, Angelo blew softly and lifted the receiver to ask Miss Medici to put a call through to Michael Innerhofer. The journalist answered after the fourth ring.

"I've just had a conversation that I find rather disturbing. What developments are you seeing among the German community? Which way are they swaying?"

"It's not good, Angelo. And there's been an incident with Hofer and the VKS."

Angelo winced. That word again. *Incident.*

"Would Signora Conti be free this evening?" Innerhofer asked.

Angelo hesitated. Gina's sons were visiting, and he was staying away from both her and the villa. "That's not certain."

"It would be important for her to join us. Chiara and I have—"

Angelo gripped the receiver. "No. I don't want them in the same room."

Michael cleared his throat. "Signora Conti is invited at Chiara's suggestion."

This took Angelo aback. It was serious indeed, then.

His and Chiara's annulment had finally come through. Angelo and she were no longer married in the eyes of the church, but that did not mean that bygones were bygones or that she simply accepted Gina Conti's presence. The emotional and caustic last few months had led to several unpleasant altercations. The priest had first unjustly accused Chiara of being unchristian and had suggested she forgive her husband for his sins. Chiara had exploded. Angelo had then gone back alone to confess his entire story to the priest, and he'd begged the man to write an official letter of apology to Chiara so that they could continue the process in relative cooperation. If she now wanted to see Gina, then this was important.

"What time would you like us there?" Angelo asked.

"Eight?"

"I'll see what I can do."

He was surprised to see his clock read six. Miss Medici had already left. He put the call to the Conti villa himself, but the housekeeper said Gina and the boys were still out. They were expected shortly. He asked that Signora Conti ring him at the ministry, and then he absorbed the time by reading and editing a report to the electrical society about the progress on the Reschen reservoir. The next time he looked up, it was half past seven.

He left everything as it was on his desk, grabbed his coat, and hurried out the building. He hailed a taxi to the Conti villa. They passed the military base, and Angelo saw that the buildings of the Semirurali settlement were almost completed. Laundry was strung up between two of them already, a sure sign that the first inhabitants had arrived and settled in.

The taxi pulled up to the Limoncello-yellow villa. Angelo stepped out and asked the driver to wait. He buzzed at the front gate and recognised the housekeeper's voice. When she opened the door to him, she paled and placed a hand over her mouth.

"Minister Grimani, I'm so terribly sorry. Signora Conti and the boys were running late. It was chaotic, and I simply—"

"No matter. Please tell her I'm waiting."

He led himself into the front parlour as the housekeeper

scurried away. Angelo called the sitting room the White Room, for all the white furniture, white carpeting, white plasterwork. But someone had arranged sprays of red, orange, and fuchsia dahlias throughout the room in black and white vases.

Gina's voice soon echoed down the marble hall. "Nonsense," she scolded the housekeeper. "You show him directly to the dining room next time. Especially if you've forgotten to tell me he rang."

Gina walked in wearing a simple and elegant periwinkle dress with a single wine-red leaf print angled from her left hip to her right breast.

He apologised for disrupting. A joke about Eve in the garden of Eden was on the tip of his tongue, but he could see the shadow of the housemaid on the wall opposite the hallway. "We've been called to Innerhofer's. Chiara's requested you be there."

"You're not serious? You are. Allow me to make my excuses with the boys. We were running late. Constanza is usually so reliable."

Angelo told her he would wait in the taxi. Gina appeared a few moments later, and he opened the door for her. She sat down next to him on the backseat and clutched her bag.

"How are things with the boys?" he asked.

She raised her chin. "I told them that you and I have been spending quite a lot of time together."

Angelo's neck popped with how fast he turned his head. "Really?"

She gazed at him. "Really."

"And?" He felt jumpy.

"They said they were happy for me but that perhaps I should wait a little longer before telling Filipa. She's going to have her final exams this year, and she ought to at least focus on that before dealing with this."

"She's still pretty sore about last year?"

Gina made a face. "There's something you ought to know."

Angelo waited.

"Marco contacted her when he arrived in Rome."

The surprises never ceased. "And?"

She shrugged. "I think it was real, what they had. I think Marco had honest feelings for Filipa, and honest intentions. If he'd not been so hell bent on getting back at you, I don't think poor Annamarie would have been the object he tried to hurt you with."

Angelo nodded. "Then let's hope it works out for them."

"Filipa will find it unforgivable if her mother is being courted by her beau's father."

"Yes," Angelo said. "Then we will continue to keep it discreet."

"I'm not sure I want to." Gina settled back into the seat. She took his hand and squeezed it.

Angelo squeezed back.

"So what is all this about tonight?" she asked.

"I'll give you one guess."

She sighed. "No rest for the wicked."

They pulled up to Innerhofer's house, the leaves on the maple in the front yard bright even in the fading light. Angelo paid the cabdriver, then lifted the knocker. A cowbell was hanging next to the door, and Gina winked and yanked on it.

Chiara and Michael formed the welcoming committee behind the door.

"Signora Conti, very good of you to come." Chiara stepped forward.

The women shook hands, and Michael led them into the study. There were chairs set out around the oven and a table with coffee and biscuits. Angelo realised he'd had no dinner yet, and his stomach grumbled.

When they were settled, he subtly studied Chiara. She wore her good-sport expression, one that said she not only would but could stand above this all.

"We are in need of your insights and your contacts, Signora Conti," Chiara started. "I wanted you to hear this all from our side, direct from the horse's mouth so to speak, so that you can make an honest assessment." She glanced briefly at Angelo. "I believe you are familiar with the game Silent Post? The more often the message is filtered down, the more it loses its original meeting."

Gina folded her hands in her lap. "Indeed."

Michael leaned forward. "Peter Hofer invited me to join him and a delegation of VKS members at the *Reichssicherheitshauptamt* —that's the main security offices of the Third Reich in Bolzano— to complain that this Option between Hitler and Mussolini is against all that is sacred to the NSDAP."

Angelo sighed. "They want Hitler to claim the Alto Adige as German soil."

"Blood and soil," Chiara said. "German blood and soil."

Angelo nodded. "And?"

Michael and Chiara exchanged a look before he spoke. "They did not get far. As a matter of fact, I am glad to be sitting here right now without any bruises. The officer lay into us. How dare we question the Führer's decisions? Every German, regardless where he lives—so he reminded us—has the obligation and duty to follow the Führer's every order. He nearly called us traitors to the fatherland." Innerhofer scratched his head. "Except by the time he was finished, I honestly had no idea whether he meant traitors to Italy or Germany."

Gina frowned. "I'm not following. Start at the beginning."

Michael explained that the delegation had been made up of both German League members and VKS members, who were now united in one thing: to have Hitler annex the territories to the Third Reich. To the *Reichsführer*, they complained about the alliance between the Reich and Italy and about the decision that now faced them: swearing their allegiance to the Führer, whose decisions they did not support.

"The *Reichsführer* then shouted at Hofer and said who did he think he was that—as the rest of the German nation was prepared to spill their blood in places like Poland to gain new territories—the Tyroleans are unprepared to make this small sacrifice to appease the most powerful ally we have."

"Which sacrifice?" Angelo asked.

Innerhofer looked at him. "South Tyrol."

"German blood belongs to German blood," Chiara said. "That's what the commander told Hofer. He also claimed that Germany would gain land in the Crimea, in France, and that where there are Germans, it will be considered German soil."

Gina straightened. "Except South Tyrol?"

Michael and Chiara glanced at each other.

"Except, for the moment, South Tyrol," Michael said.

"For the moment," Angelo repeated.

"The Crimea?" Gina said. "Is that what he said? And France?"

The room was quiet. After a moment, Angelo said, "So these will be the aims of his war. And Hitler's dragging Italy right into it."

"What else did this *Reichsführer* say?" Gina narrowed her eyes. "Why am I here?"

Again, Michael and Chiara looked at each other before Michael said, "He told Hofer and the rest of us that the migration would take place with or without our votes. But if we make any move to *prevent* the people from this migration, there would be consequences. Hofer then assured him that if this was the way the Führer wished to handle the debate about South Tyrol once and for all, then the VKS and the German League would support the Option and vote for Germany. The *Reichsführer* then *ordered* them to achieve a result of no less than ninety percent."

Angelo blew softly. "Ninety percent? Choosing to leave?"

"Minimum," Michael said.

Chiara looked at Gina. "He wants the Tyroleans to leave their land so that Italy can keep it and have rights to its claim. The

Reichsführer also told the delegation that he would inform Rome of their visit, with a list of their names. When Hofer reminded him that they were an illegal assembly in the eyes of the Italian regime, the *Reichsführer* said—"

"Not any longer," Michael interjected. "Now we're called the *Arbeitsgemeinschaft den Optaten.* The committee for the optants. And it is—with Rome's blessing—now our duty to make certain that we convince everyone to migrate."

Angelo laughed. "You mean spread propaganda."

"And Rome knows about it," Gina said.

"They know about you," Chiara answered.

Angelo frowned.

"They know me?" Gina asked slowly. "My name came up?"

"Yes," Michael said. "At the very end, he looked at me and said that I should pass along a message to you."

"That being?" Gina's tone sounded amused, but her smile wavered.

"They have their eye on you. And your presence in political business is unwanted."

Chiara leaned forward to Gina. "Signora Conti, when was the last time you were in touch with Tolomei's secretary?"

Gina frowned at the same time as Angelo. She turned her head and thought for a moment. "A fortnight?"

Michael nodded, as if she'd given him the correct answer. "He's been missing for a week now."

"Tolomei's secretary? Missing? What is the meaning of this?" Angelo asked.

Michael tipped his head. "Signora Conti, did Tolomei's secretary provide you with something that you should not know about?"

Gina shook her head. "We were discussing the revisions they were making to the bill. The fact that it still had not found the support Tolomei was hoping for. And other than that..." She shrugged.

Angelo knew she was holding something back. "Surely this man is not serious," he said. "It's just a scare tactic."

Michael tapped the arm of his chair with his fingernails. "I believe you should keep a low profile, Signora Conti."

"More than I have been?" she mocked.

Michael eyed Angelo. "This is serious. Now is not the time to be making enemies. On either side. Please be careful."

Gina sat back, then slowly rose. "I will give all you say careful consideration. If you will excuse me, however, I left my meal abruptly, and my guests. Minister Grimani? If your rumbling stomach is of any indication, you have had nothing to eat at all."

Chiara cleared her throat, but when she rose, her smile was gracious and apologetic. "Thank you so much, to both of you, for coming."

When they took their leave, Gina said they should walk and find a taxi in the centre. "I'll ask Constanza to warm something up for us when we get home."

When we get home. "Are you not concerned about Tolomei's secretary?"

"A little."

"What did you last discuss?"

Gina made a noise in the back of her throat. "There is another plan if the bill does not pass. And…" She picked up her pace.

Angelo hurried to keep up.

She hailed a taxi near the train station, and it pulled up.

"And?" he pressed.

Gina stepped into the waiting cab and settled in before facing him in the dark. "Ciano is falling out of grace."

"Why do the Nazis know your name, Gina? That's what I want to know."

She looked at him. "Chiara and Michael are sniffing up the wrong tree."

"What do you mean?"

"You're not going to get anywhere with the Reschen Valley

338

people if the former mayor's son hangs." Gina folded her hands. "David Roeschen won't hang now."

Angelo watched her looking at the road ahead, her face a mask. *Don't ask unless you want to know.*

He had no further questions.

22

RESCHEN VALLEY, OCTOBER 1939

K atharina hurried out of the bedroom and headed for the stairs, whipping the shawl over her shoulders. The door to Manuel's room was cracked open, and she caught her son sprawled out on his stomach, reading.

They were going to be late for church.

"Manuel, we need to get going. Come along now."

He sighed heavily and closed the book. Before taking the stairs, Katharina checked herself in the mirror atop of the linen chest. She was shocked by the lines etched around her mouth. She puckered her lips a little, then curled them beneath her teeth. She let go, but the lines were still there. How? When? They'd probably been formed by all the words she had forced herself to hold back all these months. Years, really. She nearly laughed at the idea. And when was the last time she had smiled? Really laughed? When had any of them?

Manuel sidled out of his room, pouting. He hated it when she interrupted his reading. And these days, when he had so many extra chores, that was often.

She placed a hand on his head, but he kept his eyes on the

stairs. She drew him to her and kissed the mess of hair. "After supper I'll take care of your chores. You can read. All right?"

He nodded against her just as Florian called from downstairs and told them to hurry.

A light snow had fallen, and deer tracks crisscrossed the road as she walked down to Graun with her family. The stakes had been pounded in all around the valley. Florian called them death markers. The workers from MFE were working on diverting the Etsch River, and before Katharina descended into Graun, they could just make out the excavators and other heavy machinery near the river bed.

They entered St Katharina's just as the bells stopped tolling. Katharina made the sign of the cross, then followed Florian and Manuel to their usual pew in the second row left. The Foglios were in the pew before them. Usually the family sat way in the back, with Klaus being so tall. Actually, she reminded herself, ever since they had changed their names from Blech to Foglio, they had taken to sitting at the back of the church. But not this Sunday. This Sunday the Foglios were front and centre, including Sebastiano. He'd always been sweet on Annamarie, but from what Katharina knew, he was now courting a young woman from the Italian district, named Rosa. Everyone was talking about it, and not in the nicest of terms on the Tyrolean side of town.

Father Wilhelm led them through the Mass. It was his last week as their parish priest. Turning seventy on the following Saturday, he could no longer fend off the bishop from sending him into retirement. With Father Wilhelm's imminent departure, the parish faced yet another loss. By the new year, a new priest would arrive. Though with the reservoir and the uncertainty of where anyone would be in a few months, nobody counted on him being around for long.

After Communion and the final benediction, Father Wilhelm approached the pulpit again. The parishioners settled back into the pews. He pushed against the lectern, straight armed, and looked over his flock.

"You're expecting me to announce news about your new priest. I'll save that for Saturday's supper. I've been asked to keep you all here, as *Podestá* Ghirardelli has an announcement to make."

Everyone turned their heads as Ghirardelli made his way to the front altar. Captain Basso came from the right and beckoned in Katharina's direction. Before her, Klaus Foglio rose and edged past his family to the aisle, clipboard in hand. People shifted and murmured, the sound of anticipation rising like steam poured onto hot stones.

"We now have the details for the voting process," Ghirardelli started.

"What does Klaus Blech have to do with it?" Toni Ritsch called.

Katharina did not have to turn around in order to recognise Toni's voice. He was the only one who still called Klaus by his former name.

Ghirardelli's eyes flashed contempt. "He's your new mayor, that's what."

Everyone began whispering. Katharina twisted to Florian. He, too, was surprised.

Klaus cleared his throat and raised the clipboard. "My first duty as mayor," he began in Italian.

Toni Ritsch shouted in German, "Quit speaking Walsch, and tell us what you've got to say. I'd be interested in knowing whose—"

"Toni!" Father Wilhelm warned. "Sit down and shut your mouth. This is the house of God, and I have given these men permission to speak in it. You are welcome to leave if you wish."

Toni grumbled, but when Katharina twisted in her pew to have a quick look, he had not moved to exit.

"As you have all heard," Klaus said weakly, "our government—"

"Not our government!" A collective outcry. It was an unfortunate formulation on Klaus's part.

"Rome and Berlin," Klaus began again, "have come to an agreement. You have been presented with the option to identify yourselves as citizens of the Reich or citizens of Italy by the end of the year. To make your choice official, there are two forms." He held up the clipboard and pulled a page from it. In his left hand, a white form. On the clipboard, a red form.

"White," he said, "is for those of you who choose to become Italian citizens. Red is for those who choose to go."

"Choose to go?" Martin Noggler's voice came from two rows behind Katharina.

She turned, met Jutta's look, and glanced at Hans. Both their faces were unreadable.

"I thought," the blacksmith continued, "that if there are enough of us who want to be recognised as German citizens, we'll be annexed to the German Reich."

Klaus looked sheepish and turned to Ghirardelli. They whispered with each other whilst Basso—as usual—kept an eye on the parishioners. Klaus straightened, but his beefy face was flushed with embarrassment. "If you choose German nationality, you will be relocated somewhere within the German Reich."

"Somewhere? What about our homes?" Walter Plangger called. "What about these letters of intent. If I vote to leave, I can't fight these ridiculous prices."

Katharina turned. Jutta was craning her neck.

"You must sell off your properties," Klaus said.

"To whom?" Jutta demanded. "The prices are unfair, and there's nobody we know who could afford to buy another farm."

Ghirardelli stepped forward, but Klaus put up his hand.

"That's right," he said. "Nobody here could afford another farm. But the—"

"Sold or taken, Klaus?" It was Florian. "You know that the values are wholly incorrect."

Klaus folded his arms. "Florian, those prices will be supplemented by subsidies—"

"Not if Italy goes to war," someone else protested.

"*Vendere*," Basso shouted. He looked at Ghirardelli.

"*Vendere*," the *podestá* echoed more firmly.

"Sell," Klaus repeated. "Sell, and let the Führer take care of you."

Katharina scoffed. Manuel looked up at her just as Father Wilhelm stepped to the side of the pulpit.

"Now they've got us in their pincers," their priest announced. "The Berlin-Rome axis, folks! That's what you're in."

"We are Germans," Toni shouted. "We're going home. The shepherd goes where his sheep go."

"Where? Where are you going, Toni?" Hans said. "Tell me that. To the Carpathians again? Like you did in the war?"

Katharina turned. Hans had his arms folded, the hands tucked away beneath his armpits. His beard trembled.

"I'm a sheep farmer, Toni," Hans said, his voice rumbling over the parish. "Tell me this. Since when does the shepherd follow his sheep?"

"And what if we don't want to be German or Italian?" Jutta called to the men at the front. "What if we want our autonomy back? What colour form do I have to fill out for that?"

There were a number of people who clapped, and someone cheered.

Klaus held the clipboard like a shield before him. "The water is coming, Jutta. Whether you like it or not. If you want to move up the mountain, that's your choice, but then you'll be doing it as an Italian national."

Ghirardelli stepped forward, the tassel of his fez trembling as he pounded a fist into his palm. Katharina had never seen him lose his temper like this.

"Option one or option two." Ghirardelli shouted in German. "There is no three! *Basta!*"

Two new words circulated through the valley that week: *Dableiber* and *Optanten*—those who chose to stay and those who opted to leave.

The *Dableiber* so far were predictably Dr Hanny and Iris, who submitted their white form the day after church. The next day there was graffiti on the walls of the *Schlößl* in Reschen. *Verräter! Wälscher!* The day after that, Iris's ginger cat was found in a sack in the Etsch River, drowned. She had loved that cat.

The Foglios were not spared either. They heard an explosion on Tuesday night and awoke to a fire in their courtyard. The perpetrators had burned Sebastiano's automobile.

Graffiti on the wall of the school celebrated Hitler's steady successes of winning back occupied territories with hopes that the Tyroleans would experience a similar plebiscite result. *Heute die Saar. Wir über's Jahr! —Today the Saare. The rest of us within the year!*

Katharina learned that Henri Roeschen—to his parents' shock —immediately opted to leave with his family. Then came an offer from the investigating magistrate in David's case, and a day later Georg Roeschen went to the town hall with Lisl, both of them broken hearted as he filled out the red form for his family to leave.

Jutta then explained to Katharina that David's release happened on the condition that the entire family choose to migrate.

That was Thursday morning. Katharina was in the garden out back, and after Jutta left, she spotted all four Ritsch children sitting outside on the front stoop, with long faces. Toni and

Patricia were fighting inside, their voices reaching all the way across the two farms.

Martin Noggler showed up to shoe the horse. Florian began speaking with him about the latest news, but Martin seemed to want to avoid the discussion entirely.

Thursday night, Katharina overheard Toni tell Patricia he did not care what she wanted—his voice was the only one that counted. He had the right and the responsibility to decide for his wife and children. He then stormed out and stalked down the road to Graun as Katharina ducked behind the barn.

What would Florian choose if it meant Bernd would no longer have to attend the military academy? Katharina weighed that against prison and remained silent. Bernd was at least getting an education. It was not the same with David or Andreas. She felt horrible about the decisions Patricia and Lisl faced. She hoped desperately Florian would not now decide to show a strong hand.

Late that night, someone pounded on the Steinhausers' door. Katharina threw it open and found Jutta shaking and sobbing.

"What's happened?" Katharina ushered her inside, and Jutta pressed a sheet of paper into her hand.

"I was closing up," she said angrily. "And four masked men with rifles came right in. Handed me this."

It was one of the poems that had been circulating about. Katharina read it—a call to be true to their German lineage, to the Reich, and to honour their homeland by leaving it behind and fighting for German soil.

"We'll win back the South Tyrol when we've shown the rest of the world our strength," she read incredulously.

"They made me read it," Jutta hissed. She snatched it from Katharina. "Under gunpoint, they made me read it aloud. And if my voice wavered, they made me start again."

Katharina went to the kitchen cupboard where she kept the

schnapps, poured two glasses, and handed one to Jutta. The clinked glasses and downed the shots of liquor.

"If I hadn't been so angry, I wouldn't have gotten through it," Jutta said.

"Do you know who it was?"

Jutta's face fell, and she looked as if she might cry. "No. They just marched off to the south." She then scoffed. "Take a wild guess though. It can only be—" She pointed in the direction of the Ritsch farm. "They thought it was all a funny joke, him and his gang. Said I shouldn't hold it against them and they'd see me tomorrow. Then as soon as they left, another gust blew in Thomas Noggler and Sebastiano Foglio. They also had a flyer for me, one for the homeland. They caught me at a bad time." Jutta looked sheepish.

Katharina anticipated what came next. "You tossed them out on their ears, didn't you?"

Jutta sighed. "I might have pummelled Sebastiano. They're normally good boys. But I'm sure they're sorry they met me this night."

"Why don't you close down the inn for a few days after Father Wilhelm's birthday party?" Katharina said. "Get some rest, and get out of their way."

She fetched Florian out of bed to walk Jutta home, and he did not return from sitting with Hans until it was time to milk the cows the next morning. When Katharina asked him, he said that Hans and Jutta would likely stay. And still he had not shared with Katharina any ideas of what would happen to them and the Katharinahof. It was his vote. His signature. His decision to take. And soon enough he would find out about David or about Andreas possibly being released from prison thanks to Toni's red form. And then Florian would seek a way to get Bernd released, and her name would end up on a red page.

Throughout that week, there were arrests for the graffiti, for the door-to-door visits, for the harassment. Basso hung a notice that it was illegal for anyone to try and convince someone to stay. The *carabinieri* turned a blind eye to those who encouraged opting out, thus giving Toni and his friends free rein to terrorize the valley folk. And then on top of the *Tantegedichten*—those nationalistic poems—other flyers appeared. *Dableiber* faced being relocated into regions much farther south or even to the African colonies. *Dableiber* would be heavily fined for speaking German on the streets. *Dableiber* were prevented from getting to their jobs at the quarries or the logging companies, where they worked for extra money in the late fall and winter.

By Friday Katharina was jumpy as she made her way to Jutta's inn. She caught sight of Iris coming out of the bank, hurried to her, and embraced her.

"Will you come with me to Jutta's?" Katharina asked. "You look miserable."

"Going to my sister-in-law right now," Iris said pensively, "is not what I would prescribe for my current mood."

"Come. We're preparing for Father Wilhelm's celebration. Join us."

Iris sighed and gave in.

As they were about to go up the steps, Alois came out with cabbage scraps for the chickens.

"Tante Iris," he greeted. "I'm glad to see you. So many people want to leave, but you'll stay, won't you?"

Iris's face read surprise as he threw his arms around her waist. He was the only one who accepted her as part of the family. Alois unwrapped himself from her. He then hugged Katharina and called her *Tante* as well. He led the women into the kitchen.

"*Mutter*, look who's here to help."

The kitchen was hot and steamy already. Jutta stood over two bowls and wiped her brow with her arm before casting Iris a quick look. Her expression became one of reluctant assent.

"What can I do?" Iris asked in German. "I could make a lasagne or a ragú."

Jutta propped herself on the table and looked at Katharina disbelievingly.

"What's on the menu?" Katharina asked hopefully.

"Cabbage," Jutta said.

"And wild game," Iris added, pointing to a stack of seasoned venison cutlets in the roaster.

"Iris, you could help with the cake," Katharina said.

"Lisl's coming to do cake," Jutta mocked cheerfully. "Iris, you can do the cabbage. Alois has started cutting it up. You can finish it and then fry it up."

Iris wrinkled her nose, examined the knife Jutta handed her, and moved to the pot. Iris threw her a half smile and dove in, and Jutta relaxed.

Katharina narrowed her eyes at her. Jutta could really be devilish sometimes. She knew darned well from Dr Hanny that Iris had a great aversion to the smell of cooking cabbage.

Katharina began cleaning the pile of potatoes.

"Have you and Hans decided to stay?" Iris asked Jutta cautiously.

None of their decisions were easy, and what Katharina saw in Jutta's eyes were the bruises of hard discussions with her husband.

"We've got less than ten years to pay off the mortgage on the farm," Jutta said. "Hans doesn't want to start all over again. With the sheep and the inn, we'll manage."

Iris nodded. "And you, Katharina?"

"We haven't decided yet."

Iris looked saddened. "Florian and you have made such an effort to try and help us here. And if you leave now? What happens then?"

Katharina swallowed, tears rising. She hurried into the pantry and grabbed a large pot.

"And what about this with David now?" Iris said as Katharina came out. She leaned against the counter. "They want you gone, the Fascists. What they did to Georg and Lisl like that… Don't let them."

"Annamarie will have to choose as well," Jutta said to Katharina. "Do you know what she's going to vote for?"

Katharina slammed the pot down. Last she had heard from Annamarie, she would be returning to Innsbruck. That was all. If both Annamarie and Bernd wanted to be German nationals, then Florian would likely submit. "No."

The two women turned back to the counter.

"We wanted to be near family," Iris said.

Jutta glanced at Katharina and turned away from pounding the venison. "Your family? Are they all coming up here from the south too, then?"

Iris whirled around, the knife tip pointed at Jutta.

Jutta went back to pounding the meat, but when the kitchen door flew open, everyone jumped.

Lisl stood in the doorway. "The boys are back!"

"David?" Jutta asked.

"All of them." Lisl rushed in and grabbed Katharina by the arm. "David. Andreas. And Bernd too."

There was whooping and hollering outside the kitchen window as three figures zipped past the inn's garden and into the churchyard. Katharina clapped a hand over her mouth. She squeezed past Jutta and Iris, who were already heading for the door. The boys skidded on the snow-covered road. Bernd was dressed in a military greatcoat.

Katharina ran down the steps and to the gate, the wind biting her cheeks. She called to her son. All three boys, with wide smiles across their cold, ruddy faces, bounded towards her.

"Mother!" Bernd flung himself at Katharina.

Before she could ask, David reached into his coat and withdrew a red form. Signed. Stamped. Approved. "We've been released!"

Katharina pulled away from Bernd. Lisl stepped around her and took the form from her son.

"Our families have opted out," Andreas said. Like Bernd, he was taller, edgier. Harder. Katharina could see that his hands were rough and strong.

"Your families opted out," Katharina repeated. Her blood chilled. "But we haven't…"

Bernd grasped her arm. He was taller than her now. "They let me out for the semester break. To return home and convince father to vote German. If he does, I don't have to return to the GIL."

Katharina tried to smile.

"I'm leaving for the German front tomorrow," David told Lisl.

"And I'm going with him," Andreas said.

"But you're not old enough," Katharina protested. "You and Bernd, you're only sixteen yet."

"They don't have to know that," Andreas said.

The way Bernd looked sheepishly away from her, Katharina shook him. "No. You are not. Bernd, we're going to make this decision as a family. Together." Her smile was strained. "Manuel will be so pleased to see you."

Jutta stepped forward. "Bernd, what do you believe you're doing by leaving?"

Bernd frowned. "We'll win the war, and Germany will be our new home."

"And what of our home here?" Katharina asked.

David looked at the women standing at the garden gate. His eyes stayed on Iris. "There'll be nothing left for the Italians to take here anyway. Let them plough the rocky plateaus. We're going to be rich on Saarland soil!"

$\sim$

They had five weeks to make their decision, but with Bernd's return, the dam broke. Florian and she left the boys in the *Stube* to catch up and went upstairs to their bedroom. Their discussion was short.

"I want to be where we are safe," were Florian's first words. "Where we are respected. Where we have a chance at a good life. Where I can provide for my family without the government breaking my back."

"What do I have to do, to say, to convince you to stay?"

Florian's face crumpled, and he shrugged.

"The writing is on the wall," he said. "We're going to lose the farm, and frankly"—he pointed to the window outside—"half the people in this valley have disappointed me so much that I don't really feel the need to fight for them. Katharina, you wanted your family back together. Moving to Germany, that's how we keep everyone together."

She went to her side of the bed, crawled beneath the sheets with her clothes on, and told him to turn off the light. A part of her was dying. The other was saying he was right. She closed her eyes and sank into a disturbing sleep.

In the morning she put on her mucking boots and joined Florian and the boys in the stable. She filled the stalls with fresh hay. A few minutes later Alois and Jutta showed up to collect her.

Alois called out and waved to Bernd. "We have to extend the *Stammtisch*, Bernd. Everyone's coming to Father Wilhelm's party. And Hans has to bring some extra chairs from his attic. You should tell him to bring an extra chair for you." Alois smiled broadly at Katharina, his eyes squinting behind his glasses. "Even Bernd came for Father Wilhelm's party."

Florian deposited two milking cans outside the stable door and gently took the pitchfork out of Katharina's hands. "Go on. I'll finish this and come down later." He rubbed her upper arm. "One thing at a time."

Katharina followed Jutta and Alois down to Graun. The air

smelled of snow and dead leaves. There was a bright-blue sky, and the sun provided a fake sense of warmth that did not quite reach beneath the skin, especially after the heat of the animals in the barn. By tomorrow they would have another layer of snow.

She took in Alois's manly gait. Ever since he'd moved up to Arlund and now helped Hans with the sheep and his farm, he seemed to have blossomed with a new independence. It made her smile.

"I know a joke," Alois said suddenly. "I heard it from one of the border guards."

Katharina could not imagine it would be appropriate.

"I certainly hope you were not the joke," Jutta said.

"All right," Katharina ventured. "Tell us."

"In German or Italian?"

"German," Jutta said.

Alois giggled. "A Tyrolean woman is walking along the Adige River—"

"The Etsch," Jutta corrected.

"The Etsch. And she wants to get to the other side, but there are no rocks, no wood, and no bridge. On the other side of the river she sees another Tyrolean woman and says, '*Scusi*, how do I get to the other side? I cannot find a bridge, I cannot find any rocks, and there is no wood to cross over.' The other Tyrolean woman scratches her head and—"

"Why does it have to be a Tyrolean woman?" Jutta said. "You tell jokes in Italian that make fun of us?"

They crossed the road to enter town. Katharina waved at Sebastiano near the miller's, but he did a double take when he saw Jutta, hunched into his coat, and walked swiftly away. She threw Jutta a knowing look.

"You really did him in, didn't you?"

Jutta rolled her eyes. "I'll apologise to him tonight."

They came upon the town hall. Katharina stopped in her tracks. "Would you look at that?"

They stared up at the red-black-white swastika flag hanging from the left window of the town hall. Below it was a sign that read Official German Immigration and Repatriation Office.

Alois shuffled between them. "Can I finish the joke now?"

Absentmindedly, Katharina said, "How does it end?"

"'*Scusi*,' says the first Tyrolean woman. 'How do I get to the other side?' The other Tyrolean woman scratches her head and says"—Alois stepped in front of them and threw his arms out to the side—"'but you are on the other side!'"

"Option one or option two," Jutta muttered. "*Basta*."

23

INNSBRUCK, NOVEMBER 1939

It took weeks for Annamarie to put her things in order for her trip to Innsbruck. Annamarie and Sepp had waited for Riefenstahl to return to Berlin, to somehow pick up the pieces and explain how everything had shattered, but when she did not return, neither Annamarie nor Sepp heard from her. Charlotte met them one day and Annamarie learned that Leni had hurried back to Poland to take part in the victory parade. Annamarie gaped at the photos of Riefenstahl and Hitler together—Leni in her element as part of the Führer's entourage—as if nothing the horrors they'd all witnessed together had never happened.

Afterwards, when Annamarie, Sepp, and Charlotte met for coffee, they could not understand it. Had Riefenstahl informed the Führer about what his Wehrmacht soldiers were up to? That was all the woman had talked about during that last leg of the trip to Warsaw. *Wait until our Führer hears about this!* Charlotte suggested Riefenstahl had done exactly that, told the Führer, who had likely had those soldiers disciplined.

"That has to be it," Charlotte said with finality.

Annamarie and Sepp looked at each other, and Annamarie decided she did not care. She was going home, and Sepp was coming with her, and they could leave this behind them. At least for a while. Everyone was saying the war wouldn't last long anyway. And the timing was right either way. Sepp had to move out of the dormitories at the university, and Annamarie's own room at the boarding house would soon be occupied by someone else. She was running out of funds, and Charlotte suggested the two of them do what they needed to do—she would stay in touch and inform them when Riefenstahl might continue with the *Lowlands* film.

As much as Annamarie was anxious to get back to the Reschen Valley, it was clear that Sepp and she had to make a stopover in Innsbruck. Their citizenship vote was one thing they wanted to take care of, but it was Sepp who insisted that Annamarie meet with Lisi. With a stopover of some four hours in Innsbruck, he argued it was a good opportunity as any to do so.

"I want to see her," he insisted. "And you should find closure with what happened to Veronika and Lisi. And let's not forget Max's role as well."

He didn't say it, but Annamarie also had to officially give up her position at Division Five. That would mean facing Margit too.

The day they left Berlin, Annamarie was so anxious she could not eat breakfast. The coffee only soured her stomach more. Sepp dozed as Annamarie read the newspaper, surprised to find how much of what was written felt so wrong, so inaccurate, compared to what she had experienced within the Reich. The propaganda reminded her of a time when she'd had to prepare a presentation in school about Dante. He was Italy's national hero to the generations before her, and hardly any of her classmates in the Reschen Valley cared.

But her mother had helped put together the costume. Her father helped build the props. Annamarie even borrowed something from Bernd, though she could not remember what, only that an argument had ensued. The day before her presentation, Annamarie's mother popped her head into her bedroom and asked whether Annamarie was nervous.

"The students don't know anything about Dante anyway," Annamarie had replied. "So all I have to do is make it entertaining."

"Are you sure you've prepared for everything?"

Annamarie had thrown the covers over her head. "What they don't know, they won't miss."

Except that her teacher had found the presentation lacking in factual and historical content. Her classmates, on the other hand, had delighted in Annamarie's storytelling performance. She became the most popular student for months afterwards.

At the German border, Annamarie lowered the newspaper and Sepp opened one eye. "What they don't know, they won't miss," she said.

He frowned a little and closed his eyes, tucking his hands beneath his armpits. "That's very profound."

Annamarie smiled to herself.

A few hours later, they disembarked in Innsbruck, gathering the cases containing their possessions. Sepp straddled two of them and looked at the clock.

"You want to do this then?" he asked. "Here?"

Annamarie waved at a porter, who came with a cart. "I do. Let's put these into storage, buy our tickets for the afternoon train, but I want to get myself stamped out of the Reich for good."

Sepp paid the porter a few coins after he rolled into the station's lobby and left the cases near the check-in counter. "What if your parents don't vote Italian?"

Annamarie threw him a dubious look. "There is no way they will leave home. No way. Besides, my father sold his house in Nuremberg. He'll give in to my mother and stay."

They purchased their tickets and stepped out onto the city street and walked to the immigration office. Annamarie and Sepp requested the white form, and after she filled hers out, she handed it back to the officer behind the desk. He took it, his face a mask. Neither approval nor disapproval. And why should he have any opinion at all? Rome and Berlin were in the same pot of soup. If Sepp was right, all of Europe was in the Führer's gunsights and Italy was holding the rifle steady. But Sepp had instilled in her an even stronger urge to return home and the conviction that they needed to register as Italians.

She watched as the Tyrolean official stamped her form, signed it, and handed that and her passport back.

"You'll need both of those to cross into Italy," he said.

"What if I change my mind?"

His eyes pierced her, though the rest of him remained straight faced. "Then do it now."

She turned to Sepp. "Your turn."

Sepp handed him a white form as well, and the man hardly reviewed it. *Stamp. Stamp. Stamp.* Sepp held his documents again and grinned uncertainly at Annamarie.

"Enjoy Italy," the official said flatly.

Annamarie picked up her case and followed Sepp out the building. They had a while before they were to meet Lisi in the Hof Garten café. Making their way to the market, Annamarie braced herself for the next big question, but it wasn't until she was paying for a bouquet of white mums and white roses that he asked.

"What are we going to tell Lisi?"

To her annoyance, Annamarie's stomach lurched. "I think you should tell her whatever it is you feel comfortable telling her."

Annamarie and I have become very close. Annamarie and I are growing intimate. Annamarie and I are holding on to each other and trying to make sense of what we witnessed in Poland.

Sepp cocked his head, his eyes on the bouquet. "Lisi and I were never anything, you know. I adore her. I worship her. I care about her deeply. But don't misconstrue that as romantic love."

He slid a finger beneath Annamarie's chin, lifted it, and kissed her cheek.

"The question is," he murmured, "what are *you* going to tell her?"

Annamarie pressed the bouquet to herself. He was fishing. "Nothing. You told me to let her talk and I should only listen."

Sepp smiled. "Yeah, that was my suggestion, but you have a mind of your own."

When they arrived at the café, the Franciscan church bells tolled ten. One quick look at the tables and Annamarie could see Lisi had not yet arrived. Sepp chose a spot in the sun, pulled his coat tighter around him, and ordered two coffees. The bouquet smelled sickly sweet.

When a woman with a pram appeared next to the table, the first thing Annamarie saw was the baby. Strawberry-blond fuzz. Inquisitive blue eyes. And a wide, bright smile. Not lopsided like his father's, but straight and honest and pure. Karl Rainer. But Lisi was right—he was a Charlie.

Annamarie then looked up and registered the new Elisabeth Rainer.

She wore a dark-green coat and a black scarf, and her face was fuller. Her gorgeous auburn hair had been forced into a style that made Lisi look like she'd taken on the role of a matron. She had changed in countless other ways, but the pearl necklace around her throat might as well have been a symbol of her incarceration. Elisabeth von Brandt had transformed into the kind of woman Annamarie had always pictured Margit would become. It was eerie.

Sepp rose and hugged Lisi tightly, but her posture remained rigid. Annamarie also stood and Lisi offered her a cool, gloved hand in black leather before withdrawing it quickly. Sepp pulled out a chair, and Lisi seated herself, one hand still on the pram. The baby gurgled and waved a rattle in his fist.

"So this is Charlie." Lisi's look darted to Annamarie and back to the table.

"He's a beautiful boy," Sepp said. He cleared his throat and called the waitress over. He ordered for Lisi before turning back to her. "Your son is really—"

"Stop trying to make me feel better," Lisi said briskly. Once again she barely looked at Annamarie, but Annamarie sensed she was pleading, almost desperate. "I can't bear this. I really can't. Please tell me you are both staying here in Innsbruck. I have nobody."

Annamarie sat back in her chair. "We're on our way home. To South Tyrol. Our train leaves at one."

"We can stay a day or two, Lisi." Sepp reached over the table and grasped Annamarie's fingers. "Can't we?"

Lisi stared at their hands for a moment, then smiled so sadly, Annamarie pulled her hand away.

"I see," Lisi said. "Is that true?"

Sepp squirmed in his seat. "We have tickets."

"Lisi," Annamarie began. She wanted to tell her to be normal. To be herself. "What is it that we can do?"

Charlie gurgled and shook in the pram. Lisi lifted him out just as the waitress brought their coffees and thick slices of apple strudel with a pot of cream. In Lisi's lap now, Charlie twisted about this way and that as his mother fussed over him.

Her smile was strained, her eyes agitated. "You know, I'd actually always pictured you, Sepp, being godfather to my children. Charlie's baptism is on Sunday. You should be there. Both of you. Naturally, Maximilian said there was no other choice but Fritz and Margit as godparents."

"You know I could not come," Annamarie said icily.

Lisi's smile disappeared. "No. Of course not. Of course I couldn't ask you to do that. What was I thinking?" She looked pleadingly at Sepp. "My husband is heading for Berlin on

Monday. I'll be alone. You two could come and stay with me for a week or two. God, Sepp. I have no life left. And my friends—since Veronika's disappearance—have all abandoned me. Like you."

Sepp now grasped Lisi's arm. "I did not abandon you. You know why I had to leave."

Lisi shifted the baby. "Everyone fears me."

Sepp chuckled gently. "They've always somehow feared you, Lisi."

Lisi shifted toward Annamarie, her expression contorted. "Would you have married him?"

Annamarie squeezed her eyes shut, held her breath.

"You would have, I think," Lisi said softly. "I imagine Sepp has told you everything."

Annamarie opened her eyes, but the tears rose anyway. When she spoke, it came out in a strained whisper. "I'm sorry. I'm so terribly, terribly, terribly sorry." She dabbed at her eyes with the napkin. "I'm sorry for everything, Lisi. For all the lying. For the mistrust. For not asking why you were being so distant with me. For not knowing that you were in such pain. I can't even imagine…" God, she loved her. Lisi had saved her when she arrived in Innsbruck, and Annamarie loved her.

Lisi sniffled and bounced Charlie in her lap. "Obviously neither of us had as wild an imagination as we'd believed." She turned to Sepp. "What about you? Did you have that kind of plot line in your head for us? For us all here?"

Sepp hung his head.

Lisi looked off toward the garden, her face a mask. "This is it, then."

"It's not," Annamarie insisted. "It really is not." When Lisi did not respond, Annamarie toyed with her spoon. Nobody had touched their coffee or their cake. "I have to go to Margit and tell her I'm not taking the job at the division. What I really want to do is give her a piece of my mind."

Lisi scoffed. "I'm really surprised that you won't take the position. It was what you were living for."

Annamarie shook her head. "Not after Poland."

"What Sepp wrote to me, it's... Annamarie, it's my fault that you got involved. I curse the day I introduced you to the Rainers..."

"I chose to go. I wanted to earn money. I thought it was the only way to get to what I wanted. Harmless, right?"

"Harmless," Lisi said in a low voice. "Nothing about this regime is harmless. Veronika simply disappeared. I can't get any information. Number one, my *husband*"—she said the word as if it were acid in her mouth—"has forbidden me to go anywhere near the police station or the Gestapo. Before the baby, I was there every day. They made me sit and wait and told me they had no information on her."

Charlie reached for Lisi's water glass, and his mother shifted the baby away. Sepp put his hand up, and Charlie grabbed his pinkie and held it.

"You want to hold him?" Lisi suddenly asked. "I mean, you don't have to. Only if you want to."

Sepp took the baby and cradled Charlie against his chest. "We won't get another train to Nauders until Monday. Annamarie? Is that all right with you?"

Annamarie agreed. They drank their lukewarm coffees and hurried with their pastries and paid the bill, and Annamarie took Charlie from Sepp to help get him back into the pram. When Lisi finished tucking him in, she reached for Annamarie. The embrace was long, and Annamarie tightened her hold, sighing.

Later, they walked through the garden, leaves blowing across the gravel paths. The smell of winter laced the air, but the sun shone, and the crisp air revived Annamarie. Sepp pushed the pram ahead of her, the mums and roses on top of the carriage.

"Thanks for agreeing to stay for a little while," Lisi said, kicking at the leaves.

"How are you managing with Maximilian?"

"When someone is ashamed, Annamarie, it's easy to manipulate them. The trouble is, I am also deeply ashamed, and Maximilian is the first to smell weakness. So you can imagine how it is."

Annamarie remained silent.

Lisi laughed softly. "Look at Sepp, navigating that pram. He's so fearless. So...you and Sepp?"

Annamarie bit her lip. "We share that tragedy in Poland, you understand?" She had not told Sepp how she felt about him—did not know herself really, and her reluctance to share her musings with Lisi surprised her. Before Poland, Annamarie would have gushed about her insecurities, told tales, or at least called attention to herself in some way. Now, she did not want it. Now, all she wanted was an intimacy that belonged only to Sepp and herself.

"Sepp is a very good person," Lisi said firmly. "Loyal. Smart. Kind. And resourceful. He'll make you the best person you can be. I always believed that."

Annamarie took Lisi's hand in hers. "Who ever thought?"

Lisi squeezed. "Who ever thought?"

Sepp turned around briefly and smiled before pushing on through the garden.

"Are you going to be okay?"

"Yeah," Lisi said. "I'm going to be okay. I'm an actress, you know? And this is just another role. That's what I keep telling myself."

As promised, Sepp found Annamarie and himself a place to stay until the following Monday, with old friends from the State Theatre. On Friday, Annamarie made her way to the BDM headquarters. She would make her resignation official, and not just to Division Five.

Margit sat at her desk and was on the telephone when Annamarie stepped inside. Margit put a hand over the receiver, stared at Annamarie, then quickly excused herself and hung up.

"Annamarie!" She rose, but her look was wary. "I heard you're back."

Annamarie's blood raced, but she forced a smile. "I am."

"Good, good." Margit folded her hands before her. "Are you here to see about your job?"

"I'm here to visit Lisi."

Margit's expression wavered and then became unreadable again.

"I've also come to tell you that I'm returning to South Tyrol. Home. And then there is this…" Annamarie retrieved her party card from her bag, her BDM badge that she had unstitched from the good blouse, and the other badges and paraphernalia. She placed them on the desk one by one.

Margit's eyebrows arched before she lowered herself into her chair. "So that's it, then?"

"Yes."

"You'll live to regret it. Good day."

Annamarie hesitated. That could not be all. But Margit wrote something on a pad of paper and lifted the receiver again, then cast Annamarie a questioning look. "Is there anything else?"

"No." Annamarie turned and left. She had no idea whether to feel relief or fear.

After they crossed the Reschen Pass and had a view of Reschen Lake, Sepp pointed out the window of the bus. "What's all that?"

The heavy machinery in and around the river and lake, the

excavators, and the red-tipped wooden posts caught Annamarie off guard.

"They're building some kind of reservoir." She pointed to Graun Lake on the horizon. "They're going to connect those two lakes."

"And the plateau? All these fields?"

"Under water."

Sepp blew softly. "Wow."

Annamarie considered how all these years she had given the impacts and the consequences so little thought. Now seeing it through Sepp's eyes, she imagined it all gone and her throat clenched. As the bus rolled past high hills of excavated earth, she could see it all now. This was another war here, and the tanks lined up for battle were already here in her valley in the form of all these massive machines. She turned her head to take it all in and did not face the front again until they reached St Katharina's church. The bus stopped at the Post Inn, and the doors folded open. Annamarie cautiously stepped onto her home soil for the first time in over a year and a half. The sundial on St Katharina's tower showed it was twenty past one. She looked at the inn.

"Some things," she said with relief, "simply don't change."

Sepp shifted his rucksack onto his left shoulder. "This is it?"

She pointed up the hillside just beyond. "Arlund is up there." But she led Sepp up the stairs to the inn, where they stood in the dim hallway. To her right, the door to the post office was locked tight. Next was Jutta Hanny's apartment door, followed by the staircase to the rooms upstairs. She'd hidden on the landing there once, spying on Marco and Angelo Grimani.

A din came from the door behind the empty registration desk, and Annamarie heard dishes clattering and could smell pears and sugar baking.

Across from Jutta Hanny's apartment was the door that led into the *Stube*. With Sepp following her, Annamarie pushed it open, and the heat from the tiled oven hit her face, dry and comforting. The round *Stammtisch* to her left was full. Empty soup bowls and breadcrumbs had been shoved to the edge of the table to make room for the cards.

The first person Annamarie recognised was Hans Glockner, the biggest man at the table, with the bushiest beard. He barely glanced up from his hand of cards, did a double take and put the hand down. Everyone looked up then: Martin Noggler, Walter Plangger, and Sebastiano Foglio, who nearly knocked over his chair as he leapt up.

"Annamarie?" he cried.

Jutta came bustling out of the kitchen with a steaming pot of something, with Alois behind her carrying a basket of bread. "Who wants another helping of—" She stopped in her tracks, and Alois nearly ran into her.

The chatter began.

"Where have you been?"

"How did you get here?"

"When did you arrive?"

"Do your parents know you're here?"

"Can we take you up to Arlund?"

Annamarie tried to answer their questions, tried to introduce Sepp, and the moment she pointed him out to the group, heads bobbed up and down, examining him from head to toe followed by gazes directed back to her, then to him, and back to her. Deciding the community would make their own assessments, she ignored them and pulled a chair out and had Sepp sit down as everyone made room for them.

Jutta sent Alois to fetch two bowls.

"We've just come from Innsbruck." Annamarie poured herself a glass of water from the pitcher. She handed it to Sepp. "And Berlin. Sepp and I here...we heard about the Option. We came back. We're Italian now."

By the way their eyes dropped, the way their breathing stilled, Annamarie had to set her glass on the table.

"What?" she scoffed. "Don't tell me you're all choosing to be German citizens."

Sepp reached for her hand under the table.

Hans spoke slowly, as was his way. "We've still got a few weeks. Not all of us have made up our minds."

Martin Noggler's face flushed, and Annamarie noted the silver strands amongst the copper hair.

"I'm leaving. Thomas and his family too," he said.

But Walter Plangger's conviction sounded stronger. "We too."

Annamarie looked at Sebastiano, and he gave the slightest shake of his head. Of course he and the rest of the Foglio family were staying.

She squeezed Sepp's hand, afraid to know the answer to her next question. "How many are choosing to leave?"

Jutta sat down next to Hans. Annamarie spotted a thin gold band on her ring finger. So the two of them had finally done it and gotten married.

"About seventy percent so far," Jutta said softly.

Annamarie covered her mouth. "So many?"

Sepp looked around the table. "Why?"

Everyone looked agitated.

Sebastiano stood up. "I need to go. Good to see you all."

The men muttered their goodbyes.

Sebastiano hovered near Annamarie. "A lot has happened since you were last here." He threw Sepp a glance. "A lot."

Annamarie turned back to the rest of the group at the table. "Where are you all going, those who are leaving?"

Everyone around the table remained still until Jutta said sharply, "You men let me know if I've got it wrong. The Leavers are returning to the fold, so to speak. Following resettlement—how was it that Hofer and the Tyrolean People's League put it?" She feigned to be searching her memory. "Yes, following resettlement, German life on the banks of the Eisack"—she looked at Sepp at the mention of his home territory—"and the Etsch will be no more."

"We'll be resettled as a unified group," Martin Noggler said. "Hofer and our representatives—"

"Your representatives," Jutta huffed.

Hans moved as if to shield his wife.

Noggler was not deterred. "Hofer will examine the regions that the Reich is putting at our disposal for resettlement."

"Is that so?" Jutta said, her voice higher than normal. "Have you seen any of this territory? Have they been anywhere to actually look?"

"It will be beautiful," Walter Plangger said. "Possibly even more beautiful than here. And so much land, they're saying, that even our fourth sons will have farms of their own."

"Poppycock," Jutta shouted.

Annamarie regretted starting this. "What about my parents?"

Jutta made a noise and clamped her mouth shut.

Hans shrugged. "No decision yet. Like I said, we've got a few weeks yet."

The tension at the table was so thick, she pictured needing a saw to cut through it. She glanced at Sepp, and his face was unreadable. They had made a mistake. They had assumed their people would never choose to leave. And people who once seemed to be like-minded were now divided. This was new.

Annamarie nudged Sepp subtly, and he stirred. They should leave before anyone asked what their experiences in the German Reich would be. The discussion would be too hot to handle.

They said goodbye, and Annamarie asked Jutta about the next bus to Meran, where Sepp would then find a connection to his valley. It was coming on Wednesday, the day after next, which gave them a full day yet. Hans offered to bring up their boxes later, and Sepp and she headed out after thanking Jutta for the soup.

The hike did not take more than twenty minutes, but the trail was muddy from earlier rains. Everywhere she looked, Annamarie spotted wooden stakes with red paint on their tips. Ahead of them, smoke rose from the Ritsches' chimney. The closer they got, the more effervescent her insides felt. Before reaching the Katharinahof, Annamarie paused at the walnut tree. They were just around the corner from the house. A few steps and she would be in the front yard. Sepp gazed at her patiently.

"I'm scared."

"Take your time."

Annamarie took in a breath, shook her head. "I have to do this —now or never."

It was Manuel she saw first, outside the workshop, winding rope. He was twice the size he'd been when she'd last seen him. He lifted his head as Annamarie and Sepp crossed the space between the tree and the fountain out front. He cried out her name, and the rope slipped from his hands and coiled onto the ground.

Throwing her arms around her baby brother—now taller than her—Annamarie laughed.

"Mani." She grinned. "You're practically a full-grown man!"

She introduced him to Sepp, and then Manuel called to the rest of the family.

Annamarie's father stepped out of the workshop. Bernd hurried out from the stable, frowning, and Annamarie gaped at her brother. How was he home? When her mother—at last— came out from the house, a German shepherd puppy nipped at her heels.

A new chorus of questions, even more joyful than the last, followed. Why had Annamarie not informed them she was coming? How did they get here? Who was Sepp? This last question was asked more cautiously.

"Sepp..." She searched for his hand. "Sepp is a very dear friend. We were in Innsbruck together, and in Berlin by chance. We..."

Her family waited, and when she did not say anything more, her father opened his arms once more.

"We're so very glad you're here, Annamarie." Her father started to dust off the discomfort. "Sepp, you're welcome—"

"We stopped at the immigration office," Annamarie burst out. She had their attention now in either case. "Sepp and I, well, we were up in Poland. After the invasion, that is. And when we returned to Berlin, we decided it would be for the best to change our citizenship to Italian."

Mother burst into tears. Florian shuffled and cleared his throat.

Predictably, Bernd made the most noise. "Should have known. Why would she even ask her family what they were planning to do?"

"Surely you are not even thinking of resettling to Germany?" Annamarie said. "Mother? You're the last person in the world I would expect..."

Sepp placed a hand on Annamarie's arm.

"We're losing the farm anyway." Her mother rubbed her eyes.

One look at her father and Annamarie knew it was he who was taking control of the situation.

"It's not just the reservoir, right?" Manuel said. "Bernd would be released from the GIL if the family chooses to resettle."

"Let's go inside," her father said. "Sepp, please. You're welcome. Come inside."

Annamarie followed everyone in but felt like pulling out her hair.

Her father stopped her and embraced her, whispering, "You've been old enough to know your mind long ago. You do what you think is right. I have to make decisions for the rest of my family." He pulled away, jerking his head toward Sepp, who was already being served with something to drink. "Is he a good man?"

Annamarie swallowed and nodded. Her father clapped her on

the shoulder and drew him to her, steering her to the table. Little had changed in the house, but Annamarie felt as if she were amongst strangers.

Somehow Annamarie got through supper, and when her mother showed Sepp to Manuel's bedroom, and Annamarie went to her own room, she was happy to shut herself in. She threw herself onto the bed, devastated. She remembered the immigration guard telling her that if she was going to change her mind, she should do it now. He had not been serious. She could still—she could remain with her family. But the last thing Sepp had told her was that under no circumstances—regardless what his family chose—was he going back to the Reich.

"And I hope you feel the same, Annamarie," he'd said. "I hope you… You know? Together, we could…"

But then her mother came with fresh bed linens.

What if Riefenstahl should call? Or Charlotte, to inform Annamarie that there was another chance waiting in the film industry? Would she go back then? Annamarie threw herself onto her stomach, scooping the huge feathered pillow to her. There was the rustling sound of paper. She patted around the headboard, and her hand landed on something. She sat up and lifted the pillow to find an envelope beneath, addressed to her. Annamarie recognised her mother's handwriting.

She folded her legs beneath her and held the envelope in both hands, her heart thudding dully. She was not sure she was ready for a confession. She turned it over. The envelope was sealed. She pulled at the right edge, then slid her finger beneath it before removing the pages.

Dear Annamarie,

It is with great sadness that I write this to a house empty of you. You are everywhere I look. I picture you at the stove, daydreaming, dressed up in some new costume and scalding the milk. I miss the laughter you brought into these rooms. I even miss coming in from my chores and finding that you have once again taken flight. The difference is, I always knew you would return. Now, I am no longer certain. But that is not why I am grieving. I am grieving over the lost chance I had to hold you in my arms, to dispel all your doubts and fears, your pain and disappointments. To let you know that what happened was never your fault and that I have failed you in the act of trying to protect you. I have heaped this shame upon you by hiding the truth from you.

Many years ago, I wrote a letter that I had decided to keep for you. It was not addressed to you. It was addressed to Angelo Grimani, and it would have been my way to share my story, and his story, and eventually your story with you. But after you left us, and after rereading that letter, I realised how tremendously trite it would come across to you. It would also have been a cowardly act not to face you and tell you the story. You have suffered so much loss, and I know that you must believe that we hold a grudge, or anger, or disappointment in you. We do not. Your father and I regret nothing. I love Florian, and I have great respect for Minister Grimani, but it is Florian who is your father and always has been. And it is most important for you to know that both of these men only wish the best for you. Florian and I wish you true happiness, the security of family, and good health and fortune. You are my daughter. You will always be, no matter where you are or what path you choose.

I am and always will be,

Your Mother

Annamarie closed her eyes, but the tears spilled over.

At the sound of a soft knock, she pressed the pages to her and swiped at her face. It had to be Sepp.

"Not now," she choked.

But it was her mother's voice on the other side. "May I come in?"

Annamarie said nothing, and her mother appeared in the

doorway. She glanced at the letter in Annamarie's hands before closing the door softly behind her.

"I didn't think you would find it so soon," Mother said. "I imagined that one day you might return, and that—like last time —you would be gone before I could share anything with you."

Annamarie felt a sense of calm come over her. She sat up straighter. "Did you ever write to him about me?"

"I wrote to him. But not about you at first. I was…I was forced to write to him in an official capacity. For the valley."

"About the reservoir?"

Her mother nodded.

"And when did you finally tell him about me?"

Her mother moved to the bed. "Not until you were in Bolzano. That's when I asked for his help and, I pleaded with him to accept some semblance of responsibility. At least help me find you."

Annamarie placed the letter off to the side as her mother lowered herself onto the edge of the mattress.

"Everything in that letter is true. It is what is in my heart."

"I need time."

"Time," her mother said wistfully. "Yes. I wish we had more of that."

Shifting to face her better, Annamarie grasped her mother's hands. "For the love of God, I cannot go back to Germany. And neither should you."

Her mother took in a deep breath. "We'll lose Bernd to the military."

"You'll lose him to the Wehrmacht."

"What's happened to you, child?" Her mother brushed a hair away, and Annamarie leaned into her hand.

"So much."

"Then begin at the beginning."

Annamarie drew in a shaky breath. She pulled in her knees, hugged the pillow to herself, and told her mother everything.

The next morning, her mother awoke her early. Annamarie sat up, the room still dark. Her mother switched on the lamp on the bedside table. Her father was also standing there, in the middle of the room, looking stern.

"Tell him, Annamarie. Tell him what you told me."

That afternoon Annamarie left Sepp at the *Hof* to walk down to Graun with her mother and father. Inside the town hall, her father knocked on the secretary's door. Inside, behind a row of tables and chairs, were two men, one dressed in German garb, the other in Italian. Several townspeople Annamarie recognised were at the tables, huddled over their documents, though it could not be made more obvious what each family was choosing. Four red forms. One white.

Annamarie's father handed the German officer the red form out of his coat pocket. She saw that it was already filled out.

"I want to change," he said in a low whisper to the official.

Four heads popped up behind the tables, and pencils stopped scratching. Annamarie stared until each of them looked away. Except for one. The banker's son, Marius.

"Are you staying, Steinhauser?" he called cautiously.

"Are you certain you want to change, Herr Steinhauser?" the German officer asked.

"We're sure," Annamarie's mother snapped. "Give him the proper form."

The Italian secretary offered Annamarie's father the white form.

Without answering, Father took a seat and began writing. Annamarie and her mother stood over his shoulder.

"What does this mean for our son Bernd?" he asked after he had finished.

The secretary shrugged. "He must go back to the military academy."

Annamarie jumped when Prefect Ghirardelli popped his head

through the door. He gazed at her father, then his eyes darted to the document in the Italian secretary's hand.

"Everything all right in here?" he asked.

The German official looked away.

"Steinhauser"—the secretary pointed—"wants to be Italian."

Ghirardelli's left eyebrow cocked, the tassel on his fez shaking. "Benito will have to go back to the GIL."

"After New Year's." Annamarie's mother turned on Ghirardelli, hands on her hips. "He can go after the final results are in. He knows, he understands, and we will comply. But"—and she punctuated each word—"we are staying."

Annamarie moved to stand next to her mother, crossed her arms, and gazed at Ghirardelli. "That's right. And my brother's name is Bernd. Italian or not, that is his Christian name."

The next day Annamarie walked back to Graun with Sepp. Sadly, she watched as the bus drew up to the Post Inn. Sepp turned to her, embraced her, and kissed her before drawing her against him again. He felt like a safe haven.

"I have no idea what's ahead of us," he muttered into her hair in Italian. "I'm going to check with my family, do the same as you and get them to stay if I can. Then I'm going to Rome. I'll see if I can get started there, and as soon as I can, I'll send for you. I'll send for you, *d'accordo*?"

She could not answer.

"I'm going to miss you," he sighed. "I really am."

I love you.

When his bus pulled away, Annamarie watched it until it disappeared on the road south, then she turned to Graun Lake. She walked along its shore until the cold wind froze her tears dry.

24

BOLZANO, DECEMBER 1939

T wo words in the message. *She's here.*

Katharina had kept her promise to keep Angelo informed of Annamarie's whereabouts. When he responded, asking whether he should travel to see her, Katharina's reply came straight away: *There is much to get through before Annamarie would be ready to face you.* In other words, not a good idea.

From his office, he sent a telex saying he understood, but once he'd sent the message, he decided he would travel to the valley either way and around the new year. He and Ghirardelli had reassessments to make, the appropriation letters to argue about with the engineering corps. There would be details to discuss with the committee, plans to put back into place after the resettlement vote. He and MFE had already received provisional authorisation to begin with the construction of the dam. *Avanti gallopi*—urgently, without delay.

Besides, if children were left to decide when they were ready to confront the adults who had pained them, nothing would ever happen. Angelo was determined to meet his daughter, to discover who she was, and to apologise.

Miss Medici buzzed him. "Signora Grimani is here."

Angelo frowned. "My mother?"

"No, Minister. Your…"

My ex-wife. "Send her in."

Chiara had never come to his office, not even when they were married. He went to the door to open it, but she beat him to it. She was dressed in a navy-blue wool coat, cream-coloured leather gloves, pleated navy-blue woollen trousers, and boots. She looked as if she were in uniform, prepared to lead a battle.

He took Chiara's coat and led her to a seat. She looked around the office.

"It's nice here," she said. "Very modern."

Angelo nodded. "How are you?"

"Fine, Angelo. I came to tell you that I am leaving Bolzano to accompany Michael Innerhofer and a delegation of the Tyrolean People's League to Rome."

"Really? The Tyrolean People's League? Sounds suspiciously like the German League reinvented."

"Right you are," she said. "Count Rath is the head, with Susi at his side."

Angelo's masked his surprise. "The count and countess are back?"

He wondered what Susi was like now. He had not seen her in years, and as annoying as she could be, he did find her entertaining. Count Edmond Rath was another issue altogether. He was an earnest man, and Angelo could imagine the politician was looking for a way to slip into a greater position of power.

"Edmond is running things from Innsbruck, and"—Chiara leaned forward—"he says all this information about resettling the South Tyroleans to the colonies in the south? It's coming from Berlin. From their Ministry of Propaganda. Rome must understand what the consequences will be if Il Duce does not take any action and put a stop to these rumours. Mussolini must make an official announcement. Over sixty-five percent have voted for resettlement so far."

Angelo rubbed a hand over his head. He had not even asked Katharina what the figures were like in the Reschen Valley. He suddenly wondered whether the Steinhausers were really able to keep the committee together at all.

"Chiara, I'll be attending the city Christmas party. Is there anything I can do?"

She narrowed her eyes. "Mastromattei will be there. Nobody trusts him anymore. Look what he did."

"But Mastromattei announced that nobody will be deported south."

"His denials," Chiara said indignantly, "are having the opposite effect. Look what he did to the people in the Reschen Valley. When they did not take up his offers the way he'd hoped, what did the magistrate do? He simply removed the proposal from the table like a child with a temper tantrum. And the water rights notifications? The details about the barracks and the roads and everything the people had every right to examine and question? They staked out the ground before anybody had accepted the letters of intent! No. Mastromattei has lost any credibility he might have once had. And he's done this all across the province. Nobody knows where the man stands."

Chiara folded her hands. "Angelo, if we're to have any hope of preventing the loss of a quarter of a million Tyroleans, then Il Duce must dispel the rumours. He has to assure the Tyroleans that they are safe here."

Angelo had to agree. "And Marco?"

"I'm picking him up in Rome, and he'll come back with me for Christmas. I wanted to ask whether you would please check on my father on a regular basis."

"Pietro? Of course. Thank you for asking."

She fidgeted with her purse. "I know you have to be careful. I know you have to keep up appearances. But we need information."

"I'll see what I can find out at the party. I'm certain the Option will be all anyone talks about."

Chiara nodded and again looked as if she were prepared to leave.

"Annamarie has returned to the valley," he said cautiously.

She pressed her lips together and seemed to be holding her breath. "Will you see her?"

Angelo shrugged. "I'd like to, but... Anyway, not yet."

Chiara looked around the office once more, her expression turning curious. "Angelo, do you..."

She was looking at the photo from the Gleno dam break. Stefano Accosi might have taken that photo, but Angelo still kept it framed on his shelf, his constant reminder of where his principles now lay. She rose and went to it. What was she seeing? The river of mud? The remnants of the foundations where once stone houses had stood? The horse turned over on the cart?

She turned back to him. "Do you still have those nightmares you once told me about? The one where you always felt there was someone who needed saving?"

He shook his head. "Not for a long time. Haven't thought about it, anyway, in a very long time."

She came back to his desk and folded her arms. "There is the matter of Christmas. Have you plans?"

"No."

Chiara looked surprised for a split second, then smoothed her face. "Then come to Villa Adige. It will just be the three of us, and my father, of course. Angelo, it might be his last."

"Pietro's?"

She nodded, and her cheeks turned bright pink, the way they did when she was trying to keep from crying.

"What about Marco?" he asked softly. "He's not going to be thrilled."

"We are his parents, Angelo. We know what's best for our children." She sniffed. "You should go and see her. When you're ready, anyway. And with the parents' permission, of course."

It was not until after Chiara had left and he was packing his things to leave the office that he stopped and looked at the photo. The last time he'd had the nightmare—the lakes cracking, rising, the earth disappearing beneath the surface, the sense that he had to save someone—had been before he'd left Bolzano to search for Annamarie in the valley. Not once since then—not that he could remember—had the nightmare returned.

～

"Happy birthday, Angelo." Pietro waved a hand from the wheelchair as Angelo walked into the sitting room. The voice was weak, thin. It gave Angelo a start.

"You remembered?" He embraced the old man.

"Of course. I might be weak in body, but my mind…" Pietro smiled wanly. "Chiara reminded me."

Upstairs, hurried footsteps crossed the sitting room floor. Chiara would have to come down soon if she was to catch her train.

"Are you here to see them off?" Pietro asked.

"I thought I would. I also wanted to see you. I promised Chiara to keep an eye on you while she's away."

Pietro waved a dismissive hand just as he began to cough. He reached beneath the blanket over his lap and removed a kerchief. Angelo waited until the old man had wiped his mouth and tucked the kerchief away. Angelo had to agree with Chiara. This might well be the man's last Christmas, and he was touched that Chiara had invited him to join the family.

Michael Innerhofer appeared in the hallway and came in.

"Angelo, good to see you. Signor d'Oro, how are you feeling today?"

"What should I be feeling at my age and in my condition?" Pietro feigned annoyance. "Every day I am able to do less than the day before."

Michael shook the old man's hand. "I wanted to talk to Angelo here. Do you mind?"

"Status update?" Pietro asked.

"Afraid so." Michael winced. "Mind if I smoke?"

Pietro waved to the veranda doors. "Take that cigarette and the politics out there and keep me out of it. I've washed my hands of it all. Life is too short."

Smiling, Angelo followed Michael out. A light drizzle fell. The gardeners had cut the grapevines, and they were bare, lined up like a row of shrunken dwarves holding hands.

He turned to Michael. "Do you believe you're going to get an audience with Il Duce?"

"My hope is that Rome will understand the looming threat here. There is a distinct possibility that Il Duce will see that this will result in a depopulated region and one for which he will have to pay a fortune for."

"How so?"

Michael inhaled and waved his cigarette, blowing smoke towards the vineyard. "A fortune for property they received for free after the war. They will never see it revive and flourish as it is, not after they reimburse the citizens' assets at that ridiculous exchange rate the Nazis negotiated."

"I tried to talk to Mastromattei again."

Michael raised an eyebrow.

"I have the impression that he is conflicted." Angelo sighed. "He had his agenda, but when the foreign minister pulled him into that meeting in Berlin, I think Mastromattei realised what he was up against."

Michael leaned against the pillar and drew deeply before adding, "None of the decision-makers have any idea how serious the Tyroleans are about removing Rome's influence. Look what Germany's general consul predicted. One to two thousand would leave at most. That's what he said. Then Mastromattei added his ideas." Michael's voice went an octave lower. "Let's resettle the so-called fifth column, our magistrate said. Ten thousand Germans and ex-Austrians. Twenty to forty thousand undesirables. Hell, Angelo, undesirables? He probably meant me. God knows I've irked the man more than a few times."

Angelo chuckled appreciatively before turning serious once more. "He meant the blue- and white-collar workers."

"No. Priority number one are the criminals and white-collar workers first," Michael corrected. "Especially the intellectuals. They make the most noise, have the most contacts beyond the borders. Sure, Mastromattei needs the blue-collar workers to go too, because they are the easiest to replace with Italians from the south. But what about the farmers in the mountainous regions? Please tell me which Italian on the plains is going to want to farm rocky, steep land?"

"He never expected the farmers would vote to leave." Angelo stepped out of the way of Michael's flabbergasted exhale. "Look at it from Rome's standpoint, Michael. There are the economics to consider as well. Italy's goal is to redeem the resettlement assets with foreign exchange and free the assets that we've had frozen in Austria since the Anschluss."

"I do see the economics behind it." Michael bent and stubbed the cigarette against the veranda overhang and immediately lit a second one. "They're all beneath the bedsheets together. The German Reich is suffering a catastrophic shortage of foreign reserves, so they've targeted South Tyrol's assets in exchange for raw materials that Italy needs, and badly if we're to go to war. The Nazis are clever though, right? How they wheedled the foreign-exchange rate for the Reichsmark. It's unbelievable. One Reichsmark was worth almost eight lire—eight, Angelo!—and now it's four and a half."

"With a cap of one billion lire," Angelo reminded.

Michael snorted. "Yes. Sure, when you take the general consul's prediction seriously of only two thousand leaving. Maximum. But we have to add up Mastromattei's plan to raise that to sixty thousand. And the Reich's demand that the Tyroleans *all* leave, or you are a traitor to the Führer." Michael paced, shaking his head. "I did the math. Don't have to be an expert in Italian or German to be able to do that. Angelo, listen to this. If we have over one hundred sixty thousand South Tyroleans already choosing to resettle? One billion is not even one-fifteenth of the value of their assets. In fact, according to my calculations, and you know I'm right—you're dealing with these figures with the Reschen Valley as it is—it's closer to one-twentieth...one-twentieth!...of the estimated value of all assets for the German-speaking population." He stared at Angelo.

"And that's why you're going to Rome."

"That's why we're going to Rome."

"Mastromattei catches wind of this and he's going to feel undermined by this new Tyrolean People's League."

Michael laughed bitterly and shook his head. He scuffed the veranda's floorboards with his foot. "Yeah. And I hear you're going to a party."

"What makes you think Mastromattei will listen to me?"

Michael pointed the cigarette at him. "Not only Mastromattei. Tolomei. The Colonel. Everyone you can get to listen to you. Pit them against Göring, Himmler. They're the ones behind this mass exodus. I have it on good authority that Karl Wolff, the personal adjutant to Himmler, is doing whatever it takes to make sure everyone—and I mean everyone—is out of South Tyrol. He's aiming for one hundred percent. If he catches wind that we're on our way to Rome..." Michael winced.

"That will never happen."

"It can't happen."

"I'm wondering how I'm going to package all this at a political Christmas party," Angelo said.

"Present them with a gift they don't want."

He wasn't sure what the journalist meant.

Michael put the second cigarette out and held both stubs in

his palm. He weighed them in his hand before extending them to Angelo. "Unpack it for them. Twenty billion lire for a province they got for free? Not very sexy, is it?"

Angelo watched Castello Roncolo rise in the distance. The taxi turned onto the road that led to the fortification on the hilltop. Even from this distance, Angelo could see that the castle walls had been decorated in Christmas lights, and festive wreaths hung from the turrets. Torches lined along the outside added a medieval aura. As the automobile climbed the hill, he looked out the window to his left. The Talvera shimmered beneath the wintry moon as it slugged its way over icy stones. To his right, Gina was just a silhouette, and beyond her window, the Dolomites' Three Chimneys pressed up against the cold, starry sky.

Before the taxi reached the castle, Gina took his hand. "You're certain you want me by your side this evening?"

"Everyone knows about us anyway. My parents will have to come to terms with it. I've just turned fifty. Not old enough to be ornery but old enough to care less about what others think."

She faced ahead, but he saw her smile. "We're certainly going to give them something to talk about."

He doubted that. The only thing truly in the air was the Option. Their affair could very well be buried beneath it, at least among the politicians attending the party. Their wives, however, would certainly talk about Gina Conti seemingly "settled," and likely with some measure of relief.

Angelo paid the driver and stepped around to Gina's side of the vehicle. She took his hand, and one black-and-white stiletto followed the other. Instead of coming to his breastbone, she now stood as tall as his shoulder. He was still trying to decide whether he liked that. She had joked it would go easier on his half-century-old spine when he bent to kiss her.

They walked through the entrance and, after checking in their coats, were told to follow through to the inner courtyard. Angelo greeted familiar faces as he helped Gina out of her cloak, revealing her dress—a deceptively simple silhouetted black gown, with ribbed weave and a corded bodice. The collar was V shaped, and the sleeves notch capped. In her high heels, Gina looked magnificent.

As they entered the inner courtyard, they were surprised to find mounds of snow and ice that had obviously been brought down from the mountains and built up into a torchlit winter wonderland with flutes of champagne and Christmas punch lined up for the taking. He and Gina both chose a glass of champagne before entering the Great Hall. Candles and chandeliers, wreaths, baubles, and orchestra music hit Angelo's every sense, and he enjoyed it for the short moment before hearing his father's laugh.

In front of the enormous fireplace, the Colonel and Angelo's mother were standing with a group of well-dressed couples. The Colonel wore a smoking jacket instead of his usual military uniform, and once again Angelo realised how much his father had aged. As had his mother, but she was fighting it with all she had. She wore a glittering emerald dress with a sagging collar, and her hair had been done up to hide the silver by pinning orchids across her coif. She brought to mind an old china doll tossed into a corner. That was precisely his mother: in everything she ever did, her one objective was to outshine the neglect she had always felt in her marriage to the Colonel. Angelo loved his mother, felt sorry for her, and he was going to lose her without ever really knowing what had ever made her happy.

He glanced down at Gina. "Are you ready?"

"They're with Senator Tolomei," Gina said.

Now Angelo noticed the short silver-haired senator. He'd

been hidden by the Colonel's girth, but as Tolomei moved out of the circle to greet and pull Mastromattei into the round, Angelo now noted, "They're all in one place."

"Don your gloves," Gina muttered.

She floated next to him, hand outstretched to Tolomei before Angelo even stood abreast his father. She cornered the senator almost immediately. Angelo nodded respectfully to Mastromattei before kissing his mother's cheeks, but she was staring at Gina with such distaste, he thought she would spit. Meanwhile, Gina conducted rounds with the remainder of the party. When she landed at Mastromattei, Angelo's mother sniffed.

"She has four children, Angelo. It's scandalous really."

"They're all grown," he reminded her. *As am I.*

When Gina reached his mother, she coolly kissed the woman's cheeks.

"As I was saying," Tolomei stressed, flashing Gina and Angelo a look as if to say their disruption was unwelcome. "This resettlement agreement will rid us of the German contaminants that dominate the region. We'll send the Tyroleans beyond the Brenner Line, where they belong, thus putting a stop to the pollution of our nation. The Option provides us with the eternal guarantee we have always sought for our alpine border. I was the one who spoke to Hitler about the idea in the first place, back in twenty-eight, in Munich. And I'm not the only one. There is this Tyrolean People's League, who I hear support the resettlement."

Gina widened her eyes in mock surprise. "Is that so?"

"Have you heard otherwise?" Tolomei chuckled ruefully. "What exactly do you believe to understand, my dear?"

Gina would never sabotage the group's efforts, but Angelo still felt compelled to interject.

"I find the idea of voluntary resettlement surprising," he said. "After all, as Magistrate Mastromattei once spoke with me, people do not choose to leave their homes if they do not have to."

Tolomei threw the magistrate a challenging glare.

"I did say that once," Mastromattei said. "I see things differently now."

Tolomei scoffed. "The Tyrolean People's League understands that the ethnic Germans in the Alto Adige must sacrifice themselves for the alliance with Italy. Without Italy, Hitler does not have a chance to succeed in his ambitions. Also, it is what their Führer wants. That is what he expects of them. One united German nation. Good. Then they should go."

Angelo turned to his father. "Come to the bar with me."

The Colonel scowled but moved to join him.

"What are you drinking?" Angelo asked him. "Whisky?"

"No more spirits."

"Wine then?" Angelo signalled a waiter carrying a bottle of Lambrusco and ordered himself a whisky.

When they'd toasted, the first jab came from his father. "Signora Conti appears intent on provoking suspicion and mistrust. It's a shame, really."

Angelo hid his grimace behind the drinking glass. "Tonight? She's hardly said a word."

"I'm not talking about tonight. I'm talking about every night. Everywhere she appears, she shares a little more about her diverging political interests. The word through the grapevine is that it's time to clam up when she is in the room."

Angelo swallowed his whisky. "What I wanted to say to you, in private, is that what you and Mastromattei did up at the valley in July was unjust. The people had a right to those fourteen days."

The Colonel shrugged, eyes front. "The leaders are the ones running things."

"Nationalists who have no regard for laws."

"You've been missed at the party meetings. You should be aware that certain members are expressing real doubts about your...allegiances. Or is that Signora Conti's influence?" The Colonel nodded at a couple as they passed by.

"I never cared for the party," Angelo said tersely. "And you know it."

"Now is when you should. That is, if you want to keep your job. Of course, the divorce is a double-edged sword. On the other hand, many of us are relieved you have separated yourself from a Communist wife, but…"

Angelo cleared his throat. "Chiara is a Christian Democrat, not a Communist. And keep her out of this."

The Colonel chuckled. "All right, Angelo. Fair enough. Now you have a different problem. Gina Conti has lost her subtlety. And her desirability. Her choice to stay true to you does not leverage the power she once had over men's lips."

Angelo clenched his jaw but relaxed when he saw his father's eyes flash with satisfaction. Instead, Angelo snapped up a canapé and indicated to the bartender he needed a refill.

"What's the news on the Reschen Valley project?" he asked his father.

"Stefano is doing a fine job. Barbarasso has an eight-year tenure to run the company, and then the board has instructions to hand the reins over to Marco should he want it. It will go into good hands."

"Marco does not want to be a civil engineer," Angelo said.

The Colonel whirled on Angelo. "The boy doesn't know what he wants. Either way in eight years he may reconsider. And when the company is doing well, he will have his future and his legacy to secure."

The bartender handed Angelo another whisky.

"I find that this Option is going to help spur the momentum to our advantage," his father said loudly. "Stefano tells me the morale in the valley is quite low and the propaganda has done its damage. So many Germans will be leaving, so delighted to be leaving, in fact, that—"

"It will be like scavenging a battlefield," Angelo chided.

"Well put." The Colonel lifted his wineglass to the light, then looked at Angelo. "It's the business of war."

～

When they had returned to the villa, Gina whipped off her gloves and went into the sitting room, then tossed her coat over the back of a chair. "When are Chiara, Michael, and the group supposed to be granted an audience?"

"Early next week. Tuesday, I think."

"I overheard something."

She might have been falling out of grace with the old guard, but Gina would find other sources of information, Angelo was certain of that.

"I'm listening."

"Karl Wolff has caught wind of an attempt to put a coup on the resettlement. He's already called Rome."

Angelo groaned. "Now what?"

"I could call the foreign minister."

"Ciano?"

Gina looked thoughtful. "He seemed sympathetic to us in the past. Besides, Michael was right. Money talks." She chuckled. "Their faces when you shared the figures! Did you see that, Angelo? Tolomei was livid."

"Tolomei was livid the moment he laid eyes on us."

"Such an unpleasant man," she teased. Lifting the phone, she winked at Angelo before instructing the operator to reach the Ciano household.

Angelo heard the line buzz on the other end, then a click and a woman's voice.

"Edda, darling," Gina started. "I know it's late. It's Gina, Gina Conti. Yes. My apologies. I was hoping to speak with your husband. It will only take a moment. Please, Edda. It's urgent."

The woman's voice continued, scolding on the other end. Angelo recalled the photos he'd seen of her. Mussolini's daughter was not a classical beauty by any means, but she was a dynamic-looking woman. And from the sound of it, Gina Conti was meeting her match.

Gina hung up the receiver after saying good night to Edda.

She faced Angelo. "She told me to mind my own business, and if I was referring to the delegation that 'we' had sent, they will not be received. Karl Wolff called this evening as well. She said that Galeazzo believes this resettlement is a final ethnic solution. By January first next year, there will be no issue with the minorities in the Alto Adige. They want it done. Struck off the list, is how Edda put it."

Angelo drew her into his arms. "What can I do?"

Gina took his right wrist and removed the cufflink, then undid the left one. Her eyes were shining when she dropped them into his palm. "There is nothing you can do, Angelo. You don't need to make up for anything. All we can do now is sit back and wait until the results of the vote come in."

There was one thing though. He knew that. "Gina, we should make our relationship official."

"Nonsense. You just got the annulment."

"We've been practically living with each other for months. My new flat is superfluous. I ought to do the right thing by you. I want to do the right by you."

Gina glided to the wardrobe. "Unbelievable! She told me to mind my own business."

She was speaking of Edda again.

"Mind my own business?" she muttered from between the hanging gowns and dresses. "As if I am the one ruining this country."

On Christmas Eve day, Angelo dressed in a wool suit and went to Villa Adige with three stems of long amaryllis in soft pink shades, which Gina had picked up at the market.

Chiara had everyone in the sitting room of Pietro's apartments. When Angelo walked in, she and Marco rose, greeted him, his son distant and cool but apparently prepared to put on the appearances for the sake of his mother and his grandfather. Pietro's face was waxy in colour, alarming Angelo all the more that time was limited for the old man.

Angelo pulled Chiara into the hallway with the pretence that he wanted to see something upstairs. When they were in the parlour, he sat down on one of the new copper-coloured chintz settees. Chiara had made a few new updates with his money.

"I wanted to let you know that Gina and I have decided to live together. I will be moving in with her sometime in the next month. How does that bode with you?"

"What ought I to say, Angelo?"

"Rome was not successful, I take it?"

Chiara shook her head. "Very disappointing. Although, suddenly now four days to go and there have been directives to stop arresting anyone trying to convince the South Tyroleans to stay. It's all too late, however. The figures are now at over eighty percent."

"I want to talk to Marco about Gina."

"Don't. He told me on the train that he and Filipa have grown quite serious, and he's asked me to request that you distance yourself from Gina for the time being. Filipa knows nothing about the two of you, and he would be very angry if she pulled away from him because of your affair, or whatever it is."

Angelo sighed. "Is there going to be any point in time when I can live the life I want to live?"

"You always have, Angelo. You do what you want anyway."

Angelo clutched the arms of the settee. "And how long do I have to wait?"

"He's going to be at the Contis' for New Year's Eve. And, Angelo, he's very serious about her."

"Marco's nineteen."

"Yes."

He rolled his eyes and stood. "I can wait, I suppose. I don't know for what, but Gina and I can wait."

Chiara took his arm. "Thank you. Now let's go downstairs and see to it that we have a pleasant holiday, shall we?"

Christmas passed with relative pleasantness. Five days later the result of the Option's vote was in. Eighty-six percent, according to the papers, then up to ninety in the next issue.

It was New Year's Eve. Knowing that he would not be welcome at Gina's, Angelo found himself on the streets as the fireworks went off, as people cheered and shouted and brawled outside the pubs. The Tyroleans were leaving, and he did not know who was hollering more: the Italians who had settled into the province relieved to be rid of the *allogeni*, or the Germans who would finally escape the Italian yoke.

Angelo found himself at the end of the street, the Villa Adige in front of him. He could see a flicker of light—the fireplace in the downstairs parlour. Snow began to fall. A snowflake. A second. More. He stood there, knowing Chiara was still awake. Or at least sitting with Pietro. This had once been his home. The fight about, for, and over the Tyroleans had driven them apart, and that was only a small part of it.

He knocked instead of ringing the bell, and Chiara opened the door, one arm hugging herself against the draft. When she registered that it was Angelo, she swung the door open without a word. Angelo stepped inside and into the parlour, where Pietro, head drooped, slept deeply.

"The countdown," Chiara whispered, "has begun."

He glanced at her. The countdown to midnight. The countdown until the province emptied of Germans. The countdown Pietro's heart was facing.

Angelo lowered himself onto the divan opposite his former mentor, Chiara next to him. She took his hand in hers, squeezed it, and they turned to the fire.

PART III

1940–1946

STAGE 1

RESCHEN VALLEY RESERVOIR NOTICE
OVERVIEW OF STAGE ONE

DECREE—April 6, 1940, Nr 1532, Div. XII., the Ministry of the Alto Adige Electrical Society has authorised Monte Fulmini Electrical (MFE) to begin work on the Sluderno hydroelectric power station with resource access to the lakes of Reschen and Graun with the simultaneous declaration that the work is urgent and cannot be postponed.

Initial diversions for the river have been lain. Monte Fulmini Electrical (MFE) and its consortium will now proceed with the first stage of building as follows:

a. The construction of a barrage.

b. Sand filtered.

c. Tunnels installed directing the water flow to Kastelbello power plant. This water flows across the mountains of Stilfs past the glaciers and onwards to the factories in Lombardy to provide power supply.

d. Chief Engineer Stefano Accosi is the head of the project.

This first stage shall be completed no later than January 1942.

For further information please contact the Ministry's chief engineer, Emilio Ranalli, Tel Nr. Bolzano 17-19.

25

RESCHEN VALLEY, JUNE 1940

The day Katharina hiked into town, past the churning excavators from the United States, called Budas, was a Tuesday. She passed the pits and the cement remnants "the company" used to patch together the tunnels. On Tuesdays, she delivered fresh butter and cheese, as well as the butter moulds and packets of her Katharinahof tea the sundry goods shop ordered. She turned on her heel to take another look at the monstrosity that was the reservoir construction site. In two weeks much earth had been moved, the landscape changed. Permanently. She continued on to Jutta's, but the town was eerily empty. Like Florian and Manuel, some of the farmers were already up at their *Vorsäß*, preparing their huts for the season on the high meadows. But there was a vacuum in town. Since spring, some families had begun leaving, like the Nogglers and the Prieths.

The sound of the chugging bus motor and the smell of exhaust reached her before she drew to the front of the Post Inn. Katharina halted at the sight before her. Basso and several policemen were leading guests out of the inn and onto an unmarked bus. Jutta stood on the stoop above them, hands on her hips and a murderous expression on her face.

"What's going on here?" Katharina asked.

"All tourists must leave the valley," Basso muttered. He was escorting a man and a woman with two small children to the bus.

The family was Italian—Katharina could tell by their clothes.

"But why?" She turned to Jutta for the answer, but Katharina had to step out of the way as Simeon, the fruit seller, was led out. His father had been coming to the valley for years, supplying Jutta with the needed fruit, including fig and barley coffee when all that was available was Ersatz. She called to him.

The young man looked terrified.

"They're not all tourists, Captain Basso!" Jutta pointed at the bus. "Half those people are merchants who come selling the things we need in this valley."

"Captain Basso!" Katharina strode over to the policeman and blocked the door. "Simeon stays here! He has a regular route around here."

One of the *carabinieri* hurried over and yanked Katharina out of the way.

Simeon was wild eyed behind his spectacles. "They're doing this everywhere. I knew I should have stayed at home. Frau Steinhauser, check with my family later. Please?"

"We will," Katharina called after his retreating figure.

It happened so fast that she was still asking questions as the bus pulled away. But Jutta was tight lipped, and Katharina could only follow her into the emptied inn. Even the *Stammtisch* was empty. There was always at least one or two locals at the *Stammtisch*, but the whole building felt hollowed out.

"Where are our people?" Katharina asked.

Jutta stalked into the kitchen, letting the swinging door bang back and forth behind her. Katharina followed but stopped before the pillar near the bar. Hanging on it since early spring, and curled at the edges, was the front page of the

Dolomiten. Katharina read it again, as she had countless times before.

AN IMPORTANT ANNOUNCEMENT FROM IL DUCE
to the representatives of the Alto Adige and all the valleys of the Alto Adige called upon by Il Duce.
"I solemnly declare you will stay in your old homes and on your old properties. Nobody has ever considered or would consider removing you from your homeland."

Fatherland Italy. Fatherland Germany. Like Annamarie, the valley was torn between two fathers, and forgetting that they were born of this land, their homeland. She wanted to scream it: nobody here was beholden to any regime, only to the mountains, to the alpine meadows, to the rivers, lakes, and valley. The Steinhausers, Jutta and Hans, Dr Hanny, all of them had not voted for Italy. They had voted to stay home. That was what they had chosen.

"Where ought they be?" Jutta stormed out of the kitchen, picking up the conversation. In her hand, a piece of paper. "Why should anyone want to come here when the police regularly raid my inn for one reason or another? The tobacconist just closed up his shop because he's been fined for speaking German to the tourists. From Germany. So you tell me, Katharina, where should everyone be?"

Katharina pointed to the newspaper announcement. "We can stay, he says, but only to make our lives miserable for it, or what?"

Jutta thrust the sheet she had at her. "You think the Italians are bad? They're almost saints compared to our people. You know what they did to Alois? Two men—men you and I know well, Katharina, but I'm not naming names—Alois was sitting outside the church, minding his own business, and when he stood up, these two *friends* shoved him back and forth and told him he had better wipe down the bench before moving on. They didn't want to sit where Walsch-Alois sat! That's what they call us now. You're Walsch-Katharina. I'm Walsch-Jutta."

Katharina looked down at the paper. Her skin crawled. She could not focus on the stanzas—another one of those horrid messages. It was either this, or the flyers, or the defamatory chain letters—and some were so crass, picking on a person's particular weakness—that it had indeed driven another handful of families to choose resettlement. And they were illegal. Contrary to earlier warnings that anyone convincing someone to stay would be punished, now—after Il Duce's government realised they were losing their base—it was illegal to convince someone to resettle. But the poems, the flyers, and the chain letters kept coming, an unstoppable tide. The *carabinieri* put Toni Ritsch into jail for three nights when he was caught producing the pamphlets. Andreas Ritsch had been warned and fined as well. Several others from Graun and Reschen had been hauled into the police station. And yet nobody—including the Italian officials, it seemed—took it seriously. The arrests were perfunctory. A slap on the palm with a ruler might have done more.

"I don't want to do this any longer." Jutta sank against the bar, arms crossed. "One more push, that's all I need, and I'm packing up and leaving this valley."

Katharina was startled. "No. You can't. Please, Jutta."

Jutta jabbed her finger at the paper in Katharina's hand. "This was on my doorstep this morning. Read it aloud."

"'Who will remain here?'" Katharina read. "'False Christians, old hags, egoists, and pimps, faggots, bad priests, Walsch bastards, stupid imps. Some will make millions, money got by fraud; some are afraid they could lose it all.'" Katharina looked up, her stomach clenching. "This is awful."

Jutta closed her eyes. "Read on."

"'Gleefully they go to bed with the Fascists. Bought up, paid for, avoiding the black list. While in the back of their minds, they still believe Otto Habsburg will arise and bring relief. If you counted them all—all these righteous puppets—it would add up to no more than a dozen of a hundred.'"

Katharina slammed the paper on top of the bar. "It's unjust. It's cruel and it's uncalled for."

Jutta scoffed, yanked the paper from beneath Katharina's hand, and waved it at her. "One more time. One more—"

"Lock it up, Jutta. Lock up the inn and come with us to the high meadows tomorrow." Katharina looked around the dining hall and bar, half-eaten breakfasts and dishes still on the tables. "I'll stay and help. Come get away from all of this."

Jutta threw her hands up and stalked out of the *Stube*, and when the door to Jutta's old apartment slammed shut, Katharina picked up a tray and began clearing the tables.

Before she reached the farmyard, Katharina paused beneath the walnut tree to watch Annamarie writing letters on the bench outside the house. Her daughter wrote almost daily, and letters came back every few days. From Josep Greil, postmarked from the Eisack Valley, and from Charlotte Mainz in Berlin. Then there was the actress in Innsbruck, Elisabeth, whom Annamarie refused to call by her married name. These letters were Annamarie's connection to a world that Katharina knew she would never be allowed to be part of, but she preferred her daughter's letter writing to the caged-up animal Annamarie had reminded Katharina of in the first few weeks. If it wasn't the nervous fretting, the disappearances for hours at a time, or locking herself in her bedroom as soon as the last chore was done, Annamarie had exhibited emotional outbursts, flinging nasty accusations at Katharina, at Florian, at Bernd—though, Katharina mused, the two siblings had always fought. But the only person who was a balm to Annamarie's raw wounds was Manuel. Sometimes Manuel simply followed Annamarie at a distance into the woods or up the mountain paths, but they always returned shoulder to shoulder.

Katharina crossed the yard and sat down next to her daughter, closing her eyes to the warm sun. Annamarie continued scratching.

"I just want a moment, before I pack for the alp tomorrow," Katharina murmured.

Annamarie paused in her writing. "I prepared us a cold meal for later."

Katharina opened one eye, but Annamarie was back in the world of her letter. She leaned away. "I have an idea."

Annamarie looked up.

"Let's take a picnic up the mountain."

"All right."

"Good. I'll pack, and we'll head out when you're finished."

"I'm finished." Annamarie folded the letter and stuck it in an envelope. It was already addressed, and Katharina caught Sepp's name on the front.

She went in and assembled what Annamarie had prepared—a cold potato salad, bread, two tomatoes not quite ripe but good enough, and bacon fat mixed with crispy rinds, the first of the spring onions. There were also four boiled eggs and wedges of cheese. Minutes later, they headed up the hill, and when Katharina veered off onto the path heading north, Annamarie followed without comment, until they reached the Spinners' hut.

Boiled skulls of roe deer and bucks hung outside on the wall beneath the eaves.

"Where are we?" Annamarie asked as Katharina laid the basket of food down.

Katharina went to the back windowsill and unlatched the

wooden shutters. Hanging from one of the bolts was the iron key. She returned to the front door and unlocked it. Inside, the floorboards were grey from age. Not much had changed in almost twenty years. The bed was still up against the far wall, the rough-hewn table was still beneath the window to her right. There was a new cast-iron stove in the corner to her left.

Annamarie hung by the doorjamb. "Is this where you found him?"

"It is."

Cautiously, her daughter took a few steps inside, and Katharina pointed to the floor before the bed. "He was lying right here. There was blood on the floor. I didn't know whether he was alive or dead. I'd followed the trail—well, Hund did. Do you remember Hund?"

"A little. From photographs mostly."

"She found him. I was so scared. I was scared that he was alive, and I was scared that he was dead."

Annamarie leaned against the table.

"He wants to meet you," Katharina said. "Angelo is waiting for me to tell him when you're ready."

Her daughter looked around the room, hugging herself. Then she turned and walked outside. Katharina followed her and locked the door, expecting to see Annamarie making a dash for home or somewhere else, anywhere but here. Instead, she was emptying the basket of food and laying it out on the grass. They were hidden behind a knoll so that, when they were sitting on the ground, they no longer had a view of the lake and construction site, only of the mountains across the valley.

"I'm not ready," Annamarie said before handing Katharina an egg.

They ate and returned home in silence, though it was not tense. Her daughter was simply being reflective, Katharina decided. Like Manuel did, she stayed a few steps behind Annamarie and let her be.

That night Katharina awoke to find Florian gone, and when she checked the ticking clock on the bedside table, it was well past midnight. She went downstairs and found him and Annamarie at the back of the house, a fire burning in the pit. They were sitting on the bench up against the wall, wrapped together beneath a heavy blanket and talking softly. Katharina silently wept with relief and returned to bed without letting them know she had seen them. From that moment on, she decided that Angelo would have to wait. He would have to wait until all the wounds had healed and Annamarie was strong enough, and sure enough. Sure enough to voice her own wish to meet him.

Wednesday was the day the Steinhausers, and Hans, Alois, and Jutta—who had shut down her inn for the summer—were to make the half-day trek with the livestock to Graun's Head and the *Vorsäß.*

The Ritsches were not coming—they would be leaving in less than a month. The Planggers were also not coming. They were leaving about the same time as the Ritsches. Neither family knew where to, only that the plan was for all the families to remain together wherever they were to be resettled.

Katharina rose extra early, unable to sleep. She let Bella out, and the German shepherd loped into the middle of the yard. A sheet of paper drifted down from the doorjamb, and Katharina picked it up with trepidation. It took a moment in the weak dawn light to recognise that it was a copied letter from the Nogglers, now in Innsbruck.

The blacksmith described the fanfare at the Innsbruck train station when they had arrived. He described the brass bands and the banners. His family was lodging in an apartment building, all of their belongings in storage, and waiting. Martin Noggler wrote extensively about specific job offers in factories in

Vorarlberg, saying that the western Austrian province was building up several housing units as rapidly as possible. Gauleiter Hofer made a speech about how it was the German's duty to help build up the industry there and prepare the Reich to defeat its enemies.

But the Nogglers were still waiting for the farmland that had been promised them. When Katharina read that Thomas had been conscripted into the Wehrmacht, her heart lurched. Martin Noggler wrote that the immigration office was very organised, because Thomas's family immediately received their first deployment pay. The family was fine and very much looking forward to moving to their new home. They hoped the rest of the community could join them soon. *Heil Hitler!* was written at the bottom.

Katharina crumpled the letter and tossed it into the oven, then went to the fountain outside and filled a bucket of water to warm up for washing. She lit the stove, Martin Noggler's letter alight in seconds. *Thomas is in the Wehrmacht.*

Italy was not involved in Hitler's war yet, though the newspapers reported of deteriorating relationships with France and Belgium, and Florian said it was just a matter of time. Bernd was at the GIL for just four more weeks. He had become an exemplary student, as summer holidays at home motivated him to work hard. Soon the whole family would be high up on the alp, above and away from everything. Her body ached with longing to have all her children together under one roof.

Someone came down the stairs, and Katharina expected it would be Florian. But it was Annamarie.

"Good morning." Her daughter yawned. She scratched Bella's ears before kneeling down and nuzzling the dog's thick fur. "You two are up early."

"So are you," Katharina said.

"I thought I'd help."

"Let's release the chickens," Katharina said as Annamarie

poured herself some tea. "And take care of the rabbit hutch first. Then you can help me herd the goats while your father and Manuel get the milking done."

Annamarie slipped into a cardigan and followed Katharina outside. They prepared the animals' feed and secured netting over the chicken coop to prevent goshawks and fox from hunting the fowl. Patricia had promised to send one of the children over to secure the chickens at night and let them out again. Without Toni knowing. He'd refused the Steinhausers everything. The bull this spring. Help with the logging. Help with the fields. Secretly, Patricia and Katharina met to commiserate. Her neighbour was devastated that Toni was packing the family up after the summer and leaving. Like Katharina's family, Patricia's had been in the valley for centuries, and leaving was unthinkable. Yet here they were. And Toni was hell bent on reminding the Steinhausers that they—Katharina and Florian—were the pariahs.

By nine o'clock the family was herding the cows, the goats, and their one pig up the road to Hans Glockner's. Hans's herd of sheep had already made it to the first plateau, a white cloud of mewing lambs and bleating ewes. Katharina could not help but smile. The sky was overcast and the temperatures pleasant. It was a perfect day for the hike.

At around midday, Jutta and she unpacked their lunches, and they ate as the animals grazed below them. An hour later, Hans's dogs and Bella then tore through the herds, getting the animals back onto the trail. They still had a long journey to the *Vorsäß*.

As she looked down the ridge to the valley below, Jutta joined her and sucked in a breath.

"That looks simply terrible," Jutta said.

The reservoir. The machinery. The gutted earth. The wooden frameworks strewn about like the ribs and skeleton of a gutted whale.

Florian whistled, and waved at her, hat off his head, and she recalled the first time he had ever gone this way with her. How many trails had they taken together since? How many times had he proven that he was faithful to her and to what was important to her? She might be losing the valley she loved, she told herself. She still had her family, she reminded herself. She still had Annamarie here, she still had Manuel, and Florian. And Bernd would be back in a few weeks. She would soon have all she ever needed under one roof—her family.

On Thursday morning at dawn, Hans was outside, legs spread apart, his gaze in the direction of the valley, his feathered cap cocked to the side. He twisted from the waist to look at her.

"Did you hear bells last night?" he asked.

Katharina frowned. "You mean from the valley?"

"Yes."

"No. Nothing."

He asked Florian next. Her husband had also not heard anything. Neither had Manuel.

Annamarie, who slept like a rock, only rolled her eyes. "Can't hear anything from the valley with all these cowbells."

But Hans was convinced he'd heard alarm bells. Jutta joked about it. Alois grinned and hugged Hans, patting the big man on the arm.

At midday they were all eating lunch outside when Dr Hanny and Iris appeared over the ridge. Behind them were Captain Basso and the policeman who had nearly arrested Katharina in Reschen.

Dr Hanny took off his hat and halted several steps away from their table. He greeted them all, but when his eyes landed on Hans, his expression turned funereal.

"Frederick?" Jutta rose from the table. "What's happened?"

"Hans..." the doctor started. He removed his hat and wiped his brow.

Basso's mouth turned downwards. The other policeman looked down at his feet.

Iris bustled over to Jutta, took her hand, and met her gaze.

"Tell me what it is," Hans said slowly.

Dr Hanny lay a hand on his shoulder. "Your house, Hans. There was a fire. It's gone, Hans. Your house is gone."

Jutta, Iris's hand still in hers, sank back down onto the bench. Alois squinted behind his glasses, his mouth slightly opened, that expression of distress he got when he knew something was wrong or when he was in trouble.

"Who on earth—" Katharina moaned. That sweet little house Hans had built! Their home!

Basso assured Hans that the two men responsible—two young men none of them knew, two strangers from somewhere south of St Valentin—were now detained. They'd been confronted and accosted by Toni Ritsch, of all people. The men, both with criminal records, both Tyroleans, would quickly be arraigned and sentenced in Bolzano.

"Would you like to file the formal complaint and press charges now?" Dr Hanny asked.

Hans nodded.

"Of course," Basso said, "if the two men voted to resettle in the Third Reich, there is little we can do."

There was stunned silence after Basso and his companion left. Without a word, Hans rose and went into the hut. Jutta put her arm around Alois, Iris still holding her hand. Katharina rose and went inside to find Hans packing his rucksack. Wordlessly, and to keep back her tears, she helped him but when he and Jutta and Alois left the alp, Katharina went back inside and howled.

The next morning Katharina awoke before dawn again and stepped out of the hut and into the cool grass. The cows were stirring, their bells ringing in a chorus that once signalled peace, once signalled that all was right with the world. The higher-pitched bells were the goats. They were already high above the plateau, jogging diagonally across the slope. The sheep, left in the Steinhausers' care, were still grouped together in the meadow.

The season was poisoned. Her thoughts turned to Jutta and Hans and what they must be going through as they picked through what was left—or not—of that beautiful little house Hans had built.

When her husband stepped behind her and put his arms around her waist, not even that one gesture, one Katharina had always regarded as safe and intimate, a union of partnership, could ease her despair.

"What if we're next? Why Hans? What for?"

Florian made an angry noise.

Who were these strangers, traipsing about the province, destroying property, stealing and looting? She could remember when leaving one's home was as safe as being in it. Now, nothing was safe. Nothing was normal. And nothing made sense.

"I wonder where that bus went to," she said.

"What bus?" Florian asked.

"The one with the tourists. The one they put Simeon into."

"I imagine to the nearest train station to send them all home."

Where is home? "Or not."

"Where else would they take them?"

"If I knew," she said, "I wouldn't ask."

That afternoon, she and Annamarie headed back to the valley, to the Glockners, to help pick up the pieces.

Katharina slept in on Saturday. Annamarie woke her with a hot cup of fig coffee and Jutta behind her. Jutta's face was blotched red, her eyes swollen. She perched on the edge of the bed.

Katharina sat up.

"Hans is taking us to Vorarlberg," Jutta started. She held up her palm as Katharina began to speak. "There's an institution there for Alois, one that will provide him with good care and activities, even a little work so he can earn something. A place that can take care of him while Hans and I work."

Martin Noggler's letter. The factories in Vorarlberg. The housing set up for South Tyroleans.

Katharina stretched her hand across the coverlet and took Jutta's. "What can I do to talk you out of it?"

"You cannot."

"But you could live at the inn."

Jutta grunted. "I told you. One more push…"

Annamarie stood in the doorway, her silence heavy and unusual.

Jutta withdrew her key ring from her purse. She dangled it before Katharina. "I'm asking you and Florian to take over the inn. Hans has agreed that we will keep our options open, return if we can. Right now, neither of us can stay. Hans's home was safe from the Italians, but what with the inn to be detonated for that"—she waved a hand towards the window—"monstrosity… Katharina, I simply can't be here when it happens. Besides, Hans believes our chances are better across the border…"

Katharina reached for her hand, but Jutta pressed a palm to her cheek.

"He's my husband," she said plaintively. "You know?"

Annamarie shifted in the door.

"I know," Katharina said.

Jutta sniffed. "Anyway, when it's time—when the final offers for our properties come in—forward them on to us, and we'll settle. They'll make you clear off the Katharinahof at some point soon, and if they send you off sooner like they did with Noggler, well, you'll have the Post Inn as a roof over your heads. They keep assuring us that, like the church, it will be the last place to go."

Katharina shook her head slowly. "I can't, Jutta."

"You can. You want to go into the hospitality industry, then do this now." Jutta pressed the key ring into her hand.

The soft tinkling ceased as Katharina clasped her fingers over the keys. They were cool and smelled of iron.

Jutta turned to Annamarie. "Now tell her what you've come to tell her."

Annamarie blinked. Katharina tensed.

"Charlotte wrote to me," her daughter said weakly. "It's about that film I told you about. *Lowlands*? Frau Riefenstahl has to leave the production in Spain because of the war. They're moving the set to the Karwendel mountains. That's north of Innsbruck. Charlotte says there would be room for me on the crew."

"And you want to go," Katharina said flatly.

Annamarie shook her head and shrugged. Her eyes shone. "Sepp would go with me, just up to Innsbruck. He wants to visit Lisi. He says she's not doing well. I've been worried over her letters myself."

Katharina slid back beneath the blankets. In three and a half weeks Bernd would be back, but she could not find the strength to beg her daughter to stay.

On Sunday, in church, Annamarie stood before the altar and led the intercessions and injected one more spontaneous petition.

"For Elisabeth von Brandt, we ask the Lord to guide her and protect her, and all who suffer from illness and grief."

Lord, hear our prayer.

Before the final benediction, Father Emil, a grey-haired priest with the face and features of a child, held on to the lectern, swaying slightly backwards and forwards. Katharina had not warmed to him. On occasion, she would hear him slide in a pro-German comment at the *Stammtisch*, so she chalked him up to being a supporter of Hitler. Then, another day, she would see him helping the MFE workers unloading something heavy from a truck, and clapping them on the shoulders, as if these men were not devastating their valley. She missed Father Wilhelm. At least she knew where he'd always stood. Just like her, he'd always chosen home. But Father Emil had just gotten here. He had no idea what the valley was about, and he walked about it as if it were still heaven on earth, filled with good-hearted, Christians.

Annamarie fidgeted in the pew next to Katharina, Jutta on her other side.

"You have all most likely seen the first letter from Martin Noggler that I had passed around," Father Emil announced. "There is a second one, and they wanted me to share this with the congregation." He unfolded a piece of paper.

Katharina was beginning to dread anything that came on paper.

Father Emil read. Katharina processed the information with closed eyes. The blacksmith and his family were going to a village in the Sudetenland, where a number of South Tyroleans would be assigned to farms. Two families from the Eisack Valley, one from somewhere near Merano, four others from other various valleys and towns in South Tyrol. But there was no one else from the Reschen Valley.

"The Sudetenland?" Toni Ritsch hollered. "The committee was never invited to the Sudetenland."

She heard Father Wilhelm's voice, *And there go your promises.*

Father Emil folded the paper and placed it between the pages of the *Book of Gospels.* "I believe today is the day," he said slowly, "that we give thanks for good neighbours and forgive one another for the deeds and judgments done to one another these past months."

Someone coughed, and an uncomfortable silence followed. Katharina slowly shook her head. He had no idea. What kind of job had the Bishop of Brixen done sending this naïve priest here? Had Father Emil come from the moon?

Katharina closed her ears to the final blessings, closed her eyes to the faces that walked past her and their pew. Annamarie sat at her side and did not stir until Katharina made the sign of the cross and rose. Jutta remained sitting.

"Annamarie." Jutta bent forward and looked past Katharina. "If you can wait that long, you could travel with Hans and me to Innsbruck."

"When are you leaving?" Annamarie asked softly.

"Hans will try to sell some of his sheep. And then..." She looked at Katharina. "There's not much we'll be taking with us."

Katharina left them alone and went outside. Lisl and Georg were speaking with Dr Hanny and Iris. Probably about how the Roeschens had decided to postpone their departure to help Jutta and Hans. She saw Matteo, the postal clerk, with the Grassos, the owners of the Il Dante. Toni Ritsch and Walter Plangger were haggling about something. She imagined they were discussing their journey north and what Martin Noggler had written. Three groups. Three fronts. Nobody intermingling. Head bowed, she ducked to the right to escape the crowd out front, when suddenly Father Emil stood before her. He was at least half a metre shorter than her.

"Frau Steinhauser." He cupped his soft childlike hands over hers and waited until she looked at him. When she finally did, the first tear escaped.

He dropped his eyes and let her hands slip from his. "Go in peace, child."

Katharina did not wait for Annamarie. She headed straight for home.

~

On Monday afternoon, Katharina left Annamarie at the farm and retreated to the Post Inn alone. There were crates and boxes to put into storage; others would go with the Glockners.

Katharina walked into the *Stube* and clicked on Jutta's radio, drowning out the tick-tick-tick of the cuckoo clock, then pushed into the kitchen. Italian folk music trailed in after her. She looked around. Everything was tidy, was in its place, the surfaces clean. She walked to the stove, much more modern than hers at home. She ran a hand over the iron top and scratched at a rust stain with her fingernail. She squatted eye level and noticed the uneven bumps and rings and burned crumbs that were difficult to discern from above.

Katharina went into the pantry and retrieved a bucket and found a large steel wool sponge. She filled the bucket with water and took to scrubbing simply because it felt good to hold the bristling steel wool brush in her hand. Outside the window, she saw Father Emil walking from the church towards the sundry goods store. He stopped and greeted each person, offered his hand, tipped his hat at them.

The radio crackled outside. She rubbed her forearm across her forehead and pushed through the swinging door. The announcer was describing the balcony of the Palazzo Venezia and how a crowd was awaiting Il Duce. There was applause and cheering in the background. Then a click and Mussolini's voice.

"People of Italy! Take up your weapons and show your tenacity, your courage, and your valour! In six hours Italy will be in a state of war with France and Britain."

She turned to the cuckoo clock and froze. All time froze. The cuckoo jeered six times. Glass shattered.

With a scream, Katharina ducked behind the bar and clenched the brush in her hand. She heard the guilty laughs that followed fear. Carefully, she rose and stepped around the bar. She spotted the broken window pane, the rock balanced on the edge of a table. By the time she reached the front door, she had steeled herself. She descended the stoop, two stairs at a time, went to the corner of the inn, saw nothing. She stared at the corner foundation of what was left of Martin Noggler's blacksmithing shop. When had they torn that down?

She turned back to the inn. Jutta would be coming soon to organise the boxes in the hallway. She climbed the stairs to the entry, when she noticed, on the right-hand side of the inn's foundation, splashes of red paint. She backed up and went around the stoop.

HOTEL ISRAEL

She frowned, then remembered. Simeon, the fruit seller, was a Jew.

This—this steep, slippery slope—would be one that the entire valley would descend. She was certain of that. Not her!

Katharina ran up the steps and back into the kitchen. She grabbed the bucket of water and marched back outside. The steel wool brush still in her hand, she scrubbed furiously at the wet red paint just as the bells of St Katharina tolled its herald of war.

26

RESCHEN VALLEY, JULY 1940

At least seven other families left for Innsbruck in the span of a month despite the Nogglers' information about how the families were not—as had been promised by the German resettlement authorities—staying together. Everyone grew melancholy in the days leading to her and the Glockners' departure. Hans, already quiet and soft spoken, was more withdrawn than usual. Tante Jutta was irritated all the time. Even Alois was more subdued than Annamarie had ever seen him. Only she seemed to be taking it all in stride, reminding her mother that she planned to come back.

Her parents helped the Glockners sell some of the sheep for emergency cash and kept the remainder to bring to market in the fall, where they might negotiate better prices. Jutta would still get some money for the inn, but that would be a long time in coming. Hans said he would give Vorarlberg a chance, and if they decided to stay in western Austria, he would put his land up for auction.

The day they were prepared to leave, Jutta pressed the inn's keys into Annamarie's mother's hand for good. Until the reservoir was to be filled, the Steinhausers would run the inn, or what was left of the business. With no tourists allowed now and little traffic back and forth, Annamarie's mother did not expect to be making much of anything with the place, but at least the inn would be tended to, and at least, should the family need it, they'd have a place to stay when it was time to vacate the farm.

Her days tinged with sadness, Annamarie started to believe that she, too, would likely leave the valley permanently someday. She was not prepared to leave her family for good just yet. Not when she had just managed to find her way back to them. And still, her heart beat faster when she thought of Sepp. Thought of seeing poor Lisi and sweet Charlie, and of course Charlotte! Of being back in Innsbruck amongst the hustle and bustle, amidst traffic and shops and cafés. Being in the midst of life and, most of all, on set again! Anything to keep her mind off the war.

Except, Bernd returned home in time to grant their mother the one wish she desperately had—to have her children all under one roof again. And Bernd said he felt the war as soon as Italy had declared it. When he left Orvieto to come home, he reported scenes of violence in the streets. Someone had thrown rotten vegetables at him just because he was wearing a military uniform.

A few days before Annamarie was to leave, the Ritsches came by. The Glockners were sharing supper with the Steinhausers, and Annamarie's mother set out five more plates. For one evening, everyone sat at the same table again and laughed, sharing memories late into the night. The Ritsches were leaving for the border the next day, and even though Patricia Ritsch and Annamarie's mother had never been close, they had clung to each other like sisters.

Then it was the eve before Annamarie was to leave, and in similar fashion, she and her brothers stayed up the whole night, bantering, vying to tell and share their funniest stories, recalling their nights at the *Vorsäß* and how terrified they'd been of storms, how they had wrestled and thrown one another off the beds, had pulled pranks and dressed up to put on plays and dramas. Not long before dawn, Annamarie caught her mother watching them, a broad, nostalgic smile, her eyes shining as she took in her three children sitting together and laughing. The tears came soon after.

"I'm losing you all one at a time," her mother had wept. She'd reached for Annamarie after that. "It might be easier if you were all just gone at once. I don't know."

It made Annamarie feel worse about leaving. Then Sepp's telegram arrived. He'd managed to escape the Wehrmacht, but the Italian Army had him now. He had all but two days in Innsbruck. Could they meet before he had to report to duty in Bolzano?

The fortress of Nauders protruded over the gully from the side of the cliff. Hans's cart moved slowly down the steep road beneath it. They were over the border, the rushing stream to Annamarie's right the only thing moving south. She sat back against the boards and looked at Alois, who was shuffling a pack of *Watten* cards.

"Are you going to play," Annamarie asked him, "or just shuffle?"

Alois grinned. "Shuffle. Hans taught me how. I'm practicing." He looked bored suddenly, the cards clutched in one fist as he gazed at the rocky face of the gulley. "What is Innsbruck like?"

Jutta twisted in her seat up front, listening in.

"There are a lot of people," Annamarie said. "And trams. Automobiles. People like to hoop their horns." She imitated the sound.

Alois giggled and imitated the horns with her. "I like that sound."

"Where will you be staying?" Jutta asked.

"With Tante Rosa."

Jutta gave her a curt nod. "Good. Where your parents can find you."

Annamarie chewed her bottom lip and looked over the edge of the cart again, the Glockners' items shifting and jostling along the uneven road. She gripped the sides. She would be where Sepp could easily find her, and had no idea that she could miss someone as much as she did him. His telegram made the war tangible now, and the urgency she felt, that time was running out, made her jumpy and irritable. She wanted to hop out of the wagon and make it go faster, regretting that she had agreed to travel with the Glockners instead of by bus.

The road ahead—a winding trail over the plateaus—levelled out, and she tried to relax. She leaned back as Hans urged the horses on.

It was late afternoon by the time they reached Innsbruck's city limits. Annamarie navigated Hans through impatient traffic over the River Inn and to the train station, suddenly embarrassed by the provincial vehicle and image they made in contrast to the modern city. Despite her hurry, Annamarie agreed to wait with Alois at the cart whilst Hans and Jutta went into the immigration office. It took quite some time, and the sun was setting when they returned.

"We've been directed to this address." Hans handed Annamarie the information. She was not familiar with it.

"No matter. We've got instructions," Jutta said. "It's not far from there."

Annamarie looked yearningly across the street to where a café bustled with evening patrons. "I should go. Tante Rosa will wonder where I am."

Jutta held her arms open. "This is it, then."

When Jutta wrapped her arms around her, Annamarie was struck dumb by the finality of it.

Alois tackled her next. But it was Hans who caused her to yield to tears. He was still unsmiling, that beard quivering, all the sadness in the world like a yoke across those broad shoulders of his. He took her into his giant embrace, and Annamarie sobbed uncontrollably, the memories and emotions all rising on one great wave. It was Hans for whom she had always had a tender spot in her heart, who made their parting real and final. She remembered walking on his feet, or sitting on his shoulders as they'd visited the lambs in the fields. It had been the highest place in the world. This giant—who had lived with them for quite some time—had taken up all the space in their kitchen, in their *Stube*, every corner of their home, and filled it with quiet devotion and unconditional love. Hans had always been there. And when it was time for Annamarie to return to the valley, she would not find him. Not him or Jutta or Alois. To whom would she go to reminisce? They were taking what they knew of her with them. They were taking parts of her she would never make acquaintance with again.

Tante Rosa welcomed Annamarie with a no-nonsense practicality, showed her to a well-appointed room in her spacious apartment, and then served a light dinner. Tomorrow Sepp would arrive, and they would visit Lisi and Charlie before spending the rest of the day together.

Annamarie slept fitfully that evening, anxious for more reasons than she could comprehend. When Sepp showed up at the door the next morning, the grin that broke out across his face lifted her spirits because she knew that he was as glad to see her as she was him. But with Tante Rosa right behind her, his kisses landed on her cheeks, the last one lingering enough to send a thrill through her. He squeezed her arm and then politely introduced himself to Annamarie's distant cousin.

"You know," Tante Rosa began, "I have tickets to the theatre tonight."

"Sepp and I have plans."

"I wasn't inviting you," Tante Rosa snapped.

Annamarie flushed.

"I only meant," Tante Rosa said more gently, "that the apartment would be free if you would like to…" She waved a hand around, and her eye landed on the record player. "Dance or something, or just talk. Whatever it is young people do when they are about to be separated by wars and other duties."

An exceptionally cordial Sepp thanked Tante Rosa. A moment later Annamarie was out the door with him. He yanked her beneath the neighbouring entryway and kissed her as properly as Annamarie had fantasised for days.

"What have you been up to?" he asked as he pulled away. His hands gently ran up and down her arms. He spoke in Italian. "God knows I've missed you. You're really here."

"I am. And so are you." She kissed him back, and this time when Sepp pulled away, he looked earnest, caressing her face.

"How long will you be on set?"

"I don't know for certain. Charlotte said something about a location scout team in the Dolomites afterwards. The schedule looks like I'll be here for at least two months, but around September, we'll head to Italy."

Sepp stepped out into the street, one hand on her elbow. "I don't know where I'll be stationed yet."

Three Hitler Jugend passed by them, their glances scouring them.

Annamarie cast her eyes down, switching to German. "You'll come and see me. Or I will see you. Hopefully, you'll be somewhere nearby."

"I doubt training will take long." He sighed. "I imagine they'll have me shipped off to Greece or Belgium or England before you know it."

Annamarie gripped his arm, but his mind was already elsewhere.

"Lisi's been strange in her letters to me," Sepp said. He crossed the road with her, heading for the tram stop, and stopped to purchase two tickets from the nearby tobacconist.

"I've been wondering about Lisi too," Annamarie said.

"I don't know what she's doing," Sepp muttered. "But let's get to the bottom of it."

They were meeting at the Iron Rooster, their old hangout, the first place Annamarie had encountered either of them. Sepp had been undeniably infatuated by Lisi, fawning over the redhead, and angry when Franz and his Hitler Jugend friends made fun of the theatre group.

The pub was in the cellar, and Sepp pushed through the massive oak door, blinking in the darkness. The air was heavy with damp, smoke, and stale beer. The radio played brass band music. Typically, they had come here in the evenings, but now the weak morning light lay the pub naked before her. Out of habit, Annamarie went to their usual table and let Sepp pull the chair out for her. A group of Wehrmacht soldiers smoked cigarettes and played cards beneath the cellar windows. The barkeep, an older man with a grizzled beard and a round belly that hung over the waistband of his *Lederhosen*, took their orders and waddled back to pour their two beers. A woman in a rumpled *Dirndl* stepped out of the kitchen, carrying a bottle of clear liquid in five shot glasses for the Wehrmacht soldiers. They invited her to sit with them and drink one, and slowly she perched on the sixth chair and raised a toast to the Führer.

With Annamarie facing the entryway, she saw Lisi walk in first, Charlie in her arms. Lisi set him down, one hand gripping his as Charlie toddled a few steps, but she grabbed him again with an impatient swing.

"Good to see you two," she laughed lightly as Annamarie and Sepp took turns hugging her. "Look at you both. You're like an old married couple."

Charlie slipped out of her hand and slid onto his bum near

the table. Annamarie bent down to pick him up, but Lisi halted her.

"Let him be. He can just crawl around."

Annamarie frowned but smoothed her dress, peeking at Charlie beneath the table, where he'd crawled up to the wall and was now trying to stand up again by grasping the rough limestone.

Lisi flopped into a chair next to Sepp and threw an arm around his shoulders. "How are you, old friend?"

"We're good." He nodded at Annamarie.

Lisi's smile wavered. "We're? How nice. And what's this I hear, you're off to work with Leni Riefenstahl?"

"Just as a girl for all purposes." Annamarie blushed. "Whatever she needs."

"And here I thought you'd finally hit the big screen. But you're good at doing all the little stuff, aren't you? Like at the Rampenlicht Theatre." Lisi's eyebrows knitted together. "That wasn't very nice of me. I didn't mean to say that."

"It's all right," Annamarie muttered. This was how Lisi's latest letters had also been: caustic and glib.

Lisi twisted in her seat and waved at the bartender, although he was already lumbering over.

Charlie yanked on Annamarie's hem, and this time Annamarie scooted back and lifted him onto her lap. He stuck a fist into his mouth, and Lisi hung an arm over the back of her chair and watched them.

"Look at that—he likes you. How nice. Isn't that nice, Sepp?" She lifted her glass without cheering them and took a long drink. She set it down, opened her purse, and retrieved an inhaler, then put it to her mouth and pressed. "This air," she said, holding her breath. "I have to—" She exhaled slowly and put the inhaler back in. "Anyone want a cigarette?"

Annamarie shook her head, trying to smooth her expression.

"Sepp, when will you be heading off to war? Isn't it

wonderful? All my male friends are gone to the front. Charlie and I are alone. Oh, it's wonderful, really. Not having Maximilian around, that is. Although the boy adores his father."

Lisi stood then and snatched Charlie out of Annamarie's lap. "You've held him long enough. Go to your Uncle Sepp, Charlie-boy."

Before either Annamarie or Sepp could protest, Lisi plopped the toddler onto his lap and sat back down, raising her glass.

"Did we cheer? Let's cheer." She twisted in her seat and tipped her drink at the soldiers in the corner. "*Heil Hitler*, you bastards," she whispered, then broke into a deep chuckle, drank, and sobered again. "So where were we?"

Annamarie, her cheeks hot as embers, exchanged a concerned look with Sepp.

Sepp smiled weakly at Lisi. "What's in the inhaler? Lisi? What's this all about?"

Lisi looked surprised. She touched her purse. "This? Nothing. Something Max's doctor gave me for my exhaustion. You remember how we used to have these at the State Theatre. I've just been, I don't know, tired."

"Tired," Sepp repeated flatly.

Lisi looked up at the ceiling, took in a deep breath, and gazed at Sepp, chin in her hand. "Max's doctor is a real sport. Besides, the inhalers help me stay on the Rainer family's good side." She laughed at her own joke.

By the time they finished their beers, Annamarie could hardly wait to get out of the pub.

Lisi leaned in just as they were paying, and spoke in a conspiratorial tone. "I wanted to let you two know that if anything ever happens to me—"

"What ought to happen to you?" Sepp's brow creased with the kind of worry that indicated he still adored Lisi, even with her troubling behaviour.

Lisi pursed her lips. "War. Death. It's all around. Right, boys?"

Again, she was directing her question to the soldiers. They hardly looked up. There had been a time when, no matter what Lisi had done, she had brought attention to herself. Not today.

"Anyway," she continued, "I'm here to tell you that I signed my last will and testament today. While I'm still sane."

Sepp looked as shocked as Annamarie felt, but Lisi smiled broadly, like someone who had just pulled the biggest prank and gotten away with it. "And you two have been named as Charlie's guardians. If Maximilian gets killed in the war, if I disappear, you two, well, you two could be his parents."

As Sepp sputtered, Annamarie stood up and clutched her purse to her bosom. "I think it's time to go. Sepp and I only have the day together, so we're going to move along now. Lisi, it was great seeing you and Charlie."

Sepp was more hesitant. "Lisi, I… What… Are you going to be all right? Is there anywhere you want us to take you?"

Lisi's laugh was nonchalant. She took the child from his arms and kissed Sepp's cheek again. She then turned to Annamarie and embraced her lightly.

"I'm going to be just fine," she said, surprisingly sober. "It's just a precaution. All right? No worries. But—" She pinched Annamarie's arm. "If the Rainers or my family try and change my wishes? I want the two of you to fight for Charlie with all you have. Understood?"

Sepp was the one to placate her. Annamarie was still too stunned to speak. When Lisi pulled away, she snatched up her belongings and headed to the table with the five soldiers. She plopped onto the seat the waitress had before, Charlie on her lap, and said, "What are we playing, boys? And most importantly, what are we drinking?"

Annamarie stared at the figure in the chair. At least this was the Lisi she remembered.

Sepp did not say anything as they walked back to Tante Rosa's flat. Annamarie chewed her lip, frustrated by his distraction. They had so little time together.

"Fine, Sepp, what else could we have done for her? Her behaviour! It's so erratic. She's like a crazy person. Lisi's been on that descent for over a year now."

"I'm going to guess it's amphetamines she's taking. We used to take those backstage sometimes, you know, to keep ourselves awake, to keep ourselves...to keep things up. You know what I mean?"

"Do you think she's addicted?"

"I know she's addicted."

"And? What can you do? I'm heading off tomorrow. You're heading off tomorrow. Are you planning on spending the rest of the day convincing her to check herself into a clinic?"

Sepp looked angrily at her, but she held her stance.

He sighed. "You're right. Can't you talk to Margit? Someone who might give a damn about her? Explain to us what the hell Lisi means to make us guardians?"

Annamarie raised an eyebrow. "That's just preposterous, Sepp, and you know it! Why don't you just send me to talk to Franz, or how about Maximilian?"

"I don't know what to make of it." But there was a gleam in his eye.

"Josep Greil, you're positively chuffed that she's made you guardian."

Sepp's face darkened. "I'd do it for her, you know? We're the only friends she's got."

Annamarie slumped against the wall of the apartment building, fishing for the key. She dangled it before Sepp. "Fine, I promise, after the Karwendel, I'll look into it. Now, shall we go back looking for Lisi, and entangle ourselves with the Rainers, or even better with her parents? Or go upstairs and .entangle ourselves in each other? Theatre tickets, remember?"

Sepp smiled sadly at her and took the key. "If you weren't so accurate, I'd call you selfish. But you're on point, Annamarie. Unfortunately."

They lingered beneath the sheets of Annamarie's single bed after making love, and she played with the hair protruding from a mole on Sepp's arm. Before she could pull it out, he yanked his arm away, and kissed her quickly. He flipped the glasses from his forehead onto the bridge of his nose and reached for something on the floor on his side of the bed.

"Are you still writing, Annamarie? In those journals of yours?"

She yawned and stretched. "Not really. Not since I returned to Arlund. Or, I don't know. Maybe a little. That is, after my mother and I spoke at great length about the accident that is me."

"I think you should. I think you need to focus on that talent you've discovered."

Sepp tossed the canvas rucksack that held his camera and films onto the bed and shoved it between them. "I want you to have these." His lenses were smeared from her kisses.

Annamarie pushed herself into a sitting position, the covers sliding down and over her middle. She plucked the frames off his face and wiped the lenses on the sheet, eyes on the bag. "Why, Sepp?"

"I can't take them with me, can I? Not where I'm going."

She stared at him as she handed the glasses back to him. "But you're nothing if you're not creating, filming—"

"You have to hang on to the equipment for me. Please? Keep them safe. And use them. You're going to be in spectacular places with Riefenstahl. Play with them." He wagged a finger at her. "Just don't break them."

"At least take the Leica. Take the still camera."

Sepp traced the curve of her arm. "Where I'm going, Annamarie, I won't have any use for taking photos. I'm supposed to shoot the enemy."

Goose pimples ran up and down her arm when his fingers left her skin. It was so fatalistic. So unlike him.

The clock in the dining room chimed ten. Tante Rosa would be home soon. Annamarie rolled on top of Sepp, kissed him, and buried her face into his neck. He held her tight. It was coming to an end all too soon.

"Promise me," he said, "you'll keep working on your stories."

She nodded against him. "I will."

The only other person who could possibly understand Annamarie's conflicted heart was Charlotte. Tearfully, Annamarie saw Sepp off at the train station and waited the three hours in the café across the street until the crew arrived from Berlin. Sepp's canvas bag leaned against her shin, and she wrote in a new notebook.

They were easy to spot, the crew, with all the trunks and cases and luggage. She grinned at the sight of Charlotte stepping off the train without looking, because she had her clipboard to balance her, though she talked a mile a minute to whoever was behind her. It turned out to be Riefenstahl herself.

Both greeted Annamarie with genuine warmth, and when Annamarie explained that Sepp had already gone, Charlotte squeezed her arm reassuringly.

"You'll be so busy, you'll hardly have time to think of him."

Annamarie threw a questioning glance at Riefenstahl, directing the crew's next steps.

"Yeah, she seems to be her usual self," Charlotte said. "At least more so than last winter. She's been kind of buoyed by this project. Spain was a pain in the behind with a truckload of complications. But she's happy to be here." Charlotte paused and tipped her head. "She did say she's finished with documentaries though."

Annamarie watched Riefenstahl glide across the platform. "You don't say."

The bus waited outside the station, and they boarded for the two-hour drive to the Karwendel. Their hotel, Charlotte announced, was in Hinterriss. The scenery was as familiar as home—towering limestone peaks, lush green alpine meadows, a scattering of villages with church steeples mimicking some fifty main peaks in the mountain chain. When they got off the bus, they were met by the sound of rushing streams and the echo of the wind bouncing off the mountain faces.

The Hotel Post was a large four-storeyed hotel with balconies in the back overlooking the stream, and with views of the range. Annamarie shared a room with Charlotte, and they spoke about everything, including Lisi and the suspected amphetamines she was taking.

"I know so many actors who take the stuff," Charlotte said. "Keeps them awake, but it makes them agitated, not to mention a bit crazy."

"Erratic, right?"

Charlotte nodded.

"I just feel horrible for Charlie."

"Her situation can't be easy if she's between those two families, as you say."

"It makes my family drama seem harmless," Annamarie claimed.

"Amphetamines is a good guess," Charlotte yawned.

Annamarie turned out the light, but after some time, she realised she could not sleep. She was wound up herself. She missed Sepp, and she was anxious about the next day. Charlotte was breathing deeply when she rose and slipped into a blouse and skirt. She padded down the stairs and entered the hotel dining room. There was a light on in the guesthouse *Stube* and she recognised the soft clink of glasses. The clock on the wall read 2:00 a.m.

Except for a bartender drying and putting away wineglasses, Riefenstahl was the only person in the room. At a round table, Riefenstahl sat with half a glass of wine and an empty schnapps thimble as well as what seemed like dozens of sheets of paper spread around her. She looked up as Annamarie approached.

"Mind if I join you?"

"Couldn't sleep?"

Annamarie nodded.

"Excited?"

She shrugged. "A lot on my mind."

Riefenstahl tore her gaze away, hands on the piles of paper. "Sometimes I feel like this movie simply does not want to be made."

"What's the problem?"

"Actresses. That's what. My lead actress is now no longer available." She raised her palms. "Extenuating circumstances. War, right?"

"Is there anything I can do to help?"

Riefenstahl rose and went to the bar, reached over it, and returned with a bottle of schnapps and a glass. "Have one."

Annamarie did not say no. She raised her glass when Riefenstahl had filled it, and they drank, Riefenstahl knocking her shot back.

"What have you been up to?" she asked before Annamarie had finished hers.

Annamarie put her glass on the table. "Where to begin?"

"How about at the beginning?"

"I just left my family again. I'm not so certain it was the right thing to do."

"You're an adult now. It's time to forge your own way."

Annamarie nodded. "It's just that my family is facing extreme hardships."

"Where are they?"

"The Reschen Valley."

Riefenstahl folded her arms. "That's right. I forgot. You'll be coming to the Rosengarten location with us."

"I will?"

"Yes. And before you do, stop over there. We're here for six weeks, then down there. Take a couple of weeks. See how they are. Then join us."

"I might do that."

"Good. Because when we move into the studio in January, I have a part I want you to play."

Annamarie's eyes widened. "A part?"

"Yes. It's a small one. I was going to play it myself. God knows with this war on, it's getting more and more difficult to find good people. So I can't play that minor role, because I've just decided this evening that I'm going to play the lead role."

"The dancer? Marta?"

"Yes. If I don't do it, who will? Oh, look at your face! You'd jump at it, wouldn't you? You're too young, Annamarie. I have the experience." She paused. "I used to be a dancer, you know?"

For the first time, Annamarie looked at Leni Riefenstahl more closely.

"You think I'm too old." She poured another shot of schnapps for each of them.

"No."

"You are bold, but you're not a good liar. I certainly hope you're a better actress."

After emptying her thimble, Annamarie muttered, "People have been telling me the opposite my whole life."

Riefenstahl set her schnapps down, scrutinised her, and then laughed.

Annamarie did too.

27

SEPTEMBER 1940, BOLZANO

This was no ordinary day at the Bolzano train station. There was a mob. An ocean of families, friends, strangers all shouting, calling, and chattering in German. Women tugged their children the way men lugged their cases, weaving and bumping their way through the crowd. On the tracks, the trains chugged and hummed. Conductors blew whistles, and with each shrill the swell lifted up and another wave of movement—faster, more urgent—began.

Angelo stood beneath the overhang, almost afraid to get caught in the stream. As the passengers boarded, it was like watching a river diverted into one of his designs, except this was the core of economic substance they were draining.

There were few farmers amongst the travellers. This was only the second wave of resettlement. The first had been made up of *Reichsdeutsche*, the Germans and Austrians who had taken up residence in the Alto Adige. The next to leave were the *Volksdeutsche*, or people who fell under the title of entrepreneurs, the self-employed, professionals, and the social elite. Mastromattei called them troublemakers who'd found their way out by filling in the white form. In other words, the magistrate considered the *Volksdeutsche* to be the greatest dissidents.

For months reports had been that around 250 people were leaving each day. These were the ones who did not own property. Or no longer did, like the families leaving the Reschen Valley.

Within minutes the platform was emptied, and the train yanked and tugged the cars past him, heading north to the Brenner, to the border. Angelo shook his head. Michael should be here now with a photographer. This ought to be recorded.

A few moments later, from the south, another train appeared. Angelo checked his watch, guessing it was the one from Rome. Not bad. It was only a half hour late. He stayed put until it chugged to a stop, brakes squealing, then stepped out from the overhang to keep an eye out for Marco.

They had last seen each other in January for Pietro's funeral. After his Christmas break, Marco had had to do an about face almost as soon as he'd arrived in Rome. And now Marco had phoned home to tell Chiara that he'd received his marching orders. Their son was twenty now, and in four days' time, Marco would be stationed somewhere on the Mediterranean. Angelo did not yet know whether Marco's unit would support the front in Greece, or the invasion that had started in North Africa that past Tuesday. But Angelo had brushed up on his knowledge of modern aircraft engines.

His son had a real fire in his belly for flying, but after a physical endurance test in the air, the medical examiner declared Marco unfit to be a pilot. He suffered from episodes of vertigo in the cockpit. Angelo was relieved, but he did not want to be like the Colonel, celebrating his son's failures. Instead he prepared to sympathise with his son, to show him real support by sharing in his disappointment.

Marco was one of the last to descend onto the platform. Dressed in uniform, he swung his gunny sack over his shoulder and spotted Angelo almost immediately. It was a light embrace, and Angelo clapped his son on his shoulder.

"Good to see you. How was the trip?"

"Long."

Angelo led him through the station and walked across the park to the city centre. "So, the Mediterranean?"

His son shook his head. "Belgium."

"What? Your mother told me—"

"I've been reassigned to the CAI, *Corpo Aereo Italiano*. We're supporting the *Luftwaffe*. The division is brand new. Just received my instructions two days ago."

Angelo was astounded. The Blitz on London had started the weekend before. "But the Nazis are terrorizing civilians."

"Father…"

Marco had not called him that in years. Angelo stopped. They were at the edge of the park.

"I'm just a mechanic—"

"I know, son, but—"

"I'm a mechanic, so I see a lot of paper. And on paper, our air force shows just a bit over three thousand machines." Marco glanced away, and Angelo saw him swallow hard. The sugary scent of roasted nuts filled the air from the candied almond vendor. Angelo followed his son's look. A child begged his mother to buy him some, and she yanked him away.

Marco continued. "I work on those engines, on those machines. I can tell you right now, we don't have a modern aircraft that matches the *Luftwaffe*. And we don't have one that matches the RAF. Sure, Britain sold us their engines, America sold us their engines, even the Germans have tried to provide technological assistance, but we don't match up. And we don't have three thousand aircraft fit to fly."

"We've got the Fiat and the Macchi," Angelo said. "Modern aeroplanes."

Marco expressed surprise, then blew softly. "You read up."

"I read up."

"Did you read that we have no long-range fighters? No night fighters? We're no match for the Brits."

"But the bombing raids in France," Angelo said. "We carried out over seven hundred missions."

"And had little effect."

"What are you saying, son?"

"I'm saying that I'm going to Belgium." Marco strode across the road. They passed the Laurin Hotel.

"You know," Marco said, "I've never even been to your new flat."

Angelo cleared his throat. "That's right. You haven't."

"I'd like to see it." Marco glanced at him.

He was testing Angelo, so Angelo tested back. "How's Filipa?"

"I've just seen her. We went to the sea for two days. She has a job at a news agency, typing copy. But you probably knew that." Marco watched him intently when Angelo stopped at the corner.

Angelo waited for the traffic to clear before crossing the road and ducking into the passageway that led to the piazza. He waited until they were in the arcade. "Marco, I've moved into Signora Conti's place."

Marco nodded. "I was wondering whether you would tell me."

"And?"

Marco shrugged. "Filipa doesn't know yet."

"How did you know then?"

"Mother."

"Ah."

"She wanted me to be prepared." He shrugged. "It's fine. Who knows what will happen?"

They walked in silence to the square. It didn't sound as if Marco was wholly convinced about Filipa as he'd perhaps once been. Or maybe it was Marco's way of presenting a truce. But when Marco flashed him a tight-lipped grin, Angelo recalled what it had been like for him in the Great War. The recruits' excitement and bravado had soon dissipated in the structural chaos, the realisation that they lacked proper equipment. He could still remember when a small unit from the navy arrived to fight in the Alps, followed by the quick promotions of officers wholly unqualified to do the jobs. The Great War—the one Angelo had fought to end all wars—had been a farce. They'd learned nothing. The country had learned nothing. His son was now marching out to repeat their failed history.

When they reached the piazza, Angelo saw that the espresso bar had its door wide open.

"Want a coffee?"

Marco paused. "Sure."

"Or something stronger?"

His son checked his watch. "It's not even eleven yet."

"Is that a no?"

"One beer?"

"Beer? Since when do you drink beer?"

"Since now."

The barista waved at Angelo.

Angelo stepped in. "Vittorio, have you got beer?"

"Moretti. Förster. On tap. Which do you prefer?"

Marco joined him in the entryway. "Moretti. Two. I'm buying." His son pulled out a seat at one of the tiny tables against the wall. "I'm buying if my father tells all about his experiences in the Great War."

On Sundays the Hotel Laurin served a midday meal for families, starting right after church. Angelo skipped services, leaving Gina to it and taking some time to get work done in the hotel lounge. Afterwards, he was to meet with Chiara and Marco before the train would take him to Milan, where he would then catch a flight to Antwerp.

Angelo was busy scribbling notes at the bar when Michael appeared.

"Minister." Michael took a stool next to him. "I was looking for you at your office on Friday."

"I took some time off. Marco's here and only until this afternoon. He's been assigned to the front."

Michael pursed his lips. "I see."

"How can I help you then? Or am I too late?"

The journalist chuckled. It was their private joke now. "Too late," as in how Il Duce had been too late to squelch the German propaganda before the Tyroleans' final vote. Berlin's and Rome's political games had jeopardised all that Angelo, Michael, Gina, and Chiara had worked for, but even more disconcerting was how Mussolini pretended he'd had no idea what had been going on right beneath his nose.

"Rome appears quite disenchanted with Berlin," Angelo said and closed his notebook.

"You read my article then."

"I was pleasantly surprised to find your byline in the Italian paper."

Michael fished out a cigarette, lit it, and ordered a coffee. "Thanks, I guess. So this little deal on the exchange rate is quite a thorn in Il Duce's side. Germany is not meeting their deadlines."

"I was at the station to pick up Marco. It seems that there are plenty of people leaving. Plenty who have received recompense for resettlement."

Michael shrugged, flicked his cigarette into the ashtray the barkeep slid over along with the coffee. "It seems that way. But what was intended to improve relations has become a bit of a smouldering incendiary device. Numbers are falling, and Berlin is stalling."

"Well, to be fair, they are a bit involved in starting another world war."

Michael blew smoke up towards the gilded ceiling. "Seems the

'Tyrolean question,' whatever it was, to be frank, has still not been answered. But I'm onto another story."

Angelo raised an eyebrow. "And you're sharing?"

"Mmm…" Michael jammed the cigarette into his mouth and fished out a small notebook from his other jacket pocket. "Remember how you asked me to research those letters of intent that the Veterans Administration drew up with MFE? You wanted to know where they were getting their stats?"

"Yeah. From the valley's records. What was left of them anyway, after that fire at the town hall."

Michael withdrew his cigarette and clicked his tongue. "Nope. They were going on stats drawn up from another resource."

Angelo leaned against the bar. "Another resource."

"Plots, forests, field, livestock, etcetera, did not match up with the registries, right? And you thought it was MFE doing it. Seems there was a mathematical formula I came up with."

"Not really."

"Not really. But practically. Anyway, the root of that formula? I'll let you guess what it is."

"Tolomei."

Michael pointed the cigarette at Angelo, winked, and stamped it out. "That's it. And his sidekick."

"Colocci-Vespucci."

"Via…"

Angelo stared at him. He sighed. "Colonel Grimani."

"Almost. Your old friend."

Angelo's jaw dropped. "Accosi? Stefano Accosi? That son of…"

Michael cocked an eyebrow. "Who worked with…"

Slowly, Angelo said, "Ghirardelli and Basso. Oh, that's beautiful. They fudged the information. Who paid them to do it?"

Michael cocked his head. "Better question. Whose pockets did they have to line for Rome to look the other way? Because they've all been signed, sealed, and delivered now."

"Damn it," Angelo hissed.

Michael waved the barkeep over. "We'll take two… What do you drink at this time of day, Minister? Grappa or schnapps?"

Angelo waved a hand, his mind still sifting through the muck of corruption. "Whatever your preference is."

Michael ordered two schnapps and handed one to Angelo. They clinked glasses and Angelo drank his down in one swallow.

"So that little ditty has led me to something new."

"And you're sharing," Angelo quipped again.

"I found a whole hell of a lot more going on behind our current administration."

"All right."

"Bribes from the great industrialists around the world. Industrialists from the free world who are now supporting the Fascists. Take Adriatica. You know why we're fighting so hard in the Mediterranean? Because we're selling parts of the sea—sea that does not yet belong to Italy—to the industrialists for drilling oil. Because we're going to need oil."

"For those aeroplanes my son works on," Angelo said quietly.

"And there's more where that came from." Michael tapped the notebook against the bar. "This one might get me the Pulitzer."

From where he was sitting, Angelo had a view into the hotel lobby. A great crowd was building up, with crates and luggage brought in by trolly. People bustled in and out, followed by shouts from outside. He craned his neck to look over the bar and out past the diners on the front terrace. He saw paparazzi running past and camera bulbs flashing.

"Who's here?"

"That?" Michael threw a casual glance. "Leni Riefenstahl is filming somewhere nearby. New film. Spanish, I think."

"Riefenstahl? Is that her film crew?"

"Film crew. Actors too, I suppose."

"Michael, hold that thought. No, listen. I want to help you. And we begin in our corner. I need to do something but let's pursue this later." Angelo lay a few lire on the bar and hurried into the lobby. There was a green autobus chugging outside where a crew was unloading luggage and equipment. The media crowded around, and two hotel personnel tried to keep them at bay.

Angelo went to the reception desk. "Do you have a register of the incoming guests?"

The receptionist—an immaculately dressed young woman with a plump figure—threw him a *you know better* glance. "We do not give out such information."

"Of course. I understand. I'm just wondering. You see, my… my daughter, Annamarie Steinhauser, she is supposed to be with this crew. And I'm supposed to meet her here."

"Did you check with that young woman there?" The receptionist pointed to a woman with a clipboard. She had a round face and light-brown hair.

"That one there?"

"Yes. She's in charge."

"Thank you."

Angelo thanked the receptionist and hurried to the woman, but when she saw him coming, she put her hand up. He halted a few feet away.

"Sir," she said in German, "please move out of the way. No media now. We'll have an official press conference at four o'clock this afternoon."

"I'm sorry," Angelo replied in German. "Do you speak Italian?"

"Only a little."

"I'm looking for Annamarie Steinhauser."

The woman cocked her head at him. "What for?"

"I'm a…I'm a friend. An acquaintance of hers. *Freund. Bekannter.*"

"No. She's not with us."

Angelo deflated. "I see. I was told she was part of this project."

The woman hesitated, seemed about to say something, but

her eyes raked over him. Something transformed on her face. "Not any longer."

She smiled swiftly, then turned away, clipboard tucked beneath her arm. She was lying. But why?

When he returned to the lounge, Marco and Chiara were pushing their way through the onlookers who had gathered along the windows and the terrace.

"Angelo," Chiara said breathlessly, "did you see that crowd out there?"

"I did." His heart thudded, as if it were winding down. He hadn't realised how excited he'd been at the prospect of finding Annamarie here. And the disappointment now made his blood turn sluggish.

Marco frowned. "Are you all right?"

"Michael's here," Angelo said, to take his mind off it. "Let's get a drink before lunch."

He cast one more glance in the direction he'd come and caught the young woman still studying him. The next moment, she slipped into the crowd outside.

STAGE 2

January 1941
RESCHEN VALLEY RESERVOIR
OVERVIEW OF STAGE TWO

With the successful completion of Stage 1, Monte Fulmini Electrical will proceed with the next stage as follows:

a. Main embankment dam and upstream blanket will be constructed across the main valley.

b. Tunnels will be built for diversion purposes

c. Impervious blend

d. Transition zone—fine granular fill

e. Drainage zone—permeable ground

f. Filter—fine gravel and sand

g. Upstream shell, granular fill

h. Downstream shell, coarse granular fill

i. Impervious blanket

j. Slope-protection, force draining into fields

k. River redirected through the tunnels

Projected timeline for this stage: 5 years.

For further information please contact the Ministry's chief engineer, Emilio Ranalli, Tel Nr. Bolzano 17-19.

28

RESCHEN VALLEY, SPRING 1941

I t was the espresso machine that saved the inn. That was what Katharina wrote to Jutta, in either case. Coffee brought in the MFE workers in the morning, who then returned in the evening to drink wine. It took a while for the regulars to accept the influx of new customers—customers the valley folk deemed the "enemy"—but Katharina made it plain and clear: those who had chosen to remain would now at least keep their opinions to themselves if they could not play nice, or they would have no Post Inn to come to any longer. But she did not write the details of that to Jutta.

I seem to have slipped into your pair of shoes well enough, she wrote. *But of course, I could never replace you. Lisl is exceptionally helpful, of course. But she and Georg will be leaving soon as well. We're rationing, like you, but we've never gone hungry. A lot of us barter. One way or another, we'll manage. We miss you.*

What she also did not admit to anyone, not even to Florian, was that the coffee machine—as big as a locomotive and hissed like one, too—had saved Katharina as well. And it was Angelo who was responsible.

He'd returned to the valley in late fall to lead one of the inspections before the next stage of developments. As the reservoir work crept closer and closer to the remaining homesteads, Angelo stopped in to visit the Steinhausers. Over cups of *Ersatzkaffee*, he diplomatically told them about an acquaintance of his who had opened up an espresso "bar" unlike any in Bolzano, and it did a brisk business selling exceptional coffees. Since then, several other proprietors in Bolzano had copied the model, but Angelo had remained loyal to his barista. Katharina had quipped that she hardly believed coffee could save the inn's lack of revenue.

Angelo had sighed. "You're probably right. Which of these workers on the reservoir are really dying for a good demitasse of espresso anyway? Besides, there is the Il Dante."

"Who also can't get their hands on anything but *Ersatzkaffee*," Katharina had defended.

When a large box arrived at the inn along with a ten-kilo sack of aromatic coffee beans, there was a note from Angelo enclosed. "I know you'd never accept this as a gift. I'm only letting you borrow it. If you don't want it, send it back. Otherwise, the bill of receipt is inside."

With a sigh of annoyance, Katharina had stood with her hands on her hips and wondered how in the world she would ever get the contraption going. Matteo abandoned his duties in the post office to help Florian and Georg. By the time Katharina was grinding beans, a crowd had formed around the bar, inhaling the air as if they were all drugged. Word spread fast, and within a few days, a line formed outside the inn before every morning shift. The contraption paid for itself within the month, and Katharina transferred the money to Angelo along with a hefty order for beans.

Katharina sealed the letter to Jutta and rose from the table only to catch Signor Grasso of the Il Dante lurking outside the inn. She suspected him of spying again, another aftermath of the espresso machine. The Grassos drew the workers in with their cheap Italian meals—something Katharina could not compete with—but those same patrons then drifted to the Post Inn for the afternoon digestif. She frowned and looked at the clock, realising that his frequent appearances seemed to coincide with the arrival of the post. She leaned towards the window and waved at him, and he scurried guiltily away, tugging at the ends of his moustache.

The next day, when a parcel arrived for Signor Grasso, Katharina could appreciate why Jutta had coveted the power of being the official postal address in town. Almost twice as big as Angelo's had been, there was a box, which Matteo helped the driver carry in. They placed it in the middle of the mailroom.

"Very clever," Katharina muttered, eyeing the threat. It took up nearly the entire space. The timing could not have been worse. It was the last weekend of carnival, and this was how the Il Dante was going to pull in the patrons for all the music and dancing.

Matteo shared a knowing look with her. "Competition," he said.

"Yes. So I see."

"New model, likely."

"You think?" She tapped the box with the tip of her shoe. "We'd need the entire reservoir just to run this thing."

"Mmm."

Katharina crossed her arms "Well, what now? I can't very well hide the darned thing until Lent. Look how enormous it is."

"Celebrate."

"Celebrate?"

"*Sí*, celebrate. You have a reason to be innovative. To negotiate new business for yourself."

"But I just did, with our espresso machine. I just found a way to get customers in."

Matteo rolled his eyes up to the ceiling. "Find a way to do

business together. One hand washes the other. Having good neighbours is a good thing."

"Mmmm," she mocked.

"You're right though, Signora Steinhauser. We can't hide this thing until Lent."

Katharina rolled her eyes. "Come along, Matteo. Let's deliver it."

"Together?"

"Yes. I want to see it when they unpack it."

Matteo ducked beneath the mail counter, and Katharina fetched a wheelbarrow out of the garden shed. They lifted the heavy box and rolled it to the Il Dante, where Katharina rang the Grassos' door. Signora Grasso leaned out the window above her. Her hair was loose around her face—all silver and black—and Katharina was afraid her bosom would fall straight out of her morning robe.

Katharina pointed to the box.

"*Col cavolo!*" Signora Grasso cried. "Nico! It's here!" The woman disappeared, though her voice—as if to alarm the valley of a fire—shrilled on from above.

A moment later, both of the Grassos stood in the doorway, Signora Grasso wringing her hands, her hair tied back in a hurry, and her blouse only half tucked in. She alternated between greedy looks at the box and sheepish looks at Katharina.

Signor Grasso cleared his throat and profusely thanked Katharina and Matteo for delivering the package. He moved to take the wheelbarrow's handles, but Katharina jumped before him and told him to point the way. Nervously, Signor Grasso unlocked the door to the tavern. Without further ado, Katharina rolled the wheelbarrow right in, muck and all, to the first table broad enough to hold the contraption.

Over and over, Signor Grasso thanked her for bringing it by, and Katharina stepped back and waited.

"Do we you owe you postage, Signora Steinhauser?" he asked.

"I'm not sure. Matteo? Is there postage due?"

"No." Matteo looked highly amused. "But I do believe Signora Steinhauser would like to see the machine."

"Oh! *Sí, sí!*" Signor Grasso began moving about the box, undoing the strings as his wife made excuses as to why they ought to not yet unpack it.

The moment of truth arrived. Katharina and the Grassos, along with Matteo, all peered into the box to behold the newer, bigger, and better model of Katharina's espresso machine.

Beside herself, Signora Grasso cried giddily, "It makes macchiato as well!"

"Macchiato?" Katharina asked.

"*Milchkaffee,*" Signor Grasso said.

Katharina snorted. "What do you need a machine for to make a coffee with milk, please?"

"Come," Signor Grasso said. "Sit down. I will show you."

Katharina shook her head. "This is going to take ages, and I really do need to get back."

"Nonsense," Signor Grasso said. "We'll be done in a few minutes." He indicated to Matteo that he ought to help with the machine.

Katharina did not sit down. It had taken them half the day to set up hers. "You call me back when it's ready," she said to Signora Grasso.

She had hardly reached the church when Signora Grasso came huffing and puffing behind her, calling Katharina to stop. She should return for a macchiato, immediately. Reluctantly, Katharina followed her back, unable to believe that the machine was already operable. But when Katharina returned, Matteo was already drinking a coffee and the air was saturated with the aroma of freshly ground beans.

Matteo raised his cup to her. "*Zum Wohl.*"

Katharina threw him a suspicious glance.

Signora Grasso led her to the machine. It had several extra features that Katharina's did not. Signora Grasso poured milk into a small tin jug and held it beneath one of the spouts. There was a lot of steam and noise, but when Signora Grasso showed it to Katharina, the milk was warm and frothy. She spooned a few tablespoons of milk on top of Katharina's coffee and handed it to her with a flourish and a wide grin. When Katharina reached for the spoon, Signora Grasso shook her head.

"Signora Steinhauser, only sugar. Do you want sugar?"

"No, thank you."

The woman's eyes were shining with anticipation as she gestured for Katharina to drink it just so.

Katharina drank. The foam, the milk, sweet on the palate as the espresso hit it. *My goodness!* She lowered the cup, masking her surprise and pleasure, but Matteo chuckled and winked at her.

"Mmmm," Katharina said drily to him. "Interesting," she added, just as drily, to the Grassos.

Signor Grasso tugged at his moustache.

She drained the rest and placed the cup on the bar. "Thank you very much for sharing that with me. I'm off to work then."

As Katharina drew up to the Post Inn once more, she stood at the back gate and eyed the garden. If Florian built a pergola back here, and maybe a new stoop for easier access to and from the kitchen, they could build a beer garden out here. Allow the guests to eat outside on nice days. Maybe even cut a window in so that she could call guests to pick up their own drinks and meals.

She patted the wooden gate before opening it. Yes, she would talk to Florian about it tonight.

~

The week before Easter, Florian finished Katharina's beer garden, and on Easter Monday, after milking the cows, Manuel helped her prepare for the *Frühschoppen* that would take place after Mass. They had just completed assembling several boards of sliced ham and bacon, hardboiled eggs, slices of cheese—*antipasti*, as Signora Grasso called them—and baskets of Easter bread before the church bells called them to the service. Katharina and Manuel hurried over, Florian and Bernd appearing just then, also running late.

Inside, Lisl and Georg were already in their usual pew.

Katharina bent to Lisl. "Everything's ready," she told her. "I'm going to slip out right after Communion."

Lisl nodded, and Katharina took her seat just as Father Emil started the service. Katharina twisted to see the Grassos in the pew across the aisle. Signor Grasso bent his head, and Signora Grasso grinned and waved enthusiastically.

For weeks the two inns had competed with one another for the largest available group of patrons: the workers from MFE. When Katharina and Lisl concocted a simple but filling lunch menu, Katharina reopened the guesthouse for lunch on the days that the Il Dante was shut. When the Il Dante set out a board with specials, Katharina did the same and added dessert. When Katharina shoved and yanked tables around in the garden to create the most ideal seating plan, the Il Dante set out tables and chairs outside the front door of their business. A few days later, Katharina had to defend herself when the Grassos marched over and asked how dare the Steinhausers put in a complaint about the Il Dante's tables and chairs were breaking regulations.

Katharina went to Captain Basso with them to clear the air, and Captain Basso admitted that it was his police officers and nobody from the town who had reported the violation. The tables and chairs were six centimetres too far into the street. Signor and Signora Grasso climbed up to Arlund that evening with a bottle of wine and flowers for Katharina and apologised. Katharina and Florian showed them around the *Hof*, and Signor Grasso was duly impressed with Florian's workshop. A week later, Signor Grasso appeared again, this time to see Florian, and put in an order for smaller tables.

When Katharina told Matteo this, he chuckled. "Competition. It's good for business, no?"

It was on Good Friday that Katharina had convinced the Grassos to take part in the *Frühschoppen* by uniting efforts. Each inn contributed food, wine, and their own touches of hospitality in a combined celebration with the entire valley. The Grassos were delighted when Katharina proposed it. Signora Grasso suggested putting all the tables into one large square in the garden, instead of keeping tables and benches apart. This way, she said, everyone could see one another, everyone could feel as if they were sitting at one large table together. Katharina thrilled at the idea. When Iris appeared on the Saturday before Easter, she jumped in and arranged flowers. Everyone that passed by volunteered to help, even some of the workers from MFE who came looking for a cup of coffee.

By the time Easter Monday service was over, it was as if the party had already begun. Father Emil stood outside the church, greeting the congregation members, and folks drifted to the inn, where Katharina was ready and waiting with the Grassos, Lisl, Iris, and Florian, all having slipped out after Communion. The garden was bursting at the seams within moments, and people laughed and clinked large mugs of beer and glasses of wine, calling *Zum Wohl* and *Salud*. By afternoon, when everyone was sitting at the tables and scavenging the remaining pickled vegetables on the boards, or dipping slices of bread into olive oil to soak up the next *Maß* of beer, Signor Grasso surprised Katharina by appearing with a guitar. Sebastiano Foglio dashed off to the butchery and returned with his harmonica. His girlfriend, Rosa, and one of the Tyrolean girls stood side by side with Iris, each taking a turn at a song—one in German, one in Italian. And the *carabinieri* closed their ears to it, raising a glass instead.

When Katharina closed down the inn—Florian and the boys long gone to tend to the livestock—only Iris, Lisl, and the Grassos were left. Signora Grasso smiled slyly, hand behind her back, before she presented a bottle of grappa, wagging it back and forth.

"I couldn't," Lisl protested. "I'm exhausted."

"Eine geht immer noch," Signora Grasso said. There's always room for one more.

The women laughed. Katharina pulled a chair out for Lisl. "I've got cows to milk in the morning," she said. "You don't. Sit yourself down."

"You know," Lisl exclaimed, "you're becoming just as bossy as Jutta was."

Katharina smiled wistfully. "Then let's drink one to Jutta. And Hans."

"And Alois," Iris said.

"And Alois," Katharina agreed.

A week later, Katharina stood in the post office staring at the two stacks of letters in front of Matteo. The return address on one stack was *Corpo Reale del Genio Civile.* The Royal Corps of Civil Engineers. These were the final offers on their land and the remaining homesteads. The envelopes bode only trouble. The second, in red envelopes—always a bad sign—contained the detailed valuation of the properties. Their resettlement compensations.

"This is it," Katharina muttered. With these letters, the remaining families who had chosen to leave would be able to. They would finally be able to settle the sale of their lands.

The bell rang at the front door of the inn, followed by Lisl coming into the post office. She was almost always the first.

She pulled up at the sight of Katharina and the postmaster. "They're here?"

Katharina stepped aside.

Matteo reached behind the counter and presented Lisl with two envelopes, one from each stack. "These are yours." He looked at Katharina and riffled through the first stack of letters from Angelo's office. "And this one is yours."

Katharina sighed and closed her eyes. It was addressed to Florian. She and Lisl looked at each other and shrugged.

At the same time as Lisl was opening her letters, Katharina slid Florian's open with her finger and unfolded the page inside. She noted the date was strange before comprehending that it included the year of Fascism: *15.IX.41 XIX.* The nineteenth year. *Address of the office: Via Dante 3, Bolzano Telephone Nr. 17-19.*

The letter listed out the assets, plot numbers, number of cattle and livestock, the value of the property. Katharina laughed bitterly. "He told me to expect this. He told me."

Lisl took in a great breath. "Minister Grimani did?"

Katharina nodded.

The bell rang on the door again. Georg appeared. Lisl whirled around as he came to her, and she handed him the letter. Matteo stepped back to the farthest corner.

As he glared at the paper before him, Georg's face reddened.

"Is it bad?" Katharina asked gently.

Georg dropped the page to his side. "Not even a tenth of what we are due."

"They don't want you to leave, do they?" Matteo said, taking a step forward.

Katharina turned to him, eyes widened. "Do you think that's what it is?"

"Rome is angry with Berlin. The resettlement is taking too long, not bringing in enough money, and Il Duce is still unhappy that it was the Germans who started all those rumours about Sicily and Abyssinia."

Katharina grimaced. "You may be quite right. Georg, look, if you do not accept their offer, they will prevent resettlement."

"And what alternative do we have?" Georg growled.

"To remain here and start over," Katharina said. "I think that the Italians will make a better deal for us to stay put and rebuild just as we were planning."

Georg ripped into the envelope with the offer on his property from the engineering corps. He guffawed and shook his head. "David is already at the German front. Henri and his family—our grandchildren—are already in Vorarlberg. Jutta and Hans are in Vorarlberg. Our families are all there."

"Frederick is here," Lisl said quietly.

Georg turned to his wife, his face contorted by conflict. "You would put your brother over our children? Our grandchildren?"

Lisl dropped her head.

Katharina threw Matteo a knowing look. "Come with me. I've got soup on. Let's talk about this."

By afternoon, when all the letters had been delivered, the air in the valley had soured. Each Tyrolean family had been trapped into a corner, and a representative from each family appeared at the Post Inn to discuss it. When the evening shift on the reservoir ended, a group of workers—men Katharina now considered regulars—noisily filed into the *Stube*, dusting off their caps and about to sit down, but when they spotted the residents, they grew quiet. The men around the *Stammtisch*, half of what they used to be, moved to the edges of their seats, menacing in their silence and stares.

Katharina hurried to the workers and shovelled the group out the door again. "Not tonight, boys. Tomorrow. Maybe tomorrow."

That evening, Katharina returned home and fell into bed next to her husband. Usually she fell into a deep sleep, but on this night, she lay awake, and when Florian stirred out of bed and rose in the half-dark, she sat up and fluffed the pillow against the headboard.

He paused in his dressing. "Did you get any sleep at all?"

"You noticed?"

He perched on his side of the bed. "What happened?"

"You mean besides the letters?"

He grunted.

"My hopes were too high after Easter. I really thought we might be able to live and work together."

Florian sighed and placed a hand on hers. "There's this idea I've had brewing in my head," he said. "Something some of the proprietors in hospitality used to do in Nuremberg."

She leaned forward. "I'm listening."

The apparatus consisted of forty numbered compartments, fashioned out of wood, each with a slit big enough for coins or paper money. It was large and heavy, but it would fit on the wall next to the door of the *Stube* at the inn. Florian and Bernd had needed a week before they presented it to Katharina. Manuel had stencilled the numbers in gold-coloured paint.

"Let me see if I have this right," Katharina said, admiring the *Sparschrank*. "Our patrons can register for one of these compartments, right?"

"Yes," Bernd said, eyes bright. "It's like belonging to a club."

"All right," Katharina nodded. "And they drop coins—"

"Leftover change or whatever they want," Manuel said.

"Which they can either use to pay for their drinks or meals," Katharina continued, "should they have no have money, or which is then donated to a cause that the forty members agree to."

"Yes," Florian said. "For a family who falls on hard times. Or for the school. Or even for a festival or celebration for everyone. If we talk to the Farmer's Bank, we might even get a good savings rate. I left a place here"—he drew a finger over the top—"for a plaque so the bank can advertise. Meaning, the monthly amount the patron has gets a small interest rate."

Katharina stroked the compartments. "I like it. I like it a lot." Most of all, she liked the idea behind it. The owners of the *Sparschrank* would return to her inn because that was where their investment was.

Eight regulars signed up for a compartment on the first day. Matteo and a further twelve MFE employees jumped at the prospect the next day. Over the course of the week, all forty compartments had owners, and Katharina wondered whether they ought not make another one, but Florian told her to just wait.

"Demand is what makes the deal sweeter," he said and kissed her forehead.

A few weeks later, as the lilacs scented the night air, Katharina walked home and heard laughter and music in the direction of the Il Dante. She had not seen the Grassos in quite some time. With the breeze still carrying the day's earlier warmth, she turned into the street that led her to the Italian quarter and the pub. She smiled at the song of an accordion and a guitar. Signor Grasso had to be playing tonight. She pushed the door open and immediately spotted familiar faces. The boys from MFE, Sebastiano, Federspiel's youngest. Katharina clapped with the music and walked up to the bar, where Signora Grasso was pulling the tap, and leaned against it.

"Good evening, Katharina," Signora Grasso said. She lifted the glass she was filling and indicated the wall to the right of the bar. "It's beautiful, what Florian has made."

Katharina gasped. There, a virtual copy, gold paint and all, was another *Sparschrank,* but with the numbers forty-one to eighty.

Signora Grasso smiled broadly as she leaned in. "I heard that at least a few of the owners of these little boxes have one at your place too. I asked them why, and they said because they want to distribute things fairly. 'Signora Grasso,' they said, 'we like you both so much, we want to make sure you stay.' And you know who that was?" She pointed over Katharina's right shoulder.

Katharina turned around and scanned the crowd of singers. Facing her, Matteo waved and winked.

29

SARNTAL, SUMMER–WINTER 1941

The *Lowlands* production was in chaos, and the extras—farmers from the Sarntal—were rebelling.

"What do they want?" Charlotte cried. She tossed her clipboard across the hotel room. "Those farmers out there are setting back the film schedule."

"They want to go home," Annamarie said. "They've got fields to tend to. They were supposed to be here for three days, and they haven't seen the camera at all. Riefenstahl is holding them hostage."

"They get the best food right here," Charlotte said. "We're spending millions of Reichsmark on this production. They get paid—"

"They have farms to tend to," Annamarie repeated.

But Charlotte was on a rampage and was not listening. "I'm handling complaints and gossip from everywhere, even Goebbels. Nobody is happy about their wages, and everyone seems to have forgotten they signed a contract!"

Annamarie wanted to remind Charlotte it had been like this since the first day. The morning after she'd drunk schnapps with Riefenstahl, Annamarie had hiked up to the alp only to discover the producer was having a fit about how the houses in the "Spanish village," which had been transported and built from the filming location in Spain, were placed too far apart. Riefenstahl demanded to know if her set designers had all gone mad. Her planned camera angles would not work with such distances. How was she supposed to shoot her precisely planned scenes in such a setting?

But it was the Sarntal peasants who were providing Annamarie her first up-close and personal experience to how very obsessed and selfish Riefenstahl could be about her work. The few days she'd brought the farmers up turned into a full week, and still dissatisfied, Riefenstahl demanded they stay on set and do it all again. So the men rebelled in a way that Annamarie could appreciate. They returned to the set with shaved-off beards in hopes of no longer appearing adequately "peasant" for Riefenstahl's picture. They were wrong. As their fields remained unharvested, and the country suffered from food rationing, Riefenstahl instructed Charlotte to order the makeup department to create fake beards and plaster them on her extras. They would continue shooting the next day.

Annamarie left Charlotte to pound her pillows in frustration and went to the dining room, where she found Riefenstahl arguing with six of the farmers again. Annamarie joined the group and shared a commiserating smile with the farmers.

"Frau Riefenstahl, you do understand where they are coming from, don't you?" Annamarie asked.

The director glared at Annamarie and yanked her away by the arm. "Are you undermining my authority now?"

"Not at all. I just meant to help. I come from a farming family. The crops don't wait, and these farmers have to make the best of the weather available to them. We have food shortages in all of Europe—"

Riefenstahl pointed to somewhere beyond Annamarie's

shoulder and said, "Your agricultural expertise obviously overrides your artistic one. What are you doing here? Still?"

Annamarie was not certain what Riefenstahl meant. Should she leave? Pack her things and go home? As she walked out of the dining room and back upstairs, she considered the fact that a similar scene took place in the movie. The peasants in the film were to come and tell the marquis that his new canals, which he built to water his prize-fighting bulls, have left their fields dry. And if they did not turn in a harvest, they could not pay their taxes. The marquis closed his ears to them and told them if they did not pay their taxes, they would be thrown off the land. In their world, however, Riefenstahl cared only about getting her reels.

Annamarie slammed the door.

Charlotte sat up. "What's happened?"

"I suppose I've just been fired."

Her friend jumped off the bed. "Why?"

Annamarie told her what had happened.

"Go hide behind a stack of cables or something tomorrow," Charlotte said. "And just wait until I smooth things over."

But Annamarie was not certain she wanted Charlotte to smooth things over again. She wasn't sure whether she'd prefer to return to the fields herself—back to Arlund—and help her parents make hay. But Riefenstahl calmed down and took her shots the next day, ordered Charlotte to pay the farmers a bonus, and sent them back to their farms.

Meanwhile, the film crew headed to Krün, Germany. Annamarie and the crew enjoyed a short respite until Riefenstahl returned from a scouting trip, where she'd been looking for extras that would fit the "Spanish look" of the villages. She returned with a bus filled with the saddest lot of men, women, and over a dozen children that Annamarie had ever seen—sad because they all looked as if they had been dragged through the mud, starved, and beaten—and still, as they stood in awe of their mountainous surroundings, Annamarie recognised the glaze of hope on their faces.

She asked Charlotte who they were and where Riefenstahl had dug them up.

"Some place called Maxglan," Charlotte said. "Near Salzburg. I heard they were penned in like cattle. They've been there for years. They're all Roma and Sinti gypsies. They look good though, no? Like real Spanish peasants."

Annamarie frowned. "They look like they could all use a good meal."

"They'll get that," Charlotte said brightly. "There's more coming too. From outside Berlin, when the city cleared them out for the Olympics five years ago."

"Cleared them out?"

Charlotte nodded. "They just put them all together into one camp. They were all living on the street anyway."

Annamarie recalled the BDM race lectures. Slavs, gypsies, Jews. *Untermenschen.*

Charlotte rumpled her nose. "You don't seem to be too happy about that. Then you won't be happy about this either. Frau Riefenstahl needs someone to look after the children. I told her that as a BDM girl, you'd led youth groups. She said I should put you on duty. You're to keep them busy and entertained, and most importantly, out of the way until it's time for them to be on set."

"I'm to be a child-minder now? But, Charlotte, I thought we were shooting the scenes where I might be playing a role—"

"Not until Prague. The castle scenes will all be shot in Prague now." Charlotte put a hand on her shoulder and shook her. "Don't worry. I've got it covered when it comes to that. Trust me. But today…" She faced the group of children, girls mostly, dirty faced and dazed by the landscape or the strange two-dimensional village facade or both. "Get those Spanish urchins something to eat."

The children, between ten and eighteen, were sweet. They were playful, and despite their skin-and-bones condition, energetic and eager. The other gypsies were also friendly with her. One claimed how being on set and taking part in the film was the best thing that could have happened to them. But when Annamarie shared that with one of the Austrian extras, the woman said, "Certainly it is. Do you have any idea where they came from? I can't imagine how good it must feel to not see a fence or a German guard in sight."

Maxglan was a detention camp then. She had thought it was just a place where the gypsies met and inhabited.

Annamarie led the children on short hikes around the area, and the children collected flowers that they then brought to "Tante Leni." Annamarie showed them how to play cat's cradle, and they taught her a silly game where all the participants had to spin on their axis for a period of time, then stand very still. The last to collapse from dizziness was the winner. Their favourite game, however, was "egg filching." They collected rocks into a basket and placed the basket on the ground, explaining to Annamarie she had to guard it and protect as many of the "eggs" as possible. The children then scattered about the mountainsides and hid, and Annamarie went looking for them. In the meantime, the children dashed out of their hiding places to try and filch a rock out of the basket. The winner was the one who collected the most rocks.

One beautiful teenaged girl named Rosa caught Annamarie's eye. She was the fastest runner and reminded Annamarie of a wild filly. It was as they were resting in the field, everyone just lying in the sunshine on their backs, that Annamarie realised she could get them to practice being in front of a camera.

She ran to her tent and fetched Sepp's equipment. She made a game of it. "Everyone now laugh," she directed. The children smiled at first, then giggled, and soon it was contagious and they were all laughing.

"Now cry," Annamarie said, pointing the camera onto Rosa. The children boo-hooed but soon broke into laughter again. Annamarie impersonated Leni Riefenstahl. "That's not crying. I'm going to have to do that again. Now cry!"

The children broke into further peals of laughter.

"What is all this chaos?"

Annamarie whirled.

Riefenstahl stood before her, formidable and beautiful, the white blouse, the silk white scarf around her neck, and the long boots. "Annamarie Steinhauser, I'd say you were either mocking me or trying to be me."

Annamarie sputtered, but the youngest children encircled Riefenstahl with excited chatter. Rosa stood next to Annamarie, arms crossed and sulky.

"It's time." Riefenstahl clapped her hands, her smile transforming into all business. "They're on, Annamarie. They should get into their costumes. I need to change myself, then we begin shooting."

Annamarie nodded.

She eyed the camera in Annamarie's hand. "I'd like you to work behind Albert's third camera. Just hang back and watch and stay out of the way."

She had not forgotten! After all this time, Annamarie was certain that Riefenstahl had forgotten or simply refused to keep her promises. Quickly, Annamarie herded the children to the makeup tents, Rosa following her.

"I don't think you're in this one, Rosa," Annamarie said.

She called Charlotte over, who confirmed that Rosa and the other teens were in the next scene. Rosa scuffed her foot along the ground and turned away. Annamarie considered letting her just watch, hang around, maybe even show her how to use Sepp's camera, as she had expressed fascination with it earlier, but the children were overly excited, and Annamarie had her hands full.

The upcoming scene was taking place in the village, when the dancer Martha—Riefenstahl—and her father would pull into the town square in their covered wagon. The "street urchins" were supposed to dash after the wagon, and when the wagon stopped, peek inside and watch Martha pulling out accessories and castanets, getting herself ready to dance in the local tavern.

Charlotte and Annamarie went over the instructions with them, as the children were dusted with makeup to make them even dirtier looking. When they were ready, Riefenstahl met them on set, dressed in her dancer costume, in barefooted elegance. The children bounced on their tiptoes and chattered until Riefenstahl clapped her hands like a schoolmistress. Annamarie looked for the camera director's third man, found him, and asked where she should stand to observe. He positioned her, and Annamarie shivered with anticipation.

The camera was set up so as to capture the children as they appeared at the rim of the wagon to watch "Marta" preparing. Annamarie caught sight of Rosa and a few other teens watching them, and waved. Rosa raised a hand. She seemed wary, even sullen in comparison to the last few days, but Annamarie turned away, concentrating on what was happening now. The children were placed into position.

It was gruelling work for everyone involved. Riefenstahl often stopped, checked the shots, and ordered take after take. She had close-ups of the little girls' faces shot over and over, and Riefenstahl teased further smiles out with sweets or surprises or tricks. It was hours before the producer was satisfied.

Annamarie thanked her for allowing her to observe.

"Did you learn anything?" Riefenstahl asked her.

"I think I did."

Her gypsy bracelets jangled. "Good. Good. Now, can you tell Charlotte to come see me? We're going to squeeze in one more shot with the teenagers. She should have gotten them into costume already."

Annamarie led the children away. "Come along. We'll pick a pretty bouquet for Tante Leni as a thank-you."

But Charlotte hurried to her and stopped her. "You know this Rosa? One of the Sinti gypsies?"

Annamarie said she did.

"I can't find her."

"She's probably with the adults. I think she gets bored rather quickly with the other children. Did you check with them?"

Charlotte was irritated, wide eyed. "Of course, I did."

"I'll go look for her."

But Rosa was nowhere to be found. Moments later Annamarie was standing before Riefenstahl, telling her she had last seen Rosa watching them as they'd set up the last scene. Riefenstahl straightened and stalked over to some of the crew standing along the sides. She spoke with them, and two of the men left, heading down the road and back to the village of Krün.

Days later, Annamarie heard that Rosa had been found by local police and taken to the jail. Riefenstahl disappeared from the set, and everything was on hold once more. It didn't matter anyway. A storm broke over them, and they were eventually driven back to town, where the cast and crew got rooms, Charlotte and Annamarie sharing one. The extras—those from Maxglan and from the detention camp outside Berlin—were put into a large stable and under guard.

Shortly before dinner, four days after Rosa had disappeared, Charlotte slipped into the room and fell onto her bed, sighing. "Well, that's over."

"What is?" Annamarie asked. "What's happened to Rosa?"

Charlotte winced. "She made Riefenstahl very angry. Frau Riefenstahl went to the jailhouse and told her that if Rosa apologised, she could come back on set. Apparently, Rosa's mother was also there. Rosa refused to say she was sorry, refused to promise she wouldn't run away again. So."

"So?"

Charlotte blinked. "I don't know. Something about returning."

"To Maxglan?"

"Uh-huh."

It wasn't until later, much later, that Annamarie heard Riefenstahl had yelled to the guards that the women—both mother and daughter—should be sent to a concentration camp if they were so ungrateful.

Annamarie fell out of love that day.

Just before they were to pack things up in Krün, Charlotte came around delivering everyone's post. Annamarie riffled through the envelopes, finding one from Sepp that had looked as if it had gone through a wringer. It was dated three months before.

My dear Annamarie,

Africa is hot. I'm feeling a bit like a Wienerschnitzel *in hot oil.*"

There were a lot of blacked-out words and lines, and even when Annamarie tried to hold it up to the light, she could not make out what was beneath. She had to take the information in bits and pieces, and part of her wanted to write back that Sepp should stop provoking the censors, or no mail would get through, or he'd be put on some kind of list of dissidents. But part of what she loved so much about him was exactly that—his firm principles.

She stroked the camera and deciphered further. He had tried to tell her about the men he was with, but at the mention of the divisions, how they were formed, the censors had rubbed out the information. There was, however, one clever part that even the censors could not have understood was code, as she had not at first either. He spoke of his weapon and said it reminded him of his fierce dog on the farm in the Eisack Valley. She mulled this over. She knew his dog. He was a cripple with just three legs who shat where he walked "as if he has permanent dysentery," Sepp had told her. And then she understood. The situation was not good.

She pressed the letter to her nose and inhaled it. It smelled of nothing and it smelled of everything she did not know, everything that the censors had blocked out.

Nobody amongst the cast and crew knew how the war was going for Italy, only knew that Germany had provided Italian units with support in Greece.

The next letter was from Arlund, and it was thick with letters from her father, from her mother, and from her brothers. There was also a letter from Margit with a request on the envelope to forward it to Annamarie.

Annamarie was delighted by her mother's retelling about an espresso machine, and she sobered when her mother shared news about Hans falling ill. Her mother wrote, *I can only fathom that he is still broken hearted by the loss of his home, his land, his sheep.* David Roeschen had fallen. That was the next news. Annamarie teared up at this. Despite what he had done with the VKS, despite David having been one of the reasons Bernd had been led astray, she could not forget all the summers on the alp with him, how kind he had been to her, how devoted to their livestock. She'd known him all her life.

Naturally, Georg and Lisl now don't know what to do, her mother wrote. *Whether they will continue with their plans to resettle or stay here.*

Her father wrote to Annamarie about the farm, and then she opened the letters from her brothers. Manuel's script and prose was so vastly different to the few lines from Bernd. Manuel always told her about the landscape, the farm, the animals, his hikes with Bernd, his discoveries. It was like reading poems. She always wrote more to him as well, always revealed just a bit more than she did to the rest.

It was Margit's letter she opened last. Margit got directly to things, and Annamarie's vision blurred as she read of Lisi's hospitalisation. She scanned the next lines.

Charlie is with us now.

Franz is concerned about his sister, naturally. As Charlie's next of kin...

The doctors say...

The one thing that baffles me is that Elisabeth repeats yours and Sepp's names. But there is little that either of you can do for her now, with you in the filmmaking industry and Sepp in North Africa. So we want to assure you that Charlie is in good hands and will stay so for as long as needed.

The psychiatric hospital was near Innsbruck in the mountains. As long as they were in Krün, Annamarie was close enough to go visit. If she moved on with the rest of them to Prague, however, who knew when she would be able to visit Lisi?

A few days later, Annamarie knew she was facing her last chance to abandon the production. They were to head out to Vienna the next day, but some of the new cast members were still trying to catch up, delayed by late trains and other war-related impediments. Among the new arrivals, Annamarie recognised Frida Richard, the Austrian actress who would play the matronly, no-nonsense head servant Josefa. They had run into each other in at least two other productions whilst Annamarie had interned at UFA.

Frau Richard joined her at a table and grasped Annamarie by the hand. "Charlotte tells me she's trying to get you a part at the table where all the servants are teasing Pedro," she said after they'd greeted each other.

"She is?"

Frau Richard shrugged. "That's what she said."

Annamarie fingered a tiny vase containing wildflowers. "I don't know if I should go on to Prague."

"How do you mean?"

"There's just…I don't know. I'm not sure what it is I should be doing right now."

Frau Richard chuckled. "How old are you?"

"Twenty. I'll be twenty-one next January. I wanted to be an actress, but there doesn't seem to be any direct way for me to get there."

The actress smiled. "I always knew I wanted to be one, but I didn't go straight into acting either."

"You didn't?"

The older woman shook her head. "I taught English for a while. It wasn't until I married Fritz and we moved to Berlin that I ever got on stage. And then it never really stopped. I'm apparently everyone's favourite supporting actress."

Annamarie smiled sympathetically. "I wouldn't even have any lines."

"But you would be on screen." Frau Richard pointed to Annamarie's stack of notebooks. "What are these?"

"My journals."

"I saw you sketching the other day. And filming with a camera."

"I guess I do a little bit of everything."

"Like Frau Riefenstahl. Also a very multitalented woman."

"Yes. I thought about directing, producing. I love everything there is about filmmaking."

"So why not pursue it?"

"I don't know. I don't see how. My boyfriend, Sepp—he's in Egypt right now—he wants to film documentaries. He worked as a lighting engineer at the Innsbruck State Theatre."

"Really? My best friend lives in Innsbruck."

"She does?"

"Yes. Her husband is the editor of the *Innsbrucker Nachrichten*."

Annamarie nodded, looking down at the vase again. "I never expected to be here, that's for certain. I never, ever believed things would end up like this."

Frau Richard scoffed. "And you thought I woke up one morning and said I'd love to live through two wars?"

Annamarie set the vase back in its place with a clunk and sighed. "I wonder if I should just go home. Wait for Sepp. Or, I don't know. Just…"

"The only way forward is forward. Not backward. Wait for nothing, child. If there's anything I've learned, it's this—life is no straight line. You will be tempted to take detours and be distracted by things, and that is all right. Take the opportunities presented. Goodness knows, for women they are limited enough."

"Sepp thinks I should go into reporting or journalism. Or write, in either case."

"Do you allow him to read your journals?"

Annamarie nodded, remembering him opening the books against her naked stomach and reading her words aloud. She flushed.

"Even Riefenstahl tried war reporting," Frau Richard said.

Annamarie swallowed. "I was with her once."

Frau Richard narrowed her eyes a moment, then leaned back. "You could give it a try, reporting. From the ground up, of course."

Annamarie shrugged, and before they could continue the conversation, a group of the cast walked in and surrounded them, and they were all on the move once more.

Annamarie awoke the next morning after once again dreaming of a child's scream, the shot, the silence, the slow-motion way the German soldiers killed and tortured the Jews of Końskie.

Before she could change her mind again, Annamarie asked Charlotte what decisions had been made for Annamarie's "roles" in Prague.

"I still can't promise anything," she said.

"Good. Then you won't miss me."

Charlotte blinked, her cheeks turning pale. "What in heaven's name do you mean?"

"I need to leave this for a while," Annamarie said in one rush of breath. "I'm going back to Innsbruck."

"And what?" Charlotte huffed. "Be a BDM girl again? God, Annamarie. You are the most impatient person I know. You just expect things to fall into your lap—"

"No I don't, Charlotte. And that's exactly why I have to go. I don't know yet what I'm going to do, but a friend needs me. And she needs me now."

"I need you." Charlotte stamped her foot, her clipboard slapped against her hip. "God, You're the only one who keeps me sane here."

Annamarie flung her arms around her friend's neck and kissed her cheek. "You know I love you, but if anyone is going to be okay standing up to that woman, it's you. Honestly, I don't know how you do it."

Charlotte blushed. "Practice, I guess. She's going to blow her stack when she finds out."

Annamarie laughed. "I doubt it. Half the time I feel she hardly remembers my name."

"Of course she does," Charlotte said earnestly. "After Poland…"

Annamarie felt numb, but Charlotte was right. The two of them, and everyone who had been there and witnessed that horrible day in Poland, would forever be bound to Riefenstahl.

Saying goodbye was not easy but Annamarie was taking the first steps, and the momentum propelled her to seek out Frau Richard. She found the actress on the pavement just as the bus pulled up to the hotel.

"May I have the name of your friend and her husband?" Annamarie asked.

Frau Richard smiled. She took the notebook from Annamarie, wrote in it, and handed it back. "I wish you good luck. And remember, sometimes you have to do the things you don't want to do in order to get what you're really after. Take it all, Annamarie. If nothing else, and when the time comes, it will make you into a most excellent actress."

As Annamarie watched everyone file onto the bus, she felt someone standing behind her. She turned around.

Riefenstahl, dressed in her trademark white blouse, a yellow vest, and flowing beige trousers, narrowed her eyes and indicated the bus and scene. "You've spent your entire life working for this."

"My entire childhood, yes." Annamarie swallowed. She thought of Sepp, about his decision to switch to the camera and filmmaking. "Sometimes there are different routes to get to where you ought to be. But I think you know that."

"Charlotte told me not to lose my temper. I'm not going to." Riefenstahl shifted her case into her other hand and waved it in the direction of the bus. "But get on. We'll at least give you a lift to the station."

By afternoon Annamarie arrived in Innsbruck, things looking bleaker than ever. The banners that had once hung welcoming the South Tyroleans had been removed. Graffiti on the walls, like when she'd first arrived, expressed the locals' displeasure of having to make room for the influx of new settlers. Landing before Tante Rosa's front door once again, she wondered whether her mother's cousin would even take her in, but Tante Rosa did just that, setting out tea and giving

Annamarie what was left of the bread she had—mostly made of chaff.

The next day, Annamarie appeared outside of Margit's apartment, bracing herself for a full confrontation, but Margit answered the door coolly, Charlie in her arms.

"I saw you coming down the road," Margit said. "Karl and I were just heading out."

"I'll come back," Annamarie said. "Or walk with you."

But Charlie kicked his little legs, stretching out a hand to Annamarie, and when he wriggled out of Margit's arms, sliding to the floor, she sighed heavily.

"Fine, Annamarie. Come in. I suppose the shops can wait."

Annamarie stepped into the apartment. There were photos of Franz and Maximilian, each in their Wehrmacht uniforms on the console next to the telephone. Margit stalked into the dining room and pulled out a chair before taking a seat in the other one. There was a jug of water on the table, and she poured a glass, placing it before the second chair as Annamarie followed Charlie in.

"Tell me about Lisi," Annamarie said.

Margit folded her hands on the table, keeping her voice low. "She was out of her mind, Annamarie. Simply out of her mind. We found her unconscious with those inhalers all around her, and Karl, well, Karl was covered in his own excrement."

"How is she?" Annamarie asked.

Charlie wandered over to a toy box and dug through it noisily.

"I certainly don't barge into Maxi and Lisi's apartments just like that," Margit went on. "I know they're just next door, but she never wanted me around anyway, not unless Franz was here. Well, I heard Karl screaming through the walls. I had to go in, hadn't I?"

"Of course you did."

"Thank goodness I did!"

"How is she?"

Margit looked caught out. She shrugged. "How should she be?"

"Is she speaking to anyone?" Annamarie asked patiently. "Can I go see her? Is she lucid or—"

Charlie came away from his playthings, holding a truck out to Annamarie, but Margit stood and intercepted him, scolding him for dashing off with an untied shoe lace. "How many times must I remind you, Karl?"

"I'd like to go see her," Annamarie said.

The fear that wavered in Margit's expression, the quick jerk of her head, reminded Annamarie of something—when Lisi had said that if anything should happen to her, she wanted Annamarie and Sepp to be Charlie's guardians. And by Margit's reaction—her mention of Lisi asking for Annamarie and Sepp—Annamarie knew that Margit was aware of something to that effect. Something substantial, at any rate.

"She's not allowed to take any visitors," Margit said. "Not yet, anyway."

Annamarie doubted that. With a flash, she suddenly saw what Margit feared most: Annamarie taking Charlie to the Reschen Valley. The idea was both terrifying and so appropriate that Annamarie nearly leapt out of her chair. She forced herself to stay calm.

"I understand. I'll wait for you to let me know when I can."

Margit looked taken aback. "I'll write—"

"Thank you for taking the time, Margit. I'd love to stop and visit Charlie and you on occasion. Maybe we can do lunch."

"Wait a moment. How long are you staying in Innsbruck?"

"If all works out, for quite some time."

"If all works out?"

Annamarie collected her purse. "I'll tell you all about it at my next visit." She went to Charlie and kissed his head.

At the door, Margit's smile was artificial. "Do call ahead next time. I mean, so that we can maybe plan with refreshments, or the like."

"Sure. That will be nice." Like hell she would.

The next thing on Annamarie's list was to find a job, which she also needed if she was to help Tante Rosa. After that, she would have to register her new address in order to receive ration books, but one step at a time. First, a visit to the *Innsbrucker Nachrichten* offices was due. The tram stop was almost directly before the newspaper's building. Annamarie stepped off and gazed at the three-story corner building before bustling in and asking for Herr Alexander Lackner.

"I'm sorry," the woman at the desk said. "He's not available."

Annamarie opened to the page in her journal where Frida Richard had written the names along with a personal note. The woman read it, read the signature, and lifted the telephone. In moments Annamarie stood in Herr Lackner's office.

"Well, I certainly don't know where to put you."

"The ground floor," Annamarie said quickly, "will do just fine. Even delivering the post. I'll prove myself, Herr Lackner. I really will."

"But why not continue with the film industry? Working with Frau Riefenstahl must be the biggest honour a young woman like you could possibly achieve. Why here? In Innsbruck? Why not Berlin? Or Vienna?"

"Frau Richard does not have a friend who is an editor in Berlin or Vienna, and in regards to the film industry, yes, it was incredible working for Frau Riefenstahl, but, sir, if I may? I believe I would prefer the drama of journalism."

He offered her a job on the obituary desk, finishing with, "It's small doses of drama, but then again, we do have a war going on." He wiped his glasses with a handkerchief before setting them back on his nose. "And it is better than delivering the post."

Three weeks later, with horribly mixed feelings, Annamarie appeared at Margit's door, but this time to pay her respects and help her formulate an obituary worthy of her Maxi. An unheroic death—a motorcycle accident while on furlough, killing both him and a Polish woman nobody in the family knew. Annamarie helped cover up the details with a tribute almost worthy of an Iron Cross.

"I'm going to see Lisi about this," Annamarie said. "Unless you want to do it."

Margit looked horrified as she stared at Charlie and shook her head.

"How is she?" Annamarie pressed. "Would she understand? Would she register it?"

Margit cupped a hand over her mouth, and nodded slightly. It was all Annamarie needed to know. Though Lisi was under medication, she was lucid.

Annamarie spoke with her, and a few days later, she escorted Lisi to the funeral services. After that, Annamarie allocated one day a week to visit her friend, and they spoke about Charlie and how if the hospital or the Rainers did not release her, Lisi wanted Annamarie to be the child's official guardian.

A month after Maxi's death, Annamarie rose from the obit desk and took the tram, then a bus to the psychiatric hospital. Franz's name had appeared on the list of the dead. He'd been on the Eastern Front. Each visit had been essentially the same up until then. Lisi would talk to Annamarie, they would converse, but Lisi was emotionless, which Annamarie almost expected when it came to Maximilian. But at the news of Franz, Lisi turned her head towards the window overlooking the garden, closed her eyes, and said nothing. Later, she refused to go to the funeral, and this affected Annamarie.

She had begun to fear for Sepp daily. Knew she would not

find out about his death for weeks, if not months afterwards. With each letter of his—and they came so infrequently—she felt a great surge of happiness and relief. He cheered her on with the newspaper job, joking how macabre it was for her to be working on the obituaries desk and then broken hearted for Lisi when she shared the news of Max and Franz.

St Niklaus came and went, and two days later the United States joined the world war. Annamarie made her weekly visit to Charlie then to Lisi. And finally Lisi reacted. She showed Annamarie the will that stated she and/or Josep Greil were named the guardians to Karl Maximilian Rainer. When Margit and the Rainers continued petitioning that Elisabeth von Brandt was not of sound mind and body, Annamarie pulled off her gloves, called her mother, and announced she would be coming home for Christmas, but what would the family think if she became the guardian of a two-and-a-half-year-old boy?

"Annamarie," her mother said, "do what you think is right."

"Tante Rosa feels I should pursue it."

"And what about your job? Your plans?"

"That? Yes. I've been promoted."

"Promoted?"

Annamarie smiled. Above the telephone console was a mirror. She gazed into it as she made her news official. Looking back at her was a good-looking—beautiful, even—young woman, dark curly hair, bright dark eyes, and dimples. "*Mutti*, I wanted to wait and tell you at Christmas, but I may as well tell you now. I'm moving to the Arts and Culture desk right after Christmas."

Her mother replied that Annamarie should find a good lawyer to help make her case for Charlie's custody.

"I have something to share with you," her mother said. "I wasn't sure whether you would want to know, but I feel you should."

Annamarie bit her bottom lip. Was it about Bernd again? Something about Manuel? Or was it—

"It's about Marco Grimani."

Annamarie's heart stopped.

Her mother hesitated. "Do you want me to share such information?"

"Go ahead." Annamarie's voice was flat from forced control.

"He was in Ethiopia—"

"Was."

"When it fell to the British. He's been taken to Malta as a POW."

"He's alive then?"

"Yes. Apparently he's an aeroplane mechanic."

"Well," Annamarie breathed, "if he's alive, then I suppose that's good. I can't imagine the Brits will do anything worse to him than what he did to me. So goodie for him."

"I knew I shouldn't have told you."

"But you did, and that's fine, Mother." Annamarie took in a breath. "It's fine. Really. I'm relieved that Angelo Grimani still has his son."

Her mother made a noise on the other end but said nothing more. Long after the line went dead, Annamarie clutched the receiver, tapping it hard against her breastbone.

30

BOLZANO, NOVEMBER 1942 – SUMMER 1943

Michael was lingering in the ministry's stairwell when Angelo stepped out of his office to head into his next meeting. He took the thick envelope out of Michael's hand.

"Have you got it all?"

"It's all there," the journalist said.

In the conference room at the end of the hall, the enormous table in the centre was hidden by bustling officials, representatives from the Building Works shaking hands with secretaries of the society, serious members of the consortium, and Stefano Accosi for MFE. Mastromattei's voice rose above it all as he called them to take their seats. It was a veritable hornet's nest.

"You'd better get going," Angelo said. "Before they spot you and zero in on you. It's enough that I'm putting my head on the chopping block."

Michael grinned. "Good luck. I hope you get what you're after."

Angelo shook his hand and left him, the envelope tucked beneath his arm. He walked in, found his seat, and placed the envelope beneath his file. He quickly made the rounds, greeting everyone. It was quarter after two, and he was certain the meeting would go over the hour they had planned. Business as usual.

"Minister." The man from the consortium shook Angelo's hand. "How is your son? We heard he's in Malta."

"As can be expected. The Brits are keeping the prisoners busy, and he is occasionally allowed to play football. His mother sends him regular parcels over the Red Cross, and he does get them. It's a small comfort but one we appreciate."

The man smiled amicably. "Shame, really. With North Africa lost, we're exposed to invasion. The Germans are nervous. Have you thought about reactivating your service?"

Angelo's smile was dry. "I am in service."

Mastromattei ordered again that they open the meeting. "Gentlemen, we have several important points to discuss today," the magistrate began. "But the two most important ones are the registered royal decree, and secondly"—he nodded toward Angelo—"we will share an update on the resettlements."

Angelo shared the details of the concession decree for the construction of the two power plants that would harness the electricity from the Reschen Lake reservoir. It stated the electrical installations would serve the economy but above all support the self-sufficient war industry in the interest of the national defense. As Mastromattei—and Angelo's father, for that matter—had always envisioned, it would primarily go to the industrial areas of the Lombardy, most especially to supplying power to the Bolzano Industrial Zone.

Angelo eyed Stefano Accosi and signalled Miss Medici to hand out the booklets he'd drafted. "These are the provisions that MFE will have to take into account. The king's instructions are expressly shared here. The State Building Office and the Public Works Administration will find that Article 9 provides explicit regulations for the two installations."

He waited a moment and allowed the men to flip through the

pages. "Gentlemen, if I may have your attentions directed here." Angelo rose and went to the board to unveil the first of his visuals. "In its introduction, it is stipulated that the concessionaire must take responsibility for all infrastructures surrounding the reservoir, such as road construction, rail construction, and so on."

He pointed to the detail on the map. "The first point regulates the flow of water in these particular courses. The second concerns the state roads of Stilfs, of the Val Müstair in Switzerland, and of Reschen. The third point concerns the interests of the Merano-Mals railway line. The fourth point concerns irrigation, agriculture, industry, fishing, hygiene, and other matters. If in the course of the excavations, the water supply in the affected areas changes and the necessary water for daily needs is lacking, MFE has to supplement the water by other means."

Everyone leafed through the details except Mastromattei. The magistrate's hands were folded on the table, and he was watching Angelo with keen interest.

"With the United States having frozen Italy's assets," Accosi complained, "how do you plan to subsidize all this as ordered?"

Angelo tapped his pointer in his hand and strode back to his seat, eager to reveal the contents in Michael's envelope. *Not yet. Not just yet.*

"I believe the magistrate can better answer that question, and I am certain he shall return to it."

Mastromattei nodded, looking relieved. Angelo smirked to himself. He had no idea what was coming.

"But before my part is done today, I'd like an answer to a different question." Angelo sat and withdrew his stats sheet. "And that's the status of the resettlement. Perhaps the magistrate can help us to understand why, to date, only about fifteen percent of the applicants who have chosen to resettle to the Third Reich have received their final appraisals?"

Mastromattei narrowed his eyes. "Minister Grimani, I feel you are out of line and outside of the scope of your interests, as well as your powers. Step away from your pulpit."

"I will do no such thing." By the slight nods and uncomfortable looks, Angelo knew it was a question everyone here wanted answered. "Even Himmler is demanding that you speed things up."

"The Tyroleans refuse to accept our offers."

"Because they are unjust and they are unfair."

"And"—Mastromattei's tone was dangerous—"they claim to be waiting for the final selection of a contiguous resettlement territory."

"That's the new general consul toeing the party line, and you know it. He's doing everything possible to delay resettlement." Angelo looked pointedly at Mastromattei. "We don't have access to the funds, do we?"

Mastromattei's jaw muscles flexed. "The United States froze not just our assets but the Germans' as well."

Angelo indicated Accosi. "Yes, but MFE here is not interested in that. They can't start construction until the Tyroleans have received payments. From what it looks like on the surface..." He stressed the last word. "On the surface, there appears to be a serious cash-flow problem. But beneath?"

The room was quiet. Looks diverted to files before them, anywhere but at Mastromattei or Angelo. Only Stefano Accosi watched Angelo with interest.

"If I may make a suggestion?" Angelo opened the envelope and unfolded the pages. If Michael was anything, he was organised and detailed. He held the first page. "Let's see here. Yes, Signor Turina, I believe this is a copy of a contract you have signed with a particular US oil company for oil in the Mediterranean? I believe that has lined the pockets of your enterprise quite well." He went to the next page. "And Signor Morandi? These orders here for pistons, gaskets, and other parts for aeroplane engines? I believe your supplier is also in the United States?"

Mastromattei straightened, rigid in his seat, but he was paying close attention.

Angelo continued riffling through the papers. "I have here proof for almost every single one of you for your dealings with British, US, and Middle Eastern companies for the raw materials, resources, and parts. And I find it to be exceptionally interesting that almost all of them are states with whom we're at war." Angelo let that hang in the air. "I will not take any further excuses as to why we cannot provide, first of all, the appropriate finances for the necessary infrastructure we must build around this reservoir and the two power plants, and secondly, why MFE cannot provide fair and just prices for the homesteads that have yet to be expropriated."

Angelo looked at the consortium member next to him. "Sirs," he said acidly, "I believe it's time you reinstate your services to the state. Or be labelled as traitors. My job here is done."

Mastromattei nearly knocked his chair over, he stood so fast. "In my office, Minister Grimani. Now!"

Angelo's blood did not simmer down after taking a walk along the river. It was late, the town clock ringing quarter to midnight before he finally veered in the direction of home—to Gina. Now what? That was what Gina would ask him. She was going to be furious that he had nearly put himself at stake, but he had proven Mastromattei that he had enough information to blackmail them all. For the time being, he could keep his job. It was almost over, and then he would jump ship. An activist, that was what he'd once debated with Pietro. Angelo was not a politician but an activist.

As he turned into the next street, two men spun away from

the corner of a building, hats tilted over their faces. They brushed past Angelo, and his insides jumped. He tossed a look over his shoulder, but the men were heading down the hill at a normal pace. Angelo waited a moment before following the bend in the road and was on the street leading to Gina's villa. It hit him that he often thought of it as Gina's, that he still felt as if he were simply a guest. But not tonight. Tonight something drove him to hurry home. To his home. To their home.

From the bottom of the road, he saw that the villa was alight. All the lights were on. All of them.

Angelo paused, fear pulsing through him. He heard a noise and whirled around. A cat slunk off across the street from beneath an automobile.

He hurried up the gentle slope to the yellow-and-green house. The gate was open. He stepped through, forcing down the panic. The door was closed, but pale light streamed through the windows onto the hedges below. He tried the door. It was not locked. All those warnings, all those hints that she was walking a fine line, ran through his head as he cautiously entered the house. Or it was him they were after. He was at fault.

The room to the left was the parlour, the white room. First thing he saw was the vase of flowers strewn across the white carpet. The books were scattered around the shelves as if an earthquake had shaken them out. The lounge and dining room were next. Chairs upturned. Crystal and china shattered on the marble tiles. His study had suffered a hurricane of perpetrators, the drawers, shelves, and cubbies spewing out parts of newspapers, his documents, his files. Angelo called her name, each call more urgent, louder. He rushed upstairs, the panic flooding him now. He did not want to stop it. He needed the adrenaline to open the bedroom doors. Each room—each of the children's, each servant's, and Gina's bedroom—looked the same: the mattresses had been uprooted from their frames. Papers, trinkets, jewellery, socks, doilies, underwear—everything—were strewn about on the carpets and rugs.

A door opened and closed in the foyer below. Angelo stepped cautiously into the hallway, edged his way to the landing. The light steps of soft-soled shoes. Two sets.

Angelo looked over the edge of the landing. Downstairs, two men. Hats tilted and angled. He could not make out their faces. One had a revolver in his hand. The other ducked into the doorway of the white room, clicked his tongue, and stepped out.

The one with the gun looked up the stairwell. Angelo ducked away.

"Minister Grimani? We know you're here."

Italian. But with an unidentifiable accent.

"You should come down now."

"We have copies of all of it," Angelo warned. "Anything happens to me, it will be printed in the newspapers."

There was a pause.

"We want to talk to you about Signora Conti."

Angelo pressed himself against the wall. *Damn it!* "Where is she? What have you done to my—" Wife. He wanted to say wife. "To Gina?"

"Minister, it's best if you come down here, with your hands up. We're armed, but we don't want to hurt you."

"That's not the answer to my question!"

"We don't know where she is. We were hoping you would know."

Angelo sucked air in through his teeth.

"Minister? Please come to the top of the stairs with your hands up so we know that you are unarmed. We're friends."

Angelo moved, but a creaking sound stopped him. The service stairwell! He spun around, looking for any kind of weapon. He saw the swift movement of the arm, and at impact, Angelo's last thought was, *These men know what they're doing.*

When he came to, all he saw were the lights and dim shapes

beyond the fabric over his head. A pillowcase? He did not know. It was a dark colour, however. He was bound to a chair. Was that a belt they held him with?

"Welcome back." It was the voice of the man who'd called from the stairs. "We're terribly sorry about that, but we had no idea whether you were armed. We didn't want a showdown."

Angelo's hands were tied behind a chair. "Who are you?"

"Friends. That's all we're going to say, so stop asking."

"Where's Gina?"

"We don't know. It could have been the Fascists who were through here, or it could have been the Nazis. Signora Conti was not very careful about covering her tracks as of late. We've been concerned about her for some time."

Angelo could still not pinpoint the accent.

"Minister, we came to warn you. You're being watched. Your ex-wife is being watched. And that journalist—Michael Innerhofer—he's likely to be next. There are very unhappy administrators at the moment."

Angelo groaned inwardly. His head throbbed.

"Listen very carefully."

The man bent down before Angelo, only a silhouette. Angelo heard the other one move behind him, and winced. *Just don't crack me on the head again.*

"Signora Conti is a valuable asset to us. We're going to find her. We need you to just stay out of the way. All right?"

Angelo shook his head. "I don't trust you."

The man sniffed. "If we'd wanted you dead, we'd have already killed you." His shadow moved away. "Stay out of the way, and make sure your ex-wife and the journalist have been warned. Understood?"

Angelo struggled against the bindings. "You have some nerve—"

"Good night."

Something came down sharp on his head again.

The ringing stopped in his head, and Angelo awoke in the middle of the dining room floor. His hands had been untied. He ripped off the head covering—indeed a pillow case from a sofa cushion—and stumbled out into the street. The sun was just rising, the sky pink. What if he was too late?

When Chiara opened the door to him, he grabbed her by the shoulders. "Are you all right?"

"Yes, Angelo. What on earth…"

He quickly explained and hurried to the phone in the hallway. He dialled Michael's number. It took three tries before Evi Innerhofer picked up and handed the receiver to Michael.

Michael said he would come to the Villa Adige right away.

Angelo replaced the telephone into its cradle and fell against the console.

Chiara looked frightened.

"Can you make some coffee?" He rubbed his head.

"Of course. Yes, of course."

When all three were sitting at the kitchen table, Angelo explained everything. He was worried sick about Gina. And he was certain it had something to do with the unveiling of secret deals.

"I'm going to the police station first," he said. He rubbed a hand through his hair, careful of the bumps to his head. "Then the German counsel. If I don't find her at either one of them, I don't know what I'll do."

Michael and Chiara shared a look.

Angelo slumped in the chair. "You don't think I'm going to find her."

Michael closed his eyes for a brief moment. That was a no.

Gina's children arrived to help clean up the mess at the villa. As days, then weeks went by with no word, no hint about Gina's whereabouts and each authority claiming they had no record of her, no arrest, nothing—as if she had never existed—fights between her children and him ensued. They hurled accusations until he picked up and moved back to his flat on the other side of the city. At about the same time, he sensed that the secret police were tailing him everywhere he went.

Christmas came and went, and Angelo tried to keep his mind on the work he had to do, and failed. He halted all contact with the Steinhausers. He stopped meeting with Michael at the Laurin. The trail was cold. Gina was nowhere to be found. And Angelo refused to accept any pity from Chiara or any of his other family members.

In late February, Mussolini went on a surprising and frightening rampage, as paranoid as Angelo had become. It suddenly became dangerous to be a member of the government, and one that had fallen out of graces, even more so. Government officials were getting fired, and others simply disappeared. Sleep eluded Angelo, and when he arrived to his office one day in late February, his nerves were already frayed. His office was in chaos, with security and police going through his desk, his files, everything. Miss Medici was in tears as she told him that the ministry was being completely restructured. Angelo was removed from his appointment as minister. The police watched as he cleared out all his personal effects.

When he returned to his flat, he unceremoniously kicked out the housekeeper. As the days, then weeks, went by, the dishes stacked up in the sink, he unplugged his telephone, and stopped going to the police stations and the German consulate.

The only place that was safe, was his apartment.

Angelo was curled up on the couch as usual one day when incessant knocking and banging on his door awoke him. He stumbled to his feet. A glass fell to the floor and rolled beneath the armchair. He was in his underpants and checked himself before opening the door, finding a pair of trousers slung over a dining room chair. He slipped into them, his head throbbing, the room dark. He turned on the light.

He flung the door open to Michael. By the sun slanting through the hallway window, Angelo realised it was the middle of the day.

Michael pinched his nose. "Christ, Angelo."

"What do you want?"

Michael dropped his hand. "To talk to you. We're worried about you. We haven't seen hide nor hair of you in weeks. And I have news."

"Gina?"

Michael shook his head warily.

"Is the war over?"

"No, Angelo, but there are developments."

"You're a reporter," Angelo grumbled. He left the door open. "You always have news."

Michael came in and grumbled and complained about the state of the scene around him. Angelo opened the shutters to the street and was blasted by the cold winter air. A bird sang in an ivy of an oak. Angelo squinted at the light and at the life below the street. How? How was anything happening?

He threw himself on the couch and indicated the armchair. "What do you want?"

Michael tossed a newspaper onto Angelo's lap before taking a seat.

Angelo turned it half-heartedly and shrugged. "I told you. I'm done with politics."

"Then I'll summarise it for you. Several of Italy's marshals and commanding officers have been brought back from abroad. Now, if I wanted to raise the alarm—and Angelo, I don't—there appears to be a shift going on within the royal halls. The king has only been keeping his own counsel. And we have a few who appear ready to play with the winning side, such as Castellano and Carboni."

"Castellano and Carboni? But they are—"

"Not exactly great supporters of our esteemed Il Duce."

"Wait a minute." Angelo stared at Michael. "Do you mean to suggest they might be talking to the Allies? Where are you getting your information?"

Michael tapped his nose. "Little scents. Here and there. My sources are dripping in information, and I am putting together the puzzle. This article here? Ciano's been removed from power."

"Mussolini removed his own son-in-law?"

"Does that make you feel better? Or not so special any longer? You're not his only victim, right? Yes, Ciano is out, and Il Duce is not showing good colour."

Angelo sat up now, unfolded the newspaper, but could not concentrate on the words.

"Apparently he's been showing signs of illness."

Angelo scratched his head. "A sign of weakness," he muttered. He put the paper down. "Gina had mentioned Castellano and Carboni to me once. A long time ago. Of course we know them in the military. She spoke of saboteurs and a shift within the palace. A slight one, but a shift nonetheless. Our military has certainly proven that it's not behind the Axis as much as Il Duce has been."

"What are you getting at, Angelo?"

He rose, went to the window. "I don't know. I just feel as if…"

"Gina? You think Gina is somewhere, supplying information?"

He nodded but did not face Michael. It was likely just his last grasp at straws. "Anything to keep me buoyed, damn it."

From where they stood, they could see part of the gardens of the cloister next door. It looked peaceful.

"Stranger things have happened, Angelo. But here's the bit that is quite terrifying."

Angelo faced him.

"Out there, there's word that the Germans are mobilising

extra troops north of our border. Can you imagine, if the Allies capture the south of Italy, how swiftly the Germans will come rushing down this countryside to meet them? If Italy falls to the Allies—"

"Then there will be little to stop them from invading Austria and Germany."

"Exactly." Michael jerked his head over his shoulder. "Get this apartment cleaned up. There's plenty to do. You come and see me when you're ready, all right? And let's hope that Marco returns home safe and sound soon, that this bloody war finally ends."

Angelo turned to the paper on the table. A shift. A coup? Perhaps. Perhaps not. Either way, Michael was right. The war could not come to an end soon enough.

In July the Americans landed on Sicily and took it soon enough, reached Rome. Everyone expected the Nazis to swoop down into the Alto Adige to secure the northern territories, but two weeks later, nothing happened. Grateful, and hopeful for the first time in a while, Angelo picked up his mother and took her to church for the first time in a long time.

His sisters both looked surprised when he walked in. Though Francesca made sure to scowl an *it's about time* look, Cristina smiled warmly and embraced him, patting the spot on the pew next to her. Angelo greeted his brothers-in-law and nieces and nephews, feeling surprisingly good about being with his family.

"Where's Father?" Cristina whispered.

"Not feeling well. He stayed at home."

A few moments later, he felt a tap on his shoulder and turned to Chiara.

"Nice to see you." She looked at him with grave concern. "I received a letter from Marco. He's fine. But why don't you come to the villa and have lunch."

"I'm going to my mother's," Angelo whispered. "Why don't you join us?"

Chiara tucked in her chin but nodded.

Angelo's mother nudged him. "I can't tell. Are you two married or not? Why didn't you just stay together?"

"She's right behind you," Angelo said.

Maria Grimani smacked her painted red lips and folded her hands back into her lap just as the priest started the procession. Angelo lost himself in his own thoughts for the entire Mass, remembering Gina at the front altar at her husband's funeral, remembering Gina the first time he'd seen her at church with her small children. He prayed for her.

When Mass was over, Angelo escorted his mother through the front entrance, and Cristina encouraged Chiara to come to lunch, stressing that she was welcome.

"Give us a minute," Angelo told his sister. "Go on ahead, and we'll join you."

Chiara threw him a warning glance but agreed to Cristina's invitation. They stood on the pavement and waited for the rest of the family to leave them, Francesca hooking her arm around their mother's.

"What has Marco written?" Angelo asked when they'd gone.

But Chiara could not answer him, as a huge cheer broke out amongst the churchgoers. A crowd surrounded the priest, and one man waved his hat into the air. Angelo's heart nearly stopped in anticipation.

"The war. Is it over?" Chiara asked incredulously.

The two of them hurried back to the crowd, and one of the parishioners explained to Angelo that Mussolini had been arrested. "Marshal Pietro Badoglio is the new prime minister," he said, his mouth quivering into an uncertain smile.

People hugged one another, and others wiped tears with the back of their hands. An old widow covered her cheeks and stared at Angelo in amazement.

Angelo took Chiara by the elbow, glancing at the square across the road. "Vittorio at the espresso bar has a radio."

When they reached the little café, bodies were packed around the narrow entrance at least six people deep.

Angelo stood on tiptoe. "Vittorio!"

Vittorio was standing on something to reach the dials of the radio on the shelf above. He waved at Angelo. "Minister Grimani! Move aside, folks. Let the minister in."

"Ex-minister," someone shouted from the crowd.

Angelo halted, chilled as scowling faces turned to him. Chiara pushed forward, apologising as she did, but someone tugged on Angelo's coat.

"Black Shirt," came another growl. "It's over for you. For all of you."

Did they truly mean him? Angelo was stunned.

"We know who you are." A strange man jabbed a finger into Angelo's chest. "You and the Colonel, we know who you are and your part in it all."

But Chiara had pulled him through, and Angelo was up against the counter in the next moment. All around him were the faces of working men, but when he tried to make eye contact, their expressions were menacing and threatening. Chiara now noticed it too, and her face blanched.

"They mean to turn on you," she whispered.

"Vittorio," Angelo shouted in a friendly tone above the din, "I'm as happy as everyone here. Tell your customers, will you?"

Someone shouted that they couldn't hear what the radio announcer was saying.

Vittorio waved a hand over the crowd and turned down the radio. "Shut up, all of you. And listen! The Grand Council of Fascism passed a vote of no confidence. Il Duce has resigned and has been arrested!" Vittorio turned up the radio again.

Someone shoved in close to Angelo, and when Angelo looked down, an older man elbowed his side.

"You can try denying it now," the stranger growled, "but we'll get you yet. Don't you dare fall asleep tonight or the nights after. We're coming for you."

"Angelo, we should go," Chiara said, and this time she yanked Angelo's arm to lead him out of the bar. Reluctantly, he followed her. All around the piazza, people were cheering and celebrating the news. Next to the café tables lined up along the back of city hall, a group of Tyroleans was dancing. Angelo turned back to Chiara, ready to take her to the Grimani apartments, but her expression was one of pure terror. Angelo followed her gaze.

On their side of the piazza, the mood and the focus were shifting. Straight ahead of them, a convoy of trucks and vehicles rolled past the church and into the piazza, squelching what Angelo now understood as premature celebrations. Each vehicle was decorated with the Nazi swastika.

The vehicles disappeared behind city hall, and the nose of the first one appeared at the edge of the front entrance. If Angelo led Chiara now to the Grimani apartments, they would be able to see the spectacle from the front, as one Nazi military vehicle after another stopped before the city hall and stormed it. But he, like the rest of the crowd on the piazza, were frozen to their spots.

Two men suddenly appeared before Angelo, hats pressed closely to their heads. They stopped and lowered their eyes. Angelo's heart leapt when he recognised the men from Gina's villa the night she had disappeared.

They paused as if to stare at the piazza like the rest of them, as if they were just two bystanders in the crowd, but they blocked Angelo's way. Then from the two Juliet balconies where Angelo's office used to be on the third floor, the French doors were flung open. On each one, a soldier stepped out and—like a choreographed dance—simultaneously unfurled Nazi banners.

One of the men in front of Angelo turned on his heel and muttered as he walked away, "When you have a moment, Minister Grimani."

He watched them head in the direction of the Laurin Hotel.

Chiara frowned. "Who was that?"

"Go home, please," he said. He remembered the threat against the Colonel and glanced down the road. "No, go to my father's and have them lock their doors. Then get out of there. Just in case. Go home and stay home."

Chiara began to protest.

He bent to her. "If I don't show up—"

"Who were those men?" she whispered.

"If I don't show up, send word to Michael. I don't know who they're with, but they did not kill me last time, so they—"

"Last time?"

"Go now. I'll be fine."

Angelo followed the street that led to the Laurin Hotel, but under one of the arcades, he caught sight of the two figures, who'd apparently been waiting for him. They walked on; he followed. It wasn't until he was near an alleyway in a residential neighbourhood that they stopped. They opened a door, and he slipped behind them into the kitchen of a tavern.

"Gentlemen," Angelo said, "I assume you're not here to hit me over the head again?"

"In there." The one with the funny accent opened the door to the pantry.

Angelo stepped inside. A chain rattled and a lightbulb went on.

"Hello, darling."

She was blonde.

Angelo stared at Gina, his face contorting with emotion, from relief, to sheer anger, to love, to pure sadness. She looked as good as she ever had. Healthy and beautiful. She wore khaki trousers and a sleeveless blouse, but her hair...

"The colour," he said, "really suits you."

She laughed, that head tipped back, but when she looked at him again, tears welled in her eyes.

He threw his arms around her, pressed her to him.

"I'm so sorry," she muttered against his chest. "I'm so sorry I had to put you through that."

When they unravelled, he waited, still dumbfounded.

"I had to make the regime and the Nazis believe that one or the other was at fault."

"It was a setup?"

"Yes. I sent these two men to you, as part of the decoy. I needed you to be desperate, darling, so that nobody would suspect you."

"My God, Gina, you could have sent a message earlier. Your children are devastated. They've been blaming me somehow." The accusations at Vittorio's bar now truly got under his skin. "Damn it, Gina, it's been nearly nine months!"

"And we've done a lot in nine months."

"We," he scoffed. "Who is we?"

"Did you hear the news?" she asked with a wicked grin.

"I knew you had a hand in this!"

Gina shook her head but was still smiling. "Believe me, there are a lot of us. We're not very well organised, but we are everywhere."

"Who?"

"The resistance." She winked at him and pointed at the door, where those two men were, he guessed, standing guard. "My British friends have done more than I ever could from here."

Of course! Brits! Those were the accents he'd not been able to place.

She kissed him and then rubbed his arms, as if to get the blood flowing again. "So," she said, "now that you have been freed from your ministerial duties, we could use a good engineer and veteran commanding officer."

Angelo pulled out of her grasp. "Me?"

"As well as Chiara and Michael." She lifted her chin, and her eyes flashed. "Soon enough the northern and central parts of Italy will be overrun by Nazis. But with everyone's help, we will make sure that it is only temporary. Your ex-wife and the journalist have a record as German sympathisers. We're going to use that to our advantage."

Angelo's head swam. Neither Chiara nor Michael would balk at the idea of espionage. Everything that they had done, everything that Michael and Chiara, and then Gina, and he had risked, led to this moment of truth. And Angelo was convinced they had a good chance of succeeding.

"What do I need to do?"

Gina's smile spread slowly across her face, but her eyes did not lose their determination. "You know the roads, the mountains, the entire infrastructures in the alpine zone. Tell us how best to sabotage them."

ORDER TO STOP ALL WORK ON THE
RESCHEN VALLEY RESERVOIR

NOTICE OF PROJECT TERMINATION
RESCHEN VALLEY RESERVOIR
August 1943

This valley is now under the occupation of the German Reich. All work on the reservoir has been ordered to a full stop and the company Monte Fulmini Electrical (MFE) and its employees are ordered to evacuate the premises immediately.

31

GRAUN, SEPTEMBER 1943

Katharina was not even out of the rabbits' pen when the goshawk swooped down. The cry came like a distant memory. She spun around to see two of the bunnies scatter in opposite directions. The grey one made straight for the black currant bush, but the bird fell on it before it could reach safety. Meanwhile, the spotted one dashed straight for her and the dog. The way the German shepherd pounced on it, she must have been waiting all her life for such an opportunity.

"*Aus!* Stop!" Katharina screamed at the dog, at the bird, at both.

But the goshawk hopped, flapped its wings, and airlifted its prey over the bushes and into the air. Bella, her jaws about the second bunny's back, shook her victim violently before tossing it over her head and catching it again. When Katharina charged at her, Bella dropped the dead animal and slunk away, lay down in the distance, and rolled over onto her side as her act of contrition.

"It's too late, you beast," Katharina cried.

Manuel and Florian rushed around the corner of the house but they were also too late. Manuel tried to soothe Katharina, promising he would hang up a net. They had two bunnies left. Florian checked the sky. From the walnut tree, a rook called, and several others answered on the fringe of the wood beyond.

Katharina swiftly tied the dog to the bench out front, yanking her by the collar to let the dog know she had not forgiven her, and Bella whined when Katharina turned away without her.

"I need a walk," she called to the men.

She took the back road and stopped at the wayward cross. Below, the valley floor lay silent. The Buda's were lined up and as still as death. Everything around the dam was quiet. The MFE workers had all been sent home, and nobody was allowed to work on the reservoir. However, the Germans were still going ahead with the construction of the rail line between Mals to the south and Landeck, north of the border. That, the Nazis had decided, would be useful to transport soldiers, machinery, weapons, fuel, and food to the front in the south.

A few weeks after they discovered the railway was still under construction, her hopes rose, thinking that she might get an influx of workers into the valley again, but Florian told her that the Nazis were using prisoners from a POW camp out of Trient. In other words, they relied on slave labour instead of offering jobs to people who needed them.

To add to that, the Germans relationship with the new Italian government was tenuous at best, with theories of the Axis falling apart. According to news reports, Mussolini was imprisoned in a secret location and his family under house arrest. But the Nazis practically force fed the Tyrolean population with news of Germany's great progress. The monstrous Allies, the local newspapers claimed, were bombing and destroying German cities, killing women and children, but the Wehrmacht was enjoying great victories on the Eastern Front. But then one of the regulars sat down at the *Stammtisch* at the Post Inn and whispered about the Germans evacuating Sicily. About the Allies landing in Messina. About Soviet troops recapturing Kharkov.

It could go any way now, this war. Despite the buffer of mountains around the valley, Katharina felt they were another pawn in the political games. Her daughter was still in Innsbruck. When Bernd turned twenty in February, he was immediately conscripted and was now fighting somewhere in Greece, on an island called Kos. And Manuel? If this war continued, if the Nazis were indeed winning, they could conscript Manuel in just two years' time. She'd have one son in Italian uniform, another in Wehrmacht. If the Axis did not stick together, Katharina could only guess what a situation they would have. She had seen what had happened with the valley during the Great War, emptied of its Italian workers, who'd had to retreat south, pick up their weapons, and turn them onto their neighbours and former employers. But now South Tyrol was occupied by Nazi Germany and the Steinhausers, the Foglios, even the Grassos, were Italian citizens with sons old enough or nearly old enough to fight. Others were German citizens, also with sons. Military age or otherwise, it did not matter—if the Axis fell apart, she could already anticipate how each family here would accuse the other of being the enemy.

A week later, news reached the *Hof* that the Wehrmacht had another reason to celebrate. They had beaten off the Allies at Rome and had control of the city. Katharina returned to Graun to check how everyone was faring, but the roads were empty. The only movement she found was coming from the Third Reich's flags blowing in a stiff mountain breeze. The Nazis had stamped their presence everywhere in the valley. On the town's notice board, the German eagle was neatly printed on every document, including the one that ordered the halt of the reservoir, and Katharina stared at it. Was it really over, this nightmare? And all for nought? With so many of the people they loved already relocated far away? Unshakeable was the feeling that she had experienced all of this before. The starts. The stops. The hopes. The disappointments. She walked by the buildings, the Italian names of the buildings already switched back to German with a simple banner over the hand-painted signs: *panificio* was now *Bäckerei* again. *Beni vari* was now *Güter und Waren* for the sundry goods shop, and even the Post Inn also had a banner. It was no longer the *albergo* but *Gasthaus*. The occupying regimes could do what they want. She was sick with the feeling that her Tyrol was forever gone.

As she stuck the key into the back door, she could hear Kaspar Ritsch—Toni's deceased father—and her own Opa, their beer mugs thunking dully on the *Stammtisch* table.

"Tyrol!" Kaspar would be the first to exclaim. "Autonomous for one hundred years!"

Yes, she could remember that. She had always been present during those discussions, but never quite aware of what they all meant back then. Now Katharina was wide awake, and when the arguments broke out amongst the townsfolk again, she wearily asked herself whether she had always been naïve, believing that those loud voices over schnapps had never really been about polite disagreements buffered by a strong value for community, but truly hate waiting for its moment to raise its ugly head and take control.

Heavy-hearted, Katharina entered the kitchen of the empty Post Inn. A fly buzzed above the counter, and she waved it impatiently away and turned on the radio. Excited chatter filled the space, a radio announcer interviewing Italian police. When the fly dove for her head, she angrily searched for the swatter.

"...amazing crash landing on Gran Sasso... Dozens of gliders... A feat never heard of before ... Parachute jumpers... Mussolini... The most daring breakout ever."

Katharina stopped trying to swat the fly and turned to the radio, but the announcer signed off. She turned the dial—static, static, more static. She clicked off the radio, heard the buzz of that elusive pest, and searched for it. She jumped when someone knocked on the door.

Father Emil peeked in. "Katharina, have you heard?"

"I'm not sure. Heard what?"

He shut the door behind him, his voice low. "The Nazis just pulled off the most daring rescue mission."

She frowned, still searching for the fly. "Rescue?"

"Yes! They flew onto Gran Sasso in gliders, landed on the mountain where Il Duce was, and got two hundred *carabinieri* to stand down. Not a shot was fired, and the Nazis just flew off with him. Il Duce's headed here."

"To the Reschen Valley?" she gasped.

"No, but somewhere in the area. Berlin will certainly want Mussolini to reestablish the Fascist government."

The fly buzzed near her head and landed on top of the counter across from her.

Swat!

Katharina dropped the swatter, drained. "I thought that would feel more satisfying."

"What?"

"Being rid of that nuisance."

Father Emil winked. "The fly or Mussolini?"

Katharina gaped at him. The morning's tension evaporated, and she laughed.

～

"It's a very thin line," Florian said gravely.

Georg Roeschen arched an eyebrow. "What is?"

Katharina placed the tray on the bar and took a seat next to her husband at the *Stammtisch.* Georg and Lisl were side by side across from her, their hands folded on the table, as if about to lead grace. Dr Hanny and Iris, like family bookends, sat on either side of the Roeschens.

"There's a very thin line between fear and respect," Florian said.

"You say Katharina and I are making our decision to stay based on fear, but I feel it is out of respect. You can say what you want about Angelo Grimani, but he fought hard for the new offers."

"Very well put, Florian. Very well put," Iris said softly.

"The fear, really"—Dr Hanny eyed Georg and Lisl and pointed to the window—"is that if you hold out any longer, the offers will be handled by the new Republic of Salò. And it could be that everything Grimani did for us will be thrown out if Il Duce comes back to rule in Rome. But I lay my bets with the new Italian government, the one committed to working with the Allies. I bet they will eventually knock Mussolini off his feet. If we just wait…"

Lisl glanced up, the uncertainty, the grief, the pain etched deep into her brow. How much more did the woman have to take, Katharina wondered? But this was too important.

"It's the last thing Angelo Grimani did," Katharina urged, "before losing his job and disappearing. Look at what has happened these past months. There was a change, a real change. And it will come again. We can't believe that the Nazis or this new Fascist government are going to succeed. The Allies will have to win, and if you are not here, who will take your grievances to the proper authorities for you?"

Georg gazed at her, took in a breath, and patted the tabletop. He glanced at his wife before rising. Lisl slid her hands into her lap.

"We'll stay here," Georg said.

Lisl's expression transformed into one of sheer surprise. Katharina could not help but smile, though she understood the loss the Roeschens were feeling. The Steinhausers' farm had also fetched a mere tenth of the price of its real value, but she and Florian had accepted the terms, certain that come what may, they would manage to rebuild, and Katharina harboured a secret need to see Mussolini topple.

"Have you sent the valuations to Jutta and Hans?" Dr Hanny asked her.

Katharina nodded. "Went out yesterday. We haven't heard from them in quite some time, but I hope we will now. Thank you again for your help in getting at least a little money to them."

Iris winced. "Hans is still devastated by the loss of his farm and his sheep, no? I cannot imagine what it must be like for him to work in a factory. And that institution that Alois is in, apparently it cost more than they had imagined? Isn't that what you said?"

Katharina nodded. "We must all have faith."

The Hannys and the Roeschens took their leave, and Katharina decided to lock up the Post Inn until the next day. She wasn't doing any business, anyway. The townsfolk—what were left of them—had essentially retreated to their meadows to finish off the summer. She and Florian had to get back up to Graun's Head the next day and bring what was left of their herd. They would sell a few more of the cows, the last of their goats, if they could manage a good price and fetch what they could for their valuables, bit by bit. What hurt the most was that the reservoir plans were at a standstill and still the land had to be vacated by the following year. Not even the Nazis could prevent that, not with Mussolini now ruling his puppet state from Salò.

Shortly after she arrived home, Manuel came down the stairs, one slow step at a time. Katharina looked up expectantly.

"Papa?"

"What is it?" Florian lowered his paper.

"If the war doesn't end soon, will I have to fight as well?"

"No," she said quickly. "It will be over before you're old enough."

Florian cast her a look. "Your mother is probably right."

"And what if she's not?" Manuel asked, now leaning against the tiled oven. The fire crackled inside. "Would I be Wehrmacht? Or Italian Fascist? Or Italian Royal Guard?"

Florian coughed into a fist. "Good question, Manuel. We have no idea."

Katharina looked at him, remembering how Florian had laughed drily at the news of the new republic. "Only ones who recognise it are Germany and Japan," he'd said. And she knew he'd said it to reassure himself more than even her.

Two weeks after the Roeschens had decided to stay in the valley, and the herds were back down from the meadows, and Katharina walked back to Graun to check on the inn. At the top of the road, she saw a strange sight. One vehicle after another—the black-red-white swastika flags stuck on both sides of the front—were coming down from the pass. When she scanned the town, she saw another line of vehicles coming from the south, also German. What was happening now?

It was when the bell tolled—a tone that collided with itself in a deep, mournful announcement—that Katharina stopped in her tracks. War. It was announcing war. Again? Then she understood. Italy was now at war with Germany.

The two German military convoys met each other in Graun. She wrapped her cardigan tightly around her and hurried back home. Florian was already coming around the corner of the house, his face stunned.

"Did you hear that?" she cried. "Did you hear that?"

Florian nodded. "I'm going into town with you. This is not good."

Katharina was breathless. No. It was not good. If Italy had joined the Allies and declared war on the Third Reich—and the Republic of Salò—she and her family were in occupied Germany now.

❧

The troops moved in fast. There was no stopping them. Florian and Katharina stood off to the side of the road with Father Emil,

Georg and Lisl, and the Grassos. The vehicles parked in the square outside the church and alongside the town hall. Soldiers were escorting the disarmed *carabinieri* outside and lined them up alongside the vehicles. An officer slowly slid out of his sedan and scowled at the muddied street. When the doors of the town hall burst open again, Captain Basso and Prefect Ghirardelli were shoved outside and brought before the German officer, who said something to the two Italian authorities. Katharina could imagine how many of their former townsfolk would have cheered to see Ghirardelli and Basso in custody, but Katharina only felt dread.

A Nazi second-in-command in a brown uniform shouted at the crowd. "Who owns that inn there?"

Eyes darted over Katharina. Florian and she stepped forward at the same time.

"We don't own it," Florian said in his Nuremberger dialect. "We're leasing it. How can we assist you?"

"We're going to need beds for our men here, and food. You have a key?"

"Certainly." Florian turned to Katharina, and she led the way to the inn. With that, the crowd dispersed.

As she unlocked the door, the telephone at the reception desk rang, as if it had been doing so incessantly. She opened the door for the officer and wanted to answer it, but he stopped her.

"I'm Feldwebel Heinrich Mayr," he said.

"You sound Tyrolean," Katharina said nervously.

"From Innsbruck. How many beds do you have here?"

The phone stopped abruptly.

"Thirty-two," Florian answered. "There are two dormitories with eight beds and six rooms with double beds. The rest are single rooms."

Mayr looked him over. "German. Veteran?"

"Great War," Florian said. "France."

Mayr approved with a sharp nod. To Katharina he said, "We'll take all the rooms. Breakfast, lunch, and dinner?"

Katharina stammered. "I will need to get some help, but yes, we can manage, though supplies—"

"We'll provide what you need. And we will need receipts for everything you are able to get your hands on."

Men marched into the corridor, carrying bags and equipment.

"*Stube?*" Mayr pointed to the door.

"*Sí,*" she said. "I mean, yes."

He narrowed his eyes at her. "Name."

"Steinhauser," Florian said. "Florian and Katharina Steinhauser."

"Good, Herr and Frau Steinhauser. And this door here?" He pointed at Jutta's old apartment.

Hands shaking, Katharina eventually found the correct key and unlocked it. From the front desk, the telephone rang again.

"Excuse me," she said, "I should answer that."

Mayr lifted a hand. "It can wait. The only thing you *should* do now, Frau Steinhauser, is make sure that this house is safe for my men."

Katharina opened the door to the apartment, and the staff sergeant strode in, checked the bedroom at the back, opened the cabinets—Katharina caught sight of a bottle of Jutta's renowned hazelnut schnapps—and closed them with some finality.

"It will do. This is now Gauleiter Franz Hofer's district."

Katharina frowned. Wasn't that the Gauleiter from Innsbruck? Florian and she followed the officer back into the hall, the phone silent once again.

The little brass bell rang each time the door opened, and soldiers shuffled in and out between the *Stube,* the hall, and the stairwell to the rooms, but Katharina pulled up at the sound of one voice.

"It's good to be home again!"

She whirled around and stood face to face with Toni Ritsch. Behind him, Andreas grinned.

Toni narrowed his eyes and flicked his gaze to Florian behind her. "Look at that, Andreas. Two of the *Dableiber* are right here. We don't have to go far to find one. They're coming right out of the woodwork. I told you, Steinhauser"—Toni glowered at Florian—"the Führer would come back for us."

"*Schutze* Ritsch," Mayr called. "There will be plenty of time to interrogate the locals about who is who."

"*Jawohl, Herr Kommandant!*"

Toni sneered as he and Andreas pushed past with their duffels and weapons.

Katharina fell against the wall, hugging herself. The phone again. A third time. It had to be important.

She indicated the telephone to Mayr, and he stepped away so she could get to the desk.

"Hello?"

"Mother? Is that you? Finally!"

"Annamarie, are you all right?"

"No! I am not all right! We're at war with you."

"I know." Katharina rubbed her forehead. "Can you come home? Can you get to the border?"

"It's too late." Her daughter sobbed on the other end of the line.

Katharina took in a deep breath, looked up at the ceiling, and gripped the receiver. "Listen to me. We can—"

"Mother," Annamarie cried. Katharina could tell she was trying to collect herself. "I just read the wire. Tell me again. Where is Bernd?"

Katharina's mind whirled. Florian was heading to her, concern on his face. Soldiers continued flooding into the inn. Someone was asking for keys to the rooms.

"Kos," she finally said. "It's called Kos." She waved at Florian to start sorting out the keys.

Annamarie breathed into the phone. "Mother, he's in great danger."

"What's happened?"

Annamarie hesitated. The line crackled. Katharina turned away from the oncoming flood of soldiers gathered around the desk. Florian stepped around her and collected the room keys to pass out. She pressed the receiver harder into her ear until it hurt.

"...five thousand massacred. Someplace in Greece called Cephalonia. The Germans were supposed to just disarm them. Five thousand Italian troops. Mother, the Nazis are just killing them off!"

Katharina went cold. The muscles in her arm, the one holding the phone, cramped.

Annamarie sobbed again. "And Sepp. I don't know where he is. I really don't. Greece. Yugoslavia? I haven't heard from him in weeks."

Katharina turned back to Florian, grasping his arm. Jogging down the stairs, past the soldiers heading upwards, were Toni and Andreas.

Andreas placed his index finger beneath his nose and lifted his right hand in a salute.

Toni, behind him, cocked an imaginary gun in her direction and pulled the trigger.

"Traitors," he murmured as he passed her desk.

In her ear, Annamarie was outraged as she wailed, "Those traitors! They're massacring our own people!"

32

INNSBRUCK, JUNE 1944

hy do you care so much about a country you left? And
W *voluntarily?*
But if I didn't care, where do I then belong? It's my home. I will always care. Just because a daughter marries and leaves her family does not mean that she stops concerning herself with her parents. That's it then. Italy—South Tyrol—is my parent.

Annamarie shut the journal and placed it on the desk, straightened her blouse, and hurried downstairs. Tante Rosa would wonder what was keeping her and scold Annamarie again for forgetting her. Ever since the bombings on Innsbruck last December, her aunt had lost her aloofness and self-reliance. She was as skittish as a young goat. No matter how often Annamarie tried explaining how writing caused time to fly twice as fast, the woman would wave a dismissive hand and snap, "Nonsense. It's your attraction to chaos!"

In the kitchen, Annamarie quickly put the hot water on, opened the larder, and pulled out the two boiled potatoes left over from the night before. She quartered them, snipped chives over them, and set them onto two plates.

Tante Rosa limped into the kitchen, her cane shaking as if she were prepared to thrash it.

"Late again," she grumbled. She laid a stack of envelopes onto the counter. "The post's already been here. The carrier complained again that the letters addressed to AL Greil only serve to confuse him."

"He'll get used to it." Annamarie set the plates back down and riffled through the letters. Not a single one with Sepp's handwriting. Her heart made a swan dive until she found the one addressed to AL Greil, postmarked from Rome. The letterhead read *Noi Donne*.

Tante Rosa slid one of her signature disapprovals down her nose. "Tell me again how you came to that name."

"Annamarie Louisa for AL, and Sepp's last name is Greil."

"But you're not even married. What if they ask for your full name?"

Annamarie ripped open the envelope. "It's called a pen name, and this way they can't tell whether I'm a woman. Steinhauser is a mouthful. I think AL Greil sounds poetic, exotic. Certainly mysterious." What she wanted was to honour Sepp, who had encouraged her to pursue writing and even a bit of photography, and because she was submitting some of his own photos.

"Mysterious like your Sepp?" Tante Rosa's countenance was gentler. "Still no word from him?"

Annamarie shook her head as she unfolded the letter. At this point, she wanted to believe that no news was good news.

"Well, at least we know where Bernd is."

Annamarie glanced at her and scowled. "Fighting with the Germans. What else?"

"It saved his life though, switching sides. Maybe if your Sepp had done the same…"

But Annamarie was busy reading, the smile spreading slowly across her face. She pressed the paper briefly to her chest before holding it out for Tante Rosa to read.

"It's in Italian," the woman complained.

"Sorry. Of course. It says they've accepted my story."

"Who has? Be specific. I swear, you're carrying on as if you were some double agent."

"The magazine *Noi Donne*. It means *We Women*. Look. It's signed by both founders and editors. I wrote to them when the magazine was still in Paris, but now they've moved to Italy."

"Slow down, Annamarie. Which story?"

"The one I wrote about working with Leni Riefenstahl. And look here." Annamarie jabbed the line with the amount of payment.

"A thousand lire," Tante Rosa murmured. "Or is it thirty-two hundred? Well? Which is it?"

Annamarie grinned and waited a moment. "Both. A thousand for the story and the rest for the four photos I sent them. But the payment for the photos is for Sepp."

"That's still a thousand lire." Tante Rosa's eyes widened. She scanned the page again. "Why that's—"

"Around one hundred Reichsmark!"

The cane stopped shaking as Tante Rosa straightened. Her smile was slow, luxurious, that hint of regality surfacing from beneath the wreckage of war.

"That would at least put some butter on those potatoes," she determined. She patted Annamarie's arm. "I like this AL Greil. I like him very much. Can we finally have breakfast? Where is that tea you were going to make?"

After breakfast, Annamarie hurried into work, excited to share the news but not quite daring to yet. She scanned the theatre section for her review and read it quickly, then prepared her notes for the upcoming assignments. Her editor approached her table and handed her a flyer. She took it from him absentmindedly, but he held on to the other end until she looked up.

"There have been more bombing raids, and there's a warning

that Innsbruck might be under attack again, soon. Everyone is to study the nearest air-raid shelters in their vicinity. Understood?"

Annamarie frowned. "Yes. Fine. I heard you."

"Annamarie. Pay attention. You can be really chaotic sometimes."

She huffed. Second time in one day someone accused her of not being orderly. She made a show of studying the page. "Got it. There's one near Tante Rosa's place at the monastery, and for the newspaper we're in—"

"Around the corner," he said pointedly.

"I'm organised," Annamarie whispered, sweeping a hand over her desk. "Look at this. I'm organised."

"Looks can be deceiving."

"I'm leaving early today."

"Again?"

"Lisi. Every other Monday."

"Is it really Monday?"

She smiled. "Always after the weekend. You really ought to stop working seven days a week."

"In case you didn't know, there's a war on. Tell them to stop fighting, and I'll stop working."

"You're the arts and cultures editor."

He raised his arms and sighed. "And the shows must go on."

When he'd left her, Annamarie went back to work, and before she knew it, it was eleven. She grabbed the cardigan she had on the back of her chair and checked the windows outside. The sky was still overcast, and she took her umbrella with her.

The convalescent home was on Lansersee, the von Brandts having spared no expense in making sure Lisi was comfortable. Getting there always took Annamarie a long time, but Mondays were her slow days at the paper. She took the pathway to the front of the building and checked in. Lisi was beneath the overhang out in the garden, a blanket on her lap.

Annamarie kissed her cheek in greeting.

"I always wonder why you bother to come," Lisi said.

"Nonsense. Why wouldn't I?"

Her friend looked off into the distance. It had begun to rain, and Annamarie breathed in the scent of jasmine and hyacinth. They sat together, quiet and contemplative, Annamarie in an outdoor armchair, Lisi, pale and fragile looking, in a wheelchair the hospital staff used to shuffle her from one area to the next.

"Do you want to walk a little?" Annamarie asked.

Lisi looked at her as if she were daft. "It's raining."

"It's spring."

"I'm not really up for it."

Annamarie bit back her frustration. Lisi had made herself into this, had weighted herself down with grief and bitterness and drugs and disappointment to the point where she possibly no longer could stand. About Sepp, Annamarie rarely broached the topic because she feared Lisi would end up prostrate in bed.

"Then let me take you back to your room and do your hair," she said instead.

Lisi agreed to that, and Annamarie tried to lighten the mood by putting flowers in the crown of braids and reciting lines from various plays with her. Lisi awakened after that, laughed a little even. Her skin was sallow, her cheeks sunken, but something brightened in her eyes. Those occasional moments were the reason Annamarie regularly returned.

Annamarie was about to leave, when someone knocked on the dormitory door. Margit peeked her head in, but Charlie burst out from behind her at the sight of Annamarie and flung himself on her.

"Look at you," Annamarie said happily. "My goodness, you're growing up."

"You always say that, Tante Annamarie."

"It's because I'm your Tante that I say it." At almost five, he looked like Maximilian more than ever.

Margit stood in the doorway, stiff and immaculate.

Annamarie rose and greeted her, but Margit stuck her hand into her purse and withdrew an envelope, waving it as if it were a knife.

"Is this your doing?" she shrilled.

Annamarie retreated a step. "What is it?"

"What is it? What is it? Oh, I'm quite certain you know what it is. I knew you'd be here, and I wasn't going to wait until your next visit to Karl. How dare you?"

Lisi raised a hand and stroked Charlie's hair, and he held her other hand. "It was my doing," she called to Margit.

It was the strongest, most confident voice Annamarie had heard Lisi use in perhaps years.

Margit looked astonished. "Your...you did this?"

"Did what?" Annamarie asked.

Lisi looked at her and slipped her hand from Charlie's. "I had my solicitor draw up the papers making you and Sepp the official guardians for Charlie. Now. Not at my death or"—she glared at Margit—"disappearance."

Margit deflated, stammering about the injustice of it. "We've been taking care of Karl all this time—"

"Please be quiet," Lisi said flatly. She motioned for Charlie to move closer to her. He did so, and she whispered into his ear. Charlie looked serious when she was through, but he nodded. Lisi turned back to Margit. "It is my wish, it is my will, and if Annamarie agrees to it..."

Charlie went to a drawer where Annamarie had been doing Lisi's hair earlier and pulled out a blue envelope. He put it into Annamarie's hand.

"You will sign it, if you agree to it," Lisi said.

Tears sprang to Annamarie's eyes. "But Sepp—"

"Will turn up," Lisi said. "I pray he will. And even if he doesn't, I know that my son will be in good hands."

Annamarie exhaled, her bottom lip quivering. "But, Lisi. I'm... I'm..."

"You're what?" Lisi demanded, the tiredness coming back into her eyes.

"Chaotic!" It slipped out.

Margit made a noise and leaned back, as if everything were settled in her favour.

But Lisi smiled wanly. "That you are. I want you to take Charlie away from here, Annamarie. Get out of here before the war comes to a head."

Margit's voice was shrill. "What right do you have to—"

Lisi cocked her head, her eyes sharp again. "Did I ask you to speak?"

Margit marched over to them and snatched Charlie's hand, but Annamarie snapped up his other one and held on tight. Charlie whimpered between them.

"Let him go," Annamarie growled.

"Yes, Margit," Lisi said. "Let my son go. Now. Or I will have you forcibly removed from this building."

Margit let go of Charlie's hand, as if to use the opportunity to point at Annamarie. "She is not the guardian yet. We will take this to court before that happens."

Lisi arched an eyebrow. "'We,' meaning you and your parents? Yes, Margit. Do that. But you're not going to earn your motherhood medal from the Führer with my son. To hell with you."

Annamarie yanked the document out of the envelope, hurried to the chest of drawers, and withdrew a pen from her purse. Without reading it, she signed the bottom. She would do this now and figure out how later. She'd chosen the wrong word. Chaotic, she was not. Perhaps impulsive, but not chaotic.

"There." She handed the document back to Lisi with a flourish. "I'm more than happy to do so."

Margit clutched her purse to her, once again trying to reach for Charlie. "Elisabeth Rainer is not of sound mind and body," she said.

"But I am," Lisi taunted. "It states so right here." She held up the papers. "Charlie, your aunt Margit is going to take you home now, but when the time comes, when your Tante Annamarie comes to fetch you, I want you to be a good boy and go with her. You're going to be—" Lisi's breath hitched. "Safe with her, you understand?"

Charlie's eyes were wide, but his trust in his mother was absolute. Annamarie could not know how Lisi had won it, but she had.

Lisi looked at her and then Margit. "This will go to court for confirmation. Annamarie, you'll be asked standard questions if they decide to call you in. Do whatever you must to make sure this happens."

Margit glowered. "We'll see about that."

"Yes," Lisi said, sitting back, her gaze steady on Margit. "We shall."

The sirens ripped Annamarie from the typewriter, the letter to *Noi Donne* expressing her gratitude only half through. Annamarie's colleagues rose with little comment, only slight murmurs followed as they filed their way to the doors. Annamarie ripped the letter out of the typewriter, folded it, and stuffed it into her dress pocket. Her editor stepped behind her, calling to everyone to stay orderly, to move calmly.

Outside, the sirens were louder, piercing Annamarie's anxieties.

"I have to get to Tante Rosa," Annamarie said to nobody in particular. She hurried down the street but felt someone yank her back. Her editor.

"You won't make it."

"If I hurry."

"You won't make it, Annamarie."

The sirens stressed his urgency.

"You stay with me." He shoved her back into the stream of fleeing citizens.

The air-raid shelter already stank of fear. It was the first thing Annamarie registered. The next was the rumbling beneath her feet from a distant explosion. Again, hardly anyone said a word. Her colleagues and the others from the neighbourhood huddled in the lair, the sirens screeching as if muffled beneath pillows, the air vibrating with a distant drone and then the occasional blast. Even more distant were the repeated bursts of gunfire. The Wehrmacht forces were positioned all around the city, in the centre and on the outskirts.

Annamarie pressed against the wall, staring at her feet. She imagined Tante Rosa with that cane, the one she now required since the last air raid. She pictured the neighbours helping the woman get to the monastery. Of course they had. They all knew Annamarie worked, that she left the house every Monday through Friday and sometimes on Saturdays. They would check, wouldn't they?

When her lungs felt as if they would explode, she released the breath she was holding. Her editor looked at her, and she noticed the bags beneath his eyes.

"We sold our souls to the devil," he muttered.

Annamarie did not know what to say to that.

"I bet those pilots were destined for somewhere in Bavaria. Munich maybe. But there's poor weather up there. So we're the suckers to carry the brunt. Need to offload those bombs somewhere."

She hoped not on the monastery.

Margit. Charlie. Lisi.

She squeezed her eyes shut, her heart pumping tar at the thought of any of them being hurt.

Another rumble. Another one. And another one.

It did not last long, but the damage had been done. As soon as she was out of the shelter, Annamarie stood on the street. Smoke rose in pockets beyond the city, but nothing appeared to have been hit in the centre.

"Looks like the marshalling yard's been hit," one of the reporters said.

Annamarie had no idea on whom to check first. She decided Tante Rosa. A reporter accompanied her, amid another chorus of fire trucks and ambulances. Some civilians stood dazed before their buildings, while others searched frantically for loved ones, calling to each other. What would normally take her fifteen minutes to reach Tante Rosa's neighbourhood now took her over half an hour. She stopped to help a woman lift her screaming child into her arms. Annamarie led a dazed old man to a safe place to sit and wait for help. But everyone she asked said there were no casualties and the city looked intact.

She and the reporter hurried to Tante Rosa's street. And there she was, standing in the middle of the road, staring at the apartment building in bewilderment. Annamarie rushed to her and scooped her into her arms.

"Are you hurt? Are you—"

Her aunt pulled away, holding on to Annamarie's shoulders as if they were a lifeline.

"You survived. With all that noise, I was sure I'd come out to an apocalypse. But it's there, isn't it? The whole building is still standing."

"Anyone injured?" Annamarie hugged Tante Rosa to her, then asked into the crowd, "Any casualties?"

"We're all here," a neighbour confirmed. "Just shocked and frightened."

It was the same when Annamarie reached the Rainers' home. They were already back inside, and when Margit opened the door to her, Annamarie swore relief flitted over her face.

"They hit the marshalling yards," Annamarie said when Herr Rainer appeared behind Margit.

"And the Wilten monastery," Margit said.

"It was a precision bombing," Herr Rainer said. "Those sons of—"

"Father," Margit said quietly.

"Are you all right?" Annamarie asked. "Charlie?"

"He's upstairs," she said. "He's asleep."

Annamarie took in a breath. "Can we talk about him? About the guardianship?"

Margit glanced back at her parents but did not move from the door. "We've decided we'll see you in court."

The door clicked softly on Annamarie's face.

"Where is this Josep Greil?" the judge asked, flipping through the documents.

"We're not sure," Annamarie answered truthfully. "Perhaps in a POW camp. We don't know."

"The blasted Allies," he muttered.

She felt it was necessary to clarify. "If he's in a POW camp, it's because he's been captured by Germans."

The judge frowned. "But Josep Greil is—"

"He's South Tyrolean, like me. He was conscripted into the Italian Army."

The judge's mouth moved, and he glanced at the documents again, seemingly to avoid looking at her. Annamarie turned slightly. The von Brandts, unified with the Rainers and Margit, stared coldly back at her.

"Where do you live?" the judge asked.

"At the address provided. Currently. But I will be taking Charlie to South Tyrol, to the Reschen Valley, where my family is. At least until the war is over."

He did not look pleased about this. She did not care.

"Job?"

"I work for the *Innsbrucker Nachrichten*."

"How do you plan to provide for the child in South Tyrol if you are not working?"

"Like any woman without a husband."

The judge met her look, and his lips twitched. He pointed to the Rainers, the von Brandts, to Margit, who was fastened to Charlie. "The Rainers are well known here. They can provide for the child—"

"With all due respect, that is not what the mother wishes for him. Last I checked, the von Brandts were also a very well respected family here, and yet the Rainers feel they have sole rights to him. Besides, should the Allies win, these two families—"

"You traitor," Margit screeched.

The judge examined Annamarie again, and something shifted on his face. "Based on the court's earlier ruling that Frau Elisabeth Rainer is of sound mind and body, I see no reason to disregard the mother's wishes. The court honours the guardianship to Fräulein Steinhauser and Herr Greil as final."

Margit's parents popped off the bench, protesting, but the judge raised a hand. "It's wartime. Let the woman take the child to where he's safe." Without further ado, he gathered up his documents and left the courtroom.

Annamarie extended her hand to Charlie, and he stepped away from Margit and took it. "This is what your mother wanted. Is this what you want, Charlie?"

He raised his eyes at Margit, then back to Annamarie. "Yes, Tante."

To Margit she said, "Are his things packed?"

Margit dropped her eyes. The Rainers and the von Brandts fumed behind her.

Annamarie faced them. "I'll come back with him. I promise. When it's safe."

Her words affected them. It was as if these selfish and

ridiculous people finally understood that Lisi had not necessarily done this to punish them but to protect Charlie.

Margit lowered herself to Charlie's level, and he let her wrap her arms around him. Then Annamarie prodded him to his grandparents. When it was time, she led him out of the courthouse.

Herr von Brandt called to her. "I've arranged a car to pick up his things and deliver them to you. Please." He looked embarrassed. "It would break my wife's heart to never see her grandson again."

"I promise," Annamarie said. "I will make sure he knows who you are." And because Herr von Brandt had always been the least nasty to her, had on the rare occasion revealed a sensitive side of himself, such as now, Annamarie added, "I didn't know my real father when I was growing up. By the time I met him, it was a catastrophe." She bit her trembling lip. "I sincerely regret that. I wouldn't do that to Charlie."

Herr von Brandt smiled slowly. "Thank you, Fräulein Steinhauser. I hope Herr Greil turns up soon."

She left with Charlie in tow, and when they reached the apartment door, Tante Rosa flung it open, her face a mask of dread, as if she had been preparing herself for comforting Annamarie. At the sight of Charlie, she looked dismayed.

"You won?"

"I won."

Tante Rosa smiled slyly and led them into the parlour.

"This calls for schnapps," she called over her shoulder, and Annamarie laughed. The woman only called for schnapps when she had to calm her nerves.

"You're coming with us, Tante Rosa. And I want to leave soon. Before another air raid. Mother doesn't know yet, but I will call her as soon as I can get a line."

Tante Rosa returned carrying two thimbles and a bottle of clear spirits. "I don't know about that."

Annamarie waited until the woman poured, then sat and pulled Charlie into her lap. There was a plate of stale biscuits, and she gave him one. "I insist. Kicking and screaming, if I must."

Tante Rosa tut-tutted. "I don't even kick and scream during air raids. I will certainly not be putting up a fight for this."

Annamarie smiled and bounced Charlie, hugging him close. "Hear that? She's coming with us."

"I didn't say that."

Annamarie cocked an eyebrow. Tante Rosa smirked, raised her glass, and tapped the bottom of Annamarie's before drinking the shot.

"You'd better get packed," Annamarie said. "The train leaves day after tomorrow."

The next day, Annamarie went to the newspaper and quit her job. Her editor stood before her, arms crossed over his broad chest. There was a grease stain on the pocket of his shirt.

"I had high hopes for you," he said.

"I'll keep writing. Maybe send you something that you can pass along to the news desk?"

"A real reporter. Is that what you want to be?"

Annamarie sighed. She had no idea what she wanted to be. This war was not allowing her to make those decisions on her own. He seemed to read her mind, because he dropped his arms, as if capitulating.

"You're young. I suppose there's still time, Annamarie. Whatever you do, stay safe." Then he embraced her. "You've got the stuff. Stick with it."

When it was time, Tante Rosa locked up the apartment, leaving a key with one of the neighbours. "For when I come back," Tante Rosa said. "And I will come back."

Inside, the telephone rang. When Tante Rosa turned the key in the opposite direction, Annamarie put a hand on hers to stop her.

"We're going to be late. It will simply have to wait."

"But we don't know who it is. It might be your mother."

Annamarie sighed with exasperation. "The train, Tante Rosa. Now."

She lugged their cases and then a wooden chest Tante Rosa insisted on bringing with her. The taxi driver packed them into the automobile. As it was, they barely boarded before the train pulled out of the station.

Annamarie and Tante Rosa stumbled between train cars, trying to find their compartment, and twice Annamarie thought her aunt would collapse. Charlie was excited about being on board, touching all the doors, waving to the passengers. They finally fell into their compartment, and Annamarie arranged their purses and Charlie's bag around them before finally throwing herself onto the bench. They were already outside the city limits, and it was here that they could see the devastation of the bombing raid.

Charlie pressed his face against the window, both hands smearing the pane. Annamarie leaned back and smiled.

"They're going to love him," she said.

"Charlie?" Tante Rosa asked. "Yes, they are."

From Landeck, they boarded the bus, and Annamarie paid one of the train personnel to transfer their baggage to it. The initial joy of travelling had worn off on Charlie, and with the starts and stops, they were delayed. With it likely they would miss the last bus, Annamarie fretted about having to walk to Graun from the pass, but where would they leave their things?

As it turned out, they made it in time, but the German border guards refused them entry until they had investigated their baggage further. Annamarie tried to reach her mother at the inn but could not get a line.

"They'll know that we've been held up," Tante Rosa tried to assure her. "And won't worry for a while."

Annamarie was concerned about the crossing at the border. They were in Nauders, and Annamarie was glad she knew the guesthouse owner, who allowed them to sleep in the barn at no cost. Annamarie traded a good vest and a good pair of stockings for food that night.

The next morning, they waited again until finally someone decided they were not spies, or child-nappers, or anything but refugees.

When her passport was stamped, she pointed with it to the south and said sarcastically, "If you're still not sure and change your mind, I'm right over there, in Graun."

The guard scowled at her. "Next time maybe you should think twice before choosing to be a citizen of the enemy."

Annamarie's shoulders slumped. So that was what this was about. She nodded, words bubbling to the top, but she bit them back. Who did he think he was? What did he know what it was like to live in this province?

Tante Rosa must have sensed Annamarie's anger, because she pushed her forward, calling cheerily to Charlie. "Look, we're in Italy now."

Behind them, Annamarie heard the guard hack and spit.

"*Cretino*," Annamarie muttered.

They had to wait again for a bus. Annamarie could have done the rest of the trip on foot, but not with Tante Rosa. Or that trunk. It was long past midday before they puttered up the pass and stopped at the border control centre. Annamarie greeted the driver and helped him to load their things before she climbed aboard, tired and sweaty.

They passed the carved-out landscape of an abandoned construction site, and Annamarie tried to explain to Tante Rosa the significance of the reservoir, but she was only halfway done when the bus pulled up before the Post Inn, pulled its brake, and turned off the engine.

The town felt abandoned. Annamarie dashed up the stairs to the door, but a sign hung on the front. *Closed for Business*. Annamarie frowned.

Where was everyone?

She recognised one of the elderly townsfolk, dressed in black, and hailed him. "Where is everyone? Do you know where I might find my mother?"

The man halted and pointed to the church. "The memorial service. I imagine she's already in church."

"Oh."

He eyed her suspiciously and then moved on.

Annamarie turned to the bus driver. "I guess it will be all right if we just unload into the garden there." She pointed to where tables had been set up in a beer garden. She told Tante Rosa that everyone was in church.

"Who died?"

Annamarie shrugged. "I don't know. He didn't say."

They waited until the driver had unloaded all their things and stacked them neatly against the house. They crossed the garden and went out the back gate to the church. Annamarie pushed inside and let Tante Rosa and Charlie go through, then scanned the pews, looking for either her mother or father. She spotted Manuel first, in a broad stance, his hands gripping the pew before him.

He was the first to turn around as the door fell shut behind Annamarie, followed by the rest of the congregation, less than half of what the church once contained.

Embarrassed, Annamarie quickly took Charlie's hand and headed for her family's pew, trying to ignore the penetrating stares, the questioning looks. But it was her mother's sad face, her conflicted expression that made Annamarie stop in the middle of the aisle and take a closer look around her.

On top of the altar, not more than ten steps away, was a propped-up portrait of Bernd in his Wehrmacht uniform. Annamarie felt someone gently tugging at her and looked down at Charlie, gripping her hand. She burst into tears.

33

The air in the courtroom was so thick with curiosity and anticipation that not even the opened windows brought any relief. Angelo was seated at a table before the cage normally used to hold prisoners, but he was not a prisoner. He was here before the panel of nine judges on his own volition.

Angelo loosened his tie and waited for the officiating judge to finish writing on the docket. He heard whispering behind him and turned to see Michael Innerhofer speaking with Gina. Chiara sat on the opposite end of the gallery in a soft grey suit and light-green blouse. In between them sat Angelo's former comrades from the resistance. Michael stopped talking and nodded at Angelo with an encouraging smile.

The judge finally put the pen down, then cleared his throat. "And the activities of this Committee of National Liberation—this resistance group—included?"

"Sabotage of railway lines," Angelo said, "roads, bridges, any line of transport to prevent Nazi troop movement really, and of course for supplies getting to and out of the area. I was in charge of the plans as such, as I was quite familiar with the structures, roadways, and construction, thanks to my former position at the ministry."

"And the actual work of sabotaging those lines? Were you involved in planting any explosives, derailing any trains, blowing up any bridges, or in any destruction of civilian properties and/or casualties?"

"No, Your Honour. I had what one might call an administrative position. I was the planner and delegated the orders."

"So you were an officer?" the judge asked.

"Your Honour, many of us are veteran officers of the Royal Italian Army," Angelo said. "We served in the Great War. I fought on the Marmolada and was responsible for the explosives unit that tried to burrow into the mountains."

"Yes, it says here you were a captain in the Great War." The judge peered at him over dark-rimmed glasses. "And were you giving orders to this resistance group?"

"Yes, Your Honour. I led a small division and communicated with the head of the First Alpine Group, led by Mauri."

"That was his nom de guerre," one of the other judges interrupted. "He is referring to Major Enrico Martini."

The officiating judge nodded, returned to Angelo. "You abandoned the Fascist party, you say, but held on to your party card?"

"Your Honour, my position at the ministry—"

"As the minister," the judge said, as if to remind him. "Appointed by the former regime."

"As the minister, yes, I was required to have that party card."

"Indeed. You could not have been appointed had you not been a member."

"Yes, Your Honour."

"It is very unusual for someone to petition an investigation to the High Court of Justice for himself."

"You investigate any collusion in the Fascist regime. I have been unjustly accused by private parties—"

"Though nothing has been submitted to this court."

"No, Your Honour. But I would like to continue with my life, with my name intact, and to also put my activities in the resistance on public record."

Behind him, Angelo heard Gina whisper something that sounded like approval.

"What baffles me," the judge said, "is that Minister d'Oro—whom I knew quite well, by the way—was your father-in-law." The judge's sentence ended on a question mark, as if he could not believe what he was reading.

Angelo bowed his head. "It was a political coup. It had never been my intention to replace him and certainly not to oust him."

The judge shuffled in his seat, put his elbows on the table, the sleeves of his robe sliding down as he folded his hands before him. "You presented us with your defense brief and requested to be questioned for the purposes of clearing your name. Your character witnesses and the testimonies shared come from your comrades-in-arms from the resistance as well as, most unusually"—he looked pointedly at the group behind Angelo—"your current wife as well as your former wife…"

There were nervous chuckles from the gallery.

"I daresay," the judge continued drily, "to be able to bring both women in to speak highly in any man's favour, well, I don't know how the rest of my esteemed colleagues up here feel, but I for one now have great hope that we may achieve lasting peace. We may be dangerously French for it, but—"

Laughter erupted.

The judge tolerated it and waited until the courtroom settled down. His tone was much more serious when he proceeded. "Do you mind sharing that story? About your wives?"

"Your Honour, it is a long one. But many people in Bolzano know that my former wife was always an activist. She was a member of the Christian Democrats and joined the committee when I informed her that I would be assisting the Underground. She was able to use her connections to the Tyrolean community, those who were against Fascism and the Nazis. She and Michael Innerhofer, who also spoke on my behalf, were able to work the German side of things, made flyers and leaflets, and often helped us with translations."

"And Signora Grimani the Present?"

Angelo smiled appreciatively. "She was the reason I joined the Underground at all. To my knowledge now, she had been working with many of those close to the king. Her disenchantment with the Fascist party came soon after Mussolini took office as prime minister. By that time she realised she was not alone. Many of the elite and former military commanders that she knew over her deceased husband—"

"General Conti, yes."

Angelo nodded. "It was clear to anyone who had served in the military that Italy suffered from a lack of proper equipment. Sabotuers abounded. In hindsight, it is also clear to me now that many Italians never really supported the Fascist regime, like the Germans perhaps had with the NSDAP. We had poor equipment —often leaving the factories faulty already—because nobody really wanted a war. On the other hand, I had a son in a POW camp, and I wanted to do my part in bringing an end to this war as quickly as possible. And getting the Germans out of northern Italy."

There were grunts of agreement, and someone clapped softly.

Angelo continued. "When the Fourth Army disintegrated in Piedmont, our unit helped them with information in order for them to achieve the kind of success they then had with guerrilla warfare. In return, they supplied us with much-needed weapons."

"Was your group specifically related to any of the official anti-Fascist party? The Italian Communist Party, the Italian Socialist Party?"

"No, Your Honour. As you can see by the shaking heads of my comrades here, what united us was a fierce will to rid ourselves of the German occupiers and Mussolini's puppet government. Our lives were in danger. Everyone's was. Whereas to the south, the Allies were disbanding Italy's armies, the Republic of Salò intended for us to march and fight against the Allies for our own land. Nobody here wanted that."

There was soft applause again in the background, and the judge waited. He leaned back in his chair and nodded at Angelo. "Continue, please.

"My comrades here shared plenty of their own stories already, Your Honour. Besides our ties to Martini's division, we were wholly or mostly an independent mishmash of former veterans, political activists, engineers, journalists, and scholars. Our work mostly took part in the OZAV region, the part under Franz Hofer's administration. Many of the men who joined us were those trying to escape the new republic's draft. Nobody wanted to fight for Mussolini any longer. Our job was to carry out acts of sabotage, guerrilla warfare—"

"You suffered many losses."

"Yes, Your Honour."

"And today? What do you intend to do with yourself today?" The judge looked pointedly at Angelo. "Are you hoping to be reappointed to the ministry?"

Angelo shook his head. "I plan to attend my son's wedding first, Your Honour. To spend time with my wife in peace. And then we shall see what happens."

"You understand, Captain Grimani, that any decision made here will be final and cannot be appealed."

"I do, Your Honour. That is why I am here."

The judge closed the file before him, scrutinised Angelo once more, and nodded to his other colleagues. The panel rose and filed out of the courtroom to convene behind closed doors.

~

Gina awoke him with a kiss, and he was startled to see that the room was already quite bright. It had to be nine, maybe ten o'clock.

His wife was already dressed in a pair of flowing brown slacks and a cream-coloured blouse. And her hairstyle was new.

"You look like Valentina Cortese," he said.

She slapped his thigh. "You saw me snip out that photo before I went to the hairdresser, you tease."

"It looks good. But if you're back, then—" He checked the clock on the bedstead. It was past one o'clock! "How did I sleep so late?"

Angelo sat up and heard the clinking of silverware and plates. The breakfast tray was at the foot of the bed and included two glasses of Prosecco.

"Is it our anniversary already? Did I sleep that long?"

"It's only Friday, but you obviously needed the lie-in. And this happened while you were dreaming." She waved two papers before him, the *Dolomiten* and the Italian *Alto Adige*. "Michael's been trying to reach you since yesterday evening. I told him you were dead. He said that was a shame because he'd have liked to see the two of us in German-language classes."

Angelo frowned, muttering, "What on earth for?"

"That's why I brought the Prosecco. It might help our addled minds and loosen our tongues."

She plopped the newspapers onto his lap, and he snapped the *Alto Adige* open. His smirk turned into astonishment.

"The Austrian foreign minister and our esteemed prime minister," Gina said as he scanned the headline: *Gruber and De Gaspari sign historic agreement granting the Alto Adige autonomy*!

"They have granted the German-speaking population of *Südtirol* the right to autonomy, the right to preserve its cultural identity and customs, and have made both German and Italian the official languages."

Angelo waved the newspaper, a smile creeping across his face. "Is this a joke? Did you go to the presses and have them write this to fool me?"

Gina laughed and handed him one of the glasses of sparkling wine. "You look like a fish out of water. Drink. *Zum Wohl!*"

The gardens at the Villa Adige had been transformed to host the thirty-two guests for the wedding reception. Chiara and Evi Innerhofer had pulled together a troop to cut back bushes and clear out space for a small dance area with a spot for the musicians to play near the oleander bushes. It was a beautiful summerlike day for mid-September, and the garden looked better than it ever had.

Angelo led Gina through the rows of grapevines where Chinese lanterns hung between the golden, green, and autumnal-red leaves. Large muscat grapes dangled in black-purple and green. They reached the veranda, crowded with tables and chairs, the head table at one end. Chiara had already warned Angelo that Marco had requested Gina sit with the other guests rather than at the family table. Weddings and funerals. They brought the worst or the best out of people, and most certainly the family drama to the forefront. He had sworn to avoid it at all costs.

Gina agreed to be accommodating. In either case, she was putting on a good show, though on the surface she wore a thin sheen of disappointment and hurt. She would never be wholly accepted or part of the family, and she knew it.

Chiara had suggested that when Marco and Geraldine had their own children, it would give Marco yet another push toward reconciling with his father. Angelo had waited this long, and upon recalling the day that Marco had returned home, he felt the wave of relief again—still felt the pain in his heart caused by that enormous swell of love.

Through the muslin curtains of the parlour, Angelo saw Marco pacing in a black suit. Angelo patted Gina's hand and left her at one of the tables.

Marco halted when Angelo walked in. "Father."

"Hello, son."

The embrace was stiff on Marco's side. Angelo patted his shoulder and let him go. "Nervous?"

"A little." Marco's eyes darted to the veranda door, where Gina stood gazing at the garden in the full-skirted burgundy gown.

"Thank you for inviting her," Angelo said.

"She's your wife. When Filipa broke off our engagement, I decided there was nothing to stand in the way of your happiness. It's simply that…" He gazed out the window at Gina. "It's a lot to take in. Still."

Angelo sighed. "Be kind to her. That's all I ask."

"I want to escort Mother to church." Marco's gaze was intent. "And let it be her day."

"I understand. We'll stay out of the way." Angelo checked his watch. "Where is she, by the way?"

"Being emotional?" Marco suggested.

"Did you tell her your decision?"

"I couldn't. Not yet. It would ruin the whole wedding for her."

"The Colonel saw to ruining that when he made his proposal known. I think she needs to know now. Do you want me to?"

"Subtly? Gently? I really don't want anyone thinking I'm not going to show up, and if you make her cry, I'll likely be late…"

"Is she upstairs?"

Marco nodded. "It might help."

Angelo smiled and waved at the veranda outside. "Before things get too crowded out there, I just want you to know, I couldn't be happier for you. Geraldine is wonderful. She truly is. You're lucky to have found each other."

Marco looked thoughtful. "I guess something good came out of this war after all."

"See to Gina, will you? It would mean something to her if you would just speak with her a little, thank her for coming."

Marco hesitated for a split second, peered through the muslin curtains, and clapped Angelo's shoulder. "I'll take care of it."

Angelo went upstairs and knocked on Chiara's bedroom door.

"You're here already?" She was breathless. She turned her back on him. "Could you please button this?"

He did up the two buttons on the seashell-pink gown. She faced the mirror.

"I saw what you did outside," he said. "You must have been working day and night."

"Evi was a life-saver." Chiara looked past her reflection. "I've gotten old, Angelo."

"Nonsense. What should we say when we look at my parents?"

"Your father is hanging on for all its worth, anyway."

"He still does not have an heir for the company—that's why."

She looked stunned. "Marco turned him down?"

"He did."

Her face fell. "Then our son will move to France with Geraldine."

Angelo placed his hands on her shoulders. "You must let him do what he thinks is right. He's a grown man now."

Chiara sighed. "He at least chose well."

"Charismatic, sharp sense of humour, and a good soul," Angelo said fondly. "She'll keep him on his toes. Most of all, he seems to have gained real clarity with Geraldine. In fact," he added gently, "she reminds me very much of you."

Chiara smiled, her eyes darted away, and she swiped at a tear he just managed to see. "Thank goodness for the Red Cross, then."

"The south of France is not far," he soothed.

Chiara sighed, straightened, and smoothed her dress. "Is Marco ready?"

"He's waiting for you downstairs. Skittish as a colt." He offered his arm. "He'd like to escort you to church so that he can show off his mother."

She blushed at this. Angelo kissed her cheek tenderly and led her downstairs before handing her over to their son.

That afternoon, Angelo watched Marco and his bride hand out slices of cake to the guests. Evi Innerhofer had set up a table in front of the rose bushes. Marco and Geraldine made a picture-perfect couple, what with Marco's dark, handsome looks and bright-green eyes, and the blonde Geraldine, slender and almost regal the way she carried herself. However, as soon as the young woman spoke to anyone, her manner was down to earth, genuinely kind, and she seemed always ready for fun.

Geraldine smiled warmly as the family complimented the parachute silk dress. The gown was simple and elegant, tailored at the bodice before blossoming into a billowy skirt and train. Geraldine's mother had sewn it after Marco got the idea from a pilot friend of his. All the women had been delighted by his resourcefulness. With rationing in full effect, luxury goods—like wedding gowns—were hard to come by. But somehow the families, and most especially Geraldine, had been creative enough to scrape something together for a proper celebration.

"Your son has found himself a stunner."

Angelo faced the Colonel. "And much more."

"I suppose I understand why he'd want to follow her to France. Though I try to picture Marco in a field of lavender...a farmer. I left that life to create a better one for all of you, and he returns to the land."

"Full circle," Angelo said, not biting.

The Colonel gazed at him, left eye drooping—a new addition since his mild stroke.

"That does leave me in a lurch."

Angelo cocked his head. "What are your options?"

The Colonel glanced over Angelo's shoulder. "Because you're suddenly interested in taking over?" His eyes darted as if to check, and Angelo saw the spark of hope.

"I just cleared my name. How would it look if I took over the company of the man who is facing his own enquiries now?"

His father cleared his throat. "It would look as if you were coming to clean up the place. You don't actually believe the ministry will have you back?"

Angelo laughed softly. "Who said I was interested in the ministry?" He caught Gina's eye when she turned around with two cake plates in hand. Her eyes flashed to his father and back to him.

"No more business talk. I have other plans." He patted the Colonel's back and headed to meet Gina.

"Angelo," the Colonel called.

Angelo sighed but faced him again.

"I'm going to give it to Accosi. To Stefano."

"Good. Do that."

The look of surprise made Angelo smile broadly.

Before Gina could reach him, the small group of musicians began to play.

Marco broke away from the cake line and strode over to Angelo. "May I have a word with you in private?"

Gina handed Angelo his plate. "Go on. I'll be sitting over there with Michael and Evi."

Angelo stepped closer to the veranda, and Marco followed. "What is it, son?"

"It's Geraldine. She has a special request. I just, well, I don't know if…" Marco looked down at his feet, his hands folded before him. "She would really appreciate it if you would—"

Angelo felt that prickling sensation when he felt something dreadful coming on. "You want me to leave? Have I done something? Is it Gina?" He was prepared to defend her once and for all.

Marco shook his head. "Look, my wife would like to know whether you would do her the honour of... Her father, you know? He passed away, and he should have had the first dance."

Angelo straightened, turned, and looked over at the bride. Geraldine was in the middle of a sentence, but noticed him. She beamed and gave a little hitch of the shoulder.

Without hesitation, Angelo pulled Marco in and kissed him on both cheeks. "Thank you, son."

He strode across the garden to his daughter-in-law, and Geraldine stepped around the table when Angelo offered his hand.

"Will you do me the honour of the first dance?" he asked. The band began to play "La Mer."

His daughter-in-law accepted his hand and walked out onto the makeshift dance floor. With the first steps, Angelo knew that it would not take a grandchild for his son and him to reconcile. This woman—this beautiful woman—had managed that for them in this one simple gesture.

STAGE 3

March 1947
RESCHEN VALLEY RESERVOIR
NOTICE OF RESERVOIR PROJECT REINSTATEMENT
OVERVIEW OF STAGE 3

(Translation in German follows)

The Swiss company Elektrowatt has invested 30M Swiss francs to the Reschen Valley reservoir project. In return MFE is to supply Elektrowatt 120M kWh of winter energy to Switzerland for ten years.

Upon review of the current status of the construction project, a new schedule has been established. The completion of Stage 2 as initially outlined will lead immediately to Stage 3 without delay.

Stage 3 will focus on completing the embankment dam, as well as the new roads from the pass to the south, as well as provisional roads around the north, east and southern tip of the reservoir.

The reservoir will now absorb the lakes of Reschen, Graun and Haider. The entire village of Graun, a large part of Reschen, as well as the hamlets of St Valentin, Spinn, Haide, and Arlund will be flooded.

A total of 163 houses and buildings will be detonated. 523 hectares of land will form the reservoir floor.

The remaining homes in the immediate vicinity and those affected by this phase will be evacuated and the families relocated to barracks located in an area above the reservoir's construction site (projected date: winter 1947). Farmers with fields and property that will not be affected until the reservoir is to be filled will be allowed to continue planting and farming through the harvest season of 1949.

Final projected completion is 1949 with initial flooding planned in 1950.

A detonation schedule of all buildings in the area will be posted on this notice board before proceeding to Stage 3. The company and the government have taken into consideration the residents' request to detonate St Katharina's church last and neither sees any reason not to grant the residents their request.

34

RESCHEN VALLEY, SUMMER 1947

K atharina followed the old path over St Anna's hill and stopped at her family's graves. Manuel and Charlie watched as she placed the fresh flowers into a vase, threw out the old ones, and ran a hand over Bernd's name etched below her mother's and father's. Like her father, Katharina's dear boy was also not really here. Bernd's body was somewhere in Yugoslavia, her father's somewhere in western Ukraine. On the memorial the communities had erected in honour of those who'd fallen in the Great War, was also her father's name. Now it would include the names of the men and boys they lost in this—*What? When that was the Great War, what would this one be called?* Josef Thaler and Bernd Steinhauser. The space they occupied in this valley would be all but etched in stone. She never wanted this.

The children left her to pray, and when she was finished, Katharina rose stiffly and saw Annamarie sitting on the bench outside the chapel. Not knowing where Sepp was, not having heard a word one way or another, had made her daughter reflective but also unable to go into the cemetery, unable to mourn for her brother properly. Katharina sensed her daughter was struggling to keep up her strength, spending a lot of time writing in her journals, letters to Lisi and to Charlotte. Even to Tante Rosa, who'd returned to Innsbruck.

Katharina followed the trampled grass that led to the new settlement, the path already growing worn from all the traffic. Hammering and sawing accompanied the landscape of skeletal houses. The framework of the Post Inn was up, and now the men were on the roof. She recognised Florian's figure hammering nails next to one of the Italian workers. Behind the new settlement's foundations, the Karlinbach rushed down the ravine with last night's rain. Ahead of her, Manuel ran with Charlie down the hill just as the church bell tolled twelve, its sound distant on this side of the valley.

Katharina went to Annamarie and offered her elbow, and her daughter rose and hooked her arm into Katharina's. They'd been spending much time together, and bit by bit she was getting the picture of the young woman Annamarie had been and, most of all, was now becoming. From Annamarie's experiences with the League of German Girls and the rhetoric the Nazis had indoctrinated about race and Aryan entitlement, to the traumatic events in Poland, to the set of *Lowlands*, her daughter spent time writing in her journals and said they were bringing her closer to understanding herself, and her world. But, she told Katharina, her entries also left her with great foreboding.

"Why?" Katharina had asked.

"Because of how we became what we were. And that we will never find our way back."

Katharina halted and slipped her arm out of Annamarie's. The path took a steep turn at this point, and Annamarie went first.

"I wonder," Katharina said behind her, "whether we will ever be the community again that I once knew and loved."

Annamarie shook her head. "I can't imagine, Mother. Those who opted to settle and return, like the Planggers, and the Nogglers? They were duped, and then when the Allies told them that the Austrians were the first victims of Nazi Germany, well now they're just full of righteousness. They feel they're entitled to all recompense. Sebastiano Foglio told me how his old friends sit with him, drink beers, and swear that the Nazis were worse than the Fascists. What do the *Dableibers* know, they ask. You never had it as bad as we did. Can you imagine?"

Katharina frowned. "That's awful."

Annamarie shrugged, took the basket from Katharina, and held out a hand to help support her. "Not really, Mother. If you think about it, they're all lugging back bucketloads of shame with them. Take the Nogglers. Imagine, you arrive in the Sudetenland and you're allocated property—a house, the furniture, the farmland, the animals, everything!—and you know that property was taken from the locals? Imagine waking up in that house day in and day out knowing that what you've just done is the same damned thing that the Italians did to you."

"Don't swear, Annamarie." But her daughter was right. And if that was the case—if they knew the malady—then it was quite possible they could find a cure. She could hear Dr Hanny's voice in her head, however. *There are no herbs for that one, Katharina. No tea you can just magically concoct.* No, it would take a lot of work. Shame was a scummy, slimy, crusty thing to rid oneself of.

They reached the Post Inn together, and Katharina waited until Florian had another beam in place before setting the basket of sandwiches and bottles of *Almdudler* soda onto the makeshift table. Annamarie began unpacking and distributing the food.

"Mayor Steinhauser," Katharina called. "It's time for lunch!"

Florian swiped his hat off his head and wiped his brow with his forearm before peering down at her. He whistled to the other four workers and waved them down from their ladders and out of what Katharina called "the trenches."

Charlie ran up to Florian and showed him the rocks he'd collected on the shore of Graun Lake.

Manuel examined the house. "Father, don't you want me to help you this afternoon?"

"Of course," Florian said.

"And me?" Charlie cried.

"No, Charlie, you'll come back with me and Oma," Annamarie said.

Katharina smiled at the boy, always thrilled when Annamarie referred to her as Charlie's grandmother.

"I've got something he can do," Florian offered, "if you want to stay, Charlie?"

Charlie nodded into his sandwich with a pleased grin.

As the crew assembled around the table, the hammering on the other sites stopped one at a time. Katharina shaded her eyes as she saw the men from the house above clamber down for their own meals.

"There's Walter Plangger," Katharina muttered to Florian just as he bit into a thick slice of bread. "And Toni. Those two have become inseparable."

"It's a shame," he said quietly, and winked. "I always liked Walter."

Katharina laughed. She tilted her head toward the rest of the crew eating, but Florian shrugged, and she knew he meant that the workers didn't understand German anyway. And that was what made Toni and Walter so sore with Florian. When he had hired Italian workers and Slavic refugees to help with the building, once again the Steinhausers were the pariahs of the community.

"I don't know why the two of them hold anything against you," Katharina said softly. "What were you supposed to? Find workers from Tyrol? From Austria? We could hardly get the ones we have here."

She glanced at the men—dark faced, dark haired, hungry. They worked hard. They did what Florian told them to and then disappeared into their barracks to return the next day for work. At the end of each week, they bought a good meal at her inn and sent money home to their families.

"Walter and Toni have their ways. I have mine," Florian said.

Manuel jerked his chin at his father. "Yes, and you were appointed mayor because the majority appreciate your ways. Not theirs."

Florian brushed a hand over Manuel's head and took his next bite.

"Nah, I'm mayor because I'm pure German," Florian winked. "That's what they wanted."

Katharina rolled her eyes and sighed with exasperation.

The men looked nervously at her. They thought Florian and she were arguing. Katharina smiled, and that seemed to set them at ease. She ate in silence, discreetly studying one of the men from Yugoslavia, mulling over her conversation with Annamarie. She wondered whether he, too, had lost all his property, his family, his home. The Tyroleans were not the only ones returning with their dreams dead in their hearts, and especially now that it was clear that South Tyrol would remain part of Italy, regardless of the promised autonomy. They would never be a part of Austria again, and that rankled all those who had chosen to resettle. It had taken a lot for these people to come back, and still there were great gaps to fill in the community. Katharina was certain Annamarie was right: shame stood in the way of reconciliation.

"And what are you two doing this afternoon?" Florian asked Annamarie.

"I don't know what Mother's up to, but I'm writing back to Charlotte."

Florian grunted. "I have a feeling you're getting itchy feet again. You're a gypsy child."

Annamarie pulled a face, and Katharina laughed a little, but anxiety seized her.

"She is, isn't she?" she tried lightly.

Katharina glanced at Charlie. Would Annamarie take him

with her? She was due to visit his grandparents and his mother soon anyway. The anxiety spread its tentacles.

Florian ruffled Charlie's head, and the boy jokingly scowled. "Well, young man? Shall we put a hammer into those hands of yours?"

Charlie's face lit up. "Really?"

Florian jerked his chin at the hillside above. "Let's see if we can beat them today in putting that roof on."

Charlie nodded and shoved another piece of bread into his mouth.

～

"What are you doing here if you don't even speak German?" Toni Ritsch shook a finger at the *carabinieri*. "It's the law now. You want something from me? You speak German!"

Katharina hurried out of the garden gate and into the churchyard. "What's wrong, Toni?"

"Damn *Walscher* wants something from me? He asks for it in *German*!"

"What do you want from him?" Katharina asked the policeman in Italian.

"I am here about his son," the man replied indignantly. "He got into a fight with some of the men from MFE."

Toni spit at the policeman. "Damn right he did!"

The officer's neck reddened. In one swift move, he had Toni in a chokehold and on his knees.

"Let him go!" As Katharina said it, she realised she was defending the man who was provoking the situation in the first place.

The policeman twisted around and raised a hand in warning. Down the street, she saw Florian step out of the Foglios' butchery. He took one look and sprinted for them.

"*Per favore, liberate quell'uomo,*" Katharina said. Please, free the man.

Florian arrived, hands raised. "*E' davvero necessario?*" Is this really necessary?

The policeman grudgingly released Toni and backed away.

Florian reached down and offered Toni a hand, but Toni spit on the ground.

"Toni, this has got to stop," Florian said warningly. "Give me your hand."

But Toni managed to get onto his feet.

The policeman looked contemptuous. "This man here tells me I can't be here? Who is he? You're the mayor, Signor Steinhauser!"

"Learn German," Toni shouted.

"I was here before that agreement was signed," the policeman snapped. "And you? You just got here!"

"Seven months," Toni shouted. "Seven months is how long you've been here and me? On whose property are you, you son of a whore?"

Florian stepped between the two, but Toni was already in motion, swinging. His fist met the right side of Florian's face. Katharina screamed. The policeman shoved Florian aside and wrangled Toni down again. This time he had Toni under control.

"You just hit the mayor," the *carabinieri* shouted. "Mayor Steinhauser, do you want to press charges?"

Florian shook his head but glared at Toni. "Just put him in the holding room and let him calm down. Toni, you had better sober up—"

"Or what?" Toni screamed hysterically. "You going to take my land away?"

Florian made a dismissive motion, and the policeman dragged Toni to the town hall.

Katharina tested Florian's cheek, already swelling. There was a small cut beneath his right eye.

"For heaven's sake," she muttered. "That's going to be a bad bruise. I have some arnica at the inn. Come with me. That man has a real problem!"

"To be honest, I think everyone is tired of all the empty promises. Toni is right—we have a right to our language, and any officials they send up here to work should be able to speak German. This is not the way to go about things, signing agreements and then only following the points that are convenient."

"Now I really don't know what to say," Katharina muttered. "That officer was here before the agreement was signed. So? What should he do? Pack up and leave just like the Grassos because it's uncomfortable?" She still missed them.

They slowed down at the sight of the post bus puttering around the corner to the front of the old inn. It stopped, and the driver honked his horn. Annamarie stepped out a moment later, the key ring jingling in her hand.

Katharina noticed passengers moving to the front of the bus. Tourists? Two people waited at the door, and Katharina released Florian from her hold. First a shrunken version of Hans Glockner stepped out, then he turned to help Jutta down. Her dark hair was streaked with thick swaths of grey and white.

When Katharina looked at her husband, Florian was also gaping.

They hurried the rest of the way, Katharina throwing her arms around Jutta first. The woman stumbled back a step, and Katharina held tight.

"Why didn't you call?" she cried. "Or write and tell us you were coming?"

When Katharina let go, Jutta looked at Hans.

"We had nowhere else to go," Hans said quietly.

Florian smiled lopsidedly, the right side of his face swelling rapidly now.

"What happened there?" Hans asked.

Florian scoffed. "Toni Ritsch."

"Nothing's changed then." The joke, dry as it was, was uncustomary for Hans.

Katharina turned to Jutta, who had not yet said a word but was hanging on to Katharina's arm as if to a lifeline. Katharina scanned her face, but Jutta would not look her in the eye. Annamarie came to embrace them but threw Katharina a concerned look.

"Jutta?" Katharina stepped back and examined the bus. "Where's Alois?"

Jutta's eyes pleaded with Hans, and he stepped forward, pulling his wife into him. He led her slowly to the inn.

"Hans?" Katharina asked softly. She was scared. She had never seen Jutta like this.

They followed them up the stairs, but Hans stopped and turned to face Katharina as Jutta disappeared into the inn. "They killed him. Alois is dead."

Katharina muffled the wail, and Annamarie's face darkened.

Florian was crestfallen. "Who did, Hans?"

"That institution he was in." Hans turned to face them, his beard trembling. "The Gestapo came and said they were evacuating them. They put Alois and all the patients onto a bus, drove them to God knows where... The institution led them there."

Hans raised a shaking hand to his beard and wiped it, but the tears were spilling. "They murdered Jutta's boy," he croaked. "They murdered the only son I've ever had."

Katharina sobbed and hugged Annamarie to her. Her daughter was shaking.

Hans squeezed his eyes shut, as if to rid himself of the image. "It took us this long to find out what had happened. We went to Innsbruck to find answers. I decided it would be best to bring us here afterwards. But now? I'm not sure..."

Katharina squeezed her daughter's shoulder. *Bucketloads of shame, Annamarie, but also grief. Mostly grief.*

It was September, normally the time of year that herds of livestock came down from the alps, the girls and women leading a wreath-crowned heifer or goat, the men carrying huge wheels of cheese or transporting them in handcarts. It was normally the time of year that they held the market, the Swiss villagers came to buy their cows, and everyone celebrated. But the valley—save for the hammering behind St Anna's hill—was quiet and sombre.

And then the Swiss did come, because now Elektrowatt was the reason the construction of the Reschen Lake reservoir could proceed.

Outside the bank building, Katharina watched as two men— one on a ladder, the other holding a brush and paint can— marked off the bank's foundation with white paint just beneath the roof. A third man stood behind a surveyor's theodolite.

"What are you doing?" she asked the man with the paint.

He squinted at the bank, then back at her and scratched his head. "Uh, well…"

His colleague came down the ladder. "We're marking off the water levels," he said.

Katharina looked disbelievingly at him. "The water is going to be that high?"

"That's right." He showed her the marks on the next three buildings.

"And what do you need to mark them for?" she asked stiffly. "They're all going to be detonated."

His colleague swung the paint can to the hillside above them. "So we know where to build the road."

It was higher than she could have ever guessed. Katharina

walked slowly away, her legs leaden. What had she imagined? Certainly not this.

Katharina was at the reception desk when the bell was disturbed by the opening of the door. She recognised the lilt of Swiss dialect before even looking up. Stefano Accosi walked in with two other men, the source of the Swiss Italian she'd heard. Katharina narrowed her eyes.

"Herr Accosi." She greeted him in German. The man was half-Tyrolean anyway. "To what do we owe this exceptional pleasure?"

"We'll need a room for our business partners here. This is Signor Crameri, and this is Signor Merlo. They'll be here for three nights."

"Room and board?"

"Yes."

Katharina provided the men with the registry, and Herr Accosi asked to speak to her off to the side.

"I have been informed," he said quietly, "that there have been official letters sent to both the foreign minister of Austria, Mr Gruber, as well as to the head of the Italian Communist Party?"

Katharina looked impassively at him. "From whom?"

Accosi pushed his glasses up his nose. "The mayor. Whom you know well."

"And what would you like to know from me?"

"The Ministry of Public Works and these gentlemen from Elektrowatt have finally negotiated and signed a contract that will move this project forward. Will you be so kind and inform the mayor that if he keeps this up, MFE will sue the towns of Graun and Reschen for all damages related to any further postponements caused by your inhabitants. Furthermore, one more attempt to appeal the process, and MFE will demand the state pay every cent back for the work we have already done as damages. That should get the Communists to sit up."

Katharina took a deep breath just as Annamarie stepped out of the kitchen. Her daughter looked at the men and then at

Accosi with Katharina. She greeted the two guests, then moved to where Katharina and Accosi stood.

"Are these the Swiss representatives?" Annamarie asked him.

Accosi looked curiously down at her. "What's it to you?"

Annamarie smiled sweetly. "Because I've been trying to get an interview with them for weeks about what happened in Splügen. But apparently they are staying here, is that correct?"

Accosi could do nothing but confirm.

Annamarie turned to Katharina. "Give them the best room, Mother. Nothing like having them right under our roof. Make sure there's an extra seat for me at the table each night." She winked at Accosi. "Thanks so much for bringing them right here."

Annamarie went back to the two guests, introduced herself, and added, "Your secretaries have certainly informed you that I rang. AL Greil. How do you do?"

Both Swiss men frowned and seemed to want to grab the register away from her.

Katharina gaped.

"Interview them for whom?" Accosi scowled at her.

Annamarie shrugged. "Whoever pays the most for the story."

Jutta came out of the apartment and glanced down the hall. As Accosi and the two men moved upstairs, she took tentative steps to Katharina.

"Trouble?" Jutta asked.

Katharina shrugged. "I don't know. But Annamarie is really interested in the reservoir and the story. She's asked everything about what I know, what Angelo has done, you know?"

Jutta nodded. She seemed to be eternally tired, and when she spoke, she muttered. "And where is Angelo now?"

"Campaigning for the Senate of the Republic."

Jutta's eyebrow shot up halfway, and she tipped her head toward the kitchen. "Good to have her back, isn't it?"

She meant Annamarie. Katharina rubbed a hand over the

woman's shoulders. "It is, Jutta. It is. I finally have my children with me..."

They looked at one another. *Except Bernd. And your Alois.*

Later, when the Swiss did not show up for dinner, Katharina, Iris, and Annamarie sat around the regulars' table. Jutta walked in and slid onto one of the chairs and folded her hands. She'd remained reserved, tight lipped these last weeks, but she joined them every night at the *Stammtisch*, the round table having given way to a woman's round each night, as the men hardly ever had the energy to stay up after working all day.

Annamarie was fingering the playing cards. "Listen, they're raising the lake by seventeen metres more than in the original project proposed."

"That was ages ago," Katharina reminded her.

Her daughter nodded but still focussed on the playing cards. "The current government is going to be interested in how all that got slipped past the Fascists via Grimani Electrical at the time, right? We still have the right to appeal."

Iris frowned. "But your mother said that Accosi threatened to sue if the project is cancelled."

"MFE will demand compensation from the state," Katharina reminded her daughter. "Do you know how much money that is?"

Annamarie shook her head. "A lot though."

"I remember," Jutta said, her voice unsteady, "how the ministry promised that the inhabitants of Graun and Reschen would never have to leave their homes. Can't we take this to court?"

"What happened in Splügen?" Katharina asked Annamarie.

Annamarie set the cards down. "There was a proposal for an electrical power station to be built in the Swiss Rheinwald. But the residents of Splügen, those who would be affected, resisted, and the Federal Council did not grant the concession. That's when Elektrowatt turned to MFE, asked if they could take part in the Reschen reservoir. And made quite a deal."

"In other words," Iris said, "Splügen will still be affected, but now by the concessions from the Italian state?"

Annamarie sighed and nodded. "Talk about a back door."

"Who *are* you writing this story for?" Katharina asked.

"I wasn't lying," she said. "Anyone who will buy it."

"Who will buy it?" Jutta snapped. "Nobody's given a damn about any of us here. Why should anyone care about a Swiss village the size of a thumbnail?"

Annamarie smiled broadly. "Good to have you back, Tante Jutta. You're starting to sound like your old self. Let me worry about that."

Jutta huffed, then stilled. She looked slyly at Katharina. "It's good to have her here, isn't it? You can be proud of that girl."

"I'm sitting right here, Tante Jutta."

The women chuckled.

The bell outside the *Stube* sounded, followed by slow footsteps. Annamarie put a finger to her lips, her eyes still bright. "That must be them." She rubbed her hands in anticipation.

"The Swiss?" Iris asked.

Annamarie nodded.

But Katharina shushed them. It didn't sound like two men. It sounded like one, but had Hans's gait changed that much?

All their heads turned when the door opened. First, a crutch. Then, a man.

Annamarie jumped out of her chair, clamping a hand over her scream. "Sepp?"

Katharina's heart tumbled. Josep Greil was back.

35

RESCHEN VALLEY, SUMMER 1947

Annamarie's magazine and newspaper clippings lay on the table before Sepp and her. Everyone else had cleared out. She sat alone with him, catching up, the cuckoo clock ticking away as they talked. Because he wanted to know about her first, Annamarie told him how she'd come to the valley with Tante Rosa.

"She went back last year. Her building had suffered damage in the last bombings, and she's living with her sister-in-law near Innsbruck."

"And Lisi? Why is Charlie here?"

Annamarie looked down at her folded hands. "Lisi was in a bad way before the end of the war. She wanted Charlie to stay here at least until it was over, and when it was over, she showed up at her parents', and she got her hands on... Sepp, she got worse. They had to put her in a psychiatric ward, and she passed last year. Right before Christmas."

Sepp hung his head. He had deep lines around his eyes and around his mouth, and his fingernails were chewed to the quick. She wanted to take his hands, to touch him, but he seemed so removed, so far away, she didn't dare.

"Anyway, the families agreed Charlie was better off here with me. It wasn't easy, but they're rebuilding their lives, and the Rainers and the von Brandts—well, they were questioned for their activities." Softly, she said, "Now tell me about you."

It took Sepp a few moments before he said, "When Italy joined the Allies, my unit was moved to Greece. We were there to defend the airport in Rhodes. But the Germans were everywhere. We didn't stand a chance. A unit surrounded my platoon and started mowing us down..."

He yanked at his collar and exhaled. "I was captured."

A glass clinked in the kitchen, but Annamarie gazed at him, willing him to go on.

He rubbed his face, groaning quietly. "Of course, as soon as they found out I came from Tyrol, the Wehrmacht commanders offered me the chance to fight for Mussolini again. I said Mussolini no longer ran my country. Their response was to intern me in a prison camp on the island. I was there for a little while. They asked me again to fight for the Axis. I declined. Twice more, and they shipped me off to Germany."

"Prison? Or concentration camp?" Annamarie asked quietly.

He bobbed his head, then opened his mouth, looking at the ceiling. His tongue pressed the side of his cheek, but the tears welled anyway.

Annamarie fought to keep her emotions at bay. They had only begun learning about the horrors of those camps. She wanted nothing more than to throw her arms around him, take him upstairs to one of the rooms, and to nurse him back to health.

"We were called IMIs. Italian military internees," he said, breathing deeply. "When I refused to fight for the Wehrmacht or the Italian Social Republic, they sent us to a detention camp in Germany. We were military internees—guerrillas—so that they wouldn't have to grant us rights as stated in the Geneva Convention. After that, we were called civilian workers, and that's how the Nazis assured that not even the Red Cross could protect us."

Sepp leaned towards her. "Every time I thought I might have a chance to finally send word, they moved me or redesigned the type of prisoner I was, and took another set of fundamental rights away. They considered us traitors, and nothing more. I was sent into forced labour to work with heavy machinery."

Annamarie clutched her hands. "How did you—"

"Lose the leg?"

"…Manage."

He removed his spectacles and chuckled drily as he rubbed his eyes. "Just before the accident happened, I'd been asking myself that very question. Men were falling dead around me. We were starved. We were sick. The conditions were miserable. Oddly enough, some things were perversely clean and nice. Everything was run in tiptop shape. Music on Sundays. We performed cabarets, those who could. When word got around that I'd been in the theatre, I spent months in one stalag running a small group of singers and dancers. And I got extra food for it… I did," he croaked, then grimaced. "I ate it all myself. Some shared any extras they got. They usually died. Others killed for any morsel. But me? I watched for myself. No hero here." He shook his head, as if he could not believe it.

The cuckoo clock made a heavy tick, and the bird popped out and shrilled. Sepp jumped, and Annamarie grabbed his hand and bent forward. She stared at his leg. The trouser was pinned at the knee.

"And the leg?" She sat back up.

"Actually, Annamarie, I think that's the easier story to tell you, because I truly believe that accident is what saved my life."

"Was it traumatic?"

Sepp shrugged. "Did I think I was going to die? No. Did I wish I would? Yes."

He told her then about how manufactories were moved to

secret underground locations all around the Reich. He was helping to unload big machines that were to produce electronics and other components needed for industry.

"One of the guys had not hitched it properly to the suspender, and when the crane lifted it into the air, it slipped. I stumbled backwards, but not fast enough. I was knocked to the ground, and the damned thing landed on my leg."

He told her that after the operation where they eventually removed his leg, he was transferred to the Ilag in Liebenau near the Lake of Constance.

"The French liberated the area, but we were kept in captivity for some time after the end. By that time..." He reached for her hand. "Well, it had been over a year, and I had no idea where you might be, what you were doing. How you would have changed..."

Like he had, was what he meant. Annamarie took his face in her hands and gazed at him.

"All I wanted was for you to come back," she said. "All I wanted was for you to survive the damned war."

He told her how he'd eventually been transferred to Rome, but the hospital was so overcrowded that the doctors discharged him and told him they would contact him when a prosthesis became available. The list was long, so he returned to the Eisack Valley.

"I went home." He shrugged.

Annamarie shut her eyes so that he could not see her disappointment. "How long have you been back then?"

Sepp took in a deep breath. "Three months."

Before he could give her some weak excuse about how she might not have accepted him, how he'd lost some part of himself that did not include his leg, she said, "If you'd written, I would have come to you. Immediately."

"I wasn't sure you would."

"Immediately." She kissed both his cheeks and then his mouth.

The clock ticked. He took her hands in his. Annamarie fought the surge in her chest. She had to be strong. She had to be brave. She was surprised when he smiled at her.

"I've got a job," he said. "That was the other thing. I wanted to wait until—"

"Where?"

He looked sheepish but was grasping her hands tightly. "In Rome. It's the new daily newspaper, and they needed a photo editor. I practically begged. Them taking me on, Annamarie, it's not something I take for granted." His eyes dropped to his lap beneath the table. "When I get fitted, I'll be staying there."

Annamarie's fingers went cold.

He said in a rush, as if trying to convince her of something, "As long as I can still think, Annamarie, as long as I can still create—up here, in my head—then I am far from finished. I will have to learn to do things differently. Different is not death. Different is simply different."

"Will you marry me, Josep Greil?"

He looked taken aback. "It would be no life for you, taking care of me like this. I couldn't expect you to…"

Annamarie choked back her tears. She understood he was trying to be selfless, but Sepp was the only person, the only man who had not only understood her but inspired the best version of herself.

"Listen to me," she pleaded. "I have an idea. It's just an idea, but it will make us all happy, I'm certain of it. We won't get married. To hell with marriage. But we are all going to live together. You, me, and Charlie. We'll find a suitable apartment for us all, and you will be the brains of our operation, I will be your hands, your confidante, your advisor, damn it, Sepp. I'm going to be your partner. And you won't feel as if you are beholden to me, or cutting me short, or holding me back— whatever it is your blasted mind is telling you to stop doing— because it's my decision with whom I live, and it's my decision whom I choose to love, and if you still love me, even a little bit, then I want you to take a chance on us."

Sepp looked down at his lap. "How do you plan to take care of an invalid and a young child, and work?"

"Because I can work anywhere. As AL Greil, I can work from anywhere. Please, Sepp. Please let us be together."

A slow, broad grin spread on Sepp's face. "You want to live in sin, in Catholic Rome?"

"Well," Annamarie chirped, "if the Communists have anything to do with setting up the next government, it will all be fine and dandy anyway. Business as usual."

Sepp laughed. She rose, smoothed his hair back, and kissed him to seal the deal.

Telling her mother was going to be the hardest thing she would have to do. She awoke next to him and kissed his shoulder before slipping out of bed. As she padded downstairs to the kitchen, she could already hear her mother preparing breakfast. Sheepishly, Annamarie slid in and leaned against the doorjamb.

Her mother turned, the knife held aloft. "Child, you scared the daylights out of me."

Annamarie went to her and kissed her cheek. "Can I help you?"

"You stayed here then, I take it."

Annamarie shrugged. "Is it so bad?"

Mother arched an eyebrow and tilted her head toward the window. "Don't let Father Emil catch you."

Annamarie smirked.

"How is he? Sepp? You had a lot of catching up to do. Is he going to be all right?"

Annamarie plucked the knife from her mother and began slicing the cheese from the wheel. "He'll be all right. He's been offered a job." Annamarie told her about it and a little about his POW experiences.

Her mother leaned against the counter and sighed. "Rome. I see. And how do you feel about that?"

Laying the knife down, Annamarie wrapped her arms around her mother's waist. Her mother hugged her back, took in a deep breath, stiffened, and then released it slowly.

"I should have known there would be a day my daughter would leave us again," she said sadly.

The swift tears surprised Annamarie, and she held on to her mother tighter. "I'm going to go with him, to help look for a place for us, and to also find a job. Can Charlie stay with you until then?"

"I don't know if I could stand losing both of you at once. He can stay as long as he likes, as long as you need him to be here."

"I will come back for him," Annamarie said.

"Of course you will." Her mother stepped away and wiped the tears. "Now, I've got to get breakfast done and will set an extra plate for you at Sepp's table. Then we'll see to getting you packed up."

Within a couple of weeks and after a visit to Sepp's family in the Eisack Valley, Annamarie and Sepp were in Rome, searching for an apartment. Sepp received assistance from the newspaper, and he visited the hospital once more to see if somehow he could expedite the prosthesis. He was in luck and received an appointment for the following week.

The apartment was a small service cottage located next to a villa in Pietralata. Nearby was a park with the Aniene flowing through it. It was a fifteen-minute bus ride for Sepp to the newspaper and only one stop. Annamarie visited the new offices of *Noi Donne* and received a freelancer's commission to write another article, this time about the revival of the cultural scene. The editors sent her off with a "Let's see what you can do," and

Annamarie decided right there she would do all she had to in order to become a permanent writer on their staff.

Once Sepp was fitted with a prothesis and began working, Annamarie hit the streets. It was on the day that she was visiting a bombed-out church where a group of artists was putting up an installation that Annamarie met a South Tyrolean journalist.

"Where are you from?" he asked when she told him for whom she was writing.

"Alto Adige. The Reschen Valley."

The journalist looked astonished but quickly recovered, sticking out his hand. "Michael Innerhofer. I've been there."

"Have you now? For what?"

"That reservoir. Years ago. I wrote a piece about it. What did you say your name was?"

"I write as AL Greil, but I'm Annamarie Steinhauser."

Innerhofer's eyebrows shot up, and a chill prickled along Annamarie's back. He switched to German. "Not really. Katharina and…Florian's daughter?"

"How do you know them?"

"I was involved with your brother's case in Bolzano, for one. I was sorry to hear that he fell."

She frowned. "How did you hear about that?"

The journalist seemed to be at a loss. He turned on his heel and patted his pockets, eventually pulling out a cigarette case. He indicated the front entrance.

"Mind if I go out and smoke? Join me?"

Annamarie frowned and laughed a little. "Half the building is gone, and you want to step outside?"

But he was already heading for the entryway. Annamarie followed him.

"Tell me again," Innerhofer started, "what you're doing here in Rome."

"Tell me first how you know about my brother being killed in the war."

Innerhofer grinned appreciatively, lit his cigarette. He was good looking, with dark hair and dark eyes and tufts of grey spattered about.

"All right, I suppose I can't get out of this one. I'm a friend of Angelo Grimani."

Annamarie's jaw dropped.

"Via his ex-wife. We grew up together. She was one of those transplanted Italians back in the day when South Tyrol was just Tyrol. Anyway, I knew you'd be upset, but I wish you wouldn't be."

Annamarie shook herself. "This is a weird coincidence."

He blew smoke out and offered her the cigarette case, but she declined.

"Yeah," he said. "Strange it is. So, your turn. What are you doing in Rome?"

"My, umm, boyfriend—fiancé I suppose—he and I are here to work as journalists. He has a job, and I'm freelancing."

Innerhofer pointed to the church. "Arts and culture for…"

"*Noi Donne*."

His eyebrows shot up again, and he nodded with the cigarette stuck in his mouth. "Wow. That's a great magazine."

"You know it?"

"Yeah, I know it."

"I'm hoping to get a permanent job with them."

Innerhofer flicked the ash of his cigarette and regarded the church. "I'm on the hunt for a good story about the future," he said. "Trying to get a handle on what this government means to do with South Tyrol."

"What do you mean?" Annamarie asked.

Innerhofer put out his cigarette. "Well, it's all over the place. If you're Tyrolean, certainly you can't miss it. Gruber. De Gaspari. All these discussions about regaining our autonomy permanently."

Annamarie huffed. "Yeah, you're not telling me anything new. I grew up with all of that. The whole great debate."

Michael stepped away from her, straddled the upper step, and crossed his arms. "Your family's right in the midst of it all, anyway."

That was an understatement. If he only knew how much. And in the next second, she wondered if he maybe did. Which was why when he asked whether she was finished and had time to grab an espresso at a nearby café, Annamarie hesitated. He stood and waited, then leaned forward, as if to share a secret.

"You know, sometimes you have to take these coincidences as they come. I think it's more serendipitous than coincidence. Join me. I'm a seasoned journalist. We can just talk shop and leave all the personal stuff out."

She agreed and followed him to the espresso bar, where he ordered two glasses of red wine and then, because it was almost dinnertime, a plate of olives, bread, and oil. Innerhofer carried them to the table, set them in front of her and retrieved another cigarette.

"All right, Annamarie. So how did you get your foot into *Noi Donne?*"

Annamarie treaded carefully at first, saying she had worked with UFA and Leni Riefenstahl and wrote a piece about her experiences with her. Innerhofer listened, and looked impressed, then asked interesting questions. By her second glass of wine, she'd essentially told him the entire story from the time she'd fled over the border into Austria.

Innerhofer tapped at the full ashtray, looking thoughtful.

"So any wise words from the seasoned journalist?" Annamarie asked, half joking, half hoping. She'd impressed him, and now she was earnest.

Innerhofer smirked and looked up from the table. "Yes. Here are my words of wisdom. Your career track is not like a railway. You can't see where it stretches ahead of you. Sometimes your breaks come in the strangest"—he pointed a finger at her—"and weirdest ways."

Annamarie frowned, and he leaned forward.

"You and your Sepp Greil, you sound like the kind of people who might care to know and document what Monte Fulmini Electrical has in store for the valley. You already said you've been digging up dirt on the Swiss."

Annamarie folded her arms and sat back. "Go on."

"Last year I wrote a piece for *der Volksbote*, demanding a review of the technical documentation and criticising the planned volume of the reservoir. One hundred twenty million cubic metres is what they plan. The problem is, the basin cannot be filled in times of low rainfall, and some of the water would have to be drained off for irrigation. In addition, the originally planned dam height was increased in an inadmissible way. The original height of the dam would not have resulted in the flooding of Graun and Reschen, nor of such a large area of cultivated land. In other words, the dam is dangerous."

"And did they review it?" Annamarie asked.

Innerhofer shrugged. "Supposedly. But there was a tragedy, back in twenty-three. Your...you're likely familiar with it."

Annamarie shrugged and shook her head. "Hardly."

"The Gleno dam break? Also an MFE—well, back then they were called Grimani Electrical—but an MFE project. Minister Grimani—" His eyes shuffled to the side as he threw her a glance. He was testing her, Annamarie realised.

"Angelo Grimani," she said flatly.

"Minister Grimani has quite a story about that, and the last thing that he wants to happen is for history to repeat itself. Again."

"How again?"

"He fought in the Great War. Saw a second loss with the Second War."

"Technically, Italy won."

Innerhofer pursed his lips. "Barely. We were lucky."

Annamarie nodded, understanding. "What is he doing?"

"Who?"

She threw him a glance. He knew whom she meant.

Innerhofer smiled. "Running for the senate. For exactly that reason."

That night, Annamarie spoke with Sepp, and as she was talking, Sepp stopped her.

"You started this story already, Annamarie. What if we..." He squinted and pushed his glasses onto his forehead. He pinched his nose.

"What is it? Are you in pain?"

Sepp looked up, that slow, broad grin again. "Annamarie, what if we document the reservoir? And all the people left? I could take photographs of their houses. We could do a whole series. We could film it. Take down oral histories. Get it all on record."

Annamarie gaped at him. She sputtered, and Sepp reached for her hand and drew her to his lap. She remembered what he'd said in Berlin, about wanting to document things as they were happening.

"We need to get settled here," he said to her. "We're going to have to plan this carefully, seek funding. How much time have we got?"

"A year? Two?"

Sepp beamed. "Plenty of time to make the connections we need to, plenty of time to find support."

Annamarie rose, but he pulled her back.

"Where are you going?"

She kissed his nose and pushed the glasses back to where they belonged. "I'm going to call my mother and let her know we're coming to get Charlie, but she can expect our visits to be much more frequent than she thought."

36

BOLZANO, MAY 1948

Angelo's shoes clicked along the well-worn wooden floors of city hall. He was back in his old building, but now his office was on the first floor and marked as *Senator Angelo Grimani, Senate of the Republic*. When he opened the door into the foyer, it was abuzz with people. Telephones were ringing, and someone was banging away at a typewriter.

"Senator," cried one junior clerk.

Another young man boisterously shook Angelo's hand. "Congratulations!"

Angelo took in the broad smiles, shook hands and accepted their congratulations, and thanked people he did not even know, people who kept reminding him—as if he were not aware —that the Christian Democrats had won by a landslide. And it was no wonder. With the world terrified of the escalated confrontations between the US and the Soviets, and most especially the latter's intentions, the Popular Democratic Front —a unification between Italy's two previous socialist parties— had not stood a chance. Before the election, over ten million letters from Italian Americans had arrived in Italy, urging the Italians to not vote Communist. US agencies interrupted radio broadcasts with short-wave propaganda and funded books and articles, warning the Republic and its citizens of the consequences of a Communist victory. Angelo had switched parties just in time, and Chiara had remained tight lipped since. Their friendly relationship was once again on the rocks, and now she displayed her feeling of betrayal by not allowing Angelo to visit the villa when Marco and Geraldine arrived with their new son.

"Senator, there's a call for you," a young woman called from behind the typewriter. She had not stopped typing and cradled the receiver tucked between her ear and a thick shoulder. She was a big, round woman with a mane of black hair flipped onto one side of her head. He thought all she needed was a cigarette jabbed into her mouth and the picture would be complete.

Angelo thanked her and sidled through the crowd into his office. He closed the door and glanced at the boxes and cartons neatly stacked around his desk for unpacking. A photo lay on top of an opened one, and Angelo plucked it out. Geraldine and Marco with their new son, Jules, in their arms. They had named the boy after Geraldine's father, and Angelo could understand why, but it still stung.

He lifted the receiver. "Prime Minister, Angelo Grimani at your service."

"That's good to hear, Senator Grimani," came Alcide De Gasperi's voice. "I'm calling to congratulate you. And to see whether you are ready to get to work."

"I am, Prime Minister. Thank you very much."

"It has come to my attention that you have a particular connection to the German speakers in your province."

Angelo winced and loosened his tie. "I do."

"After the adjustments we've made to the frontiers in France and Yugoslavia, I'm now looking at the city of Trieste and their demands for some kind of free territory. That has opened a particular Pandora's box. I've granted the Alto Adige autonomy in regard to bilingualism in government and schools, but it seems I've given them too much already."

"I am aware of that, Prime Minister."

"Now they want the whole province to be autonomous in more ways than one, and barring further demands to be reunited to Austria." De Gaspari sounded contrite but also amused.

Angelo lowered himself into the office chair and leaned back.

"I've been in touch with Foreign Minister Gruber in Vienna," De Gaspari continued. "It is clear that we will have to officially take steps in hearing out the Tyroleans' wishes or we run into having the same troubles we've had since 1920, and that's a sincere wish to be annexed by Austria. That is not in the Republic's favour. Therefore, I am setting up a committee to hear out their grievances and to begin negotiating some semblance of more autonomy. Trouble is, Senator, there are a few prickly points. Some of those points have to do with a number of open projects coming from your previous ministerial job."

"The Ministry of Civil Engineering, you mean."

"Exactly. I'd like you to be a part of this committee and help us to start smoothing those out—without, Senator, us losing a single one of those projects. They must be pushed ahead."

Angelo took in a breath and winced at the sharp stab in his head. He marvelled for a moment. "Sir, I don't believe the Tyroleans are the greatest hurdle in getting those projects completed. Everything that was tabled is being tabled mostly because of our lack of resources. We don't have the raw materials needed. And nobody is prepared to enter into new alliances with old...enemies."

De Gaspari cleared his throat on the other end. "What about Switzerland?"

Angelo winced again. "Yes," he said slowly. "Switzerland might work. The electrical association came through for the reservoir when MFE was looking for financiers."

"Except," De Gaspari added, "there appears to be a thorn in

that tale as well. As far as I have heard—and perhaps you know more about it than I do—a certain Stefano Accosi has been shafting the Swiss company and breaching contracts on that reservoir in... I forget which it is."

"The Reschen Valley, sir," Angelo said.

"I want you to get a handle on this Stefano Accosi at that company—"

"MFE."

"MFE. I understand you have a personal history with it."

Angelo glanced bitterly at the telephone. De Gaspari knew exactly how and why Angelo was involved with the company and the reservoir. He imagined files of secret police reports piled up on the prime minister's desk, spelling out one thing: Angelo Grimani was entrenched in this story for life.

"Get that man under control first," the prime minister said. "I want him to stop stoking those flames I was talking about."

Angelo laid the phone down after saying goodbye, picked up the photo of his grandson, and silently congratulated Marco for getting away from it all.

The next day, Stefano Accosi sat impassively across from Angelo's desk as Angelo reviewed the stats.

"You received a loan from Swiss Elektrowatt for thirty million Swiss francs last summer, in return for supplying Switzerland with one hundred twenty million kilowatts of winter energy. Meanwhile, in three years your costs have exceeded twenty-five billion lire. You've got seven thousand workers. Thirty-five kilometres of underground tunnels have been built. You've used one-point-five million tonnes of cement. Ten thousand tonnes of iron. Eight hundred tonnes of explosives. The highest costs projected were for razing the town of Graun and part of Reschen, and that does not include the money allocated to the reconstruction in progress in those higher positions."

"For which you negotiated," Accosi threw back.

Angelo grunted.

Accosi cleared his throat. "I don't understand the objections, Senator. The residents have not put up a fight, we're moving ahead, and yes, the Swiss company is not delighted by our slow cash flow, but we've applied for government subsidies and hope to remedy it soon."

The locals were not resisting, Angelo thought, because the two previous regimes—Hitler's and Mussolini's—had effectively divided and conquered them.

"What I find curious here," Angelo said, "is that supplies stopped coming in months ago, and yet the walls here…" Angelo pointed to the photos below Graun Lake. "These are completed. But the inspectors have red-flagged them in this report attached here."

Accosi pressed the bridge of his spectacles and shifted in his seat. "We're looking into that. It will be up to standards as soon as—"

Angelo sprang from his chair, walked to a box across the room, and riffled through it. He found what he was looking for, turned, and brought it back to his desk, dropping it unceremoniously into Stefano's lap. Without a word, he returned to his seat and waited.

Stefano glanced up from the photo.

"You took that," Angelo said. "We were there, witnesses to the ruin of that valley. If you do what my father did, if you cut corners, Stefano, I swear to God, you will not survive a tribunal. I will personally see to it that you never enjoy another day of freedom again."

Stefano rose, his hand shaking as he carefully placed the photo onto Angelo's desk. His face was turning pink. "It is not my intention, Senator, to repeat the mistakes of the past."

"I want to meet with your contacts at Elektrowatt. Set up a meeting, and we'll see to it that you get the subsidies you need."

There was a flicker of relief in Stefano's eyes, but it was again replaced by contempt before he retreated to the door and disappeared.

Angelo's secretary appeared. Mona Fontana filled the doorframe. In less than twenty-four hours, he'd learned to appreciate the woman. She was the dragon he'd always wanted and needed at his front door.

"*Die Volksblatt* is here to interview you."

"Michael Innerhofer? Great. Have him come in."

Signora Fontana frowned and blocked the doorway with both arms. "No, Senator. It's an AL Greil here to see you."

Angelo quickly checked his calendar, and there it was indeed. The name rang a bell, but he wasn't sure why. "You're sure? For *Die Volksblatt?*"

"Yes, Senator. Shall I see her in?"

"Her?"

His secretary moved aside, and Angelo saw the Dutch cap, the long dark hair, the slender hands gripping a notebook, and a pencil stuck between straight teeth.

"Senator?" Signora Fontana asked. "Shall I—"

But Angelo was already halfway across the room, and he watched the young woman glide in, her eyes cautious and determined all at once.

"Annamarie," Angelo said. "Welcome."

EPILOGUE

Reschen Valley, August 1949

A rustling sound outside the bedroom awoke Katharina. She threw the covers off, ready to jump out of bed and pound on the walls. "Do you hear that, Florian? What is that? Are those mice? Marten?"

But Florian was not in bed, and outside the window, dawn was breaking. She squinted at the clock on the dresser, trying to make out the hands in the dark. Almost five. But there were no cows left to tend to. Their farmland now had a road going straight through it, but her husband could not seem to get out of the habit of rising before dawn.

Sighing, Katharina got out of bed, the scent of the new pine floorboards a fragrant reminder that they were no longer in the old farmhouse but in the new inn. She pulled a shawl over her shoulders and slid her feet into slippers. Down the hall, she could hear Hans snoring lightly and hoped he would not awaken everyone else. Annamarie and Sepp were in the next room. Charlie was sleeping in Manuel's room, but those boys both slept like stones. Hans's snoring grew louder and sputtered before falling back to a rhythmic snuffle. At least there was one person who seemed to have that up-by-dawn out of his system.

She followed the rustling sound and found the source in the first room before the stairs. Katharina had stored their boxes and, at some point in time, was supposed to go through them. Florian was rummaging through one, and next to him Bella sat on her haunches, watching expectantly.

"What are you doing in here?" Katharina whispered.

He turned around, the electric bulb from the ceiling swinging when his forehead hit it. The light fixtures were delayed, just like a whole lot of other things were these days.

He straddled a box between his legs and lifted something out of it. "Look what I found."

Patting Bella's head, Katharina stifled a yawn, but at the sight of the trousers in her husband's hand, her eyes widened. "For heaven's sake, did you get up to look for those?"

"Can you believe this?" Grinning, he lifted a second item, the jacket he'd worn when he'd first arrived to the valley. "Do you think I'll still fit into them?"

Katharina laughed and went to her husband, one hand rubbing the slight paunch he'd acquired despite all the manual work he did. "I'd sure love to see you try."

He tilted the traditional carpenter's trousers to her, red piping and all. "I found the hat too." He placed the wide-brimmed black hat onto his head, and Katharina remembered the first time she had seen him in that costume. He'd been on his *Wanderjahre*, travelling from place to place, offering to do carpentry work in return for lodging and food only. He was supposed to have returned after a year, except that he'd met and wooed her.

"I suppose you could wear that to carnival," she said.

"Nah, I thought I'd let Charlie have it." He examined the hat again. "Although…"

"Good thing you never returned to Nuremberg."

"Why?"

"You would have had to nail a hole through your earlobe, remember?"

He exclaimed mockingly, raising his left index finger where he'd nearly sawed it off. "The piercing would have been nothing compared to this."

"Give the trousers to me. I can likely use the fabric and adjust it for Manuel."

She folded the trousers over her arm. Bella came to her and sniffed at the pant legs. Taking her hand, Florian switched off the light and led her back into the hall.

"Let's share a cup of coffee before everyone else wakes up," he said.

With Bella leading the way down the two flights of stairs, Katharina followed Florian to the kitchen. He put the coffee on, and she went into the *Stube* with the dog. Florian had built a wide, long room adjacent to the rest of the inn. The tables and chairs were neatly lined up in rows, and the room was still dark in the half-light. It would be at least an hour before the sun came over the ridge. She went to the doors that led to the outdoor terrace and took Bella to the side garden. After tying the dog up, she stood on the far edge of the terrace, and pulled her shawl tighter over her shoulders against the cool morning air. The new Post Inn was located on the south end of the tunnel, which had been drilled right through St Anna's hill. If she stood right in front of the tunnel, Katharina could see through to the old town. The new road ran right between their inn and the newly constructed Eagle Inn, located just below St Anna's chapel. Beyond that was Graun Lake and a muddied path leading to old Graun.

Katharina tipped her head and frowned. She could hear the water lapping the shores of the lake. There wasn't any wind. What was stirring the water so? Before she could further consider it, lights appeared in the tunnel and a lorry sped by.

Katharina exclaimed under her breath. She would never get used to living this close to traffic.

When Florian returned with two steaming cups, Katharina pulled out a seat for each of them at one of the outdoor dining tables. They sat together quietly for a while before Katharina said, "Do you think the tourists will really come?"

"Not before I get those fixtures installed," Florian joked.

She sighed and reached for his hand, and he kissed her fingers.

"We'll have more than just Annamarie and Sepp visiting us every summer for two weeks. It will be all right, Katharina. Promise."

There was a lot that was not right. There had been a lot of promises too. Everything seemed to be delayed, from cash flow to construction. But Florian's words gave her comfort because unlike the government or the authorities, her husband did keep his promises.

"Annamarie told me about the article she wrote for the paper in Switzerland," Florian said. "On Splügen."

Katharina was proud of her. "It created quite a stir. There was a letter from the editor afterwards, and he sounded pretty indignant that not all the families are being provided with a suitable plot of land."

"Well"—Florian raised an eyebrow and sipped his coffee— "Mastromattei did make us an offer, if you remember."

Katharina rolled her eyes. "Anyway, her story landed like a bomb on the Swiss residents."

"Unfortunately it's all a bit too late for that," Florian said.

"It wasn't too late for her though." She gave Florian a knowing look. "She credits you-know-who for leading her to the right source, getting her in to talk to the Swiss authorities in the first place."

Florian winced. "Angelo never did like doing the dirty work.

Rather convenient, don't you find? Got his daughter's forgiveness and sent her to the lion's den."

Katharina sighed. Angelo also could not take credit for blowing the scandal out into the open. There was that.

"Either way," she said. "Our girl has really made her way, don't you think? If only Sepp would marry her and do right by her."

Florian smiled and reached for the sugar bowl. "He will."

Katharina looked sharply at him. "Did he talk to you?"

"He made me promise not to say anything. It's supposed to be a surprise."

She beamed, but her husband put a finger to his lips. "Quit smiling like that, or you'll give it away before she even gets out of bed."

To get him back for keeping the secret from her, she was about to scold him for using too much sugar, when the bells at St Katharina started up. Florian's brow furrowed, and she tilted her head. It wasn't even five-thirty. And then she listened to the tone.

"Florian—"

"Flood. But we've had no rain in weeks…"

They stared at one another in disbelief for a second before Katharina, still in her slippers, jumped up and rushed out onto the road. Through the tunnel, the peals were clearer and more urgent. Florian was already loping across the street, heading straight for the lake, and Katharina followed. But someone called her name, and she turned to see Jutta and Hans, also in their nightclothes, standing in the front entrance. Katharina waved them over, Florian already dashing up the path ahead of her. He'd obviously seen something, and when she peered after him, she saw why her husband had wings on his feet. Water was seeping into the streets of old Graun. She turned to the lake and saw the water already well over the shoreline. Hans grabbed her by the shoulders, almost bowling her over where she'd stopped.

"The sluices," he said. "They must have opened the damned sluices! Katharina, go back and call the authorities."

"Which authorities? Who's going to stop this now?" she cried after him. But Hans was gone.

Katharina spun around to see Jutta catching up. "How could they? How could MFE have opened the sluices?" The remaining farmers had been guaranteed this summer to bring in their crops, but now water would be seeping up and into their fields. MFE was flooding their fields.

"I'm going into town," Jutta muttered.

"I'm coming with you."

Jutta pointed at Katharina's feet. "You're in nightclothes. At least go put some shoes on."

The bells were now ringing from the tops of belfries and chapels as well.

"Wait for me?"

Jutta agreed, and by the time Katharina had thrown on clothes and a pair of shoes, Annamarie was up and getting ready to go with her.

"Sepp, give me the camera," her daughter called. She returned from her bedroom with one of Sepp's still cameras.

Manuel teetered sleepily in the hallway. "Mother? Annamarie? What's going on?"

"They're flooding the fields," Annamarie called. "Get dressed and meet us in the town square. Sepp will come when he can."

By the time Katharina rejoined Jutta, men were running back and forth, some coming out of their barns with pitchforks and others with tools like sickles and scythes, like a scene from a medieval uprising. Sebastiano Foglio, armed with a sledge hammer and an enraged expression, took up the front and waved Father Emil over. The water was already as high as the tops of their shoes.

"I woke up this morning," Sebastiano cried, "like the rest of you to find the fields absolutely flooded. We're marching on MFE. We're marching on Reschen!"

The crowd of men—Katharina counted some two dozen—

roared. Father Emil waved an arm, and the crowd turned to follow him up the north road. Katharina, Jutta, and Annamarie followed at a distance, passing by Sebastiano's wife, Rosa. She stood wide eyed at the corner of the butchery. The Foglios' youngest son, Pepe—Charlie's age—gripped his mother's hand.

They were heading to the MFE barracks town, where the company's workers and office were located. Walter Plangger and Hans were pushing ahead to lead the company of men. Katharina spotted Georg as well. It had taken them all but perhaps twenty minutes to get organised, and the church bell in Reschen tolled quarter to seven when someone cried, "They're trying to escape!"

Katharina turned just in time to see the back of a black sedan pass between two houses on the dirt road below them.

"*Figli di puttana*," Annamarie cried.

"Annamarie!" Katharina gaped. "Is that the kind of language you learn in Rome?"

But her daughter was not listening.

"Over there," Annamarie cried. "They're going to have to come back up to the main road over there!"

Katharina stepped aside just in time, as the men veered and began running back towards Graun. The vehicle—with whoever was in it—had no choice but to veer back onto the one road that would get them out of town, north or south. Jutta tugged on her arm, more spry and vibrant than she'd been in years. Together, they hurried after the crowd, just in time to see several men blocking the road and surrounding the vehicle. They pumped their makeshift weapons into the air, and someone landed a blow to the car. Katharina screamed. Others followed in an angry frenzy, the sound of shattering glass mixing with the shouts.

"Get out, Accosi! Get out of that vehicle right now!"

Katharina cried out when someone grabbed her, but it was Florian.

"You shouldn't be here." He pointed in the opposite direction. The *carabinieri* were coming. "Go call the authorities. Hurry."

"Whom, Florian? Whom should I call? They are the authorities."

He looked flustered. At the crossing, the mob rocked the vehicle back and forth. Behind her, the police blew their whistles and charged past her.

"Call Angelo," Florian said. "Now. Tell him this is a state matter now. He'll know what to do. I have to get in there and stop this before it really gets out of control."

He left her before she could argue that it was too late, but then Katharina spotted Annamarie snapping photographs. She called to her, but her daughter—lean, strong and brave—was absorbed in the task of recording their dark history.

Two days later, the air was still charged and explosive. MFE took emergency actions to drain the fields, but it was too late. Rough calculations figured that over eighty percent of the crops were damaged. Stefano Accosi and his men barricaded themselves behind police and border guards, and protestors still threw bottles and rocks against the barracks. Katharina feared that more arrests would be made. Hans was one of four people who had been taken to Mals and held in custody. Father Emil, Walter Plangger, and Toni Ritsch were the other three.

At the new Post Inn, Katharina sat with Annamarie and Jutta, waiting for word from Angelo. Katharina had found him at Villa Conti after remembering that the senate was in summer session, and not too soon. He and Gina were on their way to the Adriatic for their holidays. Now, she waited for word from him as he headed to Mals.

"I just don't know what's gotten into him," Jutta said for the tenth time in two days. "My Hans..."

They sat around a table in the dark *Stube*, with an untouched platter of antipasti.

"He's angry." Annamarie slapped the table. "Look what happened to your home up in Arlund. Look at what they're going to do to the old inn. Besides, Hans was going to help bring in the harvest for a little cash."

Jutta nodded and patted Annamarie's hand. "I know. I know. But it's usually me who loses her temper and Hans who keeps his cool."

Katharina rested her chin in her hand, exhausted. She had nothing more to say and no energy for it.

Charlie charged into the room. "Tante Annamarie, can I go play with Pepe?"

"Where?" Annamarie asked. "The streets are all muddy and—"

"Let him go play," Katharina said.

Above them, she heard Sepp's familiar footfall coming down the stairs, and it reminded her of Hans's sway when his hip acted up.

"Go ahead, Charlie," he called, then threw Annamarie an apologetic look before sitting down.

Annamarie rubbed Katharina's arm. "Why don't you go upstairs and have a lie down? You look exhausted."

"Angelo should be calling any minute."

"I'll come get you."

"It's all right."

The telephone rang, and Katharina pushed herself up, Annamarie's and Jutta's faces expectant. Sepp reached for a slice of cheese and salami.

At the telephone, Katharina heard the familiar clicks and whirrs and then Angelo's voice.

"I've got them all," Angelo said after greeting her. "They've all been released." He lowered his voice so that Katharina had to strain to hear. "Father Emil's not been treated well."

Katharina moaned. Their priest was one of the last people she'd have expected to get the brunt of the authorities' anger. Then again, he had been the one to reach out to the pope about the reservoir, and that had not made him any friends with the Italian authorities since.

"I'll be there tomorrow," Angelo said. "Can you call a meeting with the residents for eleven the day after tomorrow?"

Katharina said she would. "I'll have Florian and Sepp put the word out."

"I'll be in the valley this evening with the men. I'm meeting with Stefano Accosi tomorrow."

"I'll have a room ready for you." She hung up, and her hand hovered over the telephone. It was odd. Angelo Grimani would be their first official guest at this inn. She walked back to the table and sank back into her seat. "Day after tomorrow. Eleven o'clock. He's gotten everyone out of jail."

She looked meaningfully at Jutta. "Father Emil seems to have been a bit mishandled."

Jutta clicked her tongue, and Annamarie's face darkened.

"That's not fair," Sepp said.

"Typical." Katharina shook her head. "Pick on the most vulnerable."

She imagined the new *Stube*, filled with angry people in two days. She looked at Jutta. "Why don't we do this at the old inn?"

Jutta winced. "That would mean having to take all the supplies over there."

"Manuel and Charlie can load up the Foglios' lorry."

When Jutta agreed, Katharina rose. "I am going to take your advice, Annamarie. Sepp? Can you and Florian get the word out?"

Sepp said he would, and she threw him a grateful glance. Then because eventually he would be her son-in-law, Katharina kissed the top of his head.

Upstairs, Katharina lay down but could not fall asleep, her mind playing over the events. She wondered what Angelo would tell them, and she imagined the confrontations and anger that were certain to erupt. This was not what she and Florian had built the inn for, not what Hans and Jutta had returned for. Not like this. Worried now, however, that the old inn was certainly not set up to serve people drinks and at least something light to eat, she rose. Below her, voices came from the *Stube*, and she recognised Florian's and Manuel's. Not wanting to get bogged down by more talk, she let herself out through the kitchen.

Instead of crossing the road to the lake where someone in the inn might see her, she took the steep path up the hill to St Anna's. She passed the cemetery that was also under construction. Next spring, the church would exhume the bodies out of St Katharina's cemetery and move them here. Nobody was happy about that, but there were no other alternatives.

She took the switchback to the muddy roads that led into Graun. St Katharina's clock tower showed it was going on four o'clock. Ahead of her was the old Post Inn, and she spotted Manuel and Pepe at the corner of it, bent towards the foundation, and then Pepe stretching up on tiptoe. He had a piece of chalk in his hand and was making a mark.

"What are you two doing?" She peered at the white lines they had made. Water marks and mud had reached nearly the wooden facade, just about to where Pepe had strained to reach and draw the last line.

Pepe spun around and stuck his hand behind his back, a look of guilt on his face, but Charlie was enthusiastic.

"Look, Oma, the water reached here by midday the day they opened the sluices, then it was up to here by afternoon. And there it was, all the way up here before they started draining the fields."

Katharina stared at the marks. They had no idea. This was just a game to them, she reminded herself. She looked up into the *Stube* windows above her, but from this vantage all she saw was the wooden panelled ceiling and a bit of the tiled oven. It looked hallowed out. The Post Inn had lost its soul. How many dances? How many weddings? Funerals? Debates? Discussions? Anger?

Happy times? Celebrations and fights had she experienced in that inn? Her chest constricted, and she had an irrational need to just sit down on the stoop and cry her heart out. Then she remembered something.

Divide et impera. Divide and conquer. That's what the Fascists had tried to do. And they had nearly been successful.

Katharina whirled around, facing the tunnel, facing the new Post Inn. Only a corner of the foundation was visible. No. They would not meet Angelo at the old inn. It was time to turn a new leaf, to stitch this community back together. It was time to change the way the residents of this valley did things, and it would begin in the new town, at the new inn, in the new heart of this valley. That much she would make certain.

On her way down from the upper floor, Katharina met Angelo in the hallway. Voices rose up the staircase from the front entrance, the bar, and the *Stube*. They stopped on the last landing together, and she turned to Angelo behind her.

"Are you ready for this?"

"They're going to crucify me, you think?"

"Not in our inn."

The door from the kitchen opened, and Florian stepped through but looked alarmed when he spotted her. He jerked a thumb over his shoulder. Stefano Accosi was here. They were sneaking him in.

"Wait here a moment," Katharina said to them all. "Let me just get everyone into the *Stube*."

Annamarie was already doing that, directing everyone inside. Katharina went through and greeted everyone, saying she was happy to have them here, that this was going to be the inn's baptism, and she hoped—wished for—a peaceful resolution. The residents seemed taken aback, but good manners prevailed, and they congratulated her and then Jutta, who came bustling out with trays of drinks and baskets of bread.

At the front tables, Annamarie was relieved to see Hans and Toni with Father Emil, relieved that they were back, but she was shocked by the bruise beneath Father Emil's eye. He assured her he was all right, but there was a flash of sheer disappointment and even anger when he looked at the front table set up for Florian, Angelo, and Stefano Accosi.

It took another twenty minutes to get people settled in. The dining room served fifty guests, and it was crammed with people lined up along the walls. Manuel threw open the terrace doors to let some air in, and some of the menfolk filtered outside, already lighting up cigarettes or pipes.

When Jutta passed her again, Katharina whispered to her, "Water down the beer and wine, will you?"

Jutta looked aghast. "Do you think this is my first time?"

Katharina laughed, realising how nervous she was, and why not? She'd seen what this crowd was capable of doing.

When Florian arrived with Stefano Accosi and Angelo, he was holding the little goat bell they used at the reception desk. He walked through the crowd, ringing it. "All right everyone, all right. Let's get started. We're going to let these gentlemen talk, and we're going to figure things out. Agreed?"

Katharina watched her husband shake hands with some of the people, clap a hand on the shoulder of others. Angelo and Stefano took their positions at the table up front, obviously uncomfortable with each other by the way they avoided looking at each other.

The questions started immediately, or rather, the accusations. Florian held his hands up and moved to his seat between Angelo and Stefano Accosi. Katharina found a spot at the back, and someone bumped up against her. She turned into Iris's embrace.

"So glad to see you," Katharina whispered. She squeezed Dr Hanny's hand in greeting.

Iris leaned into her. "Where are your visitors from Rome?"

Katharina pointed out Sepp and Annamarie, standing next to each other against the wall in the middle of the room. Annamarie had her notebook in hand, and Sepp had the still camera hung around his neck. Iris smiled broadly and gently jabbed Katharina in the ribs.

At the front, Florian was still trying to get everyone to quiet down. He rang the bell and raised his voice, starting and stopping until the room stilled.

"I appreciate everyone coming on such short notice. These two gentlemen, Herr Accosi and Senator Grimani, spent a long evening together discussing the details of the events that occurred. Now, before anyone raises their voices again, I mean to run this in an orderly fashion. Senator Grimani has asked Herr Accosi to join us today so that you can air your grievances. In matters regarding the flooding of MFE, it has been agreed that MFE will be compensating each farmer for their lost fields."

There was an indignant roar from the farmers in the room, but Georg Roeschen's hand went up.

"Florian, what about the homes and shops we still occupy?"

"Those too," Florian assured.

Stefano Accosi pressed the bridge of his glasses.

"As for other grievances and matters, Senator Grimani has promised to take all your concerns and deliver them to the prime minister in Rome personally."

This time there was a collective sigh and groan of disbelief.

"More promises, Florian?" someone shouted. "Is that what those two *Walscher* are here to give us? More empty promises?"

Florian glowered. "I would really appreciate you respecting the order in which we are conducting this. This is not a boxing ring, nor is it a street brawl. You have been invited as guests here to this inn to listen to our other two guests here, these two gentlemen. I will not tolerate derogatory remarks made to any of our guests here. Now, I have a few people who have asked me that they speak first. Everyone will get their turn. Senator Grimani has assured us that we have as much time as we need, and he will be sharing the final plans for the reservoir with all of you. He assures me that MFE will avoid any further uncertainties and accidents."

Angelo rose, one hand undoing the button on his suit coat. "Thank you all for coming here. Many of you know me, and many of you know that I have been working and doing my best to oversee this project. I understand that you feel you are victims of a plan that began under a totalitarian regime... Now, wait a minute, before you protest again..."

Florian rang the bell again. Someone in the back of the room screamed that Angelo should speak in German. Katharina clicked her tongue.

"We are no longer at war," Angelo stressed. "You are all recognised citizens of Italy, and our government, our prime minister, who—if I may kindly remind you—worked swiftly to reestablish your right to the German language, and autonomy in this respect, to schools and the government. Now, he has sent me here today in his name. He assures a smooth transition into your new homes here and for the reservoir to be filled next summer. But I beg you to allow me to share everything with you—"

Mutterings and jeers, but someone rose.

It was Sebastiano Foglio. "Mayor, may I go ahead?"

Florian indicated he should, and Angelo took his seat again.

"MFE provoked us, and they know it. And the *carabinieri*? What do they do? Protect the people who have destroyed our properties. You say that we have some semblance of autonomy again, but the police are quick to arrest those of us who have painted graffiti"—he threw a look at Andreas Ritsch—"and persecute us for standing up for our rights." He pointed at Father Emil, then towards the terrace.

Katharina looked outside. A group of four policemen milled on the terrace together.

"But those policemen," Sebastiano said, "are in MFE's pockets. Still! You say we're no longer at war, that we're no longer under a Fascist regime, but you have not rooted them all out. And we still have a lot of very bitter people in this community—"

"All right, Sebastiano," Florian called over muttered protests. "Tell us the story you shared with me, Son."

Sebastiano widened his stance. "You all said that I'd be digging my own grave if I took a job with MFE. You all warned me here not to go work for them, but I did. Senator Grimani, I worked for Herr Accosi here this past spring. I had to practically beg for work, and the locals here, well, they gave me a lot of grief about it, but I have a young son, a wife, and another child on the way—"

Someone patted Sebastiano's back, congratulating him.

"Well, I dug my grave all right," Sebastiano continued. "Nobody here looks me in the eye. It's not enough that my wife gets harassed, and you know who you are, with your comments and slurs. But I needed work to support my family. I worked ten hours a day, seven days a week, and when my wife was sick and I had to get Pepe off to school, I showed up five minutes late and was sacked. With no pay!"

"That's right," Walter Plangger stood up. "Accosi here came knocking on doors when their men couldn't get up here, begging us to pick up a shovel—"

"Walter," Florian interrupted, "just wait a moment. Sebastiano, are you finished?"

Sebastiano nodded and took a seat at his table.

"Let Walter speak," someone called.

Florian looked annoyed but recovered quickly. "All right, Walter, go ahead. Go ahead and finish what you wanted to say."

Walter thanked him and then explained how Accosi's bosses came looking for help. "Well, I just couldn't. I couldn't watch my fields being torn up and the wetlands being drained. They were taking my income. And that's another thing, Senator. We were told that by April we'd have the adjustments to our compensations for our lands, *adequate* compensation, and it's August now. Where is it? Where is my money?"

Accosi touched his glasses again, and Katharina thought if he continued to push them any farther up, they'd come out the back of his head.

Angelo shot the MFE man a look. "I was not aware of that, Herr Plangger. I'll look into it first thing after this meeting. I apologise for that."

Florian raised a hand. "The Senator wasn't sworn in until this spring—"

"Well, he's on summer break now. That's nice for the senator," Toni Ritsch jeered. "Meanwhile, we've lost our harvests and our fields. Our livestock is long gone. Our only chance was to sell the grain to—"

The bell again and Florian raised his palms. "Toni, I'll get to you next. Please. Walter, continue."

"So I said no to the chief engineer," Walter said. "And the next day, they're tearing up my fields. Well, I had a question. You know how our children love to play down at the willow, near the pond?"

Heads bobbed up and down, Katharina's included. That tree had seen many generations in its branches.

"Well, all I wanted to know was whether it was safe for our children to still go down there. To meet and play, with all those Budas creating quite a raucous." Walter pointed his cap at Angelo's table. "So I approached Herr Accosi here, all polite and respectful like, and the man doesn't even bother to acknowledge that I am standing there. That I have a question that deserves answering even though it's *my* land they're on."

Accosi raised his head, looking defiant. His neck was flushed pink. "It's no longer your land, Herr Plangger. We bought it from you—"

"I've dealt with a lot of people in my life," Walter said, his voice wavering with emotion, "but never have I met someone as unpleasant as this. He's on my land—it's my land, sir, until you pay a proper price for it—and I can't even ask you a question?"

Georg Roeschen stood up from his chair. "Florian? If I may, I just want to say something quickly. May I?"

Florian gave Georg the floor. "Herr Accosi, you say that the land you have been working and even flooded belongs to you, but some of us are still living in our homes in the old town, and last night, like I said, Lisl and I had water in our front entryway. I know that Klaus's butcher shop had water all the way to the glass in his cases. How do you expect us to believe a single word you say? We are being forced to evacuate our homes, damaged homes at that, without having gotten the appropriate amounts yet. And now you're going to offer us compensation for property MFE extorted from us? Senator Grimani, how is the government going to come in here and make appropriate assessments to this week's damages when we have—"

"Herr Roeschen," Angelo said. "May I just thank you for your question? It's absolutely valid, and I understand your concern. The damage done to your properties, your fields and your harvest, will be compensated—"

"At what rate?" Toni shouted. "That's what he wants to know! The rates you offered us in 1940? Tell us the damned rates, Senator!"

The room erupted once more, and Katharina widened her eyes at Florian, who was angrily ringing the bell again. Annamarie was scribbling furiously, and Sepp, his glasses perched on his forehead, was taking photos.

Angelo looked sympathetic and composed. "You're right to be concerned, Herr Ritsch," he said over the crowd. "A lot of bad things happened back then. But Prime Minister De Gaspari... Look, as soon as this is all settled, as soon as we have heard you all out, I'm going back to the senate, and this will be the first thing I deal with. I promise you."

Angelo was met with further jeers. Some people began leaving, and Toni slammed his hat against his thigh.

"Why the hell should anyone here trust you?" he cried. "Of over two hundred families that we had here in this valley, there are just about fifty left."

"About thirty are staying," Georg offered.

Katharina turned to Iris and Dr Hanny, and both of them nodded sympathetically.

Angelo rose and rubbed his eyes. "Look, I'm not supposed to say too much about this, but I want to assure you that our prime minister has your best interests at heart. He is making a concerted effort with Austria to negotiate certain points that will —he hopes—compensate for the last thirty years of oppression. And I am on that committee to help make that happen."

Toni waved his hat in the air in a wide circle. "Tell me why in God's name we should trust you?"

Cheeks flushed, Annamarie suddenly stepped away from the wall. "You should trust him because he has a vested interest in our valley. Hasn't he proven that to you already? He got you out of jail, Toni Ritsch. You and Hans Glockner and Father Emil. He got Bernd out of jail too. He's put his entire reputation on the line fighting—"

"Here we go again." Toni scowled. He wagged an accusing finger at her. "Grimani this! Grimani that! What kind of arrangement do you Steinhausers have with this man? Huh, Florian? Are you in his pocket too, then?"

"You're just a child," Walter Plangger said to Annamarie. "What do you know about this man?"

Annamarie stepped into the middle of the room. "I know him well enough."

Katharina surged forward. She wanted to shout for them to stop, shout to Annamarie to stop, but it was like watching two trains on a collision course, and she could not prevent what happened next.

"Because," Annamarie said, turning slowly amid the community. "Angelo Grimani is my father."

Katharina's heart stopped. Florian gazed at his daughter and pushed the bell toward the edge of the table before looking over at Angelo.

Annamarie had her back to Katharina, but her head was raised. "Both of these men are…"

"It's true," Florian said. "That's correct."

The room was silent. Some heads turned to Katharina, then to Florian. Katharina felt someone's hand grasp hers. Jutta was next to her.

Angelo sat down and folded his hands on the table. "I have a personal interest in this valley, and always have."

Stefano Accosi was looking at Angelo with renewed interest.

"Well," Florian said. His fingers danced on the tabletop. "I guess we'll take the next questions now. Who would like to go next?"

Sebastiano, who was nearest to Annamarie, offered her his chair just as Klaus Foglio rose and asked permission to ask a question. The room, still stunned, slowly turned their attention to Klaus as he spoke.

Ears ringing, Katharina retreated quickly into the kitchen. All these years she had been afraid of the moment this valley would discover Annamarie was Angelo's daughter. And that was it. Nothing happened.

"I told you," Jutta said, following her in. "This valley is full of unoriginal secrets."

It wasn't until half past two that Angelo and Stefano Accosi got around to sharing the detonation plan, something Angelo promised the people would change very little. For those families who had not yet started rebuilding—and there were quite a number still waiting for money—Angelo and MFE promised to build up barracks as temporary housing for them all.

By spring the demolitions would begin. The room sobered as they listed house for house, building for building, the dates and the order. The old Post Inn would be detonated a week before the church. The church was to be left as the last thing to go, and Father Emil choked back a small sob. Katharina went to him and placed a hand on his shoulder. He was a brave man, and she had been wrong to have misjudged him.

It was nearing evening, and Katharina and Florian invited anyone who wanted to stay for food, but not even the regulars seemed to have the heart for sticking around. Katharina, too, was tired. Father Emil was escorted back to the church by a group of the men, including Toni Ritsch. Not another word about Annamarie or Angelo was wasted.

Katharina heard the cork sucked out of a bottle of wine and saw Florian retrieve several glasses.

"Actually," Angelo said, leaning on the bar. "I could really use a walk."

"Me too," Katharina said.

"Me too," Annamarie echoed.

And then it was everyone. Manuel, Florian, Sepp. Her whole family, except—

"Where's Charlie?"

Annamarie looked around. "Oh, Sepp. He must have left with Pepe again."

"We'll go find him," Florian said. "Why don't you go ahead. We'll meet you on the ridge between St Anna's and…" He looked at Katharina.

"And Katharinahof," she whispered. Only there was no Katharinahof any longer.

Florian stepped out from behind the bar and took her in his arms. She shut her eyes, Angelo shifting out of view, as if to offer them a discreet moment.

She unwound herself from her husband and stepped outside with Annamarie. Angelo called that he would follow them in a moment, to go on ahead, and she decided that he too needed a little space for at least a few moments.

She and Annamarie walked up the path towards St Anna's chapel, then veered off to the right and followed the trail towards Arlund. With Bella on her heels, Katharina recalled Hund and then Hildi, and the other dogs that had gone this way before. Below, on the valley floor, they could make out the figures of Father Emil and the men, and she paused when she saw Father Emil heading into the church. The men joined him. Perhaps they were going to pray.

"Angelo's on his way," Annmarie said.

"Let's just walk a little ways. There's a spot I love beneath the pine trees. We can wait for him there."

She took her daughter's hand in hers, and when they reached the two fir trees that framed the tower of St Katharina, Katharina pulled Annamarie to her and sighed heavily.

"You have the inn, Mother. You and Jutta, and Hans and Father."

Katharina nodded, but she felt the tears choking her. "And you?" she finally managed. "This is your home too. What will you do if you and Sepp don't get funding for this project of yours?"

"We'll do it anyway. I don't want to ever forget where I came from. You know, Mother? This may be where I grew up, but sometimes the geographical place is not enough. My opportunities are different to yours. I'm following Sepp back to Rome, together with Charlie at the end of the day. He is my home. *They* are my home."

Katharina sighed.

"He wants to get married. We wanted to tell you this, but things just kind of—"

Katharina smiled and put an arm around her shoulders. "I'm so happy for you."

"Wait? You knew?"

Katharina sighed and looked out at the valley, but Annamarie smirked.

"Father can't keep a secret."

"That's not true. He keeps his promises—he's just not always very good at hiding the secrets he promises to keep from me."

Angelo reached the ridge.

"It's quite possibly something that took me this long to realise myself," Katharina said.

"What?" Annamarie asked.

"It's not the land. It's the people you surround yourself with that make it home."

"They form you into who you are, anyway."

The wind came up. In the distance, Katharina spotted the Planggers' tree, the willow's branches brushing along the surface of flooded pond. Annamarie had her eyes on it too.

"Nothing will ever be the same," Katharina said.

"Sometimes," Annamarie said, "it's not a bad thing to start all over."

"It's a blessing amongst the living," Katharina said.

Annamarie looked at her. "That's nice."

Katharina looked at her. "Dr Hanny said that to me many, many years ago."

As Angelo reached them, the bells of St Katharina began to toll, low and mournful, then a cadence of one tone after another.

"Is there Mass at this hour?" Angelo asked as he reached them.

Katharina shook her head, bewildered. "It's the death toll."

"Who died?"

Katharina stared across the valley, tears welling up. "Our valley has, Angelo."

Annamarie hooked her arm into Katharina's. "Different is not death. Different is simply different."

Touched, Katharina leaned in and kissed her daughter's cheek.

"Sepp told me that," Annamarie said. "We will all just learn to do things differently. That's all."

Her daughter pointed to the steep path below them. Climbing the slope was Florian in his black hat—the one from Nuremberg—with Manuel and Charlie following. Florian stopped, and pushed the hat back, shading his eyes against the sun. He lifted his hand, that gesture Katharina knew so well; that open, friendly hail to all who knew him and who did not know him.

Her heart suddenly swelled so strongly, she felt lifted. She waved back, wondering at this feeling. Was it hope? Was it relief? She had fought for two things for as long as she could remember. She had fought for her land, and she had fought for her family. She had always believed the two were inseparable—that one always belonged to the other. Katharina glanced at Angelo. He had never belonged to her. Nobody had ever belonged to her. Not even the land. As her husband reached them, Katharina understood what it was she was feeling and understood that it was the only thing she had ever needed, and always had. It surrounded her. It formed her. And it would continue to do so because it was given freely, and she gave it back just as freely. It was love.

GUIDE TO THE SERIES

For a list of historical notes, glossary of foreign words and acronyms, maps, and articles related to the history and culture of South Tyrol, please visit the series' online guide at https://inktreks.com/guide-reschen/.

AUTHOR'S NOTE

The Reschen Valley is a fictional name for the Obervinschgau Valley in South Tyrol. Years ago, I drove over the Reschen Pass from Austria into northern Italy and was stopped in my tracks by the sight of a medieval church steeple sticking out of the Reschen Lake reservoir near the town of Graun/Curon Venosta. That sight is what inspired the entire series. I set out to discover how something like this could happen and what lay beneath the surface.

In the past sixteen years since I first started researching the history of the area and getting to know South Tyrol intimately, I have used several resources that have been absolutely key to writing the most authentic and historically accurate story as I could. These include Felix Mitterer's TV mini-series *Verkaufte Heimat (Sold Homeland)*, *South Tyrol in the 20ᵗʰ Century* by Prof. Rolf Steininger and *Schöne Welt, Böse Leut* (Beautiful World, Evil People) by Claus Gatterer. Brigitte Mari Pircher's doctoral thesis specifically related to the *Reschensee* reservoir and the building of it was also a massively important source. Most of my research was conducted in German, some in Italian and very little was available in English. This is one of those lesser-known stories whose lessons should not—and hopefully now will not—be lost. As the tourists stop to take photos of the beautiful lake and surrounding area, and wonder—like I did—what happened here and why, I have uncovered that story through this story.

The characters in this series are completely fictional. Scenes and events were inspired by eye-witness anecdotes and accounts, historical facts, government documents, newspaper articles and academic research. The company MFE and Grimani Electrical are completely fictionalised representations of the activities of the South Tyrolean Electrical Society, Montecatini Electrical, and Edison, as well as the Swiss affiliates as illustrated in this specific novel. The actual historical figures portrayed here were completely fictionalised and include: Leni Riefenstahl (the production of *Lowlands* is based on historical research, but Annamarie's character as a part of the production is wholly fictional), Senator Ettore Tolomei, Giuseppe Mastromattei, and Galeazzo Ciano. According to personal accounts and his own diary, Ciano did visit the Obervinschgau Valley, and tear up at the sight of the valley floor when he was told that it would all be flooded.

The Post Inn is based on the Gasthof Traube Post, which did stand next to St. Katharina's church in Graun/Curon Venosta. I met with the daughter of the owners back in 2010 as well as several residents of the area who were present during the flooding and had taken up the task of preserving the heritage, culture and traditions of the valley as well as its story.

For more background information on this series, please visit the blog at www.inktreks.com. I post regular insights gained by the research I do on all my books, and tackle different aspects on the background I've done for this series.

GLOSSARY

List of Words, Acronyms, and Definitions

Ahnenpass
the Nazi party required a pass identifying that at least three generations of your forefathers were pure-blooded Aryans

allogeni
At this time in Italy, this word referred to "the others" - meaning foreigners.

Balilla boys
The youngest Italian fascist youth group under Mussolini's regime

BDM
Bund Deutsche Mädel - Germany's League of German Girls

BIZ
Bolzano Industrial Zone

Come stai
> *How are you* in Italian

coppole
> Italian-styled caps

Corriere della Sera
> An Italian daily newspaper

foehn (Föhn)
> the hot, southerly winds from Africa that blows over Europe

Giovane Italiane
> the Italian fascist's female youth group

Giovanni Fascisti
> Young Fascists

Gioventù Italiana del Littorio
> The GIL was the consolidated youth military starting in 1937

Hauptbahnhof
> train station in German

HJ
> Hitler Jugend - Germany's male youth group

Hof
> the courtyard or inner courtyard - but also referring to a large farm

Lederhosen
> short leather trousers with suspenders worn in German cultures

Monte Fulmini Electrical, or MFE

The (fictional) name of the Colonel's electrical company. In reality, it was calle Montecatini (Grimani is also a fictional figure)

Nuremberger laws

The nationalist laws imposed in Germany and within the Reich that constituted race-related oppression

ONC

Italian veteran's administration

podestá

equivalent to a prefect or magistrate in a town or district

Sauerbraten

pickled roast (marinated beef roast)

Schlutzkrapfen

very similiar to ravioli, filled with cheese or spinach

SEAA

South Tyrolean electrical society - a cooperative

Sekt

sparkling wine

Speck

smoked bacon, similar to Canadian bacon

Stube

In Germany and Austria, this was similar to a living room but functioned as a sitting room, eating room and even might have had a bed and benches to sleep on because the tiled oven was almost always in this room.

Sudetenland
A part of Czechoslovakia that was concerned a Sudeten German settlement. Germany occupied it in 1938/39

the SA (Sturmabteilung)
the Nazi assault division

VKS (Volkskämpferischering Südtirol)
the nationalist group that fought to get South Tyrol back into German hands

Walscher
derogatory name for Italians, like *dagos* was used in the U.S.

ACKNOWLEDGMENTS

My husband gets the first round of heartfelt gratitude for his inspiration, his steadfastness and the sheer faith he has in my work. To my family, my friends, and most of all, my readership for the years of support and encouragement you have given me during this enormous undertaking, thank you. Once again, Dori Harrell has helped me to shape this monster into something resembling the work I set out to do. Thank you for the flexibility in those deadlines and the encouragement that kept the wind in my sails.

And for the superb insights and commitment from the members of the Beta Team, who read the earliest drafts and provided their feedback, I especially thank Marta Aldrighetti, Renee Lewis, Martha Schaum, Rosalind Stirzaker, Trick Wiley, and Roxi Harms.

ABOUT THE AUTHOR

Chrystyna Lucyk-Berger is an American living in Austria. Her travels have taken her to many remarkable places, and she has a penchant for uncovering unique and lesser-known stories that spur her into author action. If she smells a whiff of injustice, a story about the underdogs fighting the system, she's on it and researching it. She writes full time and runs a second business in corporate communications training full time. When she is not working—which does happen—she enjoys hiking, biking, cooking, and entertaining. Chrystyna lives with her husband, and dog in a mountain hut in the Austrian Alps.

Author Homepage
www.inktreks.com

Subscribe to get news from behind-the-scenes, historical backgrounds from upcoming projects and inspiring author interviews from the historical fiction genre.

Dear Reader, your reviews matter.
Please be so kind to consider sharing your impressions with other potential fans. Or if you were not thrilled with this book— if it did not broaden horizons, surprise you with new insights, or

move you—feel free to reach out and let me know how I might do better.

Yours,
   Chrystyna

~

EXTRACT FROM "THE GIRL FROM THE MOUNTAINS"

PROLOGUE
April 1942

Magda shoved open the service door and hurried across the snow-encrusted lawn. Out of habit, she glanced at the empty deer park across the road. A gust of wind bent the tops of the cedars lined up along the way. There, they urged, pointing down the mountain, is the way out. In that very stand of trees where she had once planted kisses on a traitor, she now hid secrets in retaliation.

At the iron gate, Magda looked back at Villa Liška. The high curved windows of the dining room and sitting room were dark. The house might as well be empty inside. The yellow limestone facade had lost its cheeriness a year ago. The house remained well maintained, but the spirit was so long gone that it was hard to believe she had once felt safe and loved in this mansion.

Magda lifted the latch, pushed the gate open, and crossed the street to the granary. She was less likely to be noticed if she passed the two mines. From there she veered toward town. The clock tower rose against a grey flannel sky. Off the Ohře and Elbe rivers, the breeze carried the smell of damp laundry and stirred tiny frozen pellets into whirlpools of ice. Not hail or rain, but snow. Again.

"*April, April,*" Walter had chanted to her, "*der weiß nicht was er will.*" April, April, it knows not what it wants. He had stroked the birthmark on her left cheek, the blemish to which she had always accredited her loneliness, and switched from German to Czech. "Do you know what you want, Magdalena?"

At the time, she had been certain the answer was Walter. She wanted Walter, with his attentions, his confidence, and his teasing. But she had been too shy to utter the words. Instead she'd fled behind the service door only to peer back at him through the lead-glass window. He'd stood there for quite some time before turning away.

Now, she wanted anything but Walter. Four years into the occupation—since the terror had taken seed and grown into a strangling weed—Magda yearned to wrap her arms around something entirely different.

It took her thirty minutes to reach the walls that marked Litoměřice's old town. She passed through the castle gate, where swastika-stamped flags snapped salutes to the wind. Years ago, when she had arrived in Litoměřice to look for work, she'd swum against a current of fleeing Czechs and Slovaks. Now, the dismal reminders of a displaced Bohemia lay beneath a red, black, and white sheen. Those ruby-red flags were stationed throughout the main square too, draped along the sides of the town hall, sticking out beneath the clock tower, and stretched across the narrow streets. Triangular banners dangled over passages as if it were carnival. In the middle of these streamers, a portrait of the Führer reminded her that survival depended on loyalty and obedience to the regime. One misstep and the Gestapo could pick her up.

Litoměřice's ornamentations were still beneath it all: the gas lanterns—electric for decades—lined the cobblestoned roads or hung from an oriel. The pastry shops now featured a slice of apple strudel alongside a few traditional cylinders of cinnamon *trdelniky* and poppy-seed rolls. But the flower-stitched aprons and bell-shaped *krojová* skirts in a dressmaker's shop looked faded and unwanted.

The familiar bus puttered to a stop near the Baroque water fountain next to the oak tree. Military vehicles and trucks peppered the square. The signs on the buildings still had Czech names. The government offices had German.

Magda ducked into the bakery and stood in line behind a policeman, her heart hammering. She automatically pressed the edge of her headscarf over the ruby map on her left cheek. It was the oldest of her disfigurements, one of three that made her not only identifiable but immediately suspect. The two scars on her face were, after all, the marks of defiance.

As the policeman added his purchase to a jute bag, the woman behind the counter gave Magda a quick look. *The less you try to hide yourself, the less they'll notice you.*

Magda forced her hand to drop. The woman waited until the policeman had left before taking Magda's ration card and handing her the two extra loaves of rye bread in return.

"Will you be lighting a candle today?" she asked.

Magda nodded.

The woman added a roll into Magda's bag.

Magda stepped out of the bakery, the bag of bread clutched in her fist. When she reached St. Stephen's, she checked once more to make sure she had not been followed. She slipped her hand into her pocket and touched her talisman. Certain that nobody paid any attention to her in the streets, she made the sign of the cross and entered the church through the side. An older woman rocked back and forth as she prayed, her prayer beads knocking softly. A man Magda did not recognise lit a candle. She stepped into a pew, kneeled, and made the sign of the cross, her mind far too distracted to form the simplest of prayers beyond, "Dear God, be merciful. Protect us."

It was a long time before the strangers left. Magda rose and went to the door that led to the crypts below. She rapped twice in quick succession, paused, and tapped three more times. On the other side, the iron bolt scraped across the heavy wooden door. As soon as it was opened wide enough, Magda slipped through.

Published by Bookouture—Hachette UK
Feb 3, 2021
books2read.com/MagdaMountain

ALSO BY CHRYSTYNA LUCYK-BERGER

The Smuggler of Reschen Pass: A Reschen Valley Novella

Prequel to the series and a stand-alone psychological thriller

Reschen Valley 1: No Man's Land

A plan to flood her valley. A means to destroy their culture.

The first book in the award-winning series about a woman who fights for her homeland when an oppressive Italian government moves to eradicate her valley's Tyrolean identity and wipe it off the map.

Reschen Valley 2: The Breach

Burying the past comes at a high price.

Reschen Valley Box Set: Season 1 – 1920-1924

She wants her home. He wants control. The Fascists want both. Contains books 1 and 2 and *The Smuggler of Reschen Pass.*

Reschen Valley 3: Bolzano

On the journey to figuring out who you are, most often you discover who you are not.

Reschen Valley 4: Two Fatherlands

How do you take a stand when the enemy lurks where you thought was safest?

Reschen Valley Box Set: Season 2 – 1937-1949

Sometimes, when you're trying to determine who you are, what you discover is who you are not. Contains books 3 and 4.

Reschen Valley 5: The Rising (2024)

A homecoming like no other.

∼

Souvenirs from Kyiv

Unforgettable stories based on the heartbreaking experiences of
Ukrainian families during WW2

∼

The Girl from the Mountains

Not all battles are fought by soldiers.

The Woman at the Gates

They took her country. But they will never take her courage.

And stay tuned for more books published by Bookouture, Hachette UK

Printed in Great Britain
by Amazon

26309962R00354